Creatures of the Otherworld

PRAISE FOR
CREATURES OF THE OTHERWORLD

From the moment I opened this book, I fell deeply in love. The author draws you in with splendid visuals, great character development, and a compelling storyline.

— AMAZON REVIEWER

Brogan Thomas is brilliant; she is creative with an incredible imagination. Her world-building is phenomenal, packed with all types of supernatural components. The characters are well-developed, definitely appealing, and fascinating.

— GOODREADS REVIEWER

This story grabs you by the throat and doesn't let go. It's intense and electrifying.

— AMAZON REVIEWER

CREATURES
OF THE
OTHERWORLD

BOOKS 1-4

BROGAN THOMAS

This is a work of fiction. Names, characters, places, and incidents either are the product of the author's imagination or are used fictitiously.
No part of this book may be reproduced or used in any manner without written permission of the copyright owner except for the use of quotations in a book review.

Published by Brogan Thomas
WWW.BROGANTHOMAS.COM

Copyright © November 2022 Brogan Thomas
All rights reserved.

Ebook ASIN : B0BKCSHNT5
Paperback ISBN: 9781838146986
Hardcover ISBN: 9781838146993

Cover design by Melony Paradise of Paradise Cover Design

CREATURES OF THE OTHERWORLD

CONTENTS

CURSED WOLF	1
CURSED DEMON	263
CURSED VAMPIRE	529
CURSED WITCH	785
ABOUT THE AUTHOR	1043

For my hubby

CURSED WOLF

Loathed by those who should love her, can one fierce woman discover the secrets of her unique blood in time to be her own rescuer?

Forrest Hesketh desperately clings to humanity. Trapped in an infuriatingly inept wolf form since she was nine years old, the traumatized girl's hope of regaining her ability to shift is slowly fading. But as her abusive pack plots to kill her, her desperate act to help her kind stepbrother finally triggers the broken young woman's transformation.

Stunned that suddenly everyone wants her after 14 years of horrific treatment, Forrest struggles to relearn basic skills while dodging kidnappers and assassins. And with a powerful shifter councilman determined to claim her as a mate, even the protection of a gorgeous dragon can't guarantee her safety.

With monsters closing in, will Forrest's undaunted courage be enough to keep her alive?

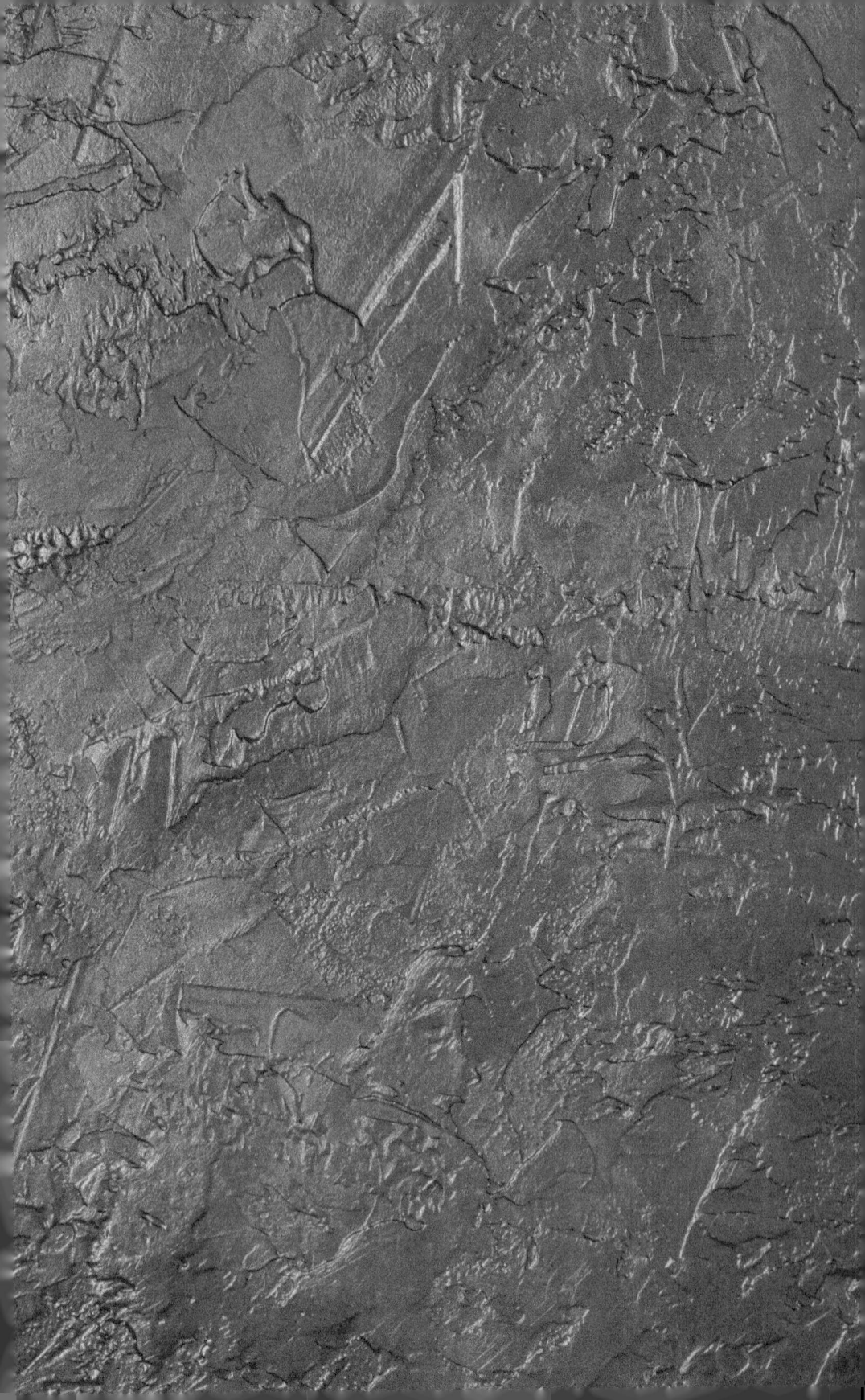

CHAPTER ONE

Head on my paws, I relax against the sun-dappled grass as the light filters through the trees above. The green light lays dancing patterns across me with the slight breeze.

I love the sun on my fur. If I felt genuinely safe, I'm quite sure I would be lying on my back, legs akimbo, doing my best impression of a dead fly with the sun on my tummy.

Sad to say, I haven't felt safe in what feels like forever, and being outside is the best I can achieve.

My name is Forrest.

On the bad days, I repeat my name hundreds of times to remind myself that I was a girl once.

A girl with green eyes and red hair. Shit, I have been a wolf longer than I ever was a girl.

"Forrest"—did I imagine her? Some days I wish I had. It would be so much easier to let Forrest go, but I'm stubborn.

God, I hate my life. I bloody hate living with the constant fear of doing the wrong thing. No matter what they do to me, I can't fight back. If I did, they would declare that I'm feral and use it as an excuse to kill me.

It's fucked up.

I do a little stretch, my claws digging into the soft ground, my bum in the air, and then settle back to my noseying. The comforting smell of churned soil surrounds me.

It's ridiculous that a bunch of shifters have the gall to treat me like a bad, unwanted dog. But what did I expect as someone stuck in wolf form?

I think maybe it's a real deep-dark fear that they all have, knowing this could happen to them. One day, shifting into their furry form, and bam, not being able to turn back. Feral, wrong, and needing to be put out of their misery. I guess I can understand why I freak them out.

Why they hate me.

I'm sure they don't realise that I'm me inside, hence the dog treatment.

A feral shifter, the nightmare scenario where the animal takes over completely, is an uncommon phenomenon, and it's not something I suffer from—I am not feral. I am the same person I'd be in my human skin. I'm in full control of myself—I am just stuck, and I don't know how to transform back. No one knows how to change me back. My magic is defective, broken.

I huff out a breath. Not being able to communicate is bloody horrible and unbelievably frustrating. Isolation and growing up trapped as a wolf—especially a wolf treated like a literal dog—has been no easy task.

A ladybird lands on my paw. I sniff at it. *Hello, little bug*...I am so fucking lonely, but I would willingly embrace being an outcast if it would mean that they would just leave me alone. Sounds ridiculous, I know. I've learned over the years that my pack doesn't have to like me—hell, I've given up trying. I only wish they didn't take pleasure in hurting me.

The days keep coming, time keeps ticking, the world moves around me, and yet here I am, never changing.

I love this spot underneath the trees, where I remain unseen but can see everything. The Packhouse draws my gaze, the ostentatious monstrosity. Temple House—as it's also called—with its five hundred acres, is located in Singleton, Lancashire. It is an extremely old house my mother built in the 14th century.

Mum was old as shit before she died. Shifters can live thousands of years, and my mum was a hard woman from a different time. She was tough on me and not one to coddle a child. Her focus was on teaching me things to help me survive. It always felt to me as if she raised me out of duty instead of love. Maybe if we had had more time...

Even so, I miss her. I miss my mum so much.

When I was little, my mum was concerned with my safety. Which looking back is ironic, as my mum unknowingly bought my current tormentors into our pack initially to protect us. Magic is commonplace, with all manner of people in our world: shifters, demons, witches, vampires, and an abundance of Fae. But there's a divide among the races—creature versus creature, with pure humans struggling to survive.

As a shifter female, I was rare and coveted—our female birthrate is low. To keep me safe, my pack didn't allow me to go to school. I was home-schooled—or home drilled, as it had felt at times. My mum had not enjoyed teaching me. Her subjects were varied and probably, thinking back, not suitable for a child. But my education was thorough, and by the time I was seven, I could speak several languages and skirmish like a proper demon.

It was kind of tragic that by the time I was nine, I would be unable to ever speak again. My mum was dead and I was stuck in my wolf form.

I hear the cars long before I see them. I lift my head and watch as two black vehicles wind their way up the tree-lined drive.

Oh, here they are, right on time. The Sunday lunch guests. Well, one guest, with her plethora of bodyguards to keep her safe. Not that I see anyone in their right mind trying to kidnap Liz. Ha, if they did, they would give her back pronto.

Liz Richardson. I curl my lip with my contempt. If you spent time with the cow, you'd understand. She's a spoiled purebred wolf shifter with an attitude. Oh, she is all smiles and niceties when she wants something. But toward unimportant people—or in my case, animals—she definitely displays sociopathic tendencies.

Getting out of the car, Liz waves away her three hulking bodyguards as she answers her phone coming towards my hiding place with her mobile against her ear. Liz is dressed in a pretty pale blue summer dress today. The colour matches her eyes, and her brown hair is styled in a perfect bob.

Liz is, unfortunately, Harry's girl. Harry is my stepbrother slash pack member. Can you call someone your stepbrother when both sets of your parents are dead? I give a mental shrug. Anyway, at a year older than me, he was sent away to boarding school when our parents died—perhaps to protect him from the feral wolf shifter at home, to make sure that what I had wasn't catching.

I don't know how many years passed—it is not like I have access to a calendar. Every day feels like a week and every month a year. I've lived a thousand lifetimes in my fur. I grew up fast; I had to. But when Harry came back, my life improved massively with his input. Hugely. I owe a lot to Harry's benevolence. I think I was going insane before Harry came back home to live with the pack.

Shit, I don't want to go back to those years—I would rather die. It still leaves me shaking when I recall them. For a long time, it was—

I shudder, close my eyes, and take an unsteady breath.

I will get to the point: they don't hurt me as much with Harry around. He is my unintentional shield and their conscience.

I open my eyes. Liz is still on the phone, and she's sauntering towards me. Shockingly I can hear a man on the other end. *Ewww, gross*—he is talking absolute filth to her. Oh, and spoiler alert, it isn't Harry on the phone. This is a real problem, as today, from what I have overheard, is the day Harry and Liz are supposed to announce that they're officially mating.

What is Liz doing...oh my God, is she cheating on Harry? Why on earth would she do that?

I scowl and wrinkle my snout with disgust as Liz finishes the call with a giggle. A little growl spills out without my permission, rumbling up from my chest. If I had hands, I would be slapping them against my muzzle about now to muffle that growl. What the heck was that! What was I thinking?

Liz freezes, and her eyes widen.

Her panicked gaze searches the garden and surrounding trees. She catches my eye, and I find myself trapped in her venomous blue glare.

Now would be a good time for the ground to swallow me up. I lower myself further down on my belly, trying desperately to make myself smaller. Liz's expression changes to a confident, cocky sneer. She flashes her teeth at me in a warning.

"Oh, this is cute. Are you spying, dog?" Liz surreptitiously looks around again, and then she smooths her blue dress and picks imaginary lint off the skirt. I have no doubt she's making sure we're alone. "What are you doing out here? Shouldn't you be in a cage somewhere?" She lets out an evil, over-the-top Cruella laugh and starts to strut toward where I'm huddling. "Bet you hate it, don't you, dog? Are you jealous that I'm visiting my mate? That I'm having lunch with your pack? Hell, you're not allowed to grace the floor in my presence. Does it upset you that I'm living my best life while you're rotting away inside? How does it feel, dog, to know that when I join your pack, your days are numbered?" Liz narrows her eyes, stepping off the driveway and into the trees. She saunters closer to me, and the foliage rustles under her ridiculous high heels.

"What you heard just now is none of your business, not that *you* can do anything." She sniffs and rolls her shoulders back. Crossing her arms underneath her breasts, she drops her voice to a whisper. "Between us, dog, the bitten shifter I'm fucking is far more fun than boring Harry." Liz regards the house with a smirk. "To get this estate, I'd mate a troll. Everything that was yours is mine now, dog. So keep out of my way and I might ignore you." She lets out another creepy laugh and glares at me again.

Huh. I tilt my head. I am sort of amazed at her impressive arsenal of nasty looks—Liz can contort her face into so many expressions.

"Fuck it, who am I kidding?" She suddenly screams as though someone's torn off her arm. I flinch in shock and flatten my ears at the shrill sound. I can barely hear the pounding of feet over her shrilling as the bodyguards come running.

Oh, shit. I try my best not to panic. I wiggle back into the protection of the trees. Squirming like a worm, I inch slowly back on my belly. *Nothing to see here, scary bodyguards.* I've made a colossal mistake —why did I growl at her? I know better than to be seen, I know better than to react. I know better than to draw attention to myself, especially with this evil woman. Stupid.

As the bodyguards get closer, Liz flaps her arms about dramatically. She then holds her hands to her chest like she's clutching a set of pearls. All the while, she is *still* screaming. Her three guards surround her protectively, and one of them literally picks her up and places her behind his bulk as he searches for the danger.

"It growled at me!" she whimpers feebly. If I weren't so pissed, I'd be rolling my eyes. But my eyes are firmly focused on the bodyguards and the three swords pointed at me. Yes, swords! The three guards have silver swords. Fuckers.

It's a little bit of overkill.

I tremble. I can smell the fear wafting off me. God, I hate being stabbed. I refuse to whine in terror. I'm still clinging desperately to my tattered pride and sanity.

"What is that doing out? I thought they killed it years ago," one of them grumbles.

"Shame, what a waste, a broken female shifter. She could have been exceptional. Her mother was a beauty."

The huge guy who's blocking Liz from my imaginary threat and my previous fear-inducing growl huffs out a laugh and puts his sword away. He shakes his head. "You were chatting with her a minute ago. Don't think I didn't see you," he reprimands, wagging his finger in Liz's face. Liz grinds her teeth, and her eyes follow his finger as if she wants to bite it off. "You know she doesn't understand what you're saying. This little wolf is too far gone. But she's not dangerous. Otherwise, there's no way the council would allow you to visit." He turns his back on me. "If she were dangerous, she would have done something when you played 'football' with her a few weeks ago." He points the same meaty finger towards the house and propels Liz in that direction. "Get inside! This shit is getting old." Liz pulls a face and digs her heels into the ground, stopping her forward momentum. I guess she hasn't finished with me yet.

"Football?" the grumbly one repeats incredulously. He too puts away his weapon, and he tilts his head to the side in question.

"Yeah, Liz thought she could kick the poor wolf like a ball." All three of the guys turn and stare at Liz.

"That's not very nice, Liz," the grumbly one chides, shaking his head in disbelief. She shrugs, glaring, probably pissed that someone knows what she did.

The relief I feel at no longer being under their scrutiny is almost cathartic. I wiggle back a little more. *Please ignore me, please ignore me,* I chant with each wiggle.

"You need to kill it!" Liz swings back, pointing at me, a snarl on her face. I freeze. *Uh-oh, oh shit.* "Give me a sword. Give me a bloody sword. If you're not going to kill it, I will!" The bodyguard closest to me still has his sword in his hand, and Liz attempts to grab it. She manages to get a good hold on his arm. She braces her feet and pulls the sword towards herself with an unladylike grunt.

"Whoa, what are you doing?" says the guard, his eyes wide with panic. They are probably matching my own.

Grabbing Liz not-so-gently by the shoulders, the huge guy turns her away from me again. Holding her elbows, he pins her arms to her sides. Liz struggles and snarls. "Are you nuts!" he shouts. "You could have cut yourself! What is wrong with you?" He shakes her a little. "A small nick and you'd be in a world of pain. You don't mess about with silver!" He's right—enough silver in the system of most creatures and it is fatal.

In shifters, silver stops the shift. As shifters, when we change forms, the magic repairs us at a cellular level. It's the whole part-and-parcel of the magic and the entire reason we live so long. So a small amount of silver in a shifter's system and we're sitting ducks. If you can't shift, you don't heal—or, as I have found out over the years, you heal human-slow.

I use the distraction to slip away.

Shit, that was a close one. God, Liz is such a psycho. I shake off my fear as I run, dodging between the tightly packed trees. Pain shoots up my spine as my lame back legs protest the fast movement. I grit my teeth. The stiff limbs drag slightly behind me, not quite in sync. I follow the line of the driveway, and I slip around to the other side of the house.

Why is she so horrible?

If Liz thinks she can cheat on Harry with a bitten wolf and get away with it—well, she bloody well can't!

What I can do, though, I have no idea—but Harry can't mate with her. Liz will break his heart. Shifters mate for life—when you mate, you form a bond. It's a beautiful, sacred thing. Better I fix this now rather than have Harry find out later.

I need a plan.

I need Liz's phone.

CHAPTER TWO

I HAVE a rough plan that involves sneaking into the Packhouse, a house I haven't been inside for years.

The back door is open—if that isn't a good omen, I don't know what is—and I creep inside. My nostrils flare as I catch the cloying, multilayered scent of the pack. It makes me shiver, and my hackles rise. The polished wood floor creeks. I freeze. My gaze darts about. My heart is pounding so hard, I wouldn't be surprised if it left my chest and splatted onto the ceiling.

What the hell am I doing...My mouth fills with sour saliva, and I clamp my muzzle closed. God, I hope I don't puke. It would be simple, easy, to turn around, go back outside with my tail between my legs and forget I ever thought of doing this.

This is a stupid idea.

Stupid stupid stupid.

I've got this crazy notion rattling around in my head, to go out in a blaze of glory. The Bon Jovi song fills my head, and I silently hum along. Motivated, I quickly pad down the wide hallway, the beat in my head.

I sneak into the dining room. I manage to get myself safely behind the dining room curtains without further freaking out.

The dense, old-fashioned red and gold curtains hang in front of a beautiful square bay window. I know from other sneaky endeavours as a child that they hide me and my scent well.

I take the opportunity to rub myself along the fabric in a vain hope that my fleas will jump off and disperse around the house, infesting the pack. Yeah, I have fleas. Plain old non-magical ones that drive me mad with the itching. My body is full of scrapes and sores. A particularly painful one at the back of my neck continually throbs. I can smell the infection as the pus oozes into my surrounding fur—I can't reach the spot. I'm falling to pieces. At least my coat isn't matted. The manky dirty, flea-ridden fur sheds without issue.

As I wait, I berate myself. Why on earth did I growl? I will be punished later. By the time lunch is over, Liz will have convinced the pack that I took a chunk out of her or something equally dramatic. It's irrelevant that Liz wanted to go all stabby on me. That growl could be the one thing that tips them over the edge. I swallow. I am the idiot who put myself in that situation in the first place. Now I'm going one step further. Here I am hiding in the dining room, trying my best to put the final nail in my coffin. And I call Liz a psycho...

I blow out a breath. I care about Harry. Harry matters to me; his happiness matters. If I can keep Harry from making a mistake with Liz, irrespective of what happens to me, it will be worth it...

God, I am absolutely nuts! I've finally lost it. I have to be honest with myself: if I do this, there's a big chance that they're going to kill me.

I lie down. My back legs make it too painful for me to stand for extended periods. I try to swallow the lump in my throat. The truth is painful to admit—but I can't live like this anymore. I'm barely surviving. I might as well die for something.

If I'm going to do this, I am going to own this shit.

I focus on the times when Harry intervened on my behalf. Maybe he doesn't remember his interference, but I do.

What he did matters to me. What type of person would I be if I rewarded his kindness by turning my back on him?

Horrible people shouldn't get away with doing bad things just because they can. If good people don't do anything, then that makes them as bad. I know that's probably a very naïve way of thinking about things.

You've got to remember, I'm not worldly.

I'm a memory of a girl.

I first met Harry when I was six years old and Harry, his two older, nastier brothers Vincent and Jason, and my new stepfather Dave came to live with my mum and me. When my mum became pregnant with Grace, our little sister, our pack of two suddenly became a pack of seven. My eyes fill with tears. *Grace*—

"So, no babies yet?" The clunking of Liz's heels on the wooden floor follows her snide question as she enters the dining room. I freeze —I didn't even hear them coming. Sloppy. "Being a human mate"— Liz sniffs, the distaste evident in her voice—"you would think you'd be trying. You don't want to miss the boat. You humans die so easily. Or has Vincent decided to wait for a pureblood female to be available? Let's be honest, your children would be next to useless—no offence— apart from the slight strength increase and a few more years added to a pathetic lifespan. They can't even shift. I see no point in anyone breeding with you."

What a cow. Liz is talking to Beth. Beth intelligently remains silent.

I mentally grumble. Liz is such a hypocrite—it's okay for her to have a bitten lover. Bitten shifters—turned human's who are always male—don't shift.

Like I said before, female wolf shifters are very rare. Female shifters are treasured, as only one in a thousand shifters are born female. Male shifters like Vincent have no choice but to mate with other races, as no one wants to live alone. Vincent is fortunate to have Beth as his mate.

"It looks good on you, by the way—the extra weight." Ugg, Liz is such a liar. Beth is gorgeous. I like Beth. When Vincent is out, she leaves the television on in the kitchen so that I can watch it through the window. She also plays music loudly so I can hear from the garden.

My thoughts drift to my estranged biological brother, John. I wonder if he has a mate and any children. John is a super-shifter, a hell-hound—"hellhound" is a name given to all fire shifters, gifted with magic. The ability is rare, and only a few male shifters get to that level of power. My brother is a total badass. He's the hero type you send in to save the world. Shifters have long lifespans and are difficult to kill, but shifters do die and all that's left of my bloodline today is John and myself.

Yeah, go John. No pressure—our bloodline now rests on his shoulders. It isn't like I am going to be of any use. I won't be popping out any babies.

I glance down at my dirty paws and sigh.

While I've been reflecting and not paying attention—again, highlighting that I'm not in the right frame of mind—I have missed the rest of the pack's arrival. They have already taken their seats around the dining table. The clink of plates, the soft murmur of conversation, and the smell of food drifts underneath the curtain.

The smell makes my stomach cramp. I am always so hungry and God, it smells good. I take a deep breath in and briefly close my eyes in appreciation. *Mmmm.* I learned a trick many years ago: when I smelled delicious food, I'd close my eyes and imagine I'm eating it—the taste, the texture in my mouth. I don't even know if my imaginary food tastes the same as food in real life. I'm sure mine is way better. I nod my furry head with conviction.

Come on, Forrest, get a grip. I take a steadying breath, trying my best not to disturb the curtain with my muzzle. I peek through a gap. I need to see where everyone is sitting.

Okay, Harry is seated next to Liz, and he's sitting with his back to me. His blond hair brushes the collar of his smart blue shirt. He needs a haircut. On Harry's right is Jason. Vincent is opposite Liz with Beth.

Vincent. My stomach tightens. He is the oldest of the brothers. He is my torturer, my tormentor, and will be the man who ultimately murders me. The monster has been killing parts of me slowly for years. He was initially assigned by my mother to protect me. Vincent and Jason were supposed to be my bodyguards. I huff. Instead, when my circumstances changed, they became my prison guards and self-appointed abusers. They're both tall and bulky, with dark hair and eyes. Jason's eyes are almost black. He is so creepy. The dread I experience when they're near is like a living thing.

I can't do this if I look at them or think about them—I will lose my nerve. I take another shaky breath and focus on the job at hand. I wrangle the butterflies in my tummy. They feel like they're going to climb out of my throat and take flight.

Luck is with me, as Liz is sitting in front of my hiding spot. The phone is sitting at the end of the table next to her fork. My whole focus of attention switches to the phone and planning my next move.

So it takes me a while to tune in to the conversation, and I wish in a way I hadn't. The members of the caring, sharing pack are all talking about killing me. Yay, fun times.

Liz places her hand on Harry's arm and pats it. "I've chosen you to be my mate. I could have chosen anybody. But I chose you, Harry. I've said that I will live with your pack—join your family, as the humans quaintly say. We're going to be mated, and our future children will not be growing up in a home with a feral wolf. Harry, it's getting ridiculous." She fake-shudders and pouts annoyingly. "Every time I visit, the savage attacks me! It is dangerous and should be put to sleep."

Huh, "put to sleep." *Really? Why not say what you mean, Liz. Dead.* Not that she has anyone to disagree with her, apart from Harry and a silent, wide-eyed Beth.

"I am sure we can convince the brother to let it go. He doesn't care about it, anyway. With enough evidence, the council will sign off on it." I am surprised she doesn't say, "It's either the dog or me." Liz sadly smiles. Wow, not only does she have an arsenal of horrible looks, but it seems as if she has a catalogue of impressive fake smiles as well. "You are selfish and cruel. Insisting on keeping that thing alive when it would be much better—" Harry is shaking his head, and I guess he's about to reply when Liz's phone rings.

Oh my.

My muscles tighten in readiness. I know it's the filthy talker—it's the same ringtone.

I make my move.

I have seconds to somehow get to the phone.

Between one breath and the next, I spring from behind the curtains.

All I can hear is my panting and my heart pounding. With more focus then I have given anything else in my life, I home in on the handset.

I need to get this right. This might be the last thing I ever do, and I need to make it count. I ignore the pain in my back legs. I just need to... My hand lands on the phone, and I press the screen to answer. With another swipe of my finger, the phone is miraculously on the loudspeaker.

"Liz babe, when are you coming back to bed. I need you..." I smile with satisfaction as the male voice echoes around the room. *Ooops, no talking yourself out of that one, Liz.* Bingo, *I got the cow,* boom, *take that, Liz. Eat your heart out, Liz Richardson.*

Everyone but Harry is ignoring the phone. I wince. Poor Harry.

They are all staring at me. *Uh-oh.* Vincent has an evil look in his narrowed eyes.

Uh-oh. Oh no.

I wobble. My legs shake as I back away from the table. My hands lift in the age-old sign of peace. I didn't touch Liz, just the phone.

HANDS. Oh my God. I let out a squeak of fright.

Oh my God!

I glance down at the tiny hands, so pale they seem transparent. My *hands*. They are no longer paws!

CHAPTER
THREE

The whole table erupts into shouting. Everybody is trying to speak at once. Shit shit shit. I freak out.

I run. Adrenaline floods my veins as I make a wobbly run for the door—a wobbly naked dash. I am so not hanging about.

I think I am in shock. No. No, I know I am in shock. Did they kill me? I bounce off the wall as I run into the hall. I almost fall, but my momentum keeps me upright. I huff out a pain-filled breath. Ow. Nope, still alive.

The shouting from the dining room is getting worse, and the three bodyguards—yes, the ones with the swords!—are rushing to the dining room from the kitchen nearby.

I keep going. Please don't see me, please don't see me. They start shouting at me to stop. Oh crap, they have seen me!

I do the most sensible thing I've done today. On instinct, on the way past the hallway table, I grab the house phone. I bounce into the toilet door and manage to get the door open. I fling myself into the tiny bathroom, slam the solid oak door behind me, and hit the lock.

Wow, who knew I had that in me?

My whole body is shaking, and my heart is pounding. I gasp. God, I can't breathe.

Running on two legs is not fun—how the hell do people balance?

My wobbly legs give out, and I slide down the closed door onto the cold, tiled floor. I shiver. I never thought I'd miss my fur...I feel so bloody cold. I pull my knees to my chest and grip the phone.

The door shudders behind me. I squeak in fright and almost drop the landline. Someone wants in here desperately. Shit shit shit. Thank God the shuddering door is solid oak and not made from a lighter wood.

I have no option but to ring my brother John. I hope he will come now—now that I'm human again. I do my best to focus and dial.

How many times have I imagined this moment...

I mentally cross everything that he still has the same mobile number. One by one, the digits pop into my head. It takes over a dozen attempts to get the right sequence, as the banging on the door is seriously disconcerting and my fingers are like useless noodles.

The phone rings, it rings and rings.

Please pick up. Please pick up.

"What! Why are you ringing from this number?" comes a gruff, angry voice.

I open my mouth to speak, and nothing bloody comes out. I want to say John's name. But I can't. Oh my God, I can't talk! My hand not holding the phone flies to my throat and my heart skips a beat.

Finally, frustratingly, I say "J—" But it's more like a puff of breath rather than a letter or word. No no no. I whine in frustration.

"Forrest? Forrest, is that you?" His tone of voice changes, gentles. Somehow he knows. My brother knows! I manage another soft whine. "I am on my way. I will be with you in just...in under an hour. Are you safe? Is the pack with you? Why haven't they called me? Shit, never mind." His soft tone of voice disappears. "What the fuck is that noise!" The banging on the bathroom door must have registered. "Is someone trying to hurt you? I am on my way. Stay on the phone. Do not shift back. Do you hear me? Do not shift back!" There's a muffled shout, like he is half-covering the phone. "Owen, get one of them on your phone now! Forrest is back. Yes, now, damn it." He comes back to me. "Hey princess, are you in your room? Somewhere safe? I am bringing Doctor Ross. Everything is going to be okay—"

I pull the phone away from my ear and squint at it incredulously.

Everything is going to be okay? Really? I have scary bodyguards...or is it the pack banging on the door at my back? Their screams echo in the hallway. I swallow back tears.

My brother is coming...

The pack wants me dead.

My brother is coming...

I feel lightheaded. I whine, and my bottom lip trembles.

The same estranged brother that I haven't seen since I shifted. John dropped me off like an unwanted puppy, and off he went to save the world without a backward glance, leaving me with monsters.

Am I safe? No, I am not bloody safe. I've never been safe, and I doubt it will ever be okay. I clamp my lips closed and hold in a sob that wants to wrench itself from my throat. I hug my knees.

The noise level in the hall drops, and finally I can make out individual voices.

"She rang John. Fuck! The hounds are on the way."

"Are you sure that's Forrest? Didn't she have ginger hair?"

"Fuck's sake, get away from that door! You will scare her and then John will rip your throats out. Get the fuck away."

This is all too much.

"Go sort your female out. Liz is no longer welcome at this time. We will deal with this problem first. Thank you for your assistance, but this is no longer your concern as you aren't members of this pack." I shudder at Vincent's smooth voice. I think he's speaking to Liz's bodyguards.

Is Vincent getting everyone away so that he can come in here and kill me? Surely he can't, now that John is on his way? Visions of Vincent crashing through the door with a silver sword make me shudder. I bite my arm to stop myself from crying out.

"Liz, don't say a word, we're leaving," says the gruff voice of the big bodyguard. "The only job you had to do was land a well-connected mate. Produce the next generation. You can't even do that properly without fucking it up. Wait until we get home—you will be lucky to leave your room. Father will be selling your ass to the highest bidder.

You better hope that we don't find that guy who called you..." His angry voice fades away.

There's shuffling, stomping, and finally, blessed silence. I think everyone has left.

"It is okay, urm...Forrest. You don't have to come out. Liz—"

Everyone but Harry.

There's rustling as if he's running his hand through his blond hair. I can picture it, as I've seen him do that hundreds of times. He lets out a puff of air. "Liz left. It's over. She was cheating. I can't...I can't trust her anymore. The phone call, you did that. You did that for me. God, it hurts. I feel sick. I am sure other shifters wouldn't care, but I'd rather be alone than that." The door squeaks—he must be leaning against it. I let out a whine, and I bang my head against the closed door in frustration. I can't talk. I can't console him.

After a few minutes, I wiggle about, trying to get comfortable. My bottom is hurting. The floor is hard, and my bum is bony. It's going numb, like the rest of me.

Glancing around the room, I spot the mirror above the sink. It feels like it's miles away from my slumped position on the floor.

But I get the most overwhelming urge. I need to see.

I don't know how I manage to get off the floor. The phone falls, forgotten.

I wobble on my feet. I brace myself against the narrow walls. My useless toes scrabble, trying to get a grip on the tiles. I lunge and grab hold of the sink. I hold on to it. Lift my head and look.

Hello Skeletor...My face is gaunt, and my features are way too big for my face. My eyes are huge and wide with shock. My left eye is an unnatural gold, and my right eye is almost gold apart from a sliver of green pooling at the bottom of my iris. The green sits at the bottom of my eye unevenly, practically taken over by the gold. But it is green. The green I didn't imagine in my head. The green I dreamed of.

I touch my forehead to the mirror.

Oh, and my hair, it's not red. No, it's a shocking shade of pink. I huff out a breath. I am a skull with hair, fucking pink hair and freaky eyes.

Fuck my life.

CURSED WOLF

Harry is continuing to talk to me from the door, and John is still talking on the phone. But it's all white noise. I am so overwhelmed. Even in my human form, I am not normal.

My skin is so pale it's translucent, the blue of my veins standing out. The black of my dog collar stands out on my pale neck. I don't understand how it shifted with me—it must be the magic in the collar. The rest of me, my body...I am supposed to be an adult, but my tiny childlike frame is hideous.

I let out a silent sob that hurts my chest. I am repulsive.

CHAPTER
FOUR

I AM SITTING on the closed toilet seat. I have used the available hand towels as padding underneath my bony bum—not that that is much use. My skeletal body aches.

It feels like hours since I called John. The phone is still on the floor by the door, abandoned. I can't make myself get up and grab it to check if he's still on the line. I can no longer hear him from where I am perched.

The constant pain from my long-ago shattered pelvis has gone, and my skinny legs show no signs of the poorly healed trauma. I'm shaking, and the toilet seat is squeaking in protest.

I don't know if all this is a dream; it doesn't feel real.

Emotionally I feel like an autumn leaf: dead but still clinging desperately to the branch and dreading the next gust of wind.

When the knock on the door comes, I start, burning my leg on the radiator next to me. I let out a little hiss between my teeth. Bloody hell, this still isn't a dream.

"Forrest, it's me, your brother. Can you open the door for me, please."

I peer at the door and nibble on my bottom lip. I take a deep breath and pull myself to my feet, using the wall and the toilet as leverage. I find it challenging to place my feet onto the floor. They want to curl inwards instead of staying flat.

Ha, it's a bloody miracle, and it's thanks to a shitload of adrenaline that I managed to get this useless bag of bones into the bathroom in the first place.

I'm pathetic.

I grit my teeth and use the wall to steady myself. I decide that I have little choice but to chuck myself at the door and hope for the best.

Oof. I hit the door with a thump. Once I am steady and in no danger of falling, I attempt a little bit of modesty. I pull the horrendous pink hair forward to conceal as much of my body as I can. Weirdly, the hair is mega thick and long—it reaches halfway down my thighs.

My fingers fumble with the lock, and it takes a few attempts to get the door open. The heavy door swings open with an ominous creak.

I nervously peek up through my hair at the huge man in the doorway. I probably resemble a pink Cousin Itt from the Addams family. John, my brother, is broader and taller than the door frame—he dwarfs me. John has to hunch over slightly to see into the small bathroom. He towers over me, frowning as his green eyes quickly take me in. He doesn't look impressed. I have a massive urge to close the door and lock it.

"You didn't bother to get her any clothes?" John asks, directing his question behind him.

"Well...urm, I can grab something of mine—Forrest hasn't got anything," Harry answers quietly. "I am sorry. I didn't think."

There's the sound of movement in the hallway. My brother moves slightly to the side of the door, and a man appears next to him. He grunts and slips a backpack from his shoulder. Unzipping the bag, he hands my brother some clothing.

John steps towards me but then freezes in place. Total horror crosses his face. I flinch. Without my seeing him move, he has Harry by the throat, pinned to the hallway wall.

Shit! What did I do?

"You put a fucking dog collar on my sister!" John growls menacingly into Harry's face.

"Not me—Vincent," Harry sputters, going red and desperately clawing at the big hand around his throat.

I freak out. My fight-or-flight must have kicked in, as I am trembling with the adrenaline rushing through me.

Heart pounding, I can't get enough air into my lungs. I take a step back.

I'm going the wrong way. I should be trying to stop my brother from hurting Harry. What am I doing? But I can't stop. I can't even stand up properly. I'm too weak. This body is too alien. Knowing all that still doesn't stop me from feeling disgusted with myself. I am a coward.

Even worse, I scramble to close the door. The shifter with the backpack blocks me. "John, now is not the time—you're frightening your sister," he says. John's head snaps around, and he drops his hold on Harry. Harry takes big gulps of air. His face is red, and he's shaking.

I'm so sorry, Harry. This is all my fault. God, I'm surprised he didn't wet himself—that scared the crap out of me. A hellhound grabs hold of your throat like that, I would sure pee a little.

"I will be talking to Vincent later," John says, shoving Harry back into the wall. Harry nods, dropping his eyes. "Now fuck off." Harry visibly deflates. He nods, keeping his eyes fixed on the floor submissively. *Please don't go!* I mentally scream as I watch Harry shuffle down the hallway. He disappears from my line of sight.

I dimly notice the other two hulking shifters, who must have arrived with John and the Backpack Hound, and they're all staring at my neck.

I jolt with the sudden realisation; I want to scream at them, *Bloody hell, still naked here, guys!* I weakly tug at the bathroom door. The hellhound's foot is in the way.

John steps back in my direction, a soft smile on his face...it looks wrong. It's that kind of smile that a predator gives its prey just before he starts eating.

Shit, he's scary.

I need to trust him. But he's scary.

He is my brother...but he left me here to rot.

My conflicting thoughts make me feel as if my head is going to pop off.

"It is okay, Forrest. It's okay." He holds both hands up to me in supplication. I flinch. "I'm sorry, sweetheart, that I lost my temper. I will try my best not to do that again. I am sorry. I want to help you get into these clothes, okay? They're going to be a little big on you, but we will make them work, right?" John's voice is soft. The backpack-shifter hands him the clothing that he dropped while attacking Harry. John holds up his hand, the one that isn't holding the clothing, towards me. I warily eye it. "Is that okay?"

I want to shake my head no.

I know I can't do any of this by myself. There's no way I will leave this house alive without his help.

I reluctantly nod.

John puts the black jumper over my head, and then, like he's dressing a child, threads his hand through the sleeve. Taking hold of my wrist, John gently guides my hand out. He repeats the process with my other arm. He then kneels in front of me and helps me with the black jogging bottoms. The clothing is ridiculously huge.

"Okay, let's get you to your bedroom. Doctor Ross can meet us and check you over." John turns and strides away down the hallway, expecting everybody to follow. I take a wobbling step forward and find myself tipping to the right. Before I can fall, the Backpack Hound scoops me up in his arms. I tense and let out a horrified squeak of surprise.

"Oh, hush now, Forrest, you're okay, I promise I'm not gonna hurt you. I promise that I'm not gonna let anyone else hurt you either—that includes you. You're gonna hurt yourself if I let you walk. So let me help you, at least until you get your legs figured out again," he says in a low, soft tone. He surprises another squeak out of me by gently stroking my hair away from my face. His humongous hands pull the mass of hair around so that it's in front of me. It pools in my lap like candyfloss. "Hush...this is hard, isn't it? Everything that is happening is some scary shit. Please ...please let me help you." His steady grey eyes are weirdly comforting; they stand out against his dark hair and skin tone. His whole expression is kind, and I believe him. "I don't know what you've been through...I know you can't talk about it. Heck, you do all of your talking with those big frightened gold eyes. Sometimes, it's better to bury the bad things until you're strong enough to deal with them, so that you can keep moving forward one step at a time to make sure your demons can't keep up. You understand?" I blink at him. "Okay?" I take a big breath, release it, and nod. Miraculously I let myself relax, and I lean into his massive chest as he lumbers down the hallway with me tucked safely in his arms.

We follow in the wake of my brother. Within minutes, we're at my bedroom door. It's kind of surreal as I haven't seen this room in, well, forever.

CHAPTER
FIVE

I SIT on the bed and glance around my old bedroom; I can't remember it being so big. It smells of dust and forgotten memories.

Everything is exactly how I left it: books on the shelves, an abandoned notepad on the table next to the bed. I was never allowed to put up posters. My mum was convinced that they would mark the walls. But if I had, they would still be here.

The room is like a time capsule.

I glimpse a silver photo frame alone on a shelf, surrounded by a thick layer of dust. It's a photo of my mum, my baby sister Grace, and me. If I could walk, I would pick it up, maybe hold it close to my chest, pull it to my nose and never stop staring at it. God, I miss them so much.

For my sanity, I force myself to look away.

Everything in here feels like someone else's life, another girl's life; it doesn't belong to me anymore.

Doctor Ross doesn't look like what I imagined. He's dressed in black fatigues like the other hellhounds, and there is no white coat in sight. With his big build, bald head, and intelligent blue eyes, he looks like a soldier.

He isn't messing around, with his extensive array of medical equipment. It's like he has brought a whole hospital with him. I have no idea why we're doing this here. This is crazy. If they're attempting to make me feel comfortable in familiar surroundings, they're doing a piss-poor job. We would be better off in the garden or far, far away from this accursed house.

The collar is removed immediately from my neck. Doctor Ross examines it, and he dictates his findings into some sort of magical video-camera-and-fancy-tablet combo. John has to leave the room for a few minutes to get control of himself when they realise that the collar is an electric shock one.

How do you stop a wolf from running away? You snap their pelvis like a Polo mint. Then you put a magical collar on them that knocks them out if they crawl too far. The fancy collar is also voice-activated and can be electrified as punishment if they don't come to call like a good doggy—yeap, fun times.

Doc R uses a complicated-looking scanner to take my vitals. He waves the thing at me and it automatically processes my height, weight, heartbeat, blood pressure, and body fat. Samples of my blood and saliva are taken and added to the data. Huh, it even produces a little chart of me on the screen. It flashes red, and my eyes widen as it beeps an urgent tone. That doesn't sound good. Doc R frowns at the screen and taps the device until it's silenced. He then examines my eyes. He uses a small penlight scanner that flashes various lights, making me dizzy. He's so close to me that our noses almost touch. Luckily his breath is minty.

My head pounds and my eyes hurt.

"Have your eyes always been this colour?" he asks me. I shake my head no.

"Forrest's eyes were the same colour green as my own. Her hair was red, and if I correctly remember, she was around the same height as she is now. Maybe an inch or two shorter before she shifted," John replies on my behalf.

"That is interesting. What age was your first shift?" Doc R asks. I start to hold up my fingers to answer him, but frustratingly I can't seem to get the digits to work, so again John explains for me.

"She was nine."

"Nine years old...that is extremely young. I've never heard anybody shifting before sixteen." Doc R turns away and adds everything to the tablet. "How long has it been since she first shifted?"

Well, that's the question of the day, isn't it? How long have I been stuck as a wolf? I observe John, terrified of his answer.

I hold my breath.

John clears his throat and rubs the back of his neck. We make eye contact. His eyes are sad. "It's been over fourteen years."

The room goes a little black, and I see black spots in front of my eyes. I am glad to be sitting down; otherwise, I think I'd be falling on my bum.

Fourteen years.

Fourteen.

"Breathe, Forrest. You're okay."

I gasp in a breath and rapidly blink. I focus on the kind grey eyes that are looking back at me with concern.

The Backpack Hound is holding my face in his hands. When did that happen? I nod. I am okay. I am okay. All I can do is nod. I take another shaky breath.

Fourteen years as a wolf. Shit shit shit.

The kind hellhound nods back at me, gives me a small smile, stands from his squat, and steps away.

Both Doc R and John gaze at me with concern.

"Forrest, are you all right to continue?" I nod at the doctor—bloody hell, stop nodding, you look like a bobblehead, your head is going to pop off. I instead give him a shaky thumbs-up. "Well, hopefully I can give you a little bit of control so you know what is happening to you. Okay?" He places the fancy tablet in my hands. Even though it's lightweight, I can't hold it up. I prop the tablet on my lap; it digs into my thigh.

The text swims slightly in front of my eyes as I try to focus on the words. It takes a few seconds for my brain to adjust. The data, the words, make zero sense.

"You are emaciated. I'm unsure why that is, at the moment. We will have to talk about your diet, as you're missing essential vitamins and minerals. I have never seen these kinds of dangerous results in a shifter." He looks at me sternly, and I find myself physically leaning away from him. Not my fault. "It is very concerning. If you hadn't shifted today, I calculate that you wouldn't have lasted much longer. The results sho—"

"What?" John barks. I flinch, and the tablet tumbles onto the bed. "I don't understand why. What do you mean, she 'wouldn't have lasted much longer'? Forrest? What the hell have you been doing to yourself!" John's whole face morphs as he bares his teeth. His rage, directed at me, fills the room.

I sit frozen on the bed as the massive hellhound barrels towards me; a deep growl resonates in his chest. My lips disappear between my teeth, and I bite down hard to stop the whine that's bubbling up in my throat. It's better to be silent. I avert my eyes. I shove the tablet further away, and I attempt to make myself smaller. I hunch in on myself, using my hair as a shield. I avert my face close my eyes and prepare for the pain.

When nothing happens, I peek through my hair, and the Backpack Hound is standing directly in front of me, rigid, blocking John.

I blow out a breath. Wide-eyed, I take in the situation. Is he...is he protecting me?

"I made a promise. What are you planning to do, John?" he admonishes.

"I wasn't going to hurt her," John snarls. He turns and stomps back across the room, his fists clenched at his sides, his shoulders tight and a muscle ticking in his jaw. "I'm too fucking busy to deal with this shit—if she wants to kill herself, she can crack on."

The Backpack Hound silently moves back to his position against the wall as if nothing happened.

Bloody hell, what...why is John angry with me? He left me here with them. It was John who didn't come back...as if I had a choice in what I ate?

Betrayed. That's what I feel, which is ludicrous. For there to be betrayal, there has to be trust, and I don't trust John.

I study my trembling hands. Wow, pack doesn't mean anything to my brother. I don't mean anything. What was John going to do if the other hellhound hadn't stood in front of me? Hit me? I was right not to trust him. I puff out a breath. I don't feel the need to scream or shout my case. Not that I can...I curl inward, a familiar feeling of inadequacy piling up inside of me. John is never going to believe me over them, so if I could talk, there would be no point—it would be a waste of words. I tense to ward off the full-body shakes and lift my chin.

Doc R, looking pained, clears his throat. "Well, it is something we will have to make a priority. From now on you will be heavily monitored, to find the cause." He drops another stern look at me. "Theoretically, being stuck in your wolf form should not have affected your growth rate." He leans over and retrieves the tablet. I flinch away, and the doctor grimaces. He steps back, clears his throat, and continues, "Your height, according to previous estimates on your medical charts as a child, should be at least six-foot. Unfortunately, as you can see in the data—" Doc R points to the screen—"you are five-foot-two, and approximately three stone underweight. Your build is also a concern—you would be small for a human, and as a shifter, it's unheard-of to be so petite." He shakes his head in disappointment. "With weight gain your overall body aesthetic can be enhanced. We can't do anything to improve your bone structure and height. It is permanent damage—at twenty-three, there is no fixing that any further." He pokes the screen again. My eyes cross. I don't bother to focus on the data. "Your eye- and hair-colour is a side effect of long-term magical damage," Doc R continues. "Shifters are not meant to be in animal form for so long. There should be a balance within us—no shifter can stay in animal form indefinitely, or the other way around, and not shift—which is even worse. To have lasted fourteen years and not lost yourself is impressive." Doc R taps the tablet again. "I am sure we will work it out as we go along. The good news is, we can improve your body weight with a controlled diet. Your natural healing will help. Unfortunately, your eyes will remain as they are, an amber-gold colour with the slight sectoral heterochromia." He points to my right eye. "Although I think your eyes are quite beautiful," Doc R says with a smile. "Your skin will improve with daylight exposure and a better-balanced diet. Your hair pigment has gone—again, a similar reaction to that of your eyes." He tilts his head to the side. "I am surprised it is pink and not white." He looks at John and then back at me. John is standing as far away as he can get. He must hate me.

"What I do recommend is hospitalisation for a few weeks." Doc R holds up a hand as if he expects me to object. "Just to get you healthy, walking, and talking. You need specialised help. Let's get you back to normal, okay?" He smiles.

I dare to peek at John, and he stiffly nods. So I nod also.

I am up for anything to get me out of this bloody house.

Fuck my life. I don't even look like a shifter. I look like an unhealthy human. It couldn't be that I was just stuck in wolf form for fourteen years. Oh no, when fate, that fickle bitch, finally allows me to change back to my human form, I'm an even bigger freak! I'm never going to blend into shifter society looking like this.

Rage and hopelessness fill me. My vision goes hazy.

I feel sick, my mouth is dry, and there's a lump in my throat that I can't swallow.

I close my eyes and simply breathe.

Shit, listen to me moaning. I need a slap. I need to get a grip on myself. I can handle this calmly. The rage can't have me. I am human-shaped—forget the height thing, forget the hair and the eyes. I am me: every cloud and all that crap.

Today I promised myself that I was going to own this shit. It's a billy bonus that I'm alive and that I'm getting away from this house and the pack. I'm getting out of this shithole, and I'm never coming back.

I should be dancing with joy, not whining like a baby.

I open my eyes. Doc R and John are whispering in the corner of the room. The Backpack Hound—whose name I still don't know, as John has yet to introduce us—is looking around my room, quietly sniffing. I tip my head to the side, curious. What is he doing?

"John, the only scent of Forrest is from today," he says quietly. Oh wow, he is a smart one. "If this is her room, why can't I smell her?"

As a unit, all three shifters turn and stare at me. Wow, they're synchronised. An old Take That song plays in my head. I wonder, can they do it again to music? I want to cackle maniacally.

Well, gentlemen, I want to say, it's because this hasn't been my room for fourteen years, obviously.

CHAPTER
SIX

We are going on a bizarre treasure hunt, like a bunch of scary pirates. Everyone is now fascinated and focused on finding out where I sleep. I'm back in Backpack Hound's arms, and like a helpful interactive treasure map, I point the way to my room.

I can hear John's teeth grind harder and more loudly as we leave the house and go further into the grounds. Come on, I want to say. You don't have to be Einstein to realise it's shit. Hello, magical dog collar.

I am kind of amused in a manic, sick sort of way at how upset they all are when we arrive, crammed into the small, dark garage. The garage is set away from the main house. It's a modern metal one, which makes it extra cold in winter and extra toasty in summer. It was purchased just for me.

I think what is causing all the drama is the main feature of the room: the silver cage that sits in the middle of the concrete floor, with the creepy drain in the centre.

Even in my human form, I can smell my scent in the air. It permeates the building—ahh, home sweet home.

"Get Vincent," my brother says quietly. "Get Vincent here now." One of his guys disappears, and we are left looking silently at the cage. Well, they're staring; I've seen this shit before.

My Chauffeur Hound—formerly known as Backpack Hound—is standing in the corner with me still in his arms. He's standing as far away as he can from the cage. He is holding me a little more tightly to his chest and is unconsciously running his fingers through my hair. It feels nice, the hand in my hair. Everything else hurts. Being held hurts. I am bony, and every bone feels like it's touching every other bone and somehow grinding together. It isn't a pleasant feeling, but I try my best to ignore it.

My brother is standing like a statue. I never thought I'd say that someone is radiating fury, but John is. He's pissed. Boy, is he pissed.

Oh, oh...My eyes widen.

Wait a minute...I blink. Yes, John's hands are on fire. Blue flames dance across his skin. Oh crap, John is radiating not just emotionally...my brother is on fire like, literally. Wow. The warm garage is even getting hotter. The lack of air makes me yawn.

Wary I peer up at the hellhound holding me. Shit, I hope he isn't suddenly going to burst into flames.

I tense in the hellhound's arms as Vincent is shoved unceremoniously into the garage five minutes later. The guy who went to fetch him wipes his hands on his fatigues with blatant disgust and steps back outside, blocking the exit. Seeing Vincent here in the place where he regularly used to hurt me...I can't stop the trickle of fear.

I don't want to be in here with Vincent. I don't want to be here at all.

I screw my eyes shut and count silently down from ten.

Be brave. I'm pretty much shitting myself.

Be brave. There's not a thing I can do about any of this.

Be brave. I'm along for the ride.

The worst is behind me and I can do this, I can control myself. The worst is behind me, and my world has changed. They see me again. I'm a girl again.

Don't look back; keep moving forward. Surely Vincent can't hurt me while the hellhounds are here? That bone-deep fear I have lived with forever slowly changes into something a little more manageable.

Be brave. I can do this. I open my eyes.

No one is speaking.

The overhead strip-light buzzes in the silence, and the heat from John's magic makes the sheet metal pop and clang. The thick dust-filled cobwebs hanging from the roof trusses sway. The minutes tick away.

John eyes the cage. Vincent nervously watches John. It's the first time I have seen Vincent nervous. A bead of sweat runs down the side of his face.

Well, this is awkward.

Doc R steps forward and inspects the cage. He's too big to enter the actual enclosure, and he's careful not to graze the silver bars. Crouching, he pays particular attention to the stained floor. The magical camera he used in my examination is recording. It bobs about in the air, following his movements.

I peek back at John as he struggles for control over his fire magic. His body shakes with the effort, and his eyes are closed. The blue flames weirdly drip from his hands onto the concrete at his feet—the flames hiss and spark. I've never seen my brother struggle with his fire magic before. Not that I know John anymore, we're strangers, but his lack of control is frightening.

The doctor turns from his inspection and switches his full attention to Vincent. I think Doc R understands that John isn't quite ready to deal with him, so he takes control of the situation.

"Why the cage?" he asks conversationally. Vincent shrugs.

My Chauffeur Hound tenses the muscles in his arms, and they bulge. He lets out a growl. It vibrates around me. The hair at the back of my neck stands up. It's a bloody scary growl. Before I can clamp my lips against the sound, a small whine escapes. With a jerk, he immediately stops growling. He gently pats my head as if to say, "There, there," and starts the hair thing again.

"Why?" Doc R asks again, his tone polite.

Vincent huffs, shrugs again, and then he surprisingly answers. "It was feral. John dumped us with a fucking feral wolf." He shakes his head. "No, you can't even call that thing a wolf—it's just a dirty dog. My father, my sister, were killed because of it, and he decided to dump it here. For us to look after, to keep it safe? Fuck that. You think I was gonna let it stay in the house?" Vincent huffs out a laugh, sniffs, and wipes a hand across his sweaty face. He turns his full attention to John, demonstrating how stupid he is or revealing to everyone that he has a death wish. "Be glad that it's alive. Thank me." He points to the flaming floor in front of John's feet. "Get on your fucking knees and thank me!" Vincent's voice echoes around the garage. His voice drops ominously. "'Cause not a day has gone past that I don't want to put my hands around its throat and strangle the life out of it." Vincent swings around and points at me, his dark eyes furious. "That fucking bitch killed my pack."

Well, that escalated quickly.

I sniff. As if we all didn't know who Vincent was talking about—no need to point. I try to disappear into Chauffeur Hound's bulk. For those few moments, while Vincent's hate-filled attention is on me, the hellhound turns me slightly away so Vincent can't see me, and more importantly, so I can't see him. I have never been more grateful. I pat Chauffeur Hound's chest, and when he glances down, I attempt a small wobbly smile. The big hellhound frowns.

The silence in the garage is deafening.

Prompted by the hellhound's frown, it slowly registers, what Vincent is insinuating. I mentally replay the conversation. The dawning horror of what he said starts to sink in. Vincent thinks I killed my mum? Does he think I'm the reason Grace died? What the fuck. Is that the reason why Vincent and Jason hate me? The reason for everything? I rub my chest. I open my mouth to explain, to shout at him that it was his precious father Dave who was ultimately responsible for their deaths. My pack is dead because Dave fucked up.

It was not me. It bloody wasn't me.

I swear on my own life I didn't do anything wrong. I followed the rules.

But the words don't come.

Instead, a raw, soulful whine leaves my lips.

Frustration and fear swirl around in my chest, cramping my tummy and tightening my throat so I can't take a full breath. Oh God, my brother doesn't believe him, does he? Is that why he left me without a backward glance? Is that why he was angry?

A horrible thought bounces around in my head. What happens if I'm wrong? What if I made everything up, and everything that happened was my fault? Perhaps my version of events didn't happen the way I remembered?

Doc R ignores Vincent's outburst and after a few minutes, calmly asks, "Has she always been in this cage? In this garage?" He looks about in disgust, toeing the cage with his boot. "Where are the claw marks?" Vincent looks blankly back at the doctor. Vincent is breathing harder, flexing his fingers. "Have you seen a feral shifter, Vincent? I have. It is such a sad and frightening thing to see. The rage..." Doc R shakes his head and brings his arm to his mouth to demonstrate his next words, snapping his teeth. "A feral would be quite happy to chew its leg off or rip its mate to pieces to escape confinement. A feral would make short work of this cage. It would smash itself against the bars, even though they are silver, without care—and do you know what?" He points at the floor. "Because this cage isn't bolted down, it would take not even a minute for a feral to get out."

Doc R steps into Vincent's personal space. He leans forward, his nose almost brushing Vincent's. In a quiet tone that sends a shiver down my spine, he asks, "Why did you cage her? A nine-year-old child? A female shifter in need of care. You said she was feral? Where is the proof?" Pointing at the cage angrily, he raises his voice, losing his calm. "Where are the claw marks? How long did you cage her? When did you put a frightened little girl unable to shift out of her wolf form. In. A. Cage!"

Vincent quickly backs away from the angry doctor.

The corner of his lip and eye twitch sporadically. "About ten years." He rubs his hand across his mouth. "I had it in that cage for about ten years. Until Harry came home from school, the kid...the kid, he urm, he got upset—"

"Ten years?" Doc R repeats incredulously, throwing up his arms into the air. "What is wrong with you?" The doctor turns away from Vincent, and he looks imploringly at my brother. "John, are you listening to this?" Doc R rubs the back of his bald head with frustration. John remains unresponsive.

I let out a sigh that's more exhaustion than frustration, much to my chagrin. Do I have to be here?

"Look, it came back," Vincent says with a snarl. "My pack didn't! I knew it was at fault. Grace died; my two-year-old little sister died. My dad died, and his mate died. You talk about female shifters—what about Grace! Why the fuck didn't the real killer, the real reason my pack died, get punished?" Vincent puffs out his chest while I try to make myself smaller. "I punished the dog, something that you fucks didn't have the balls to do. So don't start this shit." He thumps his chest. "I am not ashamed. I did what I had to do."

"I sent Forrest home so that she could be with the pack," says John. Finally, he starts to address the elephant in the room. I listen intently, my body tense with fear. Is this where he agrees that Vincent is right? Will John ask Chauffeur Hound to put me back into the cage? I peek up at the hellhound through my lashes, trying to disguise my growing horror. Will he obey?

God, I don't want to be here!

"I had no idea you'd do something as evil as this. I knew your father was rotten. I didn't realise that the rot went so deep and into his sons. My mother was adamant that you could be trusted; she was blind." I notice that the flame in his hand is now entirely in John's control. It dances across his palm, changing colours among red, orange, yellow, and blue. It's mesmerising. "I returned a traumatised child to a nest of vipers, and I didn't even visit. Except for the odd phone, call I left you to it." The flame continues its dance. "I was too busy with my vengeance, hunting down the perpetrators, to even sit down and tell you the whole story of what happened. The truth about your father and what he did." The flame jumps to his other hand. "At the time, I thought it would be better that you didn't know. That it was healthier for the pack to not dwell on things you couldn't change. I also didn't want the pack name tainted, my mother's memory tarnished." As John continues, Vincent flings his arms into the air with frustration. His head is shaking vehemently in denial. "Forrest was a child—where in that stupid fucking head of yours did you imagine a nine-year-old girl could be responsible? Is that your bullshit fucking excuse?" The tightness in my chest loosens, and I take a full breath. "I was wrong in not giving you the full story. I made a massive error in judgment. I'm going to make it right. Your pack and the whole of shifter society is going to know the truth by the end of the day. I shouldn't have kept it a secret for so long."

Apart from the flame in his hands, John hasn't moved a muscle; his eyes remain closed. I have a feeling that if John looked at Vincent right now, he would probably burn him to a crisp.

John opens his eyes. "Have you seen her, Vincent, have you had a chance to see what you have done? Look in her eyes and tell me you see a monster. Then do the same while looking in the mirror. You, your pack...you are so fucking done."

Vincent looks away, unable to meet John's gaze. He's still shaking his head in denial, his hands clenched into fists. I don't think whatever John tells him will be enough. His hatred for me is too deeply ingrained.

John turns his head and examines me. "I find out about all this, and what we have discovered so far is just the tip of the iceberg, isn't it, Forrest? The tip of what you had to suffer." His head drops to his chest, and he runs his hand across the back of his neck.

Wow, was that an apology? I'm left more confused than vindicated.

Vincent looks away with a snarl. His whole body jerks when his eyes catch the half-full bag in the far corner, near the hose pipe on the wall. He surreptitiously tries to block the bag with his body. A small sound escapes me. No one else is watching.

John turns to leave the garage, his head lowered. As he passes us, I cringe away as he squeezes Chauffeur Hound's shoulder. The hound grunts an acknowledgement.

Vincent dabs at his forehead. His knees sag in relief.

"John," Chauffeur Hound says, intervening in John's exit. "What is in that sack in the corner?" The smart hound hasn't missed Vincent's movement at all.

"What sack...what the fuck..." John turns. He clips Vincent's shoulder on the way past, pushing him intentionally against the silver cage. Vincent lets out a hiss of pain and the smell of burnt skin wafts into the air.

John stands in front of the bag; he kicks it so he can read the label. I look away, burying my head against the hound's shoulder. I have no idea why I feel embarrassed and ashamed, but I do, and my chest hurts again.

"'Working Dog Mix.'" John reads the label out loud. "Dog food? What the hell is this..." It takes just a second for everything in his head to click. "You fed my sister fucking dry dog food!"

All hell breaks loose.

John, urm, burnt the garage down. Full-on magical meltdown —he completely lost his shit. You would have thought he'd been offered a handful of dog food for dinner by his reaction.

On a positive note, at least Doc R now knows about my diet. Mmmm, dog food, crunchy and nutritious.

We all managed to scarper out before he went boom. Nobody was hurt, except for maybe John's pride at his loss of control.

I wasn't sad to see the garage burn.

If I could, I would have asked for Chauffeur Hound to break out the celebratory marshmallows so I could toast them on the flames. Maybe do a happy dance with the joy of never having to see that particular cage again. Never be forced to sleep underneath that roof. But my hound carries me into the house, mumbling something about silver particles.

Huh, silver and marshmallows might not be that tasty after all.

CHAPTER
SEVEN

THE ATMOSPHERE in this lovely sitting room is seriously uncomfortable; the cheery yellow room with delicate furniture is full of silent, angry shifters. With the energy coming off each of them, you could boil a kettle. No one is sitting down apart from me, and it's unnerving. It's as if I'm still in my wolf form, forever looking up at the angry people towering over me.

I'm all trussed up in a chair in this cosy room, waiting for the show-and-tell part of the evening to start. My Nanny Hound—formerly known as Chauffeur Hound—has tucked me into the chair with a soft fluffy throw and about ten squishy cushions. At least I feel the most physically comfortable I've been since I shifted. My tummy is full for the first time in what feels like forever. I hum. I'd have been happy to eat a scabby rat—any form of protein would have been perfectly fine to me. I ate chicken noodle soup, it was served in a bowl, and it was delicious. My imaginary food dinners...yeah, total bullshit.

I have plans, big aspirations for when all this crap is over and I'm free. I'm going to hunt myself some real chocolate cake, a whole cake to myself, as soon as possible.

John hasn't explained anything about why I'm sitting here. I'm presuming that he wants me here for some meeting or big Scooby-Doo reveal. Doc R wanted me to go straight to the shifter private hospital, but John overruled him. I don't like John very much at the moment. Even if I could speak and ask to leave, I have a feeling I'd still be ignored. My opinion doesn't matter. It's better to fight the battles that you can win and sit out the ones that you can't.

All I want to do is get out of this bloody house.

The whole pack is here, luckily on the other side of the room. I don't want to sit around in the same room as Vincent and Jason. Why would I? I'm sitting here like a target is painted on my forehead. Useless and vulnerable. I can't speak or run. I wouldn't even be able to bash someone over the head with a cushion. So fighting is out, and if it all kicks off? I'm going to hide under my cover like a boss. God, that thought pricks at my pride.

Two members of the shifter council have also graced us with their presence. I have no idea why they're here. We haven't been introduced—hell, no one has been introduced to me. I keep catching them casting me strange calculating looks, looks that I have no idea how to interpret. If they leave me alone, I'll leave them alone.

But if they come after me, I'll fuck them up. I rein in my growl and force myself not to glare at them, glare at everyone. I fidget in the chair. My strange thoughts and rage are unnerving. Yeah, I might be a tad angry and seriously unbalanced. The frustration, anxiety, and fear thrumming through my head at the moment is troublesome. Troublesome? I huff. Understatement of the century, and it's freaking me out.

Heck, I'm either so frightened I can't function, or so angry I want to burn the world.

The lost human part of me doesn't know whether to crawl away and hide, or worse, start screaming. Any minute now, I feel as if my anger is going to bubble up and I am going to snap. Break apart, and nothing is going to be left but an angry, bitter person.

My sanity is fraying.

To keep my sanity intact, I need to pack my shit up, as the hound suggested hours ago. To bury everything deep, I desperately jam the memories further and further down until they no longer exist. Pack them into boxes.

Boxes in my head that echo with my screams.

I shiver and pull the cover to my chin. It smells clean.

It's impossible to bury the memories if the two evil bastards that contributed to them are standing across the room.

I want out of this house.

I focus on the other people in the room. My brother has called in more hellhounds as backup. As well as the original three, another six have arrived. Ten hellhounds, including John. I tilt my head to the side in thought. I watch the two hounds stationed across the room, the only hounds that I can currently see from my seated position.

Hellhounds have twice the strength of standard shifters even without using their fire magic. The hounds in this room could probably start and finish a war. Natural walking weapons. It's puzzling to me that the massive shifters also feel the need to display impressive amounts of silver. I bet they carry double that with the silver I can't see. I'm surprised the hellhounds don't jingle and clink when they walk. It's all a little bit of overkill. What are they all doing here?

Nanny Hound answers my silent question.

"They are here to keep John under control. He is worried that he will either set fire to the house or kill the pack. It's a precaution, plus he hates the paperwork that killing always brings."

All I got from that was, John needs nine guys to stop him. Nine super-shifters...God, he's a total scary bastard. Why can't he control his magic? It makes what the hellhound behind me did, putting himself between John and me, more impressive. He promised to keep me safe, and he did.

John, who has been talking to the two council members, now steps into the middle of the room. Gaining everyone's attention, he holds up his hand to ask for silence.

John starts to talk. He drones on, giving a full report on what he has discovered so far. I let John's words flow over me. I sit and play with a loose thread on the fluffy cover. I focus on the thread and the movement of my fingers.

I am back to feeling like I'm not here, like this whole time, I have been dreaming.

Instead, I think about the past. Harry helped to get me out of the cage, although I still found myself in there for regular punishment. At least I wasn't in there permanently. I had the chance to breathe fresh air, see the sky, feel the sun and the rain on my fur—the grass on my paws and the dirt in my claws.

In the early years, I convinced myself that someone, namely my brother, would come and rescue me. But it never happened, and John, he never came. It took my shifting back and making a desperate phone call for John to come. Ultimately I saved myself.

I can't quite believe that it took my getting angry with Liz, my protectiveness over Harry, to force the shift back into my human form. Oh my God, when I think about it, Liz's wayward vagina helped me! I pull up the soft cover to hide my amusement. When nothing else could, it stepped up to the challenge. Go vulva magic. I bet Liz now wishes that she had stabbed me when she had the opportunity.

I focus again on John when he starts talking about the history of what happened with our pack and their deaths. He has full details, including surveillance footage—it's all pieced together like a factual police report. He goes through it in a monotone, as if he isn't talking about his mother and sisters. John has the facts, but he didn't live it, and he didn't see with his own eyes what happened.

I nudge open the imaginary box in my head and let myself remember.

CHAPTER
EIGHT

Fourteen years ago

Manchester Airport is busy. I arrive at the terminal and immediately want to find a corner and hide. People are everywhere, humans and creatures. The check-in lines are full. People with baggage trolleys get in the way of people with small suitcases on wheels. One lady runs over my toes and a man going the other way elbows me in the temple. *Oww!* I let out a growl that rumbles around in my chest. *Stop that, Forrest*, I think to myself.

I scamper past all the check-in desks, getting out of the way of the crazy, and find the blue seats where I am supposed to wait. With the people checking in and then going straight through to security, these seats are empty. I can see a clock on the flight information board, and the yellow digital clock flicks the numbers slowly.

Today has been crazy. My mum woke me up so early—middle-of-the-night early—and I automatically got dressed, like a firefighter getting ready for a call-out. I was so fast. Ever since I can remember, we have always had a plan, an emergency drill. Being a shifter is extremely dangerous when you are female—kidnapping is rife, and my mum is harsh with the whole reality of it. I have never been in any doubt that there's a target on my back. I have been taught from a young age to blend in and disappear, to go to certain busy places and wait.

The chair starts to get uncomfortable. Two hours pass and then three. I wiggle to ease the discomfort, too worried to move and traipse about in case my mum comes. She would be mad at me if I moved.

Come on, Mum, I chant in my head, bouncing on the seat.

After the fourth hour and no sightings of my mum, it's time to call in the cavalry. I'm going to ring my older brother, and by older, I mean mega old. I could ring my stepbrothers Vincent and Jason, but I don't trust them. Jason gives me the creeps. My mum adamantly declared that they were my bodyguards.

I huff. Bodyguards—what a joke. They're rubbish! If they were any good, I wouldn't be sitting here on my own.

It's now time to find a phone. I stand.

I know the scent-masker magic works for only so long, but I am hoping it's still keeping me covered. I am a wolf shifter. We do the whole wolf thing in our twenties—full furry wolf; it's incredible. My brother John is extraordinary; he can turn a single body-part wolf while keeping his human form. So he can turn his teeth or his claws. So cool, to think you'd never need a pair of scissors to open anything, ever. Just, bam, a claw and open-sesame. Not very hygienic if you're opening food, but way cool. I am so doing that when I'm older. I giggle to myself as I imagine what I could open.

I make my way towards the check-in desks, looking for some kind of phone. I should have had a spare mobile in my go-bag instead of having to hunt for a landline. But it was safer, Mum said, if I had nothing to trace me. Deciding to do the whole "I've lost my family please may I use your phone to ring my brother" routine at the information help desk, I head in that direction.

A scent hits me, and I freeze. *Demon.*

I try not to panic. So far, I have done everything by the book. I swallow down my nerves and take a deep breath. I have the scent masker on, and the airport stinks of thousands of creatures. Demons are poor trackers, and if I can blend in and use a phone and keep safe, get hold of John, then there's no reason why John can't help me find our pack. I keep moving slowly between the people. I am glad that I am still quite short. Shifters can grow huge, but at nine, I am still a tad over five-foot.

Instead of looking frantically around for the demon that I am smelling, I focus on walking straight ahead. The trick is to do the opposite of what you want to do. At the moment, I want to run and cry, grab the closest adult, and beg them to sort things out. But my mum didn't raise an idiot. She'd kill me if I did something so stupid, so I suck it up. I am going to do everything to keep myself safe and then I will find Grace, my mum, and my stepdad Dave.

I dodge a carry-on suitcase being pulled by an angry-looking human and spot a mobile phone in his jeans' back pocket. Perfect. I speed up, bump him, and stuff his phone up my sleeve.

My first thought is to get to the toilet, but to leave the busy part of the airport wouldn't be smart. I stand to the side and pull out the phone. It's password protected, but it's a simple Android handset. I hold the power button down for ten seconds, and then I hold the power button and volume-down button at the same time to factory-reset the phone. Bingo. After following the instructions on the screen, I'm now able to make a call without needing to input the password on the phone. I dial my brother's number. It rings. I glance around nervously.

"What!" My brother sounds grumpy.

"John, hey, it's Forrest—"

"Forrest, whose phone are you using?" Trust him to ask an unimportant question.

I roll my eyes. "John, that's not important. I ne—"

He interrupts again, a growl in his voice he speaks in his lecturing tone. "Forrest, you know this number is for emergencies. You can't ring me if Mum doesn't let you watch something on TV or she won't buy you some shit. I am too busy to—"

"John." I stop him mid-rant. The demon is close; I can smell him even more strongly now. The hair on the back of my neck is rising and I huff a little with panic. "John, will you listen to me—this is a bloody emergency," I whisper-shout at him, trying to cover my mouth and the phone with my hand. "I am at Manchester Airport, Terminal One, on my own. Mum, Grace, and dickhead Dave are missing. Mum woke me with a drill last night. I've been waiting over four hours at our meeting point at the airport. John, I smell a demon."

"Why didn't you start with that! I am on my way, but it's going to take me over an hour. I am going to see if anyone is closer. Give me a sec, stay on the phone." I can hear him shouting in the background. I glance around. Everybody is moving, and no one is looking at me. I turn my back to the airport concourse and lean my head on the wall. I feel so tired. So tired and so frightened.

"I have Owen, a hound who is twenty minutes away. I am going to ring you back and then you're gonna stay on this phone till he gets to you. You hear me, Forrest?"

"Yes, okay." I nod even though he can't see me.

"Okay, hang up. I'm ringing you back right now."

I end the call.

Immediately the phone starts to ring. I press to answer, and the phone is no longer in my hand.

I look up, and a scruffy human I have never seen before has hold of the phone. He puts it to his ear. "The little redhead can't speak at the moment." He drops the mobile to the floor and kicks it. It spins away, disappearing into the crowd.

Why did I turn my back? I want to smack my forehead in dejection. I have zero time to berate myself.

This guy is a human and I've got skills. I might be little, but I am fierce. He grabs hold of my upper arms. Instead of trying to pull away from him, I step into his body. I can't throw him or kick him; it would cause way too much attention. So instead, I drop to the floor. As he follows me down, trying to keep his hold on me, the position he is now in is blocking me from view. So I punch him between his legs. He lets go of me immediately with a squeak, cupping himself. As I stand up, I neatly throat-punch him.

Striding away, I shout, "That man is choking or having a heart attack. I think he needs help." A lady in a bright yellow jumper turns and takes in the situation.

"Oh my God, poor fella. Help, is there a doctor?"

Another lady with massive boobs in a cat jumper rushes to aid, her glorious chest bouncing in her excitement to help. "You poor man, I'll stay with you until help arrives, someone call an ambulance..."

I scurry away. Tilting my head, I check the airport clock. Damn it, I still have seventeen minutes before my brother's hound comes. Where is that damn demon? His potent scent, a sweetish sulphurous stink, surrounds me—it makes my nose itch.

I turn left, and another human slithers in front of me. He looks just as scruffy as the last guy, and he has a nasty smirk on his face.

Decisions, decisions—do I go through him or do I change direction? Before I can do anything, I'm yanked into a muscled chest. The scent of demon wraps chokingly around me.

"Now, Forrest, do not be doing anything stupid." The demon leans in close; his lips brush the shell of my ear as he creepily whispers. I shudder. "You want to see your pack, do you not? If you run or cause a scene, I will not hesitate to kill your mother. Do you understand me?" His whispery voice is harsh but with a very refined English accent. His cruel hands dig into my shoulders and the back of my neck. I nod, squeezing the top of my thighs. I worry I am going to embarrass myself and pee.

I don't feel brave or smart at this moment. I am a little girl who wants her mum.

Dimly I think about the hound that will be here in less than ten minutes. I need to cooperate, and we need to leave now—if the hound gets here and stops the demon from taking me, my mum will die. I can't let that happen. I need to keep calm and go with him. Hopefully the hound will arrive, see us leaving, and follow.

"I have been hunting you for such a long time, little Forrest. I've accepted an awful lot of money to procure you. A female shapeshifter, a rare little wolf, and what a pack line. So impressive. You're such a pretty little thing, with all that red hair." He runs his fingers through my hair, making me shiver with disgust. I fight the urge to slap his hand away.

"Did you know your pack line has produced the most females of any other?" the demon says as he starts to herd me towards the exit. "Your mother is a DNA jackpot ticket—the ultimate female shifter prize. Six children and five of them were female, two being twin girls, totally unheard of. So impressive, and your brother is a hellhound, as was your father. It's fascinating, such a worthy hunt. Such a shame your older sisters and father were murdered. Oh, I wish I could keep you, you'd make a fine contribution to my collection when you're older." He chuckles darkly, patting me on my head. "Although I have a courtesan picked out, and she is even rarer than you and such a beauty." He sighs. "My harem always needs new, nubile concubines—alas, they die so easily."

Are all demons this posh and pervy? I have no idea what a concubine is, but I get from the way he's whispering, it's not a good thing to be. As he's talking, he steers me outside—the scruffy guy follows behind us.

I know the rules about strangers, more so the rules about demons. But this demon has my mum and my little sister Grace. I will do anything for them, including sacrificing myself.

CHAPTER NINE

Fourteen years ago

WE HEAD towards a black range rover. Scruffy Number Two runs in front of us and opens the rear passenger door of the car with a bow—what a weirdo. I am shoved into the back seat of the vehicle, and the demon follows me inside. I take my first good look at him, and he's old. He looks about thirty in human years. I bet he isn't older than my mum. I know my mum will kick his ass for taking me, and my brother will light it on fire when he gets here.

The demon has black hair, long on the top and short on the sides. It falls into his blue-grey eyes. I think he's going for a boyish boyband look, not that it's working. He has high cheekbones and a delicate nose, and his lips appear big and puffy, especially the bottom one. His chin is strong. From what I remember of him behind me, he's tall. Although he isn't huge like a shifter, he's taller than a human. Mum would say he was elegant, elf-like. My brother would say weak, like prey. If I get the opportunity, I am going to kick his ass.

"Unfortunately I am the middleman for this transaction—you have been sold to a council member for an extortionate price. When you're more mature, once your body changes, you will drive him wild." The demon bops me on the nose. I blink at him. "I would have thoroughly enjoyed parading you in front of all the shifters. So exciting that a council member has bought you—who knows your fate. I have a feeling you will be in my care for some time. Then your owner will come in on a proverbial white horse and rescue you—that's why all this is just so much fun." He taps his fingers on the seat between us.

"I made a bargain to collect you. Your owner said nothing about keeping our bargain a secret." The demon chuckles and winks at me. "I might not be able to keep you, but I can sure mess things up a little bit. I do so hate happy-ever-afters. So you will remember, young Forrest, that everything from now on is your owner's fault and nothing to do with me. Don't be taken in by his handsome face, that's a good girl." He pats my cheek. I glare at him. I wish he would stop touching me. A council member bought me? I don't understand what he means. It's something that I'll have to deal with later and talk to my mum about. I'm a shifter, not a Mars Bar. This demon is weird.

I lift my chin and look him directly in the eye to show that I mean business. "My mum and my sister, you'll let them go, now that I am in the car with you. Ring your men, and please let my pack go." I know he said nothing of the sort, but maybe I can shame him into letting them go—it's worth a shot. He might want just me. If that's the case, I can make it easy for him to do the right thing. "I did what you asked—now let them go."

He tilts his head to the side, looking at me like I am stupid. His hand comes up, and he taps his fingers to his mouth. Once, twice, squishing his puffy lips.

"No," is his reply. I open my mouth to argue, but the look in his eyes stops me. Instead, I turn and gaze out the window. His blue-grey eyes have turned black, totally, freakily black. A primal shiver runs down my back, and I do my best to suppress the total and utter horror. I realise that I won't be kicking demon ass today.

The truth is, my *mum* would struggle to hurt him. He isn't just a demon—he is a first-level demon. I know with sudden clarity that we are all as good as dead.

I perch on the edge of the seat, spine straight, and focus outside the car, keeping my eyes wide to stop my fear from leaking down my face. I don't want to cry; I don't want to show any weakness. It would be a win to him. I might be nine, but I am stubborn, and however long I have to live, I will do so with my head held high. Being brave isn't about not being frightened; it is about being shit-scared but still doing the scary thing anyway. The right thing. If I can protect my pack, I will.

Be brave.

"Are you not wondering how I found you?" No, I don't want to know how I messed up. I watch the demon out of the corner of my eye. "My men tracked you to the hotel, but we lost you. You put a scent masker on, what a smart little wolf you are. It made me want to find you all the more. Your mother was equally tricky. Puff, she was gone"—he wiggles his fingers—"completely disappeared. But your stepfather, Dave...my my, he was too easy." The demon tuts. "With half his DNA, it is no wonder Grace is not good enough for my collection." I turn my head to look at him. "What a horrid, snivelling creature Dave is." He chuckles. "I didn't even touch him"—he shrugs, shows me his palms, and wiggles his fingers, pouting—"he was squealing like a pig. His life, his daughter's life for your mother's. For you." He raises an eyebrow, doing a fake sad face. "Such a wealth of information, so quick to tell me where he was going to meet your mother. So quick to tell me your protocols and how to find you—he even called off your bodyguards. That's why you were on your own." He shakes his head mockingly. His eyes are sparkling and finally back to their original colour. "I cannot quite believe your mother chose such a weak mate, especially after your father. That's why you are going to be safer in my care, my dear Forrest. These imbecilic wolves don't deserve you." He pokes my leg.

I want to shout at him that it isn't true, that he's lying. I know demons are said to twist things. But if I am honest, really honest, it sounds like he's telling the truth.

I don't call my stepdad "dickhead Dave" for nothing.

"Now there's you, a nine-year-old child on her own with the enemy, no snivelling, no crying, only a proud little chin held high and a single demand to release your pack. You could rule the world with that attitude, young Forrest...yes, you're very intriguing. I think I shall keep you." He nods and quickly leans forward, tapping the end my nose again. His bright smile makes me want to puke.

I am dragged into a warehouse building, Scruffy One and Two holding me between them. Scruffy One is squeezing my upper arm painfully, probably in revenge for the punch to the balls and throat. The demon is strutting in front of us.

"A pack reunion—how wonderful." I can't see around him—something for which I will be eternally grateful. Blood, sweat, and a strange cloying musty scent I can't identify fills my nose. Combined with the stench of demons and humans, the whole place smells like I've stepped into Hell.

I gag. Some inbuilt alert in my head is going nuts, and my instincts are screaming at me to run.

"Now, now, gentlemen, not something we should do to our lovely guest. Pull your trousers up, that's a good chap." The demon chuckles and shakes his head in amusement, wagging a finger at me as he turns. "Look, Forrest, at what your naughtiness has done. Your poor mother had to entertain all my men while you were running around the airport. What a bad little girl you are." He steps away, and for the first time, I see my mum.

She is on her hands and knees on the dirty concrete floor. Blood on her face, her lip is split, and there's blood between her legs. I don't understand why she hasn't got any clothes on. Perhaps she's going to shift into her wolf form to heal? That's the only reason I can think of why she would be naked. Tears fill my eyes. I can hear my little sister crying.

I scan around frantically for Grace. She's fighting with her dad, trying desperately to get to our mum. She wiggles out of her coat, leaving it behind in his grasp, and runs across the building at a speed only a toddler can do. Nobody stops her as she throws herself into my mum's arms. If I weren't being held back, I would be doing the same. I watch my mum hug Grace to her chest, and I can hear her saying to Grace how much she loves her.

My mum looks up and meets my eyes. She gives me a tearful but determined smile. "I love you so very much, Forrest. Sticking to our plan...I'm so proud of you—you have been such a courageous girl. I need you to be brave for a little bit longer. Can you do that for me?" I nod. The tears I was valiantly holding in now trickle down my face. I hiccup a sob. "I am so sorry I couldn't keep you both safe," my mum says. The desolation in her eyes almost breaks me.

She nods meaningfully.

I know what my mum wants me to do. My heart pounds in my ears, and it's difficult to breathe with the lump in my throat.

My hoodie has plastic toggles at the end of the cords that tighten the hood. The toggles are cone-shaped and are the perfect place to hide a potion ball.

"I love you too," I whisper. The lump in my throat makes it difficult to speak.

Everything after that happens so fast. Yet at the same time, it feels like a lifetime passes as I watch my mum take Grace's face in her hands. She smiles down at Grace and wipes the tears from her chubby face with her thumbs. Mum gently strokes Grace's blonde hair—a perfect match for her own—out of her eyes. She leans down and kisses my baby sister gently on the forehead.

From one breath to the next, my mum sharply twists Grace's head to the side, breaking her neck.

My baby sister slumps, dead, into my mum's arms.

The howl of anguish from my mum is chilling as she clutches Grace to her chest with trembling hands. With a look of such sadness in my direction, my mum's fingers on her right hand shift to claws, and with a quick clean motion, Mum slashes her own throat open.

The two men let go of me, rushing towards my mum and Grace.

Sometimes the last move you have is to extract yourself from the hands of your enemy permanently. With a sob, determined, I place the toggle with the poisonous potion ball in my mouth, and I bite down.

Onto a finger.

The demon has shoved his finger into my mouth.

With his free hand, he smacks the back of my head; the poisonous potion ball hits the floor, smashing. Useless.

"Naughty puppy!" the demon scolds. He keeps his finger in my mouth, and his other hand snakes around my throat. He pulls me to his chest, preventing me from moving. He shakes me a little in frustration. "Well, I didn't see that coming," he quietly says. Then more loudly, he snarls at the demons and humans in the room. "You must have broken her, you fucking idiots! Dave." He turns his anger towards my stepdad and pulls me around to face him. His finger is still in my mouth and digs into my cheek. "I am down two females. What have you to say?"

Dave, my stepdad, is on his knees, hugging Grace's coat. He shakes his head from side to side in shock, his eyes never leaving the crumpled bodies.

My mum never looked at Dave once, I think numbly. She never told him she loved him.

My suspicions are confirmed when Dave says, "You were only supposed to take Forrest. Not my little girl. We had a deal for you to take Forrest, but not my Grace, not my Grace." He rocks forward and back, stroking the coat in his hands. His expression is one of agony.

This is all Dave's fault—my mum, my sister, it's all his fault.

Dave finally lifts his eyes from the little pink jacket. "We had a deal!" he screams.

I feel the demon shrug. "I didn't kill them." He waves a hand at Dave. "Someone shut him up. Kill the useless fuck, he is getting on my nerves."

I wobble in the demon's arms. My knees go weak as the men surround Dave. His yelling is abruptly silenced with a wet-sounding gurgle.

Everything hits me at once. I failed. I've failed my mum. She would be so angry with me.

Something inside me snaps, and my body starts to shake.

I don't want to be here anymore.

I don't want to be here anymore, repeats over and over in my head.

Magic floods my body, and I embrace the feeling. I fall into my magic.

I escape into the darkness.

"Oh, for fuck's sake," I hear the demon shout, and then nothing.

CHAPTER
TEN

I CATCH John's voice as he continues his report, pulling me from the horrors of my past. I bury them again inside my head in a box marked *Do not fucking touch*.

I run my hand shakily through my hair, trying to tamp down my anxiety over the horrific memories. On my other hand, my finger is swollen and red. I have been wrapping the thread of the cover around it, cutting off the circulation. I stare at the digit in fascination.

"Forrest shifted extremely early, as you can see. Although she was only nine, she impressively managed to kill two humans and a lower-level demon before they contained her by knocking her unconscious." I lift my head, and as John talks, a 3D video of the CCTV clip plays. My mouth pops open in shock as I watch.

I watch myself attack three of the bad guys. I killed them, or my subconscious piloting my wolf killed them, which should have been disturbing. But those men hurt my mum and I managed to get a small amount of justice.

I had no idea I did that. To escape, I folded into myself and let the wolf take over. That first shift was a total blank to me, due to the whole trauma. I assumed I'd been knocked unconscious. Looking at the evidence, I have to admit to myself that I might have gone feral for a while.

I am a killer, a murderer. The angry part of me rejoices, thrilled. I want to bounce in my seat with inappropriate excitement—what a badass.

"Did she bite that demon's..." one of the hellhounds says behind me, abject horror in his voice. Oh yeah, yes I did. In my head, Billie Eilish's song "Bad Guy" plays. Huh, this is fantastic for my confidence—to see that wolf-me hadn't started out so meek, so pathetic.

"Yeah, fucking hell, looks like it."

I glance behind at the hellhounds. One of them gives me a supportive nod, while the other unconsciously shields himself. I snort. Nanny Hound gives me a little nudge to turn back around. I am such a badass I scare even hellhounds. I hum.

John continues talking about the evidence collected and the details on the demon who acted as a broker. He also explains I was held for a further week and details the rescue.

Everything around that time is hazy. I was in an awful place not only physically, but in my head. I was a mess.

John skims the room, making sure he has everyone's attention. Then he turns his focus on the pack. For the first time this evening since I sat down in this chair, I make myself look at them. I've been avoiding them. They frighten the shit out of me.

Seeing and hearing the evidence must have been extremely hard, to see irrefutable proof that Dave, their father, had been a coward. Captured by a demon, he had given away the locations of three female pack members, two being vulnerable children. The rarity of shifter females also makes the crime particularly heinous.

Vincent especially had built up his father to be the ultimate hero. Over the years, he made the Dave of his memory into someone he never was.

Beth is sobbing in Harry's arms. Jason is standing motionless, his face blank. Vincent, not bothering to comfort his mate, steps forward, his arms open wide in challenge.

"Is this a joke? So that's what you were hiding, John? Your bitch of a mother snapped Grace's neck like a twig." He clicks his fingers. I wince at the sound and the imagery that flashes into my head. "She was what, over a thousand years old, couldn't handle a bit of rough sex, so she goes and tops herself," Vincent snarls, "You heard my father—he made a deal to protect Grace. That crazy bitch didn't need to kill her. I can see as clear as day what you're doing here. Dragging my father's name down to protect that thing?" He points at me, and I can't help flinching. I wish he'd stop doing that. "Are you fucking kidding me? All this manipulative crap today, knowing what that crazy bitch did, makes me wish I'd hurt her dog of a daughter more. You want me to cry with guilt?" Vincent's hate-filled brown eyes are on mine, his finger is still pointing at me. "Get fucked. If you leave it in the same room alone with me, I will finish the job I should have done years ago. You gave up the right when you dumped it at my door." Vincent spits at the floor. His angry eyes never leave mine. He lifts his lip, showing me his teeth, and sneers at me. Nanny Hound growls behind me. I feel him move a step closer.

John lets out a dark-sounding chuckle. "Forrest's door, Vincent. Not your door."

"What?" Vincent's head goes back a little in shock at John's quiet answer, and his pointing arm drops.

"The house, the grounds, the money is all Forrest's. It has always been in Forrest's name. Everything belonged to our mother, not the pack. Passed down to her sole surviving daughter."

Vincent grinds his teeth a little, and what looks like a flame lights John's eyes, making them glow red. The hellhounds behind me move a little with discomfort, readying themselves to jump in and stop John if he loses control.

"Let me be clear. If you or anyone calls my sister *it* one more time, I am going to kill you, and I am going to do it extremely slowly." He makes eye contact with each member of the pack. None of them can meet his eye, let alone hold his gaze. Beth buries her face in Harry's chest. "Now, Jason, have you got anything to add?" John asks the usually silent, creepy shifter.

Jason looks at me, his dark eyes unemotional. The dead expression in his eyes screams *retribution*. I drop my gaze and fuss with the cover; I pull it higher and tuck it under my chin.

I don't want to be in this room. Why can't they do this without me? Jason will not lose his composure and yell like Vincent even though Jason is Vincent's puppet, his shadow. Jason is always in full control. Sadistic control.

As expected, he shakes his head *no*.

"Now, unless you make a derogatory comment about my sister, none of you are going to die tonight. What you are going to do is leave. You are no longer welcome in this house." Vincent starts to protest but John waves away his comments. John's voice drops. "I will kill you all if you don't shut the fuck up." A puff of smoke comes out of his mouth—similar to hot breath on a cold day. I blow out a little—nope, the room is warm. It's John's fire magic; he is running that hot. "You have thirty minutes to pack your shit. Take a bag with essentials only—one bag. The pack accounts are frozen, so don't bother taking your cars, either. You're hereby banished from our society for crimes against a purebred female shifter. Everyone in agreement..."

The two council members now step forward. They had been so quiet, I had forgotten about them. Which is stupid—you should never ignore the council. The taller of the two men, a golden-blond cat shifter, nods. "As a council witness, I agree."

"As a council member, I feel the sentence is too lenient. I would not be opposed to a death sentence. But as that is my personal opinion, I will witness today, and I am also in agreement," the smaller of the two men says; I think he's a bear shifter. He glares at the pack. John nods his thanks.

"Harry, stay behind. Beth, if you want to discuss your options, you can do that with me now. You do not have to stay with your mate. As you are human, I have the resources to help you. Banishment means a tough life, one you are not equipped for."

Beth gives a little nod. Still standing in Harry's arms, she says quietly, "Vinny has continued to lie to me." Looking at her mate, she calmly continues, "You told me so many horrible things about Forrest that are untrue. I know from this meeting today that they never happened." She points at the floor where Vincent had been standing. "Just now I had to listen to you equate and trivialise rape as a bit of rough sex." Beth shakes her head, her hazel eyes accusing, full of disappointment. "What is wrong with you, Vincent? If I was in that situation, would you expect me to lie back and think of England?" Her voice cracks and she starts to cry again. "I have spent eight years in this house, and I have watched your cruelty. I did nothing, nothing." Beth pokes her own chest. "I could have done more, I should have done more. I alone am responsible for my non-action. I will never forgive myself, and I will never forgive you, Vincent. May I?" she asks John, nodding in my direction. John waves his arm, giving permission. Beth moves out of Harry's arms, turns, and takes a few small steps towards me. Her eyes and nose are red from crying. "Forrest, I am sorry." Another tear rolls down her cheek, and her lips tremble. I untangle my hand from underneath the cover, and with my thumb and forefinger, I make a wobbly OK sign. Beth lets out a little sob-laugh. "Okay," she whispers back.

"You're leaving me?" Vincent says in disbelief, his face flushing red. Beth looks at him and rapidly blinks. Nervously she backs away. Once she steps back into Harry's arms, she nods. "Un-fucking-believable." Growling, Vincent turns away, his shoulders and arms tense. His hands curl into fists. If the hounds weren't in the room, I do not doubt that he would be hitting the wall or me, his favourite punching bag. I can feel his anger, smell his rage.

My eyes flick from Vincent to Beth with concern. I am worried about Beth's safety.

Yet, like the coward I am, I find myself sinking into the chair in an attempt to make myself smaller.

"Hounds, please escort these rogue shifters. Rogues, you have twenty-six minutes remaining," says John dismissively.

Vincent, with the help of a hound shoving him from behind, staggers towards the door. A visible vein throbs in his neck, and as he passes my chair, his body tenses. I huddle underneath the fluffy cover; I try my best to become invisible. Vincent bares his teeth at me.

Between one breath and the next, he roars and lunges at me.

Everything slows...

I whine in fear.

My hands tangle in the cover. I can't get them out. Oh my God, I can't get them out in time, I'm unable to protect my face. I cringe and slam my eyes shut tightly.

Warm liquid splatters my face and neck.

I take a shaky breath. The sweet metallic scent of blood fills my nose.

No pain.

I slowly open my eyes.

I blink, my eyelashes heavy.

Nanny Hound is standing over me; Vincent is standing over me.

A knife is buried in Vincent's neck. Vincent's eyes are wide open. He gasps.

My eyes widen and my thoughts scramble. Frozen, I listen to Vincent gurgle and choke; his breathing turns into a wheeze.

I pant. I can't get enough air into my lungs.

John prowls into my sightline. He casually moves up beside Vincent. His head tilts to the side and he takes in the situation.

John smiles.

I'm glad that nightmare-inducing smile isn't aimed at me.

Dimly in the background, I can hear Beth screaming, but I'm hyper-focused on the scene in front of me. I dare not move my eyes. It's like everything is silent around us, as if the entire world has shrunk down to a small bubble that encapsulates us.

John grabs hold of Vincent's arm and holds the bleeding shifter up when his legs threaten to buckle. "You didn't think I'd let you live did you, Vincent?" John whispers, that same smile on his lips; his eyes dance with sick amusement. I can't breathe.

Nanny Hound lets go of the blade. I sit frozen; I dare not move. It's macabre, seeing it sticking out of Vincent's neck. Blood weeps from the wound.

Vincent's blood is cooling on my face, my lips, dripping from my eyelashes.

"I wanted to watch you lose everything. See the acknowledgement of your utter failure. Before I took your miserable fucking life." John flicks the blade; Vincent groans. "What kind of self-respecting shifter gets off on hurting little girls? You thought that we'd be impressed?" He laughs nastily. "Thank you for making it easy for me." Another terrible wheeze comes out of Vincent. I think he is choking on blood. John lets go of his arm and roughly grabs the back of Vincent's shirt. He kicks Vincent's legs out from under him, and my stepbrother falls to his knees. John leans down to speak into Vincent's ear. "Look at that—dying on your knees as a rogue, while Forrest sits above you like a queen." John tilts Vincent's head up, using his hair. Vincent's brown eyes are glazed over, and blood dribbles from his lips. I shudder.

John braces his knee on Vincent's side, and slowly, deliberately, he pulls the blade from Vincent's neck. John lets go of his shirt, and Vincent falls onto his side with a thump. Vincent kicks and fails—his breath rattles.

Finally, his body stills in the centre of a growing red puddle.

Silence.

I stare numbly at the monster dead at my feet. The pool of his blood. It's inconceivable to me that Vincent is dead.

I was so sure Vincent would have been the one to kill me.

What the fuck just happened...

The bubble bursts and all the ambient sounds rush back to hit me at once, too loud for my nerves—Beth is wailing, her shocked cries filling the room.

"Great, I get the bloody extra paperwork," Nanny Hound mumbles. With a flick of his wrist he produces a cloth. He leans over me and proceeds to casually wipe the blood from my face. I give him an incredulous look, and he winks at me.

Jason, held between two hounds, is dragged out the door. The scary creepy shifter doesn't make a sound.

Harry, shifting his weight from foot to foot anxiously, watches as John steps over his dead brother, avoiding the growing puddle of blood on the floor. John prowls towards him and starts speaking. It's as if what happened to Vincent was nothing but an everyday, trivial thing. Perhaps to John, it was. God, he's scary.

John's voice drifts across the room. "Harry, even though you are banished and classed as a rogue, I am sure Forrest will not want to see you suffer. We will chat privately about my sister being caged and starved as you looked on." John has his back to me, but I can see Harry's terrified, pale face.

If Harry is guilty of that, then John bloody is too. Hypocritical bastard. I won't let John hurt him. The coward in me disappears, and I growl. John glances over his shoulder at me, and I narrow my eyes at him. He smirks, shakes his head, and turns back to Harry. "I am mindful that you are only twenty-four. I will allow you your belongings, including your car. You have till tomorrow to leave." Harry, in relief, closes his eyes and sighs; he nods his thanks. Hopefully he will be able to avoid my brother. John turns away from him in an apparent dismissal and starts to talk to Beth.

Harry shuffles towards me; his eyes flick around the room. Ignoring his dead brother, he slowly squats so we're eye-level. Nanny Hound gives him a small warning growl.

"Hi, Forrest. Wow, your hair is pink—that's kind of cool. I can't believe you shifted back. I am so proud of you. I also can't believe you went for the demon's crown jewels..." He shudders. "I think you freaked out every guy in the room." He chuckles, and then his smile falls from his face as he says nervously, "Once you get yourself healthy... we could maybe...urm, I dunno, go have a coffee, hot chocolate or something, chat about stuff? You're still my little sister, Forrest. I hope you know that." He rubs a hand across his face, and his eyes drop. "He was never the same after Dad and Grace died. Vincent was always difficult, and I wouldn't say he was a nice person, but growing up, he was good to me..."

Harry is hurting; I lean forward and wrap my arms around his neck in a hug. I almost make him fall over with the suddenness of the movement.

Oh, who am I kidding—he doesn't move a millimetre. I am so tiny. I nod and Harry pulls away. "Okay, well...urm...I will see you soon." He gives me a sad smile and hurries out of the room.

CHAPTER

ELEVEN

The shifter hospital is more like a medical-themed boutique hotel than a human hospital that you see on the television. I guess it's quite rare for shifters to require medical intervention, hence this fancy-schmancy hospital. If there are any other patients, I don't meet them. It's just me and a handful of rotating specialists that fly in from around the world.

I'm rapidly passed from one specialist to the next, like a shifter game of You're It.

Coincidentally, I didn't see any of these *specialists* when I was trapped in wolf form. From being left to rot to, now everyone is concerned about my health? Yeah, it's a bit of a head-fuck.

I'm a pro now at hiding behind a mask—my guise is "sweet and innocent." It matches the tiny pink-haired human I see in the mirror perfectly. Outwardly I'm small, weak, and female, the underdog. Why not use that assumption to my advantage? Huh, "innocence"—survival sucked up my innocence like the dry ground sucks up the rain. Now I play the victim to keep from being one. I'm a survivor.

Since John dropped me off here over a week ago, he hasn't been back to see me. John is under a lot of pressure—you know, saving the world—the world is way more important than his sister. Protecting everyone else is what John does; it would be selfish of me to think I'm above that.

At least the years stuck as a wolf taught me infinite patience, and I need that skill in abundance to deal with this shit-show. All this medical stuff is a joke. The doctors don't tell *me* anything—my medical file is the property of the shifter council.

I keep any questions I have to myself—what you don't know doesn't hurt you and all that. My mind thrums with the need to be left alone, and I long for normality. The only reason I stay and I'm not running for the hills is that my primal instinct screams at me to set aside my fears and accept help, and to use this as an opportunity to get stronger. It's the smart thing to do.

Hiding my anger is a challenge, and stopping the bitterness from leaking out is a constant struggle. I have to swallow it down; it makes me feel physically sick.

I'm sitting on a chair in a luxurious examination room. Jodie, my nurse, is sitting next to me. Her gentle brown eyes are warm and reassuring, and her pretty face is relaxed. Jodie, who is a talented witch, has wormed her way into becoming my friend. To kick off our friendship, Jodie snuck me a hair-removal potion ball on my first night. When helping me shower, she was horrified at my healthy armpit hair. Urm... who knew? I think I could have pulled a knife on her and not gotten as much of a reaction as a little bit of hair did. I smirk at the memory. Jodie told me I was hairy as a kitten and promptly educated me on all things *woman*, which I promptly forgot—to be honest, the whole lecture confused the hell out of me. According to Jodie, the hair removal potion is fantastic, a must-have as it even does facial hair. I had no idea women got lip and chin hair until Jodie explained it to me, in detail. Oh, and my eyebrows look nice, I guess. So unless I take a reversal ball for the spell, I will be *bad*–body-hair–free forever.

Not only is Jodie a witch and a nurse, she's also my speech therapist. A triple threat, and so far a thoughtful, talented lady. I'm not sure if I can trust her, nor do I know ultimately whose side she's on, but Jodie fascinates me. Witches are extremely impressive, and from what I can gather, they're not fighters. But with the ability to create the most incredible magic, they don't need to be. With Jodie and her coven keeping me amused with different ingenious potion balls, I have a new love of everything to do with witch magic.

Jodie's brown hair is styled into two fancy French plaits on either side of her head. My own hair is in a low, loose plait. I have been getting to grips with it after Jodie smuggled in a human hairstylist to cut my thigh-length hair into a more manageable mid-back length. The hairdresser went nuts about the light pink colour; he loved it.

My natural red hasn't hinted at a return, and I can't even change the colour either—shifters don't dye their hair. We can, I guess, but I think it's a total waste of time. You see, as part of the magic of shifting, artificial hair colour disappears when we return to our human form—same with makeup and even regular tattoos. Everything regenerates through the change—that's why shifters live for so long.

Jodie's pink scrubs rustle as she gives me a double thumbs-up, and her full mouth curves into a toothy grin. I wrinkle my nose at her antics and swing my attention back to this afternoon's doctor, Doctor Gregory; he's a cat shifter. Tablet in hand, he reads my notes with an unnerving gleam in his eye. Dr G lifts his eyes from the device and smiles at me.

I don't smile back. Instead, I watch him warily. I don't want to be rude to the nice doctor, but he specialises in shifter gynaecology. I mouth the words "vagina doctor," followed by a full-body shudder and a lip curl. Jodie's smile gets bigger. I clutch my hands in front of me and lean slightly forward in the chair—protecting said vagina.

It's his turn today to poke and prod me. Yay...the urge to tell him to bog off is huge. It has been only eight days and I'm all tested out. I feel as if my body isn't my own. In wolf or human form, I belong to everyone but myself.

I shelve my unhelpful feelings, sit up and anchor my spine, lift my chin, and try to at least look like the adult I'm pretending to be. Out of the corner of my eye, I see Jodie nod her approval. I take that as validation I did the right thing. God, it's harder than I thought it would be to behave like a normal, balanced person. I don't know the rules.

I've taken it upon myself to emulate the people around me in the hope that I will at least appear to know what I'm doing. All this is hard to comprehend, and I can't help feeling like a kid who has woken up from a bad dream and fourteen years have passed.

"So, Forrest," Doctor Gregory says, placing his tablet with a clack on the glass coffee table. He leans forward, resting his forearms on his pinstriped thighs; he isn't shy about scrutinising me. "The council is concerned that your reproductive system may have been compromised by your previous living situation. We can't introduce you to potential mates if you aren't viable." Oh, and there it is...this shit can't be ethical. I fight to keep my face blank. The anguish I feel wells up in my chest and threatens to register on my face, to knock off my mask. "This afternoon, we're going to discuss your heat cycles. Can you remember if you have had your first estrus?"

I drop my head so fast my neck twinges with pain, and I can no longer meet his eyes. I know he's a doctor, but do I have to talk about this? I don't trust him, and I certainly don't trust the council. I wrap my arms around myself.

Usually, a female Canidae shifter will have her first estrus, or heat, after the first animal shift, between the ages of eighteen and twenty-five. Shifters don't menstruate monthly like humans. Twice a year, we go into estrus. Estrus can last from two to four weeks, and only during that time we can conceive. One regular shift into animal form after the heat cycle and the unused material from the lining of the uterus is gone. The magic replaces cells so the body doesn't need to, so female shifters don't have periods—unless for some reason they can't shift.

I swallow the sour bile that fills my mouth. I wiggle in my chair and tuck my hands underneath my thighs to stop them from shaking. I struggle to keep my breathing even; bloody hell, I need to wolf-up. I can answer a simple question.

I shifted early, and I had my first estrus prematurely.
Tell him.

I take a big unsteady breath. The lemon cleaner they use on the floor makes my nose itch. The clock on the wall ticks, each second louder than the last. I rock slightly forward and back as I try to form the words. I am acting like an overly dramatic weirdo.

I clear my throat, and slowly, like I've been practising, say, "At...

about…ten." My rough voice grates. I swallow. My mouth is now bone-dry.

Stuck in my wolf form, I had to suffer through five traumatic heat cycles and the bleeding afterwards as I couldn't shift. It was a blessing and a relief when they stopped. I guess my body was too fucked up, too run-down with malnutrition. I swallow the lump in my throat, and I keep my eyes down.

My lips tremble, and to stop them, I pinch them shut with my teeth.

A memory gnaws at the edges of my consciousness. It must be a bad one—I can tell by the way it gets harder to breathe. I jam it back in its box with all the others.

Dr G is speaking, but I can't hear him above my madly beating heart. I move my hands and grip the edge of the chair; the leather is slick under my damp palms. I hold myself in place. I need to stop the rocking.

The lump in my throat is now blocking my airway, and I can no longer take a full breath.

What the hell is wrong with me?

A noise from outside startles me and the memory slams into me like a physical punch to the face. Flashes of imagery flood my senses, and I'm back in the cage:

Am I dying? Cramping pain. Star-shaped droplets of blood hit the concrete.

"You disgusting, dirty dog!" Cold water from the yellow hose blasts between my back legs.

Cold so cold. I want my mummy.

Blood mixes with the water, swirling, swirling down the drain.

No. No. No.

Long-buried shame tightens my throat. I come back to myself, and something digs into my spine. It takes me a few seconds to gain awareness and to work out that I'm wedged between the black leather exam bed and the wall. I'm curled underneath the bed, and I hug my knees to my chest. *I can't breathe. I can't breathe.* Black spots appear behind my eyes. I rapidly blink, attempting to clear my vision.

Then he's here, a big black wolf.

The exam bed shudders above as he creeps closer to me on his belly. He mournfully whines at me, his warm, soulful grey eyes full of concern—Nanny Hound. I bury my hands in his fur and place my forehead against his.

What have I done? What did I do?

Nanny Hound puffs out a breath and the hair sticking to my sweaty forehead flutters. He does it again; he breathes in and out, and I make myself breathe along with him. In and out.

I'm okay; I'm okay.

Once my heartbeat has settled and I'm no longer shaking. Nanny Hound wiggles backwards. He takes hold of my jumper in his teeth and pulls me out with him.

Well, this is embarrassing.

Ashamed, I blink up at the shocked doctor and nurse. My chair has tipped over; otherwise, the room looks the same.

Tears shine in Jodie's brown eyes, and a worried line has appeared between her brows. I mouth the words *I'm sorry*.

Jodie straightens her scrubs. She wrinkles her nose and frowns at me. "I didn't hear you. You need to try that again like we have been practising." I roll my eyes toward the ceiling, already feeling better with this switch to our regular routine.

"I'm s...s...sorry," I rasp out obediently. Jodie gives me a bright smile, drops to her knees, and wraps me in a comforting hug.

"One step at a time," she whispers, squeezing me.

After a cup of tea, I manage to give a hesitant and distracted Doctor Gregory the information he needs. He concludes his session without a physical exam. That decision is mainly due to the angry hellhound that refuses to leave my side. Nanny Hound—whose name I finally found out is Owen—is seriously my hero.

The uncomfortable doctor also let slip that there should be no issues with my ability to produce children; my weight gain should resolve my heat cycle and any fertility problems. Yay, the council will be pleased—cue eyeroll.

CHAPTER
TWELVE

I'M SITTING cross-legged on the bed in my cell. Hospital room. With my new diet, I have put on enough weight so that it doesn't hurt to be human—especially the pointy bits like my knees, elbows, and bottom. With more flesh on them, my bones don't ache or crunch against each other, and I no longer look like a female version of Skeletor. I still look childlike, but I have hope. My strength has rapidly improved, and I take every opportunity not only to stand up and make myself walk but also to stretch and make myself more flexible.

My body is adapting, and everything is less alien. I've still not gotten used to the whole not-having-fur. I'm always cold, but all in all, I'm physically doing okay.

Except my voice. Talking is more complicated than anticipated. At first, the doctors were puzzled over why I'm unable to speak. Many tests were done, and while there's damage to my vocal cords—they are shot to shit—it doesn't account for my unwillingness to speak. The problem is written off as a mental health issue. Emotional trauma. All those years I spent locked inside my head with my inner voice screaming, I would have given anything to speak. Now I find using my voice disconcerting. Hearing my voice is extremely strange and I avoid talking out loud. I am not used to expressing myself vocally with strangers. Like a wind-up toy, I force myself to speak when required. Otherwise, I'll never get out of here.

This afternoon, the doctors—the council— want me to work on my shifting; they want me to shift back into my wolf form.

I'm shitting myself.

I worry that I won't be able to turn back, or even worse, I'll get stuck in my wolf form again. The fear is a living thing inside me, eating me up. No matter what the doctors say, I'm not reassured, but I'm aware that it's something that I have to do.

I've got to wolf-up—pun intended.

I'm sure not waiting for a gaggle of doctors to stare at my naked human form, adding pressure to an already stressful situation. I've decided to shift on my own in my room.

I know, I know, I'm crazy.

I should wait or at least ask Owen for help. But the anticipation is freaking me out, and I need to get this shit over with. I puff out a nervous breath, wet my lips, hop off the bed, and square my shoulders. I glance about uneasily and remove my clothes. I don't know if it would be better for me to be on my hands and knees. But standing here feels right.

I take a fortifying breath.

I scrunch my eyes closed and think of my wolf, my fur, my paws. I start to tingle all over. I embrace the feeling. It's surprisingly invigorating, and between one breath and the next, I am in my wolf form.

I feel like I've come home.

I do a little stretch. *Oh my God, look at that!* I wiggle my bum in disbelief and my tail moves. *Wow, look at that!* I marvel at my once-lame back legs, which are now strong and sure underneath me. *No pain!* My muzzle opens, and my tongue lolls out in a happy grin. I twist in a sharp circle and gape at my strong legs. I flop to the floor, stunned. I squirm onto my back and wiggle each paw above me.

Wow. The magic fixed me...shit, the magic fixed me! I knew it would have done, but seeing is believing and I feel stunned, overwhelmed, and light-headed.

Dimly in the back of my head, I think that I'd better turn back; otherwise, I might stay as I am. Hell, it would be much easier to keep in wolf form. Simple. Unless they chuck me in another cage. I do a full-body shudder. Even thinking about it frightens the crap out of me. I can't tempt fate. I scramble to my feet.

Sighing, I again close my eyes, and I imagine my human self. My pale hands and toes, and astonishingly I think of my pink hair.

God, the relief I feel when I stand on my two human feet. I grin and fist-pump. I did it! I did it! I'm a proper shifter. I promptly burst into tears.

That's how Nanny Hound finds me—a naked, snotty mess.

"Forrest, are you alright? Did you...did you shift?" My lips tremble, and I nod. "Are they happy tears?" I wobble my head weirdly, nodding and shaking my head at the same time. Hell, I'm not sure. "You shouldn't have done that alone...do you want some cake?"

"What's wrong?" Jodie says as she comes into the room. She steps around Owen and eyes me up and down. I stand hunched and snivelling. I don't bother to cover myself.

"Forrest shifted into her wolf and is feeling—"

"Why is she naked?"

"Shifters shift naked. Clothing doesn't shift."

"Oh, I have a potion for that." Jodie rubs her hands together with a grin.

AN HOUR later and I'm in the dining room, nestled at a table in the corner, my back to the wall. I'm next to the window, which overlooks the courtyard garden. When I arrived, they thoughtfully put me in a downstairs bedroom with access to the same courtyard.

The double doors to the kitchen swing open and Karen, a skinny blonde human nutritionist, shuffles across the room. Karen gives me a nervous smile as she holds a plate of chicken, peas, and mashed potato in a white-fisted grip.

I hum in approval—it has gravy.

Karen has been hired to sort out my dietary requirements. The poor lady is so frightened of me; her distress wafts around her, filling my nose, making me want to sneeze. I wiggle in my chair and attempt a reassuring smile. The human's eyes dilate and go round. Her fear floods my senses.

I sag in my seat, pout, and glance down at the table as Karen's whole body starts to shake; a pea rolls off the plate onto the floor. I wrinkle my nose at the pea, sadly wishing it goodbye. They don't like it if I eat things off the floor. So the poor pea has to stay where it lands.

Karen places the plate in front of me with a clunk and quickly backs away. "Okay, F-Forrest, try to eat as much as you can." I mouth the words "thank you" at the trembling Karen.

I smile again, this time at the plate. I practice on the chicken and this time try to show fewer teeth. Everything at the moment is practice. I will have to add my smiles to the never-ending list, and maybe practice in the mirror.

Clumsily I take hold of my utensil. I still find it hard to hold my fork; my hands are going to be useless for a while. I grimace as I struggle to rotate the fork. I make a fist and stab down, effectively spearing the chicken. The human squeaks and scampers away out of the room. I hunch my shoulders and cringe.

For fuck's sake, why did I do that?

Owen, who is silently sitting opposite me, lets out a snort. I peek up at him. His eyes are crinkled in the corners and his lips twitch—he's fighting back laughter. I pull a face in the direction Karen ran. I didn't mean to frighten her.

He nods at my meal. "Don't worry about it; eat up." I don't need telling twice. Hell, at least I'm trying to use the fork. It would be much quicker and easier to use my hands—again, not allowed.

I lift the speared chicken, almost going cross-eyed as I watch it, until I stuff the whole chunk into my mouth. I go in for another piece.

The hairs lift on the back of my neck.

The room is unnaturally quiet, and I glance up; the few people that are around are staring at me. What are they looking at?

I pull the plate towards me as I chew.

Owen lets out a little cough. "Forrest." I meet his eyes; he's frowning at me. I must have done something wrong again—when he pulls that face, it's a good indication.

Oops, I'm growling. I stop, huff out a breath. My eyes dart about, doing a double-check to make sure that nobody is looking at my food. "Don't worry; I've got your back, no one is gonna take your lunch." I nod a thank you, trusting him, and continue eating. A happy hum replaces my growl.

With my stab technique, I finish eating within minutes. Not pretty but effective.

Owen excuses himself from the table. When he returns from the kitchen, the most fantastic thing happens: my empty plate is exchanged for a slab of chocolate cake.

Chocolate cake! I beam a smile at Owen.

I honest to God can hear angels singing; this is a heavenly cake, and I am positive the cake has a glow around it. I take a bite. My eyes roll into the back of my head.

I decide from this moment on chocolate cake: Owen and myself, we're best friends.

CHAPTER THIRTEEN

The meaty fist hits me directly in my face. Blood fills my mouth, and I snarl "You're not even trying," Owen grumbles, the arsehole, his eyes narrow the sweat is dripping off his forehead.

"I so am trying!" I bare my bloody teeth at him, and he chuckles.

"Again. This time block my strike!" He comes at me again; he feints a punch to the left. Which I catch, and I block his blow to the right. But I miss his left hand, which catches me in the stomach. I *oof* out a breath and a pained groan.

Owen steps away and circles me. He's so light on his feet for such a big guy. "Come on; fighting should come naturally to you. You're a shifter. Block me, hit me. You're fighting like a human."

I growl. I quickly dart away as he dives towards me, and I hit him on the jaw with my closed fist, finally making contact. My hand crunches. Owen stumbles backwards, and for a moment, I allow myself a little bit of pride. I made contact with his face. Go me.

My taped right hand throbs; I think his face broke my knuckle. Damn it, I should have used my palm to hit him.

Owen hits me again. "Stop getting ahead of yourself—one hit and the fight isn't over." He narrows his eyes at me; his voice is laced with frustration. "Where are the combinations that we've been practising?

The strongest part of your body is your legs, where are your kicks? Come on, Forrest, you can do better than this." Owen taps me on the shoulder with his left fist; I brace myself so I don't fall over. "Today, with me, you get it easy. It won't always be the case. Our life isn't rainbows and kittens. Even sparring, you've gotta fight hard." We go at it again.

I wobble slightly on my feet. Shit, I'm tired. But I force myself to focus. I watch his eyes, and I wait for an indication of what Owen's going to do next. I block his left and then block his right fist, which is heading again for my stomach. Owen tries to sweep my legs from underneath me, and I jump away. I go to punch him in the face with my left hand, and while he's blocking that move, I aim a palm-strike at his throat with my right. He blocks both. Owen doesn't see my left shin coming as I kick him in the side, knocking him sideways. I follow that up with an elbow to his temple. Owen goes down on his knees.

I grin. Owen's big fist hits me in the chest, and I find myself flat on the mat, unable to breathe.

I gawk up at the ceiling, gasping. It takes me a few minutes to learn how to take a full breath. Owen is sitting next to me. I roll my eyes to the side and glance at him. His dark skin is glistening, and he looks completely unruffled. Ha, I'm not glistening—I'm sure I look like I feel: a disgusting, sweaty mess.

"You did better," he says, eyes sparkling. "You need to shift to heal that hand." He nods at my now-swelling right hand. I grunt out my acknowledgement. "I will see you later tonight... movie night?" I can't move my head to nod; I wiggle my finger in confirmation. "Great, I want to introduce you to *Iron Man*," Owen says over his shoulder as he leaves. I scrunch my eyes closed. Even my hair is hurting. I think I did better today.

It has been three weeks since I was finally away from the hospital of horrors, and I'm living with the hellhounds in an apartment building owned by John. It used to be a hotel on the seafront, but when it fell into disrepair a few years ago, John bought it and had it converted.

It now has sixteen self-contained apartments. It also has a modern gym with a pool. It's a lovely building. I have one of the penthouse apartments, which has a fantastic private rooftop garden.

The building is tall, so it isn't overlooked; the roof garden is perfect; and it has the most fantastic sea views on one side and a view of the city and the ocean amusement park on the other. That side of the building is crazy busy.

I often find myself sitting huddled outside and watching the world go by, the excited screams from the amusement park a steady piece of soothing background music. It's a confirmation that life exists outside my new prison walls.

The building is magically shielded; the ward stops the uninvited or people with ill intent from entering the building. The magic warns people away, and it can even zap them unconscious. If you look up, you can see the glittering gold of the ward like a dome around the whole building. It's beautiful.

If you think about it, who in their right mind would want to attack somewhere that hellhounds live? You would have to be a complete crazy person with some kind of death wish. I am in the safest place imaginable.

The best way to describe my apartment is "modern bland." I spend most of my time on the roof, bugging Owen, or like now—a sweaty mess splattered on the gym floor.

This afternoon, I've decided that while Owen is off doing what he does while not watching me, I am sneaking out.

I want to do something on my own, venture out and buy some clothes. Everything John has kindly gotten for me is a bit naff. I am sure some department-store personal shopper out there had a wonderful time picking out all the pretty outfits. Not that I am not grateful for everything—I am. John has been thoughtful in arranging my fancy clothing. But I can't shake the urge to shop for myself and find my style.

I will probably order stuff online in the future, once I get to grips with using tech again. I need only a few things, as I want to wait until my weight has stabilised. I am still underweight but no longer skeletal. Gentle curves have replaced skin and bone, filling out my once-emaciated frame. Parts of me almost jiggle! I look like a woman instead of a child. Delicate and ultra-feminine, the outside clashes with the person I am inside, and my visage is an outright contradiction of what I imagined myself to look like, with no trace of the statuesque shifter I dreamed I would be.

At least my skinny arms have slightly more definition, and I've got good lean muscles developing.

I also want to explore the city without having my hellhound buddies escorting me. The urge to explore: to find out if there is more to the world than I have experienced so far. I want the freedom to choose.

I spent fourteen years not only being a prisoner to my pack but also a prisoner to my wolf. I have a lot of things I want to do, and a lot of time to make up for; my life will not include hiding behind bodyguards or the dictates of the bloody council. If I don't aim to gain a semblance of freedom in some form, I'm frightened that I will never learn to live. It's easy to allow others to dictate my life. But how can I grow if my dreams aren't planted in the dirt? How can I grow if I have no human experiences and no mistakes?

The security risk to my person, I think, is low.

Nanny Hound will still lecture me when he finds out that I left the building on my own. But in my defence, I haven't been working only on the walking-and-talking stuff; I have spent the last few weeks fight-training, with Owen and the other hellhounds. The fight training has massively helped improve my coordination and fitness. I might not be that good yet, nor at the standard I was as a kid. But I can handle myself. My mum insisted on fighting skills, so from the age of three, I learned the human fighting forms Krav Maga, Muay Thai, and the demon style *Fbeed znvrhnjv*.

Owen knows I'm not a pushover, and I'm certainly not a regular Princess break-a-nail-and-cry female shifter. Hell, he has spent weeks punching me in the face and throwing me around the gym. I'm a tough cookie. So I'm sneaking out.

I've FINISHED MY SHOPPING, and although I haven't bought much, I feel a real sense of achievement, shopping for myself. I guess it's a milestone. I meander down a side street away from the main shopping area. I allow my shopping bags to bounce off my leg and swing as I wander. My eyes dart to each new thing, and my blood thrums with excitement.

I grind to a screeching halt. Creatures grumble as they swerve around my motionless form...oops, I almost caused a pileup on the busy pavement. My brain has zero hope of scrounging up apologies, as my whole focus is on the glorious sight before me. My mouth fills with saliva and my face hits the window, and it squeaks as my nostrils squish against the glass. I can almost hear the angelic choir in the background. Eyes wide, I stare without blinking at the sight before me—oh my God, so many cakes! Homemade cakes.

The bell over the door jingles as I stumble inside. *Mmm, cake.* My nostrils flare with the scent of sugar, chocolate, and coffee. I've found a gem of a café; it's fantastic, small, and quirky.

My eyes swing from cake to cake, then back again. I feel dizzy and overwhelmed at the choice.

I take a deep breath, which frankly doesn't help.

I might have a cake problem.

I swallow my saliva and slowly back away from the display.

At the side of the cake counter is a colourful handwritten chalk menu, and prominently placed next to it is a board that says, "Pending food and drink." What is "pending food"? I shuffle towards the board. God, I hope reading will distract me from going into a cake frenzy. I'm at serious risk of pouncing on the counter display.

The sign on the board states: *If any person (creature or human) cannot afford to eat or drink, please pick an item(s) that someone has kindly bought in advance.*

I run my fingertips across the words reverently, and my heart misses a beat—it sobers me. I blow out a breath and the white receipts attached to the board flutter in the slight breeze.

Gosh, that is absolutely beautiful.

I know what it's like to go hungry; my circumstances have changed, but so many people are not as fortunate. This concept is beautiful, kind and thoughtful; it gives me hope that there's not just evil in the world. That kindness exists too.

After I order, I quietly point to the pending board and hand over a wedge of cash that I had left over from my shopping trip. The lady at the till blinks at me a few times in shock, her blue eyes filling with tears. I give her a shy smile, grab my order, and totter away, my cheeks undoubtedly radiating pink.

I juggle my shopping bags and glance about for a place to sit. Dotted about are ten small tables with bright, mismatched chairs. I spot a comfortable chair positioned so my back would be against the wall. I will not only see the whole café and the door, but I should also be able to see halfway down the street. I hum. It's a perfect position for people-watching. With an amused huff, I wonder if anyone else will leave a nose print on the window while I'm here.

I settle into my chair with a contented sigh, the clatter of dishes and clink of spoons a gentle background hum. I sip my hot chocolate and nibble on a fantastic slab of chocolate cake. Okay, so I am shoving great mouthfuls of cake into my mouth. But I pretend I am eating like a lady, even if I have to remind myself to chew. It's gooey chocolatey goodness. I will never go another day if I can help it without a slice of chocolate cake, nom nom.

The café's walls are clad halfway up with wainscoting, painted a pale green. On one side of the room is a whole wall full of books. My fingers itch to run across their spines. Tipping my head back, I glance up to study the ceiling, where a pink-blossomed tree branch spans the ceiling with dangling fairy lights. I love the unique, bright splash of colour. This place is amazing.

Modern life is fascinating; the humans around me are so focused on their phones. Even humans sitting with other humans are staring and poking at their mobiles, occasionally murmuring to each other without their eyes straying from their devices. People no longer engage with each other; it's such a strange development. Crap, I guess I must look like a complete psycho sitting here, staring at everyone, without a phone in my hand.

I am sure the predators are well fed.

I bet hunting humans has never been so easy. Not that I'm advocating hunting humans! Pure humans are an endangered species. Mixed-race humans are a lot more common. It's rare to find a human nowadays without a drop of DNA from some creature. In evolutionary terms, it makes sense for humans to breed to make themselves stronger, healthier, and to ensure that they live longer.

According to Owen, there are thousands of humans that petition every year to be turned into vampires; everybody wants to be a vampire nowadays. I don't think many humans want to be shifters—the conversion rate is low, and only a small percentage of males survive.

I have a council-issued mobile, which is switched off and in a junk drawer. No way I'm giving the council information or carrying that thing around with me to be tracked. Today I bought my own phone to join the modern world.

I am not the only one people-watching; there's a young wolf shifter sitting a few tables away from me. He seems equally fascinated and has not stopped staring at me. I look at him and raise my eyebrow as if to say, *what are you looking at*? I saw someone do this in a film and thought it was cool, so I've been practising. He takes the eyebrow-raise as an invitation and gets up; his chair scrapes on the floor. My pulse rate increases—shit, I don't want to talk to him! I frantically rub my mouth to make sure I don't have cake on my face. He swaggers past me, over to the door, and leaves. *Huh.* I puff out a breath in relief, although I didn't mean to scare him off. I'm glad he didn't approach me.

I drag the paper menu across the table and study it, humming. I contemplate buying another slice, and I wonder if I can purchase a whole cake to take home.

The bell above the door jingles. My eyes flick up, and I freeze.

My mouth drops open. "H-Harry," I stutter in disbelief.

CHAPTER

FOURTEEN

"How's it going, Short Stuff?" Harry strolls over to my table, a fixed smile on his lips that doesn't quite reach his blue eyes. "Can I join, and do you want anything?" He nods, indicating both the empty chair and my clean plate. Speechless, I rapidly nod my head. I can't believe he's here—wow, this is kind of surreal. My eyes feel like they're popping out of my head as I obediently poke at the menu. I bounce on my chair and grin goofily at him. How did he find me?

"So you're finally out of the hospital, then." Harry returns with another slice of cake for me and a coffee for himself. The plate clatters as it hits the table, and Harry slumps down in the chair opposite. He folds his arms across his chest and spreads his ripped-jean–clad legs wide. It's a proper wannabe-alpha pose. I barely refrain from sniggering at him, but I don't want to be rude—he's adorable. His left leg bounces slightly.

"Everyone is going nuts wanting to know about *you*, the *new* female shifter." Harry sniffs and scrubs his nose with the back of his hand. I wrinkle my nose and swallow the cake in my mouth. A new shifter? Huh, do they think I appeared overnight as a fully-formed adult? Harry's left leg continues to bounce. "Not much of a talker? Yeah, heard that too. Are you...are you alone? I can't believe you're out in the city alone. Where are your bodyguards?" He looks about as if they're going to jump out of the woodwork and attack him. I part my lips to answer, but frustratingly my throat locks up. "I heard you have hellhounds watching you?" I nod and take a sip of my hot chocolate. I hope the warm liquid will convince my vocal cords to work. "Spending time with all those hellhounds must be fun, huh?" Harry wiggles his eyebrows.

Eww, gross. Why would Harry say that? This isn't a conversation I want with him, he's my brother. I shudder. I vigorously shake my head, and if I let them, my eyes would roll back into my head and disappear without a trace. Maybe even get stuck back there. I'm not blind—I've noticed the handsome, buff hellhounds. But they are John's men, and they treat me with the utmost professional courtesy. Harry's words are disrespectful. I love Owen, he's my rock, but the thought of romantic feelings for him—for anyone at the moment, especially the hellhounds—would be wrong.

I'm not ready to have a romantic relationship—shit, I'm barely adjusting to the confusing world around me. In my head, I feel like I could be a hundred...hell, a thousand. But in this body, as a human, I feel overwhelmed and utterly lost.

"I'm sure the council has a mate picked out for you. I was chosen for Liz..." Harry's eyes light up, and he puffs out his chest proudly. He then flinches, pulls a face, and visibly deflates. Harry scans the café, avoiding my concerned eyes. "Yeah, that turned out great...cheating bitch. Now I've gotta watch while she fucks every bitten human that moves. As far as I know, she's been with half the shifters in the country...dirty bitch."

My eyes widen, and I gasp. I've never heard Harry rant like this before.

Harry sneers and holds up his hands, mockingly. "Please don't start talking about, 'time is a great healer' and all that shit...oh, I forgot, you don't speak."

The angry, bitter energy that comes off him in waves makes me uncomfortable. I open and close my mouth like a goldfish, and I squirm in my chair. I wonder if it would help if I smiled—should I smile again?

I have no idea what to do.

"Well, if you're not going to ask…if you're interested in me…I'll tell you about my shit-show." Harry points at his chest and narrows his eyes. He sniffs again, and his leg continues to bounce.

What I've failed to notice until now is that Harry looks like shit. His dark blond hair is greasy, and he has scraped it back into a dodgy-looking ponytail. Unshaven, his facial hair has grown in a bit patchy. Harry looks like he needs a good wash.

I have not seen Harry since that last day at the house. I always meant to see him; he's important to me. But circumstances and with everything that has happened, it was difficult and then impossible. I should have tried harder; I feel ashamed.

God, I am a shit person.

"After Vince got dusted, Jace split, so that left me the bad penny of society. Everyone is gossiping about my pack, my dad. I'm now known as the rogue who couldn't satisfy his mate." Harry lets out a self-deprecating laugh. "Oh, and I can't forget I'm the rogue whose father killed his mate, and daughter."

My eyes prickle with tears. I knew it. I knew Harry would have found it hard to adjust to his new rogue status, the death of Vincent, and the thing with Liz. I should have tried harder. I presumed wrongly that John would have stepped in.

I'm stupid.

Harry is hurting, and he has no one on his side. I twist my fingers in my lap. I deserve his ire; I'm selfish. I hunch my shoulders, and a small, sad sound escapes me.

"Don't pretend you give a shit. I've been sofa-surfing for weeks. Oh, don't worry, I'm not asking to stay with you and the hellhounds in your fancy-ass apartments." I open and close my mouth again, but none of the words on the tip of my tongue feel significant when compared to Harry's pain. "But if you can help me out with a few quid?" His leg stops bouncing, and his gaze becomes intense. "A deposit for a place? I'll pay you back when I'm up and running." He tips back, lifts his hips, and removes his phone from his back pocket. With a few stabs at it, he leans across the table and shows me the screen. It's an ad for a studio. "Forrest, I need a place to live. Being a rogue…it isn't safe. I've lost count of the number of times I've had the shit kicked out of me." Harry sighs and sits back in his chair, leaving his phone on the table.

Sighing, Harry rubs his hand across his face and scratches his patchy beard. The noise makes me want to cringe. "Don't worry if you can't help. It's only me." He widens his eyes and pushes out his bottom lip.

I drop my eyes and stare at his phone, contemplating. I own property around the city, and a few are safe houses not linked to my mum's estate. Harry doesn't need to stay in a grotty bedsit.

I go through my shopping bags and hunt out the box with the new pay-as-you-go phone that the girl in the store had kindly set up for me.

Harry bristles as he watches me.

"So the packhouse is on the market? I looked online…" He whistles. "That's a lot of money…you are keeping most of the land, though? That's sick—it's a great place to run as a wolf." 'Sick'? I glance up from my new phone, and I guess my face shows my confusion at the word, as Harry misconstrues my look. He angles his chin down and pulls a sad face. "You know it's for sale, yeah? I know you girls are all about the mating and the pup-making. Must have been John that put it up? Shame, that." He sniffs, crossing his arms again.

Harry is wrong; I put the place up for sale. I loathe that house.

After a few blunders, I manage to open my email. Using one finger, I haltingly type an email to arrange everything. I'm satisfied when I get an immediate reply; they can have the place cleaned and stocked within a few hours.

I nab Harry's mobile from the table, open his messages, and type in the address and door code for his new home. I hold the phone back out to Harry, and with a sniff, he snatches the phone out of my hand.

"Woah, you're joking—I can't afford this place, it's well out of my budget," Harry sputters. He narrows his eyes when I smile. I nod and tap my chest, Harry growls. To explain adequately, I show him my phone and the emails. "It's your place? Motherfucker, check you out, poor little rich girl, someone has fallen on her feet. If I had known about this, I wouldn't have been slumming it." He snarls, tapping the corner of his phone on the table. He stops and points it at me. "I have a request—can you tell your people to make sure the fridge is stocked with beer? Oh, and I don't suppose it has sky sports? For the football?" I nod. I can do that, no problem.

I give him a hesitant smile, relieved that I can do something to help him and hopefully redeem myself.

"Thanks...hey, in all seriousness, you shouldn't be out on your own. I thought with the hellhounds as bodyguards they'd be better, more experienced at keeping a female like you in check. Shifters don't allow females to walk about alone. Only slags like Liz slip their bodyguards. You don't want to get a rep as a troublemaker. Hell, you're already odd-looking. Any other issues and you'll never get a decent mate." I blink, absorbing his hurtful words. Did he mean to be so rude? "I can walk you home. Don't worry, little sis, I got your back." With a toothy grin, Harry pulls out a knife and slaps it down on the table.

What the fuck...my gaze skitters about the café nervously. Thank God no one has noticed the big-ass knife sitting in front of us.

I raise my eyebrows as Harry flips the blade into his hand and digs the tip into the table. I gawk, horrified, as he inscribes the letters *L...I...Z* into the surface.

What the hell is he doing?

I'm not normal, yet it wouldn't cross my mind to deface someone else's property.

Instinctively I smack his hand, dislodging the knife, and I glare at him. Harry shrugs and smirks. He rubs the marks with his palm, knocking the curled shavings onto the floor.

"This place is owned by humans—who gives a fuck if I scratch the table?" More like *gouge*. I think indignantly. I care. I like this café. Whoever designed the décor did so with care and attention to detail. I don't want to see the place defaced because Harry is in a mood. I can't sit and watch that.

"What a sad existence you have, from being feral to being a human-loving goody-two-shoes. Don't worry; I won't mess up my new digs. In fact, here, take the blade." Harry flicks the knife, spinning it across the table. "You'll need protection. If you won't be a good female and keep your bodyguards close, you should at least learn to protect yourself, not that it will help. Fucking hell, Forrest, you can't even talk...it's fucking weird."

My heart shudders and drops into my stomach. I want to be understanding and show compassion for Harry and his feelings, but it's hard. I still don't know the right balance between my emotions, and Harry is making me bloody cross. My nostrils flare with my growing indignation, and I stuff the last of the cake into my mouth and chomp. I better go now; otherwise, my mask will come off, and I am liable to grab hold of Harry's greasy man-ponytail and smash his face into the table.

I rub my face on my shoulder and blow out a breath and remind myself sternly that Harry saved me. This is Harry. He has earned my respect. Harry isn't a bad person, he's hurting and what he's saying contradicts conversations I've overheard in the past.

I need to explain myself. I'm nothing like Liz, and I'm nothing like the poor repressed female shifters either. I don't want to be sequestered and bred, owned, while my male counterparts do whatever the fuck they like. My purpose in life is not to be a mate, a pup-maker, or to conform to unfair standards set by the council. His words make me feel sick.

I carefully place the new phone back in its box and grab my shopping.

"Oh, Forrest, don't be like that. I'm only telling you the truth. I can still stay in the fancy house, yeah?" I give Harry a stiff nod. He scrambles for his phone, and I stomp away, heading for the door. "Do you want my digits?" he yells at my back.

It takes everything in me not to raise my hand above my head and give him the finger.

CHAPTER
FIFTEEN

I DECIDE I should get myself off home. I'm safer being on my own. When I say *safer*, I mean for others—me wanting to smash someone's face in can't be healthy behaviour. I'm not a nice person, and leaving like I did was childish. Everything was so much simpler when I was stuck as a wolf.

I stomp through Market Square, and things go from bad to worse.

I certainly didn't count on being accosted by two beefy wolf shifters. One shifter swaggers in front of me, and the other one comes up behind. For a split second, I can practically taste my fear; it floods my mouth, bitter underneath my tongue. Freeze-or-flight is my natural response to danger, but I don't see a way out of the alternative this time. The ever-present rage that simmers inside of me sweetly sings. The two shifters are trying to box me in, and I let them.

"Hello, female, why are you alone? Where are your bodyguards?" *Oh, for fuck's sake.* I close my eyes and clench my fists around the bag handles—the plastic one in my right hand rustles. I forcibly blow a breath through my nose in exasperation. Honestly, what the fuck is wrong with these idiots? I move slightly so I can keep an eye on both of them.

Both men are suited and booted, wearing black suits that look expensive. Even with fancy clothes, they look like a couple of meatheads.

Meathead One, with his shiny bald head and goatee, doesn't wait for me to answer. He instead pulls his phone from his pocket and pokes at the screen with his meaty finger. I rhythmically tap my fingers on my thigh with annoyance. The nerve of this guy, his arrogance, presuming I'm happy to stand here patiently waiting while he makes a phone call.

It riles me, and my rage bubbles.

Meanwhile, Meathead Two is staring at me like he is in wolf form and I have a juicy steak tied to my tits. He has brown hair and eyes, with a face only his mum could love.

Maybe the hellhounds or John sent these guys?

"Boss, yeah, we found the female we scented…yeah, she is on her own…yes, sir, we're bringing her in now." He jams his phone back into his pocket. "Now, girly, you are coming with us. We have been following your scent for hours."

Oh, okay, an interesting development. These two meatheads are random wolves that have decided to grab me off the street because they smelled me. That's messed up.

"Our boss would like a word with you. He is… urm… concerned for your safety." Sure he is. I clench my teeth to stop myself from growling.

Meathead One reaches towards me to take my shopping bags. I release my hold and let him take them out of my hands. Happy for him to hold them for me—for this.

"Come now. We have wasted enough time tracking you." He also gives me a smarmy, lecherous look.

What is wrong with the shifters today? Treating me like I'm not a person—it's as if I am just a walking uterus.

I am sick of this sexist shifter shit. I'm sick of being frightened, sick of behaving like I'm meek. Well, I am about to give them a lesson in leaving Forrest Hesketh the fuck alone. My overwhelming rage has buried any trace of fear, and I can no longer control my expression. My sweet mask cracks and a crazy, hungry smile crosses my face. I've got a whole lot of rage and aggression inside me, and this situation is perfect.

I let my rage out to play.

I take one of Jodie's *don't see me now* potion balls from my pocket and flick it to the ground. It breaks on the floor at my feet, unnoticed by the wolves. God, I love witch magic, and that little ball will keep us invisible to prying eyes.

I sneakily enter a fighting side-stance. The trick to this is not to telegraph my move, so I transfer my weight onto my back foot and roll the heel of my front foot across the floor. I lift my toes to turn my whole body sideways onto the ball of my foot. I point my hip towards Meathead One, who is helpfully standing at a perfect distance for this move. I lift my arms to protect my face and for balance. I spin, twisting my whole body away, and as I turn, I pivot on my back foot. I peer over my opposite shoulder at Meathead One in my peripheral vision. Spinning quickly, I jump to gain added height, and my leg shoots out at a forty-five-degree angle. I point my toes to compress my tendon, and I smack him hard with the back of my heel.

I slam him with so much force in the back of his bald head, his body crumples. The whole move takes a matter of seconds, a perfect spinning-jump heel kick. I hum.

Meathead Two blinks in shock at Meathead One's unconscious body surrounded by my shopping bags. He looks at me, his brown eyes wide with disbelief, and his mouth hangs open. "What the fuck," he whispers.

My rage purrs, and with a manic smile, I launch myself at him. He recovers rapidly, and I duck as he tries to punch me in the face. I step under his guard and towards him. He helpfully leans forward, and I use my leg as a distraction. As he goes to block the kick, I thrust my palm out, hitting him under his jaw with a palm-heel strike. I then use my elbow to hit him in the face, catching his nose; I follow that up with a punch to the throat.

Blood splatters from his nose and lip.

He makes a strange gurgling sound and drops to his knees. With a smile and a little wave at him, I bring my right leg up in a sidekick and slam him on the head.

"Night-night," I mouth.

I glance about, checking that the potion ball is doing its job. Perfect, no one is looking at us. I grin. I turn both wolves onto their sides in recovery position. I have no idea if that will help, but I feel magnanimous. I also flick sleep-potion balls at the pair; I don't want them following me.

Oh, I need to do something before I go. I liberate the mobile from Meathead One's jacket pocket and hit redial.

"Are you on your way?" a male voice asks gruffly.

"Nope," I say, popping the *p*. There's silence for a few beats.

"Hello, little wolf, it is a pleasure to hear from you. May I enquire why, and more notably, how are you calling?" the male voice purrs down the phone at me; I pull the phone away from my ear and frown at it. Bossman is slimy.

"Your meatheads are in Market Square. Please send someone to scrape them up from the pavement," I reply to Mr Slimy, my voice annoyingly rough and husky from disuse. In this instance, it's handy that speaking on the phone is so much easier for me than speaking face-to-face.

"Are they alive? What hap—" I end the call and drop the phone next to the downed wolves. I gather my shopping; I feel lighter. Almost skipping, I turn once again for home.

I get back to zero fuss. Owen gives me a nod and asks me if I got him anything. Then he tells me he will meet me in the gym in ten to work off the cake I ate. The sneaky hellhound must have followed me. Huh, he didn't interfere, so I guess I will take that as a win.

The illusion of freedom.

CHAPTER
SIXTEEN

It has been a few weeks, and I'm back at the cake café waiting for Harry to join me. I have a big mug of tea and a slice of carrot cake...urm, well, an empty plate that once held carrot cake. The plate now looks like it has been in the dishwasher, as it's so clean. If anyone insinuates that I licked the plate, I will adamantly deny it—mmm, crumbs.

A few days ago, a contrite Harry got in touch. He was full of excitement over his new place and the accounting job that he managed to bag. Harry asked if we could meet.

I'm thrilled that he wants to spend time with me.

Unfortunately, to my chagrin, my usual table is taken. So I am sitting at a table next to the toilets. It's not ideal, but it's the only free table that didn't leave me with my back to the door.

After a few minutes, Harry joins me, and as he sits, he wrinkles his nose. "Not the best table, Forrest." He indicates with his head the toilets behind me, as if I missed them. I shrug. "So kicked any more shifter ass recently?" he says with a grin—oh yeah, he thinks he's hilarious. I roll my eyes.

"So have you heard about the vampires finding that girl?" He settles into his chair, eyes alight with fervour. Harry is a big gossip and has a fountain of information on all things creature—the guy loves to talk. "They say she got bitten by a cat shifter and she got all poorly-like. The vamps found her living in a garage." It takes all my self-control not to flinch. Garages and me... we aren't friends. "Homeless, only seventeen, the word is that she made it, that she turned. Can you imagine that? A bitten human female. I wonder if she will be infertile. If it can happen to her, imagine how many other women can make the change?" He nods, his face lit up with zeal. I glare at him. "Don't worry, Forrest, I won't hurt your precious humans. I'm not going to bite anyone. I don't want any more grief with the council." Harry mock-shudders and slurps his coffee in thought. "Vamps still have her—there's going to be war if they don't turn her over."

If Grace were alive, she would be sixteen. Maybe I can find someone to help her? I make a mental note to find out if Owen knows anything about the girl's situation.

Harry appears different today; I can't put my finger on it until I realise it's because he looks clean. He is wearing smart pants and a shirt, his hair is short, and he has shaved that awful beard. I hum, pleased to see he is back to normal.

The bell above the door jingles and out of the corner of my eye, I spot a walking nightmare.

Oh, my bloody God, no other than Liz Richardson is swinging her hips towards us, a ridiculous sashay that gets every man's attention. My first instinct is to drop my eyes and focus on my mug and pray she struts past. But I can't give her that satisfaction—I'm no longer a frightened, starved wolf. So I lift my chin and hold eye contact. *Please grab a silver sword now that I can fight back, you stupid cow.* Liz snarls, showing me her teeth, and I huff out a laugh. What the hell was that? Huh, it's not just her walk that's ridiculous. I chuckle.

Oh my, Harry is here! I mentally slap myself and squirm in my chair, aware that this could end badly. Poor Harry.

Liz reaches our table. A choking cloud of perfume follows in her wake. I frown as I watch with growing confusion as Liz places one hand on the back of Harry's chair and the other on his jaw. She turns his head, and while maintaining eye contact with me, bends down and delicately kisses Harry on the cheek. She leaves her red lipstick on him and flashes me a smug smile.

"Hi, baby, so glad we could meet for a coffee," she simpers, plastering a sweet smile on her lips.

Harry goofily grins back at her. "Hi, Liz. Would you like a slice of cake?"

What. The. Fuck.

I blink. I feel blindsided. I've no idea what the hell is happening. What is she doing here?

"Oh, no thank you, I don't eat cake," Liz says with a shudder. *Psycho!* I scream in my head—who doesn't eat cake? "But I would love a triple-shot decaf skinny soya macchiato with sugar-free hazelnut syrup. If they have one," she says again, sweetly fluttering her eyelashes. I have no idea what she ordered, although I am quite sure her pretentious drink isn't on the menu. Harry scrambles away, and I watch him go to the counter. I can hear him mumbling the order back to himself, so he doesn't forget it.

Liz glares at me from across the table. I stare back at her blankly, kind of numbly. She sighs, drops her gaze from mine, and pulls out her phone. She types furiously, ignoring me. Fine by me.

Harry arrives back at the table. I watch dazed as with a flourish he places a regular-looking coffee in front of Liz. He steps back and rubs the back of his head. "It's a normal decaf coffee with...urm, soya milk, they didn't have the other stuff you wanted..." He bounces from foot to foot, anxiously waiting on Liz's approval.

"Oh well," Liz says, again sweetly.

What the fuck is wrong with her? Having her so close and her being nice is starting to freak me out. I know she's not being nice to me, but still, this whole situation is beyond my comprehension. A few short weeks ago, Harry was calling Liz nasty names. She cheated on him! Now he's presenting coffee to her like he has hunted her a prized rabbit. What happened to the whole "I can't be with a cheater"?

"We can go to a better place next time. This place is small, and it smells funny." She sniffs in my direction. Ah there she is...am I weird to feel a little relieved?

"Yeah, next time." Harry beams at Liz and throws himself down into his seat next to her. He sits slumped, with his legs and arms wide. Liz gives me a cocky smile. My bullshit detector sounds—she's up to something. For some reason, her smile makes me want to hop over the table and smash her in the face.

"I am glad you're here, dog..." Liz covers her mouth and giggles over her fake Freudian slip. *Dog.* I briefly close my eyes. It's just a word, and words only hurt you if you let them. I won't give Liz the satisfaction of seeing me react. I sit taller in my chair, fighting my natural hunching reaction, and take a deep calming breath. I cough as I inhale a mouthful of her perfume. God, did she use the whole bottle? "I know that you are *extremely* good friends with my baby and that you want to spend more time with him." She smiles the largest, toothiest, and phoniest smile I have ever seen.

I tip my head to the side. Where is she going with this? Harry is pack.

"What you don't understand is that you can't buy his affection by giving him a shitty house, especially when it was your fault in the first place that he was homeless and classed as a rogue." Liz leans forward across the table and growls. My mouth pops open in shock. *What?* "Admit that you manipulated the whole situation for your own gain and that you staged that phone call." Liz points a red-tipped finger at me, her nails painted to match the tight bandage dress that she's wearing. "Admit it. I am here to tell you that Harry is mine and that you need to leave us alone! You also need to speak to your brother and fix Harry's rogue status. Your lies will come out and you need to fix your wrongs before they do." Liz sits back and raps her coffee cup with her red nails. A smug, satisfied smile flashes across her face.

I blink. What the fuckity fuck fuck? What planet is this girl on? I flick my eyes toward Harry and scrutinise his reaction to her words. I wait for him to tell her to fuck off, but in growing disbelief, I watch as he nods his agreement. He nods his fucking head!

Harry leans forward and with consolation pats my hand, which is gripping the edge of the table. I flinch back and rub away a sharp pain in my chest with my knuckles.

Ouch. I fight to keep my face blank.

"I am sure you're upset. Liz explained everything and what she says makes sense." Harry smiles lovingly at Liz. "You have issues, Forrest." Harry makes a fake sad face and sniffs.

"Her word is no good, baby. Look, she hasn't even bothered to deny our accusations! We have to see this as a righteous intervention. Your pack kept the ungrateful dog safe. What else could you do? She was feral! Why do you think she doesn't talk? She is worried we will catch her out. No one believes her—she's a liar." Liz drops her voice. "None of this would have happened if you would have listened and had her killed when we had the chance." Harry nods his head again, hate shining in his blue eyes.

My heart is eviscerated.

I squeeze my eyes tight. I refuse to cry. I want so much to curl in on myself, but by sheer will, I snap my spine straight.

God, I so wanted to treat Harry with trust and kindness. I wanted to see the best in him. I thought he was my pack, my brother. Yet every time Harry gets the chance, he says something to hurt me, and a piece of me dies. I feel sick, my mouth is dry, and there's a lump in my throat that I can't swallow. The person I thought Harry was, doesn't exist.

I made him up.

The realisation hits me with the force of a double-decker bus—the hole in my chest aches.

I'm an idiot.

"She isn't a pureblood female anyway, right, baby?" Liz strokes Harry's face and sneers in my direction. "She is like part Fae or dwarf or something." She leans into him and whispers, "That's why she is so small and went feral for all those years." Liz runs her fingers through her bobbed hair, and her eyes sparkle with delight as she speaks. "I mean, look at her hair and eyes, what she is wearing—she's a complete freak."

"Part dwarf"—how rude is that. I'm wearing sparkly silver trainers, leggings, and a cute jumper—normal stuff. I force myself not to adjust my grey unicorn jumper. Honestly, what is wrong with this girl? Why does she hate me? The poison dripping out of her mouth is pure fabrication, and Harry is lapping it up. She's crazy, and Harry is nuts to believe anything that comes out of her mouth.

I think I prefer Liz being fake-nice.

The horrible cow can't even address me while insulting me. The least she could do is say this shit while looking me in the eye. I lift my bum off the chair with the sole intention of beating the shit out of her. I might knock both their heads together while I'm at it.

"Sweetcheeks, are you ready to go?" a rumbly voice asks behind me. I sit back down and turn to take in the shifter who has swaggered up to the table, somehow appearing from the toilets behind us. He's dressed impeccably—charcoal custom suit and matching overcoat. I examine Liz, and her face shows zero recognition.

Is he...talking...to me?

I frown. He dips his head, his full attention on me.

Bloody hell—he *is* talking to me.

"Come on, sweetcheeks. I know you wanted to do your normal thing with your *brother*, but we had better get going. We have so much to do today." The strange wolf smiles warmly at me.

I blink at him. Is everyone on drugs, or am I the only person who has not got a clue what the fuck is going on today?

He leans across the table and offers his hand to Harry. "I am Daniel Kerr, it's good to meet you, Harry, finally."

Wow, the strange wolf is good—he gives Liz zero acknowledgement. It's like the mad cow is not even sitting there. I can almost forgive him for calling me "sweetcheeks"—almost. Like bloody hell, that's annoying. Grrr, "sweetcheeks..."

Daniel doesn't even glance at Liz, even when she squeezes her ample breasts together. She's almost propping them up on the table. *Steady, Liz, if you squish those puppies any more, they're gonna pop out.*

"Yeah..." says Harry as he shakes Daniel's hand. Total confusion is written all over his face.

Daniel inspects me with a gentle smile, his blue eyes sparkling. "You are looking beautiful today, little wolf," he whispers as his hand gently cups my face. He runs his thumb across my bottom lip. I am so surprised, I don't react aggressively—I sit and gawk up at him. The gesture is so intimate, I have no clue how to respond.

How many times does an absolute stranger swagger up to you, make out that you are in a fake relationship, and start touching your face? Nothing could prepare me for this shit.

Liz is livid and has gone from smug to downright murderous. She has also gone bright red, the colour closely matching her dress and nails. Her gaze bounces from Daniel to me and back again. Liz again tries to gain Daniel's attention by flapping her hands about, frantically trying to highlight her table-boobs. She's also glaring at Harry—she wants him to do something, but Harry is also clueless about how to react.

I guess this wasn't part of their righteous intervention—fancy that.

"So you're Harry, the rogue? From the dissolved Oakland pack? Thanks for keeping *my* Forrest company, Harry. I know she doesn't talk to you, but she finds you amusing." He slaps Harry on the back, in a supposedly friendly gesture. But his big hand wallops him hard enough to rock Harry's body forward, almost forcing him from his chair. Harry winces. "If you will excuse us. We have a busy day and night ahead. Forrest, come." He takes hold of my arm gently, and I stand. I gratefully allow him to guide me from my chair and between the busy tables. Before I go through the door, I turn and make sure to give the stunned couple a snide little wave goodbye. Fuckers.

"I apologise for interrupting your conversation, but I couldn't listen to that vile girl for one more second," Daniel says when we're safely out on the pavement.

What the fuck just happened? Did this guy randomly rescue me? I look up and up. He's of course, shifter-tall—he must be around six-foot-eight. The top of my head is about level with the middle of his chest. He looks down at me, amusement dancing in his eyes. I give him a suspicious nod of thanks and a little awkward wave, and turn to stomp away.

"She is still watching, Forrest. Come on, I will give you a lift home." I look up into his handsome face. His eyes are blue and his hair is dark. He has that square jaw and heavy brow– look going on that's popular with movie stars.

I strangely allow him to take my arm and lead me towards a posh-looking car at the curb.

CHAPTER SEVENTEEN

Daniel opens the rear passenger door for me, and I slide into the seat. He closes the door and swaggers around to the other side of the car and gets in.

Why I go with him, I have not a clue. If I am honest, I don't want to give Liz the win. She tried to bring me down just now, and without Daniel's timely intervention, I would have entirely and embarrassingly lost my head in there. The only thing I lost today was my rose-coloured glasses in regard to Harry.

I grimace and rub my chest again. I could learn to live with that just fine.

I snap my seat belt into place.

The car sets off and the doors lock, I hope automatically — although the smug, nasty glower the driver gives me from the rear-view mirror suggests otherwise. The driver is male, a shifter with a bald head and a goatee. With a blatant sinking feeling, I realise he is Meathead One, the guy who I knocked out a few weeks ago.

I put my head in my hands and rub my temples. Oh, fucking hell—without being a genius, I now know who Daniel is. I spoke to Daniel once before; he is *Bossman,* the guy who ordered the two meathead wolves to track and take me.

I can't believe I got into his car. I'm a fucking idiot!

I lean my elbow on the door and nudge the electric window button. It quietly moves the window down an inch, which is a good thing. It means I am not trapped. I peek up at Daniel, and he is silently watching me, a satisfied smile on his face.

"Do you know, since our last conversation on the phone, Forrest, I have been more than a little intrigued about you. Your story, your history. In wolf form for so long, trapped. Yet despite the disadvantages, over the last few months, you have thrived. Now that I have met you in person, I am fascinated."

I think Daniel is waiting for me to reply. I don't feel comfortable chatting with a man who has more than likely just abducted me.

One thing I have noticed is, the less you talk, the more others seem prone to do so. They talk and talk. My silence makes them a little uncomfortable, so they fill in my silence with noise. It's such a weird thing that happens—even guys who generally only give one-word answers or have a grunting system open up to me like I am a priest on confessional duty.

"You are so different from other females of our species. Unique. I am almost six hundred years old and even in my long lifetime, I have never had the pleasure of meeting someone like you. It's as if you, little wolf, were created for me." *What?* I gape at Daniel with what I'm sure is a confused and horrified expression. His eyelids droop, he licks his lips. Is he trying to seduce me? *Eww*, I'm not at all impressed. He looks at me as if the sun shines out my bum. Creepy. Apart from our telephone conversation a few weeks ago, I have never spoken to the guy. Yet it's like he's starting on the path of declaring undying love. I wiggle in my seat. The way he's talking...it faintly reminds me of another car-journey conversation with a demon.

"If I hadn't seen the CCTV footage of you taking down two of my best men, I would have never believed it. I am impressed; you are a talented young woman. I'm so glad you made the right decision to leave with me." I have no idea what he wants me to say. Does he want me to give him a gold star?

He inches closer to me, turning his body so he's facing me. He reaches over and tries to paw my face in the same way he did in the café.

I growl at him. Instead of taking that as a warning, he leans further into my space with a throaty chuckle. Fear and rage flood my system, and I start to shake. Daniel takes a deep breath in, breathing my scent at the pulse point on my neck. He groans. I growl. Everything inside me screams that I need to get away, that I'm not safe.

This guy is not right in the head.

I move as far away as the seat belt will allow, squishing myself into the corner of the car. I am still growling. His right hand takes hold of my hip, and he slides me back across the leather, closer to him. He puts his hand on my seat belt, tightening it so I can't move, basically trapping me in the seat. With the seat belt across me like this, I won't be able to shift. Well, I can, but I will still be trapped. His hand is blocking the belt-buckle release.

Becoming frantic, I lift both my legs up to try to kick him away from me, but he blocks the movement with his body weight, pinning my legs to the seat. Daniel is almost entirely on top of me. His right hand has managed to grab hold of both of my wrists. I watch him wide-eyed, panting.

I grapple with my rising panic.

What the hell is happening? I try again to escape him, and his grip becomes painfully tight—the lack of room a problem.

"You're not getting away from me again. You. Are. Mine," he snaps. I flinch at the venom in his voice, and he immediately calms. His tone switches to cajoling. "There's no way out of this, Forrest. Hasn't today proven your poor judgment and that you are not safe left to your own devices? Little wolf, no one will appreciate you as I will. No one will keep you safe as I can." I try to squirm away, unsuccessfully.

I don't know why he's doing this.

The softness now in his eyes is disconcerting. Daniel is the worst kind of villain. He thinks he's doing the right thing. Delusional wanker.

My mouth is too dry to speak, my brain too confused to form words.

Daniel leans forward, and I shudder. He smiles against my cheek and my skin ripples in disgust at his closeness. "Little wolf, I can't wait to be inside you."

Oh my fucking God! I freak the fuck out.

I lose control of myself for a few seconds. The primal fear screaming through my body stops me from thinking clearly. I whine, and I struggle desperately to get away. In those short moments, I forget all of my training. I need to get away!

The meathead driving laughs.

He. Laughs.

I force myself to stop and breathe, to think.

To Daniel, it might look like I have given up or exhausted myself. But I am desperately trying to get hold of my instincts. I am no way used to a grown-ass man talking to me like this. He's got me trapped almost underneath him in a moving vehicle going God only knows where. Does he think it's okay to talk dirty to me in this situation? Maybe some girls would like being trapped helpless with a handsome wolf. But that's another type of story, and this is mine.

I spent years trapped. I dealt with and took so much shit as a wolf. I am not going to deal with this shit as a woman—no fucking way. I have no idea where he's going with this, but I am not a bloody victim, and I am not hanging around.

This is not bloody okay!

My anger triggers another response, and my shifter magic reacts beautifully. My fingers shift into wolf claws for the first time.

Daniel drops my wrists in shock, mumbling the word *magnificent*.

I don't think—I react. Owen's voice screams directions in my head, and I use my claws in one quick move to not only slash the seat belt, setting myself free, but at the same time swiping them viciously across Daniel's neck and chest.

The sudden pain forces him to move away from me—although Daniel, the weirdo, looks back at me with a thrilled appreciation. I take advantage of his distraction, and I smack the window-down button. Before the window has opened fully, and before he decides to try to restrain me further. I shift into my wolf.

I leap through the window, escaping the still-moving vehicle.

I am on the left-hand side of the car, so I don't have to contend with any other vehicles. My shoulder collides with the pavement hard, and I roll with the force of impact.

I shake it off. Apart from my pride, I am unhurt. I run.

Luckily for Daniel, he doesn't follow, as I am so bloody angry I could rip his throat out and chew his nose off with my teeth. I am that cross. I hate feeling frightened. I know it's unrealistic, but I'd stupidly hoped that I would never have to deal with that kind of fear again.

God, am I always destined to be somebody's victim?

The lack of respect he showed me is mind-boggling. I don't know if it's just my opinion, but men shouldn't jump on you like that. Did his mother not teach him not to assault random women, or is it the case that he's so good looking he has never dealt with rejection?

I didn't say *No* or *Get off me you fuck*. So maybe it was my fault—perhaps I should have used my damn voice? Why didn't I use my voice! Harry is right on one thing—I'm bloody weird. I have a voice. I need to use it. What the hell is wrong with me?

Bad things happen if I don't talk.

But Daniel is a shifter, and he must have smelled my fear. He knew I was frightened, yet he continued anyway. He didn't back off, *but he didn't touch me inappropriately either*, a horrid little voice says helpfully in the back of my head.

After I get my bearings, I realise he was taking me out of the city. The car was on the main road leading to the motorway. I was lucky on the timing of my jump, as the speed limit on this road is only thirty.

I know where I am, and I also know Jodie's coven shop isn't too far away. I need to talk to my witch friend. I need a friendly female point of view, so I get my furry ass moving to Jodie's.

As I run, I wonder if it's me and my circumstances that make male wolf-shifters react with zero respect. So far, all that I have been met with is scary misogynist beliefs. They seriously think that they can do what they want to me without consequence.

For fuck's sake, I just jumped out of a moving car to get away from that prick Daniel.

The freaky fuck probably thought it was some kind of foreplay.

I huff. Shit, I was better off sitting in that café taking nasty digs from Liz, and that's saying something...why the hell did I get in that car?

I have spent so much time in my wolf form learning about life from catching the odd TV show through the kitchen window. I have no idea how to behave as an adult shifter. I got lucky just now—the size of him compared to the size of me.

I am not letting myself deeply analyse all the crap that just happened. Being upset, hurt, and frightened isn't going to help. Nor is acting in anger and chewing Daniel's face off, unfortunately.

I have to think of things rationally. If I start thinking like a terrified woman, I'm going to make a mistake and get hurt.

It happened, I am okay, and the best thing I can do is learn from my mistake.

So I shove all this bullshit quite forcibly to the back of my mind. I push it into another mental box, this one labelled *Deal with Later*.

At least today shouldn't get any worse.

CHAPTER EIGHTEEN

It doesn't take me too long to reach Jodie's, as I set an excellent loping pace. I arrive at the shop, and it smells heavily of herbs and magic. I haven't been here before, but Jodie gave me an open invitation to visit. God, I hope Jodie is around and not working at the hospital. I desperately need to see a friendly face.

The magic shop, with a sign written in bold letters above the double frontage, proclaims: 'Tinctures 'n Tonics' - Specialists in Portable Potions. The store proudly sits sandwiched between an art gallery on the left and hairdressers on the right. Housed in a modest-sized building rendered in cream with an old bank sign engraved into the stone above the door, it is situated on Birley Street, a pedestrianised street in the middle of the city.

I plop down in front of the closed door. I lift my front paw and give the door a tap-tap, being mindful of my sharp claws and that they don't mark the paint. After a few taps, a young witch in a blue school uniform answers. She swings the door wide in welcome.

"Forrest, how are you doing, come in, come in. Jodie! Jodie! Forrest is here, and she is all wolfy!" The young witch, Heather, squeals her excitement and gives me a huge welcoming smile. I met Heather at the hospital when she helped Jodie bring in a potion order. I find the young witch adorable. "Forrest, can I stroke you? Please, please, please?" Heather wiggles, waving jazz hands at me with a big grin on her face, her short blonde curls bouncing. "You are just so cute."

In response, I nod my head, my tongue flops out, and I give her my best wolfy grin. Heather squeals again in delight. I flop down on the wooden floor, and Heather throws herself to the floor next to me.

Heather gently strokes the fur around my head and ears. She runs her hands along my back. It's sooooo lovely. I've never had my fur stroked before. Thinking about it, I've never known a kind touch in this form. With each stroke of Heather's hands, I find myself relaxing further into the floor.

I glance around the shop with interest. It's brightly lit—natural light filters through the big windows at the front. Fascinatingly, dozens of magical globes of light float in different corners of the room. As the light in the shop changes throughout the day the floating orbs will move to where they're needed. One has already made its way above Heather and myself. So cool.

I notice that the wooden shelves are filled to the brim with wonders. The tingling hum of energy from the magical artefacts fills the air, and the almost-overwhelming smell of herbs stings my nose.

I close my eyes. Life isn't so bad if you don't focus on the negatives.

"Come on now, leave her alone, you crazy child. She is a woman underneath all that fur." I open one eye, and Jodie is standing in front of a door, for what I presume is the back employee area of the shop. A genuine smile is on her pretty face. "Forrest, so nice to see you, pumpkin. If you change back, I will make you a cuppa." She turns and trots back into the room behind her.

"Aww, I never get to see shifters in animal form. I wanted more time...your fur is so soft." Heather whines her complaint as she scrambles up from the floor and stomps away.

I huff out a wolfy laugh and get up with a stretch. I make my way over to the door, my claws clicking on the floor. I peek in.

The room is large but cosy, decorated in warm tones of green that appeal to me. It has a proper wood-burning stove and a comfy seating area at one end and a beautiful, big, industrial-sized witches' kitchen at the other, with a table that can seat twelve in the middle.

As I enter the room, I allow the shift to take me. The magic transforms my body from wolf to my human form in seconds. It doesn't hurt, and it feels natural. It's not like the human-made racist werewolf films, where the bones break, strange fluid grossness comes out, and the werewolf screams in pain. It's a blink-and-you-miss-it kind of transformation, pure, beautiful magic.

Magic is breathtaking in its complexity. For example, witches handle magic differently from shifters. There are so many branches of magic some witches are potion specialists like Jodie and her coven. Other witches specialise in elemental stuff.

My point is, witches *manipulate* magic. Shifters *are* magic.

One interesting fact I did find out about witches from Jodie is, witches have the opposite issue from the shifters: male witches are extremely rare.

Jodie has her back to me and is making tea. Wow, she is pulling out all the stops. Jodie has arranged delicate teacups, saucers, and a beautiful teapot on a tray. She places on it a little milk jug and a sugar bowl, with actual sugar lumps...so fancy.

I dig out the potion balls from my pockets. I might as well get Jodie to check them, as I am not sure whether the shifting back and forth has ruined them. The shifting magic Jodie gifted me with at the hospital makes my clothing part of the transformation, so I retain my clothing when I change back. It also shifts my weapons—how amazing is that! The only thing it doesn't shift with me is tech, so I am not sure if it will like other magic coming along for the ride. I love not having to strip naked to shift.

"You can put them in the bowl on the side table, I will check them in a bit." I huff. Jodie still has her back to me. *Freaky witch*, I think with amusement. Grinning, I obediently pop them into the bowl.

"Sit down," she says, carrying the tray of tea things to the table. "So tell me, what is wrong? It isn't like you to be carelessly running around in your wolf form."

I sit and chew my lip. I bet half the shit that happened today wouldn't have happened if I'd opened my bloody mouth. I can't let this control me anymore. I place my head in my hands and rub my temples. Where do I start...

"Use your words, Forrest. It's just us here. Please explain to me what has happened." She smiles at me with encouragement. Her brown eyes are warm and reassuring, so I open my mouth, take a big breath in, and tell her.

I explain what happened with Harry, with Daniel. At first, Jodie is livid with Harry and all swoony over Daniel's timely rescue. But the more I elaborate, the angrier Jodie becomes. Jodie is furious on my behalf. I feel so lucky to have such a good friend. I also feel a sense of relief that my friend knows the details about today and agrees with most of my conclusions. Jodie doesn't think I overreacted to either situation. She gives me the impression that I should have acted sooner.

After she calms down on seriously wanting to maim Daniel for the car incident, Jodie finally decides against giving me an exploding dick potion. I think.

"Here, this one is a male impotence potion." Jodie hands me a bright red ball. "It is a witches' version of pepper spray; not only does it make it impossible for a man to get it up for weeks, it also incapacitates even a shifter for about twenty minutes, so you can either escape or as an alternative stab him." She grins.

I stare at the small innocuous ball on my palm and blink up at my friend. I hope she hasn't sneakily given me the scary one. As if Jodie can read my mind, she bursts out laughing. "Your face..." She laughs so hard, tears stream down her face. I watch her with bemusement. When she can speak, Jodie says, "I promise it's not the exploding one, Forrest." Jodie cackles again, slapping her leg, her eyes sparkling. "With this potion, if an afflicted man goes to any witch for help, she will know and will probably extend the life of the impotence potion. So be careful and only use it in a situation like today, as it is a very effective punishment." She rubs the tears from her eyes.

Wow. Note to self: don't piss off a witch.

"Thank you," I say with a cautious smile. The wrath of Jodie is a beautiful thing. I dramatically shudder, and Jodie starts giggling again.

"I wish you had smacked Liz about a bit..." Jodie says wistfully.

Daniel inadvertently stopped me from kicking Liz's ass, which did me a favour, I guess, in the long term. "I just have a new slimy stalker to contend with." That sobers my friend up, and she gives me a sad smile.

"Okay, well, we're going to have to do something about the shifters being able to track you so easily. I do have a few things that will be perfect...give me a second." Jodie claps her hands, jumps up, and starts rooting around in her stock room. After a good fifteen minutes, she producers a gorgeous bracelet. "Now first, this bracelet," Jodie says, putting it on the table in front of me. "If you decide to use it, it's not just pretty; it's also incredibly complex magic. When you wear it, you will be impossible to track."

Use it? I stuff that sucker on my left wrist so fast, Jodie hasn't even finished telling me about it. Jodie gives me a bright smile and shakes her head at me. She pours me another cup of tea and continues. "It is scent-masker magic. It will change your scent entirely and regularly. So even standing directly in front of a shifter, you will smell like a regular mixed human. Oh..." Jodie springs up and returns with an old box, which she places on the table with a thump. "By the time I'm finished with you, these wolf shifters will not know that you're standing directly in front of them. Even your hellhound friend won't recognise you with this next beauty."

"Ooh, is it a glamour?" I ask cautiously. Jodie rolls her eyes and shakes her head.

"No, not a glamour—a lot of strong creatures can see through them. Nope, what you need and what I have here, Forrest, is disguise magic," Jodie whispers conspiratorially. Ooooh.

I leave Jodie's shop hours later, a scrap of paper with a phone number clutched in my hand and my pockets full of shiny fun-filled potion balls. On the good-news front, after checking, Jodie confirmed that my other potion balls had survived my shifts. Which is fantastic news as it tells me that my new magical bracelets will also shift with me without an issue.

On my left wrist, I have my fantastic scent masker, and on my right wrist, I have the disguise bracelet. The disguise magic isn't active all the time, unlike the scent-masker magic. With the disguise bracelet, I have to put my fingers on it and say the word *Betty*—which activates the spell.

It was hilarious, choosing what I wanted to look like. There's nothing like giggling at yourself while looking in the mirror and you have a giant nose and a massive chin. Spending time with Jodie lifted my spirits. I feel lighter.

In the end, because my voice is so deep and husky, we decided on an old-lady disguise, and "Betty" is perfect. I still have my build, height, and hair colour—blue rinse used to be a thing, so why not pink? Popping my hair into a bun, I will be good to go. The less we alter with magic, the less chance of the spell being discovered. Brown eyes, a sharp nose, and lots of wrinkles, happy human wrinkles. Like a lifetime spent laughing and smiling. Shifters don't show our age with lines like humans; our age isn't stamped on our faces and bodies. No, age is measured by the level of power that radiates beyond normal senses. Once a shifter hits their natural maturity, their prime—normally a human-looking thirty to forty years—the body doesn't age. Shifters don't care about age; it's all about power.

With a little bit of artistic dressing up, even if it's just a coat, Granny Betty will be good to go, the perfect disguise.

CHAPTER NINETEEN

When I arrive back at the apartment building, I find out that John has been in contact and wants to speak to me immediately. Apparently, he wants to discuss what happened today with Daniel and the whole kidnapping thing. I've no idea how he found out so quickly.

When John answers my video call, he looks livid. For a second, I'm pleased to see how upset he is on my behalf.

That thought ends up being *hugely* presumptive.

"I had an interesting telephone call with *Councillor* Daniel Kerr." I freeze and my face blanks. Oh bloody hell, stalker Daniel is a council member. Fuck my life. I observe John with growing trepidation.

"You do realise, Forrest, that having a member of the council calling me about my unruly sister is completely unacceptable. What the fuck have you been doing to piss off one of the most important shifters in the country!" John roars.

Shock fills me, and in response, my magic tingles and my fingers partially shift to claws: off-camera, Owen grunts in surprise. I grimace. This conversation isn't supposed to go this way. I bite my lip and twist my hands in my lap. The claws on my left hand inadvertently dig into my thigh, and the scent of my blood permeates the air. Owen promptly takes hold of my hand in silent support, and more than likely to stop me from further shredding my leg.

Unaware, my brother continues to berate me. "The councilman explained what happened today in detail." John rubs the back of his neck and growls, "We decided the whole incident was your fault, clearly due to your lack of life experience. I am so disappointed in you, Forrest —you behaved like a manic child. You obviously misinterpreted the entire interaction with the councilman. Our mother would be ashamed of your erratic behaviour."

My stomach jolts when he mentions my mum. The memory of my mum that day at the warehouse tries to smash into the forefront of my mind. No, that flashback shit is not happening. I grab the memory and stuff it back into its box. No, hell no.

John is wrong; I know in my heart that my mum would understand, unequivocally.

"Daniel Kerr was not trying to kidnap you or do anything inappropriate. Bloody hell, you stupid girl, the notion that a council member would try to capture *you* is utterly ridiculous." John shakes his head and curls his lip; his disgust with me is apparent, and it is written on every line of his furious face.

I gather my courage and open my mouth to respond to his unfair accusations. The determination to stick up for myself throbs through my whole body.

"He—"

"No! I'm talking." John cuts me off with a snarl and holds his hand up to silence me further.

My eyes burn as I stare at my brother, silently communicating my hurt.

"Daniel said you assaulted him. Forrest, you assaulted a council member! He could have been seriously hurt. He also mentioned that prior to the assault, he had to intervene in your attack on an innocent female shifter. What the fuck is wrong with you! You need professional help! I convinced the councilman not to take any legal action, and lucky for you he won't be involving the hunters. But we decided between ourselves that you cannot be trusted." Confusion swirls inside of me, and my heart hammers in my ears. It takes everything in my power to sit quietly and not react. Owen squeezes my hand as I struggle to remain outwardly calm. I draw in another shaky, painful breath.

"Daniel was also concerned about how you left his car in such a dangerous fashion. The window, Forrest, really?" John continues his lecture. "Daniel has offered, at his own expense, his well-trained shifters to take over your bodyguard duty. From now on, when you want to leave the building, they will accompany you. The hellhounds are too busy to deal with you and your shenanigans." John shakes his head in frustration and disappointment.

Daniel has played John well. What a manipulative bastard. I've not got a clue how I'm going to deal with this. Well played, Daniel, well played.

"I did decline the invitation for you to go and live with him." Well, that's real magnanimous of him, refusing my kidnaper full-time access. "I feel as if you've had enough upheaval. But I'm warning you now, Forrest Hesketh, one more mistake and I will wash my hands of you." He meets my gaze, and another growl slips between his teeth. John is terrifying when he loses his temper, and at the moment, he is holding himself together with the thinnest of threads. "You need professional help. Daniel will be arranging that for you. I don't know how you got so fortunate, gaining his favour. Especially after everything you have done." John shakes his head. "The councilman is a better man than myself." John rubs the back of his neck again.

In a quieter voice, he says, "What did I expect from a feral wolf? You behave like an animal, and I will treat you like one. If I could put you on a lead, I would." I suck in a breath. Wow, fucking harsh, a lead? Really, John? Why not get me another electric collar while you are at it? "Now, you've wasted enough of my time. I've got to get back to work. Behave yourself." John ends the call without a goodbye.

I sit in the chair feeling numb. I huff in frustration. Why the hell did I mention that today couldn't get any worse? Bloody Murphy's Law.

Fuck my life.

I close my eyes and repeatedly bang the back of my head on the seat. That whole conversation escalated quickly. Technically I did claw

Daniel in self-defence, but what the fuck! He did the assaulting. Now John has invited this powerful and dangerous man further into my life.

If I hadn't spoken to Jodie today, I might have been persuaded that I'd overreacted. The cruel things John said… "One more mistake, and I will wash my hands of you." So easy for him to say, and to believe Daniel's bullshit.

To not ask me for my truth.

I appraise my bleeding leg. The cuts are shallow. I sigh. I have ruined my leggings.

Daniel, the bastard, has manoeuvred us all around like chess pieces and has gotten his own way. A tear rolls down the side of my nose, and I use my shoulder to wipe it away.

I need to hit the gym. I need to beat the crap out of something, and after I am a sweaty mess, I need to spend a few hours meditating. If I don't, I am liable to go hunt Daniel, that fucker, down and show him what assault really looks like. While he's on the floor bleeding, I want to scream and shout at him for frightening me in that car, for turning my brother against me.

No. I bet he's counting on me reacting like that, without thinking. Going after him with all guns blazing will play right into his hands. Acting like the animal that John claims me to be.

A sob wrenches itself out between my lips. I screw my eyes closed tight.

The best thing I can do is play it smart, keep my head down, and don't react. I am not bloody playing Daniel's sick game.

Daniel needs to think I am scared prey, weak, without friends. To enforce that belief, it might be best if I didn't leave my apartment. With my years stuck in wolf form I have a history of being left in a horrible situation. So this is what he would expect anyway. A predictable pattern of response, to lull him into making a mistake—and given enough rope, he will hang himself.

I think about my brothers and the pieces of my soul that they have destroyed today. I have grown up with neglect and constant pain from my supposed loved ones. Hell—I shake my head—it's easy for me to acclimatise to the callousness of this world, as I expect to be kicked while I'm down. I've dealt with this shit before. Mental and physical abuse—yeah, we're well acquainted.

Life is bloody unfair.

It's how you deal with it that defines you, and I refuse to be a bitter, horrible person who's ruled by my rage.

Why do the men in my life do this? Why are they so fucking cruel?

"That was a bit unfair," Owen says. I open my eyes and blink up at him. I realise we are still holding hands; he has been so quiet, letting me think. Huh, not all the men in my life. I squeeze his hand in a silent thank you. "Will you please tell me what happened?" I let go and poke at my claws. I peek up and give my friend a sad smile, and another blasted tear rolls down my cheek. As I did with Jodie, I start from the beginning.

After I've finished, Owen's angry energy rips around the room. He sucks in a sharp breath, then lets it out in a huff. Eyeing me, he growls.

"John needs to be told—"

"Please, he won't believe me. You heard him. Please, Nanny Hound, you don't have to fight with my brother or Daniel. I...I won't be anyone's burden." The wobble in my voice is pathetic. "It will play right into Daniel's hands. I need to pick my battles and not show my hand." I then go on to explain my thinking and theory.

I meet Owen's gaze; there's fear and anger in his grey eyes. Owen cares about me. I try to convey how grateful I am. My eyes sting and my chest burns. He visibly swallows, scrubs a hand over his face, and manages a surly grunt and a stiff nod.

"Okay." Owen then checks me over; he nods once when he's reassured I'm not an inch away from death. He ruffles my hair like I'm a kid. I then get a whole ten-minute lecture on why getting into a stranger's car is so dangerous. The normality of being told off pulls me away from the teetering edge of hysteria. The warm hug after the stranger-danger talk also helps.

Owen agrees that both the scent masker and disguise magic is a good idea. The less my movements now are tracked, the better.

We both decide that I'm on lockdown and I can't leave my apartment, let alone the building. Not with the new set of shiny henchmen, erm, I mean the *bodyguards* that will be patrolling. Heck, how much are you betting it will be the Meatheads on guard duty? As I am planning sneaky ways to escape, perhaps learning to abseil, Owen tells me about portal doors.

"We have portals? How did I not know that portals were a thing?"

"They are a witch-created gateway system attached to other portals all over the world, using ley line magic," Owen explains. "You have to have permission to go anywhere and know the gateway codes. Otherwise, you're gonna get an unpleasant, possibly even fatal greeting by a ward on the other side." There are local portals all over the city. Owen promises to give me the local codes and the world-gateway portal map later to memorise.

The laziness appeals to me, never mind the stealthiness. The thought of being able to go anywhere in the world instantaneously is mind-boggling. The world is a small place with magic.

Unfortunately, I'm not allowed to play with the newly discovered doorways, because this building doesn't have one.

Owen takes his phone out of his pocket. "I have a lady friend who is a gateway witch." I grin at him. "I can call her—"

"Oh, you have a friend..." I wiggle my eyebrows. Owen is mortified at my teasing. Which encourages me to run my fingers through my hair, flutter my lashes, and pout my lips in a poor impersonation of his hypothetical lady friend. He grimaces in abject horror. I laugh and make grabby hands for his phone. Owen places his big hand on my face and holds the phone out of my reach.

"Stop it. I thought you were having some kind of epileptic fit—don't do that again. Not that kind of friend, Forrest. I can get her to come and install a new gateway in your apartment this evening. The expense will be ridiculous but worth it. Thank God you're rich. I have another witch that owes me a favour, who should be able to come and install a ward after." I bounce on my seat. Whoop! My own portal. "The apartment ward will be extra security; I am thinking to keep this Daniel out of the building will prove impossible. He's a council member with high status. That makes him almost untouchable. It doesn't help that John owns the building and apartments. I could still talk to him...?" I shake my head. "Okay, *we* pick our battles and not show *our* hand." Owen repeats what I said before, meaningfully. "So setting the building ward to blast Daniel or his people, although amusing, would be foolish. So we set a ward to keep them out of your apartment and stop them from getting to you. Meanwhile, you can pretend that you are sitting in your apartment, sulking. It will give us time to find a solution to this mess." Yay. We have a plan. Owen stands and pulls me up from the sofa. "We will use your roof garden for training—using the gym will be out for some time. Starting now, you're on lockdown.

"Right then. Come on, Forrest, get changed. I'm gonna drill you on pressure points, eye-gouging, and your ground game. We also need to make sure those claws don't keep popping out willy-nilly."

CHAPTER
TWENTY

When I was leaving Jodie's shop earlier, she stuffed a slip of paper into my hand, insisting that I needed it. On the paper was a phone number for a group that helped creatures in trouble. Jodie swore they were the real deal and that if anyone had any unbiased information on shifter law and how to deal with problems like Daniel, these would be the people to badger. I took the number to be polite. I originally had zero intention of phoning. Jodie must be psychic.

With my stalker slash kidnapper biting at my heels, I have to do something proactive. I have no real allies. Of course, Owen is on my side. But I can't expect him to put his career and his life on the line for me. What kind of person would I be if I did that? The same goes for Jodie. I've made the sad decision to keep away from my witch friend until this thing with Daniel has calmed down. I don't want to get the witches involved. This isn't their fight. Daniel is too dangerous.

I ring the number, but I don't get a response.

A few hours later, after the witches have installed my new ward and portal, I'm making a cup of tea and my phone rings. I glance at the handset curiously. *Who the heck is calling? No one ever calls me.* Staring at the phone like a weirdo won't give me that information, so I think, *Fuck it,* and answer.

"Hello?" I say cautiously.

"Forrest? I'm returning your call...you seem to have a council-member problem? Are you okay?" I pull the phone away and blink at it. *Huh.*

"Everything's a little bit of a mess," I say guardedly.

That's a massive understatement.

"Yeah, I get that. Let me introduce myself. My name is Ava, and I'm a security expert. I'm sorry I didn't get back to you sooner. I normally vet my callers before speaking to them, and sometimes that can take a while. In your case, I spent the time productively, gathering available evidence. I am happy to tell you I have footage of today's kidnap attempt."

"You have...footage?" I whisper disbelievingly. "How did you know...what type of footage?" I close my eyes and bite my lip. *Please be ringing to help me. Oh please*, I beg to the universe.

"Yes, of both kidnap attempts. Don't forget, Councilman Kerr has tried this twice now." I can hear the faint tapping of a keyboard down the earpiece. "Camera footage from the lights when you jumped out of the car, footage from the café. Oh, and my pièce de résistance: surprisingly, I also have footage from the car."

"Oh my God." I make a sort of gurgling noise. The sound gets stuck in my throat and turns into a whine. I wobble and almost drop my tea. I manage to slide the cup onto the counter before I sink gracelessly to the floor in the middle of the compact kitchen.

Who is this person? Can I trust her? What does she want in return?

"There, I've sent everything I have to your email address. Now, instead of going to your hellhound brother with this information, I think we should aim a little bit higher, don't you think? If you're up for it and if you can trust me, let's sort out this nightmare once and for all."

"I want to trust you," I whisper. My voice wobbles only a little. "I've had a shitty day. I don't know what to say...Ava, this is too good to be true. But I will trust you. Thank you, thank you."

Ava chuckles, her voice warm. "Jodie will be pleased. It is not going to happen overnight. I will have to arrange a meeting, and in the meantime, Forrest you must keep your head down. I can't protect you until I get this evidence to the right person. That's, unless you want to disappear? I can help with that if you don't want to fight. I think you have an excellent chance to clear your name. But I can help you run instead..?"

"I want to try." I'm so glad she's on my side—I hope. I can't believe that she's got hold of all this information and she knows everything without me telling her. It's awe-inspiring. Maybe Ava is a computer hacker? Is this too good to be true? I have everything crossed and have faith that she will not try to fuck me over. "I will keep my head down and stay here. Ava, thank you. If I can help you in return, you only have to ask."

"It's no bother, Forrest, it is what I do. I will ring you when I know more. Take care." After we've said goodbye, still on the kitchen floor with my whole body shaking, I check my email.

Ava came through.

The camera footage is damning. This is what I needed; I hope it's enough.

I think I've found my rope.

I AM STANDING outside my portal door. I shift from foot to foot and wriggle as if I have ants in my pants. I am kind of bricking it. I tug my coat into place and with my fingers comb the loose strands of hair back into my bun. I've been procrastinating on using this gateway for weeks. I'm hesitant to leave the safety of my apartment, frightened that either Daniel or John is going to grab me and lock me away. So I've locked myself away in my apartment—how is that for irony?

I'm also nervous I will hit the wrong gateway symbols and end up somewhere I shouldn't. I regret telling Owen I didn't need his help when it was first installed. In reality, I should have done this weeks ago.

I laugh when I remember the gateway witch and her disgust, which was overflowing when I told her I wanted my portal to be inside my walk-in wardrobe—come on, who doesn't want a portal in a wardrobe? Hello Narnia.

She spent hours doing her amazing portal magic to connect my apartment to the ley lines. The witch was seriously not amused when for fun, I asked her if I could send out some of the clothing I didn't like through a random portal, to give someone a present. The *no* was said forcibly, the look of utter incredulity on her face was priceless. The ward witch was much nicer.

I have been spending my time avoiding Daniel's goons, training with Owen, and reading every book that I can get my hands on. Time has disappeared; it has fluttered away while I've been hiding. Now I need to use the portal, and Owen isn't here to help. Owen, along with the other hellhounds, has been sent away—some important council thing that's all hush-hush. I have a terrible feeling Daniel is messing about in the background, but that might be me being paranoid although I doubt it.

The Meatheads and other guards have been outside for the last few weeks, and I have avoided them like the plague. I have been getting my food delivered, but since the hellhounds' departure, my food deliveries have stopped. It's as if I'm in my castle, safely locked in the tower, and Daniel's sieging, trying his best to starve me out. The prick.

Ava got video evidence of the Meatheads accepting and promptly destroying or eating my food. The bastards ate my bloody chocolate cake! My cake! So in cake desperation, I'm going to take the Betty disguise out for a spin.

I need to be brave.

I bounce on my toes and examine the gateway with apprehension. I know the codes and where I need to go. I just don't know what the portal looks like on the other side, and it's freaking me out.

I take a deep breath, and with a shaky hand, I start to input the code.

The codes are magic symbols; they look similar to Egyptian hieroglyphics but are closer to cuneiform in structure, a magical language not related to human history—the witches call them "runes." There's a fancy big-ass name for them but don't ask me, I haven't a clue. My magical education ended at age nine.

The first three symbols are like an area code, and the next six are for the portal itself. The one I am inputting *should* take me to a portal door in an alleyway a few streets away from a bakery I want to try. I also need to start talking to strangers more, so I can use this trip as speech and portal practice.

I am stalling. Here goes nothing.

I finish the code, hold my breath, and step through.

That wasn't so bad—I am alive, and huh, it felt like I was plodding through a regular door. So anticlimactic—I expected a little bit of tingling or a flash of light, something. I glance about, pleased to see I am in fact in an alley—hopefully, the one I wanted.

What is a little bit interesting and not expected is the two vampires that are standing in front of the portal door as I step out. I almost careen into them. Hopefully, they're using the portal and not guarding it. I shuffle sideways and give a wary nod in greeting. I don't like vampires.

It's not the undead thing or the blood-drinking thing; it's a shifter thing. My nose is so sensitive, and vampires smell like dead stuff slowly rotting. I think it's the start of decomposition before the human body turns, but it also might be what vampires smell like, as a base scent. Rot. Either way, they always make me feel a little sick. I try not to breathe through my nose or flare my nostrils at them in disgust.

Both vampires look like regular humans. One is fat with a horrendous comb-over, the other is skinny. If I squint they look a bit like Laurel and Hardy—all they need are little bowler hats to complete the look.

"So what is an old human like you doing, using the gateways?"

Huh? Human? Oh yes, the scent masker and "Betty"...perfect! It works on vampires—that's good to know. Well, if I am going to use today as practice, I might as well use my voice. Hopefully, they're not going to want to try and eat me. Kicking vamp ass because they wanted to use me as a walking blood-bag doesn't scream "incognito."

I clear my throat and say huskily, "I apologise for almost walking into you gentleman. If you will excuse me, I'm on an errand."

They both look me up and down. "Maybe you can be of help, human. We're looking for a female shifter. Pink hair, gold eyes. I don't suppose you know of anyone with that description?"

Oh, crap, the vamps are talking about me. They are looking for me.

I give a shake of my head and squint at them with what I hope is a confused and worried expression.

Shit, shit, shit.

"I have never met a female shifter before. Is she a criminal?" I do a little shudder, hoping that will disguise my accelerated heart rate.

"No, but she has an outstanding arrest warrant. She has gained someone's interest. Like I said, pink hair, gold eyes, and she doesn't speak. Here is our card if you see anyone like that. You give us a ring, and we will give you some cash, a grand in cash, for a phone call." I nod my head with fake enthusiasm and take the card.

"How wonderful," I say brightly. "I would love that money so I could visit my sister, how wonderful. I will keep my eyes peeled." I pat my pink bun. "Oh, I have pink hair! I hope no one thinks I'm this shifter." I chortle.

"Do not be concerned, human. No one will mistake the two of you for each other," Comb-Over Vampire scoffs.

I wish them good luck as I make my way out of the alley. I keep myself calm, hoping the slight rise in my pulse will not give me away. I try to shuffle to make myself appear more human. I probably look like I've shit my pants. I will have to add that to my practice list: my Betty walk. Humans don't prowl.

ONCE I AM HOME, I make myself a cup of tea, and I sit in the roof garden eating my chocolate cake.

I thumb through my contact numbers. I first try to call Owen, but his phone is switched off. Before I put the phone down, it rings—Ava.

"Hi, you're home safe? Are you aware of the arrest warrant?" I scamper back into my apartment and throw myself down on the sofa. The ward will stop anyone from eavesdropping.

"Yes. What the hell! I just found out this morning. Two vampires were offering cash for sightings of me. Is it Daniel? What is he doing?"

"Well, yes. I can confirm that Daniel Kerr has instigated the warrant. He's getting impatient; it works in our favour beautifully. Involving the Hunters Guild is priceless." The smile in her voice is apparent. "I will email you a copy of the warrant, now. Fortunately, it's not a substantial amount of money. He will get some sloppy independent players trying to get some easy cash. There are firm stipulations about your health and wellbeing, so he doesn't want to hurt you. I feel the warrant is more for making you desperate and backing you into a corner, covering the bases rather than making a serious attempt at capture. Using the Guild to do his dirty work," she tuts. "This illegal warrant has bumped us up the waiting list considerably. I've managed to get you an appointment with the Guild tomorrow."

Ava gives a satisfied chuckle down the phone. "I couldn't find anything on the Guild's system—there's no official case against you. Daniel has bypassed the rules and issued the warrant without the proper documentation. The document even states that you are to be handed over to him and not to the Hunters Guild for processing. To even have a fugitive handed over to the supposed victim is a big no-no. The whole thing stinks. It is such an abuse of power.

"I'm going to use the vampires that you met today as a distraction for your bodyguards. Keep out of sight in the morning. I will make sure it is safe for you to attend the meeting to get the warrant rescinded. I'll send you a car in the morning." We end the call with a goodbye. It's a significant risk to trust her, but it feels right.

The email from Ava comes through on my phone, and I open the attachment and read. It's the supernatural warrant-for-arrest paperwork. I quickly read through the official document declaring me a fugitive.

Huh.

In my head, I see myself dashing through tunnels with Tommy Lee Jones running after me. *"I did not kill my wife!" I scream.*

Oh okay, so that was Harrison Ford. But to make the title of fugitive—even if it's a load of bollocks—makes me feel like a bad girl. I hum a Billie Eilish song, "Bad Guy," as I grab another slice of cake and flick the kettle on.

CHAPTER
TWENTY-ONE

I AM GOING to the Hunters Guild with a demon barrister, yes, a *demon barrister,* whom Ava has arranged to represent me. The demon, whose name is Mr Brown, is accompanying me for questioning in regard to the assault charges against me.

I'm feeling incredibly nervous.

My pink hair is loose, falling to my waist. The hem of the pretty high-necked white dress falls just to my knees. It has lovely ethereal 3D flowers embroidered onto it and a big bow at the back. Underneath I've put on a ruffled underskirt on that makes the skirt puff out. The dress is ridiculous, and because of that, it's bloody perfect. If I'd been tall, the dress would have looked elegant—it's a designer dress, after all. But on my small frame, it makes me appear more fragile. I seem merely like an innocent, *harmless* young woman. I pair the dress with a soft pale blue cardigan, pale blue tights, and delicate white shoes.

My wrists feel bare without my magic bracelets. Ava had warned me I would be security-scanned for magic, so it's best to leave them behind. I'm good to go.

I mince out the lobby door. The bodyguards left in a big rush about half an hour ago, so the coast is clear. Ava has given me the car details, so I feel confident in leaving the safety of the building and its ward when I see the car waiting.

My knuckles go white on the door handle. I tremble. I close my eyes, steady myself, and open the door. I slip inside and greet Mr Brown —he isn't Daniel, I tell my quaking self—with a nod and a small smile.

The demon isn't what I expect; he's thin, with wispy blond hair and pale, watery blue eyes behind thick-rimmed glasses. He's wearing an ugly brown suit. "Miss Hesketh." He nods back at me and then looks out of the window, not expecting a reply. I sit quietly. I don't put my seatbelt on.

It doesn't take us long to arrive at the Hunters Guild building. The car drops us off at the main glass doors, and we're greeted by a harassed-looking lady who rushes us through a magic and weapon screening. Once we have been security-cleared, she shows us to an elevator, where she flashes a card at the panel instead of pressing any buttons. We bypass all the marked floors and head to the top of the building. When the elevator doors open, we step out into a very nicely decorated hallway. At the end of the hall is a single door.

That is not ominous at all.

The door doesn't have a name on it. I have no idea who we're meeting. My nerves must show on my face, as Mr Brown looks down at me with a kind, confident expression.

"Now, Miss Hesketh, all you have to do is speak the truth. I will deal with everything else." I nervously nod and twist my fingers together. The lady opens the door and ushers us into the room. She stays in the hallway and closes the door behind us.

The office is massive, and like the hallway, it's decorated beautifully in browns and golds. The very masculine room has wood panelling halfway up the walls. It has a seating area with a bookcase, a leather sofa, and two wingback chairs.

A huge shifter is seated behind a desk that's situated in front of the floor-to-ceiling windows. The shifter stands in greeting as we make our way towards him. I peer up at the massive fucker, and my eyes settle on the bridge of his nose. In a world full of massive shifters, this guy is hands-down the biggest guy I have ever met. He is shockingly so much bigger than any of the hellhounds, in both height and build—although if you looked at him in a photo, you would think he was a normal-sized man as he is so in proportion. Standing in front of him is a whole other experience.

The navy suit he's wearing doesn't have a single wrinkle or mark. It flawlessly fits across his big chest and broad, round shoulders, his taut, tapered waist. Even in his suit, he'd look more at home with a broadsword in his hands. God, his shoulders are so wide! I bet he'd take your head off in one punch. He must be well over seven feet—I estimate around seven-foot-five. I know instinctively he is a dragon shifter.

The dragon's powerful energy makes my skin tingle, and all the hair on my body stands up. I don't know who he is, but I know he must be very important.

I am not too proud to admit he scares the shit out of me.

He sends my instincts into overdrive. I even find myself stepping behind the demon defensively, which is a pointless move as the dragon can still see me. My eyes scan the room, looking for alternative exits.

He is watching me. His face is not showing any emotion, but his nostrils flare, taking in my scent. His face is a work of art—chiselled, angular, with high cheekbones, a strong jawline, and a straight nose. His lips are full, with the bottom one slightly fuller than the top. The dragon's hair is long and silver; even his skin has a slight silver glow. The man is beautiful. I huff. How could he not be beautiful? He is a dragon shifter, rare and legendary, after all.

God, he's a handsome bastard. I let out an almost inaudible sigh.

The dragon's silver eyes flash, and I instinctively freeze. *Predator.* I try to act like smart prey. I don't move a muscle. I keep my eyes on him and my peripheral vision on the room as a whole. I can feel my chest tightening, and my breath puffs in and out with my panic.

I am both terrified of him and shockingly turned on at the same time.

There's a knock on the door, I jump and squeak in fright— a fucking squeak! The dragon appraises me even harder.

"Come in," he says in a deep, rumbling voice. The door opens, and a dark-haired male witch enters. Wow, a male witch. The witch appears like he's in his forties; he sneaks around the big desk and stands next to the dragon.

That's it, Forrest, focus on the nice witch and not the scary dragon.

The dragon shifter sits back behind his desk and holds out a hand, indicating the visitor chairs. Mr Brown nods and sits. I stand for a few more seconds, wanting to run like hell out of the room. Prompted by the baffled look Mr Brown shoots me, I rush and take the seat.

I scramble into the chair, the dress bunching awkwardly in my panic. I then have to wiggle around like a little girl, trying to straighten it. What makes the whole thing even more difficult is that the chairs are massively oversized, and my bloody feet are about a foot off the floor. I glance up when I finally manage to get sorted, and all three men are looking at me.

I hope I didn't flash them.

I am so glad I am wearing tights. Bloody dress. The dragon grunts.

I peek up at him. I try to ascertain whether the grunt is a good one or bad one.

"Thank you for agreeing to this meeting, General," Mr Brown says with a nod. "I am Mr Brown, and I am here today to represent Miss Forrest Hesketh in regard to an arrest warrant for assault." The dragon doesn't take his eyes off me. I refuse to move about in my chair. I lift my chin, but I can't help glancing towards the exit with my eyes.

"That is a serious charge, Miss Hesketh," the dragon says in a mesmerising, low voice. I nod, trying not to shiver. The witch hands the dragon a tablet, and he reads through the information. After about ten uncomfortable minutes, he glances up. "Okay, I am going to ask you some questions, and you are going to answer them truthfully, Miss Hesketh. Matthew, the truth crystal, if you please." The witch, Matthew, pulls a clear crystal from his pocket, and he places it carefully on the desk.

"Would you pick that up and hold it in your right hand. Keep your hand on the desk at all times," Matthew says quietly. I nod and take hold of the crystal in my trembling palm.

The dragon waits a few seconds and asks, "Can you give me your full name and age, please." I nod again, and I lick my lips nervously.

Shit, I can do this. *Please, voice, please don't fail me.* I cough to clear my throat.

"Forrest Hesketh, and I am..." I feel ancient. "I am twenty-three."

The crystal goes red. Is that bad? It went red! The dragon sighs with disgust, and I glance at Mr Brown in alarm.

"Mr Brown, your client can't even say her name and age without lying! You are wasting my time!"

"General, you have just read Miss Hesketh's file. She has been in her human form for only three months after spending fourteen years as a wolf. I believe her age might be the issue." The room is silent, and everyone is back to staring at me.

"I am sorry, sir," I say, my voice raspy and breathless. I wiggle in the chair. "I don't feel like I am twenty-three. My age is twenty-three. I am twenty-three." The crystal goes red again. I feel like thumping my head on the table. I am trying my best—bloody hell, I'm useless. The dragon is going to eat me!

"Repeat your name!" the dragon barks. I flinch and suck in a ragged breath; my heart is pounding in my ears.

"My name is Forrest Hesketh," I rasp.

"You are here today to deny the charge of assaulting Councilman Kerr?" he asks. I glance over at Mr Brown, and he nods.

"Well, no...urm...I mean, yes, I did," I state quietly. The crystal stays clear. The dragon scowls at me with exasperation.

"Explain!" He barks again, in frustration.

So I tell him.

CHAPTER
TWENTY-TWO

When I finish speaking, my throat hurts. I cough—my mouth is so dry. I told the dragon everything, from the beginning. I kept my eyes on his nose, not brave enough to meet his gaze.

The crystal stayed completely clear the whole time I spoke.

Thank. Fuck.

"Show me your human claws. Matthew, will you please get Miss Hesketh a glass of water?" I blink at him in surprise—he wants to see my claws? A shade of impatience crosses his expression. "Miss Hesketh, they are the weapon in question. If you please." Matthew places a glass of water on the table. I mumble a thank you, and I guzzle down almost all of the glass.

Oh my God, the performance pressure, to produce my claws in front of a dragon—a dragon! If I couldn't, would he eat me? My heart pounds anew. I close my eyes, and I centre myself and try my best to ignore my fear. I take a deep breath in and let my shifter magic do its thing on my fingers. I open my eyes to see—to see a blue flame dancing across my fingertips.

Where are my bloody claws! What the fuck is that!

I whine in shock, and without thinking about it, I stuff the offending hand into the water glass.

With my frantic movement, I unbalance, and with no hands free to steady myself, I squeak as I fall onto the floor in a heap. *Oomph*. My dress goes over my head.

I stay where I am, hoping they will forget about me down here. My breathing is panicked, and I am still whining with fear.

What the fuck was that! Fuckity fuck fuck.

There's movement above me and rustling. I peek up at the dragon in shock as he uncovers my face from underneath my dress. I blink. There's a piece of hair that's sticking in my left eye. I blow out a hard puff of air, trying to dislodge it. The dragon squats in front of me; he tilts his head to the side as he studies my hands. I am still clutching the crystal in one hand, and the glass is wedged on the other.

"Have you ever done that before?" I shake my head no. "I need the words, Forrest," he says quietly in his smooth chocolate voice. He brushes the annoying strand of hair away. I gulp and stare at his hands. Big hands, the biggest I'd ever seen. He's proportional, so it shouldn't surprise me. He is so close; the dragon towers over me.

"No, never, I was trying to show you my claws." The crystal stays clear.

"What were you thinking at the time?" he asks me intently. His voice is deeper, softer too. He is almost hard to hear. I lean forward, and for the first time, we make eye contact. Wow, his eyes are such a beautiful silver. He smells fucking incredible, the smoky musk of burnt wood. I hum.

"I was frightened that I wouldn't be able to show you my claws and that you would... eat me." The dragon huffs out a laugh, stands, and helps me back to my feet.

"Let us try that again, shall we, Miss Hesketh." He shakes his head at my still-full hands and picks me up and puts me back on the seat, arranging my dress perfectly around me without effort. I stare at him in shock. He pulls the glass from my hand with a wet plop and puts it back on the table.

"Okay, claws please, Miss Hesketh," he says as he prowls back around the desk and sits.

"What if I—?" I wiggle my wet fingers and make a weird flamey sound at the back of my throat.

The dragon smirks at me. "You will not."

Okay then, okey-dokey—let's do this. Instead of closing my eyes this time, I focus on my practice time with Owen. I think of the slice of chocolate cake I am going to have this afternoon.

My magic tingles and my claws come out. I smile brightly in triumph.

The dragon's eyes drop to my lips, and his eyes dilate. A rumble vibrates in his chest, almost like a purr. "Very good," he praises in a deeper and slightly gruff tone. The dragon tilts his head to the side and again breathes in my scent. I don't know if he's aware that he isn't so sneaky about smelling me. He holds out his hand across the table, palm up. My mouth pops open, and I blink at him in confusion. "Your hand please, Miss Hesketh."

Oh. I put my wet hand in his, and he frowns. "Sorry," I mumble.

Then he inspects my claws. "Matthew, please update the file to say Miss Hesketh's claws are approximately three inches in length." He taps the end of my index finger. "They are not weapon class," he says dismissively.

It's my turn to frown at him.

What is wrong with my claws? They're awesome! Not a weapon? I huff. "Daniel thought that they were," I mumble under my breath.

"Okay, if you will excuse me, stay where you are, Miss Hesketh." The dragon gets up and walks away from us. "Matthew, test Miss Hesketh for all magic, including residual. I want a full report." He disappears behind a hidden door near the seating area. Huh, It's a portal.

The room is suddenly colder without him in it. His smoky musk of burnt-wood dragon scent lingers.

The scary dragon smells so good.

I glance at Mr Brown, who nods at me. I bounce in my seat a little, relieved that my part in this debacle is almost over.

I take the opportunity to tidy up my hair, which is still all over the place from my fall. Matthew disappears into the hallway and returns with a magic scanner.

"Please put your claws away and place your palm on the scanner." I do as he asks. I have been using my claws to run through my hair like a comb. Unfortunately, my lap is now full of little pieces of hair. Note to self: sharp claws are not suitable for hair-brushing. Thank God my hair is thick—otherwise I'd be bald.

I place my hand on the scanner and watch in fascination as the scanner lights up. I saw one before at the hospital, and I know from my reading that hunters carry a basic version. This one isn't a basic one, and even Mr Brown is watching on with interest. It also pricks my finger and takes a sample of my blood.

We wait for the dragon to return; he has been gone for what feels like forever. Well, okay, a tad over two hours. But I have a date with a chocolate cake. Waiting for him is nerve-racking. It would be just my luck that the handsome bastard hands me over to Daniel.

Matthew orders tea and coffee for us while we wait. I stuff two shortbread biscuits into my mouth quickly before anyone else grabs them. I love shortbread, and this is the good stuff from Scotland. My mouth is full, and I probably look like a hamster.

That's when the dragon decides to walk back into the room.

He appraises me with a frown, taking in the scattered pieces of hair. The dragon raises an eyebrow at Matthew. "Miss Hesketh brushed her hair with her claws," Matthew explains.

The dragon rubs his hand across his temple and sighs. "Nutty," he says with a shake of his head. He sits back behind his desk and takes the tablet back from Matthew, I presume to read the magic scan report.

"So the anti–body-hair potion and the shifter–clothing-retention potion are active in her system? Traces of a scent masker and basic disguise magic also." I chew the shortbread that's still stuffed in my mouth, trying not to choke. Bloody Jodie and that hair potion! I can't believe the dragon knows about that. I told him about the scent masker and my disguise, although I didn't go into detail—Betty is a disguise, after all. I can't say to a dragon that I am planning to dress like an old human lady and sneak about.

"Who is your potion supplier?" I have almost finished eating my shortbread, but I puff my cheeks out a little to make out that my mouth is still full. I hold up a finger and point to my cheeks. I am attempting to give myself more time to think. The dragon frowns, not buying my move.

What do I say? Will I get Jodie in trouble? I scrutinise Mr Brown, and he does his typical nod. My eyes fly to Matthew, but he isn't even looking in my direction. I have finished chewing. I shake my head no. "You're not telling who supplies your potions?" The dragon asks incredulously. I shake my head again.

"Miss Hesketh, they will not get into trouble—you have not used anything illegal. You can answer the question," Mr Brown says, trying to encourage me. I still shake my head. Jodie is my friend, and I will not send a dragon to her door. Even if he employs a male witch. No way. Nope. The dragon will have to eat me. I cross my arms across my chest but uncross them quickly, as the move reminds me of something Liz would do. Matthew has lifted his head and is now looking at me with interest and a small smile.

The dragon puffs out a breath of frustration. "Lucky for you, I haven't got time to torture you for information," he says drolly; he rubs his temple again. "I have cancelled the arrest warrant with immediate effect. The evidence Mr Brown provided before our meeting corroborated your story. I have informed Daniel Kerr that I have placed you officially under my protection. I can't believe the hellhounds were not more of a deterrent." He regards me. Sternly he says, "You are a trouble-maker, Miss Hesketh, and you need better guidance. I have spoken in person to your brother. I showed him the video evidence of Daniel Kerr's attempted sexual assault." My eyes widen. *Shit*. Incredible shit—John knows the truth. He can't argue with evidence and a scary-as-hell dragon. *Boom*. I love this guy. I wiggle in my chair, almost doing a happy dance.

"After today, with you producing fire magic, he agrees that you will be better off in my care, for the short term."

So it *was* fire magic! Of course it was—I am such a divvy. I can't believe fire magic scared me so much. "Does that make me a hellhound?" I ask eagerly.

"No, Miss Hesketh. Hellhounds are warriors. It makes *you* a liability."

CHAPTER
TWENTY-THREE

That's how I found myself moving into the lair of a dragon. I wasn't listening to him properly at the end of the meeting, and all I heard was *cancelled warrant, protection blah blah blah,* and then my brain got stuck on the fire-magic thing. I may have mentally nodded off at the end.

Anyway, before I knew it, Mr Brown was standing up, and we were being shown back to the elevator.

Owen met us by the car. Which was a surprise—Owen told me the General had cancelled the mission and ordered him to accompany me home.

What I didn't realise at that moment was, I was only going to the apartment to pack my shit.

I thanked Mr Brown and asked him to send me a bill for his fee; he informed me that my guardian had paid the bill. When I had looked at him blankly, he told me the General had paid. *Huh.*

So here we stand on top of an actual cliff, the dragon's portal gateway at our backs. I stare at the view—my mouth is almost catching flies, it is hanging open that wide. Wow. Perched on the rocky cliff, hovering over the untamed beauty of the wild Atlantic, is the dragon's Irish lair—a square building that's made entirely out of glass.

It's a breathtaking ultra-modern James Bond villain house.

Shit, I hope that's not a sign of things to come.

The sound and smell of the sea fill my senses, the taste of saltwater heavy on my tongue—the waves of the Atlantic crash into the rocks below. I never thought a house could be so impressively beautiful. It must be at least two hundred and fifty feet above the sea. The sheer scale and dramatic impact of the cliff and house are awe-inspiring. It makes me feel small and humble.

The surrounding countryside is lush and green. The springy coastal grass at my feet is dotted with yellow, purple, and pink wildflowers. In the distance are mountains and trees. For some strange reason, for a split second I miss my trees around Temple House. But I dismiss the thought; I don't want to see them again. So missing them is pointless.

This is the first time I've left England, and I'm in Ireland. The land of the Fae. Typically shifters are not permitted on Ireland's shores. But the dragon, because he is a dragon, is the exception to this rule. Now so am I! How exciting.

The dragon opens his door when Owen knocks, and we enter a bright white hallway. I hide behind Owen's bulk and greedily take in the house, forcing myself not to gawk up at the dragon. I end up watching him out the corner of my eye anyway. His very presence is impossible to ignore.

Oak-and-glass stairs—the perfect blend of old-fashioned and modern—lead upstairs, and another set of stairs goes down, to what I presume is a lower-ground floor. Halfway down the hall, there's an oak door to the right and another on the left, with another double-glass doorway further ahead, perhaps leading to the living room. The smoky scent of the house is a delight to my senses. I weirdly feel like I'm home.

Owen places my two small bags on the polished concrete floor, shakes the dragon's offered hand, and then turns to me with a small smile. I look worriedly into his warm grey eyes.

"You be good. Don't be getting into too much trouble," Owen says gruffly. "You have my number if you need me. I don't want to hear from someone else that you beat up some troll or Fae creature, you understand me?" I grin. Owen folds me into his arms and gives me a gentle hug. "You're safe here, I promise," he whispers. I nod.

"I will miss you, Nanny Hound," I say, my voice rough. I wish he could stay.

"Okay, that's enough—you will see plenty of the nutty hellraiser. You can go now, hellhound Owen. Thank you for dropping her off." The dragon glares at Owen, who nudges me gently away, and with a smile at me and a respectful nod at the dragon, he leaves.

I forlornly watch Owen go.

I peek up at the dragon. Shit, I have no idea what to call him. I can't keep calling him "the dragon," even if it's in my head. Everyone has been calling him the General, but that isn't his name, surely it's his job title? Mr Brown said he's my guardian. It's all so confusing; I must try listening better and ask more questions.

I am also frustrated that my bloody brother keeps on passing me off to others without asking me first. What is wrong with him? I don't understand why John can't find the time to talk to me and ask me what I want and where I want to live. I have money and I am supposed to be an adult. I feel like I'm in a game of Pass-the-Parcel and the music has stopped for another layer of me to be removed. If this keeps happening, nothing is going to be left. Now I am staying with a scary dragon! This is happening so fast it makes my head spin.

"Come along, Miss Hesketh, let me show you to your room." The dragon has been quietly observing me. He picks up my bags, and I follow meekly behind him. "I thought you would be comfortable on this floor. My bedroom is upstairs if you ever need me." I nod politely.

The gorgeous bedroom smells of fresh paint and is at the front of the house. I am relieved that at least in this room I won't be asleep dangling over the cliff. The external walls are glass, and the internal walls, ceiling, and woodwork are painted a magnificent dark navy. The floor is oak in a herringbone parquet. The navy should make the room feel small and dark, but it does the opposite, and the two glass walls bring the outside inside, highlighting the spectacular view of the mountains. The navy blue reminds me of the first time I saw the night sky after years of seeing nothing but bars. It's the colour when the sky is clear, the short time before the stars come out and it hasn't quite gotten fully dark. The smell of paint hints that the dragon had the room painted for me.

CURSED WOLF

The bed is king-sized, and I run my hand across the mustard-yellow bedding with delicate blue flowers. There's a round mustard-yellow rug on the floor. I step further into the room and notice the floorplan narrows towards a door to the left, which I presume is a bathroom. It has open-style oak wardrobes on either side of the doorway. I glance behind the wardrobe, which is not flush to the wall, and see the reason for the narrowing. Next to the floor-to-ceiling wall of windows is a little hidden nook, also painted in the navy. I gasp as I take in the empty shelves begging for books and the substantial squishy-looking navy bean bag on the floor. It's the perfect reading nook. I want to squeal. I hold in the noise by the skin of my teeth and instead grin like a loon.

My eyes catch a familiar photo frame alone on a shelf, and for a second, I can't breathe. My knees go weak. I trace the glass with my finger, and my mum and sister smile back at me.

My eyes fill with tears.

"I hope you find the room agreeable." I spin and see that the dragon is still watching me from the door. I react without thinking. I rush towards him, throw my arms around his waist, and give him an impromptu hug.

"Thank you," I whisper into his abs. I might as well be hugging a tree for all the reaction I get from him, and wow his muscles have muscles. The dragon is solid. But I don't care at this moment; the dragon deserves a hug. I bury my face in his shirt and breathe him in. After twenty or so seconds, I pull back and glance up. "Thank you...the photo..." I say, trying to hold in a sob; I swallow it down, and my eyes shine up at him. "The room is perfect. It is so very thoughtful of you to have it painted." The dragon is standing awkwardly with his arms out at his sides, holding a bag in each hand. I step away and give him a watery, bright smile.

I don't know when I stopped being terrified of the dragon.

"You're more than welcome," the dragon says roughly; he coughs to clear his throat. "I will put your things here for you to deal with. Feel free to explore the house." He places my bags on the floor next to the wardrobes. He then turns, quickly leaving the room. As he is closing the door, he says, "Dinner in an hour." The door clicks shut.

I kick off my silver-sequined trainers, scrub my face, and wait for a few more heartbeats. I open the door, peek out of my bedroom. I don't see any sign of the dragon. I hold my breath and intently listen. I think I can hear him upstairs. The excited anticipation of looking around the dragon's lair wells inside of me, and I quietly pad into the hallway.

I poke my head into the room opposite mine and find an empty spare bedroom. Huh. It's nowhere near as lovely as mine. I can't go up, but I can go down. I ignore the room at the end of the hallway, and instead, I scamper down the stairs. A slight hint of chlorine and more of the dragon's smoky, musky scent fills the air. At the bottom of the stairs, the room opens up, and an impressive state-of-the-art gym greets me. I guess this is the reason why the dragon is so massive.

I open doors and cupboards and squeal when I find a cinema room through a door to my right.

Past all the gym equipment ahead of me, outside behind a wall of glass, I can see a pool. I slide open the glass door and step out; I find the dragon has a fancy jacuzzi, a sauna, and a steam room. The heated pool is what holds my fascination. It's incredible and made entirely of glass. I wobble and feel slightly dizzy as I stare down—I can see the sea through the glass bottom. It gives the impression that the water is flowing over the cliff edge, into the crashing sea below.

Swimming in that pool will be an adventure. Eeek, this house is phenomenal.

An hour later, I leave my room and this time head towards the smell of food. I amble into an open-plan room that has a kitchen, a dining table, and comfortable-looking leather sofas. Everything is modern and elegant—it's lovely. Like in my bedroom, the external walls are made of glass, but as the room is so big, the glass walls are on three sides.

My feet follow my eyes in an almost-trance; all I can focus on is the view. The sun is slowly sinking into the horizon. The bright colours bounce off the glass and make rainbows on the walls. It's incredible. The whole room is a backdrop of fading sunlight, sea, and sky. I can almost imagine I am flying or on the deck of a ship out at sea. The thought of being here watching a storm roll in, the sea wild and the wind gusting, thunder and lightning lighting up the sky, like the best natural show imaginable...how incredible would that be to see? I don't think anyone could get bored with this magnificent view.

"Miss Hesketh, please take a seat at the table." I turn and blink. Wow, I am rude. The dragon has put our plates on the table without my noticing. He is standing in front of a chair, waiting to sit down.

"Oh, I am sorry, the view took me by surprise. Your home is exquisite, and that view is epic." I want to ask if there's anything he needs, but that would be weird as it's his home. I clamp my mouth closed and I hurry to sit down. I aim for the chair opposite, but the dragon shakes his head. He indicates the chair he's standing in front of. Oh, he is holding the chair for me to sit, wow. No one has ever done that before. I sit with a mumbled, "Thank you."

I watch as he prowls around the table. He looks very nice. He has changed out of his suit and is wearing light blue jeans and a tight white long-sleeved top. The top is *crazy*; it hugs every muscle on his torso, so much so I could count them. It's that tight, he might as well not have it on. It reveals the most muscled body I've ever seen. It's hard not to drool. I peruse my food quickly to hide my ogling, and I don't look back up until he has safely sat down.

"What do I call you?" I blurt out.

He observes me. His head tilts to the side with his consideration. "Do you not know who I am?" He doesn't say it arrogantly; he says it as if he is genuinely perplexed that I don't know. I smile apologetically and shake my head no. I have not got a scooby who he is. "Oh...Miss Hesketh, please tell me, what do you know?" I feel my face go pink and have the urge to wring my hands with embarrassment.

"I know that you are important...urm, I can see that you're a dragon." I wave my hand about to encompass him. "Everyone calls you, urm, 'General'...I have no idea what you are a general of, but I presume it's something to do with the Hunters Guild? Mr Brown said you are now my guardian? After he told me you paid his bill. Thank you for that. I can pay you back." I glance down at my food; he has made steak. Steak, mashed potatoes, and broccoli, with a peppercorn sauce. Yum.

"Eat your dinner," he says gruffly. He doesn't have to tell me twice; I dive in.

I try my best to use my knife and fork correctly. I am getting better.

The dragon makes an odd noise. I peek up at him; he has his fork raised to his mouth and such a sad expression on his face. I glance back down at my food and continue eating. I hope he is okay. I don't like the idea that he's sad. It has been a while since I've eaten red meat, so I let my inner carnivore take over.

It's difficult to eat like a lady when you have the urge to stuff your face into your food and eat as quickly as you can before someone takes the plate away. I don't know if I will ever not have that worry, that inbuilt fear at the back of my mind. Being starved for such a long time…when I eat, I find it impossible to eat slowly. I unconsciously hug the plate towards myself, my arms circling it protectively. Huh, at least I didn't growl.

"You were starved." Momentarily I come out of my frenzy, and I peek up again to see him watching me with an indescribable look of compassion in his silver eyes. I drop my eyes and shrug. I guess that explains the sad look from before. It isn't something I want to talk about.

Now that I've had a few bites—well, okay half the plate—I can try to control myself and slow down a little. I listen intently as the dragon starts to talk. His voice rumbles around the room, much like the ocean below us.

"Yes, I am a dragon shifter. My title is General. I have a long and boring history of being a warrior and commander. I currently oversee the Hunters Guild, and the hellhounds are also under my jurisdiction." His big but elegant fingers tap the table. "Mr Brown is correct—as you are under my protection, I am classified as your guardian. You may call me Aragon."

CHAPTER
TWENTY-FOUR

AFTER DINNER, I'm horrified to find out he doesn't have any dessert, *nothing*. Who doesn't have dessert! At the abject horror on my face, the dragon, urm, Aragon, roots around in the freezer and finds a sad-looking tub of vanilla ice cream. It's an icy lump frozen solid to the bottom of the container. But I sit happily stabbing at it with a spoon while sitting cross-legged on Aragon's leather sofa.

Aragon talks about his rules expectations, and we got to the real reason why I'm here.

It isn't all about keeping me safe from Daniel.

"When you first went to the hospital, there were several issues raised," Aragon says. "The front part of your brain is called 'the prefrontal cortex,' and it hasn't developed properly. It is the area responsible for planning, prioritising, and controlling impulses."

So basically Aragon has medical data to suggest my brain is stuck in teenage mode.

Huh.

I want to moan that I have no issues with my impulse control—the number of times I have chosen not to do something reckless is mounting up to impressive levels. I am an absolute fucking guru of control. But I don't say a word. I am smart enough not to argue with a dragon and his medical data.

Ha, perfect control.

I smell bullshit, though—there's nothing wrong with my brain.

As well as my teenage brain...cue eyeroll. "You are stronger than an average shifter," Aragon continues in his mesmerising, low voice. "Even with your small stature, you are at a level of hellhound strength." Smugly I bounce on the sofa. I am a super-shifter! "Nutty..." The dragon mumbles as he rubs the bridge of his nose in frustration. I stop bouncing. "The onset of your fire magic has raised serious concerns. Miss Hesketh, shifters should not develop that type of magic until they're at least six hundred years old, if at all, as it is such a rare gift. To have the ability to partial-shift at twenty-three is also unfounded. I believe your brother was over a century. Combined with your shifting at a young age, you are a complete anomaly. A magical and medical conundrum." *Way to go, Mum, and your lotto DNA.*

Aragon assures me that there's a slight possibility my brain could develop adequately over time. But I'm not that worried, or that bothered. There's nothing bloody wrong with my mind.

Of course, I think I am a little crazy, but come on—who wouldn't be, with my history? I've been through Hell and come out smoking. What all this testing comes down to is an excuse to control me. They can't let me go wandering about and not have control of me. I narrow my eyes at him. Being a young female shifter with fire magic, I understand now why I've been parcelled off to Aragon.

"Who better to keep an eye on me and keep control of me than you?" I say, raising my eyebrow.

"I assure you, Miss Hesketh, that I will do whatever it takes to protect you. I want nothing more than to keep you safe. The council isn't aware of your fire magic. I'd like to keep it that way. I'm officially your guardian. It is a task I have not entered into unadvisedly or lightly." The immense burden contained in Aragon's gaze just then is disturbing. It freaks me out. He clearly believes what he's saying. Has appointing himself my guardian put him at risk? Am I that much of a danger? Aragon's expression is heart-wrenching, and something inside me rips wide open. I hate this. I drop my chin to my chest and scrutinise my hands, unable to meet his intense gaze.

"Okay, well, thank you," I mumble around a lump in my throat.

No matter what the dragon believes or what I want to think, I have to get it into my head that I am on my own. I am a survivor, not a victim, and I'm not just going to accept my circumstances. I can't. Eventually, I'm going to find a way to gain control of my life.

It's not going to happen overnight, and I can't allow myself to mope like I have been doing for the past few weeks. At the moment I have a bloody scary, powerful dragon claiming that he wants to protect me. Daniel can go swivel, and John can also fuck off.

I have loyalty to Owen and Jodie. Ava has also earned my respect and trust. But the only person whom I can rely on is myself.

I AM BACK in my room, getting ready for bed. I have showered and changed into my PJ's, which are workout shorts and a t-shirt. Since I got control of my shifting at the hospital, I have been sleeping in my wolf form. I can't sleep in my human guise as I feel vulnerable. I am used to sleeping as a wolf. Also, beds are too soft, my skin is too cold, and even trying to sleep on the floor in my human form doesn't help.

Ultimately what makes me choose to sleep furry are the nightmares that plague me. Strangely, they don't find me when I am a wolf.

I pad towards my hidden nook and place the photo frame on a lower shelf. I allow the magic to transform me. Aragon wants us to run at five a.m. I am sure he thinks I'd object, but I enjoy training, and the early time doesn't matter to me. It isn't like I have to drag myself out of bed.

I curl up in a wolfy doughnut, my nose on top of my fluffy tail. I face the silver frame; *I love you both so much*, I say to my long-dead pack. Each blink gets a little longer as I try to keep my eyes on their happy faces until I fall asleep.

I RUN behind Aragon as we follow a thin strip of a track, worn away naturally bare from previous footsteps. The morning is dry and fresh. The path takes us through a wood, heathland, and peat bogs that surround the base of a mountain. The landscape is breathtaking.

As the miles disappear under my feet, it becomes apparent just how remote Aragon's home in this part of Ireland is. Interestingly, I discover there isn't even a road leading to the house—Aragon must only use the portal or fly, I guess. I feel as if we could be the last people on Earth. Even with my excellent hearing, all I can hear apart from animals and the crashing ocean is the crunching of our feet.

Oh, and the freaky buzzing of Aragon's ward.

I didn't notice the ward yesterday when I arrived, as it's miles from the house. I am astonished to see it this morning. Instead of covering only the house, it circles out and covers miles and miles. It isn't the gold colour that I'm used to seeing either, like the ward at the apartment. No, it's multicoloured and glows and crackles in the dark. You can feel it buzzing through you, deep into your bones. No one could say that they missed seeing this ward if they stumbled up to it. It's the magic equivalent of a laser field. I'd hate to see what it would do to anyone unwelcome.

The sky lightens as we dash across the wind-whipped cliff, the waves rolling endlessly below us. Aragon points out that the coastline has tiny coves and natural swimming spots protected from the full force of the Atlantic by a reef. He explains the different flora, the delicate sea champion, cat's ear, and sea pink.

We continue for a good hour at a fast pace. I've never run with anyone before as a human or as a wolf, and it's terrific. If I had been my wolf, I would have had my tongue hanging out and a silly wolfy grin on my face. As it is, I don't think I stop smiling the whole time. My cheeks hurt. It's epic.

When we return to the house, the sky is just lighting up further with the dawn. Aragon tells me to be ready to leave by eight a.m. and to help myself to breakfast.

I fret over what to wear, and in the end, I wear black leggings and a cute green jumper. Aragon informed me last night that I couldn't wear my magic bracelets—that I am under his protection blah blah blah and he needed to be able to track me. So I wrap the scent masker bracelet in toilet paper and put it into the handy pocket of my leggings, and the Betty disguise bracelet, I put around my ankle so it's nicely hidden. Time for breakfast.

The bloody dragon's kitchen is made for a giant. I huff, prop my hands on my hips, and glare.

All the countertops are higher than standard; luckily, he has almost everything in the lower cabinets. But the strawberry jam is in a big larder cupboard, and it's on the top shelf about a hundred foot in the air. I tip my head back and glare at it. I am sure it's okay if you are a humongous dragon that can also fly, but for me being five-foot-two, it's like mission impossible.

I hum the "Mission Impossible" theme tune as I scale the counter in my socks. I balance on my tiptoes and lean across the gap. My fingertips can just brush the jar, but I can't get hold of it. I growl at the jar in frustration as I plan my first free-the-jam attempt.

I am going to jump and grab it.

Just as I am getting ready to make my first jump, Aragon appears by my side, scaring the ever-loving shit out of me.

I let out a shriek at his sudden appearance, and my sock-encased foot slips.

Oomph. I find myself in Aragon's arms as he catches me.

"I was drawn by the incessant humming. You should have called me to get that for you," he says gruffly.

"Oh, urm...nice catch, sorry about that, you, urm... scared the shit out of me," I squeak out. I gawk up and meet his beautiful silver eyes—he doesn't seem angry—his eyes are dancing with mirth.

His forearms hold my weight with ease.

My proximity to Aragon confuses the hell out of me. But it doesn't frighten me the way it would have with just about any other person. Instead, I brace my hands on his chest and lean forward. All the way forward and brush my nose against his neck.

I inhale.

His smoky, musky scent fills my nose. I shiver, and my stomach flips.

I hum.

Shit, it feels good in his arms. Why does it feel so good? I know he's dangerous, and it isn't hard to assume that he's one of the most powerful shifters on the planet. When did I stop being frightened of this huge man?

I groan deep in my throat.

Since I first laid eyes on him at his office, it's like every dormant hormone in my body has awakened at once—all clamouring for my guardian's attention.

Aragon turns his head, and I feel his breath on my lips. I open and taste his exhalation.

Goosebumps break out on my skin. I am being inappropriate. What the hell is wrong with me? I straighten up, my face burning.

"Urm...sorry. Sorry! I've never done that before. You...urm...caught me at a bad time. I'm in a hunger mood. I'm urm...hangry..." Gibberish. I'm flustered, I've no idea what I'm saying. I cringe and try to keep my eyes from looking crazed.

Why did I sniff him!

"You are absolutely nutty. What will I do with you?" Aragon sighs as he gently lowers me to my feet. My body brushes against his on the way down. A shiver wracks me; it leaves me strangely breathless—warmth pools deep in my tummy.

Wow, oh...urm. My heart feels like it is beating out of my chest, and my stomach flips again. I like being close to him. Aragon smells so good.

Aragon disappointingly moves away. I sigh in frustration. He keeps his hand on the back of my neck as he easily reaches for the jam. He places it on to the counter next to the toaster.

"Nutty, please don't climb on the furniture. Hurry, you have five minutes." I grin at the nickname: *Nutty*. He squeezes my neck gently, and then he prowls out of the kitchen.

I watch him leave. He is wearing a dark grey suit today, and it looks good against his silver hair and skin. I let out a breath, and my hands tremble as I finish making my toast.

God, that was hot.

CHAPTER
TWENTY-FIVE

Aragon takes me to work with him, how weird is that? We arrive in his office through the portal. "Okay, Miss Hesketh, it looks like you will have to entertain yourself. Please let Matthew know if you need anything."

"Is there anything I can do to help?" I ask, excitement budding inside of me. I bounce on my toes a little and my eyes flick around his office. "Any work that you need doing? I am sure I can help out with the Hunters or even help with paperwork? I can answer the phone?" I smile and nod encouragingly.

My thoughts drift away slightly as I imagine myself saving the world, and I have an urge to practice my shocked look for when the Hunters Guild honours me with a medal for my bravery. I hum.

Aragon tilts his head to the side with a frown. "Miss Hesketh, do you even know how to read? Your records do not give any indication of your literacy skills." My mouth drops open, and it's my turn to blink at him. How rude—of course I bloody know how to read! I was nine when I was trapped in my wolf form, not three. It's not like I forgot the alphabet.

I growl at him.

Then I reconsider. Of course my education wasn't a priority for the council—who cares if a walking womb can read or write? Lucky thing I was home-schooled. Aragon doesn't know the details of my mum's schooling agenda, though.

"Please don't be offended; it is an honest and genuine question." I screw my face up and give him a sharp nod that he must take as confirmation. "Well, I have a bookshelf full of fascinating reference books." He waves his hand towards the seating area and the full shelves. "Why don't you start there?" He smiles encouragingly and leaves.

Bloody handsome nobhead!

I don't want to read boring shitty books. I love books, but not those type of books. I want to do something fun! I huff, closing my eyes and tapping my foot. I need to suck it up. I do need to learn more about shifters. I don't know anything about my race apart from the basics I learnt as a kid. Nothing useful.

Ideally, I should at least learn the laws, not only to keep myself out of trouble but so I don't have others taking advantage of my ignorance. If I know the code-of-conduct rules inside-out, I'll know when I can kick someone's ass and when I can't.

I seriously need to find a solution to what is turning out to be a massive clusterfuck: my life.

I know that I cannot trust the council or the dragon, even if I have a strange new sniffing fetish. It's only a matter of time till I fuck up and Aragon gets rid of me. Hell, if my own brother—I close my eyes. *Don't think about it.* I worry the end of my hair. At least I had the foresight to bring the bracelets with me, because I have a feeling that given the opportunity, Aragon would make them disappear. If I know anything, I know that.

I glance at Aragon's bookshelves.

I meander over, dragging my feet with a total lack of enthusiasm, and start to read the titles. Bloody hell, I need a help book to navigate this shit. Do they have a handbook—*Shifters for Dummies,* or something similar? I have to learn as much as I can about *everything* as quickly as I can. I wonder if he has a book on fire magic. I hum. If I can learn to control my fire magic, it would be difficult for some bad guy to kidnap me.

Especially while on fire and screaming. I grin, imagining lighting

Daniel's pants on fire. I rub my hands together and do a mental *mwahaha*.

A few books catch my eye, and they're surprisingly perfect. Nothing on fire magic but the books do have the information I am looking for. I grab six of the most essential and settle down on a chair to read. I am back to humming "Mission Impossible."

The vast law book has blacked-out text that draws my attention. My dry eyes widen in horror as I make sense of the passage I'm reading. I nibble on my bottom lip and do a full-body shiver.

The place where the shifter bites is blacked out, but from what I can gather, there's a way for one shifter to control another. It freaks me out. Mind control! I cover my mouth. It's banned mate-slave magic.

Oh, that's bad.

Oh my, it's not banned because it's sick as fuck and highly immoral—no, it's forbidden because if a male shifter does the biting and he dies, the female he has bitten will follow him into death. I shiver again, and the hair at the back of my neck stands on end.

That's it. I think whoever wrote this book, the council who made our laws, are missing a huge point. It's fucking slavery! Evil. What the hell is wrong with shifters? I huff out a shaky breath and slam the book closed, disheartened. Female shifters are screwed—no wonder we're so rare. You can't fix stupid.

Shifter society is rotten.

"Miss Hesketh, I am free for the rest of the day—nothing pressing needs my attention. We shall be going out for something to eat. If you are agreeable?" I glance up, and Aragon has returned with Matthew at his heels.

"Yes, sure," I say, my voice glum. I spring up and put the books that I have finished back on the shelves. The law book, I poke with my finger and give a snarl.

That thing needs burning.

Aragon nods at Matthew, and as we head for the portal, I give the witch a friendly wave. I follow quietly behind Aragon. I try not to skip in excitement. He is taking me out for food. My first date!

We make our way to a small restaurant in the city. It looks like a nice place; they specialise in gourmet burgers. Aragon opens the glass door for me and follows me inside. His big hand curls gently around my neck as he guides me to a table. My heart skips a beat. I enjoy the heavy hand on my neck, a bit too much.

We sit opposite each other at a two-seater table, made smaller by Aragon's bulk. He has no choice but to stretch his long legs underneath my chair. I can't help but enjoy the feeling of our legs touching. As it's early for the dinner crowd, the restaurant isn't busy, and most of the tables are empty.

My whole focus is entirely on Aragon. Who has removed his suit jacket and is now in the process of deviously rolling up his sleeves. With each turn of the fabric, he slowly uncovers more of his muscled forearms. How can one innocuous body part be so attractive? I have no shame in watching his yummy forearm striptease.

Our human waitress is equally fascinated with my dragon's forearms. She doesn't acknowledge my presence as she runs her hand through her hair and along her collarbone, fluttering her lashes at him as if she's attempting to get those fuckers to fly off. I frown at her. Aragon is his usual polite self, and his gaze doesn't linger.

The handsome bastard needs a bag over his head.

I don't read the menu when I order; I just pick a random burger. I cough and glare at her to get her moving.

"So how was your day?" Aragon asks me in his low, rumbly voice.

"Good. You haven't got a lot of picture books," I say petulantly. Aragon rubs the bridge of his nose and sighs.

"I am sorry, Miss Hesketh, I spoke out of turn. Please forgive me." A line appears between his brows and his beautiful eyes become distressed. I keep my sad-face for a few seconds longer. But I can't stop the cheeky grin from slowly spreading across my face. I wave away his apology.

"It is fine; I'm only messing with you...your books are...urm, scary. The shifter laws in regard to women are shit." I wiggle in my chair and debate with myself about whether I should say anything.

Aragon tilts his head and raises an eyebrow. I wave my hands about and word-vomit my anger. "My purpose in life is not to be a bloody pup-maker. I'm more than my womb! The world I have experienced so far? It isn't a world that I want to bring my children into. If my DNA is so unique and I do beat the odds and have little girls, do I want them to be born into a world where their whole existence is about what is between their legs? To be fought over like little pieces of meat and sold like property?

"I'm an orphan; my father died before I was born, trying to protect my mum and three sisters. Only my mum survived. Not even ten years after that tragedy, I had to watch while my mum killed herself and my two-year-old little sister, Grace…" I lower my chin to my chest with sorrow. "She would be sixteen now. Aragon, that's just *my* pack. Five females that died for nothing—nothing! This shit needs to stop. The laws protecting us are non-existent. You are strong, can't you do something?"

Aragon gives me a pained look. I drop my eyes and take that as a no. Why did I even bring it up? I lift my head and my bottom lip trembles. I sigh and square my shoulders. Fuck it, I will do it myself. It isn't in my nature to ignore injustice and go down without a fight, even when things seem insurmountable. "So, urm, when do you want to teach me about—" I lower my voice to a whisper—"my fire magic? The sooner we get started with training, the better." So I can start helping others.

Aragon shakes his head, and before he can answer, our food arrives. The waitress literally throws my plate down in front of me. She must think I'm human, or she's crazy.

I wrinkle my nose in disgust and scrutinise my burger with growing horror. I let out a pained whimper. I have somehow ordered a veggie burger. I am so disappointed. I cut it into quarters and poke at it. I have eaten excellent vegetarian stuff, but this burger isn't a good one. It's falling apart, looks dry, and it's a strange colour. I give it a surreptitious sniff; *eww*, it doesn't even smell like food.

Not long ago, I was eating dog food. So I should count my blessings that it's warm and just eat the thing. I lift my top lip and snarl at it.

Aragon watches me with fascination, his eyes sparkling. *Yeah, yeah, dragon boy, laugh it up.* His double burger with bacon oozes cheese—it looks so good. Aragon methodically cuts his burger into quarters. Without saying a word, he takes my plate and exchanges it for his. I glance down at his plate, my new plate and the yummy burger.

My heart swells, and I am now feeling just as gooey as the cheese.

"Thank you," I say while trying and failing to get a whole quarter into my mouth. Aragon just gives me a nod and a warm smile. He eats my veggie burger without saying a word of complaint, but I catch the odd wince.

I focus on the seriousness of eating. Once I have practically inhaled my burger, I try to bring the conversation back to before. "So, the fire training?" I ask Aragon again.

He sighs, throwing the veggie burger back onto his plate and wiping his hands with a napkin. "There is no rush, Miss Hesketh. Hellhound Owen has agreed to continue your self-defence training. Once you are up to a good standard, we can address the subject of your magic again." I huff out a frustrated breath. "It takes a lot of mental control. You have dealt with a lot of challenges over a short amount of time." He meaningfully raises his eyebrow. "There is plenty of time to master your magic." Aragon gives me a gentle smile; his eyes are open and honest.

"Your brother has been trying to get hold of you," he says, changing the subject. I flare my nostrils at him and stuff an onion ring into my mouth. Aragon patiently waits, his head tilted to the side, watching me.

Oh, bloody hell. I wiggle in my chair in discomfort. "I know it is childish. But I don't want to speak to John." I examine my plate and choose another onion ring. "The whole Daniel thing? He said some horrible things..." I close my eyes. "I just need some time." Aragon puts his big hand on mine and squeezes it.

"I will explain. You don't need to speak to him until you're ready. If it is any consolation, he is aware that he has made a serious error in judgement." I shrug. John keeps believing the monsters over me. One time is forgivable, but he keeps on doing it. I will never trust him. I will try to forgive him for my mum's sake. But it's hard—to be honest, I'm not the forgiving type.

When the waitress returns to our table and we both order dessert, another button on her top has become undone!

I think I am going to scream. I know we're not on a real date, but she doesn't know that. *Oi, you, blondie,* I have the urge to say, *why don't you take a seat if you are that interested in him? Pull up a pew and grab yourself a bite of rancid veggie burger. While you are sitting down, would you like my lemonade? Why don't I work your tables while you tell the dragon what your star sign is.* I growl until she scurries away.

I'm growling as if Aragon is food and I'm starving. What the hell... am I...am I jealous? I turn the idea around in my head. Huh. I have never felt jealousy before. I have no reason to feel like this; Aragon isn't mine. I scratch the back of my head. Even surrounded by attractive hellhounds and shifters, I have never liked anyone before.

It's disconcerting.

I huff. I can't understand how he has not picked up on how inappropriate she's being. Maybe he likes her? *Shit.* I clack my teeth.

I don't like that thought.

I get down to the serious business of cake-eating, so I don't notice while eating my hot chocolate fudge cake with cream that Aragon hasn't started his. Okay, I lie. Of course I bloody noticed. It's chocolate!

Again he makes the plate exchange, my empty plate for his full one. He gets a beaming smile, and I happily hum as I eat my second dessert.

Aragon has set the date bar high. I don't even feel the need to guard my plate. *Not when you're guarding Aragon,* my snide, not-so-helpful internal voice pipes up.

I finish, and I swear I have a little food baby going on. What a relief that I'm wearing leggings and I don't have to undo a button.

The blonde waitress is back to clear the table and to ask if Aragon wants a coffee, and she unbelievably just gives him her number. It's like I am not even sitting here! Who does that!

"I swear, Miss Hesketh, if you growl at our waitress one more time, I will put you over my knee, in front of all these people, and spank you, and we will see just how well you do with being a brat." I blink up at him in shock. I cut off my growl.

When the wannabe Aragon-stealing waitress sashays past our table again, I let out a growl so loud that it frightens her and she drops the plate she's carrying. I bounce happily on my seat and watch the mayhem I've caused. I have zero regrets. I peer up at Aragon from underneath my lashes and grin cheekily at him. He rubs his forehead and shakes his head. I'm sure the forehead rub was a tactic to cover his smile.

CHAPTER
TWENTY-SIX

Aragon stalks outside, muscles rippling along his bare torso. His black swim shorts sit low on his hips. *Oh, my bloody God.* I grip the edge of the pool.

"You don't mind if I join you?" he asks in his low rumbly voice that's currently made of liquid chocolate.

No, I am not dreaming. When we got back from lunch, I decided to hit the pool. It seems like Aragon had the same idea.

I shake my head vigorously, almost smacking it on the glass side. I bite my lip—fucking hell. Aragon is lean rather than bulky, but there's so much of him—I didn't know a body could have that many abdominal ridges. I fight to keep my gaze on his face, not his beautiful body. He looks chiselled from stone.

Bow-chicka-wow-wow. My mind wanders, in a rude direction...my imagination skids to a halt as some figmental voluptuous female dragon shifter tries to drown me for looking at Aragon in *that* way.

Without thinking, I blurt out, "Will your girl not get mad that I'm living here?" Shit, shut up, oh hell. I drop my eyes and rub the edge of the floor tile with my finger. I can feel my cheeks going red.

"No," Aragon says softly.

No, she won't mind? Or no, you haven't got a girl? My brain prompts my mouth. I so want to ask, but I swallow the question.

Aragon steps down into the pool. The steam off the warm water wraps lovingly around his body.

"So, are you single?" Fuck it. I come out with the words. They almost speak themselves. *Shit, don't look at him.* I can't look. I shouldn't look. I do.

He has moved to the opposite end of the pool. He surveys the view. His face in profile is a marvel. So perfect. A stunning symmetry. The dragon is so beautiful—defined jaw, pronounced cheekbones—all that incredible silver skin. What the hell is wrong with me?

"I currently do not have a female. Do you have a male?" I drop my head and grin, I giggle, I meet his serious eyes. Oh, he isn't joking. Isn't that in my file? I make a gesture of weighing tough options with my hand. Aragon scrutinises me and his eyes narrow. I giggle again, and I shake my head no.

I let myself float on the water, looking at the sky above. I wonder if this pool can be used in winter. The whole pool area must be freezing that time of year, but as I'm floating, I can see the shimmer of magic, I guess to keep the entire area temperature-controlled. Magic is amazing.

I get bored, so I hum the music from *Jaws* as I do handstands and rolly-polys, entertaining myself. I also attack Aragon's toes. After a while he leaves me to it.

As I'm bellowing "Part of your World" from *The Little Mermaid*, Aragon returns with a towel. His eyes sparkle, and his lips twitch.

"Come on, Nutty, it has been hours." I grin at him and scramble out of the pool, and he envelops me in the towel.

The rest of the week goes the same way; we run together in the mornings, and then we go into his office. Mostly we stay until lunch, and then Aragon will work from home—although a few times we have spent the whole day at the Guild. Owen comes every other day for my combat training. I am disappointed that I have not been able to do anything at the office but read. I spend my days pretending to be engrossed in the stuffy books, making mental notes as I can't be arsed to jot anything down.

When we get home, I pop the current text onto the shelf in my reading nook. I need to go for a run in my wolf form and afterwards I need to do some training. Owen has set me a new kick combo, and I will have to spend hours working on it to get it perfect.

Aragon's fancy, well-equipped home gym has everything I need. The heavy bags are hung a little high, but they're actually at a perfect height for me to practice my overhead kicks.

I haven't asked if the dragon will spar with me. Could you imagine? God, I wouldn't want to take a hit from him. But I would love to work on my ground game. I don't hold out much hope. Pervy girl. My hormones are raging out of control when it comes to Aragon.

I shift and go for my run.

The dragon is quietly waiting for me when I return. "No fur in the house, Forrest," he says sternly. Oh, I am "Forrest" now? Huh. He has called me "Miss Hesketh" all week.

I let my magic turn me back into my human form, I start towards the gym, and his voice stops me. "Forrest," he says, "I would like to talk to you about something I am concerned about. Please go into the living room." I nod. I don't like the expression on his face; it's a look that makes me revert to being bratty. This is usually about the time when I get in trouble. I want nothing more than to either salute him or maybe stick both middle fingers up at him and shout *fuck you*.

I sigh...and they say I have poor impulse control. I manage to dawdle into the living room quietly and sit. Aragon must know about the bracelets. I find myself wanting to fidget as he prowls into the room. I watch him out of the corner of my eye; I am unwilling to look at him directly. I pick at a loose thread on my leggings.

"Forrest, when we're at work, I have some Fae come into the house to clean—they are brownies." Okay, where is he going with this? I had wondered who did all the cleaning. Is this when he shows his hand and maybe admits that the brownies went through my stuff? Looking for my magic? "I have been informed that your bed remains unslept-in. So my question is, where do you sleep?"

What? I stare at him. I didn't expect him to go with that. What on earth am I going to say? Will he use it against me? Probably. I keep my mouth shut and shrug.

"I know you don't leave the house at night."

I study my hands. The best thing that I can do is not answer him. I can feel him looking at me. I bet his face wears a fake mask of concern. What does he care where I sleep?

"Forrest, why are you sleeping on the floor in wolf form?" I peek up at him at that. "The brownies found your fur on the floor," he explains as I nibble my lip. "You will answer me."

No, I bloody will not.

"I had a whole chocolate cake ordered for you…It would be a shame for the order to be cancelled." *What! Nooooooo!* No, he can't do that, it's so mean. I glare at him. "Chocolate cake is for good girls who answer questions." He raises his eyebrows. Is Aragon going to hold a chocolate cake over me as a hostage? Damn it. I haven't had a bit of chocolate all week! I have to give him something.

I wrinkle my nose. "I get cold. I find beds strange," I tell him honestly.

"I can understand you find sleeping in a bed strange, but it has been over three months since you shifted back—you need to adapt. No fur in the house from now on, Forrest." I glare at him, but I shrug and think it's okay because I will sleep outside.

"Also, no sleeping outside. You will sleep in your bed." He leaves the room. A single tear falls down the side of my nose, and I quickly wipe it away. This is shit. Why does it matter to him that I sleep in my wolf form? Controlling bastard.

I go into the gym, and I work out like a crazy person. When he calls me for dinner a few hours later, there's a bag on the table. I look at it without interest. It isn't cake-shaped. "I bought you something that will hopefully make you feel less cold," Aragon says from the kitchen.

I peek into the bag and see something fluffy. I pull out what turns out to be fluffy pyjamas and some equally fluffy bed socks. I stare at the thoughtful gift in shock. "Thank you," I say, my hand stroking them; they're so soft. The long-sleeved top and bottoms are covered in little pink unicorns, and with the socks, they should cover me completely. It was a good idea; it was also very kind. I give Aragon a small smile.

CHAPTER
TWENTY-SEVEN

I haven't slept for three nights; I have started stumbling and knocking into stuff. Running this morning, I opted to run as a wolf as my poor coordination couldn't handle two legs.

I am so fucking grumpy. I want to bite the dragon on his bubble-bottom for making me do this. Food has started to turn my stomach, and I've almost stopped eating. The only thing I can force down is the traitorous chocolate cake.

Aragon hasn't said anything to me, but I can see his frustration building. I am sure the dragon thinks I am stupid, stubborn. I haven't told him how sleeping as a human makes me feel, and I haven't explained about the nightmares. Perhaps if I did, he would let me be?

It's too late now to even try and explain; in my experience, he probably wouldn't believe me anyway. John certainly wouldn't.

I am sitting at the table, pushing my food around the plate. My head occasionally dips down towards the table, nodding, as I force myself to stay awake. Aragon snaps and his big hand thumps down on the table; the plates jump with the impact.

"Forrest, this is getting ridiculous. You have lost weight, and you look ill. You are leaving me no other choice but to get you a sleeping potion!"

"What?" I look up at him, suddenly wide awake. Oh my God, I can't think of anything worse—the thought of being magically put to sleep in my human form, lying in bed vulnerable.

It absolutely freaks me out.

Would the potion trap me into my nightmares? So I wouldn't be able to wake up? I can feel the utter panic take hold of my body, and I desperately shake my head no. My eyes plead with him as I hunch in my chair, enveloped in the scent of my fear.

"What will you have me do! You will sleep tonight, Forrest. As a human in your bed, or tomorrow, I will get the potion and use it without your permission."

I spring up from the table, my chair screeching across the floor. I narrow my eyes at him; I am shaking in fear and anger. The only good thing is that the high level of adrenaline in my body is making me feel almost normal.

"You are a monster!" I shout at him. I turn and run to my room; I dramatically throw myself onto the navy bean bag in my book nook. I wrap my arms around myself and curl into a ball and silently cry, my head almost on my knees.

I don't want to go to sleep in this body! I don't! But I am so tired, and I can't risk him forcing a sleep potion on me.

Most of the time, when I'm awake, I can convince myself, force myself, to believe those bad things didn't happen.

Except in my dreams.

In my dreams, the boxes in my mind that are stuffed full of bad memories rattle, and the lids loosen. The memories creep out across my mind and plague me.

At the hospital, when I first started getting the nightmares, Owen would hear me screaming and gently shake me awake. He would then sit up and talk to me until I felt safe. It was Owen who suggested and encouraged me to try sleeping in my wolf form, and it worked. I never had a nightmare again. But now...I should have told Aragon the truth. I stare at the photo of my mum and Grace.

I'm a silly coward. The bad dreams can't kill me.

I shower and then put the stupid fluffy cute unicorn pyjamas on with the socks. I eye the bed with disgust. Pulling the duvet, I get in.

The bed is so soft it's like sleeping on a cloud. I hate it. I pull the cover up to my chin, close my eyes, and try to quieten my mind. I huff, chuck one of the pillows onto the floor, and thump the remaining one to flatten it. I start a simple meditation exercise, and before I have finished, I fall asleep.

I AM in my silver cage in the garage. I am naked, and my skin is cold.

My mum is with me. I can't quite believe she is here with me and that I am not alone. It has been such a long time since I have seen her beautiful face. God, I have missed her. She sits upright, leaning against the silver bars, and I can smell her skin burning.

"Mum," I whisper urgently, "your skin is burning. Please, you need to move away from the bars." I take her wrist and try to pull her away, but she won't move. Mum has a doll in her arms. The toy has blonde hair, and it looks familiar. She starts giggling strangely, hugging the doll to her chest.

"You have to be quiet, Mum; please stop laughing. If Vincent hears yo—"

"If Vincent hears what?" A voice comes from the darkness, I start to shake in fear, my teeth chattering I cover myself the best I can with my arms.

Why am I naked?

Vincent steps forward, the yellow hose in his hand. Cold water suddenly blasts into the cage. "You are such a dirty and disgusting thing, look at the mess you have made!" he roars.

My mum continues to giggle, and I watch in growing horror as her throat slowly starts to open up, and her blood pours from the wound down her chest. The blood is bright red in the darkness. The cold water from the hose hits her, the water and blood mix, splashing red against my face. I put my hands up to her throat to try and stem the bleeding. But this causes the wound to open further, and her head rolls from side to side, her neck unable to support its weight.

The doll falls into my lap as my mum takes hold of my wrists and squeezes them. "You are..." over the pounding of the water, I can't hear what she is saying, so I lean closer. "You are such a disappointment. Why didn't you die like you were told? You are cursed." My mum pushes me violently away from her.

Her throat is gaping, and she makes a horrible gurgling sound. She is no longer bleeding. Her chest stops moving, as she slumps to the side. I know she is dead. Heartbreaking sorrow grips me, and I sob. I feel like my heart is being slowly ripped out.

"Mum, Mummy," I whimper.

The doll in my lap suddenly starts to scream, making me flinch. I realise my mistake—that it isn't a doll, it is my baby sister, Grace. I look down at her, and with trembling fingers, I move her hair from her face. I meet her wide glassy dead eyes. Grace is dead, but she still screams...

"Forrest, Forrest, wake up. Wake up!" My eyes fly open, and I am sobbing, my throat is hurting, I've been screaming. My wrists are held in Aragon's grip. I don't understand why he is holding me so tightly until I notice the flames.

My arms are shockingly on fire. I am on fire!

The flames light up the room in hazy blue. The smell of smoke fills my nose. My once-fluffy unicorn pyjamas are burned black, and my bedcovers are smouldering. I sob harder. What have I done? I have ruined everything. Aragon waves a hand, and the small flames around us die. He scoops me up into his arms and takes me out of the room. He rushes me through the house, and we go up a flight of stairs.

"I am sorry, I am so sorry, I didn't mean to, I didn't mean to ruin the lovely things you bought for me. Nev—" I sob, "—never happened before. Just the dreams, never the flames. I am sorry..." I mumble over and over through my sobs. The shock of everything makes me cry harder, even more than remembering the horror of the nightmare.

"I need to get these off; then you can shift to heal." Aragon carefully starts to strip me out of my damaged pyjamas. The top has melted, and pieces of the fabric are embedded in the skin of my arms. Aragon painfully picks out the material, which makes my arms bleed.

"This is the reason I was concerned about the witch magic; messing with something you don't fully understand is dangerous. Without the potion in your system, you could have shifted. I have no idea if it will stay in your skin if you shift now." He finishes quickly, "Shift, Forrest."

I transform into my wolf, and I don't want to turn back. Aragon holds my furry head in his large hands, with a firm voice and pleading silver eyes—almost with his will alone, he forces me back to human.

I return to human naked and shaking, but thanks to Aragon, I am completely healed. Aragon grabs a long-sleeved t-shirt from his bed and tugs it over my head. He folds me back into his arms. I am no longer crying, but with his stillness, I can feel how much I am shaking.

He gets into bed and pulls me with him so that I lie on top of him. I struggle. What happens if I burn up again? I'm going to end up hurting him. Aragon ignores me and firmly holds me to his chest. I belatedly realise that his torso is bare.

"I am a dragon, and I am fireproof. Be still." I am too exhausted to fight him, and he feels warm, he smells good. I rest my cheek on his chest and close my eyes. I breathe in his smoky, musky scent. I listen to his heartbeat, and it calms me further. He cups the back of my neck in his massive palm, holding me to him. His other hand runs up and down my spine gently. My heart starts to slow, the rhythm no longer pounding in my ears. My body slowly stops shaking. I've never been held before, and I soak up his affection.

"Have you had bad dreams before?" Aragon asks quietly. I nod. "Is that the real reason you didn't want to sleep in this form?" I nod again. "Do you want to tell me about your dream?" I shake my head; I really really don't want to think about it. "Sleep, Forrest. I will watch over you." He pulls the covers around us; I don't think I will ever sleep again.

But in his arms I feel warm and safe. Lying on top of his hard-muscled form is the most comfortable I have ever been. My body fits on top of his like a perfect puzzle piece.

I AWAKE MORE comfortable than I've ever been in my life. Warmth surrounds me. My face is pressed to warm skin. Aragon. I open my eyes. My eyelashes brush gently fluttering butterfly-kisses across his skin.

I've moved in my sleep, and I am straddling a warm naked silver torso. My legs are on either side of him; he is so broad they don't touch the bed. One of my hands is resting on his chest, the other has gone rogue and is wrapped around his long silver hair. The hair is so soft; it's like silk.

I reluctantly let go of his hair. I raise myself slightly on my hands, using his chest for balance. I peek up into his face. It is then that I realise his warm skin is *everywhere*. My eyes widen in shock—I haven't got underwear on! I am straddling him. My breasts that were happily pressed to his chest a second ago gently scrape across him as I move and my nipples go hard. The intimacy steals my breath, and I let out a little gasp as his energy tingles along my skin.

Aragon meets my gaze. His eyes are heavy-lidded and his pupils are dilated. I panic and try to scramble off him. But his hand gently grips the back of my neck; his other hand wraps around my thigh underneath the T-shirt so close to the curve of my bare bottom, and he presses me back down onto him, keeping me in place. He slowly sits up, and leaning forward, he brushes his nose against my ear. His warm breath tickles the back of my neck, making me shiver. I let out a little moan. He breathes in my scent and lets out an appreciative growl.

The hand gripping my neck has now moved slightly and is cupping the back of my head. He tips my head back, his eyes on my lips. His thumb gently rubs my cheekbone. My tummy flips as he moves closer, his lips almost touching mine, and he pauses. My lips part, and we breathe in each other's breath.

His eyes close, Aragon groans deep in the back of his throat, chest rumbling under my fingertips.

He sighs sadly.

"How do you feel?" Aragon rests his big palm against my forehead, his fingers smoothing back strands of my hair, thumb caressing my skin.

"I'm okay…"

Aragon pulls me back into his chest, my head tucked underneath his chin, and he holds me close like he never wants to let me go.

CHAPTER
TWENTY-EIGHT

We are outside, and I nervously bounce on my toes. My dragon is going to teach me how to use my fire magic. After last night—I'm shitting myself. My hands are twisting around my grey unicorn jumper, and I'm gnawing on my lip.

"Nutty, what are you afraid of? Your magic won't harm you. The fire magic is a part of you, just like your wolf magic." Aragon is trying hard to waylay my fear. I don't know who he is kidding. I blink up at him in wide-eyed disbelief. So he tries a different tactic. "Without proper control, you could hurt others, and we can't have what happened last night happen again. I couldn't bear it. So I'm going to teach you how to control your fire magic. I should have done this weeks ago. Now, as a precaution..." Aragon pulls a beautiful silver necklace from his pocket. "It's platinum." With two fingers hooked underneath the delicate chain, Aragon dangles the necklace for my perusal. It spins and sparkles, the light reflecting from the teardrop diamond's many facets.

"It is beautiful," I husk out.

"It's Fae magic, and it will help you gain control."

"What...How? Will it stop me from hurting people? Will it stop me from burning down your beautiful home? I'm so sorry about—"

"Forrest, I'm the one that's at fault. I let you down. I should have respected your decisions." Aragon pulls my hair away and places the necklace over my head. The chain is long, and the diamond settles warmly between my breasts. "I let you down. I should have realised that there was more to this sleep issue." He kisses the top of my head. "Now close your eyes and let's begin." I close my eyes; I can still feel the slight imprint of his kiss. Aragon moves behind me. In his deep, low voice he says, "Relax your mind, feel your magic. The fire magic will be hotter than your wolf. The magic will feel different, pulsing. Bring it forward gently in your mind." I feel for my magic.

The almost playful tug of my wolf magic makes me smile. Behind my wolf magic is a flame. Hot. Angry. Scary. My whole body starts to shake.

My fear makes my wolf magic rush forward, and I shift.

I huff my disappointment. Aragon smiles down at me. "Shift back and try again. I promise you can do this. Please don't be frightened." Disappointed, I turn back to human. "Now, close your eyes…"

I AM at the Guild office, and because of my constant begging over the last few weeks, I have been allowed to help Matthew. It's my first job! In the first few weeks, I found coming to the Hunters Guild so dull. But now that I am allowed to do something productive, the time here goes much quicker.

If given a choice, I'd be on the street kicking ass as a hunter— chasing down warrants and catching bad guys. I find the work that the hunters do for the Guild fascinating. My imagination goes a little nuts with the excitement of it—*Hunter Hesketh*— oh my God, how good does that sound? I repeat it back to myself a few times, nodding. I will have to think of an appropriate theme tune.

Between phone calls and running around, I practice my fire magic. After weeks of solid training, I can handle my magic without much thought. I practise so much that I can make a small flame dance in my hand and make it skip from one hand to the other. I privately think that with my skills, I put John to shame. I can shape a flame in the air, and today I am working on a butterfly; it's going to be epic.

Aragon is encouraged by how quickly I've picked everything up. In a few decades, he says, I should be able to use my fire while in wolf form and light myself up like a proper hellhound!

Flaming fur! Oh my God, how cool is that!

Aragon is the real reason I have picked everything up quickly; he is an impressive teacher. It helps that he has total control of the element. Aragon can not only control his fire magic but that of others as well, and ordinary fire.

I munch on a giant chocolate chip cookie that has appeared on my desk as if by magic. Matthew must have left it for me—he is so thoughtful. It tingles strangely on my tongue. I spin my office chair and roll it across the room to answer the ringing phone. Why walk when you can roll…"Good afternoon, the Hunters Guild, how may I help you?" It's Friday afternoon and I haven't seen Aragon for hours. He has been busy with meetings all day.

"Ms Hesketh? I'm so glad I caught you. I have a buyer for the house who wants to discuss the opportunity to purchase more land than the listed ten acres," the lady on the phone says, taking my grunt of surprise as confirmation that she has gotten the right person. Huh, a call from the estate agent who is selling Temple House. I have no idea how they got this number. I drum my fingers on my desk. I had earmarked the five hundred acres to keep, but do I need all that land?

"I could probably sell a bit more land." It would be good to get Aragon's advice. Maybe John should have input too? Although I still haven't talked to my brother, since the Daniel incident. I know it's petty of me; I should do the right thing and give him a call. I guess I need to gather up my nerve to return his calls. "I need to think. Can I call you back on Monday?"

A wave of dizziness hits me, and with the heel of my hand, I rub the aching spot between my eyes.

"Ms Hesketh, the reason for my call is that the buyer is unfortunately looking at other properties and will only be available tomorrow for a viewing. She's adamant that she will only discuss the purchase in person, with yourself. She's a cash buyer, and if she loves Temple

House as much as I think she will, the sale could be finalised within the month." The fee for the agent was astronomical, so you would think they could deal with this without having to involve me in the viewings. I groan and huff down the phone. I open my mouth with the intention of putting the agent off, but I find myself agreeing instead.

"I guess I can meet her at the house at…urm, midday?" I shrug to myself. It will be fine. Realistically, I want to see the back of that house as quickly as possible. Left up to me, I would have burned the place to the ground. But Temple House is my mum's legacy, so I should at least take the time to sell it to a proper custodian. Besides, my head is spinning and I don't want to negotiate—I just want to get off the phone.

Once she gets my agreement, the estate agent quickly finishes up the call. God, I hate that house. I am not looking forward to tomorrow.

I push off from the desk, roll into a clear space, and spin again. Instead of a butterfly, this time I'm going to aim for a little dragon.

Thinking about dragons, disappointingly I have yet to see Aragon's dragon. Aragon is incredibly private; I don't think anybody has seen his dragon form in centuries. I yearn to see his shifted form. I am not brave enough to demand to see the other part of him. I wonder how huge he is and if like his human colouring, he is silver.

The flaming blob looks nothing like a dragon; I scowl at it.

I can't wait to go home; today has been boring. *Only 'cause you want to go back for cake and then bedtime,* says that helpful snide internal voice. I huff and go red at my inner monologue. God, I'm such a weirdo.

Yeah, so at night Aragon insists I join him and sleep human in his arms, so he can keep me safe. I spend my nights curled on top of him, wrapped safely in his muscly arms. Unfortunately, Aragon is a total gentleman, and he makes sure to cover me from head to toe in fluffy pyjamas so the incident that shall not be named doesn't happen again. Urm, you know, the whole naked-parts-of-me-on-naked-parts-of-him incident. Oh my.

Thinking about it, I have yet to have my first kiss. Nonetheless, I've moved to the unplanned impressive level where my bare vulva sat on a dragon shifter's eight-pack. Since the incident, I can't help thinking more naughty thoughts. I regret not pressing my lips to his.

But my experience in everything is so lacking; I have zero chance of making the moves on anyone, least of all a legendary dragon shifter. Could you imagine? What if he said no? Of course he'd say no! Then I'd die of embarrassment.

As if thinking about him has conjured him up, Aragon prowls through the portal. His jacket buttons are undone and his hair is dishevelled, as though he has repeatedly been running his fingers through it. Aragon's brief smile and tight eyes relay a lousy day, and in his wake, angry energy smashes around him like a livid wave. If I didn't know him as well as I do, I'd be hiding underneath the desk.

"Are you okay?" I spring up and rush to him. I reach out and rest my hand on his forearm. The wariness within him sets me on edge.

"Yes, I'm fine thank you, Forrest." Aragon washes his hand across his face and closes his eyes, and when he opens them, his crashing angry energy has dissipated. He holds up his arm, and I nestle underneath. "I apologise. A meeting didn't go my way. I will not bore you with unnecessary details." Aragon hugs me to his side and kisses the top of my head. "My schedule has become inundated, and I have to work later than planned. Would you like me to arrange for Owen to escort you home?"

"No, that's okay, I can go by myself." Aragon runs his thumb across my cheekbone, a soft expression in his eyes. I beam him my best smile. "Oh, the estate agent called about my mum's house. I have a viewing —" The office door slams open, and Matthew hurries in, his hands full of paperwork and a harassed, crazy look in his eyes. "I can see you're busy—it can wait. I'll see you at home." I stand on my tiptoes and kiss his cheek, then wiggle out from under his arm. I almost sprint to the portal. No way I'm helping Matthew with all that shit. "See you Monday, Matthew," I yell.

CHAPTER
TWENTY-NINE

The taxi drops me off outside the main gates. It's so strange being back here; memories whisper through the trees as I meander down the driveway. My boots crunch on the leaves that have fallen unchecked, and more red, orange, and yellow leaves swirl around me. The light breeze also tugs at my hair and teases strands from the fancy side plait.

Initially, I hadn't known what to wear; it's the middle of November, and although it isn't too cold, I still get cold. I was going to put on jeans but then thought better of it. I appear young, and the buyer might be difficult if I don't at least look like I own a big-ass manor house. So I chose a warm black jumper dress, thick black tights, and boots, and I topped off the outfit with an expensive long red wool coat.

I tug my coat closer around me and bury my cold hands in my pockets as I amble towards the house.

Something inside me doesn't want me to go near the place. Maybe I should have cancelled the viewing...no, it wouldn't have been fair to the lady wishing to view the house.

I can see that the buyer is already here; their empty car is parked by the front entrance. I presume they're looking at the grounds.

I wish Aragon or Owen were here. I made the mistake of leaving everything to the last minute, and my head has been kind of fuzzy. I rub the aching spot between my eyes.

I guess I've not worked on the whole time-management thing; today, lazily, I was relying on my missing dragon to do all the planning work for me.

I didn't leave home till eleven, and it takes a good thirty minutes to get to this house from my old apartment portal. I had hoped to spot a friendly face at the apartments, to beg one of the hellhounds to drive me and play bodyguard. When I didn't find a handy hellhound and Owen didn't answer my call, I got a taxi and fired off a text to Owen to explain. I still haven't told Aragon I have a viewing today—he's inundated with work, and he left for the Guild early.

I didn't sneak out intentionally, and I scribbled a note. I bet I will be back home before Aragon anyway.

I unlock the main door and leave the door open behind me as I traipse into the house. I glance around with a shiver; it feels like a lifetime since I have stepped foot here. All the pack photos and portraits have been removed and safely stored. The walls have a fresh coat of paint, the floors have been freshly waxed. I appointed a cleaning company to make sure the house remained pristine.

It isn't as scary as I remember, but the past still echoes in its walls. I know on some level it wasn't the fault of the house—what happened to me had been the result of the actions of two men. But it still makes me a bit sick, and I feel uncomfortable being here. My instincts scream at me to leave, to run.

My phone rings and I fish it out of my coat pocket—Owen is returning my call. "Hello, Nanny Hound," I say brightly.

"Forrest, where are you?" Owen demands, his voice urgent. I hate it when he uses that tone; it means I'm in trouble.

"I am at my mum's house, meeting a buyer. Is every—"

"Forrest, get out of that house now! I am on my way; you need to leave now! I will meet you up the road from the house. Head towards the village." He disconnects the call without saying goodbye.

Oh, crap. Owen is pissed, and Aragon is going to be pissed.

I don't know what I'm going to tell the buyer.

I turn and rush back down the hall towards the entrance, my keys in my hand, ready to lock the door. I grind to a halt.

Liz Bloody Richardson is standing at the door with a sick-looking smile on her face. *What the fuck is Liz doing here?* In greeting, she gives me a strange little finger wave. I shake my head at her and scrunch my nose in disgust—God, she's a loon.

"I can see the persuasive magic worked. Did you enjoy the cookie?"

What? Oh no! Before I can tell her to fuck off I am grabbed from behind; my head hits a hard chest, and my arms are pinned to my sides.

I react without thinking. I drop and shift my weight to the side, which handily opens up my line of attack onto the idiot's groin. I slap my hand with the keys back hard, nailing him; it makes him flinch with pain and gives me room and a few seconds to twist out of his grip.

I should now run like hell, but I am pissed. He tries to grab me again, and I drop the keys to the floor and throat-punch him. I then do a little skip and use my elbow to strike his temple. As he goes down, I recognise him. It's Meathead Two, the one with the brown hair. Oh, bloody hell. I knee him in the face for good measure. He flops to the floor, out cold.

I turn to leave, and Liz is standing right in front of me. I don't see the knife in her hand until she stabs me with it.

"Why?" I gasp.

"You killed my lover Paul with your stupid dinner stunt. My brother found him and killed him. Now, dog, any time I get even a sniff of your happiness, a hint that things are going well for you, I will be there to fuck it up. Harry says hello..." She jams the blade deeper into my side to make her point. She grins. "I hope that hurts."

The wound burns, which indicates that the knife must be silver—the crazy cow. I keep my face blank, not giving her any opportunity to revel in my pain. The silver will slow me down and stop me from shifting. But I lived in a silver cage for ten years, so while I'm not immune, I have built up a tolerance to its effects.

I punch her in the chest, and she's knocked away from me. With a sucking sensation, the knife pulls free. Liz still has the bloody blade in her grip, and she waves it at me, a snarl on her lips. I narrow my eyes and follow her. I dart to the side, cup my palm, and slap her hard across the face. I kick the knife, knocking it from her hand, and with satisfaction, I hear her wrist crunch. Liz drops to her knees, holding her broken wrist to her chest; she starts wailing. I scoop up the blade.

I stumble past her and out of the house, clutching my side.

"What the fuck, Liz, you were supposed to be a decoy, not fucking stab her with silver. That's my mate you have just marked up," a voice chastises. I glance up, and Daniel Kerr is there, looking like a textbook villain in a custom black suit. He swaggers towards me.

I slide the blade into my coat pocket, and I don't react when Daniel grabs hold of my arm. There's no fighting my way out of this. He has a group of twenty shifters at his back, and I am bleeding all over the fucking steps.

I'm starting to feel the effects of the silver, and it isn't pleasant. Everything around me echoes and reverberates like I'm underwater. I shake my head to try and clear it. I almost fall to one knee, but Daniel's grip on my arm stops my descent. The pain in my side shoots to the tips of my fingers. Slowly my skin grows numb and cold, marking the paralysis of the whole left-hand side of my body. Fuck, that can't be good...well, at least it doesn't hurt anymore.

"Forrest." Daniel pulls my head back by my hair. If he didn't have a grip on me, I would have fallen. "I have missed you, little wolf. Look at you, all elegantly dressed up." He is such a dickhead. Wordless snarls erupt from my mouth, which he ignores. "Let's go into our house and get things sorted. Try not to get blood on my suit." He chuckles and pulls me back around. Daniel half-drags, half-carries me back into the house. We pass Liz, who is still crying on the floor. "You lot, wait outside! I don't need an audience for this. Marcus, Ron, come. I want you to watch the office door."

Daniel drags me into the small downstairs office; he must have been inside the house before. I am struggling to stand, but at least the bleeding is starting to slow. According to my research on silver poisoning, it should be out of my system within the next ten minutes or so if I am lucky. I can then shift and chew his nose off.

Daniel smiles at me in triumph; he lets go of my arm and leans towards me. I take a small, unsteady shuffling step back. My bum meets the wall, and I use it to prop myself up.

"It has taken me months to get you away from that fucking dragon. Yesterday the council permitted me to pursue my claim. I told them that you were my mate. He let the vote pass."

He what? I don't believe him. Why would Aragon do that? I brace my knees and lift my chin. The back of my head smacks against the wall. Daniel is still a delusional wanker.

"I know that fucking dragon isn't going to let me near you—he will burn every favour he has to keep you away from me. So I thought I'd up the timeline. I don't need his permission; I have the council's." Daniel snarls, "I know he's been fucking you for months." He yanks me away from the wall and into his arms and spins me so that he is standing behind me. "I forgive you for that, Forrest." I attempt to turn my head to keep my eyes on him, but my vision is swimming with black dots. I feel like I have taken several punches to the head. It takes everything I have to keep on my feet.

Daniel pulls me to his chest and takes hold of my right wrist, pulling it away from my wound, where I had been applying pressure. He pulls my arm across my body. The silver is making me slow, and I don't react as he does the same to my other arm. He holds both my wrists firmly. Daniel kicks out the office chair, sits, and hauls me onto his lap. His breath is on my neck.

I hear him open his mouth, the slight click of the jaw, but nothing prepares me for him biting me.

He must have shifted his teeth. He bites the back of my neck, his upper and lower canines on either side of my spine. I let out a pained whine.

It hurts. It hurts. It hurts.

The sheer pain cuts through the effects of the silver. I manage to struggle for a few moments, but it's useless. He continues to bite me, and everything falls away. It is as if I am trapped inside myself, unable to move at all. Dark and twisting, I feel his rancid mate magic ooze through my blood, into my head.

He finally lets go of my neck; I come back slightly to myself, my breathing shallow. My heart is beating too slowly.

My neck feels wet and what I presume is blood from the bite

trickles down my back. *Daniel has bitten me*...the words bounce about my head as I try to remember the significance.

Daniel stands, and he shoves my shocked, useless body across the desk. Putting his hand underneath my coat and dress, he starts lifting everything. "I have to make this quick as we have to go. I won't leave here without finishing our mating—I have waited too long." He painfully rips my tights and knickers down; I still can't move. "Look at that fucking ass—fuck me, you are fucking perfect. I am a lucky bastard." He slaps my bottom, and he laughs. My heart has sped up and feels like it is now beating out of my chest.

In my head, I am screaming.

His fingers brush between my legs, and I suddenly wake the fuck up. I find my voice. "No." It comes out as a whisper; I say it louder. "No! Get off me, this is rape," I croak out.

"Oh, sweetcheeks, you silly girl. You can't rape your mate. I know you are not going to enjoy this, but I will." The scraping descent of his zipper brings tears to my eyes.

No God, no, I won't survive this.

I flinch, and the knife wound pounds rhythmically, waves of agony in tune with my frantic heartbeat.

Energy suddenly slams into me from out of nowhere. It fills me, and I know the silver is finally out of my system. I want to sob in relief.

Whatever the bite has done to me, will not stop me.

I fling my head back, catching him in a head butt. Daniel is knocked away from me. I roll off the other side of the desk.

The idiot laughs. "I love it when you fight."

"Then you're going to love this," I rasp out, "but not as much as I will." Daniel won't be laughing soon.

I slip the silver knife from my coat pocket into my hand. I then let my returned fire magic heat my palm. I send the flame up the blade and push the heat level to violet, my hottest level. The silver knife quickly starts to melt.

Daniel pulls me towards him, and he smiles in sick excitement.

I bring the knife up, and I press the melting silver blade to his face.

Daniel screams. I smile.

I don't have time to do anything further or see the damage I have done. I adjust my underwear and tights, shift into my wolf, pounce on the desk, and hit the window of the office.

The window shatters. I run. I run so fast.

I hear shouting behind me. Daniel has stopped screaming. What is it about that asshole that has me jumping out of windows to get away from him?

A vindictive, cruel part of me knows there will be no healing the damage to his face. Silver scars; it scars horribly. I can imagine that Daniel's face now matches who he is inside. He isn't so pretty anymore. The thought makes me smile and gives me some measure of peace.

CHAPTER
THIRTY

I have to wait for only a few minutes and a car arrives. There's an electronic whirring as the boot opens. I exhale out of my nose, and my body sags in relief as I smell Owen's scent on the air. I creep out from underneath the thick hedging where I've been hiding and spring into the back of the car. The boot closes electronically behind me with a click, and the car sets off.

I shift back to human and climb into the front passenger seat. As I move, I shed little bits of crusted blood and glittering specs of silver that were clinging to my coat and dress. Owen grips my hand and squeezes it in relief. That relief turns to concern when he catches the scent of blood.

"What the fuck happened? I got your text message at the same time as a phone call from a contact. He said that Daniel was on the move with a load of heavies and it had something to do with you...?"

We head back towards the city.

I settle into the seat. "It was a trap, an ambush. Liz Richardson stabbed me—silver knife to the side. I will be fine." My voice sounds cold and robotic to my own ears. I warily watch Owen's reactions as I curl sideways and lean my weight back against the door. My right cheek presses into the leather and I huddle into myself.

Owen's nostrils flare. "What the hell was that nasty cow doing there? The wound will scar. Are you feeling okay?" Owen flicks his eyes from the road and glances at me with concern. I smile sadly; he has entered nanny mode. "You shifted, so it must have cleared your system. Are you feeling dizzy or sick? Is your breathing okay?" I nod as he continues to give me a visual once-over. I ignore his worried questions; they aren't important at the moment.

"What happens when a male shifter bites a female's neck," I ask dully.

Owen slams on the brakes. I brace a hand on the dash as the tyres squeal on the tarmac. The car skids to a stop. Owen turns in his seat and grips my chin gently in a shaking hand. "Let me see." I peer up at him with dead eyes, unwilling to dip my head for him so he can inspect the back of my neck. Owen starts to growl.

"Who? Did Daniel do that? Did he bite you? Mate you?" Owen growls out the words. My eyes fill with tears that I refuse to shed. If I start, I'm never going to stop. "It forces a mate-slave bond, makes the female more willing. Easier to control. Real archaic and illegal. Did... did Daniel bite you?" His grey eyes beg me to say no. I wish I could. I force a stiff nod. Owen roars and slams both hands on the steering wheel. His left fist smashes into the dash, and the plastic crumples.

For a few minutes, there's silence.

In a quiet, horrified tone, he says, "Daniel will be able to track you. Is the bond entirely in place?" I look at him blankly. "Forrest, did Daniel....did Daniel rape you?"

What Daniel did was rape—the bite, his touch—but I know that isn't what Owen means.

"No," I whisper. Owen's whole body sags. "And he won't be able to track me for a while." Owen's eyes are glowing red; his hellhound magic is raging inside him. I reach across the console and place a trembling hand on his arm. "I stopped him, burned a silver knife into his face. He should be down for a while." I say this matter-of-factly, not elaborating that I used Daniel's face for anger-management therapy. But Owen gets what I'm saying, and he stops growling. He takes hold of my frozen hand.

"The bond will be only partly formed, then. If the bond is consummated, you will be stuck with him. Till death do us part, in the most literal sense. Fucking hell, Forrest, we can't let him near you. I don't recommend we kill him either; I have no idea what it would do to you. It could kill you too."

"Can the bond be removed?"

Owen turns away from me and stares out of the window. The worry and anger are evident on his face. I don't think he can bear to look at me.

"No...yes, theoretically. It is attached to your wolf; if you're willing to give up your wolf, I know of a curse. The curse will cut you from your wolf. In Daniel's mind, it will be as if you have died." Owen lets go of my hand and grips the steering wheel. "It will make you human. Cut off suddenly like that from your magic, it's not healthy...it's risky. Without shifting, you will age. *If* you live that long. It's a curse for a reason..." Owen restarts the stalled car, and the vehicle moves off.

I contemplate his words. The bite mark feels sore and heavy on my neck. I curl my lip with disgust as I skim the back of my neck with trembling fingers. I trace the ragged scar with my fingertips; it seems as if slave-bites, like silver wounds, don't heal from shifting. I huff out a breath; I am glad I messed that fucker up.

I glance at my hands, and in a split second, I decide it's what I am going to do.

I want out. I want the curse.

To choose this, after the trauma I have just experienced, is crazy. I must be insane. But when is the right time to make this choice? I want out.

I'm ruined. I let out a self-deprecating laugh; I'm half-bonded to a fucking psychopath. He won't stop till he has full control of my body and mind. Daniel will never stop coming for me, and if not him, there will be other Daniels.

I realise that my mum is no longer the winning *DNA EuroMillions ticket*. No, that's me.

In my nightmares, my mum told me again and again that I was cursed. All this time, have I been prognosticating?

My heart has just one instruction left— run.

I let out a strangled laugh. What the fuck had I been thinking!

Floating around in my happy bubble. My childish, pathetic antics, the embarrassing shit attempt at being a sweet, happy, lovable person. That stupid childish kitchen-climbing, chair-spinning idiot died in that office when Daniel bit her. I scrunch my nose, and my lips turn up in self-disgust.

I let out and nurtured every spec of childish hope that I had hidden away from the rotten parts inside me. I believed my own lies. My innocent, sweet mask got so wedged onto my face, I forgot for a while that it was just a guise. I forgot I'm rage, hate, and ruin.

Sometimes the people you love aren't safe for you, and sometimes it's you who are the toxic one. I am not safe. I'm cursed. Will it take one curse to end another?

I should never have been let out of that cage.

I forgot for a while that I was never meant to be safe in this world. The illusion of safety, of freedom, of contentment, of fucking love. It is all a cosmic joke, and I'm the biggest joke of all, with my stupid childish dreams. I thought I could make a difference. I naively thought I could alter perceptions. Help others. I can't even help myself.

I run unsteady hands over my face. I feel utterly overwhelmed and exhausted.

My fingers creep to the chain miraculously still around my neck, to the diamond Aragon gave me. Aragon...I think about him, and my heart flips. Devastation slams into me and my eyes fill with tears.

How is all this happening?

Aragon and the meeting yesterday. The council meeting. The reality of what Aragon has done makes me sick to my stomach. It was a meeting about me; it was about my life. He didn't even bother to tell me, to warn me about Daniel.

My head drops back on the window behind me, and the cold glass touches the bite mark on the back of my neck.

I love him—stupid naïve lost wolf—I have fallen so hard for my beautiful dragon. A life with him, to even contemplate it? To dream it? Loving Aragon, and him loving me back? The idea is preposterous. Impossible.

God, it is a selfish muscle—the heart.

I rub my face again, refusing to cry. Aragon will forget me. I have previously been forgettable. For fourteen years, I was forgotten. Now I will be again, perhaps remembered as collateral damage from the council's scheming.

I am so tired of being used and so overwhelmed with trying to work out different people's motivations.

I close my eyes. *Be brave.*

I am a cool calm void.

The strange calm that I feel spreading through my mind feels less like acceptance and more like the calm before a storm, made up of pure, unadulterated hysteria. I let out another strangled laugh.

Fuck, I will do this. My fear will not stop me. Without my wolf, it might be a slow death sentence, but I will be free. Freedom is the only thing that matters now.

"I want the curse," I say quietly. More strongly I say, "I have a plan. I need to speak to my friend Ava. Can you help me?" Ava once offered me a chance to run. I'm going to take her up on that. I open my eyes and give Owen a pleading look. "Will you help me?" Owen shakes his head and runs his hand through his hair in frustration. "Do you trust me, Nanny Hound?" I meet his conflicted gaze; I swallow down my sadness and my shame as I look at Owen, I beseech him with my eyes.

He growls at me— a real snarl— then scrubs a hand over his face, muttering unintelligible things to himself. His hand drops and some of the fury dims.

"Yes, I trust you." My heart hurts; Owen has faith in me. That's when I start crying. Big body-wracking sobs leave my lips, and Owen folds me into his arms. So much for being brave. "I don't want to," he says quietly into my hair, "but I'll help."

CHAPTER
THIRTY-ONE

NORTH-WEST NEWS. Police are appealing for information to identify a woman who was witnessed falling into the sea this evening at around nine o'clock. Police were called after witnesses reported seeing a girl jump from the sea wall in a presumed suicide. The coastguard will take up the search for the missing young woman in the morning, as sea conditions have made it impossible to search for her this evening.

The police have asked the Hunters Guild for assistance, and foul play has not been ruled out. A police spokesman said, "We will know more about the circumstances when the woman's body is recovered, but a curse or mental influence has not been ruled out at this time. Please call 111 with any information. We would like to identify this young lady and inform her family. Thank you for your help."

The police, with the help of a local technical expert, have released the following CCTV footage to piece together the woman's last movements.

Some viewers may find this disturbing, and viewer discretion is advised.

The footage shows a broken-looking girl in a red coat at a bus stop in Singleton village. She's captured on the bus's CCTV and on the local fire station's camera that's located near the bus stop. She gets on the number

75 bus and pays her fare. She gets off the bus forty minutes later in the town of Cleveleys, and the cameras track her movement through the town via the police CCTV system and also through a few local shop cameras. She looks like she's sleepwalking. The girl isn't moving as if she's injured, but there's a dark patch and a hole in her bright red coat.

She doesn't interact with anyone, nor does she react to anyone around her. She just traipses towards the seafront and the promenade.

We see her clearly on several CCTV cameras walking across the road, across the tram tracks, and towards the sea wall. The waves pound the sea defences, and when the sea spray hits her, she doesn't react.

Her long distinctive pink hair catches the street lights as it's whipped around by the wind. She removes her red coat and drops it to the floor at her feet. She then climbs up onto the sea wall.

The camera pans to the savage bite mark on the back of her neck.

She takes one look behind, a glance, so her face is caught one last time on film. Then she turns, and with one step, she falls, disappearing into the sea.

A clear photo of the woman flashes up on the screen, asking the public again for their help.

NORTH-WEST NEWS. Police have identified the woman who was witnessed falling into the sea yesterday evening at around nine o'clock. Police were called after witnesses reported seeing a young girl jump from the sea wall.

In a presumed suicide, the woman has been identified as Forrest Hesketh, a wolf shifter. The woman's pack has been informed.

The shifter community has responded with shock, disbelief and sorrow, the loss of such a rare female a blow. The police have thanked the public for their assistance and request any further enquiries to be directed to the Hunters Guild. The police are also warning that the promenade has been closed to vehicle and pedestrian access. For the time being, all humans should avoid the area.

Reports of a silver dragon aiding in the search have also been confirmed.

CHAPTER
THIRTY-TWO

Sunshine warms my face. It glows orange behind my closed lids. I blink my eyes open. I move, and the white duvet cover underneath me stirs the dust motes into the air. I watch them dance and twirl through a beam of sunlight.

I blink. I gasp as the general awareness of yesterday immediately bludgeons me. It hits me so hard I want to curl into a ball and wail.

Don't look back...be brave.

I don't allow any of the terrible details into the forefront of my mind. I stuff everything again into another fucking box.

Soon there will be nothing left but boxes rattling around in my head.

A tear runs down the side of my nose, and I angrily swipe it away.

I instead focus on the moment. On the here and now.

I sit up and knock a thick envelope that has been left next to me onto the floor. I scoop it up and tear it open. Contained inside are my new identification documents.

I sit on the side of the bed, my body slumped. Physically I feel okay, tired and slightly sluggish, but not as horrendous as I'd expected. I am disappointed that I can no longer feel my fire magic. It looks like the curse took both wolf and fire.

I huff and shrug. I lived my whole life without access to magic, so to be trapped in my human body is less challenging than being stuck as a wolf. I guess it's a different side of the same coin. I had access to magic for only six months, not a long time in the scheme of things.

I thumb through the documents. According to my new identification, I'm eighty-three–year-old Betty Green. I huff out a breath, and a morose smile pulls at my lips. I prod at the disguise bracelet on my ankle and notice that my scent masker is back on my wrist.

I'm in Ireland.

I grip my thighs tightly and hunch over in an attempt to stop the pain from crushing my chest. I'm in Ireland. I haven't a clue how Ava managed it. It's risky; shifters aren't welcome here. I will have to be extra careful, although with the curse, I am as close to human as I possibly can get. Being so close to my dragon, yet so far away, is going to be a challenge. I swallow down the rising bile. I'm dead to him, and I know he isn't my dragon anymore. It's something I will have to get over.

Don't look back...

I'm now living in County Sligo. I stand and lug myself away from the bright bedroom. If I don't leave this room, I will pull the covers up over my head, as if they can protect me from the world and I'll never leave. I unenthusiastically explore. The traditional Irish cottage is lovely; it's modern and set over one floor. Ava must have spent a lot of money on making this cottage perfect. The bungalow style consists of one large bedroom with an ensuite bathroom and open-plan living room, with a beautiful farmhouse-style modern kitchen. There's a hallway linking both the front and the back doors with a small utility room and another bathroom. The cottage is also in the middle of nowhere; my nearest neighbour is about six kilometres away.

The tiny little blue car in the driveway is a shock. I have an Irish driving licence, yet I have not got a clue how to drive. The cottage came with a kitchen full of supplies, so I am not going to be hungry anytime soon. But being so remote, I decide that my priority must be learning how to drive, with hitting YouTube as my first port-of-call.

If I had any light in me, it would be exciting. But I feel dead inside.

CHAPTER
THIRTY-THREE

It's a cold April morning, and I decide I want to go to my favourite café on the seafront at Strandhill. I love the place. They serve the best ice cream in the country, but I want to grab a hot chocolate and a slice of chocolate cake. I haven't left the house in weeks, so I do my best to make an effort. The stray dog I found in December isn't for moving; he hates leaving the house. He takes it upon himself to be my perimeter guard and gets miffed if I make him leave the garden. He's a character.

I spotted the big beige dog, alone with his head in some bushes, sniffing about quite happily. I whistled to get his attention, and he turned to me and growled. I growled back.

The dog blinked as if trying to work out who the heck I was—his expression hilarious. He's big, a giant breed, well over 100kg, and after a few internet searches, I found that he's a Caucasian shepherd.

I love his company, and he's delighted with his new living arrangements, especially as I will not under any circumstances feed him standard dog food, for obvious reasons. The bloody dog, whom I name Lucifer, eats better than I do. He's an exceptional guard dog, and we get on tremendously, especially when the opinionated monster realises that I'm in charge and he can't get his way.

I set off in my little blue car.

When I arrive, the parking spaces are almost empty. I imagine that when summer finally comes, it will be difficult to park. There's already a steady stream of surfers, braving the Atlantic all year round, so I can only imagine how busy it will get in summer.

I order my drink and cake at the counter and find a table. The traditional ice cream parlour has a warm beachy theme. The walls are a mix of blue and grey, with a black and white checkerboard floor; there's even an old wooded surfboard attached to the wall. I find a seat with my back against the wall. As I sit, I slide the block of wood with my order number onto the distressed-wood table. I can see little grains of sugar that have fallen through the cracks. I stroke my hand across the wood and feel some of the grains; they're rough underneath my fingertips.

I'm sitting next to a big picture window with a view of the sea. I watch the waves rhythmically crash into the sea wall, and my mind wanders to a different location. I'm glad it's the same ocean—I miss Aragon's glass house terribly.

I keep myself busy, but even with Lucifer's help, I still feel alone. Should I care that the solitude that broke me as a wolf now brings me solace as I'm stuck as a human? Without using my rage, which is the only emotion left inside me, I'm nothing but a numb shell.

My body and senses have turned human-slow; I don't need to try to walk like a human anymore. I lost that shifter prowl. I also find that I sleep more. Mercifully I don't have many nightmares, but I wake in the middle of the night or early morning with the feeling of Aragon's arms around me. In that time between sleep and wakefulness, I let myself for a few heartbeats imagine I'm in his arms. I live for the imaginary moments. When I awake fully, I feel like my heart is being ripped out of my chest. I think missing him is the worst part of my new life. I wonder if he misses me, but I know that is wishful thinking.

A chair scrapes against the floor, and I glance up to find two strange men sitting down. One of them sits on the chair next to me, blocking my exit, and the other sits opposite me.

Their whole attitude screams aggression, and they aren't human.

Even though I no longer have my wolf senses, I can tell the guy opposite me is an influential, powerful, older Fae. With shock and fearful trepidation, I realise that the guy sitting next to me is a wolf shifter. That alone scares the crap out of me; his nostrils flare as he picks up the fear in my scent.

I take a deep breath in and close my eyes. Why is my life so fucking shit?

I can't get away from them—even in Ireland, the shifters manage to find me. Without my fire magic and the strength of my wolf, I'm in real trouble. I open my eyes turn my body so I can keep both of them in sight, and I wait. I wait for them to make the first move.

The waitress comes up to the table with a smile and drops off my order. I smile at her with thanks. I'm too frightened to say the words, and there's no reason to put her in any danger by attempting to run.

The Fae opposite me is elegant and deadly. Enormous pale blue eyes and pointed ears betray him as a full-blooded Aes Sídh, a warrior elf. His black hair is long as is their custom, styled into intricate plaits. I know enough to recognise his warrior markings—they look like human tattoos, and they start at his right hand and go all the way to his neck. He is dressed in all black, combats.

I'm so fucked.

The wolf isn't as big as the hellhounds back home, not that I have seen him standing, but sitting, he still towers over me. The expression in his eyes is hard, and he screams "old shifter." He looks as if he has been to Hell and back. His light hair is shorn to his scalp, and his eyes are brown. Both men are looking at me like I have stolen the last slice of cake. Maybe I have?

"You're not human—I can see the witch magic all over you, covering your identity. You shouldn't be using appearance-altering magic in my territory," the elf points out acerbically. He narrows his eyes at me, but all he gets back is a blank stare. I shrug. What does he want me to do? Remove it?

"I demand you remove the magic."

Okay, then. I glance about to try to work out how to get away, but my options are limited. I've stupidly cornered myself.

"You are not going anywhere. Whatever you are, you are dangerous, especially if you have had to alter your appearance."

"This one is unusual or stupid, as it is more frightened of me than you. How strange. It reeks of fear," the wolf says in a growling voice. He lifts his top lip and shows me his teeth—*my, what big teeth you have.* It hasn't been that long since I was last called *it*. Instead of it making me want to rage, my stomach flips and the sadness gets me for a few heartbeats. I shake it off.

Not having much of a choice, I reach for my ankle. The elf pulls an iron blade on me and points it in my face. The wolf growls. I glare at the pair of them—they either want me to remove my disguise, or they don't. Can they make up their fucking minds? I hold up my hands to show I haven't got any weapons, and I roll my eyes when they both look pointedly at my ankle.

The elf puts his big-ass knife on the table with a *thunk* and pulls my foot towards him, almost pulling me from my chair. I let out a squeak of protest, and the fucker pulls my leg harder. I want to scream at him, *my bloody legs aren't that long, you prick!* In the end, he seems to come to the same conclusion, and he ducks underneath the table.

He pulls my leggings up and my boot off. He finds both my disguise- and scent-masker bracelets, and I feel the magic disappear. The wolf's eyes widen as he takes in my young face and gold eyes. He makes a slightly shocked sound, which causes the elf to spring up from underneath the table, his iron blade back in his hand and pointing at me.

He too stares at me with absolute shock on his face.

"What the fuck? I wasn't expecting that," says the wolf.

I sip my drink as they continue to study me. I am not wasting it—it's hot chocolate, plus it gives me something to do with my shaking hands. The wolf leans towards me, sniffing.

I glare at him. Fucking rude.

"She still smells wrong, of magic," the wolf grumbles. "I can't believe she's a wolf shifter. How old are you, kid? You look about...twenty? Where the fuck have you come from!"

"She has a curse on her," says the elf. Just like the wolf, he's looking at me with fascination.

"What type of curse? Why are you alone, kid? What the hell are you doing in Ireland?"

I ignore his questions and continue to drink. I also stare longingly at my slice of cake, which is on the edge of the table. The wolf grunts and slides the plate closer to me. I nod my thanks to him. I have no idea why—sometimes I can be too polite, but my mum drilled manners into me, and it's an excellent habit.

"A curse to stop her shifting. It has blocked her shifter magic completely. It's killing her," the elf says matter-of-factly, tipping his head to the side as if he's studying a strange bug. "Why would someone curse you?" I pick up the cake, ignoring the fork, and stuff half of it into my mouth.

The wolf lets out a really angry growl that makes me, embarrassingly, squeak. I spray little bits of cake onto the table. I glare at him. What a dramatic reaction to a few unanswered questions! I'm trying not to cough; my eyes water a little. I feel like I have inhaled some crumbs—what a bloody waste of cake.

He ignores me, his focus behind me. He grabs the back of my chair, dragging it around till he can get a good look at the back of my neck. I wonder for a split second what he's looking at, what is so—the ragged bite mark. My stupid mate-mark. I want to slap my forehead; I can't believe I forgot about it. I hunch my shoulders and quickly move my chair away from the nosy wolf.

I am not going back.

I hunch further into myself. I worry my chapped lips with my teeth, and the taste of blood fills my mouth. I need to get back to the cottage for my dog. Fuck. I won't look at either of them. I try my best to stem my rising panic. I don't want to have to fight them. I know there's no way I can win. I remember a quote: "Appear weak when you are strong, and strong when you are weak." By Sun Tzu, *The Art of War*.

I sit up straighter and wolf the fuck up. I will do whatever is necessary, even fight them if I have to. My dog needs me.

I peek at my cup, contemplating what would happen if I threw my cup of hot chocolate in the elf's face. He might spring to his feet; then I could grab his big-ass iron knife off the table and shove it up his left nostril.

"Well, we now know why she is wearing a disguise and why she is hiding out in Ireland," the elf says matter-of-factly. "Runaway mate? You shifters can be barbaric."

The wolf growls, "Says a member of the Aes Sídhe. She is still innocent, and I can't smell a full bond on her. The evil bastard bit her—that shit isn't right. I'd like to use my teeth on his throat, to rip it out. Female shifters are rare and should be protected, not fucking mauled." I glance down at the table and notice his hands are balled into tight fists. "What about the curse?"

"It's a bloody awful crude thing, presumably to stop him from tracking her?"

"Yeah, I guess? You said it's hurting her?" The wolf shifts in his chair.

"*Killing* her."

"What the fuck, kid. The wolf that almost chewed the back of your neck out, he that bad you'd rather die?" I finally look up at the wolf. I let the sadness show in my eyes; I don't hide it from him. I nod. "Fucking hell. Madán, we can't leave her like that. Must be something in your fancy magic box of tricks." The elf, Madán, shakes his head.

"It is none of my business, none of yours. We came to check out a threat. She has been warned not to use witch magic." He narrows his eyes at me. "Do not use disguise-magic, wolf." I nod. He pockets my bracelets and gets up. That's it? God, I hope so. Madán strides away, and just as I am about to sigh in relief, he looks back at me. "No shifters in Ireland. Even ones that can't shift. Out of courtesy, I will give you a few weeks to leave. If I see you after that, it won't be a curse that kills you." I nod.

Maybe if I get online shopping and never leave the house, I will be fine. I stuff the last bit of cake into my mouth. I've had worse odds; I am not leaving. I have nowhere to go.

"I will talk to him," the wolf says gruffly; I don't respond. "My name's Mac." I blink up at him, nod, and give him a small smile. "In case you need anything." Mac flicks a business card onto the table and follows Madán out the door.

CURSED WOLF

"Goodbye, Betty," I whisper.

I glance at the card; it has his name, number, and the bold claim of *Warrior*. I pop it into my pocket. I have no intention of calling him.

I grumble as I hunt for my discarded boot underneath the table.

CHAPTER
THIRTY-FOUR

I FIND it impossible with my new shitty driving skills to tell if anyone is following me. So instead of trying to drive while keeping an eye in the rear-view mirror, I just drive around for a bit. I also fill up with petrol.

I get back, and Lucifer is barking at me like a nutter. I know I am not wearing my Betty disguise, but he's used to me without it. He spends ages sniffing around my car, barking at it. My only thought is that some other dog has peed on the tyre.

I'm feeling so down I don't bother eating—I just feed Lucifer and go to bed early.

The morning comes, and I ugg like a zombie to the toilet with my eyes still closed, not wanting to wake up from my dragon dream. I know I'm a bloody idiot, but my sleeping brain will not behave.

Lucifer is going nuts at the back door, barking as if he's ready to kill something. It's still dark out, so I flick on the outside lights. Hopefully, the light will scare away whatever creature is upsetting him, before I let him out. We have a young fox that likes to come to wander about and pee in Lucifer's territory. I quite like him for his boldness but not for his driving Lucifer crazy, as some nights I can be fast asleep and then the damn dog is going mad with his barking. There was also a badger that Lucifer fought with—the badger won. He kicked Lucifer's ass. I had to take Lucifer to the vet in the town to get a couple of shots and his leg stitched up. Lucifer has his own massive first-aid kit now...well, we both do, as I can't shift to heal.

I open the door and he runs out like the house is on fire, continuing to bark, so I slip on my wellies and pop outside to make sure he's okay. He's using his big angry warning bark.

I stand in my driveway looking at the two men I met yesterday—they're outside my gate. Really? Couldn't they have waited till it got light?

Well, I am doomed now that they know where I live. I can wave goodbye to the home-delivery idea. I grab the keys for the gate and let them in; I might as well get this over with. It's not like I can hide under the bed.

As I pass the car, I remember Lucifer's behaviour towards it yesterday, and I want to smack my forehead for being so stupid. They must have put a tracking spell on it—something that six months ago I would have been able to pick out with my own nose. I also wouldn't have been taken by surprise this morning. Being human is shit.

Madán is looking me up and down—of course he is, I am in fluffy pyjamas. I just got up and wasn't expecting an ambush.

"Cute PJs," Mac remarks. I growl at him.

Lucifer continues to bark at them from behind the safety of a tree. His beige fur and black muzzle don't camouflage well. Even in these circumstances, he makes me smile. He's supposed to be a scary guard dog, but he's way too smart to come close and take on these two. It makes me oddly proud of him; he's a good dog.

We go into the house, and I excuse myself by indicating that I need to get dressed. I get changed and return to both men looking around my home.

"Your place is nice," Mac says gruffly when I catch him looking through my kitchen cupboards. I point to the kettle, and he nods. I politely make us all tea, with Mac happily telling me how they take it. We all sit in the living room; this is so weird.

Lucifer has gotten braver and is barking at them through the window. I keep my mouth shut and wait for them to tell me what they want. According to Madán's get-out-of-Ireland-and-I-won't-kill-you speech, I still have thirteen days left.

Madán starts the conversation. "Do you know what I am used to? Begging. You tell a grown man that you are going to hunt him down and kill him, and they either run, or they beg. The amount of begging..." he sighs. "Even the most insane beg, trying to appeal to my sensibilities. You get the idea." He takes a sip of tea. "Then there is you, a pink-haired girl on her own in a hostile country, with your sad, angry eyes. Unbelievably just giving me a shrug and a nod. You at least could have cried." He shakes his head. I narrow my eyes at him. Is he disappointed that I didn't cry? What. A. Wanker.

"It got me thinking, Forrest..." My stomach drops when Madán uses my real name. They know who I am, which is just great. "You look good for a dead girl...although it won't be long until you die for real with that curse. Is that what you want?" He widens his eyes at me, mockingly. "How long are you sleeping at the moment, around twelve hours?" It's more like sixteen, but why does he care?

"I have an old friend who turned England inside-out in your name, Forrest. Do you know what has been happening while you've been dead?" Madán has my full attention. Shit. I feel sick. "The council has been decimated. England almost had a shifter civil war. Replacing the council, a new assembly has been founded, with members voted into power. Their first official act was to introduce an emergency law to protect all female shifters—'Forrest's Law.'" Madán raises his eyebrows. I carefully keep my face blank. "Forrest's Law"? Oh my bloody God, I wonder if they will amend the name once they find out I am still alive and kicking? "The shifters' old laws are in the process of being updated or changed. Modernised. It has had a positive knock-on effect on shifters all around the world. The other races are looking on with interest." Madán drops the information bomb on me as if he is talking about the weather. He sips from his cup, his eyes never leaving mine.

I wiggle in my seat. I feel a tad uncomfortable and a bit like a fraud. It was never my intention to be a martyr. I selfishly ran.

Will this new assembly fix the rot in shifter society? I'm unsure, but anything positive is a step in the right direction. I think about Madán's words: *the council has been decimated.*

"The Hunters Guild, Aragon? The General, is he okay?" I husk out. My heart beats faster. Worry hits me full-force in the chest. I haven't got the energy to care about myself, but what about Aragon? My dragon.

"Shit, you *do* talk," Mac says happily, smiling at me. "Yeah, the dragon is fine. He kicked everything off, knocked heads together, set up the whole assembly, and then disappeared." I puff out a relieved breath to hear that my dragon is safe. The world is a better place with him in it. Thank God.

I make a mental note to check on Owen, and indirectly, my brother John.

"Killed over half the council, is more like it," Mac says with a laugh.

"You might be interested to know that your mate is still alive," Madán says. I wrinkle my nose and narrow my eyes. Does he mean Daniel? He's no mate of mine.

"Fuck me, kid, you did a number on that fuck-pig—you burned half his face off. He looks like Harvey Two-Face from *Batman*." He shakes his head, chuckling, "You have some impressive skills, or you did...." Mac says, looking me up and down. He frowns at me. Yeah, I look like shit. I admit it, the curse is eating me alive. I shrug, unconcerned.

Madán continues, "Yes, well, Aragon left him alive after spending a few hours questioning him. I think the dragon was happy to leave him with his life as a warning to others. Especially after the punishment you gave him. Though Aragon cut his right hand off and pulled out all his teeth...I'm sure they returned with his shift, but it must have been an unpleasant few hours." Madán looks at me, a curious expression on his face. "I didn't understand why he had left him alive, until now. I don't believe Aragon would have risked killing him if there was any chance that you could be alive. He didn't find your body...well, for obvious reasons."

"It is safe for you to go back now, kid," the wolf shifter says. "The new laws will protect you."

I am so glad, so proud that Aragon made changes to help others and the whole of shifter society. The council had ruled for too long; the laws had been for a different time. I feel overwhelmed, knowing what has happened—gratified that I made the right decision in leaving. Aragon did all that because I wasn't there to be a toxic distraction. I am still better off dead.

"I can't," I say huskily, looking at my hands. "I don't want to," I say quietly. I peek up and meet Madán's eyes. "I can beg." I will go on my knees if I have to. His eyes widen, and mine plead. *Please don't send me back; please don't. I want to die free.*

A muscle ticks in Madán's jaw as he continues to stare at me. "Aragon misses you." I shake my head in denial. Madán sighs. "He is going to murder me...Okay, Forrest. I can see you are not for changing your mind. I will help you. Foremost, we have to remove that bloody curse..." When I shake my head in panic, he holds his hand up to stop me. "And the half mate-bond. I will link you to my court as a warrior, like Mac." He tilts his head towards the wolf shifter. "The magic is omnipotent; it will clean up all that fragmented magic." He scrunches his nose and waves his hand around, indicating me. "It also means that you will be able to stay in Ireland without any repercussions. As a warrior of the court, you will be asked to help out on low-level missions, similar to being a hunter in the Hunters Guild. I will not ask for any more than you are willing to give. I offer protection, and you commit to a minimum of twenty hours a week. I will contract you for three years, to which you must commit. It isn't a permanent position—after three years you may leave. I must be getting soft in my old age," Madán says, tucking his hair behind a pointed ear. I sit in shock; the Aes Sídhe can't lie.

Mac gives me a big smile. "What do you say, kid—no dying, no psycho-mate bond, and you can have your wolf back, and a job where you can help people. You do any more hours than twenty, and you'll even get paid." Mac winks. I nod in agreement.

"Thank you," I whisper.

Madán's offer is more than I could ever dream of. I glance down at the cup in my hand. It's more than I deserve. "If you're willing to help me, it would be an honour to serve the court and help others." I lift my eyes and meet Madán's pale blue gaze. "I will not hurt the innocent, but if you point me at the bad guys, I will be good to go—I have a lot of repressed anger."

"I'm able to ascertain why he is fond of you," Madán says gruffly.

"When do I start work ?" I ask. A small, repressed voice at the back of my head whispers that I will need a theme tune.

"You need to recover from the curse; we can do the warrior link now. I am worried that if we wait any longer, we might be too late." I nod. Wow, I guess I am so not dying today, and I get my magic back!

"I will need to put my hands on your neck. Is that going to be a problem?"

"No, that's fine."

Madán moves closer and puts both of his elegant hands on my neck. They easily wrap around; he holds me gently. His eyes close, and he starts to chant in a language that I don't understand. His hands heat up, and even my human nose can smell the scent of grass and flowers. A light breeze from the magic ruffles my hair. My vision goes slightly cloudy, and my right arm tingles.

Once Madán releases me, I pull up my sleeve, and we all look at the silver markings on my arm. I blink up at Madán. The surprise on his face is a tad concerning.

"Warrior markings," he says quietly, with awe.

"Is that normal?" I ask, poking at them.

"No," he replies, knocking my prodding finger away with a frown. He pulls my sleeve up further. Of course, my strange magic has to act up and give me proper Fae-warrior markings when it shouldn't. The markings are silver and not black, so they're different. I wonder if they do anything. Another Forrest record-breaking feat, which is freaking Madán out. I hope he doesn't put the curse back on. "Would you please remove your jumper." I nod and wiggle out of it.

My warrior markings are on my right arm; they start at my fingers and go up to my shoulder. At first, I presume that they're a random pattern, but after staring at them from various angles, Madán deems that the markings depict the tree of life.

Instead of worrying about them, I will embrace my inner freak—as long as Madán and the other Fae don't get angry and try to kill me, which could still be a possibility. My eyes start to close of their own volition. The magic has drained me.

"All right, Forrest, you are going to need a few hours of sleep to recover. We shall see ourselves out. Mac will be in touch to let you know when your training starts. Do not mess with the markings," Madán says firmly. I nod in sleepy confirmation, and he leaves the room. Mac takes hold of my arm and guides me into my bedroom and to my bed.

"Sleep, kid. When you wake up, you're going to feel so much better. You will be running as your wolf this afternoon." I mumble a thank you, my eyes already closing. I sleep.

CHAPTER
THIRTY-FIVE

It has been over three-and-a-half years since Madán removed my curse and that godawful mate bond. I have my freedom, and I'm healthy.

I'm also haunted by the nagging voice in the back of my head—the voice that gets louder late at night, whispering Aragon's name. Half the time, I convince myself that Aragon wasn't that special and that eventually he let me down, or at least he failed to give me enough information to protect myself. I try to convince myself that I am still not grieving the loss of him.

The warrior training was brutal. My first week, the guys on my course (all no shorter than six-foot) made jokes about me being the token shifter mascot—the pet freak. I am sure that in their eyes the five-foot-two pink-haired shifter was a joke. They thought they had every reason to mock me. I didn't rise to the bullying—I mean, come on, I have handled so much worse.

At first, hidden deep inside I was devastated. Who doesn't want to be liked? I found their gibes and nasty comments hurtful. Mac was furious, but I made him promise that he wouldn't interfere. I kept my chin high acclimatised and got over it.

I proved my point and got payback a week later when we started physical training.

One class, my favourite, was fight-training. In one afternoon, I kicked the absolute fuck out of every guy in my class. I was so aggressive that by the end of the day, the training staff decided to pull me from sparring, for my classmates' safety. Funnily, no one talked about my mascot status again. Mac spent the whole afternoon clapping and laughing.

The Fae I worked with became warier of me. I guess I should have stuck with being the joke mascot instead of the psycho shifter with the creepy dead eyes, fire magic, and stolen warrior markings.

I wore another mask and learned it was better to be feared than liked.

I couldn't kid myself that I would fit in, and part of me didn't care.

Fuck them. I'm dead inside.

My soul is lost in buried memories.

The best parts of me remain with a dragon. I'm just the remaining shell.

I made sure to keep my chin held high and to walk with extra swagger. My new warrior theme tune: "Broken People" from the film Bright, playing in my head.

Years later—after they realised that I wasn't going anywhere, I think—I slowly earned their respect.

Always the hard way.

Being a warrior is a tad anticlimactic. It isn't how I thought it would be. Sometimes you want something so badly you get caught up; you lose yourself in the dream. You find out that what you wanted isn't what you initially thought it would be.

It's December, and ugg, today I am training an idiot. I huff out a frustrated breath, yawn, and scratch the back of my head. I'm glad I opted to have the magical cameras, as no one would believe this shit. I've set them to track my movements. It's like your own film crew following you around. The magic cameras film everything that's happening, circling above and below, getting the best angles. It helps with information-gathering and prosecution. Some warriors choose not to have them. But it's something I don't mind. At first, they were something that Madán had insisted on. But over the past few years, I've come to be so glad he did, as they have helped to exonerate me from many claims of excessive violence. No guy likes the idea of a tiny female warrior taking him into custody, so they claim loads of fake shit. The cameras are so small; it's almost impossible to see them, even with my eyesight.

"What is that!" The new warrior-in-training shrieks in a total panic. He's freaking the fuck out, and it's amusing. The Slime Monster he is screeching at is an amorphous, shapeless, gooey creature that's leaving bits of itself on the pavement outside my favourite ice cream place—the same place where years ago, I first met Madán and Mac.

The newbie warrior pokes his iron blade at the blob-monster, and the knife just disappears. Huh? I have no idea where it goes, but there's a kind of sucking sound as it vanishes.

"I wouldn't get too close to him, Noel," I say helpfully, licking my ice cream—what? It honestly would be rude not to grab one while I was here. A yummy waffle cone, even if it's freezing today—I have a scoop of Belgian chocolate and a scoop of cherry. Yum, the best ice cream in Ireland. Noel screams and dives away from a tentacle of goo; I roll my eyes.

He then produces a flame. He has a fire gift, which is why I have had him dumped on me. "Noel, don't use a flame on him, fire doesn't work." Noel has just fallen on his bottom as he has tripped over a bollard that he didn't notice behind him, as he's so panicked. He flails on the floor. I frown as Noel screeches in a pitch higher than I could ever hope of achieving. My ear that's closest to him rings painfully. I frown and rub it on my shoulder. As he cries, Noel throws his flame at the Slime Monster.

I wince and rub my forehead. With a *whoosh*, the whole monster is now alight and is dripping not just goo, but flame-y goo all over the pavement.

Noel screams again, the sound grating. I finish my ice cream and decide to rescue the situation. I circle the monster and make my way to Noel, who is still on the floor wailing.

I smack the back of his head. He finally shuts the fuck up and turns to me, his eyes wide in panic.

"Get up, you idiot. Noel, you need to listen better. You haven't even noticed that the creature is not trying to hurt you; he is just standing there!" I huff out a frustrated breath and point at the flaming goo monster. "You have set him on fire for no reason at all, apart from your total lack of control and your fear." I march up to the scary-looking Slime Monster, wave my hand, and call the fire that surrounds him into my control.

I have learned a lot over the years, and the fire listens to me as if it's my own. I wave my hand again, and the fire dies completely.

"Hi, Bert, thanks again so much for helping with training. I appreciate your time. Sorry about the fire..." Bert, the Slime Monster, nods his head, burps, and the missing iron knife tumbles to the pavement. "Tell your family hi from me." Bert gives me what I interpret to be a slimy wave and goes off to his car.

Bert and his family are so helpful. They help a lot in training newbies to react to a situation and not to what a creature looks like. It's usually a good lesson—unfortunately, it's one at which Noel has failed miserably.

I scowl at Noel, who is still on the floor. His mouth is opening and closing. He's doing a good impression of a goldfish as he watches Bert leave.

"You let him go? He is getting away!" I roll my eyes; this idiot needs a miracle to pass his training. Thank God I got this on film. I chuckle evilly.

CHAPTER
THIRTY-SIX

I AM PLAYING bait this evening, as we're hunting some big bad. The evil bastard has been killing young girls; we presume it's a male solo predator. He has moved across the country, killing as he goes. He has murdered fifteen young girls, and three girls are still unaccounted for. He started in Dublin, and it didn't take the local police—the Garda Síochána, more commonly referred to as the Gardaí or "the Guards"—and the Fae warriors long to connect the dots. The public is pissed. The human papers are blaming the Fae, and the Fae are biting back, with everyone pointing an accusing finger at everyone else. It's turning into a total clusterfuck, a nightmare of epic proportions.

All I am focused on is the big bad, and I let the higher-ups deal with the shit that's going down. The state of urgency demanded from everyone is nothing compared to the pressure that, as warriors, we put upon ourselves. We need to find this guy, and quickly.

For some reason, he doesn't mind who he picks—human or Fae, it doesn't seem to matter much. He does have a type, though: he likes the girls young and delicate-looking. So it stands to reason that I'd volunteer to be the bait to try and catch him. We know he's heading to the Sligo area, but we don't know when, so this week my evenings have been filled with me sashaying around Sligo town centre in a pretty dress looking irresistible. We have yet to get him, and I've become disheartened. On a plus note, we have already arrested three idiots who thought it was a good idea to try and take advantage of me.

The self-control I have mastered in the past few years is impressive; I don't have the worst record for beating the crap out of the bad guys. I want nothing more sometimes then to punch a few predator dickheads in the face. Women should feel safe to go anywhere after dark, without risk. I hate that in our modern multi-creature world, that isn't the case.

Tonight is Saturday night, and I'm wearing a lovely gold dress. It has long sleeves and a high neck. It's mega short, and I have to keep reminding myself not to tug at the hem. I am bloody freezing, as I am not wearing a jacket. Apparently, young humans like to freeze when they go for a night out. I am twenty-seven and find it ridiculous. A coat would be nice. I hate the cold.

"Peter, ya burger, did ya want cheese?" Arrah, I bloody hate having these idiots in my head. Bloody mind links...luckily, it's a spell used only on these kinds of assignments. But the guys on duty with me tonight, all they have done is eat.

"Yeah, and bacon." I huff out a cloud of hot breath. I am cold, and now I am fucking hungry.

I wander to the next pub and grab a drink and a snack from the bar. I find a great place to sit, in the corner, where I can watch everyone and get myself warm.

I am also isolating myself, screaming: *Hey predators, look at me, the easy prey, oooh all on her own, looking lost.*

Two members of my team keep up the chatter about food. Mac tells them to shut the fuck up, but not until after he orders his meal. Such a bunch of twats. My tummy rumbles in agreement.

I like this pub. It's situated next to the River Garavogue in Sligo town. It's the right mix of traditional Irish and modern. I love that it's still privately owned, with its character intact, and not owned by a pub chain. There's a long bar running down the left-hand side of the room. Small wooden tables are scattered around, with half a dozen booths along the right-hand wall. Chart music is playing at the moment; the live music has finished for the evening. The majority of the customers are braving the cold weather in the beer garden, which is the smoking area outside.

I sip my half-pint of Guinness and blackcurrant. I also nibble on a bag of salt and vinegar Tayto crisps. Obstinately I allow my crisp-crunching to echo in my thoughts. *Crunch. Crunch.* Mac groans—he hates food noises. That will teach them to have burgers without me.

"Hi, you on your own?" A guy takes the seat across from me, without asking—creepy fucker. I have to remind myself that I am playing bait. I peek up at him from underneath my lashes and smile in what I hope is a timid way. I always wonder if they will notice my dead eyes and realise I'm not what I pretend to be. But I have this down to a fine art, and they see what they expect.

"No." I shake my head, and then I shrug my shoulders and let out a little sad-sounding laugh. I lean forward and glance around as if I don't want anyone else to hear me. "Sort of, I guess. My sister has my phone and my purse. I went to the toilet, and she held them for me, and she wasn't around when I got back. I searched for her; I couldn't find her, so I thought I would come to this pub to see if I can find her here instead." I shrug again, tucking my hair behind my ear. "She always comes to this one. I don't think her friends like me too much." I widen my eyes in fake horror, then glance about again, searching for my non-existent sister.

The creepy guy nods. "I can help you find her if you like. A beautiful girl like you shouldn't be on her own." I nod and give him a smile, dropping my eyes coltishly back to the table and my drink.

"Thank you," I say, and he smiles at me, showing a little too many teeth.

He is a troll, although he's attractive in a greasy-hair, slicked-back, 80's-troll kind of way. Trolls usually are quite easy to like. They're big and dumb, and they work a lot in security. But this guy, even if he isn't our killer...he's bad news. My creepy-bad-guy warning alert is pinging like crazy. You know that feeling? The female lizard brain that warns you, someone or something is dangerous and to run? I think mine is a bit defective, as it always encourages me to run *at* them and punch them in the face. This creep makes my hand itch with the overwhelming need to slam the heel of my palm into his nose.

"Please, could I borrow your phone? I might ring my dad and ask him to come and get me," I say shyly.

"Sure, beautiful." The creepy guy pulls out his phone. He looks at the screen with a mock-sad face, waves it at me, then taps the phone on the side of his head. "No signal. We will have to step outside." I give him a sweet, timid smile, gulp down my Guinness, and get up. I let myself wobble a little as I stand.

"Oh, room spin," I say with a hiccupping giggle. Creepy takes hold of my arm and instead of leading me to the front of the bar, he puts a hand around my waist and muscles me towards the emergency exit at the rear.

"It's a go, leaving out of the back exit. Please be ready for my signal," I say, pushing my thoughts into my team's heads. They confirm.

"Thank you so much for helping me. My name is Mellisa, by the way," I say as we stride out into a back alley. I stumble a little; then I turn towards him with a small smile on my face. I hold my hand out for his phone. "So if I could just use your phone?"

He leans towards me and puts an arm above my head, resting it on the wall at my back. He looks down at me and flashes his teeth in a sinister smile. "Sure, beautiful. Gosh, you are a tiny little thing...so perfect." He hands the phone over to me, and I take it. I try to keep my attention on him instead of the phone, but as soon as my hand grazes the handset, I lose focus.

"What the hell..." A spell comes over me, and I realise my touch on the handset activated it. It takes only a few seconds for my magic to burn through it. If I were human, as I'm pretending to be, I'd be in serious trouble.

But a few seconds is all the creep needs. He grabs me and *steps* us to somewhere else.

Oh shit.

CHAPTER
THIRTY-SEVEN

Adrenalin rushes through my system, and my heart picks up its rhythm. Well fuck, that is interesting—a troll shouldn't be able to *step*.

Stepping is like the gateways but without a portal. Powerful Fae can step; they usually have to be as old as shit. It's like how you would imagine teleporting to be. We had been unaware of how he moved his victims—at least now we know. Creepy must be our guy.

I let Creepy think the spell is working. I slump against him, which is totally gross, but when you are playing the part of prey, you have to go with it. I am not surprised when we end up stepping into a basement.

Not knowing where I am is disconcerting. I hope I'm still in Ireland.

I keep my eyes down, feigning disorientation, and use my other senses. I can smell blood, vomit, and some seriously scary scents that I won't put a name to, for my own sanity. I can hear crying and four other heartbeats. My tummy dips as I feel a monumental sense of relief that Creepy has bought me straight to the missing girls.

Thank God.

Surreptitiously I roll my head back and to the side, throwing in a moan for good measure. My eyes dart about the room. Creepy has everything set up, a serial killer's paradise: chains on the walls in various metals and half a dozen iron cages, the whole shebang. I hope this fucker doesn't attempt to put me in a cage.

I will lose my shit if he does.

You know you're messed up in the head when you feel relief when the serial killer you're hunting only handcuffs you to a wall. Attached to the wall, I sag in my chains, the substantial steel chains heavy and biting on my wrists. He leaves me, murmuring that he will play with me later when I wake up as I'll be no fun if I don't scream. Fucker. The door slams behind him.

I am so glad that playing human is working out for me this evening.

I stand straight and roll my shoulders to loosen my stiff muscles. I twist around in my chains as I take in the basement. One door in and out.

"Jenny, Sarah, Mary?" I say in a calm, gentle tone. The girl who's crying stops. "I am sorry, I don't know who the fourth girl is. My name is Forrest, and I'm a warrior with the Fae Court. I'm going to do everything in my power to get you all home. Can you tell me if that creepy bastard is working alone? Have you seen anyone else?"

The sobbing girl answers, surprising the hell out of me. Brave girl. "My name's Sally. He took me this evening. I haven't seen anyone else."

"Okay, thank you, Sally."

"He is working alone," a quiet voice says; she's in the cage in the corner. "I have been here for a while. It feels like forever. He rapes and k — he kills. I think he eats; I think he has been eating us. I am Mary..." She makes a heaving noise. When she gathers herself, she crawls to the front of her cage, a bitter smile on her cracked lips. "What are you going to do? Chained to the fecking wall! Who is going to rescue you? We needed a proper warrior, not some girl." Mary bangs on her cage and whimpers as the iron burns her hand. "This is a bag of shite...ya rippin' the piss," Mary mumbles as she turns away, nursing her hand. The other two girls don't respond.

I know from the files that he has had Mary who is Fae for around three weeks. I won't take her words personally.

Mary won't be the last person to underestimate me, and she's a scared kid. I'm kind of proud of her angry words—it gives me hope that she will have enough piss and vinegar to get through this experience.

I listen for any movement outside the room. Sweat drips down my back and makes the gold dress stick to me like a second skin. I cautiously send my flame into the handcuffs, delicately destroying the locking mechanism. I am convinced that all the girls are victims, and I feel the time is right to get this shit sorted. I desperately need to check on the two unresponsive girls. The cuffs rattle as they fall from my wrists and hit the wall.

"Mac, have you got a track on me?" I direct my thoughts, with no answer.

Well, shit.

I rub my wrists. Now comes the difficult decision on whether to unlock the girls who are awake, or leave them. If I undo them and they panic, it might be an issue, but if I leave them and I get taken out...fuck that. They need every opportunity to try and rescue themselves.

I undo Sally's chains, whispering to her to keep still and silent until I tell everyone to move. I kneel in front of Mary's cage door. The concrete digs into my knees and shins. My flame makes short work of the lock and the cage swings open.

I channel Owen, and some of the first words he said to me pop out of my mouth. "Mary, I can see that you are frightened and that you have been through Hell. I can also see the fire inside you. Keep using that fire—your anger. Don't let it go inwards. What has happened to you is not your fault. The blame rests on him, not on you. Do not let him win and don't let him take any more from you. Sometimes it's better to bury the memories until you are strong enough to deal. It's going to be hard, but you need to keep moving forward one step at a time. Do you understand?" Her eyes meet mine, and we take stock of each other. She nods. "I need you to trust me. Stay in this shitty cage for a while longer, just until I kick the sicko's ass. If anything happens to me, I'm trusting you to grab Sally and run like hell. Got it?" I hold out my fist to the girl, who is still huddling at the back of the cage. I wait. Slowly she lifts her arm and bumps her fist to mine.

I miss my friend Owen; he's always in my thoughts, like an

emotional ghost. I regularly ask myself the question, *"What would Owen do?"*

I close the door and move on to the first unconscious girl. She's naked, badly hurt, and is bleeding profusely. I stroke her dirty blonde hair away from her face. Her breathing is shallow and her heartbeat is weak. I remember her name from the files—it's Jenny—and my heart aches for her. I slip my hand underneath my dress and dig about in my bra for the little tubes that hold condensed Fae tracking-magic and a sleeping draught. I need these girls to stay asleep; I can't afford to add any more variables to this shit-show. I tip the plastic vials and let the magic seep into her chest; I then place my fingertips on her collarbone. My warrior mark starts to glow; the silver light bleeds through the fabric of my dress. Pulled directly from the Fae Court, the healing magic rushes into Jenny. I wait and listen. It isn't long until I can hear that her breathing has become better and that her heartbeat has returned to a normal rhythm. The bleeding stops, and the wounds that I can see heal. I bow my head in relief.

We were all a little surprised when my warrior mark turned out to be defensive magic. The marks channel innate magic—healing, shields, wards, and a whole host of cool defensive stuff.

The last naked, unconscious girl is Sarah. The dark-haired girl has a nastily broken arm. I use the sleeping draught first, I pour the vial and wait for a few seconds, and then get myself into position. I brace myself. I cringe as I grip her wrist and shoulder. My warrior mark lights up again as I sharply pull the broken limb. It crunches, snapping back into place as it heals. I blow out a shaky breath—I will never get used to resetting bones. I'm glad she was asleep for that unpleasant job. Sarah's face relaxes from a pained grimace into a peaceful expression.

I heal Sally and Mary; I also put a tracking potion on all of the girls, so if the worst happens and I can't rescue them, a member of my team will still be able to track them—or at the very least, locate their bodies. I shudder and swallow the bile that's doing its best to crawl up my throat. I close my eyes for a second. I take a breath. Rage, panic and determination fill my lungs in place of air. I need to save these girls. I can't fail.

I hustle back to the wall and get back into position, looping the broken handcuffs back around my wrists. As I wait, I analyse what has happened to these girls, and I can't help thinking about my situation, my past. I have been running forever. I huff out a sigh and grind the back of my head into the wall. I'm happy to fight for others, but I have never once fought for myself. Never. I always run. I still love Aragon. My self-inflicted broken heart has never healed. I've just learned to live with the cracks.

The job I do is dangerous, and perhaps I need to meet my internal demons head-on once and for all. I can't have my trauma define me; maybe it's time to open and deal with my boxes? Deal with Daniel and tell Aragon how I feel.

CHAPTER
THIRTY-EIGHT

It isn't long until Creepy arrives back. The basement stairs creek ominously with the troll's footsteps the evil bastard slams the door open. It hits the wall and bounces closed. Sally and Mary both shudder. I stand against the wall and glare at him. I can't have Creepy paying attention to the other girls; I need him to focus on me. I'm hoping my defiance will do the trick. Creepy smiles.

Showtime.

He flashes his pointed teeth. I tip my head to the side, wondering if I can knock a few of them out. He swaggers towards me, and I let him get close enough that I smell his rancid breath.

I keep my face carefully blank and my big gold eyes wide.

"Ahh, you're awake—that's good. I can't wait to show you my—" Fuck this. I am not waiting for his villain speech or for the creepy fuck to grope me. I already think this whole assignment will give me nightmares without having to listen to him. I kick my leg out and aim for his knee. I put all my strength into the kick, and I hear and feel the knee crunch. His body goes one way, the leg the other; the shock on his face makes me smile.

I grab hold of the back of his head and smash his face into the basement wall. Once: "It's not so lovely..." twice: "when your prey fights back..." three times: "creepy bastard." I let go of his head. Wrinkle my nose and wipe my hand on my dress as he slumps to the floor.

Huh, that felt a bit anticlimactic.

I was expecting a bit more of a fight. Creepy is out for the count. I give him a kick in the ribs for good measure, urm, just to make sure he isn't playing games. I'm slightly disappointed when he doesn't make a sound. I grab some iron chains from the wall and cuff his hands behind his back. I grab some more and cuff his feet together. I hum as I loop the chains and attach both sets so that his hands are linked to his feet—he is like a Fae pretzel.

Dragging his body by his feet, I pull him towards a conveniently open iron cage. With a bit of huffing and kicking him, I manage to squish him into it. I lock and then chain the door. To make sure he can't go anywhere, I place a ward on the cage with another handy bravial. Hopefully that will stop him from stepping himself anywhere. For my final touch, I send my flame out to surround the cage. The fire hits six feet in height, and I coax it into a dome. Overkill? Too damn right it is. This fucker isn't going to be hurting any more girls, not on my watch. If it were up to me, I would have killed him. But I have to stick to the law; I can't go around killing people, even if I want to. Looking at the frightened girls here, the smell of what he has done to them in my nose, I want to. God, how I want him to suffer.

I wipe my hands again on my dress; I don't want any part of him on my skin.

"Okay, ladies, let's get out of here. I need your help in carrying Jenny and Sarah. If I carry one, will you be able to carry the other girl between you?" Mary bravely crawls out of her cage, and she raises her eyebrow at the flaming cage. I shrug and make a "meh" face.

Sally needs a little coaxing. I get them to hold the previously bleeding girl, who I think is Jenny, between them, while I pick up Sarah. I dig my shoulder into her stomach and lift her over my shoulder. Luckily Sarah is only a little taller than me, which makes it easier than, say, hefting a guy.

I open the basement door quietly. Creepy was so confident, he hadn't even bothered to lock it behind him. I dance my magic onto my right palm, letting it grow more and more until I form a sword out of the flames. Holding onto Sarah's thighs with my left hand, I make my way up the stairs, leading with my sword. I am not leaving these girls in that basement for one more second with their kidnapper. They follow me, doing an excellent job of keeping close and quiet.

As soon as we clear the basement staircase and enter the ground floor, something in my head pops. I can hear my team again, and more importantly, speak to them. *"I have our big bad contained. I also have Mary, Jenny, Sarah, and Sally with me. I need clothing, healing, and urgent assistance."*

Everyone talks at once, making me wince. Madán gains control, and with a few gruff words, he has the rest of my team silenced. I grit my teeth, and my lips straighten into a firm line. Shit. It is always an issue when your big boss gets involved. The guys must have been shitting themselves when that nobhead creepy fucker stepped away with me.

As Madán talks, I quickly clear the ground floor of the house. As I am on my own and my priority is the girls in my care, I don't bother checking the rest of the house. I won't leave them, and I can't smell or hear anyone else in the vicinity. I use another vial and set up a ward in the hallway by the front door. It's a small area, with peeling flower wallpaper, and it should be easier to defend, much safer, than taking the girls outside.

I am still in Ireland, which is good to know—the cavalry is on its way. Madán steps through before the portal is in place, bringing Mac and a healer with him. He lets me know, using the mind link, so I can open the door to the house and allow them through the ward. I inform Mac that I haven't checked the rest of the house, so he disappears to do a sweep, iron sword in hand.

I leave the healer to check on the girls. Madán gives me an assessing look, nods, and then pulls out his phone. He holds up his finger at me to let me know he will be only a minute. I can hear his side of the conversation, but he has a spell on his phone that stops creatures from listening to the caller, so I have no idea who he's talking too. I presume that he might be speaking directly to one of the girls' parents, or it could be about me.

"I have eyes on her now; she is okay. Looks to be completely unharmed. Yes, not a hair out of place. I will debrief you when I know

CURSED WOLF

more. Yes, well, it was something we couldn't have anticipated. I do my best; you know I make every effort t— Yes, well, I will let you know more when I have the information. I care about her too. I will speak to you soon." Madán ends the call and marches back to me.

The other warriors have arrived. "Forrest, will you take me to the creature you have apprehended, please?" I nod and take a final glance at the girls to double-check that they are okay. Healers now surround them.

I show Madán and my team to the basement, warning them that any mind links that they have will be blocked as we move down the stairs.

We go down.

Peter whistles at the room, which is now our grim crime scene...well, it will be once we have removed the creepy bad guy. Then the whole place will be magically processed.

They all stare at my fire dome. I shrug. I ask my flame to come back to me, and it quickly obeys, shrinking back until it's a small flame. It dances across the room and comes to my outstretched palm happily. I close my fist around it, and it dissipates.

They all look from the pretzel troll in the cage to me. I shrug again.

"How the fuck did you fit him in that cage?" Peter asks. I don't even bother answering, With fucking difficulty. The creepy guy is awake, and he moans. I open the iron cage at Mac's timely arrival, and he helps me to drag out the creepy pretzel. My fellow warriors are all Fae and avoid the iron cage like the plague.

Creepy moans again, so I kick him in the head. Mac lets out a chuckle, Madán tuts at me.

"What? We don't want him stepping anywhere, and he looked like he was about to," I say calmly, without any inflexion. We uncuff him and replace the cuffs with our own, and Mac slaps a plastic magic-voiding wristband on him. As soon as it snaps and wraps around his wrist, the magic activates.

We all watch as Creepy's shape changes. Instead of a troll lying on the floor, he's now a goblin. Huh, interesting. No wonder the takedown was so easy. I glance at Madán with eyebrows raised as if to say, are we done? He nods.

"Do you need any medical assistance, Forrest?" I shake my head no. "Let's get you off home then—you have done enough for this evening." Madán holds out his hand, indicating for me to go first back up the stairs. I wave a one-finger goodbye at the guys.

"Am I in trouble?" I say when we get outside. I breathe in the cold winter air, clearing my nose of the horrors of the basement. I start to shiver.

"No. Please debrief me. I am aware that everything that happened tonight was recorded. If you could tell me in your own words what happened, I will add your statement to the report." Madán takes off his jacket and holds it out to me. With a smile and a thank you, I slip it on. It's still warm from his body heat. I am relieved to hear that the magic cameras have been filming the whole evening and that they kept up with me, even when I'd been stepped away.

I yawn, rub my hand across my face, and explain what happened in detail.

When I finish, Madán nods.

"Thank you; I will take you home myself. I shall get one of the warriors to drop your car off in the morning." He waves his hand above my head, and my team-link chatter disappears. I sigh in relief, massaging my temple—that will stop me from getting a massive headache. I also know with that wave that the cameras stopped filming.

Madán takes hold of my arm, and we step back to my home. Lucifer goes nuts—I can hear him barking in the house. I have been working for only about six hours, but it has felt like forever. It has been a long-ass week, trying to catch that evil bastard. I can't believe we did it.

"Take the rest of the week off, Forrest, you deserve it. I am so glad that you are okay and unharmed. You did me proud today—well done." I turn and impulsively hug Madán. Inside it makes me laugh, as my affection always makes him uncomfortable. Surprising the hell out of me, he hugs me back. "Go sort that monster dog of yours out—he sounds like he is trying to eat through the door. Mac will be in touch for when your next shift is." I nod, and he disappears before I can say anything else. I still have his jacket on.

I have to jump over my gate as my stuff is back at headquarters, with my car. I unlock my door with my spare key and Lucifer goes nuts, sniffing and squeaking in excitement to see me. "Hey, squeaky boy, you missed me?" Obviously not so much as Lucifer pushes past me, almost knocking me off my feet, crazy dog. He dashes outside, his fixated priority a perimeter sweep of the garden. I leave him to it. I am that hungry, I could eat a scabby rat.

Luckily for me, I have a whole chocolate cake with my name on it calling for me. I skip and bounce towards my kitchen.

Come to me, yummy chocolaty goodness; you want in my belly.

CHAPTER THIRTY-NINE

I HATE time off from work. It has only been a day, and I'm already bored. If I didn't have Lucifer, I'd be working every hour, in a sad attempt to keep busy. But I have to be home for my dog, even if he isn't arsed in spending time with me. Lucifer is content to sit on guard, watching the road and chasing birds that dare to land in his garden.

We have a red weather warning in place for storms and heavy snow. The weather is horrendous, and the public has been warned to stay off the roads and stay at home. My Irish colleagues would say it's a day for looking out, not looking in.

Being cold isn't my thing, and I think my moaning about the cold weather in the past has been slowly driving my colleagues nuts. Mac told me, when he dropped my car off, not to come back into work until the temperature rises.

I didn't know how to take that, but I handled it with my usual maturity by waving goodbye and running back into my house, giggling with glee. I hate not being at work, but I hate the cold weather more. Even though I have fancy solar-powered heating, nothing says homely to me like a fire in the log-burning stove, so I'm staying inside and having the fire on.

While I'm getting ready for bed, the snow is coming down heavily, and lightning dances across the night sky. Freaky thundersnow—I had no idea that it could do that. The power goes out. I peer out of the window and shiver; I am not even attempting to sort out the electric in that. it can wait 'til morning.

Unexpectedly I hear a tremendous bang outside and the whole cottage trembles, and what sounds like a glass in the kitchen falls to the floor, smashing. Cue Lucifer going nuts. I rush to the back door and let him out before he does damage to the door. Lucifer tears off around the back of the house, barking.

I should probably go outside and check it out. I quickly grab my big coat, and I hop on one foot while stuffing my other foot into my wellie. Once both feet are clad in my bright orange Hunters, I make my way to Lucifer, and what I see has me jumping the fence and running across the field like a madwoman.

A bloody dragon has crash-landed in my field!

A big bloody dragon! I run, and a profound fear floods through me. It's not feasible, it can't be him, it can't be. As I get closer, the dragon starts to shift.

"Aragon!" I scream, throwing myself down in the furrow his crash-landing has created. I land in the deep hole next to him.

Flakes of snow cover his beautiful face.

I brush the snow away gently, my hands trembling. He is freezing to my caress. I try not to panic as I think of a way to get him safely into the warmth of the house.

Why the fuck is he so enormous, he's so much bigger than I remembered. His heartbeat is slightly fast, but I can't see any wounds on his naked body. He must have healed when he shifted back. Tugging off my coat, I quickly cover him—not that my ankle-length coat covers much of him, bloody colossal bastard.

I send my flames out around him as close as I dare in an attempt to keep him warm. I know he's fireproof, but my coat isn't.

I jump up and scramble back up the farrow, trying not to let any of the snow and soil fall on him. I run as fast as I can towards my garden shed. I have a tarp in there that I can use to roll Aragon onto and drag him into the house.

It seems to take me forever. It's too cold and too far to drag him to the field gate, so I have to kick some of my wooden fence down to slide him underneath the rails. It's better to get him inside as quickly as I can.

I get him into the house, and somehow I manage to get him wrapped up and into bed—I am so glad that I am strong. With relief, I slump against the bedroom wall.

Shit, he is still unconscious.

I have no idea where he came from and why he ended up in my field or who hurt him. I hope to hell that he wasn't struck by lightning.

I shuffle across the wall towards the door. I need to leave the room and gather things Aragon will need when he awakens. I magically stoke the fire, and I use my warrior markings to enforce and strengthen the ward around the house as a precaution.

I can't believe he's here in my home—wow, this is surreal. I rub my face. My hands are shaking and I feel dizzy. I need to keep myself busy to prevent myself from sitting and staring at the naked dragon in my bed.

Or even worse...I have a little episode where my imagination goes positively nuts. I urm, see myself grab some hot soapy water and some tiny handcloths and I carefully wash Aragon's body, with bow-chicka-wow-wow dodgy music playing in my head.

Shit.

I go back outside. The thunderstorm has moved on, although it's still snowing. I check on my solar power and switch it onto the battery-only option; the lights in the house come back on. Sticking my head into the cottage, I turn on my outside lights, grab my hammer from the shed, and then hammer the shit out of the fence while putting the rails back on. I might as well do it now, while I am freaking out. If I don't, Lucifer will just wander off and get lost, and even in wolf form, I don't want to track him in the snow.

It's freezing, and my hands are blue, but I can't go back in as there's a bloody gorgeous naked dragon in my bed!

Lucifer watches me; he isn't bothered about the snow. He rolls onto his back ,wiggling. In the winter he prefers to sleep in the cooler utility room. Most nights, I have to drag him inside; he much prefers being outside on guard.

When I have no more excuses I go back into the house. I shed my layers of outside clothing, prod the fire again, and put another log on. I don't need the wood, but I love the smell. My hands sting with the heat. I poke my nose into my bedroom, and Aragon is still out. I decide that he might be hungry when he awakens, so I set to making chicken noodle soup.

When I have finished the broth and I just need to heat the noodles in the microwave, I have a thought: what if Aragon needs healing? Oh my God, I have just left him in my bed, unconscious, for the past hour and he might need help! Yes, he's all-powerful and probably the strongest shifter I will ever meet, but that doesn't mean he doesn't need my help. I feel like a total idiot.

I creep into the bedroom. Aragon is still unconscious, his breathing and heart rate steady. I pull the cover away from his naked chest and lean over. My warrior mark glows. I'm just about to place my fingertips on his chest when Aragon suddenly moves, and one moment I am leaning above him and the next I am on my back with him lying on top of me. I let out a whine of shock. One massive hand is entirely wrapped around my throat, and the other is gripping my arm so hard that I can feel the bones grind together. I yelp with pain and Aragon slowly blinks at me.

His beautiful eyes widen in horror, and he lets go. I roll out from underneath him and crash to the floor. *Oomph.* Well, that wasn't quite the greeting I'd imagined in my head.

My heart hurts a little. I get up, using the wall to guide myself. I nod at the clothing I had left on the bedside table and point towards the bathroom.

Then I hurry out of the room and go back into the kitchen. I brace my hands on the counter and try my hardest not to cry. I know the dragon got startled when I leaned over him, it was probably just an instinctive reaction. He wasn't trying to hurt me deliberately.

I rub my wrist, and my lips wobble.

The shower in the bathroom goes on, and then not even ten minutes later, Aragon comes into the kitchen, dressed in the standard warrior-recruit jogging bottoms and t-shirt that I had knocking about in my car. The whole outfit looks like, if Aragon breathed wrong, it would burst open like the Incredible Hulk's from all his muscles.

"I am sorry I hurt you, Forrest—I didn't mean to grab you." Instead of sitting, Aragon prowls towards me and stands in front of me.

I hide my sore arm behind my back and shrug. I can quickly shift to heal, so it's not an issue.

I stare at his chest, feeling awkward. What do you say to the guy you are still madly in love with, and who has just found out that you faked your own death? Should I shout "Surprise!" while waving jazz hands?

Aragon puts his hand underneath my chin to lift my head so I will meet his eyes. My head lifts, and his concerned, beautiful silver eyes meet mine.

"Hi, Nutty. I am sorry I crashed back into your life—that wasn't my intent." God, he is beautiful. My stomach goes all swirly. He gently reaches for the limb that's hidden behind my back and inspects it. He shocks the shit out of me when he brings my arm to his mouth and softly kisses my wrist in what I can only think is an apology. I shiver.

"Are you okay?" I squeak out.

If this is a dream, I so do not want to wake up. I cannot take my eyes off him. I greedily take him in.

I thought my memory of him was detailed, that I recalled everything about him, from the exact colour of his silver hair and skin, to the shade of his beautiful eyes. The Aragon in front of me...my memories did not do him justice. It is as if I had remembered him in black and white, and now he is standing before me in full HD colour.

Aragon's chiselled face is a masterpiece of masculine beauty. My eyes drop to his full lips, with the bottom one slightly fuller than the top. I stare at him in awe, and shockingly he is looking at me in the same way. Like I'm the most beautiful thing he has ever seen. He must have hit his head.

"I am okay... I miscalculated the storm."

My eyes widen, and I ask incredulously, "You got struck by lightning?"

"I got struck by lightning."

I giggle. Aragon smiles, ruefully rubbing the bridge of his nose, the movement stretching the t-shirt to its limits. I gulp. Every lump and bump of his chest is defined.

"Are you hungry?" I ask, licking my lips.

"I could eat."

I nod and disappointedly move away from him. It's for the best, as I have the almost uncontrollable urge to lick him, then shout at the top of my voice: *I licked it, so it's mine!*

Aragon sits at the island and watches me as I throw the noodles into the microwave. His presence and substantial size take over the whole kitchen. I huff in his smoky scent and feel safe for the first time in years.

I pop the noodles into the bowl, pour in the chicken broth, and hunt down some extra chicken that's hiding at the bottom of the pan to add to his bowl. I smugly put the bowl in front of him, *look what I made* written proudly all over my face.

I have had yet to cook for another person, so it's nice to show off. *Look at me, I can make food, I am adulting perfectly, hear me roar.*

Roar.

Aragon scrutinises his bowl with a smile; a chicken bone is floating at the top. I know the noodles are slightly stuck together and the broth is a tad salty, but it's perfect comfort food. The pink pieces of chicken are delicious, and the black bits make them crunchy. He looks up at me, his eyes sparkling, and I give him an encouraging smile. He coughs into his fist and takes hold of his spoon.

After we have finished eating, it seems that Aragon wasn't that hungry after all. My curiosity has been building to an epic level. "So how did you end up here?" I ask.

"Forrest." Aragon taps the counter. With a sigh, he ducks his head and peers up at me from under his brow. "Since fate has forced my hand, I won't lie to you." His tone drops and his eyes are imploring, "I have known where you have been this whole time. I tracked you down the night you left, but I arrived too late to divert you from your plan," he says in an almost-whisper. "I would never have stood in your way.

BROGAN THOMAS

Your friend Ava? She was going to send you to America. But I changed her mind. This is one of my safe-houses." He taps the countertop again. Huh, Aragon doesn't shout, "Surprise!" or do jazz hands either.

CHAPTER
FORTY

I BLINK AT HIM, think for a few seconds, and then nod. "Okay."

"What?" Aragon says in a strained voice. "That's it? 'Okay'? You're not angry" He searches my gaze.

I shrug. "How can I be mad when you have helped me? I ran away, faked my death...yet you let me go and continued to help me. I should also be saying, "Thank you.'"

"I have been visiting you a couple of times—"

"—A month?" I interrupt with glee, bouncing on my seat. Aragon shakes his head, a self-amused smile of mirth on his face.

"No, a day," he says, rubbing the bridge of his nose. He visits me a couple of times a day? Wow. I can't believe I convinced myself that he wouldn't care if I was out of his life. The sneaky dragon has been watching me.

I emit a strangled cough and mumble under my breath, "Stalker."

"Absolutely." He huffs out a laugh.

"Did you ask Madán to give me my job?" I reach over and squeeze his forearm, dreading the answer. I like my job, and it's important to me. I want to make the world a better place. I know it sounds so damn idealistic and naïve. But honestly, I am proud to be a warrior. If I can stop one child from having a childhood like mine, if I can take down the bad guys...it might not be world-saving, but each person I help is one more life living safer in the world. Aragon flips his arm over and takes hold of my hand.

"Forrest, no, you got your job on your own merit. Madán is extremely impressed with you. I certainly would not have picked such a dangerous career for you." He grunts. "Over the past few years, I have had the honour of not only watching you grow, but of seeing how strong, compassionate"—he grunts again—"and brutal you can be." He shakes his head. A proud smile flashes across his plump lips.

That smile makes my insides mushy.

Something clicks in my head, and I know before I have even asked the question. "Madán gave you access to the footage from the magic cameras." Aragon nods.

He rubs his chin in preparation for telling me something else.

"I do have one last thing I need to confess. You were alone, unable to shift, and sleeping a lot. I was concerned—" I narrow my eyes at him —"so I found the best guard-dog breed, and I made sure you would find him." Guard dog...Lucifer? Aragon bought me my dog! Lucifer is mine to keep, forever!

I burst into tears, big embarrassing sobs. I can't help it—I bloody love my dog. I ignore Aragon's horrified face as I lunge from my stool and throw myself into his arms. I pull Aragon down towards me. I kiss my amazing, incredible, thoughtful dragon all over his handsome face.

He gave me my dog, 'cause he wanted me to have a friend and something to care for.

"Thank you, thank you so very much. I love him. I am so happy that he is mine and no one is going to take him from me." Well, that was what I was attempting to say—it sort of came out a bit mumbled, what with all the snot and tears. Aragon nods...I think he got all that. He gently takes my head in his big hands and thumbs the tears from my cheeks.

"You're more than welcome," Aragon says roughly. He coughs to clear his throat. "There will never be another person like you, Forrest Hesketh. You are so unique. I want you to know that I never acted out of duty when it came to you. It was always personal. That first day in my office, you lit up my world as if everything before you was just darkness. You have taught me the meaning of loneliness because when I don't see you, I feel alone, and missing you is like physical pain." He rubs his chest with his other hand, over his heart. "Losing you because I misjudged a situation was the worst moment of my life. Knowing I had to let you go and not knowing if you would come back to me..." Aragon closes his eyes; he leans forward. His forehead brushes mine. "I should have talked to you. Told you my plans. I lost you because of my arrogance. You were hurt..." Aragon growls, still stroking my cheek. "Forgive me?" he begs.

"Okay," I whisper in shock.

His beautiful eyes meet mine.

"You are it for me, Forrest. I waited lifetimes so we could meet." I blink at him. That lightning has seriously messed him up. "I understand if this has come out of the blue. I know you will need time to process—" Fuck it. I grossly use my sleeve to clean my nose quickly and then I kiss his beautiful mouth to shut him up before he talks himself out of whatever is happening here. Oh my God, Aragon likes me!

"I love you, you crazy dragon," I mumble. I move away and peek up at him, checking to see that I haven't made a stupid mistake.

Aragon doesn't run away screaming. Instead, he stands, and his arms circle me. He lifts me onto the counter. I suck in a ragged breath, my heart pounding in my ears. Butterflies explode in my tummy as he stands between my legs and pulls me in close.

He growls. I bite down on my lip in response. One of Aragon's big hands wraps around my waist. The other goes to the back of my neck.

Aragon leans forward, curling around me, crushing my body against his muscley hard chest. Oh my God. My heart jumps, missing a beat, and my tummy flips with more dancing butterflies. We are so close together that his face blurs. I close my eyes. I can feel his breath on my lips. I lick my lips, trying to get any trace of his taste that might be left on them. As I do, my tongue catches his mouth. I hum with appreciation. Aragon closes the tiny gap between us and kisses me, his full lips surprisingly spongy.

The kiss at first is gentle, then with swift graduation more intense, harder, deeper. I gasp. Aragon's tongue, as if it has been waiting for an invitation, slips into my mouth and tangles with mine.

I cling to his forearms, the only things keeping me stable in my dizzy, swaying world. The stubble on his face rubs my skin, but I don't care. I groan into his mouth. He pulls his lips slightly away and whispers, "Breathe, Forrest..." I gasp in a shaky breath, belatedly realising I had neglected to breathe. Oxygen is so overrated. How can anyone kiss and breathe at the same time?

I inhale his smoky dragon scent. I want to breathe him, lick him, and eat him up.

I've had a taste, and unequivocally I realise it will never be enough.

Aragon gently kisses my gasping lips and pulls away from me.

I slowly open my eyes and blink up at him; my lips are tingling in the best way. I give him a bright smile and with a grin say, "That was my first kiss, and I am so glad it was with you." I bite my lip and bounce with excitement. "Could we please do that again? I will get better if we practice." I stop bouncing and meet his heavy-lidded eyes. "Will you teach me, Aragon?" Aragon groans. Shit, that is an incredible sound.

I stare at my knees, feeling a little shy; I am twenty-seven, for God's sake. I needed to get this whole thing down.

"Practice?" Aragon's voice is deep and smoky, "I would love nothing more than to practice *everything* with you."

Yay. I nod. I refrain from doing a fist-pump.

I give him a beaming smile, grab his hand, jump off the counter, and attempt to tug him towards the bedroom.

Do I just take my clothes off?

Or is it better if Aragon removes them?

I worry a little. Hopefully Aragon knows what he is doing. I tug, but Aragon doesn't move; instead, he reels me back into his arms.

"But we're going to go slow, Nutty. So that's enough for tonight."

What! What? Noooo. After that speech, that epic kiss—what? Well, that's disappointing. I huff, I even stomp my foot.

"Spoilsport," I mutter under my breath. We go into the living room, and I throw myself down on the sofa.

I am not sulking.

What is it about Aragon that brings out my immaturity?

Aragon shakes his head at me, his eyes dancing. He sits elegantly beside me as if he has a suit on and not the borrowed jogging bottoms and t-shirt. He takes hold of my hand and plays with my little finger.

"May I stay over? To sleep? I would feel uncomfortable leaving you, what with the storm." I grin at him and nod like crazy. Do I want the handsome dragon whom I have just kissed to stay the night? Do I want to wake up with his arms around me and the smell of him filling my nose? I am not daft—no way I'm going to say bloody no.

I jump up with a squeal and run towards my bedroom to get ready for bed.

CHAPTER
FORTY-ONE

THAT WAS the best sleep that I have had in years. It is unbelievable, how much I missed him, and since he has come back crashing into my life, I feel so grateful. I have at least a week off work, and I can spend it getting to know Aragon again.

I so need to work on this practising kissing and stuff, to add to my adulting portfolio. I admitted I was in love with him. He didn't say it back, but that's okay. I will make Aragon love me.

"What are you thinking so hard about?" Aragon says below me. I am lying on top of him, all snug in his arms, back to being the little puzzle piece that fits so perfectly with him. I feel his words rumble through his chest. I shouldn't be worrying; Aragon is here with me in my bed and for the first time in a long time, I feel safe and complete. He cuddles me to him and kisses my forehead.

"Nothing," I mumble.

"Liar," Aragon says gruffly, "I can feel that brain of yours going crazy. What has you worried?" he whispers into my ear. Aragon gently rubs the back of my neck—seemingly unconcerned about the horrible bite mark. I tip my head and look at him. He brushes the hair from my face.

"Do... do you... Aragon, do you love me?"

Aragon's whole face softens as he meets my eyes, and I see the truth shining in them.

"I love you more than anything in this world. You are my treasure. I will spend the rest of this life with you, if you will do me the honour. When we're no longer on this earth, I will spend my new existence searching for you. You are the other half of my soul, and I am only ever complete if you are in my arms."

My eyes widen with shock. I huff out a breath and blink at him. *Tell me how you really feel.* Wow. Phew, that makes me feel better.

In comparison to Aragon's words, my snotty "I love you" seem kind of shit.

"Oh, urm, okay thanks..." I whisper.

"In my office, I was in total awe of you. You were so endearing, with the dress and the antics with the water glass." Aragon chuffs and takes the rogue hand in question and kisses it. "When I read the report delving into your life, knowing what you had to endure...it was distressing. I was devastated. I wanted to make things easier for you. I have been alive for a long time, and you hadn't had any chance to live."

Aragon sits up, and with his hands on my hips he lifts me, turning me around to face him. My legs drop either side of him—he is so wide that they don't touch the bed. He tucks my hair behind my ear and cups the back of my head, meeting my eyes.

His eyes hold conviction.

I bite my lip to hold in a moan. *Oh, this is nice.* Warmth pools deep in my stomach.

"Able to partial-shift at twenty-three, and when you used your fire magic, I was so damn proud of you. It also frightened me to death. How the hell was I going to keep you safe? You'd already dealt with so many men trying to control you. You had just shifted to human it would have been inappropriate. I couldn't throw myself into the mix." He places my hand on his chest and traces my warrior mark. "You would have run a mile. So I thought if I could be your guardian, I could officially protect you, and you could get to know me and trust me. Then we could build from that. I wanted to give you what you needed at the time, and it certainly wasn't a foolish dragon."

I lean forward and kiss his chest. "You're not a foolish dragon. You might be old, ancient even. I love you for you anyway. It is more about your soul than the body that houses it, and my soul is ancient too."

Aragon moves quickly, and he flips me over onto my back. I let out a shriek of surprise. He rests his forearms on either side of my head, holding his weight above me.

"Who are you calling 'ancient'?" Aragon leans down and runs his nose across my jaw, blowing his breath gently across my skin, making me all goosey. I wiggle away, and he follows me, blowing gently into my ear. I half-giggle and half-groan.

"Now stop worrying, I have spent over four years without you. I am never letting you go." Aragon kisses my nose. I beam a smile at him; he groans deep in the back of his throat. His chest rumbles above me, vibrating in almost a purr. "Would you like to practice this morning?" Aragon, coos at me. I giggle, and then I smack my lips to his in answer.

"I HAVE to go and handle a few things; I might not be back until tomorrow morning. Please try to keep out of trouble until I get back." Aragon gently kisses my swollen lips.

Lucifer grumbles at him. My dog isn't impressed with the new man in my life. He has been grumpy all day and will not do anything that he's told.

"No problem."

"I'll come back with a car." I laugh, imagining Aragon with his knees to his chin as he squishes himself into my tiny blue Citroen. Honestly, the car isn't that small, Aragon is just that big.

He goes to pull off his top...oh my God!

I realise he's going to shift and I am getting a show. The t-shirt slowly rises and an eight-pack appears...I know conventional shifters do this all the time. But as I have already established, I am not normal, and I have never seen a man undress.

"Fuck, seriously. It's like you're photoshopped." Bow-chicka-wow-wow dodgy music plays in my head as I ogle his beautiful body. He is seriously cut; the man is that perfect, he doesn't look real. I refrain from the urge to give him a poke. Aragon hooks his thumbs into the waistband of the jogging bottoms, and he slowly reveals his lower half. I almost swallow my tongue. I gulp, I blink, and I stare at his toes.

He has excellent feet.

Okay, okay! I don't get a good look at his penis.

I'm purposefully avoiding it; penises freak me out. I have never seen a live one before, in the flesh. And Aragon's penis? Gulp. It doesn't take a genius to understand that his monster penis will be proportional to the rest of him...oh my fucking God I'm freaking the fuck out!

I think I need a paper bag.

"Coward," Aragon says with a deep throaty chuckle as he prowls past me. I get a lovely view of his bottom.

His bottom is total perfection; I follow him, trying to keep my tongue in my mouth. I have a massive urge to run at him and bite his bum.

When we're outside, Aragon gently grips my chin between his thumb and forefinger and gives me a sweet kiss with his squidgy lips.

"I love you; I will not be long." He then vaults over my fence, into the field in which he crash-landed just last night, and he shifts.

His dragon is incredible.

He must be the most exquisite creature I have ever seen. Just like Aragon in his human form, Aragon's dragon is silver. He is way bigger than our house; he's breathtaking.

Aragon's elegant head is long and flat with a rounded nose, and several impressive sharp silver teeth poke out from the side of his mouth. I can see my faint reflection in each and every one of them. He has four horns, two at the front of his head and two at the rear facing backwards. A lean neck runs down into a solid muscular body covered in silver scales that catch the light and reflect it. It's the perfect camouflage; you would never see him in the sky unless you knew where to look. The skin underneath him is slightly darker. He has four strong limbs that allow him to stand, sturdy and intimidating. Each leg has five digits, each of which ends in a pointy, curved silver claw.

Aragon's giant wings start from his shoulders, and he is holding them behind him and slightly away. The wings are bat like. The membrane of the skin is thick, and I can see the flexible bone structure through the wing. At the top of the curve of each wing is a curved silver claw. His tail, from what I can see, is substantial, muscular, and covered in the same silver scales, and it's tipped with what looks like a silver blade.

Aragon watches me as I take him in, and I realise with delight that he has been posing his various body parts for my inspection. I can feel the slight tremor of the ground when he moves. I find that I am leaning entirely over the fence. I hold my hand out, palm up, wanting to stroke him. His big head ducks and he slowly—being mindful of the fence—lets me run my hand across his nose. Wow, his head is the size of my car.

Aragon's scales are soft, like silk to my touch; for some reason, I imagined he would feel hard like he was armoured, or like metal.

"You are so beautiful," I whisper, the awe evident in my tone. He puffs out a breath that blows my hair back. I can't help but giggle. I lean forward and kiss his soft nose.

"Fly safe, Aragon, and I will see you soon. Drive carefully on the road coming back as well; the roads will be icy. Oh, and message me when you get home, so I know you're safe." Aragon huffs out another breath, and I think if he could, he would roll his eyes. But instead, he backs away and gives me a nod.

Aragon moves to a safe distance and then goes from standing to launching himself into the air with such agility, it's as if he weighs nothing. The way he moves is with such grace. I watch him go until I can't see him anymore.

I shake my head; it's inconceivable that I am telling another person that I love him and asking him to be safe. It sounds silly out loud, saying "please be careful" to a humungous dragon. But Aragon is mine.

He loves me; no one has chosen to love me before. I have decided that there's no going back for me.

These scary feelings I have...I am going to embrace the shit out of them.

The wind picks up, and I grumble as I totter my freezing self back into the house. Aragon's naked bottom has made me neglect to put on a coat.

CHAPTER
FORTY-TWO

"Forrest, wake up." I feel the whisper of my mum's lips on my cheek. I groan. My eyes are heavy-lidded with sleep.

"Mum, what's happening," I rasp.

Awareness creeps through me. I'm alone in my room, it's the middle of the night, and my phone is ringing.

Wow, that was freaky.

Another moment in time comes back to me, when my mum did a similar wake-up in the middle of the night. That moment changed my life forever. I lost my pack and my childhood as a result.

I roll onto my side and slap the bedside table in search of the handset. After a few seconds of fumbling, my fingertips knock the phone, and I grasp the bloody thing. I wince at the bright screen—the mobile is doing its best to sear my eyeballs. I close one eye and squint with the other. The blurry name comes slowly into focus. *Huh, Ava.* Something must be wrong if she's calling so late. I rub my eyes and answer.

"Hi Ava," I say curiously, trying not to yawn.

"Hi, Forrest. Are you okay to talk?"

"Yes, what do you need?"

"I didn't want to ring you, but unfortunately I've not got a choice. The case with this serial killer and the girls...it got picked up by the news. Unfortunately, it will be all over the UK media by the morning. They've named you, Forrest, and now the shifters know that you're alive." Ava sighs down the phone. I groan. My heart misses a beat, and my tummy cramps with worry. *Oh, for fuck's sake.* "I'm so sorry to be the bearer of bad news. Daniel knows that you're alive and he's on the warpath." Ahh, shit. Now I feel fully awake. My nerves are buzzing, and the excess adrenalin sloshes through my system, making me tremble. Any second now, I'm going to freak out and drop the phone, so I switch the handset to loudspeaker. Okay, this doesn't sound good.

What is it about me and my talent to tempt fate? Fate, the fickle bitch, is getting involved again big-time. I know I said I wanted to deal with Daniel when I was in that bloody basement, but come on, I wanted it for once to be on my terms, not his. That fucking wanker is never going to leave me alone.

"Forrest, Daniel's financials have lit up like crazy." Ava continues, "Over the last twenty-four hours, he has been hiring mercenaries, and paying good money, too. I wanted to let you know that Daniel is coming, and he's going to find you, Forrest. He's going to find you fast."

"Ava, how long do I have?"

"Hours...if you're lucky. The information currently shows that Daniel has at least thirty guys. Of those men, at least a dozen are well-trained mercenary shifters; the rest are paid thugs. I will send you everything I have on them and keep you updated. I can track them anywhere there's tech." *Hours.* I cringe.

"Thank you so much, Ava," I say. "I am sorry I did a shit job of keeping my head down."

"I'm sorry that I am not giving you enough time to prepare. It's been four years, and I have so many people to monitor and protect—"

"No, please don't. Ava, I royally fucked up—this whole damn mess is my fault. I should have kept my head down better." I rub my face in frustration. "I didn't think that my name would go international with the media. Hindsight is a great thing. I feel like such a fool...I told the girls my name like an idiot, a proper idiot.

"Would you please keep me updated?" I ask, my voice a rasp.

"No problem. Good luck. Let me know if you need anything."

"Thank you. Bye." I sit on the edge of the bed and put my head between my knees. After a few minutes, I dial Aragon.

"Nutty, are you all right?" His deep chocolatey voice rumbles.

"Ava called. Aragon, I've fucked up…" I explain what has happened.

"You have alerts around the house and a strong ward in place. We will know if anyone comes within miles of you. I won't let him touch you." He growls.

"Aragon, I am so sorry." My voice breaks. "I have been selfish. I should have dealt with Daniel when I had the chance, but I chose to run away from my problem. I should have stayed and fought him. I should have spoken to you. I should have done so many different things. I'm a bloody coward, and I feel so ashamed." My eyes fill with tears.

"Hey, you are not a coward. Everything happens for a reason, Forrest. The journey you have been on, becoming a warrior? That's important. You have saved so many lives, and you have grown. You did what you needed to do at the time, and remember, I chose to help you leave. It was the best thing to do for you at that time, the safest thing. The only person that's responsible for this mess is Daniel. You cannot control everything or plan for every outcome. What's done is done. If you need somebody to blame? Blame me; I left Daniel alive. When Madán broke your bond, I should have hunted him down. At the time I wanted vengeance, and killing him wasn't enough for me—I wanted to make him suffer. You think with age you gain more wisdom. That is true…but even ancient dragons get it wrong. None of us is infallible. We all make mistakes, and now, Nutty, we're going to fix this mistake together. I'm on my way."

That scary part inside of me chuckles—it's glad that piece-of-shit Daniel is coming for me. I am not the same scared girl I was when we had last met. I am now a different creature, and my magic is stronger. I am a fucking warrior, and this time I have my dragon at my back.

Urm…or not. As soon as those thoughts clear my head, my warrior mark tingles, indicating I have unwelcome company. Whoever it is has just passed my warning ward. For fuck's sake!

I dress quickly, putting on various layers consisting of my thermals and my dark combat clothing. The snow has gone—it doesn't last long in Sligo, and according to the weather reports, the temperature is going to be milder for the next few days. I plan on hunting these fuckers, and I need to be comfortable while doing so. I pull my hair into a tight plait and secure the end by threading it through the base of the plait and securing it with grips so it can't be grabbed.

I methodically go through my kit, putting different spells in different areas of my combat gear. I attach various blades in their holders, and my black Wakizashi Japanese short sword I secure on my left hip. My disassembled bow and a dozen potion-tipped arrows I carry in a padded bag on my back. My scent masker is on my ankle. Unfortunately, my fire magic isn't sneaky enough, so traditional weapons and potions are my go-to alternatives. Hopefully I won't need to use them, as I have enough sleeping spells to knock out half of my local town.

As I leave, I send a quick text to Madán out of courtesy. I leave the phone that will not shift with me behind. Daniel has that much front and so much false confidence in his abilities; it beggars belief that he thinks he can bring a bunch of mercenaries into Ireland with no reprisals, no repercussions, ignoring a thousand-year-old treaty that bans shifters from coming into the country—unless you are a dragon given lifetime amnesty or a member of a Fae court. He can't pop into Ireland and kidnap a serving Fae warrior. Madán will be furious.

Daniel's strange obsession with me, his creepy instalove, has never made much sense. He must be coming for revenge—that's the only logical explanation I can think of.

I step outside into the winter night. The cold wind whips my hair and bites at my face. I pull my balaclava over my head. Lucifer snuffles underneath the door, not liking that I've left him locked in the house. "I'm sorry, Luca. Be a good boy. I will be back soon."

I have a plan that isn't motivated by the need to run. An offensive plan. I silently turn; let's see what these idiots are up to.

I shift into my wolf, and as I do, I pull on the power of my warrior mark. When my paws land onto the stone driveway, I'm wisps of shadow. I have to fight the urge to lift my head and howl.

In this shadow form, I can cover the distance required in a fraction of time. I follow the sound of intruders. My proximity to danger sharpens my senses, and the closer I get, the more often I pause. Listening. I'm the hunter, they're the prey. About four kilometres from the cottage, I find six vehicles and a group of twenty-eight men.

I settle against a hedge to watch. Angry. My eyes flick to each man, calculating and assessing. A few of the men, a dozen or so, move like they're trained. Professionally they check their gear and murmur to each other. The rest are messing about, laughing and joking.

Daniel is nowhere to be seen.

A bald guy steps up and claps his hands to gain everyone's attention.

"Fall in on me," he yells. Oh hello, look who it is: Meathead One, with his shiny bald head, sans goatee. I growl in my mind. "You nine with me—we go right. You nine take the left, and you nine take the rear. We're here as a support team. Back-up only. The boss is taking the front at dawn. Rules of engagement—this is capture, not kill. That doesn't mean it has to be a clean capture."

"We fuck her up then, yeah?" says a grinning fool. Meathead One smirks at the guy.

"Keep out of sight. If she rabbits, restrain her. Do not let this bitch escape. This will be easy money. Observe radio silence. Any questions?" A few shake their heads. "Don't fuck up. Let's go."

Meathead's group has all the best mercenaries. I want to smack my forehead in disgust as they move off with deadly grace, disappearing into the night. What is he thinking, putting all the best-trained guys in his group—why not use them to direct the other teams? I watch the others bumble about as they shrug, point, and argue with each other. One of them drags his gear behind him on the floor.

I might as well take out Meathead's group of ten first. I know with slight trepidation that I'll have to shift back to use my sleep potions.

I move ahead and find a place to wait.

Opportunity comes when they fan out away from each other. Dropping into mostly prone positions, they settle, chests to the ground, eyes on my dark cottage. With no one watching their backs, it's apparent that they aren't expecting company. I grin and shift back. With a handful of sleeping potion balls, I set to work.

CHAPTER
FORTY-THREE

I NEVER THOUGHT I'd be at home, hunting bad guys in my woods. I feel a little like John Rambo; this is kind of surreal.

I'm in the forest that sits at the bottom of our house. Tall pine trees surround me, and I am currently hiding up in an old sycamore tree nestled within the pines. With the snow and the heavy rain, the ground is saturated. The pines were initially planted on bogland, and no matter how you enter the woods, there's only one clear access trail through. The way of going naturally herds people underneath the tree that I'm currently hiding in. If they don't come through this way, someone will have to fish them out of the deadly bog later.

I wait for the chance to pick off my last quota of the bad guys. Nineteen guys are already tucked away in bushes and dykes, sleeping. I haven't even broken a sweat. I'm after the last group of nine that have planned to reach the house from the woods, then come up through the field to gain access to the back of the cottage.

Unfortunately for them, that isn't going to happen.

Once this is completed, I can check on Aragon and Madán while waiting for Daniel to arrive. With their strict radio-silence, Daniel will never suspect his backup is snoozing.

There's movement. The group has split further, and it looks like they're now in groups of three. The three guys heading my way are not stealthy. I'm a little embarrassed on their behalf. These men are supposed to be shifters, yet here they are, crashing through the forest. They are not ninjas.

Noisy creatures.

Now if there's a smart person in the group of nine, I'd presume that they had sent the three noisy ones out as bait and then follow stealthily to sniff out any traps. I doubt it, but I'm not going to give away my position by being silly.

I wait for them to move on, and when they're almost out of my line of sight, I use my bow. The arrows strike each guy quietly in quick succession. The arrows land cleanly, and I aim for their legs in case they're wearing any body armour. Thanks to countless hours of practice, I am a good shot, even in the darkness of the woods. I smirk as two of the guys get an arrow to the bottom. All three of them go down quickly, within seconds, the sleeping potion doing its job and working immediately.

I appear from behind the pines like a ghost and grab hold of two of the guys' legs and pull both of them into the undergrowth, followed swiftly by the third. Within seconds all three men have entirely disappeared. I am feeling a little smug.

I swing back into my tree and quietly wait for the next guys. It doesn't take long until another three thugs trample past. These shifters are quieter, but not by much. I shoot them quickly. Unfortunately, one of them lets out a small cry before he goes unconscious.

For fuck's sake. I sit and wait for sixty seconds to make sure that I won't have any further company. I need to move the bodies; everything seems clear. I drop lightly onto my feet. I listen, and I hear nothing. I make my way to the three sleeping thugs and drag them into the trees.

Luckily there's a handy trench behind a row of pines. It's wet, but still a perfect area for storing the bodies out of sight. I snort as I see my growing bad-guy pile. I arrange my guys carefully—I don't want them to drown—and just as I am about to make my way back to my tree, there's a slight movement to my right. I freeze. I bring my prepared bow up in preparation to loose an arrow.

There's a sound behind me, and before I can check it out, I'm grabbed from behind. The guy pulls me into his body. His hand goes up between my breasts and wraps around my throat, pinning me to his chest. His other hand pulls the balaclava from my head, pulling out some of my hair in the process.

I keep my hands slightly out by my sides. I am still holding my bow. My other hand surreptitiously reaches for a blade strapped to my thigh; I cup the small knife in my palm.

The movement that I spotted? A decoy. I feel stupid that I fell for it, but what's done is done. The guy behind me stinks. I wrinkle my nose; I think he's a hyena shifter. He squeezes my throat and runs his other hand down my body. He spends way too much time on my boobs; he has neglected to notice the weapons in my hands.

I barely refrain from rolling my eyes.

"What have we got here, lads—look at this tasty morsel. I'm up for a bit—she's fucking tiny." He breathes me in. "Can't smell your fear—fucking magic." His breath smells of beer, garlic, and lust. He whispers in my ear the filthy things he wants to do to me and grinds himself against my back.

"Do you mind? I can feel the tip," I say with poorly veiled disgust. I breathe through my nose and out through my mouth. I force myself to remain calm and relaxed in his grip; I'm going to kill this rapist fucker.

He is going to die horribly.

He hasn't worked it out yet.

I'm no one's prey.

Surprisingly one of the guys looks incredibly uncomfortable. He is younger than the other two, and he glances about with fright, his scent distressed. The other guy is smirking, nodding and rubbing his hands together as if he's a kid on Christmas morning, about to open a present.

Nodding Smirking Guy glares at the younger guy when he starts to beg, "Barry, mate, come on, let the girl go—that kind of shit isn't right. We're here to do a job, not hurt girls. I won't let you do it—just let her go." The young guy steps forward as if to intervene.

"You're just going to have to watch then, aren't you, lad. Not my fault you're gay and you don't want to get your dick wet." The hyena shifter undoes the button of my combats, his focus entirely on unzipping my pants. His lack of focus means I can now react.

I bury my knife in his inner thigh. I pull out the blade, twist around on my toes, and put the blade through the side of his neck. It effectively keeps him quiet. I step to the side to make sure none of his blood spray gets onto my clothing.

The rapist bastard gurgles, and I smile as he falls to the floor. This is all done in a matter of seconds. I re-button my combats.

"Stay," I say as I step towards the smirking guy. I keep the young guy in my peripheral vision. He gives me a nod and then opens his arms wide, puts them behind his head, and kneels. Without overthinking and without breaking my stride, I loose an arrow into his chest. I drop the bow on the floor as the young guy falls unconscious.

My total focus is now on the smirking guy. My wakizashi short sword comes out of the *saya* with a hiss. Smirking Guy pulls his shocked eyes from the other two men on the floor and meets my cold gaze. His breath catches and he shudders and vomits. He holds up his shaking hands in a placating gesture.

"I wasn't gonna do anything, lass," he pleads. I have zero sympathy; if given a chance, he was going to rape me.

I prowl towards him. I grip the sword in my right hand and keep it pointed in the shifter's direction. At the last moment, I jump to the side but forward, dealing a swinging cut that makes the air sing. I step and half-turn, the blade drawing a fan of black blood droplets in its wake. The shifter's head topples to the floor.

I turn back to the rapist hyena shifter. I tilt my head to the side as I listen to him gurgle. Black blood seeps through his lips. "Are you not going to scream for me, Barry?" I say, kicking him in the ribs so he is flat on his back. "What a pity. Oh, look at that—least you managed to get your dick *wet*," I whisper, pointing out unnecessarily that he has pissed himself. I grind my boot between his legs. "Guess what, Barry lad, you smell of piss, blood, and fear." His eyes are wide and rolling. "I was going to cut your cock off and feed it to you. But you're not going to live long enough, I'm afraid, which is a real shame." I draw my short sword over my shoulder and bring it down, severing his head. I kick the head into the hole where the other bad guys are sleeping.

I stand in the darkness of the wood, forcing myself to take a few slow, deep breaths. My white breath fills the air, announcing my presence and frantic state. My body is singing with the need for more violence. My mind is more than on board with that. I'm twice as deadly when my back is against the wall.

If I've learned one thing, I do not want to be the judge and executioner of others—that path only leads to bad decisions and self-destruction. But today with these two guys I'm willing to make an exception. I will take the hit on my soul, knowing that other women are safer.

I clear up the two dead bodies and put the unconscious young guy in the hole with the others. I'm still feeling a tad homicidal.

Aragon appears in front of me silently. A muscle twitches in his jaw as he stares at me intently; for once, he's unable to conceal his rage. Even in the darkness of the pines with almost zero light, he spots the redness on my neck. His nostrils flare as he also scents the hyena shifter and blood.

"Are you hurt?" I shake my head no. Aragon growls and pulls me towards him. I squeak as he lifts me into his arms. I instinctively wrap my legs around him as he looks deep into my eyes as if trying to read the truth on my very soul. Aragon grunts, then smashes his lips on mine. *Oh my.* The kiss is rough, passionate, full of anger, fear, and relief.

"What happened?" he asks when he finally pulls away and swipes a gentle finger across my throat. My lips are tingling, and I feel a little dizzy from his kiss. He allows me to drop back to my feet. I wobble a little.

I nibble on my lip and shrug my shoulders. Now isn't the time. Aragon puffs out a frustrated breath. "How many?" His voice is dark and dangerous.

"Back-up guys, twenty-eight. Twenty-six I took out with sleeping potions. Two fatalities." My eyes flick to the hole, and he strides over and takes a look at the dead bodies. "Daniel is supposedly on his way."

He growls and prowls back towards me. Leaning close, he cradles my face in his big hands. "I am sorry I left you. I am sorry you had to do that. Where is your warrior team?" he says, rubbing his thumbs across my cheekbones. I look down, and he growls again.

"I texted Madán."

"Madán is an old Fae. He doesn't do text messages." I was aware of that, that's why I did it. I shrug.

"I dealt with them. I'm not sorry that I didn't get others involved. It was nothing I couldn't handle." He kisses my forehead, and I take hold of one of his hands and squeeze it.

"Daniel is twenty minutes out," he says quietly. "I flew over the cars." I nod; we'd better get moving. I planned to meet him at the house. I want Daniel to think he has surprised me and taken me unaware. Aragon pulls me towards him. "I can get us back faster." He then shocks the shit out of me and does a partial shift. Beautiful silver dragon wings appear on his back.

I gape at him. "When did you... how... I don't..." Aragon kisses my forehead again and lifts me back into his arms. I wrap my legs around him again. He folds his arms around me, one arm underneath my bottom to support my weight and the other in my hair, holding my head against his shoulder. I put my arms around his neck.

Aragon prowls away from the trees, and as soon as he clears the canopy, we're flying. He takes off with elegance. I bury my head in his chest and close my eyes tightly. I dare not move in case I throw him off balance and we end up crashing. Which is daft, as in Aragon's arms I am in the safest place I'll ever be. Within minutes we're back at the house. We land safely.

Once inside, I stumble when I catch sight of Owen, who is sitting on my sofa. Lucifer is sitting on the floor beside him with a big doggy grin. Owen is running his big hands through his fur. My dog, who doesn't like anyone, seems to love Owen.

"Owen..." I whisper in a shaky voice, "how did you get here? What are you doing here?" Owen stands and smiles at me. I throw myself at him. Aragon grunts.

"Your dog is amazing. I got a lift." Owen nods towards a scowling Aragon. *He got a lift...but Aragon flew in as a dragon...oh, wow.* "Oh, you know. Seeing as you aren't publicly dead anymore, I thought I might come and lend a hand. Chop-chop—Daniel will be here soon. Before I forget, first dibs on Daniel." Owen waves his hand in the air as if he has asked for the front seat. "I've wanted to beat the shit out of him for years."

I huff out a laugh and give his solid middle an extra squeeze. "Fine by me; I don't want to touch him. Go for it, Nanny Hound. I better get ready." I reluctantly let go of Owen, and I'm halfway across the room when he booms, "Oy, you've been boasting about your cooking, so you can feed me later as a thank-you."

I turn back and catch Aragon vigorously shaking his head, his silver eyes wide. I frown. What's up with him? "Or we can go out for a full Irish breakfast..." Owen's voice trails off as he smirks knowingly at Aragon.

"That sounds like a splendid idea," Aragon replies as he gently nudges me towards the bedroom.

I remove my clothes and weapons, shift to remove all traces of forest, the scent of the hyena shifter, and blood. I quickly change into my regular leggings and a jumper.

After we go over the plan, I use my warrior mark to make the ward impenetrable to anyone except us. Aragon and Owen disappear outside into the garden after using a few potions, including one to link our minds.

I make myself a cup of tea while I'm waiting. I've just removed the teabag when I hear the cars pull up outside the house and the *clunk clunk clunk* of the car doors as they open and slam close.

Finally, the wolf is at the door. There's no running away this time. I take a shaky breath in. Well, here we go. It's showtime.

CHAPTER
FORTY-FOUR

"Forrest, come out, come out, wherever you are. Forrest, come out to play, your mate is here for you," Daniel shouts. I roll my eyes. What a dickhead.

Aragon growls in my head, not impressed at all with Daniel's mate comment. I take my time and slip on my combat boots. I grab my big warm coat, stuffed full of sleep potions. I open the door, take a deep breath, and make my way to the front of the house.

I crunch across the stone driveway and appraise my unwelcome visitors, who stand on the other side of the garden wall. I stand with my back to the house, holding my tea in both hands. The sun has risen. I look up at the sky with a relaxed smile, pleased to see that it isn't raining. The weatherman did promise it would be mild.

"Ah, there she is. Hello, little wolf. Nice to see that you're not dead. Are you surprised to see me?" Daniel smiles, showing his teeth, and a familiar greedy hunger fills his gaze as he looks me up and down. He is wearing his custom black suit and a crisp white shirt. The men scattered on the lane around him are wearing black fatigues. Daniel slowly claps his hands. "I do have to say, bravo on your fake suicide; it was extremely realistic. You had me fooled. Was it your dead mummy's suicide that gave you the idea? I know you failed to kill yourself the first time around." Daniel smiles brightly; he makes a show of miming putting something in his mouth and then dropping it. I lock the rage I feel inside. I don't respond; it takes everything I have to look back at him blankly. He frowns at my lack of response and then chuckles. "I've come to bring you back to England, where you belong. Have you forgotten that you're mine? Now come quietly, or these gentlemen will make you." Daniel waves his arm around, indicating his men.

Within the group of ten men stand Jason and a struggling Harry. It looks like Daniel has been very busy collecting my stepbrothers—God, we just need John now for the full set. I'm glad to see that my hellhound brother isn't among them.

I pull my attention back to Daniel and make eye contact. I tilt my head slightly to the side as I study his face. I can't help the smug smile that I give him. I'm amused to see a flash of anger as I continue to stare at him—his ruined face. Daniel is missing his left eye. Thick white scars crisscross the whole left side of his face in a mass of scar tissue. By stark contrast, the right side of his face is still perfectly handsome. I take a sip of tea, showing him I'm completely unaffected and unconcerned by his presence.

If it was anyone other than Daniel, I'd never in a million years say what I am about to: "Daniel, have you got something on your face? It's just there?" I point out helpfully, making a circular motion with my finger and pointing at the left side of my face.

As predicted, Daniel goes nuts. He roars, runs at me, and bounces off my bad-guy impenetrable and invisible ward. It's my turn to chuckle. I shake my head. "Oops, are you okay? That must have hurt. I hope you guys are getting a lot of money to work with this idiot, " I say condescendingly to the men at his back.

"I want that ward down now, get that fucking ward down now!" Daniel screams. "You think it's going to stop me? You stupid bitch. You won't be laughing or making smart comments when I've got hold of you. I've got such plans. Your life is going to be a living hell." Daniel slams his palm against the ward. Aah, now there he is, the real Daniel.

I catch movement out of the corner of my eye. The passenger door of the leading vehicle opens. A foot encased in a blue high heel and the hem of a blue dress appears. I am stunned to see who steps out of the car.

Like the proverbial bad penny: Liz Richardson.

I huff and my eyes go wide: a heavily pregnant Liz. Wow, Harry has been busy.

Wearing a tight blue dress that emphasises her tummy, Liz waddles towards Daniel and takes hold of his elbow and tugs at it. "I don't know what we're doing here. We should be at home with our two boys. I can't believe that I've been forced to follow you. Just kill her so we can go home, darling, I just want to go home," Liz whines. I scan them both, and I raise my eyebrows.

I take another sip of tea to hide my confusion. I puff out my cheeks. Wow, Harry hasn't been busy at all. I blink at the pair of them. I guess Harry has had a lucky escape? My perusal of Liz makes me shudder—that could have easily been my alternative fate. I can't help worrying. I hope that their relationship is consensual—if Liz chose Daniel, that is karma at its finest. She must be an absolute pain in his ass. But Liz ending up with a monster like Daniel? I really couldn't have predicted this outcome: with all her manipulations, she ended up with a bigger monster than herself.

"Wow, Liz, you —"

"I'm not fat; I'm pregnant, you stupid cow. Why hasn't somebody killed her already!" Liz snarls.

"Wow, okay. I was going to say, 'scraped the bottom of the barrel' in regard to being with Daniel, not that..." My voice drifts away as I pull a face and indicate her tummy with a floppy hand.

"Why didn't you stay dead? Daniel, mate, kill the bitch so we can go home," Liz whines. Daniel attempts to pull his arm from Liz's grasp, but she hangs on. Her nails dig into his suit-clad arm.

"I'm a little confused. Didn't you say that I'm still your mate?" I point at my chest, widening my eyes. "I didn't know that you could have two mates at the same time...that is a little greedy, Daniel. Hey, I don't mind stepping aside," I say with a wave and smile. A few of the shifters shuffle. I bet they don't like Daniel claiming two females either.

"Dog, what are you talking about? I am his mate he's just coming here for justice. Who would want to be your mate?" Liz sneers, looking me up and down with disgust, as if I am covered head-to-toe in dog poop.

Daniel shakes Liz off his arm and shoves her none-too-gently back towards the vehicle. She stumbles. "Get back in the car. This has nothing to do with you. We're not mates; there's no bond between us, you stupid cow. I've come here for my real mate, my true mate. Who was made for me! She is going to give me daughters. Three children, three useless boys...you are incompetent. Get in the car." My mouth pops open in shock. I can't believe he just came out with it like that. The mother of his children, and calling his kids useless.

What. A. Dick.

Liz turns her attention back to me and screeches her rage. "This is all your fault." I can't help rolling my eyes. She thrusts her arm out, and a sharp nail points at me. "We wouldn't be here if it weren't for you. We're happy. Why do you always want to take what's mine?"

"I don't want Daniel. Please keep him." I shrug—my bad. I can understand where she is coming from, I guess, but that has never been my intention. I only tried to stop her from hurting Harry. I never set out to hurt Liz. Even after she kicked me and continually encouraged others to kill me and she stabbed me with fucking silver. Yet I'm the problem? She's such a psycho.

"Don't blame my true mate. It was never about you—you approached me, remember? Do yourself a favour and shut the fuck up," Daniel snarls. "Once that kid drops, I'm selling you to a hyena shifter. He knows just how to deal with women like you. He will have you trained. I might have your tongue cut out. It would be so much better if you couldn't speak. I quite like that in my women." Daniel grabs Liz roughly by her shoulders and shakes her.

I watch him with growing horror. The men around him don't bat an eye.

"Hey, dickhead let her go!" I shout. Out of the corner of my eye, I can see Harry going nuts. Usually I wouldn't be bothered, but if she is that pregnant that she waddles, Liz must be almost ready to pop.

"You were always only going to be the second choice—hell, you'll always be the last choice. I wouldn't have touched you if I wasn't grieving. I always planned to sell you. I'm not crazy enough to want you around forever. Put her in the car."

Liz screams. She tries to scratch Daniel's remaining eye with her nails. He grabs hold of her wrists to stop her. Two of Daniel's men rush forward and force a growling, spitting Liz back into the front of the vehicle. One man stands guard against the car door.

I wonder if that's the same dead hyena shifter, Barry, that lost his head in the woods? If it isn't, I will be hunting him down.

"Now the ward. I wanted that ward removed ten minutes ago!"

A guy moves into Daniel's view; he shifts from foot-to-foot anxiously. "Sir, the, urm...the ward is Fae magic, sir, I won't be able to remove it," he says, wringing his hands, his body visibly shaking.

"You're all useless," Daniel mutters. "Well, Forrest, I'm glad I brought your beloved brother with me. Liz told me about how much you care for and love dear Harry. I wanted to give you a pack reunion." Daniel waves his hand to indicate my old pack. Jason steps forward, pushing Harry. At least that explains the mystery of why Harry's here. *Nice one, Liz.*

I turn my full attention to my two stepbrothers. Jason looks at me with pure hatred. It's rare for the puppet to show emotion. I give him a small wave. *Yeah, that makes two of us, buddy—you're a dead man walking, and you don't even know it.* I frown at Harry. He is bleeding, bruised, and his left arm hangs at his side, broken. I can't do anything for him yet, but I will.

"So you have a choice, little wolf. Come out from behind your ward and come with me, or I'm going to kill Harry here." Daniel grabs hold of Harry by his hair, and one of his men hands him a silver blade.

"Hey, little sister." I want to roll my eyes at the term, but now isn't the time. "Don't you be going anywhere with these bastards—stay where you are. Better yet, go into the house, lock the door, and call for help—" Daniel wallops Harry in the face with the handle of the knife, cutting off his words. Harry groans. I cringe.

Jason continues to stare at me with dead eyes full of hatred, not sparing one glance at his younger brother. "You always were a selfish bitch. Nothing is going to happen to Harry unless you don't leave with Daniel," Jason says in a high, nasal voice. The normally stoic shifter is usually not one for talking—no wonder; his voice is worse than mine. "Do as you're told for once in your life—save Harry. Sacrifice yourself. God, it won't cost you anything apart from opening your legs, and that's all you are good for anyway." I think this is the most words the quiet, creepy shifter has ever said; it's like Vincent is speaking through him. I can't help my shiver. "I've seen you on the news playing the warrior—the Fae token shifter. You're no hero. You're a coward. Still the same feral dirty wolf that we had to lock up in a cage for years."

I ignore Jason's rant. I yawn; I couldn't care less what he thinks. Why everybody thinks that I'm responsible for everyone else's actions is beyond me. Yet it's always my fault.

I'm done giving a shit.

"What did you mean when you said I was made for you?" I ask Daniel instead.

Daniel smiles. The softness that floods his blue eye is disconcerting. He enjoys my attention. "Little wolf, you were made for me, my true mate. Everything was designed by magic to be perfect." Daniel waves his silver knife in the air. "For me. For my needs. You are my fated mate.

"I wanted the best. Faster, stronger, smarter, and look at you... forged in fire. Made of steel." Daniel pushes Harry's face against the ward and traces my outline along its surface with the tip of the blade. A strange, manic smile plasters his face; the creepy smile is slightly lopsided due to the scars on his face. "Little wolf, haven't you worked it out yet? I paid that demon to take you when you were a child."

CHAPTER
FORTY-FIVE

I WOBBLE ON MY FEET. I feel a little shell-shocked as I stare at Daniel's now-delighted, smug smile.

Daniel put my pack on that demon's radar. He caused the events of that day to unfold; it was him.

Bloody hell.

Shit, I can't believe I hadn't put it all together.

I rub my temple, and a hazy memory comes back to me: the demon in the car saying something about a council member buying me. What was it? I take a mental peek inside that box:

"Unfortunately I am the middleman for this transaction—you have been sold to a council member for an extortionate price. When you're more mature, once your body changes, you will drive him wild. Now that I have seen you...well, I have such a desire to keep you for myself." The demon bops me on the nose. I blink at him. *"I would have thoroughly enjoyed parading you in front of all the shifters. So exciting that a council member has bought you. Who knows your fate? I have a feeling you will be in my care for some time. Then your owner will come in on a proverbial white horse and rescue you—that's why all this is just so much fun."* He taps his fingers on the seat between us.

"I made a bargain to collect you. Your owner said nothing about

keeping our bargain a secret." The demon chuckles; he winks at me. "I might not be able to keep you, but I can sure mess things up a little bit. I do so hate happy ever-afters. So you will remember, young Forrest, that everything from now on is your owner's fault and nothing to do with me. Don't be taken in by his handsome face, that's a good girl."

Fucking hell.

Daniel starts to rant. "The demon took everything too far. He made a deal with your stepfather, greedy Dave, behind my back. His instructions were simple: to take you. One missing little shifter girl, I could have covered up. Not the death of a whole fucking pack. Your mother should have handed you over. I paid a hell of a lot of money to get hold of you. After a while, I realised if I wanted the job done correctly, I would have to do it myself." He stops talking and gives me that crazy, bright smile again.

"Oh, and the reason you were stuck in wolf form? Jason here kept slipping you rare, untraceable magic that stopped you from shifting back." Daniel chuckles and keeps on smiling, his silver blade tap-tapping on the ward. "I wanted you to gain access to your innate magic quicker. But to do that you had to suffer. You had to struggle. The more you struggled, the stronger your magic would eventually become. I also wanted you pliable and grateful." Daniel shakes his head, and his lips twitch into a snarl. "I was days away from rescuing you. I had everything in place. I had Jason reduce the dosage to almost nothing. Then, little wolf, you just had to go and to try help this idiot." Daniel smacks Harry's head on the ward. "You saved yourself. Thanks to that stupid bitch ruining my plans." He glances at Liz in the car with another snarl. "Little wolf, you will always be mine. I made you. I made you the only female hellhound in existence. Your fire magic, your ability to partial-shift? That is all down to me. I paid for you. Now I've come to collect." My eyes flick to Jason; his dead eyes don't show any emotion. But his lips curl up in a smug, satisfied smile. I take that as confirmation.

I blink back at Daniel.

What the hell? This is getting to be a little bit too much. I expected a hint of "muahaha," but not this!

Instead of rage or horror, the relief I feel is peculiar.

I knew I was different. Hell, stuck in my wolf form, I blamed myself. The partial shifts, my fire magic, the warrior markings. I was so worried, frightened about being a freak. But now it all makes a strange type of sense. For the first time, I know deep down that I'm going to be okay. It wasn't me, and I was never broken. It was Daniel all along.

It's all been the fault of the delusional wanker standing in front of me.

I give myself a little mental shake. I have to get back on track and wrap up Daniel's weird villain speech.

"Don't look so worried, little wolf, you're one-hundred-percent perfect. The magic inside you was left to build and is now giving you the most potent traits. You are unique. Our daughters will be incredible," Daniel continues smugly. "I'm days away from taking over the assembly—your time in Ireland is coming to an end anyway. So whether I take you today or next week, it's still going to happen." Daniel pokes his blade at Harry's neck. "The only difference is, Harry will be alive today, but he will be in the ground next week. Choose wisely, little wolf."

I tap my fingers on my cup as if I am thinking. Then I nod and say with a smile, "I think I'm going to choose option B." The chatter in my head lets me know we're a go on my signal.

"Option B...what the fuck are you going on about?" Daniel asks. He doesn't like my smile or my answer.

Aragon appears behind me. I hand him my cup and he kindly takes it out of my hand. "Thank you," I say with a small smile.

"What the fuck—" Daniel says.

"Now," I say out loud, and all hell breaks loose.

I hear the *thud thud thud* of falling bodies as the surrounding bad guys are taken out with my sleep potions. Three down, seven to go. At the same time, Owen, who is in wolf form, pops out of thin air and bites Daniel's calf.

God, I love magic.

Daniel drops his hold on Harry, and he tries to slash Owen with the knife that's still in his hand. Owen grabs hold of that arm and bites, effectively stopping his strike. Daniel shifts into a brown wolf. His clothing flutters to the floor, and they start fighting.

I call my flaming sword, and I leave the ward by vaulting over the gate.

I pull Harry to his feet and stand in front of him, then shuffle us both backwards. I back Harry up towards the wall and the safety of the ward. I twirl my sword, protecting us from anybody that's trying to get close.

"Forrest...where the hell did the fancy sword come from? You need to get to safety, Forrest..." Harry mumbles. Aragon unceremoniously grabs Harry by the back of the neck and plucks him over the wall.

"Get down on the ground," I shout. The anxious man who was supposed to deal with the ward drops to his knees and puts his hands behind his head, Six. I flick a potion at him.

"Where the fuck is our backup?" Jason screams, mashing his phone with his fingers.

"Are you talking about the twenty-eight guys who were surrounding the house?" I answer helpfully. "Yeah, they are not coming." I shrug, twirling my sword. "I dealt with them ages ago. Not bad for the Faes' token shifter," I say snidely. "You've got no backup. Do yourself a favour and get on your fucking knees and put your hands behind your head." The remaining four shifters look at each other, then completely ignore me. They start pulling out weapons.

Hello, flaming sword here! I huff. Sometimes I wish I looked scarier. Aragon clears the wall and joins me—*oh hello, handsome*. He is partly shifted, with his wings, fifteen-inch silver claws, and an impressive set of chompers on full display.

"I am getting impatient!" Aragon warns with a low growl. Smoke escapes his mouth in an intimidating fashion. The four remaining shifters immediately drop to their knees and prostrate themselves in submission.

I growl and raise an eyebrow at my dragon. Aragon shrugs and gives me a wink.

I hit them all with potion balls. I keep a careful eye on Jason, who's still standing—if you can call leaning against one of the cars and shaking like a leaf "standing." His wide eyes are fixed on Aragon. Owen and Daniel are still fighting, but Owen looks like he has the upper hand and he's just playing with Daniel.

Jason, seeing an opportunity, charges at me with desperation, a silver knife clutched in his hand. Aragon steps in front of me. His claws pierce Jason's chest.

I peek around Aragon's bulk and watch as the light leaves Jason's eyes. "Rot in hell, you evil bastard." I can't help the smile of satisfaction. God, I'm getting to be a bad person. "I had him, Aragon," I whine. "I could have done that myself." Aragon shifts back to fully human and leans down and kisses me gently on my lips.

"Nutty, I didn't want you to have to kill your old pack," Aragon says earnestly.

Jason was never my pack. He was just the guard to my cell. Jason had it coming, and it was only a matter of time before I hunted him down. I wasn't going to leave him alive after what he did to me. He would have always been a threat.

The black wolf that is Owen is standing over a prone wolf-Daniel. He has his jaws wrapped around Daniel's throat. Daniel whimpers his surrender. Owen backs away and shifts. Daniel also shifts back into his naked human form. He stands, glaring at Owen. There's a click of a car door opening, and Liz steps out of the car. Tears are running down her face.

She holds something in her right hand, cradling it between her breasts. Daniel has his back to her. Liz moves the object, and with a war cry, thrusts it into Daniel's back.

I realise too late that it's a silver blade. Liz has done what she does best: she has stabbed her supposed mate in the back. Liz pulls out the knife. Daniel makes a choking sound, and he turns to face Liz, a look of incredulity on his face.

"You can't sell me if you're dead, you bastard. I could have mated anybody, anybody! Yet I chose you. You with your deformed face! You lost power, money! Yet I stood by you. You couldn't help yourself from going after that whore, and for what? The possibility of a daughter? You are an idiot!" She ends her rant with a scream. The knife that is still in her hand goes back into Daniel, into his chest. She impales him another three times, following him down as he falls to the ground. Daniel's blood splatters across her face and neck.

The words *poetic justice* come to mind as I stand with my lips parted as Liz goes all-out slasher. Liz is also a victim of Daniel's. No, not a victim—I shake my head at that thought—a *survivor*.

Owen and Mac wrestle with her, trying to get the knife from her hand without hurting her. I give Mac a wave. I didn't know he'd arrived.

Madán strolls up, late to the party. Casually looking around, he raises an eyebrow at the manic woman. He gives me a smile and Aragon a nod.

"Status report, any casualties?" Madán asks.

"No casualties on our side, sir," Owen replies, having won and gained control of the blood-covered Liz. "But three fatalities—" he glances at Daniel—"four fatalities, thirty-six captured, plus this lady." Owen points his thumb at Liz.

"Good job. I will get them collected and handed over to the Hunters Guild for processing," Madán says with a nod. "Oh, Forrest, I have had a transfer request—a shifter called Owen? He named you as a reference? I guess that will be you..." Madán says, lifting an eyebrow at Owen. I beam a smile at him and Owen. Nanny Hound!

"Oh my God, yes, he's my friend! You'd be nuts not to take him. Please say you will? I am so excit—" I squeak in fright. Aragon picks me up and moves me away from a bloody hand that is stretching out towards me. Fuck me, that is some creepy shit. Daniel has managed to pull himself across the floor towards us, towards me.

A trail of blood follows behind him on the floor.

"You will always be mine. I've owned you since you were a child. I am your destiny, I made you." Daniel holds out his hand, and on what must be his last breath, he says, "Little wolf..."

His hand drops.

We all gawk at the now-dead Daniel on the ground—although I am kind of waiting for that classic final horror moment where he jumps up and tries to kill me. I shiver. Aragon pulls me tighter to him.

I can hear Liz telling Owen and Mac, "I'm not a bad person. You do realise this is all due to pregnancy hormones. I had no idea what that man was up to. So that you know, I've got two young babies at home to look after—they need me. Plus one on the way. I am heavily pregnant, don't you know." I can't help feeling sorry for her and I'm worried about her kids. What's going to happen to her children?

"Why does that dog get away scot-free?" she whines. Honestly, she just can't help herself.

"'Dog'? If you are talking about Warrior Hesketh, the warrior is doing her job, protecting the innocent. Now shut up." Mac growls, "The Hunters Guild will want to speak to you."

Liz shrugs at the news. "I'm a pureblood shifter. The only place I will be going is to the next male. There's a new law that will protect me. 'Forrest's law'..." I can't help my rueful grin. The new law protects shifter women impartially, even if the woman is a horrible person. I have a feeling Liz is going to be okay. I watch as Liz is bundled into the back of a car. Mac slaps an anti-magic band onto her wrist.

I really hope I don't see her again.

Harry is crouching over Jason. Harry reaches down, and using two fingers, closes Jason's eyes. He stands and makes his way towards us. He holds his hand out to Aragon to shake, and after a pause, Harry drops his hand. Aragon grunts. I don't think Aragon likes Harry.

"May I?" Aragon narrows his eyes, then grudgingly nods. Harry pulls me into a hug. "Thank you for saving my life." I huff. Harry runs his hand through his blond hair. I glance up at Aragon, and he is glaring at Harry as if he is contemplating ripping his head off.

"Harry, Harry, I need you!" wails Liz from inside the car, tapping the window with her nails. Harry gives me a small smile and scurries away. *Bye then.*

I take a moment to think, and I feel...lighter. Vindicated. Many of the imaginary boxes in my mind have disintegrated, the memories losing the power to hurt me.

Aragon leans down and kisses me on the top of the head.

Everybody clears out. Owen goes inside to get changed. Madán gives us a nod. "Statement tomorrow, Warrior Hesketh. I will sort out the paperwork for your friend. The sleeping and dead bodies scattered around will be dealt with," he says as he leaves. Yay!

"Is it over?" I ask, leaning into Aragon's warmth.

"Yes, Nutty, it is over." He kisses my cheek.

"Can we go back to the glass house?" I like this little cottage, but I miss my first real home. I will also feel safer behind Aragon's ward. I miss our runs, plus Owen needs somewhere to live, and he'll love living in this cottage.

"Anything that you want, Nutty."

"Oh, can we get cake?"

"We will always get cake," Aragon answers.

THE END

CURSED DEMON

She enjoyed life as a demon's pet. Until the cries of an innocent tore her world asunder....

Emma Case is freaking out. Being surrounded by monsters is risky enough without breaking the rules, but when the softhearted girl hears a pup in distress, she can't resist trespassing on forbidden ground. And after discovering the unfortunate creature is a wolf-shifter, she's stunned when the child's pack accuses her of the crime and abducts her for interrogation.

Tortured for information she doesn't have, Emma pleads desperately for her handsome tormenter to believe her. Yet, as the naïve young woman tumbles deeper into the realm of supernatural intrigue, she unexpectedly manifests frightening powers she has no idea how to control.

Will Emma's hidden heritage prove a blessing or a bane?

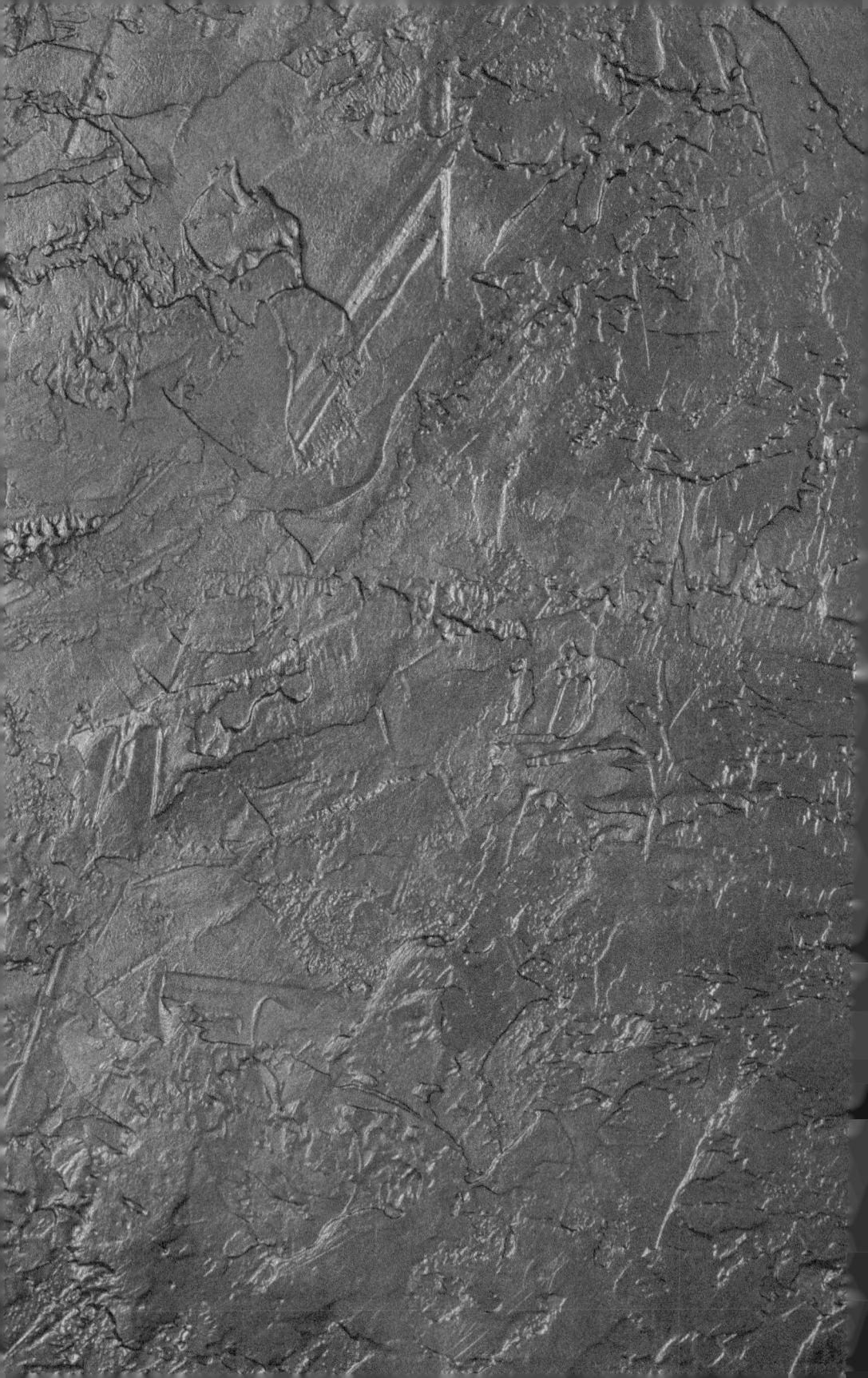

CHAPTER ONE

A LEAF FLUTTERS DOWN and he dramatically jumps to the side, his hooves scrabbling for purchase on the stone track. My heart misses a beat and for a fraction of a second my body tenses. *Keep him straight, keep him forward, chin high, breathe. Relax.* I repeat the mantra in my head over and over.

It's not helping.

Only one of us can freak out at a time, and it's never my bloody turn.

My vampire dressage trainer, Nuno, has sent us to ride around the estate to cool off after this morning's lesson. Nuno wants us to bond. Bond, ha, tell that to the snorting beast I am sitting on. Every little thing he can find is a grand excuse to spook. I'm trying my best to keep my posture elegant, pliable, to move with him and not to tense up, but I can already feel my shoulders creeping towards my ears. I let out a shaky breath and again force myself to relax.

The name on his paperwork is so fancy, it amuses me that he has the unfortunate stable name of Pudding. "Pudding," what a laugh. If you combined the energy of a fancy sports car with a hair-trigger bomb, you still wouldn't get the scary power of this horse. He feels like he is going to explode.

All. The. Time.

I love riding. But Pudding, my new gelding, is…urm…a challenge. We aren't clicking the way I thought we would. I know it's my fault as I want to ride Bob, my hairy Irish cob. I trust him and he trusts me, and we perform dressage like we are doing magic together. But I've been firmly encouraged to ride a 'proper' dressage horse, and both sides of Pudding's breeding are impeccable. He is made for dressage. I guess he just isn't made for me.

The beast underneath me shakes his head—my urge to get off is enormous. But then, Pudding would be worse with me on the ground —undoubtedly he'd stomp all over me. It doesn't feel it at the moment, but from experience, I know I'm still safer to be riding him. I roll my eyes. Bloody horse.

The day is beautiful. Morning sunlight filters through the trees above us, painting glowing stripes on the track—golden lines that Pudding keeps attempting to leap over. Yay, I'm having such a good time. *Not.*

Keep him straight, keep him forward, chin high, breathe. Relax.

The birds sing, and his hooves crunch rhythmically. I gently stroke his mahogany neck with my left hand, and he snorts out a breath.

For the first time, his head and neck start to relax. We both begin to relax. I puff out a sigh, and just as a smile touches my lips, a duck hidden behind the hedge to our left takes flight with a dramatic snap of wings and an echoing quack.

The whole hedge wobbles.

My eyes widen in horror and before the quack has even dissipated, Pudding springs into action, and we go from what feels like 0–60 miles per hour in a split second.

Oh hell.

No amount of pulling on the reins is going to stop Pudding's panicked flight. Instead, I bridge the reins in my hands so they don't get yanked from my grip, and I grab a handful of mane for good measure.

Oh bloody hell.

"Ooh, ooh, steady, steady," I say in a soft, lilting tone.

His hooves thunder beneath us, and the world is a blur of colours as it flies past at a breathtaking rate. My eyes water as the once-gentle wind batters my face. "It was a duck, silly boy, it's okay, it's okay. Steady boy, steeeaaadddy. I would never let anything hurt you, steady." Years of practice keeps the fear out of my voice.

It doesn't stop me from internally shrieking, *I'm going to die*, but Pudding doesn't have to know that.

Pudding's left ear flicks back, and his strides slow.

Oh thank God.

"Good boy, steady now, walk, whoa." His mad dash slows to a canter, a trot, then finally a bouncy walk. The energetic movement makes my boobs bounce, and my chest aches. Ow.

I fight the urge to slump in relief as I unlock my cramped left hand from its death-grip on the reins to stroke his now-sweaty neck. "Good boy, steady, walk." God, my entire body is trembling with the adrenaline that is coursing through me. I feel sick, and my mouth is dry.

But ha, I'm alive. *I'm alive.* I want to jump off and kiss the ground. Take that, universe. I'm alive. I giggle with relief. "I'm a master rider—" As soon as the cocky words leave my mouth, without provocation Pudding leaps and spins.

Oh crap.

The saddle is no longer underneath me. Catapulted, I find myself airborne. In what feels like slow motion, the ground meets my face. I crash to the floor with an *oof*.

Oh bloody hell.

Wheezing, I roll up onto my hands and knees and lift my throbbing head to watch Pudding's retreating bottom as he gallops away in what I hope is the direction of the stables. His hooves thunder into the distance, dee dum—dee dum—dee dum, without me. The urge to curl up into a ball and sob is huge.

"No, no. Oh, no, noooo," I whisper in disbelief. I scrape my gloved fingertips across the stone ground in frustration. Louder and with abject horror I shout, "Pudding, come back. Please come back. Pudding!" What if something happens to him? What if he gets tangled in his reins? "Oh my God, please don't get trapped in your reins," I cry.

I undo the chin strap and pull my riding hat off and rub my forehead with frustration. "No, no, no, no...this isn't happening. It's not bloody happening." The thought of him hurting himself, hurting his posh dressage-horse legs with his mad dash back to his friends at the stables, makes me dizzy with fear for him.

I rapidly blink to fight back my tears.

Instead, I force myself to get up. My legs wobble underneath me. Ouch—I think I've bruised my ribs. I press my hand to the sore spot and my hand also throbs in pain. My right palm underneath my glove is bleeding, although miraculously my handmade soft leather glove remains intact. I pull both gloves off and carefully tuck them into the waistband of my jodhpurs. I can't say the same for my favourite riding hat—it's scuffed and dented, and it will have to be replaced. It did its job. I give it an appreciative pat. I landed on my face; I could have easily been sporting that dent in my head instead of in the hat.

I plop it back onto my head.

I roll my shoulders and huff out a frustrated breath. The rest of me feels...okay...as okay as being chucked ten feet into the air and slammed down onto a stone track can be okay.

"Yeah, Emma, you're a master rider," I grumble. I wince as I pick a piece of gravel out of my bleeding palm. I turn and hobble in the direction Pudding fled. My ribs ache with the movement and my head pounds.

Gah, I am so stupid—I can't believe I left my mobile in my bedroom. What the heck am I going to do? A glance about, and I realise that our mad dash has taken us far away from the usual hacking route and into an area of the estate that I haven't ventured to explore before.

I shouldn't be here.

In the world I live in, magic is commonplace, with all manner of supernatural people: shifters, demons, witches, vampires, and an abundance of fae. But there's a divide among the races—creature versus creature, with humans like me struggling to survive. It is all about the strong against the weak. It is all about power.

I kick a small stone. Humans like me do as we are told. To stay alive, we follow the rules. Barely tolerated, we are an afterthought to the powerful creatures around us. It has always been that way, since the beginning of time. I'm human and weak, but I'm also an anomaly: no one knows what my human breeding is mixed with. Combined with how I look...I roll my eyes. Everyone covets beauty. In this dangerous patriarchal world, with the tricks that I can do I'm a prize. Enough of a prize to gain the attention of a first-level demon and a measure of protection. *All* I need to do is follow his rules.

Bloody hell, I shouldn't be here.

I swallow. My mouth and throat are dry. I hunch, and I keep walking. Hopefully no one will find out I ventured into a restricted area.

The trees stir with the breeze, revealing a bright-white building. It shows up in my peripheral vision to the left.

I look towards where Pudding has disappeared and then look left at the mystery building. Huh.

A niggly voice inside my brain tells me, *Go look. Get help.*

It is a terrible idea.

I drum the tips of my fingers on my thigh. I look at the building and then back at the track. Pudding will be back at the stables now, and I have at least a thirty-minute walk to get back to him. If I can find a phone and ring Sam at the yard, hopefully she can keep a lookout and grab him before anything further happens to him.

I nod; it is a good idea.

With my mind made up, I turn, grit my teeth, and barge my way through the trees. I drop my head so the dense branches scrape against my dented riding hat and not my face. My riding boots slip on the loose earth, and I almost fall as I scramble down a soft soil embankment and head towards the building. With each step towards my goal, my heart beats a little faster. It's now hammering in my ears. My breath puffs out of my mouth a little more with every stride I take.

I should not be doing this.

Why am I doing this? Pudding, that's why. God, my horses will be the death of me. I shake my head and keep walking.

The white building is large and squat-looking, with no windows. As I have some creature DNA, I can sense magic. So as I cautiously hobble toward the building, I can feel the magic surrounding it. The perimeter ward buzzes. I feel it thrumming in my bones—the witch-made magic is usually enough to stop anyone not keyed to it from entering.

A ward is a magic force field. Wards tend to be golden in colour and shaped like a dome. They can give you a nasty shock or kill you, depending on the ward's purpose. They are designed to keep people out or keep people in.

This ward is a real piece of work; it crackles menacingly and flashes different colours as I get closer. The whole building screams *keep out, or else*—it's a killer ward.

With that helpful thought, I can't help the smug smile that pulls at my lips. At least I can do this.

I walk through the ward.

CHAPTER TWO

The magic slides off me like I don't exist. I might be mostly human, but my unknown father has given me some neat tricks. Magic has zero effect on me.

The unlocked front door soundlessly opens when I pull it. I stick my head inside and take a peek.

All is quiet.

I have an excellent excuse for why I'm here. But a feeling of dread fills me. Like a good demon's pet, I am well trained. Yet I am breaking another rule. I gulp.

I step into the dark corridor and let go of the heavy door. It automatically closes behind me with a *whoosh*. I jump forward to avoid the door almost smacking me on the bum.

The ceiling lights click on automatically with a hum. The harsh, bright light makes the now-grey corridor look worse, if that's even possible. Everything is grey: the walls, the floor—I tilt my head up—yep, and the ceiling. This place is grim, and I can't help the full-body shiver that racks me.

I stand in a square pocket of light. My nostrils flare, and like a proper nutter, I sniff loudly. I can't make out any scent. Not that my nose is any good —It's not like I'm a shifter or a vampire. Those creatures have an excellent sense of smell. But like a weirdo, I do it anyway. I can smell horse. I snort out a laugh. *What a dickhead.*

I shake my head in self-deprecation. I'm glad I'm alone so no one can see me make a fool of myself.

"Hello." I cough to clear my dry throat. "Hellooo, is anyone here? Hello? I fell off my horse, and I need to ring Sam at the stables. Hello?" My voice echoes back to me and my ears strain to hear a reply. Nope, nothing.

I shuffle down the corridor. Like something from a horror film, the lights come on with a buzz in front of me, and with a click, they turn off behind. It leaves me with a single square of light so I can never see what's in front of me or what's behind. Without windows, this building is like a grey tomb.

"Gosh, this place is so creepy." I shiver again. Halfway down, I find an office and bingo, a phone. *Yes.* I make my call.

"Hi, Emma...yeah. I've got the snorting, sweaty monster. What do you want me to do with him?"

My legs sag with relief, and I slump against the office wall.

"Oh, thank God. Oh, Sam, it was horrible seeing him gallop off like that. The stirrups flapping and the reins dangling. I felt so helpless. Is he okay?"

"I found him running up and down the fence line of the mares' field, snorting and screaming for their attention. Yeah, the daft bugger is fine. I'm glad you rang; I was about to do a security alert and send the guards out to search for you. I was so worried. Where are you? Why didn't you answer your phone?"

"I left my phone in my room—I didn't think I'd need it." I nibble on my lip and ignore her question about where I am. The less she knows, the better. "Would you please hose him down and check his legs? I should be back before you've finished if I hurry."

"Yeah, yeah, I'll pamper the shit out of him, not that he deserves it. Are you okay?"

"I need a new riding hat, perhaps new ribs," I mumble, then say with a contrite huff, "I'm fine, I'm fine. It was my fault, not Pudding's. I feel like a right idiot."

"I don't know why you feel like an idiot. It's not your fault that silly old vampire told you to hack the monster of a horse out for a cooldown. That man has a sadistic streak a mile long. I knew it was a mistake for you to ride out on your own. Look, I will sort this beast out for you *if* you promise to go have a hot bath. Hopefully the warm water will help with the bruising. You don't think you've broken your ribs, do you? Ribs are the worst. I promise, Em, Pudding is fine. Please take care of yourself, and just this once let *me* help you." I assure Sam that my ribs are just bruised, and we end the conversation with my reluctant agreement to have a long soak in the bath.

I have a feeling I won't be able to stop myself from checking on Pudding later. Not that I don't trust my friend, but I know I won't be able to relax if I don't see him with my own eyes. At the moment all I can see when I close my eyes is Pudding tear-arsing away.

I shake my head with disgust. I should have at least kept hold of the reins.

I head back down the corridor to the exit. As I hobble, I force my glum mood away. It happened, and Pudding is safe. I feel like we've both had a lucky escape today. It could have been a lot worse.

I hear a strange noise; I grind to an abrupt stop. I tilt my head to the side, hold my breath, and listen.

I can hear a...a dog...I think. Yeah, I can hear a dog crying in pain. I don't even contemplate my next action. My feet instinctively follow the sounds of distress. My love of animals overrides any common sense that I might possess.

I hurry down the grey-on-grey corridor. The hum of the creepy lights follows in my wake, each square of light clicking on and off as I progress. My ears strain as I follow the cries. Goosebumps rise on my arms.

I stop when I come to an ominous-looking solid-steel door. I think this is where the sound originated. A standard gold ward wavers in front of the doorway. I swallow and nibble on my lip; I hold my breath and listen. Yes...this is the room. I've found the source of the cries.

What are you doing, Emma? Making a phone call is one thing; poking around in locked, warded rooms is quite another. Of all the mistakes I have made, this may be my worst one yet. I gulp. I should not be doing this.

This is the point of no return. I shuffle forward, then thrust my hand into the ward; it parts around my fingers. I grip the doorknob. "Please don't be locked...please be open," I whisper as I twist. The door clicks, and with a hard shove, I swing the door open.

The light from the corridor spills into the room. Cautiously —I do have some semblance of self-preservation—I keep my toes on the other side of the golden ward so it's between me and whatever is in the room. Slowly, my eyes adjust to the dim interior.

"Oh." My heart breaks at the sight of the puppy. The fluffy, cream-coloured puppy with red tips on its fur is huddled in a ball in the far corner. I rub my chest, and my eyes fill with tears. "Poor baby." Without thinking, I hustle into the room. "Oh puppy, please don't cry." The tiny puppy—no, I'm wrong, the creature's wild energy tickles at my senses—the tiny *wolf shifter* lifts its head, and my gaze meets big, soulful green eyes. Green eyes filled with pain. The shifter continues to cry as it crawls across the concrete floor on its belly towards me. My heart misses a beat and a lump forms in my throat. The cries and the fear rolling off the shifter pull at something deep inside of me. Without thought or worry that the pup is going to chew my face off, I cover the distance between us and drop to my knees. I scoop the shifter pup into my arms. I ignore the pain in my ribs as they scream in protest. This puppy needs me.

A quick undercarriage glance, and I realise the shifter is a *girl*.

Oh, no. Oh bloody hell.

I swallow the building lump of now-fear in my throat. Female shifters are as rare as rocking-horse poop. Oh heck, I've stumbled into an impossible situation. *Wars* are fought over female shifters.

The pup buries her head in my neck, digging her front paws into my collarbone as she scrambles to get closer. Each breath she takes and the subsequent cry she makes tugs at my soul. Her puppy breath tickles the hairs on the back of my neck. A frightened tear runs down my cheek, and I rub my face against the shifter's soft fur to hide it.

"It's okay, it's okay. I've got you, it's okay. I am going to help you get home, you're safe now. I'm going to do my best to get you home," I whisper, swallowing the lumpy clump of fear that is now stuck in my throat. I rock her in my arms.

Both of us tremble.

I rock her and stroke her soft fur. Finally, after a few minutes, her whole body sags, and she stops that awful crying.

I feel her trust.

Total trust. In. Me.

I grit my teeth as a quiet rage slithers through me. Fire sparks in my chest. It's my automatic response to bullying, to injustice, and a quintessential need in me to help the underdog. She can't stay here.

She can't stay here, not in this room, and not on the demon's estate. I'm...I'm a pampered pet, but others...they are not so lucky. I have to do the right thing.

This shifter needs *me*. I clutch her soft, furry body to my chest, and determination thrums through me. The need to keep her safe is almost overwhelming.

If I don't get her out of here, something bad will surely happen. Leaving her isn't an option.

That kind of black mark on my soul? It is not something I'm willing to live with.

"It's much easier to fight your way out of trouble than to fight a guilty conscience," I mumble to her. I hug her to my chest and smile sadly. Another tear rolls down the side of my nose. I *was* the girl who always played by the rules, not because I'm perfect, but because I learned to *play* perfect. A neutral, calm, elegant facade. It has kept me relatively safe.

God, I'm going to be in serious trouble for doing this, but sometimes you have to do what you think is right. Even if you are punished for it in the end.

And I will be punished.

Yep, I am breaking all the rules today.

CHAPTER
THREE

Again, my freaky thing with magic works to my advantage. As we hurry out of the building, the ward slides over us. So far, so good. I have found that the trick seems to work for anything or anyone that is touching me.

I hurry towards what I hope is the west boundary of the estate. My sense of direction is appalling, and it is even worse after my rollercoaster ride on Pudding. My brain feels like Pudding stuffed it into a washing machine on spin. With each step, the shifter gets heavier and heavier in my arms. Any time I even think about putting her down, hoping she will follow me, she cries. My arms feel like they are going to drop off, and my ribs...God, my poor ribs... *Suck it up, Emma.*

I hobble along. My heels feel painfully red-raw, undoubtedly bleeding as my handmade riding boots rub them. These boots are not made for walking; they especially are not made for tromping through trees and scrambling over walls.

We slink passed another ward, the last one—which surrounds the whole eight-hundred-acre estate—and we end up down the road at a local grocery store.

The shop is sandwiched between a kebab shop and a Chinese takeaway. My legs almost buckle with relief when I realise the shop is open.

I peer about and puff out my cheeks. All it would take is for someone who works for the estate to notice us and everything I've done so far, everything I've risked, would be lost.

I have never done anything so stupid or so brave.

As luck or fate would have it, we bump into a shifter. The pup sniffs the air and wiggles in my arms, also sensing the shifter.

The guy gives me a flirtatious smile. "Fuck, you're hot. You lost your horse, blondie? You can come and ride this—I will even let you whip me." He cups his groin and thrusts his hips at me. My mouth drops open, and my nose wrinkles with disgust.

Ewww, what an idiot.

This right here is why I prefer my horses over people—at least their shit comes out the right end.

I resign myself to fate and the fact that this horny shifter is all the help we currently have. No one else is around and needs must. I can only hope and pray that he doesn't do anything stupid. Like, attempt to kidnap me or the pup. "Can you help us?" I say in an urgent tone. "I need to get in contact with *her* pack." I widen my eyes meaningfully and nod down at the wiggling bundle of fur.

It's as if I've said the magic words.

The shifter snaps to attention. His focus switches from me and the rude stuff undoubtedly going on in his head to the female shifter in my arms. His nostrils flare, and his eyes comically widen. He promptly backs away from us with his palms in the air.

"Oh, fucking hell. Oh, fucking hell," he says, shock and panic lacing his tone.

Oh no, oh God, he looks as if he is going to make a break for it. I step forward in a vain attempt to stop him. Instead of running, he digs into his jacket pocket and fumbles for his phone. He holds a finger up for me to wait. "Sir, that missing pack you are hunting…I think I've found one of the kids."

AFTER WE'VE both guzzled down some water, I find a safe place in the shop to wait while the nervous shifter stands guard. I sit on the floor in a dusty corner with my back propped up against a buzzing fridge. In this position, I can see the door, and through a handy gap in the shelves I have an excellent view of the street.

Now that I have stopped moving, my entire body feels like one enormous bruise. My feet are throbbing and my long boots are digging into the back of my knees. I daren't take them off, so my poor feet and ankles will probably swell like balloons.

The shifter pup crawls across me and curls up on my lap. I unconsciously stroke her fur as I fret about what is going to happen to me when I get home. The anticipation. God, there is a peculiar agony to waiting, when you know something terrible is going to happen at the end.

The demon sees everything.

I regularly glance at the shop's clock. Time seems to have sped up.

I need to get out of here.

The longer I'm away from the estate, the worse things are going to be. But I can't seem to force myself to leave, not until I can see with my own eyes that she is safe.

"They are here," says the gruff voice of the shifter as three black Land Rover-style cars pull up to the kerb. I struggle back to my feet and scoop up the pup. My riding hat and gloves, I leave on the floor. I will grab them in a moment.

I watch with nervous interest and a smatter of relief, happy knowing that I can finally hand over my furball to somebody who knows what they're doing. The car doors open, and what I can only describe as a squadron of men spill out onto the pavement.

Unease skitters through me, and the small hairs on my arms rise.

Wearing black fatigues, loaded down with shifter-killing silver weapons that catch the sun and glint in its light, the men who exit the cars aren't standard shifters. No, the fatigue-clad men who exit those vehicles are in an altogether different class. A predator class of their very own. My relief turns from nervous trepidation to abject horror.

They are bloody hellhounds.

"Oh my God, you didn't tell me they were hellhounds," I say to the shifter with a squeak.

Hellhounds are powerful shifters with rare fire magic, the shifter council's elite fighting force. I've never seen a hellhound before. I don't really want to see a hellhound again. My pulse picks up, and my fear wafts off me in waves. It's something that I can't control...heck, any sane person would freak the fuck out. Hellhounds. What my now-pounding heart can attest to is that hellhounds are *scary*.

What the hell—pun intended—have I gotten myself into?

Ten pairs of eyes lock onto my position. The hellhounds fan out. Frightened butterflies crash against each other in my belly, and my heart pounds so hard it feels like it's going to explode out of my chest.

Oh bloody hell.

I have the urge to slap myself silly. I've made a colossal mistake—I know it instinctively. Alarm bells are going off like clappers in my head. I groan. Why did I think I could just drop off the shifter pup and skip back to my life?

I didn't think. I am an idiot.

I got so caught up with fear over what the *demon* will do to me, I forgot about other dangers. For my stupidity, I blame my fall from Pudding and the blow to my head.

Keep your eyes down. Try your best to be invisible. Only speak when you need to. Hand the pup over, and at the first opportunity, run.

In the big bad world of creatures, you have the powerful, and then you have the prey. Ha, I know which category I firmly fall into. These hulking monsters that prowl towards me, that tower up above me like army-clad trees, are at the very top of the power scale. They're on a godlike level.

I'd rather sit on Pudding while he bolts down a motorway than stand here with ten hellhounds advancing. Hunting.

Hunting. Me.

Oh my God. I stand trembling in the shop doorway and keep my eyes respectfully lowered. Out of the corner of my eye, I watch as the hellhounds continue to approach. The shifter that called them is bouncing from foot to foot. I wouldn't be surprised if at any moment now, he didn't drop to the floor and prostrate himself in submission.

Come to think of it, *that* sounds like a good idea. Throwing myself on the floor while wailing, "Please don't kill me." Yeah, begging for mercy might be the way to go.

My heart pounds faster and faster. Yet I force myself to stop trembling and keep still, so still. I'm afraid to even breathe too loudly.

I need to get a grip on myself. I slam my eyes closed, like a coward. I welcome the comfort of blackness to the view of the encroaching hellhounds. I hug the little shifter to me in a vain attempt at unrepentant self-reassurance. She stirs in my arms. I open my eyes and glance down. Her bright green eyes blink up at me. Her little tongue comes out, and she licks underneath my chin. "Eww, puppy spit. Thanks for that," I say with a small smile. I return the sentiment with a quick kiss to the top of her head. "You're worth the hassle of this living nightmare, pup." *I think.*

The biggest, meanest hellhound shoulders himself through the others, and they part for him like a wave. I forget to keep my head down and instead I slowly trail my eyes over his massive form as he prowls toward us. The scowl he wears makes him look *petrifying*.

God, but he is handsome—handsome in the way deadly creatures are. I take a deep breath and try to ignore how my body quakes in fear. His wild, masculine beauty only serves to make him appear more lethal. His aggressive hellhound energy hits me with the force of a double-decker bus. I'm surprised I don't see it crackling in the air between us.

This creature is downright terrifying.

"What the fuck did you do to her?"

My surprised gaze flicks up to his. Familiar but livid green eyes meet my own. His glower is like the slash of a knife. I tamp down the urge to check if I'm bleeding. Those eyes—there is no doubt in my mind that he is related to my pup. I've found her pack. Stupidly, I give him a tentative smile.

"Are you dense? I asked you a question. What the fuck did you do to her?" he barks again. I drop the smile and gulp. His face, his face is angelic, proud. He is almost too much to look at. Too beautiful, too breathtaking, too ominous...

Whoa, I'm so confused. This is not a normal reaction to a gigantic monster of a man who is so angry he's almost frothing at the mouth. Has he got some freaky hellhound attraction magic that I'm not aware of? I am supposed to be immune.

I shouldn't feel anything but fear when I stare into his green eyes. I force myself to look away rather than ogle. I know better than to make eye contact with this man.

Why the hell did I look him in the eye in the first place?

I drop my eyes to his chin.

"She smells of horse. Is that intentional? To mask her scent?" one hellhound says in the background.

"What. Did. You. Do," he growls. I jump and glance down at the pup in my arms, not understanding his question. "What have you done? How can she be in wolf form? She is a nine-year-old child."

Oh, wow. My eyes widen. *Oh, I see.* I know that born shifters do the whole shifting thing in their twenties. I can see with my own eyes that she is tiny. I want to smack myself on the forehead for not putting those two things together.

Poor pup.

All I can do is shrug—well, I try to shrug, but my rigidity makes the motion look strange. I have no idea what happened to her.

I want to hunch into myself, but I force myself to keep rigid and stand straight. His scary presence seems to require good posture. I might be mostly human, but I have my pride. I might feel like prey, but I don't have to act like it.

"I'm sorry...I don't know...I found her like this and came straight-away to get her help. I don't know anything else. I'm glad she is safe, but I need to get home." My voice drifts away into mumbles. *Gah, nice one, Emma. Very assertive.*

The hellhound crosses his arms. He taps his massive hand against his forearm in a rhythmic motion and narrows his eyes when it becomes apparent to him I have nothing further to add.

I swallow again. Pure fear is clawing at my throat.

I need to get home.

Ha, I talk a good game, but now I'm hunching for all my worth in an attempt to hide my shaking. With shifty eyes, I quickly search the hellhounds, looking for...looking for...there. Him. One hellhound is quietly watching the proceedings like a rock in a rolling storm, seemingly unaffected by the masculine rage of his peers.

I kiss the top of her head. "Goodbye, pup. Be brave, be safe, and be happy," I whisper. She whimpers as I shuffle meekly towards the hound

I have chosen and hand her over to him. He has kind grey eyes; they stand out against his dark skin and hair. He takes her gently in his massive arms. I brave a final stroke of her fur. Then I skitter away.

"Where did you find her? Where is the rest of my pack?" asks the scary hellhound as he follows me with his eyes. He looks me up and down, taking my measure, and his lip curls with disgust. Oh yeah, he finds me lacking.

I self-consciously adjust my top and the waistband of my jodhpurs. Since puberty, I have never had a man look at me with anything other than interest or poorly concealed lust. Not very nice, but unfortunately it's the world that we live in. This guy looks at me as if he wouldn't think twice about pulling my head off and using it in a game of football.

I'm a thing to him, not a person. A thing that is in his way.

I take in a shaky breath, lift my chin, and meet his eyes head-on.

I am not a thing.

"I didn't see anyone else. I hope you find your pack. I really do. I am sorry, but I can't be of any further help. I really have to go." My voice is quiet, but I'm proud to say I keep it even, strong, resistant.

I can't explain where I found her—I can't give any details that would implicate the demon. Not out of loyalty, but self-preservation. You don't snitch on the people that are your prime protection. *You don't break their rules, either,* the helpful voice in my head pipes up. *Mhm, thanks for that.* Heck, I have to get out of here. I back away as Mr Angry Hellhound advances.

He steps into my personal space, dwarfing my five-foot-six frame. The humongous man must be almost seven feet tall, and his body is every bit as pleasing as his face. Massive shoulders, each arm bigger than the span of my waist. Body corded with slabs of powerful muscle. Narrow hips.

This hellhound is made to be feared.

I throw away my moment of false pride and bravery with a wobbly smile and an awkward double-thumbs-up.

I gave the scary hellhound double-thumbs.

Oh, God, what the heck am I doing? I fold my arms behind my back. Next I will be doing jazz hands. The hellhound growls and the look he throws me is one of pure, acrimonious rancour. I can feel his angry energy as it buzzes over my skin. He wants me dead.

Bloody hell, he is going to eat me. Like a packet of pork scratchings, there is no way I won't be tasty. Crunchy.

I gulp.

Why can't he say thank you, like a normal person? I didn't steal his kid. I barely refrain from opening my mouth and pointing that fact out to him.

"You refuse to answer me?" he asks, his voice quiet—deadly. I know that I've crossed some invisible line with him.

The two of us are staring each other down. I catalogue each thick bulge of muscle, not for its beauty but as proof of all the ways that he can hurt me. Stiffening, I straighten my spine and brace myself for the consequences. Which will probably be painful.

I hear a grunt, a thump, and the scrabble of claws on the pavement. Then a bundle of cream-and-red fur barrels around the hellhounds. My pup dives between the scary hellhound's legs and throws herself in front of me.

"For fuck's sake, Owen."

Adorably, she growls and snaps her teeth.

"Sorry, John, she bit me," the grey-eyed hellhound says, poorly hiding his small smile, which is directed at my pup and her adorable antics. She turns her head and gives me a look as if to say, "Go on then, run."

I spin and run into the shop. Like an idiot, I waste precious seconds grabbing my hat and gloves—I don't want to be accused of being a litterbug. I was eyeing the back exit before, and that door is now calling my name. I need to get home.

There is a sound behind me.

Before I can turn, I feel a sharp blow to the back of my head, and then darkness.

CHAPTER
FOUR

Blood pools in my mouth. It dribbles from my cracked, swollen lips and drips lazily down my chin. John—the hellhound—paces the outside of his hand-drawn, archaic circle...a circle he thinks he has trapped me in. He snarls. I roll my head back against the pillar, grinding the back of my head into the brickwork. Wearily, I keep my eyes on his prowling form.

I don't want to be here.

If I hadn't helped the female wolf shifter, I would be home in bed. But I did, and I'm not. I huff out a painful breath.

I don't want to be here...here in a hellhound's torture chamber. Everything hurts, my body is a mess, and I know, deep inside, that...that I'm done for.

I've been internally fighting myself, fighting my fear, fighting my own body, which is begging for me to close my eyes and let the blackness take me away.

My name is Emma, Emma, Emma. I repeat my name over and over again. It's my anchor.

I want to go home. I want to go home. Please, God, why are you punishing me? I'm not magical like other creatures.

I'm not strong or unique. I'm just me, half human with a mix of some unimportant creature. Nothing special. I lick my lips. My tongue feels oddly big in my mouth.

My lack of uniqueness didn't stop me from helping the female shifter, John's *sister*. It didn't stop me from doing the right thing, and doing so sent me on a direct path to this hell.

John wants information. Information that I haven't got.

Every decision in life has good and bad consequences. That saying? No good deed goes unpunished? Yeah, that should be my motto. Crap, perhaps I should have that tattooed on my arm to remind myself to think things through before I act. That is...if I ever leave this fucked-up situation alive.

My breath rattles in my chest. John narrows his eyes at the sound. "Fuck you," I mouth without any venom. My rude words are a poor attempt at bravery. A vocal shield. A cracked, broken shield. I try to hide behind it as the thick fog of terror rolls inside me. The cracks are spreading, and soon nothing of me is going to be left to protect. His disapproving expression only deepens at my silly word. He folds his arms, content to just watch me, a look of mild repulsion on his face. Yeah, the feeling is mutual, buddy.

I hate the pretty bastard.

Gosh, I really messed up this time, and now I'm reaping what I've sown.

No.

No, I have to be honest with myself. I knew. I knew things would go to shit when I helped that little pup.

I couldn't have imagined this, though, a *hellhound*. God, I thought my demon master would have been the one doing the punishing.

Not her *brother*.

I thought...I thought the shifters would be grateful...ha, I'm so naïve. Stupid. Stupid. Stupid girl. I am a kind-hearted fool. Doing the right thing, what would be the harm? A bit of risk to get my blood pumping?

Well, my blood is certainly pumping now, all over the bloody floor.

The daft thing is...I can't blame John entirely. The hellhound has shown himself to be a primordial beast with primitive black-and-white views. If I had a family...a pack and someone had taken them, hurt them, wouldn't I do everything in my power to get them home safe?

For a person I loved…I would burn down the world.

The entire world could burn, and I would pull them from the wreckage. That makes me a bad person, doesn't it?

I also can't help asking myself the question, would I make the same mistake John has, of not recognising innocence over guilt?

Ha, that's some serious Stockholm syndrome shit right there, Emma. I have way too much empathy.

Yeah, bloody pesky empathy.

I absorb joy and stress like a sponge. My nana—my mum's mother, was an earth witch. She had an incredible off the charts ability to communicate with the world around her.

Unfortunately, I inherited nothing witchy, as my weird immunity to magic isn't a witch trait. I like to think my empathy and love of animals comes from her.

My nana died when I was four, so my memories of her are fuzzy. When I think of her…I can remember flashes of warmth and love. My nana would have wanted me to do the right thing. Yeah, what would be the harm.

My chains clink. I wish I could rub my face. My wrists throb, a dull pain compared to the rest of my injuries. Can you call something an injury when it's inflicted by someone else? I don't know; my mind is slowly shutting down, just like my body.

When I first woke up chained to the pillar in a basement, I freaked out. Luckily I was alone, so the hellhound didn't get a front-row seat to my frightened thrashing. After that, I kept my dignity for those first few hours. Only my bleeding wrists told the story of my early struggle. Once I'd calmed, I got a better idea of my surroundings and my messed-up situation. Redbrick walls, discoloured at the bottom from damp. The damp was almost the same height around the room. It was like someone had drawn a line. To keep myself from freaking out further and to gain some semblance of control, I counted the bricks. Eight. Eight rows of the darker bricks. Except in the far corner, where I counted nine.

At the top of the wall directly in front of me, a half-circle window draws my gaze away from the hellhound and the strange hand-drawn circle at my feet.

Before, the window cast a perfect half-circle of light onto the dusty, mouldy floor. For hours I watched, chained to that pillar as the curved light moved with the sun. It slowly edged across the floor until it was almost gone. That was when the hellhound returned and subjected me to his ministrations.

"Demon, you will tell me where they are, the others you stole. My mother, my other little sister. You will talk, demon, or otherwise, things are going to get much worse for you." His voice is deep, soft, tipped with barely controlled anger.

Urm, how can things get any worse? The urge to manically laugh at this idiot, calling *me* a demon...*Not a demon, dickhead*, I want to scream at him.

Beg. Plead.

But my voice no longer works. A person can scream for only so long before their throat gives out.

I live with a demon, a first-level demon. I think *he* would have mentioned if I had any demon DNA. The reason my demon master likes me so much is the mystery of my breeding. I'm like a human equivalent of a lucky dip: you don't quite know what you're going to get.

John's a shifter so why can't he smell my humanity? I guess it doesn't matter anymore.

My tummy screams at me. I pant in pain, but I bite my lip so I don't cry out. So much pain, an endless ocean of it. With waves that try to engulf me—drown me.

I take a steadying breath and try to force down my nausea. The pungent smell of mould with the undertone of urine stings my nose. I gag, and the sick burns up my throat. Suddenly I projectile-vomit over myself and the floor like a character from The Exorcist. John makes a sound of disgust and walks away. I blink in shock.

In the dim light, it's pale green. Wow, that doesn't look good.

What does pale-green sick mean? Nothing good. His knife before... it must have internally nicked something. At least I emptied my bladder early on, and I don't have to live with the indignity of wetting myself *again*.

Sick, blood, and pee...what a combination to have on my skin. I hope John is enjoying the odour.

Not long now, the helpful voice in my head pipes up. God, everything hurts. The pain is a living thing clawing at my insides.

It would be so easy to let go.

Emma, just close your eyes.

No. I grind my head against the wall. The rough scratching that is almost white noise drowns out my wicked, unhelpful thoughts and the slow pounding of my heart.

My eyes drop. I glance at a dry spot on the floor wistfully. I wish... I wish I could sit down—the concrete looks mighty comfy. But I can't. The chains he has attached to my delicate wrists to hold me aloft will not let me. My legs are now useless noodles, unable to support the weight of the bag of bleeding meat that the hellhound has made of me.

I'm such a fool.

I'm such a fool that even now after everything that has happened, I would *still* have helped the pup escape.

I'm such a fool.

John spins back towards me, and my heart misses a beat as his big body steps over the chalk line and into the circle.

A circle he thinks will keep me from accessing my *demon* powers.

The circle pulses. I don't hear it, but I feel it. It reverberates through me. It echoes deep in my bones. Whatever magic it contains doesn't touch me.

Ha, still not a demon, dickhead.

His body dwarfs my own, and I lift my eyes to his. My throat bobs and the heavy chains rattle as a full-body shiver takes me. I am so cold.

He leans half an inch closer, his bright eyes full of the orange fire that is his fire magic. Those eyes are so terrifying. Yeah, beautiful and terrifying. Even after everything, he is still painfully beautiful. His proud cheekbones and that square jaw...unnaturally handsome, a vicious sort of beauty.

What is wrong with me?

I'm so confused—my attraction to him makes little sense —it's magically enhanced...it must be.

I flinch away as his hand reaches out, and he tucks a piece of my matted blonde hair gently behind my ear. He is so close, breathing deep, so warm...I feel the heat radiating off him and into me. Scalding.

"You dare to wear the disguise of a girl...you even smell human," he whispers intimately into my ear, his low words brushing against my skin like velvet. "Yet you do not fool me, demon." The hellhound cups my face. His fingers gently brush the underside of my jaw and he tilts my face up. His gaze searches mine. He has absurdly long, curly lashes, the colour of fine gold. "Death always comes. Even to something like you, demon, there is always a way." His hand drifts down to my neck, and he rubs his thumb up and down my throat. "You are a fucking curse on the world." I don't think he is aware of the way his thumb brushes back and forth over my jugular, testing my pulse. Until his thumb pauses. He frowns as if he doesn't like the feel of my weak pulse fluttering in his grip. "Tell me about my pack."

I swallow, and his grip tightens. I freeze. The prey animal in me recognises the danger of this beautiful man and the precipice of the thin ice I stand upon. To have fire magic, to be a hellhound, he has to be an old, powerful shifter. I see the violence and age in his eyes. A thousand years of battle, war, and pain. My heart hurts for him, for the loss of the man he could have been. So many deaths, so much pain. It has turned him into a monster.

In the quiet times like this—between his violent attentions—I usually talk. I tell him everything about my life.

Everything.

Nothing is off limits. Almost every thought I've ever had in my head waffles out of my mouth. I tell him. Our time is so intimate. He knows me better than I know myself. Yet he doesn't believe a word I say. God, I tried my best to convince him. Before my screams robbed me of my voice, that is. Now I have no voice left to talk, I have nothing else to say, to prove. This hellhound has cut me open, and my secrets have poured out. He has ignored every single one, picking through them with disinterest and grinding them beneath his boots.

Who I am doesn't matter.

His presence is intense. Now that I can no longer speak, we communicate with energy alone. It vibrates around us.

When I continue to ignore him, his eyes flame with his fury. "I'll let you heal if you answer my fucking questions," John bellows. He tightens his hold on my throat and slams his fist into the pillar beside my head. My ears throb as his angry voice echoes around the room, and my insides feel like they have liquefied. I slow-blink. A mixture of blood and sick bubbles from my lips.

I try one last time.

I widen my eyes and try to plead with him, plead to the logical side of the man, the rational side trapped inside him, caged in by the monster. John curls his lip and continues to stare at me, his dislike nearly palpable.

John knows magic doesn't work on me. I explained it all to him, yet he mockingly still believes that I'm the mastermind behind his stolen pack. That I'm a demon.

"I will let you heal *if* you answer my questions..."

I close my eyes in defeat. No matter what the monstrous hellhound wants, I can't answer those questions.

How can I answer them when I don't know?

I feel his breath against my cold face—hot breath. My own breath rattles. He lets go of my throat. A click and a rattle, and with deft hands the hellhound releases my wrists from the chains.

With my hands free of the chains, my useless body flops to the floor with a bang. My head hits the unyielding concrete with a *crack*. My already dodgy, fading vision goes black.

Wow, you really do see stars, I think as my vision comes screaming back with multicoloured flashes of light. I think of all the cartoons I watched as a kid that I scoffed at, and I mentally apologise. Stars are a thing.

The hellhound growls with poorly concealed contempt.

I lie where I've crumpled. Compared to everything else, the pain from the blood rushing to my newly released wrists, arms, and shoulders fades into the background. Wow, wishes do come true. Didn't I wish for the comfort of the floor?

I settle in and watch John prowl towards the edge of the circle. Deliberately he smudges the hand-drawn lines with a shiny boot.

What is he up to now?

"No tricks, demon." Yeah, 'cause I'm so sneaky. "Crawl. Leave the circle, heal yourself. Crawl, demon." I give him a look of what I hope is total incredulity at his ridiculous demand. Crawl? Is he taking the piss? Perhaps a few hours ago, but now? What would be the point? Not that I can heal myself here or on the other side of the stupid, useless demon-trapping circle. *Still not a demon.*

Mhm. Do I attempt to crawl…offer the very last of my dignity?

No.

No, the floor is the softest I've ever felt, I'm happy to stay here.

Die here.

In response to my lack of movement—in John's mind, I guess I should scuttle across the floor like a demon cockroach —he strides back towards me, grabs hold of my ragged top, and drags me across the floor, onto the other side of the circle.

I moan in pain. I scream in my head.

"Heal, damn you," John barks. I can feel more blood soaking into my ripped top—the fabric sticks wetly to my skin. He runs his hand through his short, blond hair in frustration. He looks down at me, his legs wide apart, his big muscly arms across his broad chest. He drops his chin. John taps his fingers against his forearm impatiently. He waits.

He waits.

Bloody hell, John, you'll be waiting a long time. The breath rattles in my chest. My heart slows. I can't take a full breath.

I didn't realise that the human body had the ability to feel so much pain. A person could go mad. I thought, wrongly, that after a while, your body would shut down, that the nerves would stop firing and then everything would become one big…well, I imagined it would be like being wrapped in cotton wool. Muffled. Perhaps it's me and my creature DNA that keeps the pain so vivid?

Oh God. Oh God. Oh God, make it stop, please, please make it stop.

"Why aren't you healing?" His fiery eyes have turned green. He prods me with his foot. *Careful, John, you don't want to get your shiny boots dirty,* I think dimly.

I wonder if when the sun rises, I'll be lying in the half-circle of light...I'd like that. Will it touch my face?

I guess I'm done.

"Why aren't you healing?" He drops into a squat and pushes the hair away from my face. He stares intently at me and lets out a low growl. I can't respond —nothing works. After a few seconds, John picks up on my broken state. "You piece of shit. You fucking manipulating piece of shit."

I blink. Each time I open my eyes, the time between gets longer and longer.

If you fall asleep, you will die.

That is okay. I'm ready.

I don't notice that John has left until he returns with a potion vial. He tips the whole thing onto the skin of my throat; it trickles down the back of my neck. He might as well have splashed me with some water.

What a waste of a healing potion.

"Why aren't you healing?" he says again, and his voice has changed. Gone is the harsh whisper, and instead, I almost fool myself into thinking he is concerned.

"Why aren't you fucking healing."

Because.

Magic doesn't work on me.

CHAPTER
FIVE

I FLOAT INSIDE MY HEAD. Will I find peace? Is it over? This whole torture experience has been kind of cathartic. I guess there's nothing like a hellhound torturing you to find out what you're truly made of. A genuine fucked-up horrific experience of self-reflection. It feels as though I have lived a hundred different lifetimes with John—each one violent and bloody. I guess that is what terror and pain do to you—fast-track your soul.

Helping the pup has settled and redeemed something inside of me. For as long as I can remember, a rotten part of me has taunted, cajoled, whispered that when it came down to it, I would be exactly like her.

My mother.

Proud to say I'm nothing like you, Mum.

Ha, it always comes down to your parents in the end, doesn't it? Her lack of affection, lack of closeness, her poorly concealed hate, put a shadow over me. I was five when my mum sold me to a demon so she could jump the queue to become a vampire.

I forgive you, Mum.

"Emma, don't fall asleep." His voice...soothing and *agonised*.

I hate you, Mum.

BROGAN THOMAS

"Emma, don't you fucking dare."
I love you, Mum.
"She is not healing. We need to get her to a hospital."
I don't regret helping you, pup.

CHAPTER SIX

I WAKE. Huh, I'm alive. Oh, and now there's the cotton-wool–cloud-like feeling. I blink my eyes open to greet the world through a drug-fuelled haze. Colours sharpen enough for me to make out a face. A demon looms over me, his face still somewhat blurry.

"Arlo," I mouth. His blue-grey eyes that normally sparkle with devious delight are flat. His expression shows nothing, not even anger. I guess I've been unconscious for a while if he has gone from the spitting-mad "I'm gonna rip your throat out" stage to this calm, scary and uber-controlled phase.

I yearn for him to hold me, God, I want him to hold me. Stroke my hair and tell me that everything is going to be okay. That I'm safe and nothing will ever hurt me again, that he won't allow anything or anyone to hurt me.

The demon does none of those things.

Silly me.

Arlo runs a gentle finger down my cheek. "I had high hopes for you...you were my favourite. Look what you have done to yourself: broken. Broken beyond repair. If I wanted you broken, damaged, I would have done it myself," he says. Frowning, he rubs his thumb over his finger as if he is removing dirt from the digit, dirt from touching me. "You went and involved yourself in *my* affairs, in *my* business. Look at how that has turned out. Look what your kind heart did. You are ruined, and you did this."

I beg with my eyes for forgiveness, unable to say the words. It has no impact. Like it had no impact on John. I tremble and my tummy aches.

Arlo's eyes narrow, and his pouty mouth turns down. He steps away and walks towards a floor-to-ceiling window. My fuzzy gaze quickly takes in the unfamiliar room. It's made of glass—I feel a little like a fish in a tank. I presume we are in a hospital.

I shift a little and dull pain ripples across my torso. Ouch.

I go still. I wait for more pain but luckily, through the cotton-wool feeling imposed by the drugs, the pain remains a dull steady throb.

The demon turns, and my mind jumps a little. Did I miss what he was saying? Fuzzy. Everything is so fuzzy. "I hope you learned your lesson. I need not punish you when you did such an excellent job on your own. Your life has changed—your status in my household has dropped to the very bottom. Now you are a cautionary tale for the others. No one will step out of line for centuries. That is the *only* reason I won't kill you. I will keep you. Though I will never touch you again." He steps back to the bed, a fake, smug smile on his full, puffy lips. "I would have let you die. I don't like broken things." Arlo's eyes run across me, and he curls his lip. "The poor, poor hellhound is distraught—I can see the guilt eating him alive. Poetic really, two broken souls twisted together by fate, forever entwined." He waves his hand to indicate the room. "John Hesketh paid for all this, found a vampire surgeon that has a passion for non-magical intervention. The doctor butchered you to keep you alive."

Arlo chuckles. He leans closer and whispers, "Did John Hesketh play with you in an attempt to rescue his mummy? What secrets did you confess? Mmm? How long did it take? To destroy my pet?" He uses the tip of his nail to lift my chin. "Would you like to know something interesting, Broken Thing? While you received the hellhound's special attention..." he pauses dramatically and leans close, his icy breath fanning my face. Goosebumps break out on my arms. Arlo raises an eyebrow. His eyes sparkle with joy. "...They were already dead. His pack. Before he even met you, they were dead. Dead for over a week."

CHAPTER
SEVEN

The world is full of monsters with friendly faces and angels full of scars.
– Unknown

My surgeon, Mr Hanlon, is a miracle worker. I call him The Professor in my head. He is a vampire, short and thin with big, bushy grey eyebrows, and although his hair is short, it's wiry and sticks out at the sides. He looks like a mad professor. Quick to smile, he comes across as being quite strict, but he doesn't fool me—the man is a saint.

Most medicine nowadays is magical; medical equipment is a combination of magic and technology. Things that look like simple medical scanners are chock-full of magic. Magic is another useful tool in a doctor's arsenal. If someone breaks an arm, the bone will still have to be reset before the doctor applies a healing potion. Nobody wants to have to re-break bones when someone has used a potion too soon. Magic accelerates healing; it knits everything together and replaces tissue that is missing. Over the years, they have developed lucrative medical magic to cure most diseases and infections. Wounds that used to take weeks if not months to heal can now regenerate in minutes, lifesaving in combat or emergencies.

Healing potions work on beings of every race, even if they have ornate powers of their own. Healing potions work on everybody…except me.

Mr Hanlon says he has never met a person like me before: someone immune to magic, a magical void. Even he doesn't understand my freaky powers.

It thrills him, the challenge I present…well, after he got over his initial shock of me breaking a few of his expensive machines. Magic combined with technology can be temperamental, so add in my immunity and the hospital's fancy tech tended to implode.

The Professor was ecstatic to have performed my magic-free surgery, to dust off his training and theory. I can imagine in my surgery he had the ardent glow of a child left alone in Toys R Us with a credit card, and the words *buy whatever you want* fading in his ears. The opportunity to get his hands in and actually play around with my organs was a rare treat.

The weirdo.

He tells me at every opportunity that I'm his best work.

Of course, some people need alternative health care—mainly the rare, mostly purebred humans who are adamantly against the practice of magic, and people who can't afford treatment, as healing potions can be expensive.

When it comes down to it, it's really only humans, witches, and young shifters who need regular intervention by doctors. The other races have their own innate gifts for everyday healing.

I'm not too proud to say that I'm jealous—I wish I could magically heal.

I have been in the hospital now for over two months. For a small stab wound the damage was extensive, the knife shredded my appendix and some of my small intestine. I've had two major operations and a battle with sepsis. Frustratingly, no matter how many bags of antibiotics they pump into me, I still seem to get small, nasty infections. At one point, I dubbed myself Pus Girl as a joke. It was so gross, how much pus my body could produce. Litres of the stuff, gag.

But I'm alive.

To save my life, I have…I have an ileostomy, a stoma. Which is an artificial hole in my abdomen wall, where part of my small intestine has been pulled through, and it collects my faeces in a bag.

My Professor is confident, given enough time and adequate healing on my part, he should be able to put everything back.

The stoma sits on the lower right-hand side of my tummy. It's bright red, and it looks like a small rose. It's alien-like. The texture is like touching the inside of my cheek.

Yes, it is surreal.

Something that should be on the inside of my body is now on the outside.

I name the stoma Bert. I purposely treat Bert like a wayward life-saving pet. I won't go into details, but having a stoma can be messy. So having the mentality that it's *Bert's* fault when things inevitably go wrong has helped tremendously.

Bert is the naughty one, it isn't me. It's not me.

Everything still feels unreal. It is like I'm permanently trapped in a bad dream.

Why did this happen to me?

I guess naming Bert allows me to get over the shock of my *new normal*. Ha, "my new normal." God, I hate that phrase. I don't want this new bloody normal. I liked me just the way I was.

It's a challenge to fight the grief over the changes to my body. I guess I've lost myself a little. I've learned to be stronger in keeping optimistic about my illness, but I've lost some of my fire. I no longer feel as confident. I have a deep-seated need to not be near people. Instead of being that bubbly talk-the-ear-off-a-person, I've turned into somebody awkward.

I'm supposed to be a brave and independent woman. I rub the scars on my wrists, left over from the chains. It's one of the many strange habits and quirks I've developed. My scars randomly ache with the memory of the cold metal on my skin. I rub them to reassure myself that the shackles are no longer there.

Some days, it's like it has reduced me to a lesser person. I'm frightened all the time, and I hate myself for feeling this way.

I've always been a positive person, so I force myself to hold on to that positivity—clinging desperately to it with my fingers and toes. Any time bitterness tries to creep in, I forcibly push the destructive thoughts away.

So many scars. Inside and out.

I have to see them as life-saving. If I don't...well. In my waking moments, I don't allow myself much contemplation. I'm not so fortunate when I sleep.

The nightmares...they plague me. I have to remain brave and mentally keep moving forward. If I stop to think...if I dwell on the bad...I will undoubtedly drown in my sadness and fear.

I've quickly learned that true bravery can be just the act of getting out of bed in the morning while fighting your mind, body, and those destructive inner fears.

Eating is difficult. Food has become my enemy. If I eat the wrong thing, I either throw up or I get a horrendous stomach ache, and Bert goes nuts. It's demeaning. Gosh, I'm moaning. I must stay positive.

Mr Hanlon is doing his rounds. He stands before me and pokes at the tablet in his hands. Having been so poorly, I found it almost impossible to string a semblance of my thoughts together. Now that my head has cleared from the drug-fuelled haze and I'm feeling more like myself, I take the opportunity to ask him some *important* questions.

"No, you won't be riding your horses for quite some time," the Professor answers. He looks at me as if I'm completely nuts. I'm sitting cross-legged in an attempt to stretch the tight muscles in my legs and back without using my poor abs. I wiggle in response to his stern look. "I'm hoping that you will naturally heal so I can do a reversal operation and put everything back in its rightful place." The professor taps the tablet. "The tachycardia and your weight loss are concerns. I have to warn you, Emma, that organs don't like to be played with. I'm sure there will be many challenges ahead of you with your digestive system. The food you can eat—but that is a discussion for another time. I have no doubt you will handle it with your customary grace and courage. Let's get you home first. If your next set of test results are clear, you can go home. Ideally, once you leave the hospital, I strongly suggest *no* horse riding and also that you avoid lifting anything heavy."

"Heavy?" I ask for clarification. *Heavy* to me is a couple of bags of horse feed, perhaps a 25kg bale of shavings.

"Objects no heavier than say...a small kettle of water," Mr Hanlon replies with a helpful smile. My heart dips, and I rub my face and temple with frustration.

Oh bloody hell.

I force myself to nod. "Thank you, Mr Hanlon." I give him an overly bright smile. I nod again and cast my eyes upward in the vain hope that it will help me not to cry.

How am I going to look after the horses?

If I still have my horses, that is. I have not seen Arlo since I woke up. At the time, he purposely didn't explain what my "drop in status in his household" meant. I swallow my nerves and the constant nagging worry.

"Everything good or bad happens for a reason," I mumble.

I am grateful I'm alive. I'm grateful I'm alive. I'm grateful I'm alive.

Oh, but it hurts. I rub my chest with my knuckles. I want to care for my horses. How can I care for them when everything to do with horses is heavy? It is perhaps a silly thing in the big scheme of things. But Bob, my hairy cob, has been the centre of my world for over ten years. I can't imagine not spending time with him, caring for him. These past long weeks of not knowing if Bob and Pudding are safe has been horrendous.

Heck, I struggle even to sit up without flapping around like a fish. Because of my surgeries, my abdominal wall has been cut to pieces and all my muscles have wasted away. I know for a fact that for safety reasons, I cannot do a thing with Pudding—he is such a shithead. But I'm not *me* without my horses. I rub the pain in my chest again.

Mr Hanlon gives me a gentle pat on my shoulder and leaves the room.

Be positive. Be brave. I'm hopefully going home...if I have a home.

Arrah. *Quit it, Emma.*

I think of the potato quote: "The same boiling water that softens the potato hardens the egg. It's about what you're made of, not the circumstances."

Ha, "what I'm made of." I roll my eyes.

I'm like Frankenstein's monster.

John's monster.

I stretch my right leg out and roll my shoulders. I wonder if he is proud of his creation. As if my thoughts have conjured him, the hellhound appears outside my glass 'tank.'

John stands in the doorway. He is wearing a black T-shirt and trousers that mould to him. His unsettling green eyes take me in. Smart and clear, they evaluate everything with calm precision.

My eyes widen. I freeze on the bed. Sweat breaks out around my hairline, and my left eye twitches sporadically. Why is he here? To make an apology? "Sorry I stabbed you, Emma." This is so not appropriate. I cautiously move my hand to rub my twitching eye. I then narrow both of my eyes as I stare up at him. I can't wrap my head around the fact that he is *here*.

"We need to talk," he says.

Boom.

As soon as I hear his voice, the room darkens. Bitter-tasting bile rises up my throat. Belatedly, it becomes apparent to me that...*I'm screaming*.

In a panic, I clamp my hands over my mouth. One on top of the other to hold in the sound. My fingers dig into my cheeks. The scream is now muffled, yet it continues to bubble in my throat. A flood of frightened tears runs down my face unchecked. They pool at the top of my fingers and drip slowly down my wrists, the salty tears making a minor cut on my wrist sting.

My God, it is like all my nightmares have come together into human form.

I shake my head. No.

No to the horrified disbelief that is rattling around in my brain, that John is *here* in the same building as me, has he come back to hurt me? I don't want to talk to him. I'm a mess, thanks to the man standing before me. He wants to talk? His blasé tone does not inspire any confidence. Just bone-deep fear. Oh God, why is he really here?

John remains in the doorway, his body relaxed. A penitent expression flashes across his face. But it disappears so quickly, I think I must have been mistaken. His eyes are assessing, judging.

Judging *me* as I struggle for control.

I fight the overwhelming, demanding urge to manically fling myself from the bed and run, or at least attempt to hide, with my fingers in my ears in the vain, childish hope that if I can't see him or hear him, he will leave me alone.

Oh my God, if he takes one more step...

NO.

My panicked thoughts screech to a halt as I gain control of myself. I am *not* doing that to myself. I'm not.

John is another form of *infection* that I have to fight.

I will not let my primal fears control me. I force myself to stay on the bed, with my elbows I hug my knees to my chest. My breath struggles to escape from between the dam of my hands, and my nostrils flare as I pant. I can't get enough air through my snotty nose.

He patiently waits until I stop freaking out, then continues as if I hadn't interrupted him with my screaming. "I'm worried about your safety...the consequences of your helping my sister." The consequences of what you, John, did. "I have the means and the resources to get you somewhere safe. You're not safe with Arlo." John says the demon's name as if they're old friends, not current enemies. The smooth rolling of his voice twists my insides. Nothing in John's tone indicates any awareness that the demon was behind the kidnapping and subsequent deaths of his pack.

Of course he knows...after months of investigation, the hellhound will know everything.

"He has removed his protection—there is no longer a claim on you. It will only be a matter of time before someone makes their move."

Why the hell does John care?

"Arlo will never let you go. He will dangle you like bait to see what he can catch."

A fishing reference...how apt, considering I've lived in this fishbowl of a room for weeks.

I rock. "Don't pretend you care," I mumble around the fleshy barrier of my hands. John tilts his head.

Now that I have full control of myself, I cautiously drop my hands from my mouth. Licking my lips, I not-so-surreptitiously put the hospital bed between us as I shuffle to the other side of the bed. My abdomen sharply twinges a protest as I quickly stand. I sway on my feet. My blood pressure is still dangerously low, and as I've gotten up too fast, dizziness hits me. I blink rapidly to clear the black dots that dance across my vision. As soon as I feel steady enough, I slowly back away.

My already-stressed heart pounds, causing my neck and jaw to ache.

I keep moving backwards away from the hellhound until my bum hits the glass window and I can go no further. I wipe my hands across my face to clear it of tears and cough to clear my throat.

I take a deep breath.

It's all going to be okay—or it isn't, but that's okay too.

I can't stop my hands as they stray of their own accord to rest protectively in front of Bert. John's eyes track the movement and he frowns.

I swallow and lift my chin, and bravely I say again, "Do not pretend that you care." It comes out wobbly. More strongly, I say, "You just want to use me. I assume you have some big nefarious plan? I will not allow myself to be used, hellhound. Haven't you...haven't you done enough?"

I bite the inside of my mouth and I force myself to continue—I have my own questions. "Your sister," I say through a growing lump in my throat, a nasty lump of fear that is doing its best to rob me of my voice. I need to know —not knowing has driven me crazy in this hospital bed and only this man has the answer. "Is she okay? Did she shift back? Is she safe?"

He flinches. It's only a micro-expression, a tightening of his mouth, a flick of his right eyebrow that he can't quite staunch. "Do not talk about my sister," he growls. "Don't even think about her. Her welfare is not your concern." His gorgeous face twists into a fearsome expression and his now-livid energy sucks the air out of the room.

I shrink back further into myself. If I could, I would dig a hole right through the window at my back and escape. Isn't it normal to ask about my pup?

I point a trembling finger at him. "You are a monster, John Hesketh. I see you."

Oh crap, I've said too much. I nibble on my bottom lip. But because I'm a glutton for punishment and I can't help myself, I square my shoulders, lift my chin, and blurt out, "Arlo told me you paid for my medical treatment. Excuse me if I don't say thank you. You are the reason I'm here. Please leave. Leave me alone. Get out. Please, just get out. I never want to see you again. You've done enough."

"I will send someone to help you. Guard you—"

"No."

"You have no choice," he growls.

No, I never have.

"I hate you," I snarl, my pulse pounding heavy in my veins and my entire body shaking with fear.

John's confident demeanour slips a little at my words. I swear that for a second, he almost looks uncertain. But then his eyes flash with that awful orange flame.

"Good," he says with a cruel twist of his lips.

CHAPTER
EIGHT

AFTER THE WHOLE VISIT DEBACLE, I recognise the fingerprints of John's interference everywhere. As I put two and two together, I realise quickly that not only has he paid for my treatment, he has also purchased all the toiletries and clothing that have conveniently appeared during my hospital stay.

It is a strange feeling, being vulnerable around someone who's both hurt you and tended to you.

A tiny insistent sliver of compassion, keeps reiterating that the hellhound has lost his pack. *Lost,* what an insignificant word. John didn't *lose* his pack. The demon, my demon master, murdered his family. That tiny shard of compassion insists that John is doing his best to ratify his mistake.

No—God, I smash that shard to pieces. I can't allow myself to be that naïve.

I rub my face and weave my fingers through my hair. I tug until the strands pull painfully against my scalp. I have to force myself to not believe my own hopeful lies that John somehow cares.

He does not.

It's ludicrous of me to think so. He is using me to get at the demon. He has inserted himself into my life like some kind of virus. I was right with the analogy of him being an infection. He is the worst kind of infection.

John is *poison*.

I am not even going to pretend to understand what is going on in that man's head. At least after he demanded my compliance, he thankfully left me alone.

For the millionth time, I stare out of the window that overlooks the hospital carpark. In the world outside this insular room, drizzle soaks the ground. It is the kind of day when the cold seeps into your bones.

My blood results have come back clear. No infection. I am finally free from my pus-girl status—they have finally cleared me to go home.

Home.

I turn my head and take in all the packed stuff on the bed. "How on earth am I going to carry it all...all this stuff?" I mumble. I fold my arms and hug myself. I've heard nothing back from the estate. So I'm unsure of where I'm going.

Is the estate still my home?

I poke at the bags. The hospital has its own portal, so at least I don't have far to travel. Portals are a witch-created gateway system that uses ley-line magic. The witch magic attaches the doors to other doorways all over the world—you have to know the correct gateway code to go anywhere and you have to have permission—otherwise you're going to get an unpleasant, possibly even fatal greeting by a ward on the other side. Well, *I* wouldn't. But it would be rude and dangerous to pop out of a random gateway.

I can't explain why the gateways work for me and other magic doesn't. I guess the ley line magic is so vast, my magic is like a teardrop in the ocean—it isn't strong enough to interfere.

Only the rich and powerful have access to portals, so perhaps I'm wrong with my assumption that I will use one today. My gaze flicks to the cold, wet day outside. Heck, I might have to walk home.

A knock on the glass behind me has me spinning around. A refined and regal-looking elf is standing in the doorway. Not a nurse. She bows in a formal greeting. "Emma, my name is Eleanor. They have assigned me as one of your personal guards. Will you allow me to escort you home?" She smiles.

Eleanor is beautiful. Her enormous dark-brown eyes and pointed ears show her to be a full-blooded Aes Sídh, a fae warrior elf. Her shiny black hair is long and styled in intricate plaits, as is their custom. The cut of her clothes makes her look simultaneously archaic and futuristic. She is dressed in a loose, black high-necked long-sleeved top and pants. I know hidden underneath, on one of her arms, will be her magical warrior markings—they look like humans' tattoos. Supposedly the markings glow as the warrior does freaky fae magic.

I blink at her like a divvy while my mind takes a second to catch up.

One of my personal guards. Oh. Okay. Ha, the guards. Of course I ignored that significant detail from John's visit.

Home...I swallow and hunch over a little. I rub my arms in a vain attempt at self-comfort and gnaw on my lip. I'm sure the nurses could assist me to the portal...I could refuse. Couldn't I?

But the sensible part of me gives me a nudge to accept help.

"Do I have a choice?" I ask quietly, still rubbing at my arms.

The fae can't lie. In response to my question, Eleanor doesn't answer. Instead, she offers me a beatific smile, then glides towards the bed to gather my things.

Okay, then.

"Eleanor, it would be an honour to accept your help," I mumble politely. John confuses me, frightens me, but it isn't this lady's fault. Eleanor is doing her job, and there is no need for me to be rude. Plus, she is a scary badass warrior. I don't need anyone else angry with me, especially an Irish Aes Sídh.

Heck, I have no idea what I risk in going home; it might be handy to have a badass warrior by my side, even if she comes from unsavoury circumstances.

"Excellent. Is this everything?" She indicates my pile of bags on the bed.

"Yes. I am sorry...I can't help you carry them...I have...urm—"

Eleanor interrupts my pathetic attempt at an explanation. "I am aware of your limitations." I nod and shoot her an awkward, wobbly smile.

Instead of Eleanor grabbing the bags like I thought she would, the warrior mark on her right arm glows. The light bleeds through her black long-sleeved top, and the bags on the bed twitch and rattle. I'm fascinated. My lips part with disbelief as with an upward hand gesture from Eleanor my bags slowly rise into the air.

Wow, okay, that's a nifty trick.

Not sparing my fishbowl room a backward glance, I meekly follow Eleanor out of the room and down the corridor. The bags bob about in the air behind us as we walk. I warily monitor them—I don't want to interfere with the handy fae magic. It should be okay as long as I avoid getting too close.

Eleanor slowly leads me down the corridor after I refuse the use of a wheelchair. I'm determined to leave this hospital under my own steam. After a while I regret that decision as my body screams at me to rest, but I've done enough sitting around for a lifetime. *Push through it, Emma. One step at a time.* With my dodgy, exhausted vision, the walls of the hallway ripple. I am pleasantly surprised that I'm not bouncing into them. I take walking in a straight line as a win.

When we arrive at the portal gateway on the ground floor of the hospital, we are greeted by a massive hellhound in wolf form. I squeak and take a wobbly step back.

"Emma, may I introduce you to your other guard, Riddick. My employer has informed me that Riddick will remain in wolf form while in your presence."

Both the elf and the hellhound watch me in silence as they wait for my response. My pulse hammers away until it's all I can hear. Not another hellhound, oh God. I wonder if Riddick can smell Bert. The thought makes me hunch over, and my lip twitches. I rub it on my shoulder before my whole face starts.

My new guards stare at me. They're still waiting for a normal response to the introduction.

Come on, Emma.

I blow out a nervous breath and subject them both to my elegant jazz hands.

Jazz hands.

I cringe. *What the heck was that?* I lace my wayward, now-shaking hands across Bert protectively. Ha, to think I used to be refined.

In response to my out-of-control anxiety, Riddick drops his heavy bulk to the floor. On his belly with his head on his paws, he whines.

My mouth pops open in shock as I eye the giant wolf prostrated before me. He has a thick cream-and-red coat and the brightest green eyes. Wow, he could be related to my pup, as he looks like a colossal male version of her. I dismiss the thought as silly. I've not seen many shifters in animal form, so I've no idea if the red colouring is standard or not.

Riddick's massive tongue rolls out of his mouth. He gives me what I can only describe as a doggie smile. I can't help my answering grin—I'm a sucker for animals. Even though I know there is a giant, scary man underneath all that fur, I can't help but appreciate his kindness—he is going out of his way to set me at ease.

"I'm..." I cough to clear my throat, "...I'm sorry. You must forgive me, I'm not myself at the moment. Pleased to meet you, Riddick." My hands twist in front of me. "Urm, may I ask how long you are both assigned to guard me?" I blink at Eleanor.

Eleanor is frowning at me. She must think my behaviour is nuts. Because it is—is Arlo right, am I broken? No, I am not...I am just dented. "This assignment is a permanent position."

"Permanent." What the heck?

"Permanent? Oh, I'm sure I'll be okay with your help just today." I titter. Oh crap, I don't know how I've qualified to have a warrior elf *and* a hellhound as guards. The more pertinent question would be, what on earth have they done to gain *me* as a permanent assignment?

Colour me surprised when Eleanor inputs the gate code for the main house at the estate. I don't know how John has gotten away with having his people on the demon's estate. Being a demon, Arlo is incredibly territorial.

I keep my rogue hands pinned to my side as my fingers twitch with the need to stroke the hellhound's soft fur. I'm nuts. Who in their right mind wants to stroke a hellhound?

The gateway flashes, and without any fanfare, we step through.

CHAPTER NINE

When we step out of the portal, Doris, the estate's housekeeper, greets us in the hallway. "Miss Emma, you are back, and you have brought friends." Her voice is laden with distaste. With a sniff, she tucks her dark hair behind her ear while looking me up and down. A sly look enters her watery blue eyes. "We have moved you. The Master's new favourite is now in your old suite of rooms..."

In response, I beam a smile at her.

I'm sure Doris expects me to be rolling around the floor in floods of tears wailing, "Why me, why me. I love him." When I don't, she narrows her eyes and barks out, "Follow me."

We all traipse behind her as she leads us to the back of the house. When we get to my new accommodations, I am a tad uncomfortable—when the demon said I was now at the bottom of his household, boy, he wasn't kidding. Embarrassed, I wonder what my guards will make of this.

I shuffle my feet. God, I want to go back to the hospital, to my light and airy fishbowl.

This room is shit.

Gone is my airy suite of rooms and in their place is a Harry Potter–worthy cupboard under the stairs. The door doesn't open fully as it hits the bed—the room is big enough for the single bed, and that's it. It's an empty storeroom with no window, so there isn't any natural light, only a single, dangling light bulb.

In a house where there are dozens of empty bedrooms, this is indeed a statement. But it's okay, it's totally fine. I can work with it.

"Cosy," I say with a smile.

"I got some of your essentials," Doris says, indicating with a nod the small cardboard box and single pathetic black bin-bag dumped in the middle of the thin, sagging mattress.

"Huh, how nice. It appears I have my own Homer hole," I say with amusement as I pay homage to my favourite animated TV program. I grin at the sagging mattress. "Thank you, Doris, this is perfect, and thank you, it was very kind of you to rescue my things." Doris *humphs* crossly. She folds her arms underneath her boobs and glares.

Ha, what can I say? I'm an irritating people-pleaser. Sorry, Doris, I'm still not at the point of throwing myself to the floor and wailing.

I can't help the grin that tugs at my lips. If I had the energy to do a happy dance, I would. It's a relief, such a relief, to no longer hold the title of the demon's pet. I guess I shouldn't be thrilled that Arlo has relegated me to some lowly position and that I have to sleep in a storeroom, but until this moment, I didn't realise how much I wanted out of my opulent cage. I never saw being his favourite as a grand prize. I can't help a full-body shudder. Wow, what a lucky escape.

Everything happens for a reason.

"The bathroom is upstairs...on the *third* floor," Doris continues snidely. Riddick growls at her, and she jumps a little. I grin at him. "Did I say the third floor? I meant third door...it's up the corridor." Doris gives me an embarrassed nod, hands the key to the room over to Eleanor, and quickly scampers away. I pat Riddick on the head—*good boy*—as I shake my head in bemusement at her retreating form. I've lived in this house for over seventeen years; it's like she has forgotten I know every inch of the place.

I clap, then smile at my two guards. Conversationally I say, "Did I tell you I have horses?"

When we arrive at the stables—which are directly behind the main house, so it isn't too far for me to walk—the first thing I notice is the silence. The rain has stopped and the sun is shining through the heavy grey clouds. Instinctively I know something is wrong…it's just too damn quiet. As soon as I spot the empty, cleaned-out stables, my legs buckle. A big furry body stops me from falling to the ground. Riddick props me up.

All the horses. Gone. The horses are *gone*.

Gone, gone, gone echoes around in my head.

They have cleaned the building out. It's empty. Overwhelming panic fills me and for a few minutes, I can't think. Useless. I'm utterly powerless. "Bob…I have to find him," I whisper brokenly through a solid lump in my throat. My heart is slamming, my gut is twisting, and I can't stop shaking. My vision goes hazy. "I have to find my best friend, I can't lose him. Pudding, I didn't have time to check on him, I fell and I didn't have time to see if he was okay. Oh, God." Eleanor's eyes meet mine, and they shine with concern.

Check the field.

I rush towards the fields. The wooden post-and-rail horse paddocks are empty. The surrounding silence is deafening.

For several minutes I stand staring in utter disbelief. What do I do? I rub my temples.

What do I do? No. No. No. Bob…my Bob.

My horses are gone, Bob and Pudding are gone.

This, this finishes off what is left of my soul. I don't want to be here anymore. This world is too much. Everything is too much. My mouth contorts in grief, and I cover my eyes with my hands.

Riddick huffs out a breath and gently nudges me. Without thinking, I drop one of my hands and dig my fingers into his fur to ground me. The giant hellhound offers me comfort.

"What are you sniffling about?" comes a familiar voice. I drop my hand from my face and lift my head to meet the blue eyes of a vampire girl. She narrows her eyes, assessing me with her hands on her narrow hips. She looks almost homeless, wearing dirty jogging bottoms and a red strappy top, her brown hair scraped up into a messy bun at the top of her head. It has clumps of hay sticking out of it.

"Sam," I mumble, "the horses are gone..." I wave my hand, pointing out the obvious.

"Yeah, they were all sold within a few weeks. You *really* pissed that demon turd off. I'm sorry, Em...Pudding, that spooky shithead, was sold for crazy money. He is so talented, there was a bidding war over him. He has gone to Germany. I couldn't afford to buy him..." I nod sadly, hurt that I never got to say goodbye. "...Not after I bought your hairy cob." I blink at her.

"You bought...Bob?" I whisper in disbelief.

"Of course I did. You owe me fourteen and a half thousand pounds. Who knew Bob was worth so much? Contrary to popular belief, vampires aren't made of money, you know." She smiles at Eleanor. "I'm only eighty. Horses took over my human life, and the passion followed me into my undead one. Creatures like me will never be rich if we have horses. The fuckers cost a pretty penny—"

"Thankyouthankyouthankyou." I rush towards her, instantly snapping out of my melancholy.

"You're welcome. Just don't hug me." She holds out her hands to keep me away. "I don't want bashing with that poo bag. God, Em, I thought you'd been in the hospital. They let you out looking like that? You look like shit." She puts her hand at the side of her mouth and says to Eleanor, "Pun intended." Eleanor looks horrified and Riddick growls. I giggle and smile so big, my cheeks hurt. Only a genuine friend would take the mick out of someone that has a stoma. I love this girl.

"I love you, Sam, and I've missed you. Would you mind if we went to see my horse?"

"I can't believe it's taken you so long to ask. He's in a *shitty* stable." She grins and wiggles her eyebrows at the word *shitty*. "So don't get mad, I had to hide him somewhere. I bought him a Shetland pony as a companion. I know how much you like them." I roll my eyes. Sam knows the little ponies are a nightmare to deal with, scary waist-high monsters. I bet poor Bob has been terrorised. I'm convinced that the Devil himself created Shetlands and then went out of his way to make them extra feisty.

Sam grabs me and gives me a fierce hug. "Don't you dare pull that *shit* again. I have been worried sick. Sick. What were you thinking?" She gives me a little shake. "You bloody idiot. I'm so glad that you're okay. Whatever you need, I'm here for you—don't forget that. I charge for tough love, though, and sniffling all over me will cost extra." We all follow Sam as she leads the way. I'm so tired, I feel sick. I lean more and more against the hellhound.

There is a whinny, and Bob's head appears over the ramshackle stable door. "Bob," I shout, and he whinnies again. I rush to open the stable door. It sticks halfway and Sam has to tug it open for me. My hands shake as I step inside the stable. With wide tear-filled eyes, I take in my boy. He looks great.

"Bob, I thought for one horrible moment that I lost you. God, I have missed you so much." Bob avoids my reaching hand with a head toss. He flares his nostrils at me and narrows his eyes. He gives me an angry look, as if he has just realised something. He wrinkles his nose. Then, almost knocking me over, he swings away from me to face the back corner of the stable.

"Bob?" I say, feeling a little hurt as he presents his hairy bum to me. He peeks over his shoulder and then turns his face back to the corner with a horsey huff. "Bob...are you...urm...cross with me?" I whisper. His ears flick back as he listens to my voice. "I didn't leave you on purpose. I'm so sorry, I have missed you so much. I promise I will do my best to never be away from you for so long again. I'm so sorry, Bob-cob...forgive me?" Bob huffs out a sigh. I step to his side and scratch his blue-grey dappled bottom. He wiggles it, deliberately moving my hand to a different prime scratching spot. Once he has deemed my bum-itching time adequate, with a grumble he turns back around.

Bob's warm brown eyes take me in. He stretches his neck and blows warm breath at me. He slowly moves so his heavy head rests on my shoulder. I ignore the nagging voice in my head to be careful. I run my hands gently across his soft muzzle and rub the base of his ears. Bob huffs hay breath at me and his eyes close in contentment. "God, I have missed you. I have missed you so much." With a sob, I move forward, throw my arms around his neck, and bury my face in his long silver mane. I breathe him in. "Now I feel like I've come home," I whisper.

CHAPTER
TEN

I SCAMPER down the corridor to the bathroom with my hands full of my wash things and pyjamas. I try my best to avoid looking at myself in the bathroom mirror. If zombies existed, I would be seriously concerned, since if a guild hunter copped a look at me lately they'd so take me out. And not in a good way.

When I catch my reflection, I shudder. My skin is so pale...there isn't any pink in my lips or even underneath my nails. With my pale blonde hair and dull blue eyes beyond the obvious poorly zombiism, all I see is the ghost of a girl.

After a quick shower, a vigorous tooth-brush, and a Bert-bag change, I'm ready for bed.

"Is it okay to leave the door open?" I ask Riddick, as I rock from foot to foot in my pyjamas and twist my fingers in front of me. I feel silly, asking like a child to keep the door to my room open and the hallway light on. With no windows, the storage room is dark, and I've been living in a glass fishbowl for months. It shouldn't have been a surprise to me, but I didn't expect this room to feel so claustrophobic. The size of it and the lack of light is disconcerting. There's no way I will sleep in here without the door being open—there's no air.

Riddick replies with a small sigh, and ever so slowly he nods his head.

For what must be the millionth time in my life, I wish magic would work on me. From what I can gather, Eleanor communicates with Riddick through a magical mind-link. So cool. I wish I could talk to him.

I take his head-nod as permission and beam a smile at him. "Thanks, Riddick."

I tug the door, and it scrapes against the bed frame and bounces back. I narrow my eyes and ram the door with my left shoulder, being mindful of Bert. Oof. I still can't get it fully past the bed, but with another forceful shove, I wedge the door against the bed so it's stuck wide open. I take a step back to survey my handiwork and rub my now-aching arm. I smile with relief: it's much better. The chandeliers in the hallway flood the storeroom with soft light.

Take that, Doris. I don't mind the lack of privacy.

The bed creaks and groans as I get in. "Woops," I squeal and flap my arms about in panic as my body unwillingly rolls into the centre of the bed. Oops. I let out a snort Bob would be proud of and giggle. Oh my God, I forgot completely about the Homer hole until I lay down. The dip in the mattress makes it impossible to sleep anywhere else. I might need a rope ladder to get out in the morning. I cover my mouth with my hand and continue to giggle, then huff and wiggle as a spring digs itself into my back.

Huh, when I thought about my first night back, I imagined so many nightmare situations. An uncomfortable bed wasn't anywhere on the list of penalties for returning to the estate—the scene of my crime—after I stole the little shifter out from under the demon's nose. I thought they would relegate me to the same creepy building, the same prison I stole her from. Or perhaps I'd be kept in some deep, dark dungeon, never to be seen or heard from again.

I nibble my bottom lip.

Yet here I am with a personal guard keeping me safe. It feels almost too good to be true.

The duvet cover is soft, and the pillows are squishy. I run my fingers across Bert's seal to make sure he is nice and tight. Finally, after more wiggling, I settle on my side, my hands tucked underneath the pillow.

I peek down at Riddick. The huge hellhound is lying in the corridor directly in front of the room's threshold. I don't know what he thinks about my antics getting into bed. I grin; he must think I'm a right idiot.

The bright hallway light dances on his fur and highlights his beautiful glossy red coat, making him look extra fluffy. Underneath the pillow, my fingers twitch with the urge to stroke him. *Hellhound weirdo*, I chastise myself. His full attention is directed down the hallway as he keeps watch.

It's in quiet moments like this I think of my pup, especially as I'm looking at the hellhound. No one will talk about her—it's as if she never existed. I don't know where she is or if she is safe. The shifters are incredibly closed-lipped; you can't ask about a female shifter, it isn't safe and the one man who knows would get violent with me if I asked him again, if the look in his eyes is any indication. Even though I don't want to, I have to push her to the back of my mind. If I'm meant to help her or see her again in the future, our paths will cross. Otherwise, I have to have faith...faith that she's okay and that the shifters are looking after her. Heck, I can't even protect myself...this is crap. "Please be safe, pup," I whisper under my breath into the universe. "Please be safe."

When Riddick continues to feel my eyes on him, he sighs and turns his head to regard me. His solemn green gaze takes me in.

"'Night, Riddick. Thank you for keeping me safe." He doesn't acknowledge my whispered words, but he doesn't have to. His shifter magical energy creeps towards me. It floods the room with gentle, comforting waves.

I sigh, and my body relaxes.

He makes me feel safe. Being metaphysically enfolded in his warm energy is a different type of intimacy, a feeling of peace and protection that to anyone else would be unnoticed, underrated. I have never felt it before. I close my eyes and let it wrap around me. It might be my imagination, but I'll take it. It warms my soul. I don't understand why, but I'm grateful.

Warm and safe, I sleep.

There is a deep rumbling growl. My eyes fly open. My throat is burning and the remnants of a scream die on my lips. Immediately, I throw my hands up and cover my mouth.

Oh no. I shake as the tentacles of my nightmare slither away from me. I was screaming. *Oh no.*

I attempt to sit up, but the dip in the bed makes any movement difficult. I hear another growl and my eyes fly to the door. Riddick's gigantic form is blocking the doorway.

He is growling at someone in the hallway.

My heart slams in my chest with fear and I give a panicked wiggle, and Bert and my abs twinge in protest as I finally flop and roll enough to get sufficient momentum to scramble out of the bed. My feet hit the floor with a thud and one tiny step finds me out in the hall.

There is a disgruntled crowd of people in the hallway—most of them in nightwear—facing off against Riddick. At the head of the group is Doris.

Oh, heck, it looks like I've woken the entire house. My burning, sore throat tells its own tale. I kind of hoped that once I'd left the hospital, I would have left the terrible memories behind. Unfortunately, it looks like that isn't the case. I understand why everyone looks upset. I clutch my arms to my chest and rub them. No one wants to be woken up in the middle of the night by bloodcurdling screams.

I try to step around Riddick's bulk, but he swings to the side to block me, his soft red-and-cream fur brushing my legs. As soon as Doris sees me, her eyes narrow and her finger comes up. "You," she says furiously, jabbing her finger in my direction. "You will remove yourselves immediately from my house." Not your house Doris, our territorial demon master might have some objection to that comment.

I fidget and tuck a piece of sweaty hair behind my ear. "I'm so sorry, did I wake you? I must have had a bad dream. Please forgive me. I didn't mean to frighten anybody," I say, mortified. When all I get in response are dirty looks and poorly veiled anger, my eyes fill with tears.

I know most of these people...while they aren't my family, we have lived together for years. I have never once treated them without kind-

CURSED DEMON

ness and respect. Yet they now look at me like I am a stranger. My heart hurts.

I don't belong. I don't belong anywhere.

For a split second, Riddick takes his eyes away from the hallway crowd to check me over. His bright green eyes meet mine, and he looks haunted. Oh, no, I think I've traumatised the poor hellhound.

"I'm so sorry," I tell him.

"You will be," snarls Doris. She claps her hands. "Everyone else back to bed. I will handle this...this thing." The half-dozen bodies disappear back down the hall...leaving Doris, two guards, Riddick, and me.

I rock from foot to foot as Doris steps aggressively towards me, her pointy finger heading towards my face. I flinch. Riddick's low growl rumbles around us and miraculously it has her remembering herself, and she quickly retreats.

I know if he wasn't here, she would have hurt me.

Her face pinched with fury, Doris pulls her purple dressing gown tighter around herself and crosses her arms underneath her bust. Her eyes flash with the need for retribution.

Oh bloody hell, she is so mad.

"There is an empty room available in the barracks out the back," she spits. "It is vacant during the evenings, as the guards are on the night shift with everyone asleep during the day. That means your attention-seeking screams will have zero effect. You have no care for others, Miss Emma. Your behaviour tonight was appalling, and it proves just how selfish you are. You'd better keep quiet during the day—woe betide you if you disturb anyone else." Her pointing, jabbing finger is back and I cringe at her words. "Your dog guard will not protect you if you do." The guards shuffle and one takes a step back.

The *dog* in question flashes his teeth. I step in front of Riddick in case he bites her. Last time I checked, people don't control what they dream. But I keep my mouth tightly closed and drop my gaze to the floor, attempting to look properly chastised. Which isn't hard to do—I feel horrible. Riddick might not be here next time to keep me safe, and I have to live here. I don't want to make this woman my enemy.

321

God, I am so embarrassed. I already look a mess, and now everyone knows I am a mess on the inside too. *Broken.*

"Grab your things." Wow, we aren't even waiting for the morning. I look at Riddick, my eyes wide with panic. Oh no, what am I going to do? I dare not tell her I'm not allowed to carry anything. Surely she will think I'm making it up to be difficult.

"I will gather Emma's things," Eleanor says as she glides up the corridor. I breathe out a sigh of relief.

"Thank you, Eleanor, I'm sorry for the trouble." Gosh, not a full night has passed and I've already been evicted from the main house.

Doris huffs and stomps away. Crikey. I shiver. I think if she could, Doris would have marched me out of the main house by the ear or with her foot kicking my bottom with every step. Whew, I am so glad she didn't dare cross the growly Riddick. I never thought I would be grateful for John's intervention, but at this moment I'm grateful for my guards.

"Come on then," Doris snarls from the end of the hallway. I jump and quickly go to follow her, but I am stopped mid-step by a giant furry body. I blink at Riddick in confusion, and in response he drops his head and licks my bare toes.

"Ew," I grumble, wrinkling my nose as I glance down at my now-slobbered-on, wet feet. "Did you have to lick them?" I pat his head. "Good point, though. Let me grab my shoes."

CHAPTER
ELEVEN

The demon wants to talk to me—he has called me to a meeting. I don't want to talk to him. Just when I think I've obtained some semblance of freedom, the demon calls me back.

Freedom? Ha. I roll my eyes heavenward at the thought. I've jumped from the demon's frying pan into the hellhound's fire. There's no freedom for me.

No, I'm the pinball in the creature machine—I have a demon flipper on the left and a hellhound flipper on the right. As the ball, I have no hope of going in my own direction and have to instead just allow myself to be bashed about. Fun times.

I dress casually in hospital chic, which comprises comfy leggings and an oversized, slouchy jumper. The softness around the scars on my tummy area is key. My pale blonde hair is a sheet that falls down my back to my waist—it's the only part of me that looks good. When I dressed this morning, my pale face looked gaunt, my cheekbones stood out sharply, and I had bags under my eyes. I had hoped that the sky-blue jumper would bring out the colour of my eyes and make me look less washed out, but it didn't.

Before I step into the room, I anxiously run my fingers around the circular seal on Bert's bag, which is hidden underneath my clothes. It has become a nervous habit: tracing it with my fingertips, double-checking, always checking to make sure the adhesive of the small opaque bag is intact and that it remains tight to my skin. I shoot my elf guard a nervous smile.

Eleanor is accompanying me—when I suggested she didn't have to come, she gave me a badass eyebrow-raise, which I interpreted as, "Are you kidding, I'm your guard."

Silently she nods at the closed door and my head wobbles in response. "Nope, I am not ready," I whisper. "Can't we stay out here?" Eleanor ignores me as she knocks on the door and then opens it. I take a deep breath and step into one of my favourite rooms in the house, the library.

Opulent yet inviting, the library is the only room in the demon's house that hasn't been modernised. I take another deep breath in, and the earthy, sweet-vanilla, musky smell of books fills my senses.

Floor-to-ceiling open oak bookshelves line the walls—shelves full of wonders. Apart from the stables, this is the room where I spend most of my time. The demon is aware of that. I hope he isn't trying to ruin the space for me. I quietly sigh. Probably.

Arlo sits in a throne-like chair. The piece of furniture is bigger and more ornate than the other chairs in the room. It is an unsubtle psychological ploy aimed at manipulating anyone who isn't aware that the demon is the most important person present.

The demon is dressed impeccably in a charcoal custom suit. Most of the time his black hair which is long on top, short on the sides, flops boyishly into his blue-grey eyes. Today his dark hair is gelled back away from his face, highlighting his high cheekbones, delicate nose, and prominent, puffy lips.

Three men that I've never encountered before are sitting around him in a semicircle.

I stop in the centre of the room. "Master, you wanted to see me?" I lower my head and eyes respectfully in a formal greeting.

Out of the corner of my eye, I see Eleanor position herself to my right and slightly ahead of me. She also formally nods and takes up a protective stance.

I have to fight to maintain a serene expression. Gosh, I want to fidget. I've burning questions inside me. But I clamp my lips closed and keep everything I'm feeling off my face. I wear a blank mask. My spine is snapped straight with shoulder blades together and chin held high. I am attempting to be a picture of pure elegance, so I hide my hands behind my back, where no one can see them trembling.

The demon taps his puffy lips once, twice, and moves to sit on the edge of his chair. The energy that surrounds him thrums with excitement. His devious eyes sparkle. Uh-oh. This will not be a pleasant meeting. Arlo is too excited. Bad things happen when the demon is in a playful mood.

Why does the demon want me here?

I take in the three visitors with trepidation. From their energy, the other men are prominent in status. To be in this room, they would have to be.

Unusually, the men are all from different races: a vampire, an elf, and a shifter. If I said that out loud, it would sound like the start of a bad joke.

The vampire draws my gaze first, and my eyes fall to his nails—eww, his nails. His freaky dirty long nails, which are more like claws as they dig into the padding of the chair. He is ancient-looking, not old in a human way, but old for a vampire. He has lost that vampire vitality that they all seem to have and he looks faded...like a well-preserved mummy, a skull with hair on. He has long brown hair, secured with a bow at the nape of his neck. Yes, a black bow. That isn't the only thing strange about his attire...his black shirtsleeves are lace.

Yes, he looks like a crazy old vampire.

The elf has enormous grey eyes and long blond hair plaited in a style similar to Eleanor's. That's the only comparison I can make between them, as the elf isn't a warrior and he is wearing a suit. His regal bearing might indicate royalty. I tilt my head as I wonder which court.

The shifter is wearing more modern clothing, jeans and a long-sleeved white top that hugs his muscly torso. He sprawls across his chair, his legs wide apart in a classic alpha pose. As I take him in, he hunches forward, leaning on his elbows. His hands dangle between his legs. He hasn't taken his eyes off me since I entered the room, and when he notices my attention, he flexes his biceps. I barely refrain from rolling my eyes. Bloody shifters. I think perhaps he's a cat shifter, as he has a golden mane of hair that reminds me of a lion's. The man's energy is powerful, and before I met the hellhound, I would probably have been terrified of him. But his power level isn't even on the same scale. He can stare all he wants; he doesn't frighten me.

Huh. None of them do. My eyes snap back to Arlo. With fervour, he has started introductions. "Gentlemen, may I introduce Emma. Unfortunately, since an encounter with a hellhound..." the cadence of his voice, which is customarily marked by a refined English accent, is extra posh today..."she is broken," he adds with a dismissive wave in my direction.

"Broken? Why would we want one of your broken pets?" the elf spits out. I flinch. He sniffs, looking over at me with barely veiled disgust.

"I like broken," Crazy Vampire pipes up, clapping his hands.

The elf continues, ignoring the vampire, "What is she? I can see she could be beautiful, but why would any of us want her?" He stands, adjusts his suit jacket, and glides in my direction. He halts in front of me.

Eleanor deliberately shifts her weight. After a quick glance at my guard, the elf smirks. He doesn't touch me. But he does lean closer, so close our breath mingles. The elf stares deep into my eyes and I confidently stare back.

I am not bloody broken. I am strong and I am brave.

"Yes, she is beautiful. She looks better now with the angry flush on her cheeks. Her eyes are so unusual—multicoloured, exquisite."

My eyes are perhaps another gift from my unknown father. They are different shades of blue, ranging from light sky to dark violet. They change colour. Some days the colour can have multiple hues, depending on my clothing and also my mood.

With a final smirk at Eleanor, the elf glides back to his chair. Once he has taken his seat, the men start a discussion about me. A debate. It's as if I'm not in the room, as if I'm of no consequence.

I fight the urge to fidget, this time with anger. *Keep straight, keep eyes forward, chin high, breathe. Relax.* I repeat my riding mantra in my head. It's kind of apt for this situation. I don't move, and I don't acknowledge them. I have no control. Not yet. But I will. I'm a cool, calm void.

I don't know what has motivated the demon to chair this farce of a *meeting*. But I will not give him any ammunition to use against me.

"Emma is immortal," the demon dramatically declares. With that bold comment, he silences the men. Four sets of eyes take me in. Three now look halfway intrigued. "Yes, immortal. But she can be damaged, and she does not self-heal. I recently found out that her ornate magic allows her to fight the ageing process. My extensive tests have shown that now that Emma is twenty-two-years old, she will stay like this"—he waves at me—"forever."

Ha, that is news to me. *Immortal?* I frown and make a whatever-you-say face. Luckily I catch myself before they notice and school my face back into its blank mask.

Immortal. Why is he lying?

"What is she?"

"What was she bred with?"

"Emma's breeding is a conundrum, such an exciting mystery. She has many talents. She is an accomplished *horse* rider..." he smirks at me. My nostrils flare. The demon mustn't be aware that Sam bought my horse for me and that Bob is safe. *What a dickhead.* "...Dancer, and she speaks several languages. I believe over a dozen." I barely refrain from rolling my eyes—it's two at a push; I can speak French, badly. "Her magical talent is that she is immune to magic. Magic has no impact on her. Absolutely none. Imagine what you can do with that kind of power...she can walk through wards, and magical attacks do not touch her. It is as if the magic tries to avoid contact. She is remarkable, unique."

Eleanor shifts her weight beside me. I glance in her direction, and she returns a contemplative look. I roll my eyes and tuck a wisp of hair behind my ear.

"I could use her as a magical shield?" asks the elf. His grey eyes light up with interest.

"Of course."

"Would those traits pass on to her children?" asks the shifter.

The demon nods. "Perhaps."

"Can I give her more scars?" the vampire disturbingly chirps up. The other men ignore him.

"Now, that is interesting. I would like to see her without clothing," says the shifter. Eleanor tenses and steps further in front of me. "Girl, take off your clothes," he barks.

I lift an eyebrow. *Urm, no, you perve.* I ignore him.

Arlo tilts his head and a small smile tugs at his lips. "Emma, take off your clothes. We're all intrigued by the damage the hellhound made." He pouts with his puffy lips, his eyes gleaming with glee.

My lips part in shock. *What?*

"I like scars," the crazy vampire says with a strange giggle.

I blink at Arlo as if he has lost his ever-loving mind.

"Now, Emma."

Now? Right now, all I want to do is sink into the ground. Fine beads of sweat form on the back of my neck and I feel my cheeks heat with humiliation. The demon smirks at me.

No, no, no, this is a nightmare. I want to cry and I have to chomp viciously at my lip to stop it from wobbling, and my mouth fills with the taste of blood. My eyes desperately fly to Eleanor. Her face is blank and I know instinctively she's unable to do anything to help me. Currently, there's no risk to my body, and I guess there's nothing in her terms and conditions of employment to bodyguard my mind.

I wish Riddick was here.

This whole situation isn't normal—the demon would have never done this before. Now his eyes dance with a sick delight. This is his way of *punishing* me. And it's working.

My entire body trembles. I don't know if I can do this. I don't want these strangers to see me. Bert is private. More private than my skin and bone.

I briefly close my eyes. I can't let them win. I can't. I won't.

I am brave enough, bold enough. If I can survive the hellhound, I can do this. Let them see...let them look. I don't care what they think. People only hurt you if you let them. I will take what they dish out with my head held high.

I'm enough.

My fingertips brush the edge of my jumper...

The door behind me opens. Without looking, I feel the energy in the room shift.

I *feel* him.

Tingles rush up and down my spine, and I tense. His angry energy smashes around the room, an immense wave of crashing power. I brave a peek over my shoulder.

"Why wasn't I invited to this sale?" John asks menacingly.

CHAPTER TWELVE

John prowls into the room, his face a mask of violence as he takes in the seated males. His broad shoulders and rippling torso are highlighted by his tight black fatigues and the sun shining through the windows. My heart misses a beat.

"Gentlemen, this meeting is over," he snarls.

Oh, thank God.

My clamped-up fingers let go of my jumper, and shivers of relief and apprehension work up my spine.

Huh, relief?

I don't understand why the hellhound's presence makes me feel *relieved*. With everyone's eyes on him, I break my rigid, controlled stance and tug at my hair in exasperation.

He didn't hurt me intentionally. I remember the flash of horror in his eyes when he found out I couldn't heal...and he has taken care of me since then. I groan.

God, I'm an idiot. Am I really trying to stupidly convince myself that this is a timely rescue? Do I expect him to protect me? Defend me? Ha.

I let go of my hair as I shake my head. Am I enamoured by the hellhound?

CURSED DEMON

I'd like to at least say my apprehension is from sheer terror...but there is a sick part of me that inappropriately reacts to the low, sultry timbre of his voice.

Oh bloody hell. I blow out a breath. *Come on, Emma, you are being ridiculous.* It is one thing to be attracted to bad boys—something I usually don't suffer from. It's another thing to be attracted to bad men. John Hesketh is a really, really bad man.

At this moment, I need to be honest with myself. No one—no one has made me feel as self-aware as John.

It is like I am cursed.

I swallow and rub my chest. What does that say about me? I know —crap, I know that isn't healthy and I don't understand it. It's wrong. The direction of my thoughts where the hellhound is concerned is wrong on so many levels. What a dickhead I am. It is gross, how gorgeous he is.

I look heavenward for patience.

John glares at the shifter. "I'm too old a wolf to be fucked by a kitten." He nods at the exit. "Out." Without further ado, the elf and cat shifter quickly exit the room.

Pure indignation crosses the still-seated vampire's face. "Why?" he whines. "I want to play with the girl. Aren't we going to see her scars?"

"Out!" John roars.

I hunch in response and squeeze my legs together. I have a sudden urge to go to the bathroom.

The vampire giggles. As he rises from his chair, he snarls, "Arlo, you've disappointed me. I always expect lots of fun in your presence. Get rid of the killjoy hellhound and next time, I will arrange the entertainment." As he saunters out of the room, he adjusts his lace sleeves. On the way past my shaking form, he gives me a devious smile. "See you soon, pretty broken girl." The door clicks shut.

The silence in the room is deafening as the hellhound and the demon take each other's measure.

"Let's not lie to one another—we are beyond that now. You and I are evil men." As John speaks, he runs his thumb across his lower lip. It's unsettlingly sexy.

Quit it, Emma.

Lording it on his fancy chair, Arlo lifts his chin in response to John's words and pouts prettily. "John, John, John, you come into my territory, into my *home* without invitation." He leans forward. "You dare to embarrass me in front of my guests? You dare to threaten me? Me? Shifter, you've gone too far." Between one breath and the next, the demon drops his pretty facade. His eyes slowly bleed black.

I shiver. I hate it when he does that. Like rain, the blackness drips down until it covers his eyes entirely with endless darkness. He flashes huge fangs, and his black eyes glitter. Tilting his head, he leans back in his throne-like chair, and ever so slowly, Arlo claps his hands. "Bravo on your impudence."

In response, John's whole face lights up with a smile. A creepy, familiar, predator smile. "You owe me, demon. Perhaps you are stronger? Perhaps I am..." His eyes glow orange.

Oh crap, bloody hell, this isn't good. My heart hammers in my chest, and as no one is watching me, I take a wobbly step back towards the door. I think I need a nap.

John holds out his hand, and a bright-blue flame appears on his palm. The flame hypnotically dances. I tilt my head to the side, and my mouth pops open. Oh. That is the famous hellhound magic. Huh. I wonder if Riddick can do that.

My eyes flick around the room at all the flammable books. I rub the back of my neck. Oh heck, only *that* hellhound would have *this* showdown in the library. Oi hellhound, put the flame away.

I take another shuffling step back towards the door. Each tiny step back is, I hope, unnoticeable with the ongoing drama in the room.

"Your pathetic flame will not work on me, hellhound," Arlo scoffs. "I'm Demon. We are born within the flames. They nourish us. Please, John, lend me your strength." He opens his arms and curls his fingers in invitation. John raises an eyebrow. "Come, boy, you are out of your league."

With the misdirection of the flame, neither the demon nor I notice the knife in John's other hand. That is, until he throws it with impossible force. It flies across the room. The weapon spins end over end through the air, and with a meaty *thunk*, it buries itself in Arlo's shoulder, pinning him like a pretty butterfly to his fancy chair. I blink.

The demon makes a startled noise, and before he can grab the handle, another knife flies, hitting his other shoulder, *thunk*. John's colossal form prowls forward. I take another few steps back. His head snaps towards me. "Stay," he says in a deadly whisper.

My feet freeze. "Okay, no problem. I will stay right here, on this spot," I mumble, pointing to my feet, and then I throw him a thumbs-up.

Beside me, Eleanor lets out an exasperated sigh. Unconcerned with me and without further acknowledgement, John continues his almost leisurely prowl towards the pinned demon.

Arlo laughs. "You've been playing warrior for too long, boy. I'm older than time itself, older than this world. Which incompetent idiot told you that these demon blades would influence me? Mhm. Sadly, you have been misinformed. The symbols carved into these blades are useless. I will still be wreaking havoc when this planet is dust. You are useless, pathetic. Spending all your time protecting this world, yet you couldn't protect your pack." Arlo laughs mockingly. "Taking them was shamefully easy. You think these knives can hold me?" In answer, John slams another blade into the demon's left wrist, then another into his right. Another knife in the thigh, then another, until the demon can't move an inch. With each new blade, the demon laughs malevolently.

My whole body shudders. In my desperation, my eyes search out Eleanor for reassurance. The elf is no longer by my side. Instead, she is crouching over the sizeable oriental rug in the centre of the room. With a flurry, Eleanor flips the rug several times, revealing a circle.

A familiar circle.

My legs buckle, and I plop to the floor on my bum. My stomach screams in pain, but all I can do is stare at the circle in horror.

Oh my God.

Desperately I search for something else to look at rather than the ominous circle. I turn my head and instantly regret it as I watch in shock and growing horror as John grips the back of the demon's chair and drags it and its pinned passenger across the library floor. The loaded chair's legs scrape thick gouges into the once-beautiful parquet, and in the demon's wake, dark-green blood drips and smears onto the wooden floor.

Arlo's laughter dies when he sees his destination.

The circle.

He starts to struggle in earnest. He looks so angry, so vengeful, but behind those emotions, I see fear and panic. I hug my knees to my chest. As he struggles, clumps of gelled hair fall into his eyes. With his eyes full of hair and darkness, Arlo has never looked more human. A sob chokes out of me, and my hand flies to my mouth.

My unashamed tears fall.

He's all I've known since I was five years old. The demon ruled my life, but he never truly hurt me. He has always treated me with an odd fairness. All I had to do was follow his rules. Rules that I broke...did I set all this into motion?

Arlo showed me no love, but...but now do I have to watch while the hellhound destroys him? Oh God, I don't know if I can.

John lifts the chair and Arlo over the lines of the circle, I assume to make sure he doesn't damage them. The chair hits the floor with a wobble and as soon as it settles, the circle flashes a bright-white blinding light. I slam my eyes closed. The bright light sears the back of my eyelids. I blink to clear my vision. The symbols on the floor glow and hum.

I can sense the circle's power from where I am sitting, and it makes the hairs on my arms stand up. I run my tongue over my teeth...my teeth ache.

My eyes fly to Arlo and I watch in horror as his face morphs...it *bubbles*. I can see the bones moving as his face rearranges itself into something nightmarish. Gone is the ostentatious pout. He looks more like the pictures in the old books that depict demons. Gone is the pretty face that I have known for seventeen years, and in its place is something *other*.

"I will make restitution. You can have the girl," the demon screams. More of his blood splatters to the floor. Me? He is offering me?

"She is worthless. You were going to sell her. What would I want with the girl?"

"That was a bit of fun at her expense. I saw your guilt...you want her for yourself." The shape of his mouth has changed, so Arlo's voice is rough, guttural.

Are they talking about me?

"Guilt? What you saw was what I wanted you to see. There is no guilt, demon. Just this." John shakes his head and smiles mercilessly.

I rub my chest, God, I'm so stupid.

Arlo glares. "Haven't you worked out what she is? Yes...yes, of course you have—you knew straight away, didn't you. Come on, John —your pack, it wasn't personal; it was business. I had no intention of hurting them. Things happened beyond my control." The hellhound slams another knife into the demon's chest. I pull my knees to my own chest.

My God, where are they all coming from?

After finding the shifter pup locked in that room...I don't know the details of what happened to John's mum and sisters. I don't want to know. I have enough nightmares. But that moment in the hospital, when the demon revelled in their deaths in delighted, whispered words, I knew, without a doubt, that he was responsible.

Even with that knowledge, I still can't watch another creature suffer.

I can't. It's not in me to sit and watch someone be hurt. Not after having suffered the same fate of being subject to John's ministrations.

With determination, I place my palms on the floor, ready to roll onto my knees so I can stand, but a firm hand pushes me back down.

"Emma, no. This has been a long time coming." I flinch as the demon screams. "Do not interfere, don't you dare get up," Eleanor says.

"You used me," I whisper. My voice is hoarse from my tears. "While you pretended to guard me, you were in here making a demon circle, in his home. Weren't you?" I shake my head in disbelief. I throw my arms up in frustration. "I don't know how Arlo let this happen. It was never about guarding me; it was always about gaining access. How could you do this, why would you do this? I can't watch this. I have to help him." I attempt to rise again and she pushes me forcibly back down.

"You will do no such thing. He was going to sell you. If we hadn't interfered, one of those men would have bought you."

"No—"

"Yes. Don't be such a silly little girl. This is how the world works."

Eleanor's hand returns to my shoulder in warning, and her fingers dig in. "What do you think you could do? Against John?" She shakes me.

"I could get the guards—"

"What guards? The entire estate is crawling with hellhounds. Wake up, Emma. The demon's rule has ended. You need to pick a side. The right side. The demon would have let you die. John saved you."

I knock her hand away from my shoulder. "John hurt me," I shout. At that declaration, Eleanor shakes her head with disgust. She looks away and blatantly ignores me. "Please, don't let the hellhound do this, Eleanor." I beg, "Please make him stop, please make him stop. I don't want to be here to watch this, please?" The demon screams, and without my permission, my eyes flick back to Arlo. I look.

The floor of the circle is now awash with blood. No-no-no. I shake my head and press the back of my hand to my mouth in an attempt to stop the frightened keening noise as it spills from my lips.

Each time the hellhound uses his knife, my own skin burns.

Oh, God. I don't want to be a witness to this.

Traumatised flashes of my time in the basement superimpose themselves over what is happening to Arlo. I rock from side to side and hug my knees. I could have kept pretending that what John did to me wasn't as bad as my memories. That it was embellished by pain and trauma. Seeing this happen with my own eyes without my shock and pain to shield me, there is no burying the truth. *John is a ruthless monster.*

At the sight of all that blood, part of the innocence that I was doing my best to cling on to—dissipates.

After all the challenges I've had in my life, it comes down to the bare-bone facts. The demon has sheltered me. I heard things...I heard about the horrible things the demon had done. But before I rode out that morning on Pudding, I still thought the world was fair.

I never wanted to see the bad. I wanted to see the light.

The beauty.

I wanted the bad things to fly above me, completely over my head, unrecognised in the bright bubble of my life. I wanted to be untouched, untainted.

On purpose, I misinterpreted intentions and situations. I didn't want to see it. I didn't want to see the horrors of what people are capable of. Especially when I could do nothing to help. Powerless.

I held a silly, fixed black-and-white view where I trained myself to see only the good. To see evil and recognise it around me...I didn't want to. I thought it would break me.

Then I met a frightened shifter pup.

After I looked into those green eyes...to ignore the terrible things and to not acknowledge them, it made *me* culpable. It made *me* accountable.

I patted myself on the back for doing the right thing in helping her...when I should have been doing the right thing on countless other occasions.

It is my shame that I didn't act sooner.

Bad things do not stop if *you* don't see them or when you stop watching or stop listening to the whispered *truth*. They are still there, even when you deny their existence and put your metaphysical fingers in your ears.

I'm a hypocrite.

You don't need power to do the right thing. No, doing the right thing *gives* you power.

I struggle again to stand, and Eleanor mercilessly holds me in place.

I watch as the hellhound turns Arlo into pieces of bloody meat, destroying the once-proud demon. As I watch, I remember my pain and my fear at the hands of this man.

I cry.

I cry for the demon who nefariously sheltered me.

I cry for my own inadequacies—my uselessness.

And I cry because deep down inside I know...I know John is *right* and I *hate* him for it.

It takes a monster to destroy a monster.

When it is over, all I can hear is the steady drip-drip-drip of blood. The rough breathing of the hellhound and my own twisted, beating heart. The girl I once was has died, but by God she was clinging on. Clinging on to foolish hope. But in this world full of monsters?

There is no hope here.

CHAPTER
THIRTEEN

Glistening raindrops spatter against the window, beading the view. I trace them with my finger.

"Where do you go?"

I turn my head and look at Sam blankly. She frowns and then pokes me. "Where do you go? As you haven't come back yet. I need you to come back. *Bob* needs you to come back."

Well, if my horse needs me...

"Also, Emma? Stop stroking the hellhound, yeah? It's fucking weird. You realise there's some big, handsome, sexy, muscly man underneath all that fur...Oh?" Sam wiggles her eyebrows and gives Riddick and me a lecherous wink. "Never mind, carry on. You keep stroking, girl."

She bounces away, leaving a trail of white shavings like wooden snowflakes behind her. They must have fallen down her boots when she was mucking out and stuck to her fluffy socks.

I quickly snatch my rogue hand away and I blink at the massive hellhound that is leaning against my leg. "I apologise, Riddick. I didn't mean to treat you with any disrespect." My voice is rough from disuse. I twist my hands in my lap and give him what I hope he interprets as a contrite look. He blinks back at me. His head bumps my elbow, and when my arm flops towards him, his cold nose butts at my hand.

Huh, okay then. I put my hand back onto Riddick's head and continue running my fingers through his soft fur.

Since the move to the new house, I've been stuck in my head. John has employed my vampire friend Sam to help me with the horses. The cost of a full-time groom must be excessive, especially with only Bob and the new pony, Munchkin. Sam is used to managing a team of grooms and a yard of over forty horses. I bet she's so bored…but I don't know because I haven't asked her. I sigh and rub my face. I've been a terrible friend. I need to snap myself out of this unhelpful mental darkness.

I am grateful for Sam's help. I can't do much with the hindrance of Bert, and most days I am exhausted. The tiredness hits me at odd times, and so quickly. One second I feel as if I can do everything and the next second, bam, my energy has gone, vamoose; it's vanished like I've hit a brick wall, and there is no way around it. It is so frustrating.

Hopefully I don't have long to wait until my reversal operation with Mr Hanlon. Once everything is back in place, perhaps this horrible tiredness will end.

I shake my head. Some powerful creature I've turned out to be. Every time my mind drifts, I am back in the library doing nothing while the hellhound kills Arlo. I feel ashamed.

I could have fought, tried harder, I could have done more. I hate myself for my non-action, and I hate myself for thinking that the world is a better, safer place without Arlo. It might be true, but who am I to decide that?

Now in my nightmares, Arlo watches on as I relive my time over and over again with John in that basement. He pouts and his black demon eyes glare at me when he tells me, *"You didn't help me. Why should I help you?"*

"Sam's right. I need to spend some time with Bob," I say. I scratch behind Riddick's ear and like a giant dog, his back leg goes. I huff out a laugh. I know he is doing it on purpose to make me smile. "You are one strange shifter."

I groan as I reluctantly get to my feet. I wobble as it takes a second to get my balance. I leave the room and Riddick pads behind me. He patiently waits as I stuff my feet into my boots.

Then we both go outside. Riddick is like my faithful shadow. I don't know when he sleeps, as he always seems to be awake and one step behind me, watching me, watching out for danger. His green eyes are always watching. Instead of it being creepy, he makes me feel safe.

My shadow keeps me safe.

The house. Dear John, of course, came to the rescue. My guards moved me and Bob into a pretty five-bedroom house with good equestrian facilities. The sprawling, modern home is on a quiet cul-de-sac. It looks like a doll's house from the front, with white render and a bright red door smack-bang in the middle with windows spaced equally on either side. It's pretty. I believe, from half listening to Sam's gossip, the house used to belong to a professional footballer.

John's continued help is bizarre. I don't know why I am here. It's disconcerting to sleep under his roof and eat his food. I'm forced again to allow my enemy to take care of me. It feels wrong. The last thing I want from the hellhound is any kind of care. I can't get my head around why he feels the need to help me. He did what he needed to do. He got his revenge by killing Arlo. Surely my usefulness is at an end? Yet, here I am. I now feel like the guards are here to keep me from leaving. Ha, they're not here to keep me safe, that's for sure.

I shake my head. I'm so naïve. They've always been a method to control me...I just didn't realise it until it was too late. Arlo didn't realise it either. I shuffle my feet a bit with that thought.

I haven't even been able to look at Eleanor. She makes me sick. She's nothing like the warrior elves in the stories—they protect the innocent and fight for justice. No, she's a hired mercenary, a hired thug. At the snap of the hellhound's fingers, she wouldn't think twice about taking me out. Killing me. In her eyes, I'm filth. Demon-loving filth.

Listen to me. I annoy myself as I'm a hypocrite. I'm quite happy to hate Eleanor but I *stroke* Riddick. Perhaps it's because Riddick wasn't around when things kicked off at the estate? I've noticed he's never about when John is. I've never seen them in the same room. John has probably got something on Riddick—perhaps that is the reason he is being forced to stay in his wolf form. I flick my eyes to regard him with concern. It must be uncomfortable to stay in animal form for so long. I grind my teeth. I wouldn't put it past John to do something so barbaric.

I wander aimlessly around the small, brick, L-shaped stable yard. It has four large stables, With one room for tack and feed. I trace my fingertips across the wooden doors. The stables are immaculate—Sam has already done everything.

A raindrop lands on my cheek. I didn't think to put a coat on and it's still raining. But I don't mind the rain and the nip of the wind on my face reminds me I'm still here, that I am still alive.

Bob and Munchkin are out in the field. Bob saunters over to me when I approach the fence. He checks to see if I have anything for him to eat. When I produce nothing tasty, and his snuffling inspection of my hands and pockets leads to no result, he turns away in disgust and wanders off.

As he snatches at the grass, he gives me a side-eye. "Human, visit only if you offer sustenance," his angry chomping seems to imply.

Munchkin, the cheeky black Shetland, stuffs his entire head through the fencing and attempts to bite me. I step away from his teeth, and when Riddick growls at him, Munchkin pulls his head free, rears up, and waggles his little hooves at us. He then turns and kicks out with both hind legs and runs away with a squeal.

"Little horror." I can't help my laugh; he makes me smile. Sam has him in a tiny lightweight rug and he looks adorable.

"So you've finished moping over the demon," Sam says, wiping her hands on her pant legs as she walks towards us.

Riddick pads away, to a dry spot underneath the overhang of the stables. He is giving us some semblance of privacy to talk. He settles down, head on his dinner-plate-sized paws. I see a flash of tongue and his bright white teeth as he yawns, and then he closes his eyes.

The fine mist from the rain settles on my skin, and a piece of damp hair sticks to my cheek. I scrape at the wood of the fence with my nail. "I wasn't moping, Sam." I grumble, "The hellhound pulled Arlo's head off in front of me. It was…it was bloody grim." I swallow and rub my chest with my knuckles. "I can't sleep without it replaying behind my eyes over and over again. All that blood…" I shiver.

"Yeah, I can understand. That green shit gets everywhere." Sam shudders and wrinkles her nose. "You can't even call that stuff *blood*; it looks and smells bloody awful."

I roll my eyes toward the sky. Not quite the point I was trying to make. Gah, vampires.

"You're better off without him, though...you know that, don't you? He was an evil twat." Sam digs me in the side with her elbow to make her point.

I give her an incredulous look. "Yes, I know he was a bad guy. I'm not used to that level of violence." I lower my voice to a whisper. "I don't know what's gonna happen. Sam, I'm so scared."

"Hey, we are living in a delightful house and you've got your Bob. Just take each day as it comes, Em." She shrugs. "That's all you can do. If the hellhound kicks you out, I've got a place for you. So keep your chin up, kid. It could be worse."

I lean against the fence, my chin on my arms. "Yes, it could be worse," I whisper back.

CHAPTER
FOURTEEN

I POTTER around the stable yard and find a light job of scrubbing the automatic water feeders. They are bowls in the corners of the stables that automatically fill with water. I scoop handfuls into a wheelbarrow I've parked below to catch the water. Then I scrub the already-clean bowls. The bowls do have rubber plugs in the bottom, but they are sealed so tight, I worry that if I even managed to get the stopper free, it wouldn't go back. So I scoop.

My hands are red and almost going blue from the cold water, but I'm determined to do something. I've been trying my best to keep moving without lifting or doing anything heavy. I sigh. To be honest, I get in Sam's way.

Next, I'm going to do the horse feeds.

I hear a strange noise and the hairs on the back of my neck rise. I rub my wet, stinging hands on my jumper and pop my head out of the empty stable.

I count at least a dozen vampires outside the property line. They are heading towards us. "Oh bloody hell. Sam, friends of yours?" I shout. Sam appears from Munchkin's stable with a grooming brush in her hand. She takes in the situation and shakes her head.

"Nope, I don't have friends. Apart from you—only you seem to like me."

Eleanor appears around the corner. With grim determination, she grabs hold of my arm and guides both Sam and me into the feed room.

"Emma, do not move." There is the telltale glow of her warrior mark and with a wave of her hand across the doorway, she sets a ward around the feed room.

Whoa. Two short swords appear in her hands from out of nowhere. I watch with trepidation and a bit of awe as Eleanor goes into warrior mode.

"Vampires, you are trespassing. I suggest you leave with haste or otherwise prepare to die," she shouts as she heads towards them.

"I wonder what film that's out of?" Sam asks as she pokes at the solid, clear fae ward. It looks entirely different from the witch-made wards that I'm used to seeing. I shrug. Eleanor is so badass she can pull off the cheesy line.

"We have no quarrel with you, elf. We just want the girl," a vampire shouts back.

"The girl is my charge. If you want her, you must come through me."

"That's defo bad dialogue from a movie. Ooh, I can't wait for the heads to fly. I love a good fight." Sam claps her hands together and grins. Then she literally presses her nose against the ward. "I bet she gets at least seven before the rest run away. I wish we had popcorn."

"You don't eat popcorn," I say, distracted as the vampires invade the land at the back of the house. Hmm. I can't help thinking, *why* hasn't the house and stable yard got a boundary ward? With an established ward, they wouldn't be able to get so close. It makes little sense.

Eleanor twirls her two swords, perhaps warming up her wrists or as an intimidation tactic. Why she does it isn't as important—it's how impressive it looks.

The vampires flood the grass field and I watch as Eleanor engages them. Suddenly she begins to dance with her twin swords. That's the only way I can describe her movement and fighting skill: a dance. I'm in awe of her talent. Both swords work independently of each other, yet they still work together. The vampires don't stand a chance. Their once-human bodies, although stronger, are no match for the warrior elf as she swiftly cuts through them, one slice at a time. They fall at her feet. I cringe. It's so brutal. At one point Eleanor fights five vampires at once. Instead of it being an advantage to the vampires, they get in each other's way. It makes Eleanor's fluid dance even more dramatic, and it also makes her job easier. Slash, stab, twist. She jumps, and at one point she even rolls, avoiding a deadly strike from behind when a vampire tries to sneak up on her.

"Whoa, she is like a ninja," Sam says in awe.

I feel sick. The hairs stand up on the back of my arms. It is like watching art. Deadly, horrible art. Yet I still can't help worrying about her—the odds are overwhelming.

Even though Eleanor's impressive display and her fighting prowess are making me feel a little queasy, she is risking her life to keep *me* safe. The petty things I have felt about her fade quickly and become insignificant. I respect the hell out of her.

My silly empathy makes me sad for the vampires, though. Whoever sent them, totally sent them unprepared, and the massacre unfolding is a tragedy.

"Ooh," Sam says, her hands now pressed to the ward as well as her nose. I cringe as Eleanor serves a brutal slice across the torso of a big vampire.

"Will some of them recover?" I ask as I twist my hands.

"Yeah, if they get blood in time. As long as they don't lose their heads or get a direct hit to the heart, it's all good," Sam mumbles back, distracted by the gore outside.

There is a growl and a flash of red fur, and Riddick joins the fray.

The vampires scatter then as Riddick's fur—like he has struck a match—lights up with blue flames.

Oh my God. Flaming fur.

Sam lets out an appreciative ooh. I won't be able to look at him the same way again. And here I was wondering if he could do a tiny flame on his human hand like John. When he's got enough fire magic to light his fur on fire. Wow.

The fire magic lights up the entire garden with a blue glow. Riddick is like a mini blue sun as he burns and tears into the surrounding vampires.

Yet they keep on coming.

It's then that we hear the voices: "While everyone is busy, why don't we kill the horses?" My eyes widen with horror.

"Oi, if you harm a hair on those ponies, I will rip your ugly faces off," Sam snarls, banging her palm uselessly on the ward. A face appears, and it looks Sam up and down.

"What you gonna do, stuck behind that ward? You can't do shit. Charles, you do the little'n and I'll get the big'n. Horse blood is a proper treat." He licks his lips.

"You fuckers. Leave them horses alone. I will hunt you down, I promise. I will fucking hunt you down. Them horses are not for eating." Sam again slams her hand against the ward with a growl.

With a chuckle and a wave, the vampire stomps away. The other one has already slipped into Munchkin's stable.

The vampire's hand goes to Bob's stable door.

Without me thinking, my own hand lands on the sharp knife, the one we use to open bales of hay and bags of feed. I grab the black handle in my fist.

I'm so livid my vision has gone hazy, almost black. An inhuman growl rumbles in my chest and leaves my throat with a roar.

Whatever Sam is saying—shouting—is totally outside the bubble of my rage. At the forefront of my mind is *Bob*. My full attention is honed in, and all I can see is that vampire.

I growl again and shoulder Sam out of my way.

I step through the ward.

CHAPTER
FIFTEEN

The vampire steps into the stable. Distressed by the stranger's sudden entry, Bob backs up against the far wall. His ears are pinned back and his eyes roll wide, showing the white. Bob snorts, nods his head, and paws at the ground. Instinctively, my boy knows this vampire is out to do him harm. "Be a good boy, let's see how you taste," the vampire says with a chuckle and a smack of his lips. He moves towards my Bob.

On silent feet, I slip into the stable and creep up behind him. No one threatens my horse. I hold in the angry growl that wants to rise and rip itself out of my chest. Without thinking, I lift onto my toes. I reach out and grab the vampire's hair. I grit my teeth, jerk him back, and with a tilt of my wrist, I run the blade across his neck.

I slice his throat.

I cut cleanly through his carotid and trachea. His only sound is a sharp intake of breath, then a gurgle.

His hands fly to his throat in an attempt to stem the bleeding. I let go of his hair. The vampire turns. His panicked eyes search for the threat and he finds me. When he takes in my expression, his hazel eyes go wide with fear. With a snarl, I circle him. Protectively, I put myself between him and Bob. I let the growl I've been holding in rumble.

I. Am. Livid.

Sweet Emma isn't home at the moment.

I boldly step forward and push him. He stumbles away from me, but not as fast as I would like. I shove him again, *hard*. I force him out of the stable, away from my horse. The vampire hits the doorway on his way out, wobbles for a second, and then sinks to his knees. Dispassionately, I note that he is struggling to breathe. He wheezes and chokes, and blood bubbles from his lips.

Another growl leaves my own lips. I kick away his legs so I can quietly close the stable door. Leaving him on the floor outside, I step over his prone, gasping form.

Munchkin.

My lips curl back, and I bare my teeth.

The second vampire has had little luck with getting hold of the feisty Shetland pony. My head tilts to the side as I watch him chase the pony around the stable...until he isn't and the pony turns and chases him. The vampire lets out a squeal. "This thing is nuts. Patrick, what do I do? It's trying to bite me," he shrieks, unaware that his buddy *Patrick* is a little preoccupied. Munchkin chases him towards me, and he runs into my knife.

He runs into my knife six times.

"Emma, are you okay?"

Sunlight streams through the stable door. One stripe catches my face and arm in its golden light. I blink. Sticky, warm, dark-red vampire blood clings to my hands and arms. One hand tightly grips the black handle of the dripping blade. My other hand drifts up. I hold it up to the sunlight. The blood glistens, and it makes sticky webs as I open and close my fingers.

"Emma, are you okay?"

Blood covers me. I pant with exertion.

My eyes drift down to the body at my feet. Munchkin gives the vampire a good kick, and his head rolls to the side. I get a good look at his glassy, dead eyes.

CURSED DEMON

"Are you okay, stabber?" Sam shouts again from the feed room. Her words finally register through my slowly fading rage. The blackness clears from my eyes. I nod, even though she can't see me. My head keeps nodding on its own, it won't stop.

Oh my God. What did I do?

What did I do?

Uncontrollably, my hands shake. I must have stabbed him in the heart. I hold the knife out in front of me, extra careful not to stab myself. My knees knock together. "Bloody hell," I whisper. "Oh bloody hell, what did I do?"

Munchkin ignores me...and the dead vampire on the floor. He goes back to eating his hay as if nothing has happened.

"What the hell did I do?"

"Incoming," Sam shouts. Dazed, I walk out of the stable and encounter two more vampires. I wobble on my feet, and I clutch the blade in front of me in a tight, sticky fist.

Oh, hell. Where's the rage and the blackness now when I need them? I tremble. Oh no, I can't do this again...I can't do *that* again.

Riddick comes out of nowhere and barrels into the vampires. His teeth flash, and his massive claws rend the vampires' flesh. Blood splashes. The vampires don't have time to react. No time to scream.

My whole body trembles. I rock on my feet, heel-toe-heel-toe.

"Good job, Emma," Sam yells.

God, I feel sick.

Eleanor comes out of nowhere and gets in my face. "You were supposed to stay in the feed room," she chastises. "What were you thinking?" I continue to rock.

I wasn't thinking.

With a wave of Eleanor's hand, the ward on the feed room drops and Sam is released. "Oh, fuck—look at all the vampire bits. They're all over," Sam grumbles. Her nose wrinkles as she peeks over Bob's stable door. "Look at the stable floors. I'm gonna have to hose both the boxes down and disinfect." With her hands on her hips, she continues, "The field is also a mess. I hope I get a clean-up team to help with all the goo."

The words *vampire bits* and *goo* circle around in my head. I lean forward, and I only miss not throwing up on Eleanor by a whisker.

When I've finished, I go to rub my mouth...only to freeze at the state of my hands. My bloody hands. I can't wipe my mouth. I look forlornly at my trembling, bloody, murdering hands. "I better get cleaned up," I mumble.

"Yeah, killer, go wash your hands," Sam helpfully pipes up. "The heathens were gonna hurt the ponies," she tells Eleanor.

"Bob's a horse," I mumble.

"What arseholes. I got this, Em—I think you've had too much excitement for one day. I can hear your heart from here, it's going nuts."

"I am furious with you. Putting yourself at risk like that," Eleanor continues with a *tut*. It's as if I haven't just sprayed her shoes with puke.

"I'm sorry," I whisper. "I didn't mean to make your job harder." *I'm also sorry for the horrible things I've been thinking in my head about you.* But I don't say the words as it would only make the whole situation worse. I've been judgmental and unkind.

"Well, I understand your need to protect your horses," Eleanor says gruffly. At that moment, the vampire whose throat I first slit groans.

"Is he going to be okay?" I ask.

In response, a sword appears in Eleanor's hand. Light on her feet, she turns. There is a high-pitched noise as the sword sings through the air. She slashes the blade in a downward arc. It meets the vampire's neck at the perfect angle, just above his clutching hands. In its wake, the blade paints a fan of blood on the wall of the stable. The vampire's head topples to the floor with a squelch.

I wobble. Okay, urm, I guess that answered that. I cough to clear my throat. Pieces of loose hair that have escaped my ponytail blow in the slight breeze. I avoid looking at the vampire. Instead, my eyes fixate on the blood dripping down the wall.

My chest hurts. I killed a man today. I've stepped over a line and into the realm of being a killer.

The sound of paws padding, claws clicking on the concrete gains my attention. I lift my eyes. Angry energy swirls around Riddick. His ears are held flat to his head and his tail is tucked. He prowls towards me.

Blood covers the fur on his face. His nostrils flare as his nose meets mine. He snuffles at me. When I attempt to wiggle out of his way, his growl blows the wisps of hair back from my face, and I make the mistake of inhaling and get a mouthful of Riddick's *meaty* breath. I gag. "Eww, your breath smells of dead vampires." Riddick growls again and shows me a mouthful of enormous teeth. My entire face scrunches up in disgust, and I turn my head away. I'm sure I saw bits of vampire stuck between his teeth. "Riddy, I'm going to puke again if you don't get your bloody face away from me." Riddick huffs out another stinky breath as he continues his smelling inspection. "Stop it." I smack his nose away from Bert. "Stop it, I'm fine, they didn't hurt me. Stop breathing on me...stop sniffing me. It's gross."

"Em, fuck...urm, maybe you shouldn't smack the *hellhound* in the face," Sam squeaks out, her voice full of horror. I wave her concern away.

"I left Emma inside the feed room, behind a protective fae ward. She then left the ward of her own volition, to intervene in an attack on her horses," Eleanor says.

Riddick growls, again showing me his teeth. Not caring about my bloody hands, I grab his muzzle and close his mouth. I look into his angry eyes.

"I'm not sorry. I couldn't let them hurt Bob and Munchkin. I used the knife in the feed room, and I..." my voice drops to a whisper and my eyes fill with tears..."I stabbed them, stopped them. I'm...not...sorry." I swallow a sob, wobble and rock again. "Riddy, I killed someone." Riddick looks at me with understanding. His green eyes are full of compassion.

My hands fall away from his nose as he moves his colossal body to my side. His soft fur brushes against me, and he wraps himself around me. Warm, supporting. I take comfort in his nearness. After a few minutes, I gently pat his head. "I need a shower." I wobble away. My teeth chatter, and with each step, my body screams at me to rest. Nobody stops me. I can only assume that it is now safe. I need a shower.

This newly made *monster* needs to wash the blood from her hands.

CHAPTER SIXTEEN

I'M QUIETLY READING on the sofa, diligently doing my best to ignore Riddick, who is attempting to get my attention. Nope, it's not happening, this book is way too good. The throw cover that I have over me jerks and ever so slowly moves. Out of the corner of my eye, I see Riddick has the cover gripped between his teeth. My lips twitch. I roll my eyes, grab it, and hold on.

Ha, I don't stand a chance in a one-handed tug of war with a hellhound. Riddy does a big jerk and the cover flies from my grip and pools on the floor. His dinner-plate-sized paws stomp all over it. I huff to cover my giggle and turn my entire body away.

Way too close for comfort, Riddick moves so he stands over me. Nose in the air, I continue to ignore him and pretend to read my book. Instead, I watch him. He has a glint in his eye and an evil doggy grin on his face. From this angle he looks even larger, which is a neat trick considering that he is already huge.

In revenge for my non-action, weirdo Riddick leans across and licks my face. His great dirty tongue licks me from my jaw to my forehead, catching the side of my mouth.

I dramatically spit and scrub at my mouth. "Eww. Eww. Eww. Oh my God, you did not just do that. Eww," I wail, shuddering as I frantically rub at the rest of my wet face with my sleeve. "Riddick, you are a minga. That was so gross...you are a shifter, not a dog." I attempt to smack him with my book, almost falling off the sofa in my zeal. Riddy jumps from side to side, avoiding my blows, a smug and delighted wolfy grin on his face. "Bloody Riddick," I grumble, doing a poor job of hiding my smile.

Hellhound or not, I love the stupid creature.

"John has arranged a meeting with an angel," Eleanor says as she glides into the room.

I stop my assault on Riddick and blink up at her. I am currently hanging off the sofa. I huff and blow at a piece of my hair that's fallen from my ponytail and is now sticking in my right eye. I sit up with wobbly arms and give Bert an apologetic pat. Eleanor now has my full attention. What? An angel?

"Me? Why do I need to see an angel?"

"To heal you, of course," she replies. Heal me? An *angel* can heal me? Huh.

I wiggle and my book falls to my side, forgotten. Excitement and disbelief thrum through me. I've never seen an angel. Like demons, they have to be of a high level of power to be on Earth. They aren't native creatures of this world.

The ley lines that form the witches' transport gateway system are also gateways to other worlds. It's all a bit hush-hush. I only know this because I listened to the whispers at the estate, and I spent a lot of time with a demon. Only the powerful come to Earth, as they have to have the political clout in their world to do so.

Angels aren't like religious depictions of angels, but some believe that both races, angels and demons, had input into early human and creature history...poking their noses into our evolution, nudging us all in their preferred direction. Angels are as scary as demons. Perhaps if there is a creature that might heal me, an angel might be the one?

I scratch the side of my head. My ponytail is lopsided and more hair has come loose. To gain an audience with an angel is an impressive feat. I pull the bobble out of my hair to re-do my ponytail. I don't know why John wants to waste the opportunity on me...especially as there is a high risk of the magic not working. Then again, John is a hellhound—I shrug as I gather my hair and pull the elastic tight—so maybe he's best mates with everybody and I'm just overthinking things. Perhaps I might get information…information about what kind of creature I am.

"I will go get changed," I say with a bright smile. The thought that I might be able to go to the loo normally is a huge motivator. I stumble on the cover as I get up and use Riddick's enormous head to steady myself. "Thanks for that, big-head," I say with a cheeky grin. With a playful growl, Riddick nips at my bum as I hurry past.

"Ten minutes," Eleanor shouts at my scurrying back.

The house hasn't got a gateway, so we will have to drive to the angel. I make sure I have a fresh hot-water bottle handy. The heat will help me if I have any tummy pain on the way.

Twenty minutes later—as I had to check on Sam and the boys—we pile into the car and set off on a new adventure.

Thirty minutes into the drive, I'm fiddling with my phone, so I don't see the other vehicle when it hits us.

There's a sudden burst of impact. Time slows as my body slams into the seatbelt. My phone flies from my hand. I'm torn between protecting Bert and protecting my face. My stoma wins, and I hug my tummy protectively with my arms. Another bang. My head jolts to the side, and the pain in my side and stomach is excruciating. White-hot. My seatbelt keeps me painfully anchored in place, burning my shoulder and chest.

I whimper.

Crunch.

Weightlessness. I feel like we're in a washing machine as the car flips, over and over. I scrunch my eyes tightly closed as the window next to me splinters and glass flies, the tiny shards stinging my face.

My vision and hearing reverberate like I'm underwater as the car settles on its side. I blink and groan. It sounds distorted to my ears. My head throbs, and with a shaky hand I touch an incredibly sore spot on my temple. My fingertips come away wet with blood. I'm hanging sideways. I blink and try to focus my dizzy vision on the condition of the other occupants of the car, but both Eleanor and Riddick are *gone*.

What…where did they go?

With a *whoosh*, my hearing comes back. Outside the car I dimly hear fighting, the hiss and singing of Eleanor's swords, Riddick's growls. Then the tick-tick of the engine, the crackle of metal, glass, and plastic as the car continues to settle.

I take a deep breath to control the frantic beating of my heart. I'm unsure about modern cars and engine fires, and it might be my imagination, but I'm sure I can smell smoke.

Oh bloody hell. I decide it is safer to get out. I remove my seatbelt, grip it, and do a controlled slide across the seats until I stand on the crushed passenger door. The plastic and glass crunch underneath my feet and I use the headrests for balance. I slip my boot off and wobble on one foot as I surreptitiously use it to knock the shards of glass away from the broken side-window now above me. I feel like an idiot for what I need to do next.

I'm going to have to pop my head up into the line of fire.

Crap, it'll be like sticking my head out of a rabbit hole, hoping that a predator will not bite it off.

Boot safely back on, I tuck my hands into the folds of my jumper. Fingertips lightly on the windowsill, I take a breath, brave it, and peek out.

Vampires. Oh bloody hell, the vampires are back.

It looks as if Eleanor and Riddick have drawn the vampires further away from the car and me. I duck back down and puff out a nervous breath. My heart pounds. *Thud-thud-thud.* God, I feel sick. *Come on, Emma.* I silently count down from three. When I hit *one,* I force myself to leave the vehicle.

I somehow manage to scramble out with no one seeing me. The car roof squeals as I slide down it, and I land on the road in a heap. I slam my back against the car. Then I let out a frightened squeak as the car rocks a little with the impact of my body weight.

Oh bloody hell.

Thud-thud-thud goes my heart. I pant, and my arms tremble from the exertion of getting out of the car. My head throbs and my crazy heart rate makes me feel dizzier. The residual pain from the accident throbs through me, and combined with my overwhelming panic, it makes it hard to think.

"It's okay, you're okay." I compartmentalise and swallow down my pain. I push it to the back of my head. I know pain, I can deal with pain. I can do this. I don't have a choice. I take a deep, shaky breath and force myself to be calm. I lift my jumper and do a visual check on Bert. Luckily, my stoma has no immediate issues. God, I am lucky to be alive.

I get on my hands and knees, tuck my head, and crawl.

The car that hit us is burning, and dark, rancid smoke billows around me. Shards of glass glitter on the tarmac like diamonds in front of me, and unavoidable they bite painfully into my knees and palms. I quickly crawl away from the fighting and the car, desperately searching for somewhere safe to hide.

Out of the corner of my eye, I catch a droplet of red.

Oh no, my head wound is dripping. With horror, I look back at the small trail of blood drops that lead away from the car. Oh God, I'm leaving a ruby-red trail of breadcrumbs. I swallow a sob. What a stupid mistake, with all the vampires. I rub as much blood as I can from my face onto my jumper and keep going. There is nothing I can do about it now.

Oh God, vampires, please don't smell me.

I crawl into someone's legs. I close my eyes and hunch over into a ball. I should have stayed in the car. "There you are, pretty demon," a male vampire says.

My heart drops. Oh bloody hell, not this demon shit again.

The vampire scoops me up. I don't stand a chance against his strength. Before I even think to scream for help, his hand slams over my mouth. My nostrils flare in panic as I try to get enough air into my lungs.

As he drags me towards a generic white van parked at the side of the road, he licks the blood from the side of my face. Gag. He hums and smacks his lips as if he is at a wine-tasting. "Huh, so that's what a demon tastes like. Not as bad as they have led me to believe. See you later, pretty demon." With a last lick and a creepy chuckle, he throws me unceremoniously into the back of the van.

I hit the metal floor with a *crack*, my knees taking the brunt of the impact, ouch. The van's back doors slam closed. Waiting hands grab hold of me, and a bag...they shove a smelly black bag over my head.

Darkness. With every panicked breath I take, the thick material of the bag moves closer to my lips. I tremble as they tie my hands together in front of me. Painfully tight, the plastic digs into the scars on my wrists.

The click of chains. I shudder as a terrible memory tries to take me.

The van jerks, and suddenly we're in motion. I squeak as I'm thrown against the side panel. The impact knocks my already-sore head. I try my best to brace myself, protecting Bert as much as I can. But I slide and bump around. I let out a frustrated cry. My bruises will have bruises. Before I can slide again, I'm gripped by big, heavy hands, and I'm lifted. Warmth surrounds me from behind as I'm nestled into a stranger's lap. My kidnapper's lap. Solid thighs pin me against an equally solid chest. I shake with fear.

"I couldn't watch you bashing about anymore. You looked so pathetic. Settle down, lass, I won't hurt you. I won't let anyone else hurt you either, so just relax. This will be over soon."

"Where are you taking me?" I whisper. But this stranger with this smooth-as-chocolate voice doesn't answer. He just holds my shaking, frightened body tighter.

I'd like to say that when the doors of the van finally open with a grinding metal clank and a creak, I spring into action like a ninja and fight like hell.

But I don't.

If I hadn't been in a similar situation before, perhaps I'd be brave and be able to fight. But all I remember is the pain, and every day, all I see is the physical reminder of my last kidnaping stamped all over my body—in Bert and a network of scars.

This is all too soon. This is all too much. I can't do *this* again. I won't.

Everything fades: thought, worry, emotion. I retreat to a protective place in some deep corner of my mind that I've never found before. I stop trembling. The big guy who has held me steady during the journey guides me carefully out of the van. My body is being helped out of the vehicle, but I'm not currently here.

Like a coward, I've hidden in the dark recess of my mind.

My elbow is gripped, and I meekly follow. When I'm pushed down into a chair, I automatically sit. When the bag is tugged from my head, my eyes automatically respond to the bright overhead light. I blink.

I don't acknowledge the sound or the surrounding movement—I can't. Fingers click in front of my nose, but I don't respond. Hidden safely away in my mind, I curl into a ball.

My body sits in the chair, my eyes unfocused, my heart beating steadily in my chest. A hand slaps me across the face, and my head turns to the side with the impact.

A loud noise, yelling, crashing, banging.

Silence.

CHAPTER SEVENTEEN

Fur. Fur underneath my fingertips, so soft. *Safe*. My fingers twitch of their own accord, they flutter across the familiar softness. My head tips forward, and the darkness recedes.

I blink.

My senses rush back, the cold bite of the unyielding metal chair beneath me, the sharp smell of bleach.

I'm cold. I'm hungry. I'm thirsty. My body aches. How long have I been sitting here?

I blink. The sight of cream-and-red fur fills my vision. Riddick. He sits in front of me. There's fresh blood on his muzzle, and darker dried blood is mixed with his soft fur. Oh, no—I jolt when I see it. A silver collar is around his neck.

Shock and fear flood me, and with that potent hit of adrenalin, everything around me becomes more focused.

"Riddy," I whisper, my voice hoarse. I lick my dry lips. I hiss when I try to lift my hands to touch the collar and my wrists chafe against tight plastic. My frightened gaze drops to my hands. I can't lift them more than an inch as the vampires have secured them to the arms of the chair. I'm trapped. I'm trapped.

Oh God, I need to get out of this chair. I need to get out. I struggle in vain and thrash about until the pain of my desperate movements registers. It bleeds through my panic and I notice that my entire body is screaming in protest. Ouch.

I pause, panting. My rapid breaths whoosh in my ears and I barely swallow down a scream that wants to bubble up from inside me. I force myself not to struggle and instead I close my eyes and compel myself to breathe through my rising hysteria.

No, breathe slow. It's okay, it's okay. Save your energy. I want to scoff at my thoughts. Energy? Ha. What bloody energy? Just breathe.

This is happening. I have to deal with it. I have to be brave. I have to think through the desperate, raging panic that is clawing at my insides.

If I don't, I'm dead.

Everything happens for a reason, even the horrible stuff. *But why me?* the little voice in my head whines. Why not you—would you really want someone else to suffer in your stead? No, I would not. Riddick needs me.

God, please give me the strength to be brave. If not for myself, then for Riddick.

I slowly count down from ten. When I get to one, I take a shuddering breath in, and then I open my eyes.

Riddick limps away from me. He offers me no further comfort; he just whimpers and then curls into a ball in the corner of the room. He won't look at me. My lip wobbles and my heart drops like a stone. To see my growly, brave friend so defeated is *horrific*. He is the picture of total misery. I am suddenly ashamed, and so embarrassed at my panicked reaction. Riddick is truly suffering, while in reality I'm only tied to a chair. *You are pathetic, Emma.*

Hell, what have they done to him?

I know little about silver and its effect on shifters. I know that silver stops the shift. The memory of when I first saw the hellhounds with all their silver weaponry comes to me and only adds to my confusion. Why carry silver weapons when contact with it makes you weak? My head throbs. What is the silver collar around his neck doing to him? Can it kill him? If his whimpers are any sign, it must cause him pain.

"Riddy, are you okay? Is...is Eleanor okay?" In response, Riddick soulfully whines.

Oh my God.

As if his whine was a signal, a lock disengages and the bang of metal makes me flinch. The door opens behind me and the sound of heavy footsteps precedes two men as they saunter into the room.

The cell.

From his corner, Riddick growls.

My eyes flick about as I take in the bare cell-like space. My chair is the only piece of furniture and it is positioned in the centre of the room. I can't help the all-over body shudder that wracks me as my eyes take in and then skitter away from the drain underneath me. I clamp down hard on any thoughts on why they would need a drain. I shudder.

"Are you awake, buttercup?" Fingers click aggressively in my face. "I knew a little rub from the hellhound would get your attention." The guy who is talking has a horrific nasal voice. He isn't a vampire—no, he is a shifter, which is a surprise. Dark hair and sharp features. He gives the impression, as he looks down his pointed nose at me, that I am an inconvenience on what should have been a perfect day.

I keep my expression blank, take a shaky breath, and lift my chin. I can't help thinking: *Sorry, pal, undo me so I can leave. Sorry that my kidnapping and being here tied to this bloody chair has ruined your day.* But smartly, I keep those words firmly locked inside. I am in enough trouble.

"See the state of your hellhound? If you don't answer my questions..." He smirks, leans forward, and whispers in my ear, "I'll let you use your imagination on that one." His fingers brush against my left hand and I flinch. His eyes light up, and almost nose-to-nose, he purrs.

Oh, now he is interested in me. I lean as far away from him as I can. "Breath," I mumble, and I wrinkle my nose in distaste. His eyes flash in anger and he lifts his hand as if to hit me. There is an almost inaudible growl. I close my eyes in readiness for the blow, but it doesn't come.

"Just think, I was going to go soft on you, give you a time-out and a drink of water. Let's do this," he snarls.

He steps away. I gasp and my heart skips a beat at the sight of the trolly. He has a trolly full of *bad things*.

A wheel squeaks as it rolls across the uneven floor and the things clatter, clink and knock together. They glint in the harsh overhead light. I try to shrink away, but the unyielding metal chair I am tied to keeps me firmly immobile, as it's bolted to the floor.

I can't speak, I can barely breathe as my mind starts to shut down. More adrenaline and fear cloud my head, and I vaguely recognise that I'm going into shock.

He claps his hands, and I jump at the sound. "Oi, you disappear again and you'll never see him again, so stay with me." He nods in Riddick's direction.

Eyes gleaming, he runs his fingers almost reverently across the *things* on the tray. The shifter carefully separates each item so I can see them. Wide-eyed, I swallow.

His hands are delicate for a shifter, hands that are no doubt unafraid of getting dirty, bloody. He selects a knife, and he shows me the silver blade by waving it in front of my face. He smirks at me as he stands, his eyes now alight with cruel amusement. I tremble. His hand drops and he taps the Rambo-style knife against his thigh. It's big and solid, and the edges are serrated, with a blood groove down the middle.

Tap, tap. Tap, tap.

I nod, swallow, and lift my eyes away from the blade to his face. I look directly into his mean brown eyes. He is going to use that stuff to hurt Riddick, to hurt me. Oh, God. I shake, and my teeth chatter.

In desperation, my gaze skitters away from the threat of the man with the knife. I turn my frightened eyes away from him and focus on the other man who is in the room.

Is he safer?

My bound hands' jerk. He is John-level beautiful, but he doesn't stir me the way John's frightening beauty does. The way John makes me feel is almost magical—and I don't mean in a good way. Magical like a curse. It's like I've been cursed whenever I'm around him.

God, I hope the hellhound isn't angry when he realises his guards have failed. I worry for them if we're lucky enough to get out of here, to live through this nightmare. John is another scary obstacle to overcome. The man won't accept failure.

I drop my thoughts about John and focus back on the handsome face. Dark hair and pale honey-coloured eyes stare intently back at me. He stands quietly as he casually leans, resting a booted foot against the wall, arms folded across his chest as he observes me. I do the same and observe him right back, my head tilted to the side in contemplation. He isn't a shifter, a vampire, or a demon. I'm not a hundred percent sure, but I don't think he's fae either. The power coming off him in waves is...familiar. Even though I never saw his face, I'm pretty sure he is the man in the van that held me in his arms.

Angel? Could he be? What the hell is going on...

He pushes away from the wall and meanders towards me. The shifter backs away, giving him room. He crouches down in front of my chair. Being deliberate in not touching me, he grips the metal arms of the chair and leans forward. His honey gaze flicks up to my eyes, to the side of my head, my cheek, and then back. His eyes stop moving, as though he's focusing with everything he has on maintaining eye contact. Somehow I know he doesn't like what I presume is the smear of blood from my head wound and the bruises that are smattered achingly across my face.

"Save the hellhound some pain and tell us what we want to know," he says. As soon as I hear his voice, I know he is the man from the van.

I drop my eyes and look at my lap. I gnaw on my lip. It's a simple decision: I need to do everything in my power to keep Riddick safe. I lift my eyes. "You promised you wouldn't hurt me," I whisper. "You lied." His honey eyes flick again to my throbbing cheek. Someone, perhaps the shifter, hit me.

I push down my fear inside me and gather the tatters of my courage. "I will answer your questions...if I can. But I have one of my own." The honey-eyed man narrows his eyes in disappointment. Like someone's turned off a light switch, the softness in his eyes disappears, replaced with distrust. I shiver.

Crap, I've lost whatever rapport we had and I've disappointed him. *Way to go, Emma.*

"Go on," he growls.

Permission granted. Oh hell, in for a penny, in for a pound. I release my sore lip from between my teeth. "The warrior elf that we were with...is she okay?" I husk out.

The honey-eyed guy takes a sharp breath. I don't know why he is surprised—Eleanor is my guard, and she was protecting me. I need to make sure for my own sanity that she is okay.

"Yes. Last time I checked, she was fine."

I allow myself a deep, shaky breath of relief. "Okay, well, good, that's okay. Thank you." He stands from his crouch and moves away. He lifts his chin and nods at the other guy, the shifter.

Okay, let the questions—hopefully, sans torture—commence.

Riddick growls. My eyes slide in his direction. But the shifter with the knife, the guy who wants to interrogate me, clicks his fingers in my face to gain back my attention. "Eyes on me, demon."

Demon. I let out a sad-sounding sigh and look at him.

"Don't lie to me as this guy here will know..." He tilts his head and nods towards Honey Eyes "...and I'm very skilled in getting the truth." He smiles as he runs his fingertip lovingly against the shiny new blade of a box cutter. "Where did you come from? Who sired you?"

Oh, the straightforward questions. "I was born in Preston, Lancashire. Twenty-two years ago. I don't know who my dad is or what race he is." I shrug. My throat is so dry. I swallow the roughness and keep talking. These questions are simple. I can do this. "My mum wanted eternal beauty, so when I was five, she sold me so she could skip the vampire waiting-list. A first-level demon bought me." My wrists ache and I want to rub them, but I can't because I'm tied to this bloody chair. I drop my eyes and look. My thin wrists are red from my struggle before and the pressure of the tight plastic.

Fingers click again in front of my face. I lift my eyes. I wish he wouldn't keep doing that. "Keep talking," he snaps. When I don't answer him quickly enough, the shifter interrogator drops his hand and touches my knee. I let out a squeak of protest, and at the same time Riddick *and* the honey-eyed angel growl. The shifter looks in the angel's direction and smirks. He must see something hazardous to his health as within seconds he snatches his hand from my leg and he's backing away from me with his palms up in surrender. He lets out a creepy laugh. The skin underneath my leggings crawls from the memory of his touch. He gives me the creeps—there is something fundamentally wrong with him.

"Keep talking," he snaps again.

I lick my dry lips. I feel like I have a throatful of sand. "I was in the demon's household until a week ago. Then, Arlo, the demon died."

"Died or was killed?" the honey-eyed angel asks. My head swings in his direction.

"Killed. He was responsible for the deaths of a hellhound's pack and the hellhound took his revenge," I answer matter-of-factly, with a small, awkward shrug.

"John Hesketh?"

"Yes."

"He questioned you about his missing pack?"

I swallow and nod. He lifts his eyebrow; I guess he needs to hear the words. My whole body trembles, and my wrists scream in pain at the involuntary movement as my arms jerk. For a second, I close my eyes. "T-tortured me for the information, yes," I stutter out.

"Did you know anything about their disappearance?" God, this whole thing is like deja vu. I have answered these questions before—John's. I don't understand what the connection is and why these men want to know about John.

"Yes," I whisper.

"*What?*" The sharp-featured man snaps. Oh boy, it looks like he wants my full attention. I turn my head back towards him. He has moved closer, and the box cutter is pointing in my face.

Almost going cross-eyed with my eyes on the blade, the words spill from my lips. "I found a shifter female in wolf form locked in a room on the estate. I helped her to escape. When I handed her over, that was when I first met John…"

The questions keep coming, and I answer them. With each question, Riddick *paces*.

"Do you know what you are?"

"I'm half human."

On and on, more questions. Like some angelic lie detector, the angel interrupts for clarification or confirms to the other man that what I'm saying is the truth.

My head hasn't stopped throbbing since the car crash. The bright light and the almost-overpowering stench of bleach don't help, and my poor belly pulses with pain.

But I don't lie.

After what feels like hours, the angel finally gives me some water, and then both men leave the room. As soon as the door locks, my attention goes to Riddick. He isn't doing so good. The silver must be painful. He has stopped moving. He lies in the far corner of the room. Despondent, he stares at the wall. "Riddy," I whisper urgently.

Oh, crap. I have to get the silver collar off him. It must be killing him. Perhaps when he is free, together we can get out of here. I tug at the plastic binding me securely to the chair. Ouch.

I remember reading if you hold your hands up above your head and then quickly bring them down sharply while pulling your hands apart with a twist, you can snap plastic ties. But being stuck in this chair is a different matter.

I stare at my right wrist and grit my teeth, as this is going to hurt. I put on my brave pants and tug and twist my right arm. The plastic bites into my wrist. Blood dribbles. My poor abused abs scream at me to stop. But desperation makes me ignore the pain. I keep pulling. I keep twisting, keep tugging. Blood trickles down my wrist. *Come on, come on.* "Come on, damn you," I growl. The plastic on my right wrist snaps.

Bloody hell, I did it.

I wobbly stand up, my body screaming and my joints painfully crunching at the movement.

Ow. Gosh, I move like an old lady...I must have been in that chair for hours.

I nibble my lip; I need to be careful. With a painful stretch of my leg, I stick it out. Huh, the tip of my boot can just...just touch that awful trolly. My left eye squints as I slowly, oh so slowly, drag the handily left-out torture trolly towards me. I grab some nasty-looking clippers that I have been eyeing for hours. With a clip and a snap at the plastic on my left wrist, I'm finally free from the chair.

With a quick pants-rub, I smudge the dripping blood from my

wrist. In a shaking hand, I grip the clippers, and with determination I limp across the room, intent on nipping that horrible silver collar apart.

"It's okay, Riddy, I'm going to make you better," I whisper.

My fingertips stroke Riddick's soft fur away from the atrocious collar. Before the clippers have even closed around it, a seamless catch hidden within the collar clicks and it swings free.

I catch the collar before it hits the ground, and as soon as my hand closes around it...I belatedly realise it isn't silver at all.

No, it's plastic.

"Riddick?" I ask. My hands shake and I stumble back, my legs weak. The cutters fall to the floor with a *clack*. "I...I don't understand—" Baffled, I look from the plastic collar in my hand to Riddick. Mournful green eyes meet my confused gaze.

Riddick shifts.

CHAPTER
EIGHTEEN

Between one breath and the next, his wolf form dissipates, and a naked *John* stands in front of me. I stumble again, the shock almost sending me to my knees. John grabs me before I fall. My stomach tumbles, and my heart leaps. I feel sick. On instinct as I expect a blow, my hands come up to protect my face and quickly I back away from him. What the hell...what the hell happened?

I look *John* up and down with incredulous eyes. A naked John.

Oh, hell.

I rub my face, and my skin weirdly prickles with awareness as I stare open-mouthed at the beautiful, naked hellhound. I press my lips closed, unwilling to speak. I don't trust my mouth. It might blurt out every tangled, confused thought screaming through my head. The emotions I'm feeling are *nuts*. Even now my eyes find his abs. God was clearly biased when he made this man, because he is perfect. Every sloping muscle, every hard ridge is perfect.

Perfect, perfect, perfect.

The words bounce around in my head. I try not to think about my scars and Bert. I'm obviously *not* perfect. It makes me sad for a moment until I remind myself that there is beauty in my scars, in my imperfection. Beauty in the knowledge that I've survived.

John might be physically perfect. Yet inside he is rotten.

I tuck my hands behind my back, as I am still liable to reach out and run them up and down that bumpy torso. What the hell is wrong with me? A beautiful face and I'm enamoured—enamoured by a monster. A man who has committed atrocities against me. A man that has ruined me.

I hate myself. There is something seriously wrong with my head. There is something fundamentally wrong *with me*.

I wrestle with my libido and gather my crazy thoughts together. The question is, what is John doing here? Where is Riddick? What the hell is going on?

"Where is Riddick?" I ask. "If you've hurt him..." John drops his sorrowful green eyes and rubs his temple.

With that one look...I know.

Bam. Everything clicks into place.

Betrayal, sharp and bitter, hits me in the chest.

My heart feels like it has been eviscerated. Riddick...*Emma, you stupid cow, Riddick isn't real.* I close my eyes and rub my chest. God, it hurts. My shock is a ball of pain in my chest, it's stuck in my throat.

Ha, I dismissed the truth when it was staring at me in the face when I first met *Riddick* and I noted that he looked like a colossal version of my pup.

Of course there was a resemblance...he is her brother. Of course he stayed in wolf form; it was never about being forced.

It was a disguise to manipulate *me*.

For a second I wilt, embarrassed by my obliviousness. How could I be so stupid? I let out a deranged laugh.

Riddick is *John*.

I continue to laugh. My manic, deranged laughter echoes around the bare room. My hands flutter to my mouth to try to hold the crazy in. I can't trust myself. I survived this man. Yet, look at me...still being punished. I tug at my hair.

"What? Why?" Oh my God, *Riddick is John*. "Why? Why?" I say again, more insistently. His expression is grim. He prowls forward and takes my upper arms captive, stopping me from pulling at my hair, but his hold doesn't stop me from pushing him away. "Why?" Another push, warm naked skin. "Why?" Another push. "Why? Why? You were my friend," I wail. Now, like I have turned a tap, the tears come.

I'm angry, God, I'm so angry, and I feel so sad. So, so helpless. I bitterly laugh through my sobs. Has this all been some elaborate test? A joke.

"Riddick was my friend," I whisper brokenly through my tears and my tight, straining throat. John pulls me to him and attempts to gather me into his arms. I struggle a little more against him, but it's useless. His arm around my waist is like a manacle, shackling me to him. My body sags into his warmth. I hiccup a sob. Was I so transparent? Give me someone in animal form, even a hellhound, and I hand over my trust like an idiot. "Why?" I ask.

"I had to make sure," John says, his voice rough, deep, *agonised*.

"Make sure of what? Why would you do this? Let go of me." What the hell am I doing, taking comfort from this man? This *monster*. I finally push away from him. My breath shudders and another stupid tear, a rebellious tear, slips down the side of my nose. Gah, my eyes need to stop leaking.

My friend wasn't real...Riddick wasn't *real*. This entire time, was it all a sick game? "What? Tell me. Was it all a trick? A game?" I say mournfully. "Did I pass? Did I pass your fucking test?"

"You truly don't know," John says with a swallow, his evil eyes sad. No, how dare he, he doesn't get to feel sad.

"*I don't know what?*" I scream at him. "I told you *everything*, God, I helped your sister. I had nothing to do with anything beyond that. Didn't almost killing me satisfy you?"

"Demons lie—"

"*I'M NOT A FUCKING DEMON!*" I screech.

Silence as we look at each other. I shake my head and turn away from him with disgust; otherwise, I'm going to hit him. God forgive me, but I want to hurt him. The man is psychotic.

I rest my hand on the wall. The texture is sharp, jagged underneath my palm.

"Emma, think...your father was a demon. That means you are half demon."

"No—that's not true. No." I shake my head. "That is not bloody true." John takes my face in his hands. He gently cups my cheeks and brushes away my tears with his thumbs. "I don't believe you," I mumble.

"Please don't cry." He rests his forehead against mine.

My God, I can see the truth in his green eyes. I am a demon...how did I not recognise that I was a demon? To quote Sherlock Holmes, *"When you have eliminated the impossible, whatever remains, however improbable, must be the truth."* What a bloody silly idiot I am. I'm still that naïve, stupid little girl. Even after everything...I've yet to learn my lesson. I haven't changed at all.

"I'm part...demon...I'm a demon? Am I evil?" I mumble.

"Being a demon does not make you evil, Emma. It makes you powerful. Power corrupts. Demons as a race aren't evil, just as angels aren't inherently good. You are a lovely person. A good person." The hellhound continues to stare at me, into me, his green gaze intense. "Too good."

"All this time...all this time I thought you were wrong. I convinced myself that you made a mistake in taking me." My voice breaks. "I thought you were stupid, blinded. I couldn't contemplate how you could conclude that I was a *demon*. My God, you were right." I again push away from him. With a self-deprecating laugh, I wobble away to the other side of the room and sag against the wall. "Can I even use that word, 'God'? Will He strike me down?" My eyes drift up to the ceiling. Nothing makes sense in this world anymore.

I am bruised from the inside out.

"Why do you keep hurting me?" I whisper. "What have I ever done to you?"

"I had to determine what your involvement was in the murder of my pack. I had to ascertain that you did not know what you are. That you unequivocally told the truth."

I shake my head and laugh bitterly. "Your conclusion?"

"I absolve you. You are innocent." Oh, thanks for that, John, so kind of you to bloody *absolve* me. "You didn't know, you genuinely didn't know. Emma, how do you not know? Sam said your eyes went black when you stopped those vampires at the stables."

Sam said that? I swallow down another bitter betrayal. Wow, they keep coming, don't they? "Why didn't Sam speak to me? Is everyone in on this?"

What a fool...I'm such a bloody fool.

I rub the back of my head against the wall as my brain struggles to line up all those little puzzle pieces together. I frown and tap my lips with my fingertips. "So...so you wanted to trick me? Force me to go all demon on you...to prove you right? You believed I was faking..." I rub the seal around Bert's bag. Was it *all* a setup? My eyes widen in shock, and I look at him in horror. "Killing Arlo in front of me...the vampire attack at the house...the lack of a ward. The car crash, the kidnapping, all those questions..." My lips part with realisation. "You killed all those vampires...to, what? Test me? Why...why would you do that?" I swallow, and my heart aches. "I killed that vampire. His name...was Charles," I husk out.

I grow agitated and my voice rises. "Those two vampires...did you set it up so those vampires would hurt Bob and Munchkin, to get a reaction out of me?" I tilt my head to the side. "But...you missed it when I went after them. According to Sam, my eyes went black, and you missed it. So you set this up as an elaborate hoax...of fake torture. With your fake silver collar, so you could sit all back of the bus as Riddick and have a front-row seat to my demon unveiling. My downfall. See my reaction first-hand with no distractions. Were you expecting a James Bond-style villain speech? Well, you horrible evil bastard, are you happy that you are fucking right?" I hold my hands out. "Aren't I the most pathetic, worthless demon you have ever seen?" I laugh bitterly. "I helped your sister, yet you tortured me. Not once, but *over and over again*. Riddick was my friend, and you used that against me. You used my love against me. I loved Riddick—"

My voice breaks on a sob. John flinches. "What a stupid fool I am... did you have a good laugh? Have I finally passed your tests, or are there to be more? Now that you have your answers...am I expendable? Like the vampires? Are you going to kill me like you did those vampires? Didn't you think to ask Arlo? Before you chopped his fucking head off, but no, you didn't, did you? As you got it into your head that I was the mastermind...ha, I forgot it's always the overlooked blonde who is the evil genius."

"I'm sorry—"

"You're sorry? No—no." I raise my eyebrows and point a shaking finger at him. I rock on my toes. "You don't get to say that. You don't get to say *sorry* because you got caught."

"Emma, when I was with you as Riddick, our time together was genuine. What I feel for you is genuine." What? His beautiful green eyes plead.

The man is nuts.

I wipe the tears from my face with my dirty hands. "Genuine? You wouldn't know *genuine* if it slapped you across the face. You are so full of shit. You don't have any feelings for me, not without an ulterior motive." I turn away from him. I can't look at him; the man is pure evil.

"I still want the angel to heal you."

I huff and laugh bitterly. My sanity is fraying.

"Oh, how very magnanimous of you, let the angel fix your mess." I look at the honey-eyed guy tucked away in the corner by the door. Has he been here this whole time? "Will you do it, will you be able to heal me?" The angel's eyes widen. Yeah, I worked that shit out hours ago. The angel nods. I huff. "Thank you," I say with gritted teeth. "If your magic can put everything back, I'd appreciate it." Sorry, Mr Hanlon, I know you were looking forward to the reversal surgery.

"Just the internal stuff, not the scars." I glare at John. "If you can, please don't remove the scars. I've. Earned. Them," I bite out.

"I can unlock the rest of your demon powers—"

"My powers? I have blocked demon magic?" I interrupt the angel, staring at him incredulously.

Oh wow, there is more to come? Well, isn't that just dandy.

The angel nods and narrows his eyes. "Yes, it looks as if they bound them when you were a child. It's a normal thing to do—children are by definition difficult. It's a simple but strong binding."

"Will I hurt anyone?"

"That would be unlikely," the angel replies softly. I want to say, "*Well then, let the bitch out.*" I barely hold my tongue. I want to scream, and cry, *rage* at everyone, at the world. My head is rattled, my stupid heart is in pieces. I'm going through the motions of dealing with this shitshow.

Demon, demon, demon.

The word rattles around in my head, festering. How could I have not seen this? It has been in front of me this whole time. Now the honey-eyed angel is going to heal me, oh, and yeah, release my demon powers.

Ha, demon powers. Bloody hell.

Will my eyes go black like Arlo's, will I have scary teeth? Sharp, jagged things that will fill and poke out of my mouth? This is a nightmare.

A nightmare I'm going to have to embrace. John wanted to see, he wanted to see a monster.

Well, looky here, he has created one.

"Aren't you worried that I'll want revenge?" I ask John.

"No." Ha, he is so sure. Yet recently he was convinced that I was something evil hiding behind a human mask. Perhaps I am? I don't know anything anymore. What was up is now down…my whole life, my entire identity has been turned on its head. I'm no longer that elegant human girl, no no, I'm half demon.

"No, you are right—I don't want revenge. I didn't want to be hurt in the first place," I whisper.

I nod politely to the angel. His hands glow gold. "Okay, I'm ready." I don't want John here watching, but I don't have the strength to ask him to leave.

"You might need to sit." We both look at the metal chair. I cringe. He shrugs, and his glowing hands come closer and closer towards me. He gently takes hold of my face. His enormous hands cradle the back of my head, and his thumbs rest on my cheekbones. I blink up at his honey eyes. We both ignore John's growl. The small hairs on my arms and the back of my neck rise and my skin tingles. I shiver. Is this what magic feels like? Does everyone feel tingles and warmth? It's nice.

"So much damage, so much pain," the angel murmurs as his golden magic twists and sparkles through me. "This is a lot of healing to do at once, I didn't realise…you need to sit down—" They are the last words of his I hear as I crumple into strong, waiting arms.

Blackness.

CHAPTER NINETEEN

I WAKE. Sunlight filters through the bottom of the blinds and my heart sinks like a stone when I realise I'm back in my temporary bedroom at John's house. Am I a prisoner, or am I a guest? Oh, heck, do I have to make nice with that monster?

I sit up without pain—wow, that is a good sign—and slide from underneath the covers. Still dressed in my dirty clothing, I stumble into the en suite bathroom. I grip the sink and with trepidation, I look at myself in the mirror. I'm shocked to see the difference. Gone is the hollow-cheeked girl with the purple smudges underneath her eyes and the pale corpse-complexion. With a frown I poke at my face. I don't look like the girl I once was either.

There is a darkness, a hardness in my bright-blue eyes—a sadness that was never there before. I drop my eyes to the countertop, no longer able to meet the eyes of the sad girl. Huh, no wonder. My lower lip trembles.

When you hit rock bottom, the only way is up, right?

Right. I've got this...I look down at my tummy and puff out an anxious breath. I tap my fingertips against my mouth as I count down from three, and with shaking hands, I grip the hem of my stained, dirty jumper and lift it. I pull it over my head and allow it to drop to the floor with a *plop*. The ileostomy bag is still attached to my tummy, but Bert…Bert is *gone*.

Oh wow. I sag with relief.

I lock my knees as my entire body wobbles. I grip the side of the counter so hard, my fingertips turn white; I hold on so I don't flop to the floor.

The. Magic. Worked.

The awe I feel…wow, with a swipe of his hand and the warm golden glow of his magic, the angel healed me. It is mind-blowing. Magic has never been my friend, so it is surreal that an angel's healing gift has made this life-impacting problem disappear.

I empty the bag and then grab the adhesive remover spray, and with twitchy nervous fingers, I carefully spray and peel the sticky seal away from my skin. I tremble as I remove the bag for the very last time.

A sob spills from my lips. It's over, it is finally over.

Relieved tears stream down my face. Having Bert was lifesaving, and I will be forever grateful to the hospital and my surgeon, Mr Hanlon. I'm not sorry that because of magic, I avoided the scary step of more surgical intervention. I can finally get on with my life. I've hit a whole new level of *normal*.

Gah, I will forever hate that word. I laugh through my tears of relief. This "normal" is one that I can now get behind wholeheartedly. I hiccup another sob and allow a wobbly smile to tug at my lips.

"No more crying," I whisper to myself as I gently trace the scars on my tummy. As promised, my surgical scars and the scars from John's attentions are still there. Prominent. As I inspect them, I wonder if I've made a mistake, if I should have perhaps had a full healing.

My lips tug into a sad smile. I am at a youthful stage in my life where I should be able to safely make mistakes and learn from them. Learn what type of person I want to be. But in my world, I can't make mistakes; there is no room for error. You make a mistake, trust the wrong person, and you die.

I think I've proven that repeatedly.

I hand my trust over like it is a meaningless commodity. I can't afford to make any more mistakes. I have to be more cautious. I have to ask questions and I have to be smarter, listen to my instincts.

These scars are a visual reminder.

When my memories fade over time, which is inevitable, the scars will be here. Hopefully, they will keep everything at the forefront of my mind.

They look years old—gone are the puckered, angry red gouges that painfully pulled at my skin and muscle. Instead, silver lines crisscross my tummy. My warrior markings.

I need a shower. As I strip off of the rest of my clothing, out of habit I move cautiously, almost protectively. I shake my head and straighten when I realise I don't have to be careful about Bert anymore.

It's the absence of pain that hits me the most strongly—it is so strange. Over the months I had Bert, I thought the pain levels had improved. But I guess I'd gotten used to it. Its absence now is profound. My body silenced.

I blow out a shaky breath. Internally I have been healed, but mentally, physically, I will never be the same. What's that saying? What doesn't kill you makes you stronger...I've always believed that everything happens for a reason, even the horrible stuff. Especially the horrible stuff. It impacts us the most. It forces us to change, to grow or to falter. You truly find out what you're made of when the shit hits the fan.

The way I see it, I've always had two options: option one, I can roll around on the floor wailing, "Why me, why me." Option two: I can woman the fuck up.

I have so many things I've got to do. If I think about it too much, it becomes almost overwhelming. First step: I need to find Bob, Munchkin, and me somewhere to live. My independence starts now, this very minute.

I will not depend on that arsehole John. The demon gave me an allowance that I managed frugally, so I have money in my name. Not a lot, but enough for me to pay for Bob and Munchkin and set them up at a livery yard, and sufficient to find me a place to live.

I'm not staying here in John's house for one more minute than I have to.

In this world, power is freedom, and I'm a shiny new half-demon. I need to learn what I can do—fast. I need to protect myself. I'm going to manoeuvre myself into a position of power so that no one, *no one* can have control over me again.

I slump. That sounds great when I say it in my head. I wonder how the heck I'm going to learn my new demon powers. I rub at my eyes, and the dirt on my face is gritty underneath my hands. I'm so gross. It's not like I can say to just anybody, *"Hi, will you train my demon?"* I snort.

I need a help book…or…I need a library.

I smile. Well…well, funny that. It just so happens I know of a private collection of demon books. I guess I need to visit one library in particular. Arlo's library.

He has a substantial hidden collection. I strum my fingers on the bathroom countertop in the rhythm of a horse's canter. It looks like I will be sneaking back onto Arlo's estate.

Dodging hellhounds and guards. Whee. It will be so much fun.

I shower and change, and before I head out, I pause. Perhaps I can start with something small, like my eyes.

I go back into the bathroom, and I look at my eyes in the mirror.

I blink a few times.

I strangely hope my eyes will automatically go black, like flicking off a light switch. If I blink enough, they will change. Right? My rapid blinking makes me look a little deranged. Instead of my eyes going black, I look as if I've got something stuck in my eye.

I groan in defeat. This will never work. I strum my fingers against the sink. How do I do this? I've done it before. Huh, perhaps the colour of my eyes is linked to my emotions? When they changed, I was angry. I want to smack my forehead. Of course—anger is the trigger. Arlo never had black eyes when he was happy.

Okay, think angry…I close my eyes and I focus on the moment when Sam said my eyes turned black. My heart drops at that betrayal, but I shove it to the back of my mind to deal with later. I remember the moment clearly. Yeah, I was angry.

The vampire's hand goes to Bob's stable door.

Without thinking, my own hand lands on the sharp knife, the one we use to open bales of hay and bags of feed. I grab the black handle in my fist.

I'm so livid my vision has gone hazy, almost black...an inhuman growl rumbles in my chest and leaves my throat with a roar.

Wow, the rage I feel. *That bloody vampire.* I growl and straightaway my eyes tingle. My eyes fly open and I stare at my reflection. I blink—my vision is hazy. I gasp. Whoa.

They are black. Boom, get in.

I've seen Arlo's eyes like this countless times. But nothing prepares me for seeing my own eyes completely black. It is probably the most freaky thing I will ever see. The urge to poke myself in the eye is huge, and I almost headbutt the mirror by getting too close. They don't look real. I drop the angry energy and like raindrops the black colour bleeds slowly down. It collects and pools at the bottom of my eyes for a split second and then disappears without a trace. I shudder. Creepy.

My wide, multicoloured blue eyes stare back at me. I blink.

Wow. I need to do that again.

SAM IS CLEANING Bob's bridle in the tack room. I stand at the door and watch her as I gather my courage to ask her *the* question. I could ignore it and pretend I never found out, but I am done with lying to myself. I clear my throat. "Why didn't you tell me that my eyes went black?"

Sam turns her head. She tilts it to the side and silently regards me. "You look good. Better. The poo bag is gone then?"

"Yeah, it's gone. After John set up another kidnapping...he staged a car crash. Sam, why didn't you tell me? You told John, but you didn't think it might be worthwhile, to...I dunno, say something to me?"

"He set up a kidnapping? Who did he try to kidnap—"

"Sam, please answer my question," I implore.

Sam shrugs and looks down at the bridle in her hands. She rubs a clean spot vigorously with her sponge. I silently wait. My eyes narrow as the minutes tick by. Finally, she replies with a mumbled, "John pays well."

I flinch at her words. Oh, that's how it is?

I huff out a breath. "'He pays well'? You didn't think to speak to me...give me a heads-up? Sam, I thought we were friends." Sam shrugs again—unbelievably, she couldn't care less. I grind my teeth in annoyance. "Did you not hear me? John set me up. He staged a real-life car crash. The car flipped. Riddick and Eleanor jumped out of the smashed-up car and slaughtered a bunch of vampires." I wait for her to respond. "Do you not care?" I whisper.

Sam keeps scrubbing. I grip the wooden frame of the doorway. "I was thrown into a van and taken to what I can only describe as a cell, where I was interrogated. *Again*. They used Riddick as an incentive for me to talk...if I didn't talk, they said they were going to cut him into tiny little pieces. It was *horrendous*. I was so bloody frightened." I let go of the frame and hug my arms to my chest. I hunch and rub my arms. "Oh, and Riddick turned out to be John in his hellhound form. Did you know that? I was stroking my torturer this whole time." I laugh a little manically, my crazy peeking out.

I cut the laughter off and bite my lips closed. I need to hold all my deranged thoughts in; I need to get a grip on myself. I drop my arms and sag against the door. I close my eyes. When I have gained some semblance of control, I open my eyes and continue.

"It was all a trick to get information out of me. Ever since I fell off Pudding and helped that little shifter, the hellhound has been attempting to manipulate me into showing myself to be a raging demon—a demon that John knew without any doubt that I was, because you told him. You told *him*, not me, that I had black eyes when I confronted those vampires.

"I'm not saying that what happened wouldn't have happened anyway. I'm saying if you would have told me"—I slap my chest—"perhaps...perhaps I would have been more prepared." Sam continues to scrub in silence.

"Did you always know that I was a demon, Sam? Did you know John set everything up? He killed all those vampires to trick me into revealing myself..." I shake my head, my eyes water, and I sniff. I wait for her to answer me, but she will not look me in the eye. My heart squeezes painfully. "N-nothing? You won't say anything to defend yourself?" Sam shrugs. That's all the response I get to my heartfelt splurge of words.

I tap my fingertips on my lips and try to swallow the lump in my throat. In an attempt to get her riled up, I say, "You can get your stuff, and you can go. I don't trust you, not with Bob and not with our so-called friendship..." My voice cracks.

Sam throws down the sponge and places the bridle onto the side with a *clack*. "Look, Emma...you owe me money for buying Bob." I blink at her. That's it? That's all I get?

"I transferred the money last week. It should be in your account," I whisper through that same painful lump in my throat, my chest burning. I recognise the calculated move: Sam has neatly reminded me I owe her for rescuing Bob. Am I being too harsh? Or has my friend always been so manipulative?

"I'm keeping the Shetland," Sam says somewhat snidely as she barges past me, clipping my shoulder. I swallow down all the angry words I want to say. I've done enough damage.

"Were you ever my friend?" I ask her retreating back.

She pauses mid-stride, and with her back still to me, she quietly says, "Em, you are *the* best friend I have ever had...I just wasn't yours. I told that demon twat your every word, your every move. Then I told the hellhound." She shrugs, lifts her chin, and walks away. "I will do anything for protection, and I have bills to pay." Her last words to me whip around in the wind.

Wow, clearly all my instincts are seriously messed up: a ten-year friendship, or what I thought was a friendship, is over within seconds.

God, it hurts.

What is it about me that brings out the worst in everyone? Just when I thought I'd hit rock bottom, I instead have another meter to fall.

CHAPTER
TWENTY

The taxi drops me off between the shop where I first met John and the estate. I hunch as I walk the remaining distance to the estate boundary wall, where I plan to sneak in. I can't seem to stop my shoulders from creeping up towards my ears. The memory of that shop...the hellhounds, of first meeting John...will be forever ingrained in my nightmares. Having it at my unprotected back creeps me out and makes me shiver.

I come to a stop at the boundary wall. I tilt my head as I investigate the glowing new ward. After the angel's golden magic-show yesterday and the supposed unlocking of my demon powers—if that's even what the angel did—I'm afraid of what will happen when I touch the ward.

Perhaps he blocked or altered my strange magic. I scratch my head—it's warm underneath my wool hat. Oh, heck, what happens if my immunity powers no longer work? I bounce from foot to foot. Oh, God, I should have worked out a way to check before I came.

I let out a self-deprecating breath, rub my hands together, and then tentatively stick my right index finger out towards the ward.

I grimace, close my eyes, and wait for a nasty surprise. When nothing happens, I open one eye to see my hand completely immersed in the ward. I want to roll my eyes at my foolishness. Note to self: I have no depth perception with my eyes closed.

My grin fades, and I glance about. I've been messing around out here for way too long. Confirming with a look that the coast is clear, I launch myself at the wall. Oof. In an ungainly move, I scramble over it. I wonder, when I gain control of my demon powers, will I become more elegant and prowly? I can't see Arlo ever having had to climb over walls.

I grunt when my feet hit the floor, and I land in the middle of a dense, thorny thicket of raspberry bushes. Oh bloody hell. I roll my eyes and raise my face to the sky in exasperation. Give me strength. The bushes tangle my legs and the thorns dig into the fabric of my leggings, biting my skin.

Ow, ow, ow.

I tiptoe away from the clingy plants without damaging myself or the thicket—I only sustain light scratches to my legs and hands. I groan as the old phrase "look before you leap" pops into my head. Trust me to choose the only stretch of wall with thorny bushes.

At least this time I'm somewhat prepared and wearing the right gear. I give myself a mental pat on the back. Today for my mission I settled on dark-green leggings, a heavy dark-green waterproof military-style coat, and a black (itchy) knit hat, all finished with sturdy boots.

There are guards everywhere, so it feels like it takes forever for me to slowly, cautiously sneak my way across the estate grounds to the main house. The bright sunlight dims and, luckily for me, the weather changes—the clouds roll in, and it starts to rain heavily. The rain lashes and visibility goes down to almost nothing.

I huddle into my jacket underneath a thick, ornate bush and squint at the guards as they patrol around the house. I watch as they battle the cold, stinging sideways rain. I work out their rotation and route; it's going to be challenging to get past them. When their shift changes, a few of the guards congregate together and in proper British fashion moan about the weather. I grin and use the handy distraction.

I hustle to the side of the house and the laundry room door. The lock has always been a bit temperamental. With a long-practised jiggle, a yank, and a sharp tug, I lift the door up ever so slightly, taking advantage of the loose hinges. The barely heard *snick* of the lock as it opens reaches my ears, and I'm in. I step through the door and close it behind me. I lean against it, and then I wait. The room is empty.

My heart is beating fast, and my naff human senses are tingling. I hold my breath as I strain my ears for any sign of danger. I count down from thirty in my head. When I feel it's safe, I take a small fortifying breath and move.

I creep past the empty, silent machines and grab a towel from a folded stack of clean laundry. I crouch down, grab the handle of the internal door, and open it a tiny crack. So far, so good. I peek out from the hinge side of the door. It gives me an unobstructed view of the hallway as well as the library, which is opposite.

As I unfortunately don't have X-ray vision or a super-sniffer or supersonic hearing, I figure I will have to do things the old-fashioned way. I will have to wait until I'm a hundred percent sure that the library is empty. So I sit on the cold tiled floor. I use the towel to blot the drops of rain from my skin and clothing, and to clean my boots. All the while, I continue to squint through the gap in the door.

I silently wait.

Well, sort of silently. My panting breaths are so loud in the small room. It seems almost impossible to control them with the adrenaline flooding through me, which makes my heart pound like a herd of galloping horses. I do my best to control my breathing, but when I try to quieten it, my chest burns with the lack of oxygen. I attempt to breathe through my nose, but the damn thing squeaks on my exhalation. I roll my eyes. Mouth breathing seems to be quieter.

Every time I contemplate what will happen if I'm caught, my galloping heart skips a beat, and I have to force the thought away. If it wasn't imperative that I access the demon's hidden books, I wouldn't be doing this. I'm so nervous, my stomach hurts.

My patience wins. Not thirty minutes later, the library door swings open and two witches exit. "I thought the library would have better texts," one of them moans. She has fluffy white hair—similar to the seeds of a dandelion before you make a wish.

"Oh, I don't know, Diana. The first editions are incredible."

"Yes, but what about all the references? Surely a first-level demon would have a better reference section..." They continue their conversation down the hallway and disappear around the bend. Conveniently they have left the door open, and based on what I can see from my position on the floor, the library looks empty.

I spring into action. I throw the dirty towel into an empty machine, slip out of the laundry room, and scamper across the hallway. Once in the library, I gently close the library door.

Without intending to, I take a deep breath. The library still smells the same as I remembered. It worried me that Arlo's death might have left an imprint in the very fabric of the room, spoiled it somehow. But it doesn't feel any different.

I guess I carry the wounds of that day within me.

I fix my eyes and ignore the area where he died. I don't look to see if they have erased the circle, or if the floor has been cleaned and repaired. I can't. Not even to show my respect. Heart thumping, I hurry across the room, my gaze firmly locked on the back shelves.

Instead of heading for a dusty dark corner, where any normal person would stash a hidden room, I aim for the centre of the solid oak shelves. It is the most prominent area of the library. Who would be mad enough to put the entrance door to a secret room in such a place? A demon would.

I place one hand on the most notable square of wood, above Lewis Carroll's *Alice's Adventures in Wonderland*, and my other above and slightly to the left on another panel. I push.

Nothing happens.

I duck, cringe, and adjust my hands. I bet the two witches only went for a quick break, and depending on how fast they can drink their tea, they could be back at any second. Oh, God...I feel myself shake. I'm panicking. If I get caught...I swallow down my nervousness, move my left hand an inch, and again *push*.

Oh, thank God. The relief when the panel clicks and the shelves swing forward towards me to reveal the hidden doorway. I open it enough to give myself sufficient room to squeeze inside. The nasty, crackling ward appears as soon as I pass through—it has killed trespassers in the past. I ignore it and gently pull the whole shelving securely back into place with a *clunk*. Once the door securely closes, I hit the old-fashioned light switch and the secret space is flooded with light.

Whoa, that was scary. I take a deep breath in, roll my tense shoulders, and jiggle my arms to loosen them. I then remove my wet jacket, stuff my hat in the pocket, and place it on the hook beside the door. My leggings are a little damp, but they shouldn't affect the environment in the room.

This secret place is...was...Arlo's pride and joy. What seems like unending shelves adorn the walls—they are as beautiful as the library's on the other side of the door, containing not only books but potions, magical weapons, and trinkets. Arlo stored everything of value in here, stuff that he didn't want anyone else to see.

I look about with nostalgia. The hours I've spent in this room...I shake my head. How on earth do I choose what to take? To remove everything from here would be impossible. I let out a sad sigh. It's such a waste. To have permanent access to these priceless treasures would set me up for life.

I've been in here hundreds of times, always while the demon was present. Growing up, this was my playroom. This is the first time I've ever been in here alone.

I drift towards his desk, and my fingers trail across it. My eyes drink in its beautiful wood and the well-worn leather chair.

Sorrow hits me in the chest when I acknowledge that he will never sit here again.

I know he was a bad guy, but I still feel guilty for not trying harder to save him. I thought he was ageless, as unremovable as the mountains, as unending as the ocean tides—but he wasn't. I guess no one is. When it comes down to it, we don't know how long we have, even with the title of *immortal*. No one is unending, not even Arlo.

I don't know why that thought gives me a measure of peace. I guess I wouldn't want to live forever.

I might as well start my search at the desk. I lean down and open the nearest drawer. I sag when my eyes land on a note. I drag the chair toward me and sit, heavy with shock. I lift the letter addressed to me and place it with utter care on the desk. My fingers trace his words.

Sneaky demon.

Dearest Emma,

If you are reading this, you have either entered without my permission, or I am no longer of this earth. If it is the latter, you will be in danger as the sharks will circle. My gift to you is this room and its contents, as it is a pocket dimension—

I squeak, "A *what?*" I jump to my feet, knocking the chair over in my haste, and it clatters to the floor behind me. I back away from the desk. *Oh my God, oh my God.* I flap my hands. *A pocket dimension.* With my mouth open and my eyes wide, I spin and stare at the room, taking in the vast space with fresh eyes. I rub my face.

No wonder it is so big and has zero effect on the footprint of the house. Of course I knew it was magic, but a pocket dimension? I presume it's a similar magic to the gateways, strong enough to handle my weird demon magic and all the poking about I've done over the years. The room is a little world. An independent bubble within space and time that can only be accessed through a specific means. I glance at the doorway leading to the library. Wow.

That is how it fits into the space between the library wall and the rooms beyond. Wow, that is unbelievably…cool.

And it's mine all mine. Arlo has given the pocket dimension to *me*. I turn and stare incredulously at the letter, still on the desk. I cautiously tiptoe back towards it. I pick up the chair with shaking hands, sit, and continue to read.

— to ensure that nobody else can access the dimension, and to guarantee that you can access the space from anywhere, follow the instructions below to the letter.

The rest of the letter has instructions, and it also has the location of a reference book.

Huh. I wasn't expecting Arlo's last words to me to be anything special…hell, I wasn't expecting any last words. Yet he dropped that bombshell, signed his name, and that is it. There is no mention of my demon heritage. Not that I'm not appreciative, because I am…I'm shocked. The demon does—did—what was best for him. Manipulation, yes; outright kindness, never.

That's why I'll be finding this book, and I will make up my own mind rather than blindly following Arlo's instructions and willy-nilly doing pocket-dimension soul-tying magic. I don't understand *why* he left me this room of absolute treasures. Especially after I fell from his favour. Unless he wrote this letter a long time ago and had yet to update it...who knows? But I'm unbelievably grateful.

I hunt down the book, and when I find it, I let out a joyous laugh. I smile so big my cheeks hurt when I see it nestled within an entire collection of how-to-demon books. Well, they don't actually say that on their fancy titles, but the shelves surrounding the text on pocket dimensions have every demon book imaginable. More books than I will ever need.

Sneaky demon.

How can he be so thoughtful in death? It's nuts. I grab the book, and instead of heading back to the desk, I go to the squishy dark-red leather sofa that's tucked into a quiet corner. I settle down, open the book, and read.

After a few hours, I know everything there is about how this room works. The book doesn't explain how to make a pocket dimension, as it is more like a TV set-up manual. But it has everything else regarding keeping the pocket stable. The book talks about connecting the pocket to a permanent fixture—like the library—or having it linked to a person. As I don't have my own secret doorway and I don't want to unintentionally kill somebody by attaching it to a regular door, the best way to go is to secure the dimension to me.

The steps to do the transfer are the same ones Arlo had written in his letter.

I roll my eyes. Hours of reading and I end up doing the pocket-dimension soul-tying magic anyway.

Once I have read the steps another few times, I guess I'm ready to attempt the transfer. I get up, roll my shoulders, and march to a shelf full of weaponry. I grab a small, plain blade and a cleaning cloth. I clean the knife and then carefully nick the tip of my finger. I place the blade back on the shelf, and with the bleeding digit held aloft, I head to the doorway.

I smear my blood around the doorframe and say the words, "I bind you through time and space, I bind you to my soul, you are mine to command." I sense a tingle down my arm and a pleasant feeling of righteousness in my chest. When I step away, the ward on the door flashes and the colour changes to a smoky black.

I cringe. Oh, crap. Okay...hopefully, black is good? I don't know, but there is now a tug, a heaviness in my chest. I rub the spot. If it doesn't sound too crazy, I can now *feel* the doorway.

The book was specific: since I've attached the pocket to myself, I can now open the door into *any* room. I have to have seen the room with my own eyes, but from what I can gather, I can exit and enter from anywhere. Like...like my own personal portal. Wow, how amazing is that? I guess if I haven't messed it up and I open the door and think of my room at John's...I should be able to walk straight into that room. I shiver. That's incredibly powerful magic.

I have absolutely no idea if it'll work. What I don't want to do is open the door back into the library. So being safe, I guess I should wait. Do some more reading, take some notes. If I don't have to sneak back out of here and out of the estate, I have time.

I back away from the freaky ward. I also need to treat my bleeding finger—I can't have my blood anywhere near those demon books. Heck, I can only imagine what a mess an unintended blood sacrifice would cause. I shiver. I wonder if there is a medical kit around here, with some plasters. I glance down at my poor finger...what the heck...I squint at it, turn it around to look at it from a different angle. I squish it with my thumb...*oh wow*...yeah, the wound, it's, urm...gone.

CHAPTER
TWENTY-ONE

I check my hands and legs for the minor scrapes from the raspberry bushes. The scratches are gone. Holy crap, I healed. I healed myself...or did the pocket dimension heal me? I think back to when I was drying my skin with that towel. I can't remember the angry scrapes being there. No, the scratches were gone. I healed myself.

Bloody hell, that's amazing.

The revelation is mind-blowing. Will it be only the small stuff, or can I heal like a proper demon? I'm unwilling to test my theory and only time will tell. Ha, it was only a slight cut on my finger and a couple of scratches. No need to go crazy, but it's something.

I turn and head for the shelves and the demon books; time for some reading. Thinking of time, at least I know that time in here runs precisely the same as it does outside. Could you imagine coming into a pocket dimension for ten minutes and then leaving and ten years have passed? I shiver—magic is so dangerous in the wrong hands.

That's why I've got to be careful.

I don't know why, but that moment when I asked John if being half-demon made me evil springs into my head. He said, *"Being a demon does not make you evil, Emma. It makes you powerful. Power corrupts."*

I have to be morally incorruptible, with my own strict moral compass. I have to have rules...that's something to think seriously about later.

I spend a few hours reading. When I get hungry, I know it's time to leave. I need to bring some supplies if I am going to be spending time here.

I leave the books I've been reading on the desk—I'm unwilling to take anything with me as I can't yet protect it outside of this room.

I look around Arlo's office. With its dark-green walls and low ceiling, it's cold and drab. The only things of beauty are the objects themselves and the shelves they sit on. I wonder why it was made this way. It's like a basement or a movie office for an old detective who has fallen out of favour and the police department has put him somewhere out of the way. I wrinkle my nose. If I designed a pocket dimension, I'd make it so homey and bright. I picture what that would look like, and I sigh and shake my head...that's never going to happen. I don't even know who makes pocket dimensions, let alone has one so nice. I'd have more luck decorating a cardboard box. Which might be in the cards if I don't get a finger out and find somewhere to live.

At the doorway, I put on my hat and coat. I blow out a nervous breath...I might need to be ready to run if this all goes pear-shaped. I close my eyes and focus on the en suite door of my temporary bedroom at John's house. With that image firmly embedded in my mind, I take a deep breath, open the door, and step through.

I whoop when I step into the bedroom. I then duck down and slam my hands across my mouth. Oops. My ears strain for any movement. When neither John nor Eleanor comes running to investigate, I sag in relief.

Perhaps I need to do less whooping in what is enemy territory. I grin, wiggle, and do a silent happy-dance instead. Boom, I am a master...I then immediately freak out. Oh bloody hell, what happens if I can't get back in? My hands flap. I didn't even bring one book out with me...oh no...oh no, how could I be so stupid? No, no, no. My luck wouldn't be that bad, would it? I cringe and wring my hands. Yes, it would.

I will have to do a test.

I spin to the en suite bathroom door, close my eyes, and whisper, "Secret room, I need you." I snort, that sounds so silly, Emma. I force myself to concentrate. I don't know if the words will work, but anything to help me focus is good, right? It's not the words but the intent that matters, and it should help me focus through my panic and my thudding heart. I step through the door, and the smoky black ward clings to my skin almost lovingly. Huh, that's new. But I'm back in the secret room. Boom, fist pump. I'm so nailing this stuff.

I realise I've left the lights on—I don't even go there, thinking of how that works. The lights, the power...it's enough to blow my mind. I shrug; it's magic. I switch them off.

If all else fails, at least I have somewhere to live. Again, I concentrate and step back into the bedroom.

As I stand in the centre of the room, I tilt my head and strum my fingertips on my lips as I contemplate the bed. Huh. *If all else fails, at least I have somewhere to live*...Mmmm. I wonder if John would notice if I stole the bed.

I grin. I can so see myself dragging it through the doorway and into my new *home*. No, the key word is *stealing*, and I can afford my own bed, and the sofa in the storeroom is comfortable.

I grin wider. Stuff it, I'm going to move out. I know the secret room isn't ideal; it certainly isn't suitable as a place to live, but it would be incredibly handy and incredibly *safe*. My new home, it's perfect.

My bags are already packed. I've not been willing to get too comfortable here, and I never unpacked when I arrived from the hospital. So it takes me mere moments to gather my pathetic worldly goods together.

Oh, yeah. I smile smugly when I remember I have a room full of stuff. Important stuff. I can buy more clothing. Bags in hand, I go through the same routine of thinking of the pocket, and when I step through, I stumble.

The room has changed.

I drop my things at the door in shock, and my hands fly to my mouth. What the hell is going on? My eyes are so wide, I feel as if they're almost bugging out of my head.

Honestly, if I didn't know any better, I'd think I'd have come to the wrong place. This is not the same pocket at all—oh, all the stuff is here, so I know I've not entered some random doorway. There are still the unending shelves, my smoky, happy-to-see-me ward, but they have magically been moved to make way for a...*home*.

Total incredulity fills me as I gape at the surrounding room. I pinch myself.

Bloody hell.

All my favourite things that were hidden within the shelves are grouped together—displayed. Instead of Arlo's murky basement office, it's a homey space. The walls are a pretty, soft grey, the entire room is brighter. I tilt my head back; the ceiling looks higher.

Arlo's desk is now in the corner, and the leather sofa is now surrounded by floor-to-ceiling shelves and a reading lamp—it has been turned into a book nook. A beautiful, cosy mini library. I confirm with a glance that my favourite books and the demon texts I need are close at hand.

I stumble to an ample wooden cabinet with the word POTIONS prettily stencilled onto the door. I trace the writing with my finger and then take a peek inside. It is full to the brim with potions in beautifully crafted bottles.

Even though I cannot use these potions myself, the contents of this cupboard are worth a small fortune.

How can I be immune to potions but sneak through wards? Use the gateways and my pocket dimension without affecting the magic? I have no idea. That is the nature of magic. I smile in the direction of my book nook with all the demon books. I will do my best to find out. Perhaps with more control, I will eventually be able to use potions? I gently close the doors and continue to look around.

There's a weapon area, a kitchen. A dark-grey kitchen with a bright-white worktop and a white ceramic, deep Belfast sink. It has all the kitchen appliances I will ever need.

There are also two brand-new doorways, and when I peek into each room, I find a five-piece modern bathroom in the first room and a perfectly luxurious bedroom in the second. I stroke my hand across the bed and hum when I realise that the bed linen is super soft.

Back in the main room, I spin, my mouth agape, as I take in my new, magical home.

What the hell kind of magic is this? It is everything I imagined I would want for my own space, a proper home that no one can take away. Linking the pocket dimension to me must have caused this to happen. Wow.

I spin. I need to find that book. My eyes fly around the room, and my gaze lands on Arlo's—no, no, on *my* desk. There was a passage in that book...I rush to the desk and after a quick search I snatch up the book and carefully flick through the pages. There was an almost-offhand comment I had seen...there...*If the pocket dimension has ties with a powerful magic-user, over time the dimension can adapt within the original footprint for that magical user's needs.* Huh. I blink and look around again. Well now, that is interesting.

CHAPTER
TWENTY-TWO

I'M ALMOST in a trance as I unpack my clothing—I'm feeling a tad overwhelmed. When everything is put away, I decide I need to check on Bob. I also need to prioritise finding my boy a safe new home. It's a shame that I can't imagine equestrian facilities into being—the book said the changes had to fit in the original footprint. If I could imagine a few acres for Bob and a friend, I'd probably never leave the pocket dimension again. That would be, I guess, unhealthy.

I change into my stable stuff and step straight through the tack room door. I grin. Not the smartest thing to do, but no one is about. Bob's head comes up when he sees me. He whinnies and charges across the field. I'm relieved to see that Munchkin is still here. I grab both boys' head collars and get them in. Their stables are all ready for them. I brush both boys and leave them to chomp on their small nets of hay.

I take advantage of the late-afternoon sun and slump on the floor outside Bob's stable. I stab at my phone, which had been rescued from the car and conveniently left on my bedside cabinet, and search for a livery yard with a vacancy. Gosh, I also need to find myself a job. The money I have will not last forever—keeping one horse even in a basic do-it-yourself livery yard is expensive. Also, bad things happen to people with idle hands. If I'm planning to keep myself on the straight and narrow, I need to keep myself busy.

Bob's head pops over the stable door to nosy at what I am doing. He sprinkles the hay from his mouth into my hair. "Oi, Bob, stop it." He disappears to get another mouthful.

I shake my head and run my fingers through my hair. The little pieces of hay stuck between the strands remind me of Sam and my heart aches.

I feel lost without my cheeky friend, and I can't help worrying about her. I might have been too hasty. Was I too harsh? Mean? I didn't try hard enough to find out what was going on in her head. What kind of selfish cow does that make me? But I can't go back, I can only go forward. If she needs me, I will try my best to be there for her...*if* she ever needs me. Our friendship wasn't about what she could do for me. Being her friend made me feel good, and I'm going to miss that.

I allow another thought to whisper through my head. I miss... Riddick. Isn't that pathetic? I close my eyes and take a sharp breath as I'm hit with a boatload of pain. I miss him so much, those bright green eyes always watching, keeping me safe.

Ha, the silly things he used to do...My smile fades. I can't get my head around the fact that he was John. Who knew that John had that level of fun...that level of kindness inside him. Perhaps the wolf and John are distinctly separate entities. I don't think that's the case, but the disparity between the pair of them is so disconcerting. So confusing. Unless I ask John, I'll never know the answer.

I'm never going to ask John.

Gosh, all these changes. My life has changed so much in such a short space of time. I wiggle my bum; it's going numb with me sitting on the concrete floor. I guess I have to embrace my new life, and unfortunately, at this moment it doesn't include my friends from the old one. I hear a muffled snort, a stomp of a hoof, and finally, a lip-smacking, crunching sound above me. I tip my head back and close my eyes as more hay sprinkles down on me. Well, not all my friends. I reach up and tickle Bob's soft nose. "I still have you, Bob-cob."

I eventually find a few wonderful choices of livery yards. Most are in the northwest of England. I don't need to stay in the area where I grew up, but I think it's better to stick with what you know.

There is one expensive stable yard that stands head and shoulders above the others. It's posh and the facilities available are on par with the estate's. It's an all-singing and all-dancing yard, which means it will have an all-singing and all-dancing price tag. I gulp. It has outstanding reviews and fantastic security.

Not messing about, I ring and make an appointment with the manager in the morning.

"Emma, I didn't know that you'd returned," Eleanor says, appearing from around the corner. "Where have you been? You left like a thief, telling no one where you were going. You need to allow us to do our jobs. We didn't even know if your healing was successful," she chastises me, her hands firmly planted on her slim hips.

I avoid looking at her directly; I am still sore about her involvement in the whole fake kidnapping. I'm back to not liking her, and this time I won't allow my stupid empathy to make me feel bad. I also don't want to lie about my estate adventures this morning. If I look at her straight on, I'm sure all my sneaky endeavours will be written right across my forehead. Instead, I take a leaf out of her fae playbook and don't answer her question.

"My healing went fine, thank you. I am glad to see that you're all right," I say instead, then smoothly change the subject. "I'm going out tomorrow; I've got an appointment."

Eleanor huffs and shakes her head at me with obvious exasperation. "Speak to John. He isn't impressed that you disappeared today. How can we protect you if you don't give us the courtesy of letting us know where you are going?" I can't help snorting at that comment. Wow, really?

I raise my eyebrows and shake my head at her. She hasn't got a clue about how hypocritical she sounds. She wasn't protecting me when the vampires knocked us off the road and the car flipped. That stupid stunt could have killed us.

"Excuse me," I say as I jump up and head for the house, "I'm going to speak to John to ask for *permission*." This will be interesting.

He's in the kitchen, making some food. The smell of cooking makes my stomach growl, and I remember then that I still haven't eaten anything today. It's a silly move; I need to take better care of myself.

Don't look at his face, Emma.

Yes, I will keep my eyes away from him. I don't trust myself. When I look at him, my brain short-circuits, it goes all gooey with my hormones.

Every. Single. Time.

Every time it happens, I hate myself a little bit more. So I will avoid looking at the hellhound. If I don't look into those sad green eyes, my hate can go entirely onto him, it can rest on his massive, broad shoulders instead of on mine.

Thinking of his shoulders...the man still has a body that belongs in a different time. There is a beautiful, brutal kind of efficiency about the way his muscles cord his frame. I forgot how large he is, not having seen him in a normal setting; he dwarfs the kitchen. There is no way to ignore it, the sheer physical power of him. I shiver.

He turns towards me and the eyes that I should avoid light up when he sees me. The hellhound has a mug of coffee in his hand. The mug has a pink, cutesy unicorn on it.

He is making dinner...something so normal. In my head, I'd expect him to be in his hellhound form in some forest somewhere catching and killing and eating raw meat. But no, here he is, charming and untroubled, making food as he sips coffee. In a pink unicorn cup.

"Are you hungry? I made enough for you." Somehow this new John-on-his-best-behaviour version is scarier.

Abort-abort-abort, my instincts helpfully scream.

He smiles.

And my mind goes right into the gutter.

A man has no right to be so fiercely sexual without even trying, and now I have the hellhound's undivided attention, and it isn't frightening. It is...flattering. The way my body lights up when he turns his attention onto me. He turns me on by looking at me. I *enjoy* all that overwhelming masculine intensity focused on me.

I'm some special kind of idiot. Alone-time with the hellhound hasn't turned out so well for me.

I laugh under my breath, snort, and then laugh some more. I chuckle to myself like a loon. Perfectly mentally fit. I drop my eyes and I stare at the centre of his chest. Yeah, the hellhound will love that, he'll think I'm all submissive.

The wanker.

"How are you feeling?" I shrug; it's none of his business.

My blasé shrug looks silly when I glance down to find I'm rubbing at my right wrist. If that isn't a reminder not to trust the handsome bastard, I don't know what is. I can sense his eyes on my scars, so I snatch my left hand away and put both of my hands behind my back.

He tries again. "The healing was successful?" I can't stop my polite head from nodding in response.

Instead, I should swear at him. Scream. Smack him. Rage. But I can't force myself to do that. Screaming and shouting won't get me anywhere. I have to be smart, bide my time.

I know I need to let things go, move on. If I don't…I nibble on my lip, my eyes still firmly planted on his chest. I am not sure I will like the person I will become.

Pure hate is not an emotion I want to feel constantly. It rots. John Hesketh is not having that power over me.

"Yes, thank…you," I mumble.

He puts his coffee down and pulls off his hoodie. The white shirt underneath tugs up to reveal smooth abs before he pulls it back down again. The grey jogging bottoms he is wearing sit low on his hips. Forearms flexing, he tosses the jumper onto a nearby kitchen chair. He leans against the counter and crosses his arms over his broad chest. His top stretches tight across his broad shoulders and energy rolls off him, ferocious, alive.

I want to run my hands down that chest and feel the hard ridges of his abs.

Oh hell. I almost swallow my tongue. My attraction to him must be a mental impairment or something magical. *It's not real.* It can't be.

My thumb points behind me in the door's direction. "I need to go to an appointment tomorrow. I'm just letting you know."

"An appointment for what?" His voice changes from polite and chocolatey to deep and aggressive. I bet if I look, his eyes will be glowing orange. I have a strange urge to say, "A gynaecology appointment." Teach him to not be nosy. But I refrain from lying, even if it would be funny to see his expression.

"To view a livery yard for Bob."

"No," he growls. In John's mind, the conversation is finished. He drops his arms and turns away from me in apparent dismissal. He continues with his cooking.

My mouth drops open…how rude. What. A. Nob.

My temper flares. "Am I your pet?" I growl at his back. I try to keep the venom and the frustration out of my tone, but I fail miserably. He turns back around to look at me.

"Of course you aren't. You're a demon—you are no one's pet," he bites out.

"A prisoner?"

John shakes his head.

"That's great, then you can't stop me. As soon as I can find a home for Bob, I'm leaving."

John shakes his head at me as if I'm a naughty, disobedient child. He steps closer to me, and I'm enveloped in his scent.

I'd like to say the hellhound smells of wet dog, but he doesn't, he smells of campfires and linen fabric softener. His scent tickles the back of my nose and throat. It makes me dizzy.

"You do not understand the dangers of the world out there—"

I lift my head and meet his green eyes with a glare. The edges of his eyes glow orange. My heart misses a beat.

"Oh, don't I?" I plough on, choosing to ignore the orange eyes that scare the crap out of me. I also have creepy eyes, so John isn't a special snowflake. "Well, from the viewpoint of standing here, the world looks mighty safe in comparison." I point to the floor in front of him.

"Emma, I apologised for our misunderstanding." *Misunderstanding?* Ha, the bloody crazy hellhound…he calls what he did to me a misunderstanding?

A laugh slips from my lips and darkness creeps into my vision. I can almost sense my eyes bleeding demon black. Now that I know what it is, it takes nothing for me to blink it away. I have a lot of work to do in controlling the demon part of me, but I will not start by letting it control me.

I huff and slam down on my accusatory words that are screaming in my head to be heard. I cross my arms across my chest and glare at him. I was going to sleep at my new place and pretend to be still living here, but stuff it, I won't do it—I'm not pretending anymore. I will not be a hypocrite like these two idiots that claim they are protecting me.

I have to live my life with my rules, and I'm not pandering to this... this hellhound.

For a few seconds, I clamp my lips closed, afraid to open my mouth again in case he accuses me of being overemotional. My nostrils flare with my building rage, and between clenched teeth, I carefully say, "Look, John Hesketh, I'm not your pet or prisoner, and if you've forgotten, I'm not a minor either. I'm a twenty-two-year-old woman, not a child. Frankly, I'm done. I will not live under your roof for one more minute. I don't trust you. I have a safe place to live, but to be honest, if I didn't, I'd rather sleep in the stables or on the streets then take any more of your *hospitality*." I spit the word. John's eyes flame more with his growing frustration. "I am not asking for your permission. I'm telling you out of courtesy, but you take my good manners, twist them, and demand more of me. I've had enough. Just so you know, John, I have already moved out. I do not need, nor do I want"—I curl two figures on both hands and do the annoying finger-quote thing to make my point—"your 'protection.'" I indignantly huff out an angry breath.

I turn to leave, then stop and spin back—I have another bone to pick with him, "Also, what the hell did you do to my friend? She won't even look at me. My only friend and you had her spying on me? Reporting back to you? What happened when Sam, my only friend, told you she'd known me since I was ten years old, that she watched me grow up? Sam practically raised me. Did you not think, 'Huh, grunt-grunt. Emma isn't a demon mastermind after all'? I didn't take you for stupid, John Hesketh, so don't take me for a fool. Leave my friend alone. Oh, and while you're at it, forget about me." He moves his arm and I flinch. His eyes soften. "I was angry with you and I took it out on her, blamed her. When I should have blamed you. You manipulative twat." I drop my voice and whisper, "Why do you ruin everything?" John regards me with solemn green eyes. "Please, pay her what you owe, protect her if that's your agreement. Then please, for the love of God, leave her alone."

Now it's my turn to turn away, dismissing the monstrous hellhound.

Take that, you dickhead, I think smugly as I stomp out of the house. I slam the door as hard as I can behind me. I know it's childish, but I don't care.

I'm going to get a pizza, I'm starving. Huh, it hits me. Without Bert, I can now eat what I want without pain. Wow.

"Emma," John calls out from behind me. I jump with a squeak at the sound of his voice. Gah, I didn't even hear him follow me outside. Creepy hellhound.

I take my time in turning around. I school my face into a blank mask as I turn to face him. I do an Eleanor and plant my hands on my hips. Even though he is at least a foot and a half taller than me, I tilt my head as if I'm looking down on him. He is total scum. I am so over this man's shit.

When I look at him, all I feel is anger.

Anger is good, healthy.

"One thing I want to say in case we do not see each other again, is, if you are ever stuck, need a doctor, a solicitor, or a portal to get you out of somewhere...you know you can call me. I'll be there for you." His eyes have gone back to green, and he slumps his shoulders in defeat.

My left eye twitches at his words, and I slap my hand over it. My soft heart squeezes...No—I can't let his pretty words and solemn eyes sway me. I don't believe him for one second. His whole sad posture is a lie. He is attempting to manipulate me.

Too right, hellhound, you owe me, but it's not a debt I'm willing to let him pay. "I'm good. Oh, if you wouldn't mind letting me use the equestrian facilities for a few more days, a week at the most, until I can get Bob somewhere safe, I'd appreciate it. Please let Bob stay until I can find him somewhere, that's all I ask." John nods in agreement. Then he lifts his hands and rubs the back of his head. His top rises with the movement, flashing more toned skin and abs.

CURSED DEMON

Gah. He so did that on purpose.

"You know that won't make us even." He speaks softly, his voice warm and deep. His energy trickles around me, playful and cajoling.

"We will never be even," I whisper as I spin away from him.

"No," he says quietly to my back.

CHAPTER
TWENTY-THREE

AFTER SPENDING the night in my new home and sleeping on my cloud-like bed, I feel well-rested and confident. I arrive on time for my meeting at the livery yard. As I haven't been to the stable yard before, I couldn't zap myself there using my pocket gateway, so instead I got as close as I could and then got a taxi.

Everything was going so well until I was ushered into the yard office. "Your kind isn't welcome. You really should have been more transparent on the phone," the manager hisses at me. He lets go of my arm with a shudder and promptly pumps hand sanitiser from a bottle on his desk into his palm. Vigorously, he rubs his hands together.

What? Does he know I am part demon? Does everyone know, do I smell of sulphur? Oh my God, that must be it, I must have a demon stink.

"Our livery rates discourage humans. I have never had a human request a stable before—this is unprecedented. This equestrian centre is a human-free establishment."

Oh. Relief floods me. By my kind he means *human*. The yard is *a human-free establishment*—what a load of codswallop. I stare at him, grinding my teeth. I'm stuck, because if I tell him I am not entirely human and I am half-demon, he will laugh at me for lying, or worse, call the Hunters' Guild to arrest me.

To think I wasted taxi money to get here just to be insulted.

He is a boggart, an English fae. Sometimes people call them house-elves; in Ireland, they are called brownies. Tall, blond, and wiry, the fae sniffs at me with disdain. Even though he is wearing horse gear from head to toe, he looks like he hasn't seen or been near a horse in his life. He's so spick-and-span, the thought *"all the gear and no idea"* comes to mind when I look at him and his immaculate, shiny boots. But as he is the manager of an equestrian centre, he must have the experience, right?

What seems more likely to me is, the *human* grooms that are outside scurrying around are the ones doing all the work.

Human-free establishment, my ass.

I *almost* look back at him with a sneer, a rude reply on the tip of my tongue, but I stop myself. Whoa, what the heck is wrong with me? *My nana would be ashamed of me,* the thought hits me in the chest.

The guy is a boggart; they are renowned for being clean and tidy. That's what makes them so unique. Perhaps it's the owner of the yard that sets the no-human-client rules? Maybe he will get into trouble for even having me on the premises.

To protect myself from going all demon-evil I have to do better; I have to be morally beyond reproach. I tap my fingertips on my thigh rhythmically. The canter-strum calms me.

I need to nail the virtues...urm...when I look up what they are. Courage...and something...I squint at the thought. I think there are seven of them, or is that seven sins? I roll my eyes. It doesn't matter. In the meantime, it's time to set my rules...

Rule number one: Don't be a dickhead.

Rule number two: Be kind—always.

Rule number three: Don't lie to yourself.

Rule number fou...I need to write these down.

The boggart is looking at me as if I am nuts—I've been silent for too long. He points at the door with a glare and even taps his shiny foot impatiently.

Oh heck, it's a shame I have to break a rule right off the bat. "It's not for me," I say, scratching my nose. With a slight cringe and a shake of my head, I shove my hands behind my back and cross my fingers. "The stable is for my employer's horse. He is a demon, Mr..." I look at the guy's brown jacket that is placed carefully over his chair, "...Brown." The lie sticks in my throat, and I swallow down my nervousness. One small lie doesn't mean I'm evil...this is for Bob. "Mr Brown is a barrister for the guilds."

The guilds enforce the law and prevent crime and civil disorder. The dominant races have their guilds controlling their people, with everyone overseen by the Hunters' Guild. Which means the guilds are scary and important.

"Oh, Mr Brown...why didn't you say so?" the boggart says, nodding his blond head as if he and my made-up Mr Brown are besties. I barely refrain from rolling my eyes. "When will Mr Brown be able to come and sign the livery agreement?"

I huff out a breath, dramatically look around, and drop my voice to a whisper. "Mr Brown is incredibly busy, and he is currently off-world."

"Off-world?" The boggart whispers back, his voice filled with awe. I nod and put a finger to my lips as if to indicate it's a secret. He nods back and glances around his—apart from us—empty office. "Of course, of course, say no more."

"It also depends on whether I find the yard satisfactory. I'm unsure if we're going to stable Bob here. Mr Brown expects only the best." Oh God, am I laying it on a bit too thick?

"Of course, of course, let me show you around."

The livery yard ends up being perfect. It has sixty stables split over several yards. Some are the American-style barns with the stables enclosed under one roof, with the stable doors overlooking an internal walkway and an external window at the rear. My favourite yard is where I score an empty stable. The yard is one of the smaller ones, with only ten stables. Each large box overlooks a pretty central courtyard. Designed in a traditional brick style in a horseshoe shape, the adorable stables have a clock tower and a cockerel weathervane.

The facilities are also crazily good, with two huge international-sized indoor riding arenas and three smaller outdoor riding arenas. There is also a horse walker, a lunging ring and all-year grazing. There is also a farm ride, so like the estate I can hack Bob out without having to venture onto any roads. The place is incredible.

By the end of my visit, Stuart, the boggart yard manager, is eating out of my hand. He even arranges transport for Bob and all my horsey equipment to be collected from John's. I pay up front for the full year, and Stuart allows me to sign the livery documents on Mr Brown's behalf.

Phew.

Oh heck, I will at some point have to magic up a Mr Brown, but after reading a particularly interesting demon book last night before bed, I have a rough plan for that.

I lounge on the red leather sofa, a cover on my lap and a mug of tea in my hand, as I flick through the giant tome balanced precariously on my chest. I should do this at the desk. The book is so old that I should probably be wearing the fancy white gloves that historians wear to look at old books and parchments.

Instead, I'm sipping tea a little too close to it, and I'm in danger of dripping the liquid onto the pages. I am an idiot and I'm not thinking. My brain has short-circuited, and I can focus only on the words. The book has my undivided attention; it is absolutely fascinating. If I can do what the text indicates...if it is within the scope of my powers...I should...urm...be able to change my face.

Yeah, my face. It seems from further reading that not only can I change my face but my body type and sex...and if I want to, I could switch into an animal form, too. Wow. It's crazy.

This is one of the reasons demons are so dangerous. This is the reason John kept demanding to see my *real* face. According to this book—I tap my finger on a page—I can look like whatever I want.

Freaky.

Wide-eyed, I take another mouthful of tea and shiver. The book isn't an instruction manual. It hints at how to do things, but it doesn't give any clear directions or details. Ahh, magic users are so mean. With the whole, you could do this...but nah, I'm not telling you how because you should have proper people around you to show you. Reading between the lines, I think I have a rough idea of what I need to do. I gulp some more tea and my heart pounds in my ears.

The thought of being able to look like anyone is thrilling.

The possibilities are endless, as it's not just hypothetically shifting into a person or an animal. According to this book, it's *everything*, including clothing and weapons.

Can you imagine…

I'm in a scary situation, and bam, I look like John with all his muscles. Come on, who is going to mess with John? Or if I need to blend into a crowd or disappear into a small space? Being able to change my appearance to blend in is a game-changer. It's not like I'm unmemorable; you see my white-blonde hair and there is no missing me.

I've always been a pretty girl—oh woe is me, I have long blonde hair and pretty blue eyes, the universe is punishing me…sob…sob. Ha. I am not moaning about that, but being pretty in this world puts me at risk from the predators. It makes me an easy target. Add being half-demon without protection to the mix, and I'm doomed.

From my understanding, when shifters turn into animal form, they have to remove their clothing to do so. A friendly shifter guard at the estate once told me that shifters can use a witch's potion to shift with their clothing. But the potions are expensive and difficult to get hold of, and they're only really available if a shifter is on friendly terms with a talented witch. The guard sneered at the idea of taking a potion. I have no idea why…I guess most shifters are men and getting their bits and pieces out in public isn't an issue for them.

According to this book, demons don't need to strip. Everything… clothing, jewellery, weaponry…should shift with me. If I can just learn how.

I tap the book in thought. It all hinges on this question: was my father a first-level demon? If he was, there is a possibility that I will also have that level of power, or at least a small version of it anyway.

I have hope, as when the pocket dimension turned into my home, I realised I must be relatively high on the power scale. Why would it adapt so quickly if I wasn't?

My point is, I would enjoy nothing more than being able to go about my day unnoticed, without the risk of an inappropriate touch or comment. Ultimately, without fear.

Everything I've got to do to keep myself safe is almost overwhelming. I have so much to do. I'm so alone.

I've never felt so scared or so free.

The nervous excitement I feel at the endless possibilities, but also the stress of pending failure, gives me a mild headache. I put everything away and decide that what I need is to get some fresh air.

I need to go ride Bob and then get some food-shopping. Which is kind of exciting…I've never shopped for food before, and to me, going into the supermarket and filling the trolley with stuff is exciting. It is such a normal thing to do, a small thing that proves how controlled and insular my life with Arlo was.

Time will tell if my freedom is a good or a bad thing.

I hope I have the time to learn…as I have a horrible, nagging feeling that things are going to get worse.

CHAPTER
TWENTY-FOUR

I'VE JUST BOUGHT my first-ever load of practical food. It was a challenge, as at one point I had a trolley full of random items, stuff that I like to eat but that didn't go together. When I realised that custard, mashed potato, and olives weren't really a good flavour combination, I had to turn around and start all over again, putting things back and picking up items that would not only work together, but was stuff that I might actually cook. Ha, at least I had the epiphany before I paid.

As I am leaving the supermarket, I see leaflets fluttering on the customer notice board. I guess not everyone can afford the internet. Nosily, I turn my head and scan the ads. A flyer catches my eye. It is for a women's self-defence class at a local gym. Huh. Now that might be handy, and there is a new class tomorrow evening.

I put the trolley back and battle to free my pound coin from the locking mechanism that is holding it hostage. It has gotten dark while I've been inside, and the car park is strangely empty. I hurry away from the supermarket; I avoid the car park and stick to the pavement. As I make my way around the side of the store towards a normally busy shopping area up the road, the hairs on my arms rise and a shiver works its way down my spine. My instincts scream at me, *I am being followed.*

My eyes dart about, my heart thuds. As I pass a dark shop, I glance in the window at the reflection of the street behind me. My heart misses a beat when I spot them tailing me. Three vampires are hunting me.

I'm sure there are more.

They move so elegantly that they almost float, compared to me as I shuffle awkwardly along the street, overloaded with my shopping. I hold the bags in my sweaty, tight-fisted grip, my still-weak arms trembling. The bags rustle and my heart pounds; sweat beads on the back of my neck. Somehow I don't think they have anything to do with John... the word must have gotten out about my being a demon, or about my unprotected status. Creatures love to gossip, and I am guessing these vampires are probably opportunists looking for an easy mark. A snack.

They mean for me to see them, so I'm more worried about the ones that I can't yet see. I think I am being herded. With so many eyes on me, opening my doorway is going to be a challenge.

With trepidation, I search the quiet street. I was going to go to a shop that I know well and use their doorway, but it's further up the road. Too far up the road—I need to get out of here pronto.

Unfortunately, I can't use the supermarket doors as they are automatic and they don't have a door handle. I con-template abandoning my shopping, dropping it to the street and running, but I know the vampires will be on me within seconds.

A can clangs down the street, noisily scraping the ground as it rolls across the pavement. The sound spooks me. My heart jumps and I spin, my shopping bags painfully smacking against my legs as I abruptly do a sideways shuffle into a dark alley.

Not the smart-prey move.

Nice one, Emma. I am being hunted by vampires, so what do I do? I hop into a dark alley. I hope my crazy move will confuse the hunting vampires as much as it does me. If I'm lucky, it might gain me a few extra unseen seconds to find a doorway and escape.

I hurry past two huge bright-yellow bins full of rubbish and food waste. I breathe through my mouth so I don't get a whiff of the rotting garbage. Yuck...mouth-breathing doesn't help, as the stench is so bad it fills my mouth to the point where I can almost chew it.

The alley has rear fire doors for a takeaway and a nightclub. I head towards the closer nightclub door, which I know will be locked. However, I *hope* I can access my home through the locked door before the vampires arrive at the top of the alleyway and grab me. I've never attempted to use a locked door before.

Crap. Perhaps this is a thing I should have practised?

I jump almost a foot into the air when there is a crash, a bang, and a gurgling scream at the mouth of the alley. What the hell is that?

An echoing, angry growl reverberates off the tight walls of the surrounding buildings. A shifter has joined the party.

Oh hell, a bad shifter or a good shifter? Oh God. Oh God. I don't look back and instead I break into a run. I avoid a puddle of something unpleasant as my feet slap against the tarmac. When I get close to the door, my hands shake as I push the bag handles down my right arm to the crook of my elbow to free my hand. I reach for the handle and open *my* door.

Heart pounding, I rush inside and slam the door closed and slump panting next to my touchy-feely ward. My back thumps against the door.

Safe. God, I feel sick. That was way too close.

I drop my bags in disgust. I bought too much stuff and I encumbered myself with the shopping—that choice could have killed me. I scrub my shaking hands across my face. I need to do better.

I remove my coat. When I go to remove my boots...eww...a used condom is stuck to the bottom of my left shoe. I almost throw up in my mouth. That is *nasty*. I am so glad I have gloves and that I bought bleach. I carefully remove my boot. That will teach me to wander into nightclub alleyways, I think with a curl of my lip and a full-body shudder.

I ignore my shopping and my poor boot for now. Dejectedly I wander over to the sofa and slump down. I stare up at the ceiling. One step forward and then two steps straight back...I'm rubbish at this. I can't even do a basic shop without messing everything up. I tug at my ponytail and then rub my face in frustration.

My real strategy hung on my being able to change my entire visage or being able to run. Crap, it looks as if hoping to have a handy doorway to step through will never be a foolproof plan.

I groan. This is no way to live, and at the moment I'm a demon that feels like prey. If I don't get myself at least halfway able to look after myself, I'm going to get hurt. Dead.

I need desperately to learn some self-defence so I can at least fight if needed or stop an attacker long enough so I can run away. The whole being-stalked-by-vampires has seriously upped my deadline. I need to be able to handle myself. *You dealt with vampires before when you went all stabby,* my brain helpfully pipes up. I rub my wrist.

God, I don't want to kill anybody. But I do need to add "learning to fight" to my growing list.

Handy that I now know of a place that has a class tomorrow.

Fighting wasn't something I ever had to think about in my old life—I was surrounded by guards. Dance, horse riding...I even had singing lessons, but nothing as uncouth as fighting. It would be silly to learn an actual useful skill to keep me alive. I roll my eyes.

Gosh, I have so much to learn. It's so overwhelming.

I lean forward to plant my elbows on my knees and rest my head in my hands. I rub at my temples. There was that one time that Arlo mentioned that I was immortal...bloody hell, I need to be immortal, to get through my piling-up to-do list.

My phone rings. This pocket is so weird—the internet and my mobile phone work, but how? Just like with the electricity, I have no idea. Pocket-dimension free wi-fi and power. I just hope someday I don't get an enormous bill. I jump up, sidestep my boot, and grab my phone from my coat pocket. I groan when I see who is calling. I answer.

"Emma, are you safe? Your scent disappeared and I can't track you," John says.

Oh bloody hell, it was him. My frightened brain didn't imagine the growl...the gurgling. I shudder.

How on earth did he track me down at the supermarket? Is this another trick? A test? Gah, I want to tell him to get lost. I have the perfect rude words but I stop them from leaving my mouth, as I don't want to antagonise the scary hellhound.

Instead, I aim for diplomacy. "I am fine…" How can answering him be so difficult? Talking to him…I swallow. "Thank you for your help, but as I've said before…I'm not your responsibility. I can look after myself just fine, thank you very much." I say it primly, but my words are sour with dishonesty.

Liar, liar, pants on fire.

The truth is, I occupy a strange space between being a damsel in distress and knowing enough about the evils of this world to realise my vulnerability. I am doomed.

I know it, and the man on the phone knows it.

I am also stubborn, and I'm unwilling to allow my fear of the unknown, of what could happen, to curb me. I will have no one dictate my life going forward.

I don't want a man to come to my rescue. I want to be a hero, not a snack.

"You can look after yourself?" he scoffs, his tone incredulous. "Tell me then why you had vampires hunting you? Did you even notice them?" He lets out a patronising laugh and I grind my teeth.

"Yes, I noticed them. I got away, didn't I? Did I miss hearing the beginning of our conversation when you, the mighty hellhound, said that you'd lost my scent?" I say smugly. "So that was you? With the vampires…were you helping them?" I narrow my eyes and John growls down the phone at me.

I wait for him to answer. With a grunt, he says, "Stopping them."

"Oh, okay…well…urm…thank you?" I scratch my head and puff out my cheeks. "Do…do you, urm, know what they wanted?"

"Emma," he says, a warning in his voice.

"Oh, look at that"—a painful laugh slips out—"I can't even ask a simple question about my safety." He sighs and the phone rustles like he is smacking it against his head. "You don't have to help me out of guilt." As soon as the words leave my mouth, I realise how ridiculous I sound.

God, I want to smack my phone against my head, too. The idea of John reacting from any emotion other than anger is nuts. Ha, something as frivolous as guilt wouldn't motivate him.

"A master vampire has taken an unhealthy interest in you."

"Unhealthy?"

"Yes, for him. I am going to kill him."

Well, that is a little extreme. I open my mouth and no words come out. What can I say to that? "Thanks?" I slump against the wall and toe my abandoned shopping bags.

"I don't know any master vampires...oh, oooh, the crazy guy with the bow in his hair and the lace."

"Yes, Alexander," he growls out.

"Alexander...why? Is he going to keep sending people after me?"

"No. He will not have another chance."

"Why, 'cause he's going to be dead? Can't I talk to him, try to reason with him? You don't have to kill him."

"For fuck's sake, Emma, are you for real?" he explodes. "Do you think this is a game? He sent ten vampires tonight, and it's not the first time."

"Hang on...not the first time—"

"Look, I've got to go—"

"Was it him...did he send those vampires to the house? The ones that wanted to hurt Bob? The ones that hit the car?" Silence. "John?" I pull the phone away from my ear and check the screen. The bloody hellhound has hung up on me. I throw my hands in the air. Why is he so infuriating?

Arrrah, he is so annoying.

This is my life. Shouldn't I have some input?

I turn my phone off. I glare at the dark screen and grind my teeth. I groan, and with a throaty growl, I turn the phone back on in case the livery yard calls and Bob needs me. I can't risk missing that kind of call. I shove the handset back into my coat pocket.

I grab my shopping bags and head for the kitchen. Why does he care, why can't he leave me the hell alone? I slam the kitchen doors as I put the food away. This is my problem to deal with; it's got nothing to do with him. I got away fine and I hurt no one. I lean against the worktop. No. He will not handle my problems for me.

I spin and go back to my coat and grab the phone. I tap it against my thigh. I know two vampires; one isn't talking to me and the other... well, I've been avoiding her.

Is it wrong to call her? I hop from foot to foot. I thumb through my contacts and impulsively press the call button.

"Hello?"

"Hi, Mum, it's Emma. I need your help."

CHAPTER
TWENTY-FIVE

Like with the supermarket, I've never been to a nightclub before. The music is blaring, and the flash-flash-flash of the lights makes my growing tension headache worse. The surrounding people are happily dancing, drinking, and shouting to be heard over the pounding bass. The club smells of sweat, old beer, and cloying perfume.

I thought my skinny jeans and pretty top would help me blend, but it seems I'm way overdressed. The rest of the patrons of the club are practically naked and I'm standing out, and not in a good way.

I shouldn't be here—it's a mistake. I know it's a mistake, but a big part of my life now is about moving forward, and I can't move forward with the chains of my past dragging me down. I could continue to ignore her, I could spend a lifetime ignoring her, but my anger isn't healthy.

I'd also like to somehow stop the vampire, this Alexander...before John pulls his head off.

A twinge pinches my stomach. Nerves. Gosh, I feel so nervous. I cross my arms over my stomach. The demon...although he disapproved, he never stopped me from searching for my mother. As soon as I was old enough to understand, I searched for her online in fury, and found...nothing.

Thanks to an old-fashioned address book that I found while digging through Arlo's desk, though, I've had my mum's phone number for a week. To think it was in his desk the entire time.

I creep around the edge of the room, avoiding grabby hands, and head towards the back of the nightclub to a bar area that stretches the full length of the back wall. I spot her immediately and grind to a halt, my feet sticking to the floor with shock. Like a statue I stand and just stare at her.

As I watch her work, I fiddle with the bottom of my blouse until my stomach tightens again, and my heart flips. She smiles and serves drinks to strangers as, laughing, she tucks a piece of blonde hair—so like mine—behind her ear. Vampirism has frozen her at twenty-four and we look like sisters...heck, we could almost be twins instead of mother and daughter.

I swallow a lump in my throat. I can't force my feet to move forward.

Is this what she imagined her life would be when she sold me to a demon so she could bribe the vampires to turn her? I try to push the bitterness away, but it hangs around my neck like a heavy chain.

My mum lifts her head and our eyes meet. A bright, blinding smile lights up her face. "Emma," she mouths. She drops everything and she is suddenly there in front of me. Her hands shake and she goes to touch me—perhaps to tuck a loose strand of my hair behind my ear. I flinch away and she drops her hand to her side. Her lip wobbles.

Oh bloody hell.

It takes but a second for me to be flooded with guilt, especially when her eyes flood with tears. "Hi, Mum," I say with a wave and a matching wobbly smile.

She looks about. "Let's talk somewhere quieter," she says as she grabs my hand and pulls me with her. We weave through the middle of the dancing, gyrating bodies and head towards a door that is marked PRIVATE.

When we step inside I find it's a staff room. As soon as the door clicks behind us, the throbbing sound of the club outside fades, and the thud-thud of the music disappears almost entirely. They have pushed a table and chairs against one dark-blue wall, and a leather sofa backs against another. There is also a small kitchen, comprising a couple of cupboards, a worktop, a white under-the-counter fridge, a microwave, and a kettle.

"Would you like a cup of tea?" Without waiting for my answer and with shaking hands, she fills the kettle with water and clicks it on to boil.

She turns and perches on the edge of the sofa. Her hands settle between her knees, and she trembles. "What can I help you with, Emma?" she asks, blinking up at me. It is then that I realise that I'm looming over her. I grab a chair from the table, spin it around, and sit.

There are so many questions I have, but she looks so fragile. Her genuine, bright smile when she saw me and the tears in her eyes have thrown me off completely. She doesn't look heartless. My stomach crunches and flips. Suddenly I don't feel the need to demand answers from her. As I look into her teary blue eyes, I see worry and fear staring back at me, and it makes me feel sad. This lady is a stranger. I shouldn't have come here, and I shouldn't have even thought about involving her in my problems.

I am selfish.

"You've grown. It's so strange...like looking in a mirror." She lets out a painful laugh and licks her lips and bounces her knees. "Your eyes, though, are so different, beautiful...I thought I remembered them but not clearly enough." She ducks her head and looks at her hands. "What kind of mother doesn't remember her daughter's eyes?" she mumbles self-deprecatingly.

"They change colour," I say, to make her feel better. "Every day they are different, depending on my mood and what I wear." I tug at my top and smile uncertainly at her. "Urm...thanks for seeing me so quickly." I cringe and let go of my top and instead twist my hands in my lap. "I'm sorry that the circumstances aren't better. As I said on the phone, I found your number and I needed some information." I shrug and attempt a reassuring smile.

It doesn't work, as my mum frowns and leaps from the sofa. She busies herself with finishing the tea. I sigh and continue anyway. "A master vampire is attempting to...urm, I guess, kidnap me? I'd like to find out why. I need his contact details so I can persuade him to back off before he loses any more of his minions or his life. There's this hellhound..." I tug at my hair. "I am not worth this amount of trouble," I finish lamely.

My mum pours the boiling water into the cups, places the kettle back on the side, and turns to face me. Confusion fills her eyes, and she shakes her head. "Sweetheart, you're not that naïve. You know what he wants." She gives me a sad smile and drops her voice to a whisper. "It is what all wicked men want."

Behind me, the door to the staff room clicks open. For a moment, the loud music from the club blasts inside, and I wince and rub my temple as my head pounds painfully in protest. The door closes and I swivel in my chair to eye the newcomer.

A pureblood vampire strolls across the room. A pureblood. A born vampire. My lips part in shock.

Born vampires are entirely different from turned vampires as they were never human; they never had mortal, human failings to start with. Born-vampire DNA produces exquisite-looking creatures. They are the supermodels of the creature world. There aren't many born vampires around, and the ones that are have an almost cult-like status among other creatures—everyone seems to worship them.

As I stare at him, the pureblood, I don't see the appeal. Yes, he is handsome, with his tailored bespoke navy suit from London's Savile Row that perfectly accentuates his wide shoulders and narrow hips. His floppy blond hair has a warm golden hue compared to my mum's ice-white, and his dark-blue eyes are almost the same shade as his suit. To me, he looks fake—airbrushed. Photoshopped. Perhaps even doll-like. Creepy.

I can feel his powerful energy and the monster inside him. On a danger scale from one to John, he is a level six.

My body twitches as if it wants to automatically stand in deference, but I firmly keep my bum planted on the seat. I pin my shoulders back, straighten my spine, and lift my chin. I watch him approach with narrowed eyes.

I instinctively know that on the power scale, I'm somehow stronger than the pureblood. Huh, well, that's a recent development.

My eyes narrow further as I watch my mum deflate before me, her shoulders rounding and her body shrinking an inch at a time. He frightens her, even when he glides across the room and envelopes her stiff body in his arms and kisses the top of her head.

"Martine, who is this?" Huh, a game player. He knows who I am... unless my mum has other kids or clones stashed about.

"Luther, this is my little girl, Emma. Emma, this is Lord Gilbert, I don't think you remember, you were such a little thing..." her voice fades.

That's strange...I've met this guy before? "Hi, Lord Gilbert." I wave.

He tilts his head down, chin almost to his chest, as he assesses me. "Hello, Emma, how marvellous that you are as beautiful as your mother." He rolls his fingers in a wave of his hand and his nose goes up in the air with a sniff. "I didn't think that would be possible, what with all that disgusting demon DNA."

I huff out a startled breath.

What. A. Dick.

I slowly nod in acknowledgement of his words. My lips tug themselves into a small smile. *Oh dear, was I rude, not standing?* Yep, definitely. Arlo trained me how to greet other creatures, and not standing and giving the pureblood a formal bow is a real no-no. I know I shouldn't press his buttons and piss him off—I already have one vampire problem. But for some stupid reason, I can't help myself.

Mhm. I watch as he turns to the side, angling his body and face just so, highlighting his physique as if on a photo shoot. My eyes flick around the room as I search for the hidden cameraman. It's odd—normal people don't do that. This guy loves himself, and it's like he is in another world of his own making.

"Emma has an issue with a master vampire," my mum rushes to tell him.

"Who?" he asks me.

"Alexander."

"Ah, Alexander. The man is a lowly worm." I nod again. He narrows his eyes at me. I barely refrain from glaring back at him. I don't like this man. Something about him raises my hackles. "What is it about children? You only see them when they want something."

Huh. I squirm in my chair. The pureblood doesn't know me; he knows nothing about me. Yet I find myself looking down at my hands in embarrassment: he has a point.

I knew I shouldn't have come here. I just...I didn't want to be responsible for another person's death, so without proper thought, I jumped at an opportunity to gather information. Perhaps, being honest, I also used it as an excuse to see my mum.

No, I shouldn't be here, and I blame bloody John. I wouldn't be in this room if it wasn't for him. I'd also be more scared of the pureblood.

John broke something inside me...or...maybe he let something out? I lift my eyebrows. Wow, that's a scary thought.

Alexander is a centuries-old master vampire and responsible for his own actions. I remember the vampire's crazy rolling eyes...his giggling. You can't talk sense into that kind of person; it would be useless to try. I don't need Alexander's details, I don't need to talk to him. I'm reacting on impulse, an impulse to rebel against John and his ill-conceived protection.

If I got Alexander's details, what was I going to do? Say to him, "Please don't kidnap me...oh, and watch out for the hellhound that is coming to kill you." Ha, I didn't think this out at all. Being impulsive could get me killed. I'm breaking rule number one: Don't be a dickhead; *and* rule number two: Be kind. I'm not being kind to my mum or myself. I was wrong.

God, I shouldn't have come here.

I stand. I ignore the pompous Lord Gilbert and smile at my mum. "I can see you are busy. Thank you for your time—it was lovely seeing you, Mum. I hope we can do this again, perhaps meet up somewhere quiet for a cup of tea?" Her eyes fly to the now-stewed tea on the side. "It's okay, I will ring you. I promise." I turn to leave.

"Didn't that demon I sent you to not teach you anything?" asks Lord Gilbert.

I stop. The demon *he* sent me to? What the hell?

Heck, look at that. He made that comment without even a hint of *mwahaha*. He doesn't even bother to villain it up—he just drops that bomb without care. *Boom*. I glance at my mum. She won't meet my eyes.

Okay, pureblood, I can play along.

My chest aches as I suppress the urge to growl and my eyes burn and go hazy as I fight to stop them from turning black.

My mum's introduction to Lord Gilbert, when she asked me if I remembered him, now makes more sense—how would I have remembered him if I hadn't met him before? According to my demon master, my mum didn't know any vampires before she sold me.

"*You* sent me to?" I say through gritted teeth. I raise an eyebrow. "Huh. You make it sound if you sent me off to school. So just to clarify, it was *you*, Lord Gilbert, who *sold* me to a demon's household?" He nods his head. I shake mine in response and my nostrils flare.

Un-bloody-believable.

"I didn't need the hassle of a five-year-old demon spawn."

What is it about powerful people? How they ruin lives without a thought. Without care. My eyes flick to my mum and she is crying. Oh, Mum. Silent tears roll down her face. All these years I hated her. What a waste of emotion: she never threw me away. "So it wasn't my mum's decision, was it? It was yours." I tap my lips. "As you know...what with all my disgusting demon DNA...the last time I checked, a demon was my daddy, not you. You had no right to sell me, Lord Gilbert." I want to scream and rage at him. Inside, I am livid.

The pureblood licks his lips, enjoying my reaction. I force myself to drop the anger and instead I contort my lips into a smirk.

He starts again to angle his body and face in weird poses, and I realise belatedly that he's peacocking. If he had feathers, he'd be flapping them about. He looks me up and down, almost like he's mentally stripping me naked. Eww. His attention makes me want to go straight home and have a shower.

"What's done is done. I clearly made a mistake in sending you away. You are a lovely creature, Emma. I can offer you my protection against Alexander, in exchange for you working for me." I scrunch my nose as his tongue again flicks out of his mouth. Eww. Does the tongue thing work for him? I shudder.

Out of the corner of my eye, I catch a movement. My mum imperceptibly shakes her head no. Her puffy, tear-filled eyes scream at me, beg me, to refuse.

I keep my eyes firmly on his. "No thank you, Lord Gilbert. I appreciate the offer, but I am happy on my own." I'm not at the stage where I am ready to deal with the Devil—demon pun intended.

God, I will have to somehow let John deal with the Alexander matter. I don't want people killed in my name. But it looks like it is out of my hands. I am out of my depth.

What I can do is work out how I can get my mum alone and perhaps away from this idiot. Impulsively I step forward, and fold her into a hug. I can't help the extra squeeze I give her. "I will see you soon," I reassure her.

"Okay, sweetheart." She squeezes me back.

"Oh, Emma, you don't have to worry about your admirer. He is dead. A team of hellhounds killed him and his inner circle"—the pureblood flicks his wrist and looks down at an ostentatious solid-gold-and-diamond watch—"about forty minutes ago." He smiles at me.

I close my eyes for a split second so I can absorb that nugget of information. I'm way too late. I would have always been too late.

John must have been ready to bust the door down when he called me. I don't understand what's going on in that man's mind; it's probably got nothing to do with me and everything to do with John using me as an excuse to settle an old score or old debts. He's fooled me so many times, everything he says can be taken as either half truthful or an outright lie. It's impossible to understand John's motivations. Perhaps rule number four should be: Don't trust the hellhound. John at least falls firmly into the territory of rule number one, don't be a dickhead.

If the pureblood wants a shocked response from me, he will have to wait a long bloody time. He knew Alexander was dead before he entered the room.

Instead, I give my mum a small wave, turn, and head towards the door. I open the door and blessed silence greets me—home.

I can't help myself: I look back over my shoulder at the pureblood and I'm gratified to see the confusion on his face. It confuses him, why his club is so quiet...ha.

To hammer my point home, I let go of the tenuous hold on my eyes and allow them to bleed black. "See you around, Luther," I whisper creepily.

I step through the door and disappear.

CHAPTER
TWENTY-SIX

THE GYM IS old-school in style and based within an ancient industrial building. The place looks rough, with its dirty, marked, off-white walls. But a good sign is that it smells like lemon cleaner rather than sweat and blood.

There's a reception desk with a small shop behind it, selling things like gloves and wraps, along with an office, two changing rooms, a weight room, and a room with standard gym-type equipment like running machines and bikes. There's also a room with over a dozen different punching bags, all diverse in shape and size.

I stand in the middle of a big blue matted area with nine other nervous women. My eyes flick about as I take in the padded roof-support pillars and walls. High on the off-white walls, there are national flags from all over the world.

"Okay, ladies, I am your instructor, Scott, and this evening I'm going to teach you some self-defence," the smallish redheaded shifter says with a smile.

I say *smallish* as, come on, shifters are never small...but this guy is under six feet. His dark-red hair is brushed away from his face—a handsome face with freckled, bold features, a broad forehead, and a short beard that hugs his jaw and highlights his narrow, pink lips. He claps his hands. "Let's warm up…"

The warm-up is brutal…or it should be. The surrounding ladies are all red-faced and sweaty, but my body is nicely warm. I don't know where my wobbly arms have gone. The instructor pushes us to work harder, but to no avail; I'm still not sweating like a pig, and I should be. Huh. Is this another demon thing? As in, it's weird. I've not been fit in months, yet I feel fantastic.

They pass pads and somewhat smelly boxing gloves around, and we split into pairs. One girl hits while the other holds up a square pad. Scott barks out instructions on our fighting stances and encourages us to use our hips to add weight to the punches. "Aim not to punch the pad, but through it."

When it's my turn, I try not to pull a face when I slide my hands into the damp gloves. I punch the pad and I grin, as this is fun. To add a little motivation, I imagine John's face superimposed onto the blue foam. *Take that, John,* I think as I hit his nose and then his chin. One particularly hard hit from my right fist and the poor girl holding the pad flies through the air and lands with an *oof* on her bum.

"Oh gosh, I'm so sorry," I say as I rush to help her up. She gives me a rueful smile, but before she has time to speak, Scott is there, pushing her towards another pairing.

"You okay?" She nods. "Double opponents," he says to the girl with the boxing gloves.

He turns back to me, and with a determined, angry look on his face, he nods toward a quiet area. I follow meekly behind his stomping form, and when he thinks we are far enough from the others, he spins back around and interrogates me. "Why you here? Are you from another gym? It's clear you're not a normal beginner." His head tilts to the side.

Boom. Instead of taking offence at his angry questions, I grin at him. He thinks I'm a fighter! I refrain from doing a fist pump. Instead, I bounce on my toes. I can feel the silly grin spreading across my face—my cheeks hurt from the strain.

Eat your heart out, Rocky. Eye of the tiger.

His eyes narrow. He looks me up and down, and then he nods. "You're the new demon," he says bluntly.

I stop bouncing, and my happy grin slides from my face. It's my turn to narrow my eyes at him. When he continues to stand there, I surreptitiously flick my gaze around the gym. No one heard him. But I'm busted.

I drop my eyes and stare at my feet. I toe the blue crash mat. "I will go, no need to chuck me out," I mumble. I remove the smelly gloves and hand them over. I turn to leave, but a gentle hand on my arm stops me.

Scott stops me. "Hey, no, don't be so soft...are you kidding me? A *demon* at my gym? Hell, demon, I'll train you for free—it would be an honour to train you. Look, we are almost done anyway for today. Why don't you come back tomorrow night, and we shall work out a real training programme." He sounds...excited.

My eyes narrow. If something sounds too good to be true, it usually is.

"Look, demon."

"Emma. My name is Emma," I grumble.

"Emma, I know the hellhounds. Well, I know *of* the hellhounds, and I know that they have a vested interest in keeping you safe.

"Times are hard. I'm not gonna advertise that you come here, but word of my training you will get out to the right ears, and it will be good for business." He smiles and gives a small shrug. He seems genuine.

I find myself nodding in agreement. I need the help. "It's a deal, but I'm paying you." I'm not using him—that is what bad people do.

Rule number one: Don't be a dickhead.

He slowly nods, and an even bigger smile works its way across his face. "Great. See you tomorrow night at eight."

"You killed the vampires," I say. John grunts down the phone at me. "You can't just go around killing people."

"Why not?"

"Because...because it's morally wrong."

"Morally wrong according to whom?" Honestly. Why do I bother?

"To me." He grunts again. "I met my mum last night," I whisper. I don't know why I tell him—maybe it's because I've got no one else to tell. How sad is that?

"How did that go?" he asks gruffly.

From our time together, he knows my history better than anyone. *Cold metal on my skin.* I shiver at the memory. I stop my free hand from frantically rubbing at the scars on my wrist. I swallow.

"She's with a pureblood, Lord Luther Gilbert..." I pause, waiting for some valid input to the conversation. All John does is grunt an acknowledgement. I roll my eyes. "...I found out tonight it was him who sold me to—"

"Emma, let me stop you there. You can't seriously be suggesting your mum didn't have a say in your being sold off. Come on, Emma, what mum would hand over a five-year-old child without a fight?"

Not being able to remain seated, I jump up from the sofa and stomp across the room. I growl with indignation down the phone, "No, you're wrong. Don't you dare tell me what a woman would and wouldn't do, John Hesketh. Last time I checked, you're a seven-foot monster of a man. You do not understand what being a woman is like in this world. So shut your mouth." I grind my teeth.

Why did he have to say that? He could never be in her shoes, never understand what happened. Neither can I.

"Did she confirm he sold you? Did she say the words, Emma?"

"Well, no...but it was insinuated."

"By the pureblood?"

"Yes."

"Before or after you turned down his protection?" How did John know he offered me protection? I rub my temple. I can't remember... before, I think. I turn and stare at my smoky ward.

"I want to help her."

"Like she helped you?"

"John," I growl out, a warning in my tone.

"Emma, listen to yourself for a moment. *She is a vampire.* She isn't human anymore. She left you at the mercy of a *demon*, with no clue about what kind of creature you were. If she is with the pureblood, then she clawed her way into that position. Vampires destroy weakness, Emma. You saw what she wanted you to see. Take it from a man who's seen and done awful shit: it's pure manipulation."

"You see the worst in people."

"Yes, and you see the best in everyone. That's what makes you a beautiful person, but thinking like that, it can get you hurt. Forget about rescuing your mother. She's made her bed, and she's fine. She isn't getting hunted by creatures like you are. It's a full-time job, keeping you safe," he grouches.

"No one asked you to keep me safe."

"How is your demon magic progressing?"

I sigh. His change of subject makes my head spin.

"It's fine," I grumble.

Gah, I can't see fault with his logic, and I understand what he's saying. Did I see what my mum wanted me to see...was she manipulating me? The shaking, the tears. Or is my mum another broken woman who is doing her best to survive in a broken world? I tap the fingers not holding the phone on my thigh. I don't know.

If I don't know, perhaps I need to find out.

"Emma, you still there?"

"Yes," I grumble again. "I was thinking...my demon magic doesn't do shit." I poke at my ward magic and it twists around my finger. I drop my hand and step away. I shake my hand out with a full-body shudder. Freaky ward.

"Try harder. You can disappear into thin air, so that's a good start." I don't take the bait—I'm not explaining my pocket. I grin; I bet it drives him crazy.

"Will you stop killing people in my name?" I boldly ask instead.

"No." Ha, a short and sweet answer. At least he didn't lie.

"I've got to go." I say.

"Will you call me tomorrow?"

I groan. "Whoa, no." I pull the phone from my ear. I wrinkle my nose and glare at it. I cautiously put it back to my ear and say, "I'm not going down the route of friendship with you, John. You make a horrible friend."

There's a long pause. I can hear him breathing.

Was I unkind?

"I don't want to be your friend," he answers in a low, guttural growl. Sexy. My body clenches and my heart misses a beat. I gasp and my throat makes a strange *eeep* sound. John laughs huskily and I quickly end the call.

I throw the mobile across the room like it's a magical hand-grenade. It bounces onto the sofa and the momentum carries it over the arm of the chair. It lands with a clatter on the floor, out of sight.

Oh bloody hell.

CHAPTER
TWENTY-SEVEN

Everything was going so well. I moved Bob to his new stable yard, and I said a sad goodbye to the Shetland pony, Munchkin, who even gave me a farewell love-bite. I still have the bruise on my thigh. I will miss the little tyke.

Yes, everything was going well until Bob-cob developed a sore hoof. An abscess from running around his new field. A stray stone must have knocked his foot, causing an infection within the hoof horn. He was dreadfully lame.

Like a normal horse owner, when I got the phone call I freaked out. The world was ending because my precious Bob was in pain. The livery yard has its own emergency potions, but I am not the type of owner to allow someone to slap any old potion onto my horse without vet intervention. I waited, biting my nails, until the vet, Cathy—a talented witch— arrived to treat him.

I grin with relief as I lean against the stable door and watch a contented Bob happily munching on his hay net. Bob stands pain-free on all four hooves. My bank account will be lighter when I get the bill, but I don't care. Healing magic is incredible, Cathy is incredible. She has just left. It's late, dark, and it started spitting an hour ago. Now the rain is coming down in sheets.

In my panic to get to Bob, I didn't bring a coat. Now that I'm almost finished with my jobs and completely wet through, I wouldn't be able to put one on anyway without changing. I shrug and then wince as the movement causes the rain to trickle down the back of my neck—oh, that wasn't pleasant. Not at all. I do a full-body shiver.

With a final brush of the floor outside Bob's stable, I'm ready to go home. I empty the wheelbarrow and put the sweeping brush away and lock everything up for the night. As I am closing the feed-room door, there's a loud *bang*. I jump and clutch at my chest. "Shit, what was that?" My pulse pounds and my senses sharpen with the adrenaline that floods through me. I turn towards the sound.

Everyone else left hours ago. Perhaps it's Stuart doing a late-night check on the horses? I squint into the night. The rain and the powerful overhead floodlights blind me. "Hellooo?" I shout. I blink the rain out of my eyes and wait, straining my ears for a response, and weirdly I hold my breath. As if stopping breathing will make me hear better.

I shrug when I get no reply. I rub my face and I huff out a nervous laugh. *No one is here, Emma. What a scaredy-cat.* I berate myself for being so easily frightened.

I roll my tense shoulders, and my wet top sticks to me uncomfortably. I peel it away with a shiver. I need to get home and have a hot bath. I blink back out into the night. It must have been a horse. Bob isn't the only horse stabled tonight.

I look at Bob with a smile.

I freeze.

Bob isn't chomping on his net. Instead, his head is over his stable door. With wide, panic-filled eyes and flaring nostrils, his attention is firmly fixed on where the bang came from. My eyes drift to the other horses around us. The stables are in a horseshoe shape and they overlook a central courtyard. The other horses too are looking in the same direction, with an equal measure of fear and trepidation. All the horses are looking. One stamps, a few snort, and one horse lets out a frightened, shrill whinny.

A trickle of fear creeps down my spine and my heart speeds back up.

My body trembles as I back away from the feed room and towards

Bob's stable. It would be so easy to use the feed-room door to leave. But I won't. I can't leave Bob and the other horses in danger. I pat my phone to double-check that it's still in my pocket. Should I ring for help? What if I'm mistaken and it's nothing?

That's when the creatures come out.

Fae creatures...the beithíoch. They look like deformed cats, hairless and big. Their skin is black and blends into the night. I estimate that they are around hip height and about five feet in length. The floodlights reflect off their huge white teeth, teeth so big they look like prehistoric lions'. As they get closer, their eyes glow with a freaky blue light. My back hits the stable wall as they prowl towards me on silent feet. Six, seven—no, eight. Eight huge beithíoch.

Oh bloody hell.

The bang must have been the ward failing.

I keep my eyes pinned on the beithíoch and slowly lift my hand. My fingers scrabble around as I scrape them against the wall, blindly feeling around behind the back of Bob's stable door. I blow out a relieved breath as my searching fingers meet metal. With a deft flick of my wrist, I unhook the top door and ever so gently swing it closed. With shaking hands, I bolt it, locking Bob inside. It's my only option to protect him. There is no way those beithíoch will clamber over the door now.

I sidestep slowly to the left, to the horse stabled next door, and do the same.

The cat-like creatures watch me, not yet moving to attack. I attempt to do another stable door, but a low hiss freezes me. I swallow down a moan of fear. The creatures want me to stay where I am. The surrounding horses are silent—the poor things are terrified. Trapped, vulnerable in their stables, unable to run.

Oh God, this is all my fault. I've never heard of fae creatures attacking a livery yard. You don't have to be a rocket scientist to work out that they've come for me.

I breathe out quick, panting breaths that fog the air, it's gone so cold. The cold is especially apparent to me given the wet, frozen state of my frightened body. I stand wide-eyed and shaking. My heart thuds in my ears until all I can hear is my heartbeat and the drip and gurgle of the guttering, the patter of the rain as it taps against the window of the feed room.

Footsteps.

My stomach twists. At least three different treads are approaching.

Men dressed in black wind their way around the scary beithíoch. Their long hair and distinctive plaits identify them as fae warriors. My breath shudders.

Is this how I'm going to die?

"P...Please d...don't hurt any of the horses," I stammer out through my frozen lips. I shuffle forward and open my hands. I hold my trembling arms out to the side to show I haven't got a weapon.

One of the fae steps forward. He tilts his blond head to the side and regards my shaking form with disgust. In a soft, lilting Irish accent, he replies, "We don't hurt innocent creatures." I briefly close my eyes and sag in relief. "That doesn't mean we won't hurt you, baby demon."

Demon. I'm not surprised that my assumption was correct. Why is every Tom, Dick and Harry out to get me? I've done nothing wrong... what the heck does everyone know about demons that I don't? I shoot him a small, wobbly smile. "Oh, I know. That's okay, as long as you promise not to hurt the horses." *Urm, Emma,* my inner voice shouts at me. *"It's okay?" Are you nuts? This is not bloody okay. They're going to kill you...*I shut down my unhelpful, screaming thoughts and—

A knife is at my throat. A heavy arm around my waist pulls me into a male body. A fourth fae warrior has me in his powerful grip. I have no idea where he has come from. I jerk away from the sharp blade and my head smacks into his chest, and the warrior's blade follows my movement. I lift my hands and with a panicked squeak dig my nails into his arm in an attempt to pull it away, but the knife moves closer and with a sting, it bites into my vulnerable flesh.

Ouch. I can feel my blood as it trickles hotly down my throat. It cools as it mixes with the rain.

Wide-eyed, I stare at the creatures surrounding me. Yeah, with my one self-defence lesson and my brand-new skill of turning my eyes black, I will have no problem fighting my way through four fae warriors and eight giant monster beithíoch. Right?

Oh my God, I'm going to die.

With these overwhelming odds, I feel so helpless. I should have run when I had the chance. *Coward, fight. Do something, anything,* my inner voice screams at me.

Oh God, if I don't fight, I'm dead.

I struggle in the fae's arms and kick his shin. He doesn't even grunt at my pathetic blow. In desperation, I drop my head to bite his arm, but with a tilt of his wrist he angles the blade so it pokes underneath my chin.

I freeze.

"You are a danger to us all," he says in a gruff voice.

"A danger? Me? Yeah, I was planning to take over the world on Tuesday, as Monday—" He strikes the side of my head with the butt of the blade and my vision goes hazy. I hiss out a pain-filled breath and my ears ring.

What the hell do I do with a knife at my throat? Defeated, I shake with useless adrenaline and my body sags in his tight grip. I could continue to struggle and fight, I could scream and I could beg. But I've begged before, and I know it doesn't work. I am reluctant to go down that path again.

I know…I bloody know that I need to get mad, get angry, somehow pull the sleeping demon out from hiding, but…but I don't want to hurt anyone, kill anyone.

I see the vampires' faces in my dreams—they haunt me. They are why I have my silly set of rules. It is kind of karmic that I'm going to die with my throat cut. Isn't that what led to the other vampire's death? Me slicing his throat? Eleanor only finished what I had started.

I will forever wonder about the lives I took, the man I stabbed. Did he have a family? A wife, children who relied on him, loved him? Realistically I know turned vampires can't have children. He most likely didn't even have a human family. Yet I can't help seeing his entire family in my imagination, in my dreams. They cry for him.

I feel as if it's marked my soul. I can feel it, the tainted blackness sitting there festering.

"Kneel, demon."

"My name's Emma," I whimper through my numb lips. "If you're going to kill me"—my voice cracks—"I'd rather stand than die on my knees." The wind whips up, snatching at my words, but the surrounding fae hear me.

I guess I can die with dignity.

The blond warrior in front nods his head and the arm behind me tenses. No villain speeches for me, then—these guys are professionals.

I lift my chin.

I slam my eyes closed.

I might be brave enough to stand. But I'm not brave enough to keep my eyes open. *Maybe...maybe I will heal?* Numbness spreads through me. I let go of the fae's arm so I don't hinder his movement. I remember reading that nobles used to pay the executioner extra to guarantee a clean blow. If I have to die today...Oh God, please, I am not ready...if I have to die today I'd rather it be quick.

In my head, I'm riding Bob. The sunlight is on my face and the birds are singing in the trees. The sound of his hooves as they clop rhythmically against the ground...it fills me with a sense of peace. "I love you, Bob-cob."

CHAPTER
TWENTY-EIGHT

A FAINT, whispered *thunk*, a sharp intake of breath in my ear, followed immediately by a warm, wet splat against my cheek. The fae warrior who is holding me becomes a dead weight at my back. The knife slips from his grip and clatters to the floor. His arm becomes impossibly heavy against my neck. I let out a squeak as he drags me backwards while his body drops. On instinct, I frantically prise his arm away from my throat. I cough and choke.

"What the hell?" I gasp. I stumble when I see the silver knife sticking out of his pointed ear.

There is a thud and the sound of boots as they hit the concrete beside me. I lift my eyes to see a dark shadow. The enormous male must have jumped from the roof. With a flick of his wrist he throws another blade while simultaneously grabbing the third warrior's head, and with a sharp twist, he breaks the man's neck. Both bodies crumple to the floor at the same time. He moves between one heartbeat and the next. With a flash of silver and a blade to the chest, the last fae warrior drops. Without hesitation or pause, he has ripped through the fae like paper. The silver blades in his hands wink in the overhead light.

I gasp as he turns his head and his eyes lift to mine, regarding me. Rainwater trickles down his face, a beautiful deadly face. Rain drips from his jaw. His strong cheekbones are highlighted by the orange glow of his eyes. "John." I mouth his name. My lips remain parted in shock.

The hellhound is like a war machine. All that took a matter of seconds.

Dead bodies lie around him.

A hiss and an angry growl draws my shocked eyes away from John, just as an angry fae monster springs towards me. I let out a squeak of fright. All I can see are glowing blue eyes and a mouthful of gleaming white teeth. I lift my arms to cover my face and take a quick step backwards. I trip over the body at my feet, and I go down heavily. As I hit the ground, a sharp pain in my hip and shoulder resonates through me.

"Bad kitty," John growls as he grabs hold of the skin at the scruff of its neck and yanks it away from me. I peek through my arms. Jaws snapping, the beithíoch quickly turns its attack onto John, and he grabs hold of its muzzle.

At first, I think he is trying to clamp its mouth closed. The beithíoch lets out a whimper—oh no—as John's forearms bulge and instead, he rips the beithíoch jaws apart. Blood splatters to the floor and I gag.

The other beithíoch converge. "John, look out!" Muscles bunching, John picks up the dead beithíoch and throws its body. It hits the other beithíoch, slowing them down.

John shifts.

It's a blink-and-you-miss-it kind of transformation. The magic reforms his very cells. Intact clothing scatters around in the wake of John's hellhound form. Riddick growls harshly, so deeply, it's almost a roar. The sound echoes out into the night. Riddick. I watch wide-eyed as Ridd—I shake my head—no, *John*. As John crashes into the fae creatures.

I scramble back up to my feet, and my right hand lands on the warrior's chest. I yelp and shudder with revulsion. The whole idea of touching a dead person makes me want to puke. Bile rises into my throat. I gag again and my chest burns.

The seven remaining beithíoch circle him, their tails whipping from side to side. Each of them takes a turn at dashing in to attack the hellhound. Teeth and claws.

The hellhound is no mouse. He is bigger than the beithíoch, and his thick coat fur offers him a measure of protection that the hairless creatures haven't got. I don't want to watch him kill them. The beithíoch didn't bring themselves. Monstrous and scary, they are still innocent animals. I hate the fae for bringing them here.

John fights as if someone has hit fast-forward. His movements are so fast they are hard to track.

You are being pathetic. Do something. Help him.

I wobble on my feet and look around for the dropped knife. Oh, God, I can't see it anywhere. Instead, I turn to the dead fae and with trembling hands and a strange gurgling noise deep in my throat, I grab hold of the blade in his ear. I heave as I pull. When the knife doesn't come out, I wipe my hands on my wet pants and put my foot on his neck for leverage. Wincing, I silently apologise to my would-be killer for what is surely desecrating his dead body. I tug. The knife doesn't move. "Ew…come on…come on." I wiggle the blade as bile again creeps up my throat.

There are hisses and a yowl from the beithíoch.

I continue to half-heartedly tug at the knife still lodged in the fae warrior's head. "Please come out—I need to help him." Gah, I can't believe I am talking to an inanimate object.

A warm hand touches my shoulder. I fling my arms into the air and scream like a banshee.

"Emma, it's okay, it's me. You're safe, it's me."

I lift my eyes to see that John is next to me, and I cover my mouth with my hands. I hurriedly back away from him.

More dead bodies lie around us.

His naked body follows my frantic movement, and he prowls towards me. His beautiful body ripples with every step, and I almost swallow my tongue. I don't know if I'm more turned on or frightened. At least I'm no longer numb.

"Why did you stand there and allow that fuck to hold a knife to your throat?" he growls.

Oh, heck, the hellhound is pissed.

John growls again. "You lifted your chin for him." He reaches, and his massive hands grip both my shoulders. He drags me towards him, and as he does, he shakes me. "If I hadn't been here, you would be dead. Why didn't you fight? Why didn't you fight, Emma? You always fight. Yet you stood there...you just fucking stood there." He continues to shake me until my bones ache underneath the grip of his enormous hands. My teeth and eyeballs feel like they are rattling around in my head. "If you are ever in that situation again—you fight like fuck. Even if the odds are insurmountable. You fight."

Isn't he supposed to say, *"Do nothing—don't be stupid and don't antagonise the bad guys, Emma...call and wait for help."* I blink up at him with confusion. The rain hits my face and John moves closer. His huge body leans over mine, blocking me from the worst of the weather.

To be honest, I wasn't expecting the poke-the-bad-guys-in-the-eye speech.

Is this another trick? 'Cause if it is...I don't care how I do it, I will kill him. Dead John can haunt my dreams, no problem.

I think I am in shock. No, I know I'm in shock. This is all a little too much.

I open my mouth in an attempt to answer him and a keening, frightened noise escapes. I clamp my lips closed. Wow, where did that come from? Wide-eyed, I stare at John. The hellhound's eyes also widen and with no further words of reprimand he pulls me into his body. I bury my head in his naked chest, and his equally naked body wraps around me. His heat and comforting shifter energy surround me. The scent of him, bonfires and fabric softener, fills my nose.

His voice rumbles through his chest. "I will come for you, I will always come for you. But you don't give up like that. Even when you think there isn't a chance, you fight. You always fight, you silly fool. For fuck's sake, you didn't even attempt to run."

"Are they all dead?" I mumble into his chest. My lips brush against his hot skin and in response his entire body shivers. He groans.

"Yes. They are all dead. I am sorry about the beithíoch—I had no choice. Without the fae to control them, they would have killed all the horses." I expect him to move away from me, but instead, he threads his fingers through my wet hair and strokes the back of my neck, offering me comfort.

"Why are the fae now after me?"

"They're not. They were paid assassins. Don't worry, it won't happen again." John drops his chin onto the top of my head.

"'Cause you'll kill them?"

"If I have too."

"I'm sorry you have to," I murmur.

"Don't be sorry. The fae warriors were bad guys. No one will miss them. The man who hired them was an old business associate of Arlo's. He's dead."

"Oh." What do I do, say thank you? I should...but I hate the idea he has to come and kill people because of me. "What do we do now?"

"I will get you home safe. I have the hounds coming to investigate and do a clean-up. I will also have a better ward installed." I nod, and shiver. "Do you not own a coat?" he growls out, tucking me closer into his body, into his warmth.

"Am I in trouble? Are you in trouble?" I mumble against him.

"No, Emma, the fae are the only ones in the shit. Neither of us is in trouble." He crushes me to his chest and drops his voice to a chocolatey whisper. "I've grown to care about you in the time we have spent together."

I lift my face from his chest. "Time?" It's as if John has flipped an angry-switch in me. What the hell am I doing cuddling with this *naked* man in the rain? "What time are you talking about, John? The time when you spent hours torturing me? Or the time when you disguised yourself as Riddick?" I snarl. I glare at him.

My hands come up between us and I shove him away. I squirm out of his hold. My back bumps into the wall of the stable and I use it to prop my useless, trembling body up. "If you think about it"—I flap my arms about—"we spent many nights together while you played hell-hound bodyguard. But I'm not willing to spend any more *time* with a man who thinks it's okay to lie to me. What was all this?" I wave at the bodies. "Did you set this up too?"

John's torso tenses and he steps away from me. "I didn't set this up," he splutters incredulously. "I saved your life. While we're on the subject, I didn't intentionally set up the fake kidnapping or the vampire attack at the house. The lack of wards at the house was to encourage you to leave and to lead me to your accomplices. I didn't realise at the time that you could walk through wards."

I grind my teeth and narrow my eyes. I bloody told him I could do that when he had me chained to a bloody wall. What is it about this hellhound and his listening skills?

"The vampire attacks were Alexander. That was a real car crash, Emma, with real bad-guys." He rubs his face. "Did I take advantage of the situation? Yes. I used it as an opportunity to get more information out of you. The angel agreed to heal you and when we were ambushed, I asked him to come and get you. To set up an interrogation. I never set out to hurt you."

I huff with disgust and shake my head. His colossal body is blocking out the light, so I can no longer see his expression. "Well, you did hurt me. I sat in that chair over that drain for hours while you played with me. I can't shift and make everything perfect again. You had no idea if I had internal injuries. Yet you proceeded with your games anyway. I sat in that chair, frightened to death and in pain." I spin and undo Bob's top stable door. I open it and peek in. The fat cob is already settled and is back to eating his hay. I march over to the other stable and open its top door as well. "You, John Hesketh, are a stubborn grade-A dickhead. I have no idea what's going on in that head of yours. Thank you for saving my life tonight. Now leave me the hell alone."

CHAPTER
TWENTY-NINE

Over the past few weeks, I've made no headway with getting my mum alone and away from the pureblood idiot. Frustratingly, she no longer answers my phone calls, and the one time in desperation I tried to visit the club to see her, the vampire doorman wouldn't let me in.

I am at a loss on how to proceed. Changing my face also seems an impossible dream. I have so much detailed research and so many in-depth notes on demons, some days it feels like I am doing a doctorate in demonology.

"Come on, Barbie," Scott yells, snapping me out of my musings.

He's right...I need to get my head in the game.

"Come on, Scott, that's not original," I gripe at him. "Bloody Barbie." Grr.

"Hit the bear shifter like you mean it," he bellows unhelpfully across the room. I grimace and puff out a breath. Okay, I can do this. I nod at Malcolm, the bear shifter in question, to check that he is ready for me, and then I punch him in the face.

Crap, it's less of a punch and more of a love tap. I groan in self-disgust and rub my face with frustration. Eww. I end up with a mouthful of the boxing glove.

"Oi, stop that. Come here," Scott says with thinly veiled exasperation as he waves me over. I'm perfectly fine hitting the bags, but when it comes to hitting people...I don't know, it makes me feel all icky. Pesky empathy. "What were you thinking about that day you knocked that girl on her ass?" Scott raises a red eyebrow. He nods and points at my frowning face. "Yeah, think that." He pushes me back towards the colossal bear shifter.

My face scrunches up with confusion. Yeah, that was an epic pep talk. I square up to the bear shifter and give him a wobbly smile. Okay, I can do this. Malcolm rubs his gloved fist across the back of his head; his dark blond hair, which is cut short on the sides and fashionably longer on the top, sticks up. The light stubble on his jaw adds to his overall roughness. Malcolm's kind brown eyes dance with amusement. He nods his head with encouragement and smiles kindly back at my grimace.

John. I superimpose John's face like a target. I squint, and it's almost too easy to imagine John's face on anything I want to smash my fist into. I bounce on my toes and punch him with a left, a right, another left. I bounce and roll my shoulders.

It's John's face that I'm hitting, and each punch becomes easier.

Malcolm drops his guard as he lazily swings an embarrassingly slow punch towards me. I duck out of the way and follow it up with my right hand. I twist my hips and throw everything I have at bear-John.

Smack.

I watch in horror as the bear's head snaps to the side. He spits and blood flies from his lips, and with a not-so-helpful shout of "Timber!" from Scott, the poor bear smashes down onto the blue mat, out cold. I knocked out a bear shifter.

I blink at the bear.

I blink at Scott.

Oh bloody hell.

"Oh my God, Malcolm, I am so sorry," I squeak out, mortified.

At the same time, Scott says, "That was brilliant! When he wakes up, I think we should start you on weapons."

"Weapons..." I silently mouth.

"Yeah, you're a natural," Scott says. He grins and his heavy hand pats my shoulder.

After the particularly hard training session with weapons, Scott and I sit on the floor guzzling down water. As I pick at the label on the bottle, I get up the nerve to ask him, what he thinks and experiences when he turns into animal form.

Perhaps I need a fresh perspective.

"Well, I just do it. Like scratching an itch—it's as natural as breathing." Helpful. I sigh and give him a smile of "thanks, anyway."

Malcolm lumbers over. I say *lumbers*, but it's still more like a prowl. I guess even bear shifters don't lumber anywhere. He sits on the floor opposite me, hands on his knees, his concerned brown eyes quietly observing me. "I couldn't help overhearing. I train the cubs." My ears prick up with intrigue. I stop messing with the label and focus my full attention on Malcolm, smiling at him with encouragement.

Come on, Malcolm. Please give me something I can use.

"The cubs first shift into animal form in their twenties. I help them. At first, it's all about focus. They have to learn to meditate, and then we work on getting them to imagine themselves in their true form, their natural self." Malcolm rubs his eyebrow with his thumb. "When the time is right, they shift. They know when the time is coming…" he huffs out a laugh and his face lights up with a grin…"we all know when it's time. It's a little like human puberty—they get all obnoxious and rude. Then suddenly you have a new bear knocking shit over and scratching the furniture as they get used to their claws. We normally take them somewhere rural, like the Lake District. It's hard work because they need extra help, but it's gratifying."

"So they think of their natural self?" I ask.

Malcolm nods. "Yeah. To shift back is the same thing—we get them to imagine themselves as human. You…urm, don't need any help with a young shifter, do you, Emma?" He drops his voice and looks about. "Be careful of the shifter council—they're a nightmare to deal with. Dangerous. It's best to let us shifters deal with our own."

I lean across and squeeze Malcolm's hand in reassurance. "No, I'm just nosy. Don't worry, I'm not harbouring a rogue shifter. I'm not about to do anything silly like stepping on the shifter council's toes." I do an exaggerated shiver. Malcolm's drawn, worried expression clears, and he returns my smile. "Thank you for explaining. The cubs are lucky to have you." When his ears go a little pink at the tips, I giggle at him.

"I'm happy to answer any questions you have—you only have to ask."

"Thanks, Malcolm."

I finish my water. I can't wait to go home and try his suggestion. I need to think of my *natural self* and meditate more. Maybe I've been overthinking things. Perhaps my magic should be as Scott said, *as natural as breathing*? Everything seems to go tits-up if I overthink stuff. I've found that with my fight training, the less I think and the more I just do, the better.

With a wave at the guys, I head towards the front door.

"Emma, don't use the front door—that hellhound of yours is hanging around again. It's almost like you're his mate, the way he follows you around," Scott says with a chuckle.

My heart jumps. *John.*

I puff out my cheeks, spin on my heel, and head for the fire exit at the rear of the gym. John finds it hard to follow me, but when I'm in one place for a while, it doesn't take him long to track me down. He must have lookouts all over the city. Not that my evening trip to the gym is tricky to work out...I've been coming here for weeks and we set the time in stone.

"Thanks for the heads-up, Scott. Have a good evening." Scott shakes his head and laughs, then waves at his office.

"Use that door," he says. I turn my head and look at him. Oh, crap, does he know about my pocket? "Don't freak out. I know you are a demon, and I know you have magic. I also know that you don't walk out of here. The other day I was seconds behind you when you left, and you vanished into thin air." He taps his nose. "I am a fox. I couldn't track you—there was no scent. So I guessed you can *Step* like the fae or make your own temporary ley-line doorway like a witch." Scott shrugs.

Powerful old fae can *Step*, which is how you'd imagine teleporting to be. They just "step" from one place to the next. "It's no biggie, and I won't tell nobody. I understand that there is shit as a demon that you can do. So if you want to just Step or if it's a portal thing, you can use my office door..." He shrugs.

I don't bother with any denials—what would be the point? Scott is my trainer and, I hope, my friend. There is no point in lying, but I will not explain what I do, either.

I smile and head for his office. "Thanks, Scott. See you tomorrow." Using the office door, I open my door to home.

CHAPTER
THIRTY

When I arrive home, I can feel John's absence, the lack of his energy on my skin. John's energy is like what I experienced when I was around Riddick, inner peace—which is nuts. The thought makes me antsy. I need to learn to recognise this *inner peace* feeling as his energy, so I know when he's around and can avoid him. I've stopped answering his calls.

Yet John continues to follow me...I don't know how I feel about that.

It's all so strange. I can't help feeling safe whenever he is around. He saved my life, and in return, I was horrible to him.

Crap, when does being kind change to being a doormat? Or when does trying to protect yourself turn into unnecessary rudeness and cruelty? I don't want to be rude to him, but I also don't want him to walk all over me.

Heck, I don't want him to think that his actions have no consequences and what he did to me was okay, because it bloody wasn't.

He scares me.

My head tells me to run like hell, but something inside of me likes his attention...it tugs me back.

It is so confusing...Is it a demon thing? Is it an Emma thing? A hellhound thing?

Scott's words flash into my head. *"It's almost like you're his mate, the way he follows you around."*

Huh. I frown...demons don't have mates...do they? I vaguely remember that shifters have chosen mates, but I can't for the life of me imagine John choosing me as his mate.

There is nothing as silly as the idea of fated mates. Apart from in romance books, I've never heard of fated mates in real life. It might be some demony danger-warning system that I'm experiencing. Yet I don't feel as if I'm in any danger. It's more...contentment. Which is plain old freaky.

I stomp to my shelves and pick out *the* book. it's not like I've been avoiding this book...I just didn't feel the need to learn about demon *love*. Gag.

My life in pages...all I seem to do is read stuffy old books. It feels like I'm forever searching for answers, answers that leave me with more questions. Yay to freedom...I grin toothily. I am living the dream. *Not.*

I plop down on the sofa, still sweaty from the gym. I should have a shower, but my brain won't leave Scott's words alone. I skim the book and find what I need.

I read, and my hands shake as my brain slowly registers the words. When I've finished, I close my eyes tight.

Horror floods me.

Oh, no, no, no. I really wish I hadn't read those words. I slam the book closed, jump to my feet, and slide it back onto the shelf. I wriggle and rub my hands on my leggings.

Nope, it's not happening.

Every time I blink, the words are inscribed on the back of my eyelids, lasered onto my eyeballs, and stamped into my brain, never to be unseen.

Demons have soul mates.

Nope, it's not happening.

Soul mates.

Fate is really getting on my tits. A strangled giggle spills from my lips and I tug at my ponytail. No, no, no.

John is my *mate*. Ha, ha, mate—like in a romance novel. Insta-love. Soul mate.

Oh bloody hell.

I throw my hands in the air and look heavenward. "Okay, fate," I shout aloud like a madwoman. "What do you want from me? I will get on my knees and beg. I will roll on the floor and wail if that is what you want. What the hell have I done to offend the universe? Arrah...why him? Why bloody him? I feel so bloody fucked over." I let out my rage with a bloodcurdling scream. It echoes around the room. I pull my hair and then scrub at my face.

Nope, it's not happening.

That book, that bloody book. I lift my eyes and glare at it. It sits there innocently on the shelf. It dares to tell me how lucky and blessed I am. I grit my teeth. *Blessed*. My nostrils flare and my left eye twitches. "Blessed," I snarl.

My little mantra, "everything happens for a reason," isn't going to cut it.

My entire face twitches, and I vigorously rub it. The book talks about my symptoms: feeling his energy beyond the norm and an overwhelming attraction.

The whole overwhelming attraction on its own isn't a red flag. John is beautiful—he's on a scary level of beautiful, a walking, talking wet dream. But the book describes my strange feelings to a T.

My attraction to him has never been normal for me. I'm a reasonably sensible, well-rounded person despite my experiences and childhood. All this time, it's never made much sense —let's face it, the guy has been horrible. Yet, when I hear his voice...when I'm in his arms...I feel like I've come home. When that happens, my head screams at me to knock it off, and my heart...my soul? I gulp. Well, my soul wants to lick him.

I huff. Heck, the guy spent hours aggressively questioning me, he bloody stabbed me and my heart still happily skips a beat whenever I see him—that's not normal.

What has me worried the most is the energy thing, the ability to *feel each other's energy beyond normal senses*. I don't know...I don't want to know if he can feel my energy like I can his. His wild hellhound energy welcomes me; it is almost alive. Now that I can recognise it, I could probably pick his energy out of a crowd or feel him coming from down the street.

If that isn't enough, the book also describes a zap, a mixing of energy on the first touch. Considering John smacked me on the back of the head and dragged me away to a basement, I might have missed that step while I was unconscious. If I zapped him, John probably thought it was my bad demon juju.

I stomp to the bathroom and turn on the taps for a *relaxing* bath. I'm seething. But I smell, so I will have a bath, damn it.

While the tub is filling, I grind my teeth and stomp back to the sofa and the *love* book. "Hell's bells. I should burn it," I snarl.

Crap, that shows how angry I am, blaming a book for my situation.

I'd never intentionally harm a book: that's sacrilegious.

I gently remove the book from the shelf. I take a deep breath, ignore the mate stuff, and head for the chapter on progeny. I'm planning to never open this book again, but I just need to double-check one last thing before I forget about its existence.

Breeding with humans is best avoided. The offspring of such a pairing can be unbalanced and aggressive.

Huh. This right here is why I need to be careful and why I need rules.

Emma, the love content of the book is all about demon-to-demon pairings. No, there is nothing written that I can find about soul mates from other races. As John isn't a demon, and I'm only half...he shouldn't feel the same.

Ha, there is no way he feels the same. I know he's gone all flirty with me lately, but that could just be a normal attraction and not this soul stuff.

There's a fuzzy memory from the hospital...I narrow my eyes and tap my mouth with my fingertips as I try to remember. Arlo standing over my hospital bed, *"Poetic really, two broken souls twisted together by fate, forever entwined."* I close my eyes and groan. Arlo he bloody knew, he must have recognised the signs.

I lift my chin and square my shoulders. I can control myself; knowledge is power. This can only be a good thing. Now that I know what's happening, I can ignore the whole thing.

I am not masochistic, nor do I have Stockholm syndrome. That's at least a relief. It explains a lot. I roll my tense shoulders and take a deep breath.

I swallow down my fear of John and the...*thing*. I will not think about that again.

The book goes back on the shelf, and I drift back towards the bathroom. I take another cleansing breath. Everything is going to be okay if I follow my rules, keep myself out of trouble, be kind, and *avoid* John. Everything is going to be okay. I nod. The direction in which my life goes will be on me.

I open a bottle of wine—I'm not much of a drinker, but, well, tonight I need a drink. The white wine is sweet and refreshing on my tongue.

With my glass, I slip into the steamy bath, and I close my eyes.

Once I'm wrinkly and relaxed, I set my empty glass on the floor and think about what Malcolm said about the bears and how they learn to shift.

Think of your natural form.

I shrug. I close my eyes and think, *Natural...natural—natural—natural demon*. My mind brings up Arlo's monstrous face in the circle, and I shudder. No, not like that. I dig deep into myself, into my magic, and I mumble the words *natural form*.

I feel an unfamiliar warmth on my skin, separate from the now-tepid bathwater. I open one eye and my smoky-black ward-magic is surrounding me and the bath.

I squeak and jump. A wave of water splashes onto the floor.

What? Oh my God...Oh, not my ward. What the heck is it doing here? I lift a shaky hand and the smoke drifts gently across my hand and twists between my fingers. I want to smack my forehead.

This smoky stuff is *my* magic.

Wow. I use my big toe to pull the bath plug, not willing to take my eyes off my magic. I stare at it in wide-eyed fascination as the bath drains. Wow.

"What can you do?" I whisper to it like a proper weirdo. The smoke seems to get thicker. *Natural form.* I aim the thought at my magic. It shimmers, and from one breath to the next...I have a cape around my shoulders.

A cape.

Ha, bloody brilliant. Useless. I roll my eyes and turn my head to see black fabric. The empty bath squeals as I stand up. The cape is heavy on my shoulders and hits me mid-thigh. What the hell? I don't need a bloody cape. I know the book said demons can create their clothing, but a cape is crap. "At least it could be designer horse-wear," I grumble as I step out of the bath.

I let out a bloodcurdling scream when I see myself in the mirror.

Oh bloody hell, hell, hell. That's not a cape. That's not a cape!

Wings.

I have wings. I panic. I wave my arms about in the air, and the bloody wings follow the movement of my hands as they open and flap. Ouch.

OhmyGodohmyGodohmyGod.

I run in a circle and they follow me; they smash off the bathroom walls, knocking stuff off the shelves and onto the floor.

Ouch, ouch, ouch, that hurt.

Oh my God, they are real. Oh my God, it's not my imagination. The freaky huge black *bat wings* sticking out of my back *are real*.

I slip on the wet floor, and only a desperate wing flap keeps me from falling on my bum.

Emma, calm down.

I stand, panting. I drop my arms and the...gulp...wings...relax down my back.

It's okay. I am okay.

Oh bloody hell.

I tremble. "*Natural form*...oh, for fuck's sake." I bury my face in my hands. "Nice one, Emma."

CHAPTER
THIRTY-ONE

IT HAS BEEN two days and I've had to cancel my training with Scott as I can't go. I can't go anywhere. They will not go back in.

Oh, we're having a grand time bonding, the wings and me. I'm definitely learning the art of patience and the zen of keeping calm, as these things are sensitive.

I can't sleep. When I try to get comfortable, they do random things. Like smacking the walls, which is painful and causes bruises across the soft, silky membrane that covers the thin, bendable bones. I think I broke a small bone, but it healed before I calmed down enough to investigate. Both wings look the same, so at least it healed straight. Bones take seconds to heal, yet the bruises seem to take forever in comparison.

I have to admit my wings are beautiful. In direct light, they are purple. I sigh. God, I wish they would go away. Malcolm said to shift back, all the bears had to think about was their human selves. I close my eyes for what feels like the millionth time and *think* human. Nothing happens. Nothing ever happens. I let out a manic laugh at the entire situation. What a clusterfuck.

I'm doomed.

I breathe one deep breath in and one deep breath out. I try my best to relax. *I bet my mate can help me.* I groan at the unhelpful thought. The entire left side of my face twitches. I don't want to rub it in case my wings go nuts and pop out from the movement of my hand. I much prefer them to be still.

Yeah, the thought I can't seem to banish, that is continually running through my brain, is: *I need John.* I need his help. With his experience, he must have an idea about how to help me. I have no one else to turn to.

I can't ask Malcolm or Scott—it's too much to ask, it's too much trust to give.

There is only John. How's that for irony?

My soul m—nope. John, the monster, has been texting me, demanding to know where I am. The missing time at the gym didn't faze him. But when I called the stables to arrange care for Bob, the demanding messages came in. I haven't replied, as I don't know what to say.

But after two days with still no headway, I'm admitting defeat. Each hour that passes, I step closer to breaking rule number one: Don't be a dickhead. I promised Bob that I wouldn't leave him for long and these wings are going to make a liar out of me. So I mentally pull on my brave pants, grab my mobile phone, and message John back.

We arrange to meet at his house.

I wear jeans, but my top half is an issue. Ha, I'm screwed. I carefully rub my face.

In the books, when a character has random wings appear out of nowhere, they slit two holes into the back of their shirts and thread the wings through. Voila. Hey presto all sorted.

Oh yeah, that's okay if you've got help and your wings are not trying to knock you out. There's no chance a tiny bit of fabric is going over my giant-ass wings, not a chance in Hell. I end up wearing a shirt backwards. I button it at my neck and my waist. It is not ideal, but if I keep my hands down, pinned to my sides, I shouldn't flash anyone. At least I'm covered.

I think maybe I'm making a mistake, going to John for help. But after days of pure frustration, I have no other options left. I step through my door and appear outside of John's house. When I think of leaving my doorway, I imagine stepping out of John's door so I don't step into his home. I could, but that would be rude.

I run my fingers through my messy ponytail. I turn. The driveway stone crunches underneath my trainers. I step up to the red door and tentatively knock.

My wings twitch at my back.

Moments later, as if he's been waiting for me, John flings open the door. I fidget as we stare at each other.

Oh my, he is still alluringly handsome. I haven't *seen* him in weeks and my eyes drink him in greedily. John's gaze flicks up and down as he takes me in, from my tired eyes to my wings. With a head tilt, he studies my new appendages. My wings rustle. I smartly drop my eyes and stare at his chest. He is wearing tight black fatigues, and his black combat top is so tight it almost gives way under the strain of containing all those muscles. I swallow and fiddle with my shirt.

"You're looking pretty demony, Emma," he says as he raps his knuckles on the doorframe. I grind my teeth. Why did I think he'd be able to help?

I reach up and cover my black lips. The strange colour is the least of my problems. With all my wing drama, that little detail I pretended to overlook. At least my eyes and mouth match.

"The wings are cute. Is that the biggest they get?"

I drop my hand and my lips part with shock. Cute? My eyes flick to his, and I growl at him, insulted. "What? They're massive."

"Oh, okay..." He coughs into his hand. "So I see you have a problem." And then the dickhead dares to smile. His bright-green eyes twinkle.

My nostrils flare, and I glare at him. After a few minutes, I break the awkward silence with a cough. "Urm...can I come in?"

"Of course." John steps away from the door and waves me inside.

As I walk over the threshold and pass John, a rogue wing *snaps* out and smacks him in the face.

Oops.

That wasn't intentional, but heck, I want to give my wing a high five. I do my best to hide my grin.

When we enter the living room, he circles me and inspects my wings. They twitch. I'm sure the little buggers are waiting for the ideal opportunity to smack him again.

"This is the reason you've been MIA," John says as he rubs his now-wing-red face.

Sorry-not-sorry.

I nod and suck in my lower lip. "Can you help me? I can't...I can't get them to go back in." John pauses behind me, and the heat of him sends shivers down my spine. I can feel our combined energy like waves battling against each other. Caressing each other.

He leans in closer. His warm breath on my ear. "May I touch you?" I shiver as his whispered words tickle the back of my neck. My mouth fills with saliva and I gulp; I can't speak. I gnaw on my lip and nod my head.

Even after I nod my head with permission, John seems to take forever to touch me. So I jump when his hand finally touches my back, landing gently between the wings.

My wings fling out with a *snap*. Flap-flap-flap. "They have a mind of their own," I say with an embarrassed whisper. John makes a noncommittal grunt, perhaps because he's dodging my wings.

I wish he wouldn't touch me. I like his hands on me, and that's bad, very bad. I swallow again. I force myself to stand still and not squirm. I like it and I don't want to. He runs his hands down my back and across my shoulders and neck.

"You need to relax—"

"I have been trying to," I bite out. I roll my eyes heavenward with exasperation. As if I can relax with John touching me...yeah, that's going to happen. Ha, I'd have more chance with Freddy Krueger standing behind me offering a head massage.

"Close your eyes." I huff. "Close your eyes, Emma. Think of your wings, think of how happy you are with them...how special they are." I scrunch my face in disbelief. What has that got to do with anything? I'm not bloody happy. I sigh and force myself to do as he says.

I am happy I've got wings...I grind my teeth. So happy. I puff my cheeks out. Okay, let's start smaller: I am happy I've got magic.

I have the means to protect myself, which is incredible. Seriously, looking at my messed-up situation, it could have been worse. I've got wings...I could have had a mouthful of serrated teeth and scary nails to go with them. At least I look like me. Me with black lips and dark-purple wings. I guess it's kind of cool.

The possibility that I might be able to fly is nuts, mind-boggling. I mean...how amazing is that, to fly...crash. I gulp.

Oh heck, what goes up must come down. Perhaps I'm not ready for that step yet.

"Shush, Emma, calm your thoughts. Relax, you are safe, now relax." John's hands continue their light attention to my skin. My skin tingles in response to his touch. He touches the membrane of my left wing, and it flutters. Wow, the wing is so sensitive. I can't help the small moan that leaves my lips. I cringe at the sound.

Oh God, that wasn't embarrassing at all.

John's hands move back to my shoulders and he digs his thumb into a sore spot. The wings are so heavy and my shoulders are so sore with carrying all the extra weight. His hands feel so good. I allow myself this one moment to enjoy his attentions. I need his help and it won't do any harm just this once. I breathe in deep to fill my nose with his bonfire-and-linen-fabric-softener scent. My shoulders relax, my wings drop, and my chin drops to my chest. I let go. I let go of my fear. I forgive myself for being frightened of my wings.

I mentally release the tight grip that I have had on my magic. I let go of the ball of magic that I've been unknowingly, fearfully clutching inside me; I allow it out.

The black smoky magic pours out of me and gently caresses my skin. *Human*...I aim the thought at it. My magic shimmers, and between one breath and the next the wings dissipate. They are gone. *Thank you*. I sigh in relief.

"Well done," John says behind me, his hands still on my shoulders. He did it, he helped me.

I force myself to step away from his hands. With my back still turned, I remove my shirt and put it back on the correct way. "Thank you," I say as I quickly button it up. I turn and fix my eyes on John's chest. "Thank you for your help."

"You're welcome. Emma, why won't you look at me?" My heart misses a beat at his question. I gulp and attempt a blasé shrug.

"Thank you for helping me. I need to go," I mumble.

"Emma, what are you hiding?" My eyes fly to his, and his beautiful face almost makes me stagger. *Soul mates.* I fidget; he can't make me talk.

"I have two full days to catch up on. I need to go home and get changed and then go see Bob. Thanks again for your help."

Oh, and we are soul mates, bye-bye. I smile my bizarre, toothy grin, give him a double thumbs-up for good measure, and then with my thumbs still stuck out, I awkwardly wave goodbye. I hurry out of the room like my bottom is on fire.

The hellhound follows on my heels.

"Stay, talk to me. I want to know what you aren't telling me, what you are hiding. I know you, Emma. Tell me what's wrong, let me help."

"I've done nothing wrong," I squeak as I power-walk to the door.

Oh heck, I don't want to be in a situation where the hellhound feels the need to interrogate me. I need to get home. My heart hammers in my chest and my hands shake. The scent of my fear will be winging its way up the hellhound's nostrils.

I pant. I can't get enough air into my lungs. Oh God, oh God. Coming here was a mistake.

"What are you hiding?" He catches up, grips my shoulders, and spins me around. He deftly manoeuvres me until I'm pinned against the hallway wall. His muscly forearms land on either side of my head and I gasp as his massive body presses against mine. My blouse and his T-shirt are thin barriers between us. The clothes between us might as well be non-existent for how aware of him I am. My breasts press against him and with each panting breath and the friction it creates, my nipples harden. I feel my face turning bright red with embarrassment as his solid bulk against my softness reminds me I haven't got a bra on.

I swallow a mortified moan.

He cups my face, thumb under my chin as he angles my face until we are nose to nose. He looks into my eyes. "What are you hiding?" he growls. Something in his pupils flares and the orange flames flicker.

The clink of chains.

I shudder with fear. My body shakes as the lust that was dragging me down disappears. I feel nothing now but fear...it vibrates through his fingers.

He draws his knuckles across my cheek and I flinch. "Tell me what you are hiding."

I swallow. "You...are frightening...me," I stammer out.

"That is not what you are hiding." He glides his fingers down my throat and grips the back of my neck. His hand circles my throat. My pulse pounds underneath his fingers. No, I can't hide how much he frightens me.

"You are my mate."

Oh bloody hell.

My eyes widen with horror. No-no-no-no, *shut up Emma, say nothing else,* I scream in my head.

"You're my mate," I repeat, because saying it once isn't enough. "Demons have soul mates, can you believe that? Hahaha..." An awkward, nervous laugh spills from my lips. "Well...if you believe a crusty old book...I am not sure I do." I try to wiggle away.

If it's even possible, John moves *closer*, his eyes heavy-lidded and filled with awe. He dips his head.

"Mate..."

"No." Oh God, no. I turn my face away, John brushes the wisps of hair from my face and rubs his nose against the pulse at my neck, breathing in my scent. I tremble.

"You love me in my hellhound form...as Riddick, you love me." John speaks softly, coaxingly, his voice warm and low.

I wave my hands to the side to ward him off. I work them between us and try to push him away. I shake my head as if doing so will stop his words.

No, this is not happening. I voice my thoughts. "No, it's not happening, the soul-mate thing." I vigorously shake my head. He hasn't denied it, so John must feel it too. The awe in his eyes is freaking me out. "You aren't good...*we*...we aren't good enough for each other. Fate got it wrong." Rule number two: Be kind. "Yes, I loved Riddick as a friend, and I could have loved you too, John." My voice breaks. Being honest sucks. "Everything in me wants to love you. Yet I question your motives every second I'm with you. Even now you *scare* me."

Like I'd hit a switch, he sucks in a deep breath, and John allows me to push him away. A rueful expression flashes across his face, and my frightened brain takes in every detail. The subtle rhythmic movement of the veins in his neck, the tense muscles in his arms and shoulders, his hands clenching and unclenching. My chin quivers and I press my lips together. I can't look at him, his eyes…they are so sad.

"I don't want to frighten you, Emma."

"You do, though. You do frighten me, John. What is love without trust?" He doesn't love me, how could he love me? "Maybe in another lifetime, but not this one. I'm sorry. Too much has happened between us." I implore him to understand, and as my eyes flood with unshed tears, his face becomes hazy. "I didn't want to burden you with this. It slipped out. I am so sorry. Forget I said anything. Forget about me."

"I will not let you go. I will prove to you that we can be happy, that I can make you happy," John whispers as he closes the gap between us and his enormous hands gently caress my face. I look into his beautiful green eyes. "War is in my blood and war has moulded me. Times change for some people, but not for me. I am a full-blooded warrior— I'm expendable. I made peace with that a long time ago. But for you, I can try. I can try to change." His thumb caresses my bottom lip and dips into my mouth. The salty taste of his skin floods my mouth. The urge to flick my tongue across his thumb makes me groan. "You are the first thing that is mine."

With his words, my heart breaks and my tummy twinges with stress. I drop my head to his chest and suck up the pain.

Ouch, it hurts. God, how this hurts.

"That…" my hand taps his chest, and I slide against the wall and away from him. The tether between us stretches thin. The tears I was gallantly holding fall. "…That right there is the problem. John, you said, 'thing.' I am not a *thing*." I try to lift my chin, but my head is heavy. I shrug and my lips wobble into a semblance of a smile. A broken smile.

I am not strong enough to deal with this man.

I cringe away from the orange glow that is brightening again in his green eyes.

He frightens me.

CURSED DEMON

Rule number three: Don't lie to yourself. I am not strong enough. I know that without even trying, without meaning to...he'd destroy me.

So I walk away.

Everything happens for a reason. Pain rips through me and I barely hold in my heart-wrenching sobs.

CHAPTER
THIRTY-TWO

I DO what I always do when I feel like crap—I go and spend time with my best friend.

Bob-cob is grumpy. He isn't impressed that his human hasn't been to see him for a few days. To placate him, I feed him a full packet of extra-strong mints and spend a good hour brushing him. I scratch all his favourite spots. I even take him for a lazy hack around the livery yard instead of schooling him in the riding arena.

When we get back from our ride, I untack him and then go grab a grooming brush. I leave Bob tied up outside his stable with his saddle resting across the top of the stable door. Brush in hand, I meander back across the yard. I narrow my eyes as I watch Bob lean towards his saddle. "Bob," I say in a warning tone. He looks back at me and then gives a deliberate nudge of his nose. The saddle on the door wobbles. I speed up. "Don't you dare..." I am a step away. With a wrinkle of Bob's nose and another strong push, the saddle thuds to the floor. Gah. "You little sod, that saddle is a made-to-measure... why the hell would you do that?" I scoop the saddle up off the floor and inspect it. Phew, it's gotten away unscathed and there are no scratches.

I glare at him and he looks back at me, the picture of horsey innocence. If anyone that tells you horses don't or can't hold grudges...they haven't spent a lot of time with them. Bob seems more content now that he's got his own back.

I TAKE the saddle and my cleaning kit and go sit on a bale of straw in the hay barn. A shaft of sunlight warms my face, and the rough straw digs into the back of my thighs. I've done all my stable jobs and a smug Bob is back out in the field with his friends. It's a lovely, warm day without a cloud in the pale-blue sky. With the saddle resting on my knees, and the comfortable heat in the barn relaxing me, my mind drifts as I apply the leather conditioner with a cloth.

"You moved out then, for real?" says a familiar voice. I cover my eyes with my hand and squint into the bright sunlight. "This is a nice place for Bob... expensive...that horse is so spoiled."

So I can see her better, *Sam* steps underneath the barn's overhang.

My lips part as I take her in. She twists her riding hat in her hands and looks at me sheepishly.

"Hey, yes and yes it's nice," I say, answering both questions. I glance down at the saddle on my knees and gather my courage. "I've missed you," I whisper.

"Yeah?" She steps closer. "I'm sorry, you know, about the whole"—Sam cringes and then does the *Psycho* film knife-move, with the screeching sound effect for good measure—"stabbing you in the back and stuff." I snort and shake my head at her antics. She plunks down next to me on the bale and nudges my shoulder. "I missed you too," she mumbles and shoots me a rueful grin.

"Did he send you?"

"Who...the hellhound? No. No, I don't work for him, not anymore. I finished up riding a client's horse and saw you sat here on your lonesome." She bounces the hat on her knee. "What's the hellhound done to you now?"

I shrug.

"You okay?"

"Yeah, I'm okay. You?" Sam shrugs back. "How is Munchkin?"

"He is a shit. The little tyke is teaching kids to ride...it's hilarious." I roll my eyes. Bloody vampire. I bet their parents don't think it's hilarious. I can imagine the poor kids pinging off the monster pony, crying on the floor while Munchkin tries to kick them in the head. Fun.

We sit in comfortable silence. I run the cloth across my saddle. Sam picks at some mud that's splatted on her breaches, peeling it off with her thumbnail.

"You know you can't trust me—I can't keep your secrets."

I turn my head and look at her, my eyebrows raised. Wow, that was honest.

"You know what? I'm sick of being afraid." I smile sadly and grab hold of her hand. I thread our fingers together. "I'm fucking sick of this world. It uses us and then it spits us out. To survive...we have to turn on each other, friend against friend." I squeeze her hand. "Parents against their kids. I don't want to be afraid anymore, and I'm sick to death of running. I don't want to hurt anyone, but I will not stand by and do nothing. I am done with standing on the sidelines...*snivelling*." I curl my lip in self-disgust. *I'm done with being a victim.* "I'd rather you didn't blab Sam. But you do what you need to do to survive—I trust you not to say too much." It might be a mistake, but it's a gut feeling I have.

I debate on whether to tell her about John, about us being mates, but I think it's better not to. It's private between us, and even though I should talk to someone else about it...I'm not going to disrespect John by doing so. Instead I change the subject.

"I've got wings."

"Wings? No shit...what type of wings?" Her eyes widen, and she almost shoves me off the bale in her exuberance to look at my back.

"Demony ones—bat, I guess. They're dark purple."

"Can I see?" she asks with a wiggle of her eyebrows. I grin and nod.

This...this is something I can share. I stand and prop my saddle against the bale. I open up the tenuous hold I have on my magic and it eagerly comes to my call. My black, smoky magic appears and Sam's eyes almost bug out of her head. "Is that your magic? Wow. I've never seen anything like that in my life. What can you do with it?"

I shrug. "I have no idea—your guess is as good as mine." Sam waves her hands in the air in an attempt to capture my magic, and as soon as her hands get near, they slip right through.

I mentally call for my wings. Sam squeaks, and it's only due to her vampire reflexes that she catches herself before she falls off the bale.

I giggle and allow myself a tiny bit of pride. Like with my eyes, I've been practising. Before I came to the stables I worked on releasing my wings and then putting them back away. Once I knew what I was doing and I wasn't freaking out over my magic, it became as easy as breathing.

Sam jumps up. "These are incredible, Emma," she says with awe. "Oh..." She holds a finger up and then digs into her jacket pocket. She pulls a potion ball from its depths and wiggles it at me. "...It's a 'don't see me now' potion, so we won't be discovered." She taps her ear. "I will also listen out with my vampire hearing." She flicks the potion ball onto the floor and it activates with a shimmer. As long as I don't go near that spot, it should work fine. "The wings don't tear your clothing?"

"Oh no, I forgot about that." I groan and rub my forehead. "I've never shifted with my top on." *Damn it.*

"Oh well, even if you have to shift with your boobs out...I still want a pair. Go on then, up you go." She nods at a rickety set of stairs in the corner that leads up into the hayloft—it's an open mezzanine area far above us. "Wait one sec..." she grabs her riding hat from the floor and slaps it onto my head. "Okay, champ, now go fly." Sam smacks my bum.

"Fly? Oh no-no-no, I am not going to *fly*. Are you nuts?" I shake my head so vigorously, the riding hat almost bounces off.

"You've got wings, Emma...what else are you gonna do with them?" She gives me a meaningful look and pushes me towards the stairs. "You're a demon...it's not like you're going to die."

I approach the dusty stairs, and thanks to the encouraging poke from behind me, I take a step up. The old wooden steps creak and the whole staircase wobbles. I glance back; the movement and the heavy weight of the wings unbalance me and I almost fall to my knees. "Okay, these things need to go, at least until I am up there." My magic springs into action and the wings dissipate.

So far, so good. I take another few cautious steps up.

"Huh," Sam says from behind me. "Your top is like brand new, it hasn't got any tears in or holes from your wings...looks like your magic fixed it."

"Wow, that's great." I grin as I continue my wobbly ascent. "How cool is that? I'm so glad, as I like this top." I step into the loft. The old wooden floor looks like it hasn't seen a brush in years. Clumps of dust and rotten-looking pieces of hay and straw crunch underneath my feet. I wrinkle my nose as I catch sight of a dead, mummified rat. The poor thing is so flat, it looks like it's been squished by something heavy. Eww.

I shuffle to the edge of the platform and peer down into the barn area. The ground looks like it's miles away. My stomach dips with anxiety. Crap, I know I can heal small things...so far, cuts and small breaks. But I can't heal bruises. I swallow a lump of fear; I don't know if I will be able to heal a broken neck.

"This isn't going to go well," I mumble. In response, Sam shrugs, rubs her hands together, and grins evilly. I roll my eyes. "Sam, that is quite a way to fall. I am not sure about this..." I wipe my sweaty hands on my jodhpurs.

"Yay, I have an idea." Sam scampers away and reappears with half a dozen haynets. Directly below me, she empties the contents onto the concrete floor, creating a hay landing-pad—a crash mat. Yay. I gulp.

"I hope you're gonna refill them and put them back later, 'cause I don't want to get kicked off this yard," I grumble.

Sam flicks a rude finger at me with dismissal. "It's all good. You always worry wayyyy too much...Miss Goody Two-shoes. Live a little, Emma."

Or die. Bloody vampire, it's not her who's going to be flying.

My wings return with a thought. I roll my shoulders and do an experimental flap. With the gust of air the movement creates, the dirt in the loft swirls around me. I close my eyes a second too late and a scratchy piece hits my right eyeball. It makes my eye water. Heck, do I need goggles? I rub my eye and blink like mad.

"Okay, fly," Sam yells.

Thanks, Sam, you're such a help. I adjust the hat and it wobbles. Sam's head is bigger than mine.

Why am I doing this?

This is so like the time she made me show-jump—which ended in disaster. No wonder I prefer dressage.

What the hell am I doing?

Is this going to be another thing to add to my "never try that again" list?

"Oh, no, wait!"

My heart rate picks up at her urgency; my hands tremble and my wings jiggle.

"Oh my God, what?" I yell back. "Is someone coming?"

Sam waves her hand in the air and then digs her phone out of her pocket. She'd better not be thinking of filming me.

No, after some button pressing, a tinny sound of music comes from the phone's speaker. "Is that...'Top Gun?'" I ask incredulously.

Sam nods and gives me a double thumbs-up. "Okay, we are good. Fly."

"Bloody Top Gun," I mumble as I back up as far as I can. *Sometimes the only way to learn is to throw yourself into it...*

I blank my mind, take a deep breath, and flap like crazy as I sprint towards the edge.

"Arrrah!"

Let's say the fall down was quicker than the climb up. I land on my bum with a crunch and a puff of hay.

Ouch.

Sam stands over me. With a big, silly grin on her face, she claps her hands and bounces on her toes. "Perfect. Now do it again."

"Do I have too?" I whine.

She lowers her chin and in a deep voice says, "'Why do we fall, Bruce?'" She pauses dramatically. "'So we can learn to pick ourselves up.'"

"Batman?" I groan. *Why am I listening to her, again?*

"Yeah, love that line. Okay, again...again, more flapping...urm...less screaming. You'll give me a headache."

"Liar, vampires don't get headaches," I grumble as I scrape myself off the floor.

I go again. My wings flap like mad. I can't say for sure if my efforts keep me aloft any longer, but I fall as quick. I land on my face in the middle of the hay, and the pile doesn't cushion my landing, not at all.

I don't like concrete.

To add insult to injury, the loose hat tips, cracking me across the nose. Blood dribbles down my face.

"More flapping"—she flaps her arms—"less falling, mmkay? Wipe your face, go again."

After another unsuccessful attempt, instead of running I stand at the edge with my heart in my mouth. My breathing is ragged and even though my nose isn't broken anymore, it's bruised. It's also blocked with crusty blood. My whole body is one big bruise.

Somehow, standing on the edge is *way* worse than doing a running jump. I close my eyes and I flap my wings, begging my magic to help.

At first, I try to flap them quickly, and then when that doesn't feel quite right, I try a bigger movement. I concentrate on moving the air like it's water, catching every little bit I can within the folds of my wings. I imagine I am swimming.

Eyes clamped closed, I feel...my toes leave the wooden boards.

I hover in the air for about twenty seconds, using muscles that have only just come into existence. My wings scream in pain and then my body drops like a stone. I whoop with triumph.

Sam is jumping up and down, a grin splitting her face from ear to ear. "You did it, you did it," she chants.

"Oh my God, I did it. I can do this." I grin back. I remove Sam's riding hat and brush clumps of hay from my face and hair.

"Okay, enough for today. I've gotta go." Sam grabs the riding hat from me and bounces away. "Same time next week?"

"Oi, what about the haynets?" I shout at her back.

She waves me away. "Yeah, you better get them refilled. Gotta go, I have another horse to ride. I'll send you a bill for the flying lessons," she cackles. I slump back into the hay and groan. "Oh, and Em, you are so badass." I huff out a laugh.

"No, I'm not." I drop my voice to barely a whisper. "But I'm going to be."

CHAPTER
THIRTY-THREE

Eighteen years later

The years roll by in the blink of an eye.

I slam the door of the taxi and wave to the shellshocked girl huddled inside. I nod to the driver and mouth a thank-you. He returns my thanks with a cheerful smile and drives away from the loading bay. As the taxi disappears around the corner, I quickly check that I'm alone, and then I shift into *the girl*.

I mimic her perfectly, from her clothing to her hair. My magic is incredible. I can even remove an item of clothing and it will stay real for a few hours before dissipating, it's that complex.

No wonder John had an issue with me when we first met. The things I can do now with magic...I scare myself sometimes.

It's freaky.

John...I sigh. He's been off-world with a team of hellhounds for over a year, so I haven't seen him. The hellhound has thrown himself into work, doing more and more dangerous things; he puts himself at risk. John is more renowned, more dangerous than he ever was before. I can't help thinking I've had a lucky escape, but a niggle in the back of my head tells me I am ultimately responsible. That I snuffed whatever goodness he had right out of him.

When I don't see him or hear about his antics for a while, I can't help the fear and the worry I feel. I know he's a grown-ass man, *a man who I rejected*, even if we don't talk about "the elephant in the room," he is still my mate. We gravitate towards each other. I catch the odd flash of pain in his green eyes, undoubtedly mirrored in my own.

Ha, I'm not one to talk about risk. People in glass houses shouldn't throw stones, and what I do isn't rainbows and kittens. John isn't the only one who has thrown himself into work. Daily I mess with people's lives, and there is nothing more dangerous than that.

With that fun thought...I turn and slip back through the fire-exit door into the shop's storeroom. I enter the changing rooms and nod at Penny, who has been my vigilant changing-room gatekeeper while Jessica was making her getaway.

The shop assistant twists her fingers together. "They are getting impatient," she whispers.

I give Penny a reassuring smile and I gently squeeze her shoulder. "It's okay. Thank you so much—you've done amazingly. I shouldn't need to ask for your help again."

I have a network of people I have helped over the years who owe me favours. I don't ask for much. It might be like today, a request to use the back door to a shop that they work in so I can smuggle a girl to safety, or for them to delay a bus for two minutes. Little things that add up like puzzle pieces in a sometimes-complex scheme that involves me helping others.

In a world full of monsters, I am the light in the darkness.

Mentally, I snort and I roll my eyes. Ha, what a big head: *I am the light in the darkness.* I am so glad I didn't say that out loud. I grab the clothes that Jessica has supposedly been trying on, and her small bag.

"Oh, no," Penny urgently whispers, "if you ever need help, you've only got to ask—I'm your girl." Her big brown eyes fill with tears and her lower lip trembles. "What you do...what you did...for my brother, for me. I can't ever repay you. So anything, *anything* I can do to help you..." her whispered words fade and she shrugs and rubs at a stray tear that's escaped. Impulsively, I give her a quick hug. "I've never met a witch like you—your illusion magic is incredible."

"Thank you." I smile, and I don't correct her assumption that I'm a witch; I let her think I am, like most people. Others think I'm a high-level fae. No one has yet to suspect that I'm a demon, which is how I like it. I scoop up and void the sound-masking potion ball Penny laid before the switch. The little ball crumbles to dust in my fingers and I rub my hands on my jeans.

I almost walk into the burly shifter bodyguard who is guarding the changing room door. "Mrs Philips, it is time to go," he says sharply.

"Of course. Thank you, Briggs." The voice that comes out of my mouth isn't my own. No, I look and sound a perfect copy of Jessica Phillips. I even smell like her. The shifter in front of me would be unable to tell us apart.

It took me a while to work out my demon magic. Transforming into a person took a little bit of finesse in the beginning. If I wasn't careful, I'd look fake, or worse, like a bad illusion. I spent days sitting and observing people, their faces, clothing, and their movements. I got good at mimicking people, and when I realised I could change not only my voice but my scent, I was hooked.

The satisfaction I feel knowing that the real Jessica is already safe and on her way to an entirely new life is addictive. It is why I do what I do. It started with my pup, and then there was my mum and the frustration of not being able to help her. You don't have to beat people up or kill people to be a hero—sometimes you can uniquely, sneakily use your gifts. I am a silent hero and I don't care if no one knows. It's better that they don't. Every time I do this, my soul feels a little lighter.

Jessica is half-fae and unfortunately gained the attention of the wrong man, Henry Phillips. They met six years ago, and the cat shifter, a former member of the old corrupt shifter council, would not take no for an answer. He forced poor Jessica into a relationship with him.

No one realises what goes on behind closed doors, and with powerful creatures—especially powerful shifters—even if people know something is not what it seems, they still turn a blind eye. Too frightened. I guess they think it's not their fight.

When an associate gave me Jessica's information and told me she needed my help urgently, I didn't hesitate to step in.

I have to play the role of Jessica until I can safely slip away. The clock is ticking down and Jess is less than twenty-five minutes away from stepping through a portal into Ireland. Shifters aren't allowed in Ireland. The country is a haven for humans and the fae. It has strict rules, so I'm confident Mr Philips won't be able to track her.

Oh, and I don't just shove her through the portal. I have an entire identity established for her and a place to live, a job. Once Jessica finds her feet, she can decide what she wants to do, how she wants to live. For the first time in six years, Jessica is free.

Now I'm about to play a game to keep Jessica's bodyguards, and Henry Phillips, busy. Busy enough not to implicate any of the people that have helped me today. The game is my favourite: "Now You See Me, Now You Don't."

I follow the bodyguard, my back ramrod straight and my chin high, but my eyes are firmly, submissively fixed on the floor.

I meekly hand over the clothing to another shop assistant. "Just the white top, please," I say in Jessica's whispery voice. Mr Phillips loves the colour white. With the help of my hacker friend Ava, I have eyes all over the city, and I have done my homework. The shop assistant nods, and another bodyguard steps forward to handle the payment. Jessica isn't allowed any money of her own.

Once the guard has paid, we leave. The bell over the door chimes as we step out onto the busy pedestrianised street. Briggs tightly grips my elbow as the three other bodyguards that are waiting outside the shop join our small group.

Even though I've spent what feels like more time with other people's faces on than my own, when I catch my reflection in a shop's window, it is still jarring.

Like a living wall of shifter muscle, the five guards surround me as we head back towards the parked car. I chose this shop in particular to do the switch because they don't allow cars in this pedestrian-only shopping area, and the loading bay at the back of the store makes the perfect getaway.

When we get to the main road, which is heavy with fast-moving traffic, it's showtime. "Oh," I say. I rise onto the balls of my feet and peek around the bodyguard wall. I pretend to recognise somebody across the street. "That is my friend from school." I elbow Briggs sharply in the ribs, whip around the guards, and dash into the traffic. Chaos ensues as cars swerve to avoid me. The air fills with the sounds of screeching tyres and angry car horns. No damage.

Jessica's completely-out-of-character action leaves the five bodyguards stunned for a few seconds. A few seconds is all that I need as my feet land on the pavement on the other side of the road. I grin as I blend into the crowd.

I hurry into a department store, and I make my way through the store at a fast clip. With a wink at another shop assistant, I snatch my earpiece off a shelf and stuff it into my ear. I groan—this would work so much better if magic would work on me; a communication spell would be a godsend. I shrug. Unfortunately, using other people's magic is still not in my remit.

"They are tracking you outside. Turn left," Ava says in my ear as she follows me on the security cameras. I love this store, as it has various entrances that exit onto busy shopping areas. "Look up to your left, flick your hair, perfect...got you on that camera. The bus is at the stop and it will leave in three..." I step onto the bus and wave the bus pass at the driver. "...Two..." I move away from the doors and head to the back. "...One." I grab hold of the safety bar as the bus pulls out into traffic. "Okay, they have seen you and they are following."

I slide onto the bench seat and surreptitiously look about to make sure I have no one's attention. When I deem the coast is clear, I lean against the seat in front of me and I carefully wedge Jessica's small purse, which contains her phone, underneath the seat. I also leave the bus pass inside—dated today and dirty, with a footprint on it. It's almost as if it was dropped on the floor and Jessica conveniently found it. Fancy that.

"They're following, two cars back," Ava updates. The bus goes over the bridge. "The station is coming up in one minute—get ready." I stand, leave my seat, and make my way slowly to the front of the bus.

It is imperative that we leave a trail for them to follow. Over the next few days and the oncoming weeks, ex-Councillor Phillips will want to get his greedy hands on everything to do with Jessica's escape.

No one can be implicated. The bus rolls to a stop and with a polite "thank you" to the driver, I jump off.

I head through a mass of people congregating around the station's monitors. "Stand there...okay, three cameras have got you...that's perfect. Look at the timetable. The next train to London is at platform six. Go, quick—you have three minutes, Boss."

I rush past and dodge the many travellers, some lumbering along with their bags and others chatting and stabbing at their phones. A few people are also rushing towards platforms. I run up some stairs that take me over the railway lines and then go down another set. I am glad Jessica listened and wore flat shoes—running in heels is not my strong suit. I arrive at platform six just as the train pulls in and the doors open. I head for the closest carriage and step inside.

"Okay, train camera has you. I can take it from here." I step behind a partition, and when I'm sure no one is looking...I shift and step off the train.

I tap my walking stick against the concrete as on doddering steps I slowly shuffle away. There's a beep-beep-beep behind me as the train doors close, and a whistle from the platform guard. I turn my head and watch in satisfaction as he waves to the driver, and with a hiss, a clunk, and a grinding sound, the train pulls away.

Three huge shifters barrel down the stairs, just in time to watch the train leave. One of them picks up a bin and throws it at the departing train with a roar. The others stand there, looks of disbelief on their faces. The rubbish flutters onto the floor and track. I frown. God, I hate littering.

"It's an express train to London. No stops, she's trapped. Come on, we have three hours to collect her from the other station," Briggs says with a snarl. He turns and almost knocks me over. "Watch where you are going, you stupid old cow," he spits out. He runs past me up the stairs. The other two shifters follow in his wake, not sparing me a glance.

I hum as I shuffle towards the lift, my walking stick tap-tapping. No one sees the old lady with her walking stick as she hobbles along. "Jessica made it, Boss," Ava says. I cackle with glee. Boom, mental fist-pump. Today is another good day.

CHAPTER

THIRTY-FOUR

Stuart waves at me in a panic when I step out of Bob's empty stable. "Emma, I apologise—Bob should have already been in for his afternoon check and feed. I'm sorry to inform you he keeps running away from our staff. I even attempted to get him myself...but he would not come." He twists his hands and blinks at me with a contrite expression.

My lips twitch and I try not to laugh. Bob at twenty-eight is the same horse he was at three. The older he gets, the easier he should be, but no, he seems to get sneakier with age. "It's no bother, Stuart, I'll get him." I grab his headcollar from the hook next to his stable door, and with Stuart on my heels, we head towards the fields.

"How is Mr Brown—" Stuart puffs out. Mhm, Mr Brown, my demon barrister and Bob's *owner*...this situation right here is the reason I shouldn't lie. Eighteen years I've had to keep up the ruse. I think Stuart is aware that I'm not completely human, what with the not ageing and popping randomly out of thin air. I had to make Mr Brown up on the fly and now he is a renowned barrister who works tirelessly at helping people with guild issues.

To be honest, he is a favourite of mine. I thoroughly enjoy the havoc I can cause and the amount of good I can do when I wear Mr

Brown's face. I have others do the legal stuff, as I'm not a barrister no matter what the paperwork says. But I can be a figurehead when needed, a legal advocate for the vulnerable and the lost. "—Are the new laws causing you much trouble?" Stuart continues, his eyes glowing with his excitement. He's such a gossip.

In response, I laugh and I shake my head. Truthfully I answer, "Oh, the law-makers are the people who deal with all that. My firm is doing what it can to help. If I am honest, I keep well out of the way—it is far above my pay grade." As Emma, I officially work as Mr Brown's personal assistant and Bob's groom. I think of it as my Clark Kent disguise. I go into a solicitor's office daily and disappear in there for hours.

In reality, the practice is mine and the very best minds are behind helping me help others. They know nothing about my gifts, and to them, Mr Brown is their boss and I'm his respected right hand. I let them do their jobs while I spend all my time planning my rescues of the people I can't save within the law.

I only keep abreast of the various legal situations of the races, as when big changes happen, the innocent can get caught up.

Also, there is a certain hellhound that I have a vested interest in protecting...I can't help myself.

Stuart is still chatting away, and I smile and nod my head at the appropriate moments. When we arrive at the field gate, I shout for Bob. His head immediately comes up, and he does an adorable high-pitched whinny that I translate to mean, *"My human is here."* He thunders across the field in my direction. The true love of my life.

"Hi Bob-cob, have you been naughty?" I ask him as he skids to a stop in front of me and gobbles up a couple of mints from my palm. I smile as his whiskers tickle my hand. I then frown as I catch sight of clumps of mud that are stubbornly clinging to the side of his face. I vigorously rub his face and left ear to clear the worst of it, and I get a mouthful of mud dust for my trouble as it transfers itself onto my face. Satisfied, I pop Bob's headcollar on and lead him out of the field.

I grin as Stuart scowls at Bob, and Bob flattens his ears and glares back.

I roll my sleeves up. My phone on the side is blaring out the local radio station and I dance around the living room. I'm setting up one of my safe houses, an apartment in the city centre. Apart from Ava and myself, and the few people that use a safe house, no one knows these places exist.

The money Arlo left in my name was a vast amount, and it amuses me, how I spend it. It would have made the demon rage. I normally choose the places I buy to be in busy buildings with young, transient residents who won't notice if somebody new arrives. I rarely use houses, as an empty house on a street is more noticeable. I have dozens of these apartments all over the country, and I try not to use the same one more than twice a year. Sometimes I will move a person in and it will become their permanent residence. It takes nothing with Ava's computer skills to bury the paper trail and keep the apartments hidden.

I also use my doorway to access them when I stock up, so I don't risk being followed and have the safe houses traced back to me.

I hum. The apartment is immaculate. I have stocked it with everything I can think of to make it comfortable. Unisex clothing—as I don't help just women—in various sizes, food, and toiletries. I'm not expecting to use this place for a while, but it's ready.

There is a bang behind me and the front door shudders. I have time to stop the music, send Ava a text message, silence my mobile, and shove it in my back pocket before the lock shatters.

I tilt my head and watch as three vampires barge their way into the apartment. Huh. I raise my eyebrows. What do these idiots want? "What the hell did you do to my door?" I ask incredulously, waving both hands at my poor dangling lock. "Ever heard of knocking? Why did you break down my door?" At least the door itself isn't damaged. What the bloody hell is going on?

Instead of saying anything, a vampire rushes me. His fists are almost a blur as they fly at my face. How rude. His form would mortify Scott, as his technique is awful. I step to the side and punch him sharply in the kidney. Vampire or not, that had to hurt. I kick out his knees and with a thump, he sprawls to the floor.

I shake my head as I step back away from his reach, and I keep his groaning, twisting form in my eye-line. I turn my regard to his friends, who so far, luckily for them, aren't as brash. I raise an eyebrow, cross my arms, and tap my foot...I wait impatiently for an explanation.

It better be good.

"Is this her?" one of them asks. He is tall and thin, with a dark blond comb-over.

"Yeah, the demon bitch. Girl, our boss would like a word with you. You are coming with us," his friend replies.

I make a meh-face. If I didn't have my empathy and I was a normal demon, I would pop his head clean off for being so rude.

This rude guy is broader, with an athletic build, and his hair is cropped close to his scalp. All three of the vampires are wearing variations on cheap combat clothing—although the tall blond guy's pants aren't quite long enough and they finish halfway up his ankles, leaving a bit of skin between his boots and pant leg. He sees me looking and glares at me. I smirk back at him.

I turn my eyes back toward the chatty rude vampire. "Urm...yeah, about that. I don't *chat* with people who send their goons to break down my door. I think I'll pass, thanks." The idiots are so paying to fix the lock.

"Bitch, you don't have a choice." The rude talkative one sticks his hand in his pocket and pulls out a magical Taser. Huh. "Come quietly—I don't want to have to hurt you, but I will." He wiggles the Taser at me and in response I hold my hands up.

Crap, I don't fancy being zapped today. Sometimes they are just magic and it slides right off me; other times they can have a spark of electricity. You know how in cartoons when a character gets electrocuted, you see a visible skeleton, a flash of bones? Yeah, I always imagine myself looking like that when I get hit by one of those things. It makes my teeth hurt.

"Before we leave, we need to confirm your identity." The tall vampire steps forward with a datapad. "Place your hand on the pad. It will take your fingerprints and a drop of your blood for DNA profiling," he says in a bored tone.

"Oh, I can't touch that thing..." I hold my hands up higher.

If I touch it, I'll break it.

I can sense the magic in there—it's a fancy combination of technology and magic. The machine is like the medical ones at the hospital. A rip-off version of the ones that the guilds carry. The vampire with the pad ignores my protest and grabs my hand. He wrestles my arm down and with a heavy grip, grinds the delicate bones of my hand together painfully.

I wince as he slaps my palm against the screen and within seconds there's a beep and a burning smell. A puff of smoke comes out of the side of the machine and some poor pathetic-sounding beeps signal its death.

"What the fuck...you did that on purpose."

"I really didn't. I tried to warn you." I give him a toothy grin and shrug. "You put my hand on it." His face slowly morphs into horror and the hand holding the broken datapad trembles. I think reality has just caught up with him and he realises that I am a demon.

The vampire on the floor—whom with a smirk I dub "the Kung Fu Master"—groans and staggers to his feet.

Oh, here we go.

Like a wet dog, he shakes himself, and then a ferocious expression passes across his face. With a war cry of "Arrah," the bloody idiot attempts to rush me again.

I roll my eyes as I dodge his fist, and this time, I throat-punch him. Eyes wide, clutching his throat, he gurgles and drops back to the floor. I wince as his knees crunch. Red-faced, he sputters.

"Where on earth did you find this idiot?" I ask, looking at him with a frown. I'm not the best at hand-to-hand; even after years of practice, I'd say I'm proficient. I run my hand through my hair. Truthfully, I don't like hurting people. I will if forced to do so. But compared to Kung Fu Master, who is again rolling around on the floor, I'm practically a ninja. "He makes a terrible henchman."

I glance back up and cringe at the livid look Taser Vamp is giving me. I hope he hasn't got an itchy trigger finger. I give him a rueful smile and I hold my hands up again. I shrug. "Hey I was defending myself. You can't zap me for that."

"He's my brother," he says through gritted teeth.

"Oh, that sucks," I reply with another glance at the floor.

He nods to the tall vampire, who now cautiously side-steps towards me. He pulls out a magic void bracelet—it's a plastic magical band the guilds use. Aw, bless him, he has all the best toys today. I helpfully hold my arm out for him. With a trembling hand, he slaps it onto my wrist. With a snap, the plastic tightly wraps around. What it should do is deaden my magic. It voids magic completely, helpful if you have to arrest a magical creature.

I don't have the heart to tell them they don't work on me. Oops.

The two vampires back away and warily watch me. No doubt they are waiting for something dramatic to happen. Perhaps a good old head-spin? The third is still on the floor gurgling. I give them a toothy smile and tap my foot again...time's ticking, and we need to get this show on the road. I can't spend my entire day being kidnapped.

"Why hasn't she changed," the tall vampire says out of the side of his mouth. His buddy stares at me, his lips part, and he shrugs his shoulders haplessly.

"I dunno," he says.

I tuck a piece of my blonde hair behind my ear. "This is what I look like," I say, doing jazz hands. I rub my mouth to stop myself from smiling. Their confusion is adorable. "Were you expecting something different?"

"I didn't expect you to be so pretty," Tall Vampire mumbles.

"Oh...urm, thanks." I think. I'll take it as a compliment. At least he isn't trying to be creepy. "So your boss?" I need to get them back on track. Their dumbfounded expressions are now making me feel uncomfortable.

I've already decided that I'm going to go with them. I need some questions answered, like *how* they found this safe house and *how* they knew that I'd be here. It shouldn't have happened and I need to plug the leak. It's not just me I'm worried about. People are counting on me.

I'm also fascinated, so I will play along. I need to know *who* decided it was a good idea to come and...kidnap me? Ha.

"Yeah, our master has been after you for some time," Taser Vamp replies. I shrug. I do like a good bad-guy confrontation. Their boss doesn't know what shit he has dug up. Thinking about it, I've never done a confrontation looking like me before. I am like a walking trap. I might look like an easy mark, but I'm not...I am far from it.

"Terry, get the cameras." Terry, formerly known as Tall Vampire, scampers off to do Taser Vamp's bidding. I'm disturbed as I watch him pluck tiny cameras from obscure places around the apartment. Cameras are dotted all around. I cringe...that means someone somewhere has evidence of me attempting to twerk. I blame Sam for teaching me.

I wonder if this is the only safe house that's compromised. I doubt it. I groan. Crap, I'm not looking forward to all that extra work. At least that answers one of my questions, of how they knew I was here.

I am unceremoniously marched out of the building with the Taser poking into my side.

These guys have watched *way* too many films.

Kung Fu Master is trying desperately to intimidate me—he keeps knocking into me and growling. When he shoves me into the side of the car and I painfully bang my hip—ouch—I lose my temper; I spin around and smack him on the back of the head. "Knock it off. You're acting like a right wanker." I growl, "Knock into me again and I'll pull your bloody arm off." I poke my finger in his face. He growls back and flashes his fangs.

Oh no, he bloody didn't. If he does that again, I will pull his fangs right out of his stupid head.

Stuff it. I allow my eyes to bleed black.

His eyes widen in disbelief, and he drops them to my wrist and the void band.

He stumbles back away from me and glances about, opening and closing his mouth like a goldfish. His entire body shakes and he drops his eyes to the floor submissively.

"Your attitude is going to get you killed," I hiss at him. "Think before you act. Now get in the car." I push him for good measure and he hurries away to the front of the car and jumps in.

As I slide into the back of the car, I look up at the street CCTV camera. I give it a nod and mouth the words, "Track me."

CHAPTER
THIRTY-FIVE

"She has black eyes. This isn't good, this isn't good...she's going to kill us all," Kung Fu Master whispers as his shaking body rocks forward and back in the front passenger seat.

"Shut up, Matthew, you're doing my head in," his brother, Mr Taser, harshly replies. Cringing, I sit in the back of the car with Terry. I feel a bit like a bully; I didn't mean to frighten him.

I wiggle in my seat. Okay, I meant to frighten him, but not as bad as I have.

We drive for around thirty minutes in uncomfortable silence. Kung Fu Master can't keep still. Every time I move, he shudders and his left leg bounces.

When we arrive at a familiar building, a familiar nightclub, I roll my eyes. This place has had many revamps over the years and its owner has stayed relatively quiet. I knew it was only a matter of time before the pureblood came for me.

My various attempts to rescue my mum from his clutches were in vain, and my relationship with her was stilted as a result. I close my eyes for a brief second, it still hurts when I think about her role in my life. The mystery of her giving me away hampered our non-existent mother-and-daughter relationship.

I don't trust easily, and I guess with John's words of caution churning in the back of my mind, it was difficult to give her the benefit of the doubt. I asked her; I brought up the painful subject a few times over the years, but she wouldn't answer. She'd quickly change the subject or she would cry. Then I would be left feeling like the bad guy. No one wants to make their mum cry. So I let it go.

I suppose I could have forced her into leaving him. But what kind of person would that have made me? I would have been no better than the wicked men and women I fight against. It's a lesson I learned quickly: you can only help the people that want your help. The people that are ready to move on. Otherwise, you are wasting everybody's time.

The club is closed as it's Monday afternoon. I get out of the car with a yawn and stretch. With a hand on my shoulder, Mr Taser frog-marches me across the street. The frightened, wide-eyed brother disappears.

We pass bored-looking vampires that are standing guard outside. They have the look of elite soldiers, but they lack the menace of trained professionals. It doesn't help that their bright-red uniforms stand out for all the wrong reasons. I quietly count them as I pass. I give up when I get to over a dozen. I groan. Perhaps this isn't my best move, allowing Lord Luther Gilbert to have the pleasure of my company.

I'm shown up some stairs and we head through a door marked PRIVATE. Taser Vampire swings the door open without knocking and prods me to enter. We step inside.

The colour red assaults my senses. Glossy red tiles span the floor and gleam my reflection back at me—dozens of creepy, red, distorted versions of myself. Oh heck, that's not a flattering look. I refrain from the childish urge to grin or stick my tongue out.

I lift my eyes from the creepy floor and take in the rest of the room. I wrinkle my nose with distaste as the red theme continues. Red walls, curtains, blinds, and furniture. Instead of looking sensual, the shade of red chosen makes the entire room look tacky and gives the overall impression of trying too hard. Cheap. It's as if the designer was intent on screaming, "Here be vampires"...it's like a vampire threw up on it.

My feet squeak on the tiles as with another taser-nudge to my back we continue into the room and head towards a seating area in the centre. "The only thing missing in this room is a blood fountain," I mumble. Mr Taser grunts in response.

The floor-to-ceiling internal windows, which look out onto the club, is the only break from the colour in the room. I think they might be one-way glass, or perhaps mirrored. I can't remember seeing a window on the club side the last time I visited...but that was over eighteen years ago.

Mr Taser watches me and his eyes widen in panic, as without an invitation to sit, I plunk my bum down onto a bright-red leather chair, which is hard and unyielding. I wave his concern away as I slump back. I'm not standing on ceremony like everyone else; waiting for the pureblood to arrive can easily be done seated.

When the man of the house...club? glides into the room, I smile lazily at him. Vampires call their collectives *Houses*. Headed by a pureblood leader, the then-House rules over the smaller clans in the area. So perhaps I was right the first time with "the man of the house."

"Hello, Luther," I say with a small wave. I sit up and peer over his shoulder for any sign of my mum, but she doesn't appear. The pureblood is alone. Well, if you ignore his guards, that is...three of them flank him, plus Mr Taser. "My mum...not about today?" I ask pleasantly as I drop the wave and slump back into the chair. My elbow cracks against the arm. I frown, give it a rub, and then prod the cushion. Poke-poke-poke. I'd be better sitting on a slab of concrete or the floor. What was the designer thinking? Perhaps vampires don't have any sensation in their bottoms or lower extremities, so it doesn't matter if the furniture is uncomfortable. How on earth did they get this chair so hard? That is an impressive feat on its own. It's definitely not styling over comfort, as the chair is u.g.l.y.

"Emma," Luther says sharply. I glance up from my chair-poking to meet his narrowed, angry eyes. He takes in my overall slumped, unconcerned position on his rock chair. Was he expecting fear and tears? I haven't done that in a very long time.

"Why am I here?" I ask with an enormous yawn...gosh, the room needs a window open and some fresh air. The stale air and the smell of rot from the turned vampires in the room is giving me a headache. I rub my temples.

Yes, turned vampires smell of dead things. I never noticed it before, but over the years my senses have improved. It's no wonder that shifters, who have more sensitive noses, seem to hold their breath when around vampires —they stink.

"I've been biding my time, waiting for the ideal opportunity for you to be vulnerable. I'm a patient man. It is so handy to have eternity at my fingertips."

Yeah, yeah, you're immortal, aren't we all? Good for you.

With a dramatic sigh and an ostentatious pout, he looks at his nails. My heart misses a beat as he reminds me of—in that moment—Arlo. Although a poor version of the demon. Arlo would have done his villain speech a heck of a lot better. Luther smiles down at his nails as he misinterprets the jump in my pulse. "The opportunity presented, and I took advantage. Today I decided on a more direct approach as your hellhound protector is off-world and isn't around to rescue you," Luther continues.

My lips twitch at his words and I relax further into the chair.

I've never been, nor I have ever wanted to be, the girl who waited to be rescued. I'm a fighter, not so much with my fists but with my mind. The mind is the best weapon. I'm not a princess looking for her proverbial prince. Does he think I need John to save me? Oh boy, of course he does.

I cough and cover my mouth to hide my smile.

"You refused my invitation once before and attempted to take away my favourite toy." He lifts his eyes from his nail inspection and petulantly glares at me. Someone had his feelings hurt.

I raise my eyebrows and give his words a small nod of acknowledgement. "How is my mum?" I inquire pleasantly. "I haven't spoken to her for a while."

"She wants you in the fold. My House offered you protection with open arms and you turned me down." I barely refrain from rolling my eyes as the pureblood goes into a rant. "Do you know how many times I've offered protection in my lifetime? Yet you turned your nose up at my offer." He paces in front of me, his shiny shoes clicking across the tiles and his voice getting a little louder with each step.

Gosh, I agitate him. I do that to some people. It's a gift.

"You belong to me. You are in my House now," he declares, turning around to pace back towards me.

"How did you find me?" I ask conversationally as I trace the leather seam of the chair. My heart rate is steady, and I relax my body and belatedly ignore his manic words and pacing. Nothing upsets a pureblood more than a lack of fear or non-deferential behaviour. They love all that bowing and scraping. If you don't kiss ass, it freaks them out.

"Your new apartment was flagged in our system as having an unknown buyer. We have been monitoring the residents of that building, as a few of the clans have become…" he narrows his eyes and curls his lip, "…difficult. There is a rebel leader in that building on our watch list. When the sale for your apartment was processed, it was flagged by my security team, who ordered the cameras to be put into place. I was pleasantly surprised when you moved in today and my security team alerted me. I took the opportunity as a gift and sent my closest men to collect you."

Huh. If he is to be believed, Ava and I missed a vampire issue in the building. A definite oversight, but understandable as the politics among creatures is ridiculously complicated, and this is a small vampire dynamic in the scheme of things. If I do believe him, and I have no reason yet not to, I can rest easy that my other safe houses are…well, safe.

This rebel leader…I need to have a chat with them. Anyone willing to upset a pureblood might be someone I want to watch and possibly help. The enemy of my enemy and all that jazz.

"You could have called. Stalking and kidnapping is so cliché, Luther." *Crack.* The pureblood slaps me across the face with the back of his hand. The sound echoes around the room.

"You will address me as Lord Gilbert. You have not got my permission to use my given name—have some respect," he seethes.

Blood fills my mouth. Huh, I didn't see him move—he was fast.

I slowly blink at him, lift my hand, and run the back of it across my lips, smudging the blood across my mouth and cheek. I look down at my hand, at the evidence of his anger on my skin. I tilt my head until the dark-green tinge of my blood catches the light.

Lord Gilbert steps back and the guards in the room mumble. His eyes narrow as he stares at me. "Green?" he says with astonishment.

I tilt my head and smile. I watch him as he frantically wipes the hand that hit me on his suit trousers.

"Demon," I growl back.

He knows I am part demon so why is it such a surprise?

On purpose, I lick my lips clean. In response, his own lip lifts at the corner with poorly veiled disgust. Unable to hide his distaste, he shudders.

There is more mumbling from the guards. My blood tastes normal to me, but to a vampire, my green blood—my demon blood—tastes like shit.

The green didn't happen overnight. It started as a green glitter within the red and it became darker over time. Meh, I roll with it. I have wings and I can fly...heck, I can shift into a fly...so I decided early on not to freak out about my blood colour.

My tongue prods my lip. The cut from his blow has already healed. My lip was good as new seconds after he hit me. Shame I can't say the same for the bruising—my throbbing cheek will take a while to heal. He doesn't understand who he's messing with.

I can see the growing confusion in his eyes as he focuses on my lips, as he looks for the evidence of the damage he caused. He shakes his head dismissively. He ignores his instincts, which I presume are screaming at him, with a shake of his blond head.

All he sees is a little girl he sold.

"Your demon parlour tricks don't impress me," he scoffs. "I have watched you for years. I wanted to see what of your own volition you'd amount to, and honestly, Emma, I'm not impressed. An administrator at a solicitor's firm? What a disappointment," he sneers at me, and paces away.

I can read him like a book. He's now using the pacing as an excuse to move away from me. My overall unconcerned demeanour and my dark-green blood have thrown him. I do my best to keep the smile off my face as he starts what he thinks is an epic speech about my failings. I miss the majority of what he has been saying, but it's no bother. He sounds like a disappointed parent. A disappointed parent who lacks all the facts.

Not for the first time, I think about what kind of person I would have been if this man had been in charge of my childhood. If I stayed with my mum, lived with his vampires. I remember John's words, "*Vampires destroy weakness, Emma.*" My stomach flips as I acknowledge they would have killed me or I'd have changed into someone unrecognisable.

"Guard," he yells. I don't understand why he isn't all suave and vampy. You'd think a pureblood would know his vampires can hear everything and that there is no need to shout.

I've done my homework on this guy and he's supposed to be at the top of the vampire hierarchy, the top of the tree—at least in this area. Yet he's behaving like an idiot. No wonder his men were so gung-ho and ill-trained: his whole House is festering.

One of the elite-looking vampires marches forward. If it wasn't for the smell and the shocked muttering from before, I would have forgotten that they were in the room. It's that red uniform, with the whole red-on-red...they sort of blend into the background. "Dominic, please show Emma to the white room." I sigh at the clear dismissal.

Dominic, a guard in a neat red uniform, deferentially bows to Luther. He turns to me, and his expression is...zombie-like; his eyes are dead and void of all expression. Creepy. He snaps out his hand to indicate for me to go ahead of him. Okay, then.

I rise. As I escape the unyielding concrete torture chair, I frown and shake out my limbs. Pins and needles run up and down my thighs. I glare at the chair and give my bum a rub as it re-forms back into its normal shape. God, I feel as if my whole lower half pops back into place.

"I will talk to you tomorrow. For the rest of the day and evening, perhaps you can have a rethink about your attitude and behaviour. Tomorrow we will discuss your new role in my House." I nonchalantly shrug in response.

Huh, not if I have anything to do with it. I'm planning not to be here within the next hour. I have all the information I need.

CHAPTER
THIRTY-SIX

Aptly named, the room is white, everything is white. I wash my hand across my face and groan. Oh heck, I can see myself leaving dirty smudges everywhere. The more I try not to, the more it will happen. I'm the person who, when told to be careful while eating, gets all nervous and my face twitches and I miss my mouth. I will drop every crumb or spill my drink. Not intentionally. But the more careful I try to be, the less it works out.

Gah. I also cleaned the apartment in this outfit. Forcing a horsie demon into a fully white room amounts to torture. It's almost as bad as that red chair. I remove my boots and leave them by the door. Even with me as an unwilling visitor, some poor sod will have to clean up after me, so I can't drop my manners.

In my socks, I pad across the white carpet and look around the room...no windows. The door has a fancy locking mechanism; it is a combination of infused magic and technology. It also has a dangerous, buzzing ward over the top. I move to the closest wall and give it a tap. It clangs. I hum; they've reinforced the wall. There's a big white bed and another door leading to an attached bathroom.

I yawn. I haven't got a clue what I'm going to do about the pure-blood—I can't let him get away with this, but I can't kill him either. I don't mess around in vampire politics, and killing a pureblood is equivalent to killing a king.

Flash-flash, flash-flash. I lift my head and spot the red light underneath the security camera as it blinks rhythmically. I spin away before whoever is manning the security camera can catch my bright, beaming smile.

I dramatically flop onto the bed and bury my head in the pillows as uncontrollable laughter bubbles up inside of me—I can't help my giggles. This whole situation is ridiculous.

Anyone watching the camera feed will see my shoulders shake and probably think I am crying, not laughing.

I allow a few more minutes for Ava to do her thing, and when I'm sure enough time has lapsed, I flip over and sit up. I lift my hips and pull my phone from my back pocket.

The naughty vampires really should have frisked me.

My mobile vibrates immediately in my hand. I get comfortable and sit cross-legged in the centre of the bed as I answer. "Hi, Ava."

"Hey Boss, I'm in their systems—I have been since I got your text message. I've got you on screen." I wave at the camera. "I've looped the camera feed so they can't see you talking to me. I've gone through their systems with a fine-toothed comb and I can't find any evidence of any other safe house being compromised. No more hidden cameras. I found and deleted the one from the apartment. But just in case, I'm doing a full security check as a precaution. I'm..." the phone rustles as Ava puffs out a sad-sounding breath. "...shit, I'm so sorry Boss, I messed up." I vigorously shake my head at the camera.

"No, no, hey...you haven't messed up, don't be daft. These things happen..." I push my hair away from my face and tuck it behind my ear, "...and I appreciate everything that you do. Thank you for having my back."

"I saw the void bracelet. Can you still use the doorways?" Ava asks.

I glance down at the snap band on my wrist. Huh, I'd forgotten about it. "Oh yeah, it's all fine. I can still use the doorways—my magic is still active; the bands don't work on me. I have some clippers at home that I can use to cut this sucker off. I'm not happy about hanging around here for long—I need to leave."

"I will keep you on the camera loop, so you can leave anytime. Are you going to use your doorway?"

I grin at the camera and point at the warded door with my free hand and scramble off the bed and roll my shoulders. "Is it bad that I want to go out the front door?"

"Yes," Ava says, being the voice of reason. "I can see on the cameras that he has a lot of vampires hanging around."

I grunt in response.

I move towards the door with its crappy ward and the over-the-top magic lock. It would be so easy to walk out of this room. Going out there and beating up or frightening the vampires is going to make me feel vindicated.

In that awful red room, when I looked down at those glossy red tiles as they reflected my distorted, red face back at me, I felt inspired. It gave me such a great idea. I could shift into a demon, red, huge, and scare the crap out of them. A human against vampires wouldn't stand a chance, but a demon...

Walk away or cause a scene...apart from a bit of bruising across my cheek, I'm okay. I let them take me. I came for answers, and I got them.

But...Ava is right, it's not a good idea. I am not that person; it's not the vampires' fault that their boss is a dick.

I spin and mockingly glare at the camera, then shift my gaze to the room's bathroom door. With a disappointed sigh, I grab my boots from the floor, and like a sulky teenager, I trudge away towards the bathroom doorway. "No, it's not a good idea," I grumble, once I'm standing on the bathroom tiles and not on the dreaded white carpet. One-handed, as I'm still holding the phone in the other hand, I stuff my feet into my boots. "It's not a good idea at all. I hate you. It's not like you, being the voice of reason."

Ava snorts. "Yeah, I know. You must be rubbing off on me."

I know I'm doing the right thing. Luther has a lot of guards... poorly trained, but a lot of them. Perhaps we can take him on indirectly. "Mhm, so...what else did you find? Do we have any dirt?" I smirk up at the camera. "Of course we have dirt."

"Oh, Boss, I have access to so much dirt on this guy, I am surprised he hasn't got a team following him around with shovels. With the stuff on his computer network, he should have been more on our radar. There's a girl at the apartment building they took you from. In their communication, they call her *the rebel leader*." Ava snorts. "The girl is twenty. Bunch of idiot vampires calling her a rebel leader. I think releasing the information I have to the vampire council will help her, act as a distraction, and keep the vampires away from you. It should keep this Luther guy busy for years. I can make his entire House a priority for the guilds. He is going to be a pariah in vampire circles. It's a win-win on all fronts."

I tilt my head in thought. I'd prefer to see the information with my own eyes and plan things properly. But…we've done this so many times and I trust Ava's judgement. This situation calls for something different. Plus, he made it personal by sending his henchman to my safe house to kidnap me. And he slapped me.

Not that it wasn't already personal: the guy sold me to a demon. I nod while I rub my sore face. "Perfect, do that."

"Okay, done. I've sent the information out to the vampire guild, the vampire council, and a few Houses. I'll do the necessary explaining to the girl and get her someplace safe."

"Do you need me for anything?"

"Nope, I just need to ring the *rebel leader*." Ava snorts again. "I've already sent all the information out to the relevant parties. Lord Gilbert, your pureblood kidnapper, is about to have a very bad day."

CHAPTER
THIRTY-SEVEN

THERE IS a bang and a crash outside my office. Raised, angry voices filter into the room. "You can't see her without an appointment—" Suddenly the door flies open, the door handle impacts the wall with a crunch, and a puff of white dust rends the air.

"I don't know how you did it," he says as he stomps into my office, panting. He pauses at the edge of my desk and points a trembling finger at me.

With calm nonchalance, I gather the documents that are spread across my desk and slide them safely into my top drawer. I wave away my hovering, worried staff, rest my palms on the desk, and plaster a pleasant smile on my face.

"You disappeared from a locked room. It was supposed to be impenetrable," he whines. "You had a void band on. How the fuck did you get past five of my best guards? I stationed them right outside." He runs his hand through his hair in frustration, and his floppy blond hair awkwardly sticks up. "I had a visit from the vampire council's enforcers. Some questionable evidence has come to light. Evidence that was held on my secure servers. The information could only have been obtained by someone hacking into my computer system. Which I've been assured isn't possible. It is the same computer system that handles my security cameras, the same cameras that had you lying facedown on the bed. Yet, the entire time, the room was empty—"

I interrupt his rant. "Hello, Luther, what a pleasant surprise, it's so nice of you to visit my place of business rather than simply kidnapping me." I follow my words up with a patronising smile.

The pureblood is wearing yesterday's clothes. His once-pristine suit is now wrinkled. Perhaps I should have bided my time in sending out the information and not made it so obvious, the link between my escape and the data leak. Luther isn't certain of my involvement and he is still seriously underestimating me.

Oh heck, I am surprised smoke isn't coming out of his ears. He slams his hands down on my desk. The heavy desk squeals in protest as it is shunted a few inches across the floor towards me. I rest my elbows on the desk and prop my chin on my hands. I flutter my eyelashes at him.

He leans over the desk until our noses almost touch. "You little bitch, I am going to kill you—"

"Oh, okay. That's nice...um hm...you might want to work on that temper, Luther...eww...no one likes a spitter." I scrunch my nose, sit back in my chair, and wipe my face. "Humans use a saying: 'Say it, don't spray it.'"

"—I'm going to bleed you dry." So vampy, I almost shiver. "I have your mother—"

I gasp and press one hand against my lips and the other on my chest. I open my eyes comically wide. "Oh no, not my mum, your partner for almost thirty-five-years...whatever shall I do?" I drop my hands and give him a toothy grin.

"—and your hellhound."

Everything stops.

My silly quips freeze in my throat, and I almost stop breathing. Fear floods me. When I look into his livid eyes, the hair on my arms rise.

He has my hellhound.

"I am listening." It's not my voice that comes out of my mouth. It's throaty, dark, not human. I can feel my eyes going black. Instead of being hazy, like it was in the early days, my eyesight becomes pinpoint-sharp, magnified.

"You fix what you did." Luther prods the top of my desk with his index finger, and his voice drops into a low growl. "You send a retraction, admit liability. You tell them you lied." I've seen the evidence, and there's no retracting that shit—Luther is delusional. "Then you make sure you have all your affairs in order." He digs into his trouser pocket and slaps a business card on top of my desk. "Come to this address."

"When," I growl.

"Ten this evening." My eyes flick to the clock: it's eleven a.m....I have eleven hours. I nod and he turns on his heel and stalks out of the room.

Rein in your temper, Emma. Wield it like a weapon.

My nostrils flare with my poorly reined-in anger and I close my eyes for a second. In a poor attempt to get a grip on my wildly beating heart, I take a deep, shuddering breath. I force my eyes back to normal. Freaking out will not help John.

God, I'm so angry. I have an urge to run after him and pull his head off—with the increase in my strength over the years, I'm pretty sure I could do it.

Instead, I call Ava. "Have you got a location on John? Drop everything for a moment. I need a location on him and everything you have on this address..." I rattle off the address from Luther's card.

"Boss? That you? You sound...urm...okay. One sec." I wait. My breath rasps through my tight throat and my heart continues to slam into my chest as I wait and Ava plucks stuff out of the internet ether. I strum my fingers on the desk and rub the side of my face when my eye twitches.

It's a long time since I've been this angry, this afraid.

For John.

Our relationship is the epitome of complicated.

Over the years I've attempted to date, sort of. One guy was nice, but after a few weeks, he ghosted me. I later found out the guy had a visit from John. To be honest, it was a kind of relief. Dating is naff. I felt so guilty...like I was cheating on the hellhound. Which is ridiculous...you can't cheat on a man that you've never had a relationship with. Can you?

I guess when you have had your soul mate handed to you on a silver platter and then you tell fate to go shove that platter...I compare everyone against John and they don't stand a chance.

God, how I've missed him.

I huff. It's not like he's breaking down my door—not that he can, what with my living in a pocket dimension—and proclaiming his undying love. I glance down at my strumming fingers. In my secret, shameful moments, I daydream he'll do just that.

Whenever I need him, he's always there.

Grumpy, angry hellhound. Attempting to fix problems that sometimes don't need fixing.

"Oh, wow, oh no, John Hesketh isn't off-world. He came through a portal within an hour of your kidnapping."

Why the hell did he do that? I let out a pained moan. The bloody stubborn man came to rescue me...he knows I can take care of myself.

"Can you send me everything you have, please, Ava?" I manage to whisper. We end the call and I place the mobile carefully down on my desk.

I bow my head, and grip the edge of the table so hard that it hurts my fingers.

He has John.

CHAPTER
THIRTY-EIGHT

I STAND in front of my desk, hands gripping the back of my neck as I eye the complete rescue plan that's laid out in front of me. Ava has pulled up everything she can find about the building. The live camera feeds are unavailable as the vampires have destroyed the cameras, but I have older CCTV footage and detailed building plans of the inside. My office is overflowing with pertinent information, but frustratingly, it might not be enough.

When the pureblood left, all I wanted to do was immediately go and rescue John. Off the cuff, figuratively storm the castle and kick vampire ass. But I told myself I couldn't do that as I'm not Rambo. No, I needed a plan. Now, an hour later, I have a plan that'll work, but I have no way of pulling it off.

We've tried to contact John's team of hellhounds, but frustratingly —because of the time constraints—we can't even get hold of them, as they are all still on mission and off-world. Eleanor's on a bodyguard assignment and unable to leave her client. Ava even attempted to find the honey-eyed angel—not that I'd know if he would help, I haven't seen him since he healed me—but to no avail. If Ava can't find someone, no one can.

God, I am such a bad person. I've never bothered to find out about his friends. If he has friends outside of work, that is...I guess that like me, John is very much alone. I drop my hands and lean against my desk. I know everything about his enemies. He has a tonne of those. Yeah, such helpful information for this situation.

I huff and rub my forehead. What is frustrating is that off the top of my head, I don't know anyone I can ask to help me. I care too much to ask anyone to risk themselves in going against an entire House of vampires, vampires that I've already backed into a corner—it's suicide. I could pay mercenaries, but with the short time frame and the risk of collateral damage...heck, it looks like it's back to me playing Rambo.

I glare at the mounds of information and the surrounding plans—what a waste of bloody time.

John is my go-to person. How's that for irony? If I ever needed muscle I'd ask him, or he'd turn up uninvited with his shiny knives.

I have a better chance of doing this on my own—well, I won't be on my own, because I will have John—perhaps all I need to do is get to John and heal him. I know the only way to keep a shifter down is silver. If I can get him away from whatever silver they are using, heal him enough so he can shift...

In my cupboard, I still have lots of fancy healing potions. All I'd need to do is hand him a bottle and he'd just have to tip it...he could then shift into hellhound form and chew everyone's faces off. The pair of us might be able to fight our way out.

Gah, unless he's got silver in his system, and then a healing potion isn't going to do shit. His body has to process the silver and that could take a while. The odds aren't good.

I could hand myself over at ten tonight and hope that Luther will let John go, but when does that ever happen? Bad guys don't let men like John go.

I look at the clock. Time is quickly ticking away...every second he spends in the vampire's clutches is a second too long. I wring my hands together and dig my nails into my palms. I fight against the almost-overwhelming panic that is gripping my throat and squeezing my chest.

The little voice in my head is screaming, *I did this.*

God, I feel so guilty—this is all my fault. If I hadn't allowed myself to be taken, he wouldn't have come back to rescue me. Time and time again he helps me, and I let him.

I just use him.

I rub the back of my neck as my heart continues to ache.

I point John at the bad guys, and I use him. Memories flicker across my mind like a film with the countless times John has saved my life. It more than makes up for our poor beginning. I was so hurt, so bloody angry for such a long time, it became a habit to grudgingly accept his help and then push him away. I didn't even realise how cruel I was.

Oh God, I didn't mean to, I never thought—I attempt to shelve the disturbing thought to deal with later, as now isn't the time, but it won't go away. I use him just as everyone else does. A tear runs down the side of my nose and I angrily swipe it away.

John Hesketh is renowned in creature circles...his reputation is practically legendary. We see him as the hellhound, as an extremely deadly weapon. I remember his words on the day I rejected him: *"War is in my blood and war has moulded me. Times change for some people, but not for me. I am a full-blooded warrior—I'm expendable."*

But he is also a man.

All he has known is war and violence.

And what did I do? I showed him he is also expendable as a mate.

I sink into my chair and I tuck my knees to my chest and hug them as if I can stop the pain from leaking out of my heart. I want nothing more than to slump to the floor and let my body shake from the anxiety and the heartache that I feel for John.

I have another epiphany. I realise something quite profound, and it rocks me to my core...I'm *not* afraid of him, and I've wrongly been clinging desperately to that excuse for *years*.

I know...I bloody know he will never again hurt me. He can't. Something inside me, deep down, knows John didn't hurt me on purpose and he has allowed me to slowly torture him through the years.

Bloody hell, Emma, he's been punished enough.

God, I have been so bloody selfish. I've spent this entire time rescuing strangers when the man who needed me the most—

I grit my teeth. I slam my eyes closed and rock on my chair, as my thoughts berate me. I tug at my hair in realisation. His power terrifies me, our past terrifies me, but it's a deep-seated, instinctual kind of fear that has no hold on me. Not anymore. No, I'm not afraid of John Hesketh.

There is lust, there is always lust…and yearning. But the fear that rattled me for so long is *gone*.

I've grown. The person who I am today is different from the frightened girl that I once was. I'm not who I was years ago, and that brings me a little peace.

No, I'm not that girl anymore. I'm better, stronger.

I'm strong enough.

I almost disbelieve my thoughts…I let go of my knees and flop back in my chair in shock. I'm strong enough. I've been strong enough for *years*. Now, if John hurt me, I'd hurt him back. Yeah, that's not healthy, but I'm not human.

I'm a demon and John is my mate.

My mate needs me to fight for him. I cover my mouth with my hand and rock in my chair.

Oh bloody hell.

I am going to rescue the shit out of him. I laugh lightly through my pain; I sit up and square my shoulders. Even if I have to take on every bloody vampire in this world.

I am going to rescue the bloody hellhound, and I'm going to keep rescuing him until he is mine. *Mine*. Until he knows he's loved.

Love…wow, I do, I do love him, and I am strong enough to deal with his shit.

My eyes drop back to my plans. I just hope I'm not too late.

CHAPTER
THIRTY-NINE

THE VAMPIRE RUNS straight at me, and his meaty fists fly at my face. I block his right arm with my left forearm and jab the heel of my right hand into his nose. He staggers back. I sidekick him in the ribs and follow with a punch to his liver. He grunts in pain. Ow. My hand screams as a small bone snaps, then instantly repairs itself. My poor fist burns. I hit him in a supposedly squishy part of the body, but what the hell? His vampire muscles broke my hand. I shake my hand out and I whirl to the side with seconds to spare. I laugh at the near-miss to rile him. The vampire flashes his fangs at me and lunges. My temper flares when a punch gets through my guard and he hits me in the boob. Ow.

I grab hold of his shoulders for leverage and knee him in the side to hit his liver again. Once, twice—vampire bodies hate their organs being bashed about; it's particularly painful. The vampire clutches his side and falls to the floor. For good measure, I grab his hair and knee him in the face. His eyes roll back in his head as he goes unconscious. He won't be out for long, though.

I grab hold of his shirt and with a huff and a puff, I drag him across the hallway and prop him up against the wall. I don't want to trip over him when we leave.

It was all going so well. As soon as I arrived, I could feel John's power, the energy that is all him emanating halfway down the road. It only grew, the closer I got to him. I shifted into a mouse and squeezed into the building undetected. The problem arose when I became a little cocky and ran down the middle of a hallway without caution. I could feel John behind the door at the end of this hallway...my magic shivered in appreciation and I got excited.

A surprise attack of a stomping foot ruined my hallway dash. The boot missed me by a whisker. I had no alternative but to shift into my human form and kick his ass.

I groan as two more vampires run around the corner. The one ahead of the other comes at me with his fists swinging. I step into him rather than making space, and his eyes widen with surprise. I'm hoping the move will make it more difficult for vampire number two. Unless he wants to hit his colleague, he has to wait his turn. I grab his arm, block the blow, and land two quick jabs underneath his chin. I follow that with a kick to his side. He stumbles back but doesn't go down. I kick out again, my boot hits his chest, and the momentum shoves him down the corridor and past the other vampire.

The other vampire takes his place, barrelling into me with brute strength. For a vampire, this guy is huge. With a squeak, I try to jump aside, but his arm catches me in the throat and we both tumble to the floor. I land on my back and forget to lift my head as we crash down, and my poor head smashes into the unyielding concrete. I groan and my ears ring. The vampire is halfway on top of me...at least I manage to get my leg between us so he can't pin me. I use the strength in my thigh to shove him off me. I roll away from him and scramble to my feet. With a growl, I kick him in the face. I must have hit the sweet spot underneath his chin, as his eyes roll into the back of his head and he slumps unconscious.

I feel the movement in the air behind me. I duck and the remaining vampire's arm swings above my head. I grab his wrist with both hands, bend, pull, and twist my hip. I use my smaller frame combined with my strength to flip him over my head and onto his back with a *thud*. I boot him in the ribs twice and skip away when he tries to grab my leg. When he attempts to roll to his feet, I jump into the air and Superman-punch him with everything I have. The bones in my hand shatter as I hit his face.

Ow-ow-ow. At least three bones in my hand rapidly repair themselves. The pain makes me feel dizzy; I clutch my hand against my chest as I glare down at the bleeding, unconscious vampire. I huff and puff as I shake out my healed but bruised hand.

I hate fighting. It hurts.

Unfortunately, our fight wasn't quiet, and now I can hear more incoming vampires. The entire building has come alive, like a nest of angry wasps.

Oh, God. I bounce from foot to foot. What to do, what to do.

I can't do this all night.

Scare them. Go big or go home, Emma.

Well, it's more like "die" than "go home"...but perhaps I can shift into something scary. I allow myself a cheeky grin, and then without preamble, I shift into a seven-foot demon.

Inspired by the reflection of the red tiles, my demon comes to life with a little added theatre. Red skin, horns, the whole shebang. I wobble on my hooves and brace myself against the wall. My horns scrape the ceiling.

My real wings hurt, so I keep those bad boys tucked away and instead choose wings of fire. I make them the same size and shape as my natural wings, but without substance, so there is no risk of them getting hurt just in case this doesn't work. I am sick of hurting my hands punching vampires, so I also produce a ruddy great sword; it forms solidly in my right hand. I flex my impressive red bicep as I twirl the enormous sword to warm up my wrist and arm.

Okay, showtime.

A vampire guard in his red uniform dashes around the corner. When his eyes land on me he skids to a stop and his arms comically windmill. His eyes widen, and I see the fear ignite in their depths. He fumbles with something in his hand, and then with a war cry he throws a potion ball at me. It hits me on the chest and the glass breaks. I tilt my head down and we both watch as the noxious orange substance gets to work.

The vampire's mouth opens and closes. He makes a strange

squawking noise in the back of his throat when the potion dissipates harmlessly into the air. I shoot him a toothy grin.

He promptly wets himself.

I frown. Oh no, that's not good. Having peed myself in fright, I can't help sympathising.

He spins, and in his haste to get away from me, he bounces off the wall. As he runs away down the corridor, droplets of wee follow in his wake.

Oh crap, I feel terrible. I cringe and tap my hoof as I wait for more guards to arrive. Heck, his reaction to me makes me feel like a big bully. I know he chucked what was probably a nasty potion at me. Nevertheless, I've never made anyone so frightened before that they wet themselves. I scratch the base of my right horn. Perhaps the seven-foot demon—eight and a bit with the horns—was a little too much?

The first guard—the mouse stomper—wakes up. He takes one look at me and with a gasp, he flips onto his hands and knees and motors off down the corridor.

Wow, look at him go.

There are crying, screaming, angry voices. Should I take a peek around the corner? I lower the sword and push the point into the floor. I cross one hoof casually over the other and lean against it as if it were a cane. I can't hear what they are saying, but I can imagine the potion guard pantomiming what happened to his colleagues.

The stomping footsteps quickly *retreat*. Huh? Urm...I think they are running away from me. I shrug and move back down the hallway.

I carefully step between the two unconscious guards. I *finally* get to the door and without even checking to see if it's unlocked, I lift my leg and kick out with my hoof—I am no longer messing around. The door shatters into satisfying pieces.

I clop through the doorway.

I rapidly take in the room, and I immediately find John. You would think a year of not seeing him would make a difference, and it does. It makes whatever wicked fate-magic that pulls me to him *worse*.

With widening eyes I take him in, and my heart pounds with my growing panic.

This is worse than I imagined.

CHAPTER
FORTY

T HE DIFFERENCE between this situation and our previous fake kidnapping set up all those years ago is *huge*. They have chained John to the wall with silver. Attached to the short chains are silver manacles that have *spikes*. Like an inside out-dog collar's, the spikes dig into his skin. I did a lot of reading over the years and I now understand that silver only harms a shifter *if* it gets into the bloodstream.

He has thick collars around his neck, wrists, waist, and thighs. The nasty combination pins him literally to the wall. Everywhere the silver touches, he bleeds, and the skin around the wounds that I can see has a black tinge. To me, it looks as if his skin is dying. I swallow the bile that is attempting to claw its way up my throat and I bite my lip so I don't make a sound.

This archaic way of keeping him secured is not only stopping John from shifting to heal, it will painfully bleed the shifter magic right out of him.

He's shirtless, and his blood-crusted black pants are tucked into his black boots, which come halfway up his ankle. His hair isn't long enough to be tousled, but it looks unbrushed and messy, and dark stubble highlights his jaw. Chained to a wall, he's lost some of that killer efficiency that makes him so terrifying.

I hate this. How the hell am I going to get him out of those chains without hurting him further?

Women up, Emma.

I wave. "Hi, I am here to rescue you," I say, slurring around a mouthful of demon teeth.

John lifts his chin from his chest and raises an eyebrow as he slowly takes in my red demon form. His lips twitch and he huffs out a bitter laugh. "Why did you come?" Wow, that's it? No, "Hi sweetheart, you're looking fetching this evening. Thanks for the rescue..." I roll my eyes.

I clop closer and between one step and the next, I allow myself to shift back. Everything dissipates, including the sword. My shift leaves me dressed in leggings, boots, and my favourite black T-shirt that has a bunch of flowers and a knuckle-duster on it and the words *fight like a girl*.

I am trying my best to remain blasé, but inside I'm freaking out. A younger, less powerful shifter would have already been dead.

The muscles in his shoulders and arms tense as he leans forward towards me, and the chains on the wall clank and groan as they hold him in place.

"Please..." I squeak out, "Please don't move, you will hurt yourself." I swallow. Oh, this is bad, this is so, so bad. My bottom lip wobbles but I force myself to speak. "So you have a vampire problem? You seem to be in a bit of a pickle, John. Urm...how do we do this without hurting you further?" My voice cracks, revealing the panic I'm trying my damndest to hide.

My hands flutter. I don't know where to start. Blood is running in rivulets down his arms and neck; it trickles down his chest. This shitty situation is going to give me nightmares for a very long time. I tremble as I inspect the horrific, archaic setup. I gnaw on my lip.

Oh, God, he must be in so much pain.

John lets out a gruff laugh. "It's not me that has the vampire problem—I came to rescue *you*."

"Screw you, I rescued myself," I say back with a fake angry huff. "I'm not the one chained to the wall, Hellboy. So, the whole rescue attempt worked out well for you...I thought you were off-world. You shouldn't have come back to save me, John—I had everything in hand. What did you think you were doing?" I glance at his poor wrists. "Please tell me how to get you out of these chains." My voice breaks.

"I will always come for you," he mumbles, his eyes closed. "Get out of here, sweetheart. I am too weak. What were you thinking, coming here on your own? Go before they catch you. You need to get as far away from me as possible...I keep making mistakes. I've lost my edge and I've slowly been losing control for years. Look at me, I can't even do a basic rescue without fucking everything up...It's fucking shameful."

I ignore him as I intently study the manacles. There is so much blood on them, on the floor. John's blood. I need to get them off.

"Yeah, yeah, and you've lost man points 'cos you're being rescued by a girl...have you heard yourself? That's a little hypocritical, John. Where has my fighter gone?" I mumble.

My heart pounds in my ears. I flick my wrist and a long, thin pick appears between my fingers. I think it's better to start at his feet. I don't want to practise on his neck or wrists. As I drop to my knees, I decide I'll use the pick and my smoky magic on the spiky cuffs on his legs. It's a shame I can't imagine a key that would fit...yeah, that would be way too easy.

"Didn't you see my badass demon form? I'll get you out of here before the vampires get brave enough to intervene. I'm pre-warning you...if I have to shift and throw you over my shoulder, I will. Isn't that the way it goes when you rescue someone? The damsel always gets carried by the hero." I grin up at him and wiggle my eyebrows. "You're the damsel."

I smirk. If that doesn't motivate him to move his bum when I free him, nothing will.

"Will you find my sister? Tell her...that I'm sorry."

I clamp down hard on a sob that wants to smash its way out of my lips. No, I've got no time for that. "Tell her yourself," I growl back.

"This world doesn't take any prisoners. If you're weak, Emma, you die. Tell her our pack wasn't weak. Our father was one of the first of his kind, a hellhound. In the beginning, they called him a fire wolf." John coughs and his strong voice becomes a rasp.

What on earth is he going on about? I spare a moment to peek up at him. His bright green eyes have gone dull, unfocused.

"He was an incredible warrior..."

Oh bloody hell, my hellhound is doing his death speech. He doesn't think he is going to make it. John grimaces and black blood seeps from between his lips. My heart thuds in panic and I force my attention back to my task and focus. I narrow my eyes and bite down on my tongue, which is sticking out the side of my mouth. With shaking hands, I dig my magic and the pick into the locking mechanism.

Bloody hell, what a time to learn how to pick a lock.

"The world of shifters you know today differs completely from the world that I was born into almost a thousand years ago...nine-hundred and twenty-two-years. There was equality between the sexes, with no difference between men and women. We had female warriors and male caregivers. In those days, shifters were all about pack. Wolf, bear, even the dragons—it didn't matter. We coexisted peacefully."

"Perhaps you should save your strength—"

"My father said the beginning of the end started with a group of rogue fae. They decided the shifters were getting too strong. I was young when they started killing our females. It took us a while to notice the pattern. That shifter women were not dying in normal circumstances...no, they were being targeted. At first, it was one or two, and then dozens as more races joined in on the cull.

"In horror, we attempted to keep our remaining females safe. We adapted, and we changed for the worse. The carefree shifters became dangerous and in many ways incredibly selfish. We lost our dignity, and with that, our strength. Our women suffered the most, losing not only their friends, their mothers, and their sisters...but also their freedom. Many fought the changes and were beaten down and forced. Others embraced it, as everyone was frightened. I never experienced again the joy, the comfort of being a shifter. All I saw was pain, war, fighting, and oppression.

"Before my eyes, as a race we changed...I changed. My pack, my sisters Nessa, Clare, Gwen, and my mother became targets. Hunted not by the other races but by other shifters, because as our women became rarer—a commodity—shifters became more aggressive in their pursuit for mates. My father worked tirelessly over the years to keep them safe. Until one day on leave from battle, I came home too late, and I watched helplessly as they ripped apart my pack. I destroyed the perpetrators. But I couldn't save them. My smart, funny, incredibly talented sisters were gone. My father, who was a better man than I'll ever be, was killed. Not by an outside enemy, but by friends. Jealousy, panic, and fear rot. Only my mother survived.

"In the aftermath, she discovered that she was pregnant...with another female shifter. Another fucking problem." John lets out a sad-sounding laugh. I lift my eyes from my task as he drops his head and his eyes plead with me to understand. The spines of the collar dig further into him and I watch helplessly as more blood trickles down his neck. His sorrow is palpable and my heart aches.

"They denied me leave, so I had no time to grieve. I compartmentalised the best I could, did what I could to keep my mother safe, but I distanced myself from her and my new replacement sister. When you've seen everything that you love ripped away...I guess it's natural to avoid having to deal with that shit all over again. My mother ended up meeting another man, having *another* girl." John's fists tighten as he laughs bitterly. "I was livid. You have to understand, our remaining females couldn't produce girls. The birth of a female was rare. No amount of scientific or magical intervention worked, nothing. We were cursed—it seemed as if even Mother Nature herself wanted us to go extinct." John coughs again and his entire body shudders. I keep my eyes on my task.

"Yet there was my mother, popping out girls for fun, for all to see. Couldn't she see the world as I did? Understand the dangers? Fuck, it's not like any of the other girls lived. It's not like she enhanced or saved a dying race. I knew...I fucking knew they'd die anyway, Emma. Born to die. It was senseless. Selfishly, I couldn't take it. I avoided the problem... to my shame. If I didn't care about the two girls, it wouldn't matter when they died in the end.

"With my mother having a new pack, a new mate, I was relieved to finally be able to wash my hands completely of them. My mother's *new* pack could deal with the problem. I was done. Then as you know, it all went to shit. When they were taken, it hit me, how much I had failed them. To find them was an impossible task, the proverbial needle in the haystack. The possibilities of who could have taken them were endless. Because of our status as protectors, my team and I were assigned to the task. We chased our own tails until a call came in, a shifter claiming that he had eyes on a young female." John sags further into the chains and bitterness flashes across his face.

"Seeing her wolf form in your arms, I lost what little control I had. I could tell that you were a demon and I convinced myself it was all a trick. There is no excuse for what I did to you, and I will be sorry for the rest of my life." That might not be very long if I don't hurry. "No wonder you rejected me." John lets out a bitter laugh. "I can't keep the women in my life safe. That's why I let you go...I am a selfish bastard and I still couldn't leave completely. Seeing you safe and helping you...I told myself it was enough. It was what I deserved. All the strength that I possess, the shifter magic, the fire magic, being a trained combatant...it doesn't do shit."

With his words, I'm done for...I silently cry. I tuck my head down and hide my face so he can't see me.

"I'm an evil man. Even after you rescued her, my little sister...I...I let her go. I couldn't bear to even look at her. She survived, and I hated her. I hated her for it. I still wanted Nessa, Clare, and Gwen, not her. I wanted my mother, not the useless, weak shadow of a wolf. My fear and hate blinded me...yes, fear and panic rot. I am the most rotten of us all."

My tears drop onto my hands. I can't stop them from falling, and every tear is for John.

"Please, Emma, tell my sister I was wrong. Tell her I love her and that I am proud of her. I've tried, but...her mate said he'd rip my head off if I attempted to talk to her before she was ready. Now it's too late, but she might listen to you."

If I could swap places with him, I'd do it in a heartbeat. This is horrible. I hate how useless I feel. On the day I admit my love for him I have to see him like this, hear his confession. I can feel his energy slowly ebbing away, a wisp of pattering raindrops compared to its usual crashing wave. It's not bloody fair.

"You will tell her yourself. I promise I will speak to her, and we will have... urm...dinner."

My guilt thrums through me. *I did this*...I need to get him out of here and somewhere safe. My determination feeds energy into my magic, spurring it on, and the cuff clicks open and releases its grip on his legs. I sob in relief, then cringe as I gently peel the spikes away from his legs.

One down.

Now that I know what I'm doing, I send my magic to each lock simultaneously instead of slogging my way up his body. We haven't got long before the guards get brave enough and storm in here.

Finally, the locks on the evil silver cuffs pop open, and they tear away from his blackened skin with a squelch. At the sound, I cough and heave. Oh, God. My chest painfully tightens as John's blood rains down on the floor around us, but he is stoic and doesn't make a sound. *Be just as brave, Emma.*

I kick the cuffs away from him. His entire body sags and his legs wobble underneath him as he struggles to stay upright. I use my body weight to hold him up against the wall so he doesn't fall. "Sit down on the floor and get your breath back." He nods and I help guide his huge, muscly frame down onto the concrete floor.

John flops back against the wall. I cup the back of his head to make sure he doesn't bang it. His breathing is shallow, and where John's skin is not black, it's overly pale. He is still bleeding. "I got you," I whisper. "Remember our conversation in the rain? When the fae assassins almost killed me." John nods. I wipe the black blood from his lips with a trembling hand. "At the time, you told me I had to fight; I had to promise that I would never give up. Don't make a hypocrite out of yourself, John Hesketh," I say with a growl. "You are not dying today, I will not let you."

"You can't fucking forgive me for what I did."

"Too late. I already have."

It's then that I hear the footsteps.

The vampires are coming.

I step in front of John, blocking the door from him. If the vampires want to throw potions at my hellhound, they will have to get through me first.

CHAPTER
FORTY-ONE

To say I'm surprised when Luther and my mum appear would be an understatement. Shock radiates through me as they stand in the doorway, surveying us and the remains of the door.

"What is going on here? I thought we agreed for you to come at ten o'clock," my mum says as she toes the wooden splinters of the door with her blue heel. What? My mouth pops open as I stare at her incredulously. Oh, my bad. Sorry, Mother, how rude of me—I didn't come at the appointed time.

"Oh, I thought I'd arrive early as I was so excited to see you, Mum. Good evening, Luther. I don't suppose you have anything for silver poisoning, do you? It seems you are trying to kill your hellhound guest." I grit my teeth and grin maniacally.

"No, we have nothing like that here," she replies as she carefully steps around the door and glides further into the room. Luther follows, content to let my mum speak. "There was a report of an enormous demon terrorising everyone. One of our guards who reported in said it was eating another guard's leg." She sniffs and looks again around the room. "An illusion, I am sure."

Eww. "I didn't eat anyone's leg," I mumble for John's benefit.

The pair of them are dressed so smartly, they both look ridiculous.

Luther is back to looking like his usual put-together self in a sharp, crisp suit, and my mother is in a beautiful dark-blue dress.

"The pair of you look nice. I do have to say you're both a tad overdressed for our current location." I wrinkle my nose as I glance about the room and raise an enquiring eyebrow.

They should have condemned the entire building. The place is a hovel, although the poor state of the building didn't stop the vampires from having a state-of-the-art security system, so perhaps they wanted it to look like this—a shithole. Not the ideal place to dress in fancy evening wear, that's for sure. The amount of vermin poop I had to negotiate while I was a mouse was so gross. Luckily, most animals are sensitive to magic and run away as soon as I'm scented, so I am glad I didn't get to meet the locals. I sure didn't want a new rodent boyfriend.

They both ignore my remarks. So for the sheer hell of it I try again. "Going somewhere nice?"

My mum gives me a withering look. Her upper lip curls back with a sneer, showing her pointy fangs. I take a jerky step backwards. Oh, wow, that's a bit different from the trembling and crying that I am used to.

"You were always such a horrid child..."

Oh, here we go. I puff my cheeks out with frustration. Okay, mum, hurry up and get the villain speech out of the way. I have a damsel to save.

Now John is free from those archaic manacles, he needs a moment to rest. Given enough time, his body should be able to dispel the silver that's floating around in his bloodstream. We aren't *yet* overrun by vampires, so I will listen to her speech...oh bloody hell, that wasn't me trying to tempt fate. I groan.

"...You never did anything that you were told to do. Throwing yourself on the floor, having a tantrum, saying you were hungry. You were always hungry. Screaming and demanding. You were a horrible child and I see not much has changed."

I roll my eyes. "Yeah, as a baby I was an evil genius. You are right, I so did that on purpose." I tilt my lips up in a semblance of a smile. "Well, Mum, this has been a fun visit, but we need to go, and by *we*, I mean me and the hellhound." I nod toward John, in case they've forgotten about him.

"When Luther suggested sending you away, I knew it was the perfect solution. You'd done enough: ruined my body, ruined my life. There wasn't a day that went by that I didn't wish you didn't exist. I still wish I'd never had you," my mum continues. Her voice is utterly toneless.

I blink at her with slowly dawning comprehension. John was right in warning me about her. My mum has always been a little *off*, but she hid her hate for me well. I never wanted to believe my mum could be a bad person. For twenty-two-years I thought that she'd sold me to a demon to become a vampire, and for another eighteen years, she led me to believe it was Luther's fault. Wow. Tonight the mask has come off and she's baring her real face to me, fangs and all.

I understand that having a child doesn't automatically make that child lovable or endear that child to you. I also understand that having a kid is really hard work, that parents have the most important and hardest job in the world. I'm grateful I'm here, but I didn't ask to be born. I might have been a naughty child, according to my mum, but I hadn't done that on purpose. I was a baby.

I wait for the pain to hit me. But there isn't even a twinge. I don't know if she is trying to upset me on purpose, to throw me off track and imbalance me, but it looks like that ship sailed long ago.

Huh. I forgave my mum a long time ago, even if she doesn't want, need, or deserve my forgiveness. I did it for me. Sometimes it's okay to let the dream of someone go, to see them as they really are and be okay with that. After all, she has to be the one to look at herself in the mirror.

I need to wrap this conversation up and get John the hell out of here.

My mum continues, "Yes, it was Luther's idea, but I made the arrangement for you to go to your father."

My mouth pops open and my thoughts grind to a halt with my shock.

What. The. Hell.

"My father?" I choke out.

"Yes, Arlo, your father. It was his fault I got knocked up. At least he could deal with the consequences. Not all women want to be mothers, Emma. What would I want with a hybrid child? I thought he was in love with me and that a child would bring us closer together. But he left, as most men do. Not every man can be as powerful and loyal as Luther." She smiles at him and then sneers back at me. "Arlo took you off my hands with my promise that I'd never contact you. If you made the move to contact me...well, I promised to spare your feelings—" She keeps talking, but my head is spinning. My legs feel oddly weak. I keep on repeating her words back to myself.

Arlo was my father.

My dad.

I wasn't his human *pet*, I was his bloody daughter.

Wow. The entire time that I lived with him now makes some weird sense. Why he called me his favourite but didn't touch me...he made everyone believe he did. It was something I never disputed as he was my demon master, and I learned to be grateful. I was safe and had so many nice things. He had many, many lovers...I was relieved that he never picked me.

What was all that about, then...Arlo asking me to strip in front of his friends? In the end did he know the hellhounds were coming for him?

By human standards, what he said and what he did was seriously messed up. I mentally shrug. Even after all of my reading, I still don't understand demons as a race, not really. If I think about everything too closely, I will freak out. I rub my temple. Perhaps he said stuff to punish me? Protect me? I guess that being his pet, I was invisible; being his daughter, I would have been a target.

Bloody hell.

That's why he left me so much money, why he gave me the pocket dimension. I guess in his own way he was trying to protect me.

I thought there was nothing left to shock me. I never really thought about who my father could be as I was so focused on my mother selling me. Apart from the total mystery of what type of creature he was, I classified him as a sperm donor and didn't think any more about it.

You're wasting time. I need to get John out of here.

Another thought rattles to the front of my head. John killed my father, who killed his mum. Wow, that's messed up. Later we will have a lot to talk about.

I compartmentalise my feelings as it doesn't matter...only John matters, and I need to get him out of here.

I turn my head and my eyes fly to him. He's still on the floor. Oh, God, he looks worse. How can he look worse? I swallow. My eyes swing back to my mum. She's still talking... "Let the hellhound die. You are coming with us." Why mum? So you can use me? I believe you've made it quite clear that you don't like me. "Everyone knows he's a loose cannon—he won't be missed."

"He killed fifteen of my vampires, fifteen. He is an animal," Luther says when my mum finally stops to take a breath. "The hellhounds are irrelevant in today's world. Redundant. No one needs them anymore—that's the reason they sent them off-world. No one will miss him. We are doing the shifters a favour, getting rid of a problem." I growl at his words.

Without my thinking about them, my protective instincts kick in. I allow my eyes to bleed black and my shoulder blades tingle as my top magically parts to allow my demon wings to spread. The purple-and-black wings hang heavy at my back. I growl again, which highlights my black lips, and my smoky black magic pours from my hands. My magic snaps out towards Luther and a smoky tendril wraps itself tightly around his neck. His eyes widen and his hands scramble to pull my magic away from his throat, but he ends up scratching his neck as the smoke holds tight yet shifts away from his grabby fingers.

"Look, Luther, I don't want your hellhound-hating hard-on poking at me. This hellhound is not your concern. John has nothing to do with what is between us. You even look at him wrongly and I will rip your pureblood face off. Do purebloods need to breathe?" I snarl as my magic tightens and his face purples. Huh, I guess so. "The problems you currently have are to do with me. Instead of wanting me to join 'the fold,' perhaps you should look around you." I curl my lip with disgust. "Your House is crumbling around your ears. You're a disgrace to the purebloods."

With my mum revealing her true colours, certain things about the pureblood and his House makes sense—for an example off the top of my head, the dirt that I have on him didn't start accumulating until a few years after they'd met. I flick my eyes at my mother's snarling face and shake my head. "My mother whispering poison in your ear has made you weak."

"Emma, let him go," John says gruffly behind me. There is a sound of scuffing and a scrape of his boots on the floor as he attempts and fails to get to his feet.

What John is avoiding saying is, I can't kill Luther—if I did so, I would be dead in a week. The vampires would come after me, and I can't fight all the vampires.

I flick my wrist and throw Luther across the room. He hits the wall with a crunch. "Come near John again and I'll kill your whole House. Oh, and you're wrong: hellhounds are the pride of the shifters, and the guilds won't take kindly to you holding one of their elite prisoner."

I growl. "You." I glare at my mother. "The vampire council's enforcers are coming. I wouldn't stick around if I was you." She rushes to Luther's side and helps him to his feet. I shake my head again with revulsion. "We are leaving. Believe it or not, I haven't had to kill anyone yet—please don't make me." I turn my back and dismiss them.

My full attention is on John. My magic grows heavier behind me, screening us from the two vampires. I drop to my knees and slap my wings on either side of John, hardly feeling the sting. The light changes to purple as my wings cocoon us. I drop my forehead to his and my thumb rasps across his stubbled cheek. "Shift," I tell him. He needs to heal.

"I can't. Too much silver in my system."

Like a naughty puppy pulling on a leash, my magic pulls towards him. I allow more of it out and it eagerly rushes to John; it dances across his skin and then sinks into his chest.

Oh, that's a bit freaky...I've never seen it do that before.

Within moments the wounds on his neck, wrists, and thighs weep tiny droplets of silver. As soon as the silver leaves his body, my magic attacks it, turning it from a liquid into a cloud of dust—that floats harmlessly to the floor. Wow.

My wings dissipate.

John lifts his chin and takes a deep breath in as his whole body straightens. Using the wall to help, he rises.

In my peripheral vision, I see the horrific, torturous manacles and chains that nonchalantly rest on the floor where I kicked them. I narrow my eyes at them. The nasty spikes still drip with John's blood and skin. I wonder if I can also deal with that...my magic eagerly accepts the challenge, and it creeps across the floor, surrounding the silver restraints until they too disappear in a puff of dust.

"You're full of surprises today, pretty girl." I shrug and help him undo the laces of his boots. I know I don't need to help him undress, what with the whole dissipating shifter magic, but I want to.

He needs to shift. My magic got rid of the silver but John still needs to heal. He shucks off his trousers, and suddenly I am intimately close to a naked John.

I look because why the hell not. He is mine.

Wow...urm, yeah...the man is perfectly proportioned. I cough. "Shift," I whimper. John takes me in, on my knees, and his once-tired and pain-filled eyes shine with poorly veiled interest. With a sexy grin and a nod of his head, he shifts.

His massive, bleeding form is replaced by my hellhound. My heart squeezes as my hand reaches out and soft red fur threads through my fingers.

CHAPTER
FORTY-TWO

I SIT in a comfortable chair positioned so my back is against the wall. The café is unusual and one of my favourite places to visit. They sell the most amazing selection of cakes. I tilt my head to study the ceiling, where a pink-blossomed tree branch spans the space with dangling fairy lights. The clatter of dishes and clink of spoons is a gentle background hum.

I've shifted into Christine, a human with some fae DNA. Christine is in her early sixties. With a blonde bob, bright-blue eyes, and curvy, she is the quintessential elegant English lady. Pretty, but forgettable. Safe.

I pour more tea into my cup and take a sip. When I set my cup back down with a *clink* on the matching saucer, my hand drifts across the table to trace the upside-down indentation of a name...*Liz* has been gouged into the table. I shake my head at the vandalism. I curl my hands back around my cup, enjoying the warmth of the porcelain, and I lean forward so the steam that rises from my tea warms my face.

At first I feel him. His energy drifts into my consciousness and tickles against my senses. Instantly it warms me and makes me feel safe.

I lift my head and watch out the window as he approaches. He steps lightly, his strides sure and unhurried, an apex predator on the prowl. Predatory yet irresistible.

He is hunting me.

People on the street shy away from him. Wow, he'd be great at a concert or out shopping. He parts the hordes of people faster than... well, people can't get away from him fast enough. He screams *danger*.

His dark suit fits him like a glove, from broad shoulders and powerful chest to flat stomach and long legs.

Breathtaking. I have to force myself to breathe.

Huh, a visit from the hellhound—a suited and booted hellhound, no less. I sit up as I watch him, happy and kind of smug with the knowledge that, like everyone else, he won't recognise me. He opens the door to the café and the bell above it jingles.

I blink when his green gaze immediately locks onto me.

Me. Elegant, Christine-lady me.

John's gaze flicks up to my eyes, down again, then back up. Not good. He grins, and my heart stops for a beat.

He is almost embarrassingly handsome. Beautiful. I greet him with a low groan when he prowls to my table. "No matter what face you wear, I will always know it's you," he says. My heart misses another beat. "You can change everything about yourself but you can't change your soul, and mine will always recognise yours in an instant." There is a hint of sweetness in his eyes.

Wow. I wiggle in my chair.

"May I sit?" I nod and he pulls out the chair opposite me and folds his bulk into it, dwarfing the table.

The people around us have gone quiet—they know that there is a predator in the room. I flick my eyes to the closest table, and a red-haired witch has a cup halfway to her mouth. Her cheeks go pink and she looks away when she realises I've noticed her watching. I can't help but grin as she fans her face.

I look back at John. "How are you feeling? Back to normal, I hope?" I rescued him, healed him, made sure he was safe, and then I ran.

I mean, bloody hell; they had pinned the guy to a wall with silver. I figured he needed to get his head around his near-death experience, and he didn't need me throwing myself at him and declaring my undying love. I have to be honest with myself: I've not been the easiest woman to deal with.

My eyes take in every inch of skin that I can see. Shifters' wounds made from silver never fully heal, even after they shift. Silver scars shifters...it scars them horribly. But I'm happy to see there are no visible marks on John's skin. My magic must have destroyed the silver down to its very molecules. I can't help my smug grin, and I give my magic a mental pat on the head.

"I am fine, thanks to you. That was my first experience of being rescued." John runs his hand through his short hair and gives me a rueful grin.

I can't help but grin back at him. I lean across the table and pat his big hand. "You did so good, you didn't cry once. You were very brave." I nod my head condescendingly.

I feel safe in John's company, and silly keeping my Christine persona, so I shift back into myself with a bright smile.

John's rueful grin fades as he fixates on my mouth and eyes. I guess I don't smile at him often. In fact, I'm not sure I've smiled at the hell-hound very much at all.

He looks shell-shocked.

I duck my head and look at my hand, which is still resting on top of his.

"I had you in my arms and I lost you. I was so angry, for years. I've blamed myself, blamed you. I never took the time to go deeper," he says. I lift my head and he shrugs his massive shoulders and regards me with solemn green eyes.

"I'm just a man...I know war. Every day is a battle, and any softness I possessed was beaten out of me a long time ago. I came from a time when men didn't show their feelings, and that's something that I've never attempted to change, until now. The mistakes I've made...I can't change them. Shit, how I want to go back and change them.

"From the moment we first met, I should have taken you and my sister and run. I should have done my job as a brother...and as a mate."

He swallows and his beautiful eyes shine with pain. "I can't take back those moments, and the decisions I made haunt me. But I can try my best to never let you down, to never frighten you. I can do better. I know what you've been doing: helping others, saving people from evil bastards like me. I don't want to be the monster under your bed, Emma. My soul is lost without you. You are everything good and right and beautiful in my world. I don't exist without you. I'm half a man without you. Emma, give me a chance—one chance is all I'm asking. You help others; save me...save me from myself, I'm begging you. Bring the softness back into my life. I'm asking for *one* chance to let me prove myself to you. I love you."

Fire flares in his eyes and they burn, lighting up our corner of the room. Chairs scrape on the floor and utensils and cups clatter around us as the surrounding tables' occupants suddenly find that they have somewhere else to be.

I barely notice—I'm sure I will be mortified later. But at the moment, I can't take my eyes away from his. The fire in his eyes, it isn't rage or lust. It is more than lust, more than need. Nobody has ever looked at me like that.

Love.

He loves me.

I rise from my chair, step around the table, and reach over. My hand hits his chest. His skin underneath his suit is burning hot; his muscles tense underneath my fingertips. I grab his tie and pull him towards me.

I slam *my* lips against his.

I gasp as his mouth seals mine, stealing my breath. John stands and pulls me towards him, my breasts mashing against his sculptured chest. The heat of his powerful body burns me. He moves both of my hands into one of his and wraps my hair around his fist and claims my mouth. The taste of him floods me and my senses go haywire—it's almost overwhelming. I want to run my hands across his skin, but he holds them tight, trapped behind my back.

When some brave soul whistles, we slowly pull apart.

I lick my swollen lips and drown in his now-beautiful green eyes.

"I love you too," I tell him.

Gosh, I have so much to tell him. We have so much to sort out, so much to make up for. But I know, I know deep inside, soul-deep, that we are going to be okay. Together.

I grab hold of John's hand and lead him towards the nearest doorway. I'm taking my hellhound home.

CHAPTER
FORTY-THREE

Dinner

I TWIST my hands and John's big, warm hand engulfs both of mine to stop me from fiddling. He gives me a reassuring squeeze as we wait for the door to open. I'm the one that should be holding his hand, supporting him...but God, I'm so bloody nervous.

I haven't seen John's sister for a while—not as myself anyway and meeting his pack, his only pack, as his *mate* is scary. She's been avoiding John like the plague, but after asking Ava to make a few telephone calls, I scored the dinner that I promised him.

Inside the house there is a shout: *"I'll get it."* My lips twitch at the sound of running feet, socked feet scampering across what I presume is a wooden floor. There's a small squeak, a thump, and the door in front of us shudders. A muffled, *"Shit."*

I glance at John, and he shakes his head and smirks. I snigger. Whoever is hurrying to answer must have skidded into the door.

With a click, the door is flung open and my heart jumps. It misses a beat and I swallow and squeeze John's hand for reassurance as her energy batters against me. I lock my knees to stop myself from almost taking a step back as her shifter energy crashes aggressively against my senses. It has an innocent, playful quality, but beyond that innocence is sheer *power*. Her energy is violent, twisted.

Forrest.

A tiny woman peeks up at us through a curtain of pale-pink hair that is covering almost her entire face. She puffs and blows rapidly to get the thick, long strands out of her eyes. When that doesn't work, she bats the hair away into some semblance of order with delicate hands. I toothily grin as I take in her now-uncovered, pretty face.

Beautiful but strangely coloured eyes regard us. Her eyes are disconcerting, mismatched—they are not quite gold, and the right eye has a touch of green that the other doesn't. It's a small sliver of green at the bottom of her iris. The impact of her eyes makes it difficult to look at her directly.

But I force myself to.

Even with her mountain of pale-pink hair, the cute unicorn jumper, leggings, fluffy wolf socks, and a growing sweet smile, my demon senses tingle and my instincts scream at me to run back to the portal and go home. She's not what she seems...she is *dangerous*. The pretty facade of the cutesy pink-haired shifter is a ruse to trick the unwary.

Oh, and she is way more powerful than John.

With twinkling eyes she smiles brightly. She tilts her head to the side and looks me up and down, her complete attention laser-focused on me. On purpose, she deliberately ignores her brother.

"I remember you...you're the angel that saved me." Her voice is a shock, so rough and guttural for such a small woman. You would think it would match the pink hair, soft, girly. But instead, it matches her energy and the flashes of hardness that I catch every so often in her eyes. "I remember being frightened, broken. I was so lost in my head, in my pain, and then you appeared, with that beautiful blonde hair." Forrest blinks her big gold eyes and points at my hair. "The light from the corridor behind you made it look like you had a halo...you smelled of horses. You brought me back into the world. Pulled me out of that prison and out of my head. For years I used to dream about you. I thought I'd made you up." She says all this with a nod of her head. Tears fill her eyes and I blink my own away. "I'm sorry...I'm sorry I forgot about you," she whispers.

Like all those years ago, my heart drops and my stomach clenches and before I've realised that I've moved...I rush forward, open my arms, and wrap them around her. Forrest throws her arms around my waist and hugs me back with a strength that takes my breath away.

"It's okay, pup." The words from long ago stick in my tight throat and my voice cracks with emotion. I stroke back the mass of pink hair and gently kiss the top of her head.

Moments pass in comfortable silence. Forrest then stands on her toes and moves my hair away from my ear, and she whispers, "Ava told me it was you...Mr Brown? Thank you, Emma."

"You're welcome. I'm sorry I didn't do more," I say with another hug and a sniffle.

Forrest steps away, and more loudly she says, "You're so badass, you need a theme tune." She nods her head as if her comment is completely understandable. I frown down at her, wipe away my tears, and scratch the back of my head. My lips tug themselves into a small, confused smile. *I need a theme tune?* Uh-huh. I look at John for clarification; he shrugs and gives me a small smile. He is equally confused.

Finally, Forrest follows my gaze, and she takes in her brother, who is waiting patiently at my side.

With a curl of her lip, she growls out, "Arsehole."

It's then that a man calls from deeper inside the house, "Forrest, let our guests inside, you're being rude." His voice rumbles and the hairs on the back of my neck rise.

Oh bloody hell, this will not be a normal dinner.

Forrest's mouth forms a perfect O and with a roll of her eyes, she grabs John's and my hands and pulls us inside.

THE END

CURSED VAMPIRE

Half unicorn, half bloodsucker, all trouble. When her secret gets out, can this feisty teenager survive?

Tru Dennison's life feels like a sick joke. Barely coping with the loss of her adoptive grandad, the seventeen-year-old can't believe it when her no-good uncle kicks her to the curb. And now stuck working two hectic jobs to save up for a place, a shifter customer biting her is the last thing the magical hybrid needs...

Already battling a mysterious illness she can't seem to shake, Tru is terrified the incident will reveal her hidden bloodline to the supernatural community. And when the shock and the wound cause her sickness to intensify, frightened teen fears saving her life could only make it all so much worse.

Will Tru's rebel soul be enough to protect her when she becomes the prize in a paranormal tug-of-war?

CHAPTER
ONE

The weight of exhaustion lies heavy on my shoulders. It's been a hell of a week. My grandad is dead.

The pain from his loss now curls inside me, making a home. Somehow the wait, seeing him suffer for so long, makes it worse.

I miss him. I miss him so much, and I'm sure I always will. I smile. *He was my person.* I grip the steering wheel with both hands as my smile fades. The world is a darker place without him. Hell, he wasn't perfect, but who is? *Perfect*, I mentally scoff. *Nobody is perfect.*

I rub my tired eyes. My face feels gritty underneath my palm. *At least I got a parking space outside the house today.* Dragging myself out of the car, I bump the door closed with my hip and groan as my feet rhythmically throb with each movement. I shuffle my exhausted carcass around the car and step onto the pavement.

Work doesn't stop for my grief. I can't stop as there are bills to pay. I guess it's an achievement to stay on top of things when circumstances... *fate* wants to bury you.

I inhale, then release the breath slowly. I'm proud of myself; I got us out of the debt hole. He'd be proud of me. "I'm adulting perfectly, Grandad," I say into the wind. The late water bill is paid, nine hundred pounds gone with a click of a button, and my last twenty quid went on petrol. Super Noodles for dinner then. Yum.

Being grown-up sucks.

In an exhausted daze, I flick the latch open on the wooden garden gate. The things I still need to do before I get to relax roll through my head. My boots scrape noisily across the path as I trudge towards my front door—I've not got the energy to lift my feet. I take a few seconds to realise that my key isn't opening the front door.

Huh. I pull it out and stare at it. It doesn't look damaged. I shove it back into the lock, and my hand meets resistance when I attempt to turn it.

"What the heck," I mumble.

The hinges on the gate behind me squeak, and I turn just as my uncle smashes his way through. The poor abused gate thuds against the wall, and the impact sends a chunk of mortar to the floor. I narrow my eyes.

"Trudy," he grunts.

Gah, my name is Tru. T-R-U. Not Trudy. Why does he have to be such a prick? His lips curl into a semblance of a smile. Uh-oh. Whenever this man flashes that creepy smile, I know something bad is going to happen. My tummy flips, but I force my face into what I can only hope is an unconcerned mask.

He loves nothing more than to rile me up.

Looking at him makes my skin crawl. Now Grandad is no longer here to protect me, there's no telling what this idiot has planned. His short silver hair flops in front of his eyes, and with a thin hand he pushes it out of the way as he glides towards me.

I've worked out what's happened.

I tilt my chin and look down at him, at this moment loving my six-foot height. With growing dread and barely controlled rage, I nod my head back at the door and raise an inquiring eyebrow. "Uncle Phillip," I say through the gritted teeth of a fake smile. "My key isn't working... You changed the locks?"

This is the man who couldn't be bothered to visit his father when he was ill. When he was *dying*. This is the man who also couldn't attend or contribute to the cost of his dad's funeral. My hands ball into fists at my sides, and I attempt to curb my temper with a self-restraint that I don't feel.

One... two... three. I slowly count in my head as I wrestle with myself. My nostrils flare as I take in a deep, cleansing breath.

He's now taking ownership of my home.

This is *great*. Just fucking great.

The keys gripped in my right hand jingle as I force myself to uncurl my fists and swallow down my rage. With an angry huff, I cross my arms underneath my boobs and attempt to look calm and unconcerned. I am not.

My hands twitch. God, I want to punch him in his smug face.

"My house, my locks." With that *helpful* statement, his wind magic whips out and he snatches the keys from my hand. They slap into his waiting palm.

"Oi!" I shout. *What is he doing?* I snap my hand out and wiggle my fingers. "Give. Them. Back."

He's already changed the locks. Why the hell does he need my keys? My uncle spins on his heel and heads to the street and towards *my car*.

Oh no. Oh hell no.

"That's my car, *dickhead*. You have no bloody right!" I yell as I scramble after him.

No, no, no, no.

Adrenaline sloshes through my system, washing away my earlier fatigue. My heart pounds in my ears and my entire body shakes. Uncle Phillip opens the passenger door and leans into *my* car. "My dad's name is on the DVLA documents, so legally, it's mine. Unless you want to complain to one of the Guilds? I'm sure they'll be very interested to find out about you." He turns, braces his arm on the door, and smirks. "If you know what's good for you, you'll take your shit and disappear. You're what, twenty now?" I'm seventeen. "You need to grow up and stop leeching off old, vulnerable people—"

I swallow my pride. "Uncle Phillip, please," I beg.

He laughs under his breath, and his eyes flit about as he takes in the quiet residential street. Like a living thing, the silence stretches between us. He looks me up and down with poorly veiled disgust. "I'm not your uncle," he finally snaps out.

Pushing away from my car, Uncle Phillip takes a menacing step towards me. He drops his voice to a harsh whisper and leans so close his lips brush the shell of my ear. I shiver. "Not your family, not your anything. You're the kid he picked up at the side of the road. Like garbage."

I swallow.

He steps away, and from his back pocket he pulls out a sad-looking roll of bin bags. With a tug, he snaps a single bag off the roll.

As he goes back to my car, I move to block him, but he shoulder barges me out of the way. I watch in disbelief and a growing state of numbness as he fills the black plastic with my meagre possessions.

Once he's finished, he wipes his hands on his trousers, and with a satisfied smile, he drops the bag at my feet. My eyes drop to the bag. The plastic is so thin in some areas it looks almost grey and see-through.

"Here." He throws something small at me, and it bounces off my chest. I fumble and just manage to catch it between my fingers. I flip the cool metal into the palm of my hand.

It's a rusty key.

I lift my eyes to his.

"A key to Mr Gregson's garage." Uncle Phillip answers my silent question. "You'll find your shit, and the stuff of my dad's that I won't be able to sell, in there. The old git Gregson wouldn't take less than two months' rent, so unless you empty it, you'll have to pay him more by the first of October." He points an angry finger at my face. "That's all you're getting from me, girl, and I only did it 'cause it was cheaper than a skip. So you can wipe that look off your face... I'm no soft touch."

I curl my fists again and glare at him. The rusty key bites into my palm.

God, I have the urge to chuck it back at him.

The darkness inside me rises; I narrow my eyes and jerkily tilt my head. Perhaps it would be better to use the key to stab him in the eye, then while he's distracted clutching at his face, I can get my keys back.

Hit him. Hurt him. Punish him.

Or even the car... My eyes flick to my pride and joy. He won't be able to sell my car if it's dented and the windows are broken. I step forward and...

I close my eyes for a moment and breathe deep.

Losing my temper now will achieve nothing. Girls... We aren't supposed to be filled with so much rage. *Sugar and spice, and everything nice. That's what little girls are made of.* The crazy words bounce around in my head.

I don't give a shit what people think about me. *But* I have this daymare, a vision of me being caught on someone's phone and the video going viral: Hybrid Gone Wild or Wild Girl Rampages headlines all over the net. The thought freaks me out. It's dangerous to be noticed and isn't worth the risk. So I keep my temper in check.

How sad.

I grit my teeth. I will get him back for this, but now isn't the time. I just need to be patient.

My uncle has fucked me over.

It's already done.

Shit, and I have nowhere to go.

"He'd be ashamed of you," I say with a glare. I want him to see my hate. Instead, I have to rapidly blink to dismiss the sting of angry tears that no doubt shine in my eyes.

He barks out a laugh, and his own eyes shine with mirth. "No. No, he wouldn't. You wanna know why?" He leans in, and a manic-looking grin spreads across his face. "'Cause he's dead."

I flinch.

"Dead men don't feel shame." He continues to chuckle as he walks around the front of my car. He taps on the bonnet and throws me a bright smile.

I watch as my uncle yanks the driver's door open, and without another backward glance, he drives away.

The car has long since disappeared from my sight, yet I stand and stare down the road. I can't move. My feet are frozen to the pavement.

Move. I don't think I can. Fear plants my feet. *If I stay here, I'll die.* I need to find some courage. "Courage," I scoff.

I shake my head, and the wind whips strands of my hair from out of my plait across my face. I force my frozen lump of a left hand that's pinned to my side to lift and tuck the wayward multicoloured hair behind my ear. My hand shakes.

In this world, magic is commonplace, with all manner of supernatural people, but it's all about the strong against the weak. It is all about power. It's been like that since the beginning of time.

I hug myself. We don't have people out on the street, homeless.

You have somewhere safe to stay... or you're dead. The vulnerable are quickly snapped up, disappearing without a trace. I turn my head and look mournfully back at my former home.

Here I am. No money. No home. No car.

I raise my eyes to the clouds and contemplate the seriousness of my situation. A mad-sounding giggle rips from my lips. I stand in the middle of the street, clutching at my stomach, and I laugh like a loon. I laugh with my despair. 'Cause if I cry, I don't think I'll ever stop.

Oh, the irony.

If he'd come the day before, I would be *nine hundred and twenty pounds* richer. I throw my hands in the air. The urge to scream my pain out into the universe thrums through me. My laughter dies.

How is that for irony? Bloody fate.

God, I feel sick. I fold over and clutch myself tighter. I can't do this. I'm not strong enough. I can't do this. I can't. I'm alone. I have no one to help me.

He might as well have choked me with his pathetic wind magic.

It would have been kinder.

CHAPTER TWO

The old key still gripped in my hand encourages me to move. I need to be polite and speak to Mr Gregson before I go poking around in his garage. At this point, I wouldn't be surprised if the key was a trick to get me into trouble. My shoulders slump, and I drag the bin bag up off the ground to slog towards the garage owner's house—which is one street over.

Fake it till you make it, Tru.

I knock on the door and wait as what sounds like half a dozen locks and bolts click and slide. With the chain still attached, the door creaks open, and Mr Gregson's brown eye peeks through the gap.

His eye widens when he sees it's me. "Oh, Tru." He holds up a finger as he shuffles back and slams the door in my face. I hear the chain slide free. The door opens for a second time, and the smell of unwashed man hits me. I rapidly blink and force myself not to wrinkle my nose.

"You got the key?" he asks. I nod.

"Oh, kid, I'm so sorry." His eyes soften with concern as he takes me and my bin bag in. "If I wasn't such a pathetic old man, I could have stopped him. I was on my way to get a bit of shopping, you see, and outside your grandfather's, sure enough, Phillip was on the phone. He ended the call when he spotted me and asked if he could use the garage.

I hope I did the right thing, love? That boy…" Mr Gregson shakes his head, and the loose skin around his jaw wobbles. "That boy has never been a good person. Your grandfather was a fine man, a fine man. I don't know what went wrong with the lad. He's a real wrong'un."

"It's fine, Mr Gregson. Everything is fine." I attempt a toothy smile. Mr Gregson subconsciously flinches away, so I knock that shit off.

"You have somewhere to go?"

In answer, I lift my hand with the garage key firmly clasped between my fingers and wiggle it.

He sighs and rubs a liver-spotted hand across his face. "Oh no, that's no place for a young lady. No place at all."

In an attempt to look all sweet, I widen my eyes, and for good measure, I pout a little. "Mr Gregson, please… Will it be okay? It will just be for a few weeks until I can find something better. No one will know I'm there, and I promise not to cause you any trouble."

"Tru, your grandfather… I can't have you living in there. It's not right…" His voice fades off into mumbles, and he looks over his shoulder.

Oh heck. I know what he's about to say, and I vigorously shake my head. I can't stay with him. Not with my uncle Phillip's nasty words of me taking advantage of old people still ringing in my head.

"No, thank you, Mr Gregson. I can't stay with you if that's what you're about to suggest. I'll be fine. Everything will be fine if I can stay in the garage for a few short weeks. The rent? It's due on, urm… the first of October?" I do my best to change the subject.

"The first of October?" Mr Gregson's chubby cheeks steadily grow red. His worried expression fades, and his eyes shine with glee as a small smug smile pulls at his lips. "No, I made him pay through the nose. I told him October, but you're paid up till the first of December." He guffaws and slaps his thigh. His grey comb-over slips. It flops down onto his forehead and swishes against the bridge of his nose. "The rent is only eighty pounds a month," he continues with a chuckle. He frowns when he notices the dangling hair, and sheepishly he swirls and pats it back into place.

His dancing brown eyes grow serious. Oh God, he's going to say no. He's going to say no, and then I'm dead.

Mr Gregson huffs out a sad-sounding sigh and shakes his head. "No, I'm sorry, Tru. You can't stay in the garage. It isn't in a liveable condition, not for a young lady. The police might help, or the human council?" He lifts his bushy eyebrows. "I know your grandfather was fae, so perhaps the fae guild will have somewhere for you to stay." He steps away from the door and gestures to the landline phone on the table.

"I can call them for you. I don't like the thought—"

Overwhelming panic smashes through me, and I do something I instantly regret. "Don't think about it again. It's all going to be okay, Mr Gregson, I promise. I'm going to be okay. I wanted you to know as it's polite... but you don't have to worry about me. Forget all about it." I lean forward and whisper, "I'm not a normal girl. Don't think about it again." I then smile brightly.

I watch Mr Gregson's eyes glaze over, and he robotically nods his head. "No need to worry. I won't think about it again." He shuffles back into his house, and his door clinks closed.

I blink. Okay, that's okay.

I swallow down the guilty lump that's forming in my throat. I feel a little sick.

I'm just trying to survive—like everyone, I'm just trying my best to live in this shitty world. He would have stopped me living in the garage, and he was going to call the guild. "I am so sorry. Please forgive me, Mr Gregson," I whisper. God, I feel sick. I cough into my fist.

That's right, Tru. You get fucked over, so you go straight in and mess with a kind old man's head. I slump forward and rest my ear against the door; I listen as his feet shuffle away. *Oh crap. Nice one, Tru.* He hasn't locked the door. "Mr Gregson." I tap the door with my knuckle. "Mr Gregson, don't forget to lock up."

Behind the closed door, like a mind-controlled zombie, Mr Gregson's footsteps shuffle back, and again in a monotone voice, he repeats my words. "Don't forget to lock up." One by one the locks click and slide into place. I puff out my cheeks with a relieved sigh.

Closing my eyes, I push my forehead hard against the white PVC door. Guilt continues to grip me in its vise.

I should not have done that.

He will be perfectly fine in ten minutes. I did it for his own good.

I cringe, push away from the door, and slog my guilty ass back down the street. With hunched shoulders, I turn my head and glance back at Mr Gregson's silent house.

Liar, you did it for yourself.

Okay, so I can do a little compulsion. It's no big deal. I shrug, and the bin bag in my hand rustles. It's a defence mechanism, a defensive reaction. All born vampires can do it. It's no biggie and nothing special, and it has limited uses. If only I was strong enough to use it on my uncle.

I scratch my head with the garage key. I don't do it often, and I'd never normally persuade an old man like Mr Gregson if it wasn't a life-and-death situation.

Yes, I feel bad. But given the same type of circumstances... In the same situation, I'd do it again.

Does that make me a bad person? I cringe again. Yes, yes, it does. I pause, clamp the bin bag between my knees for safekeeping, and readjust the bobble that is falling out of my french plait. I didn't hurt him, and I am giving him peace of mind as I know he'd worry about me, and now... Well, now he doesn't have to.

Listen to me. Who am I trying to fool? I'm no better than my uncle. No, no—I am worse 'cause I took a kind old man's choice away, and that makes me scum. I force my feet to keep moving.

The alleyway behind Mr Gregson's terrace that leads to his garage is dingy and untarmacked, and the track is composed of uneven crushed stone with a scattering of red brick and broken glass. My gaze flicks around as I manoeuvre between the glass, clumps of weeds, and the pale, washed-out dog poo that's decorating them. I attempt to hold my breath as the pungent scent of ammonia—yay, fresh pee—assaults my nose. Crap, it makes my eyes water.

I've been to this garage before, a few years ago. So if I can remember right, it's just up here. I groan when I find it. Hands on my hips, I survey what I have to work with.

Gah, the garage is worse than I remembered. No wonder the rent is only eighty quid.

The faded garage door has seen better days. It's more rust than paint. Spots of different colours smatter its surface as the paint peels away. Squinting, I inspect the metal holding the door up. It's crumbling, and it looks as if the mechanism and frame of the up-and-over door has rusted tight. A small push and I bet the whole door would fall to the floor. God, I don't even know how my uncle got the thing open.

"The height of security," I grumble. Let's hope no one noticed my uncle loading the place up with my stuff. I don't need any attention.

My hand clenches the key with relief, and my feet crunch on the uneven track as I step around to the side of the garage. Thank God there's a side door.

Or not. I frown at the wooden door and growl out a curse. The door is swollen shut. I brace against it and wiggle the key in the lock. After a few failed attempts, it finally clicks open, but when I pull the handle, the damn thing almost comes off in my hand. With a jiggle and a tug, I open it just enough to get my fingers into the gap. Splinters from the old wood dig into my skin, but I ignore the pricks of pain as I tug the door. Inch by inch, it scrapes across the ground, kicking up little stones.

It wedges.

"For fuck's sake!" I scream. *I can't have a door that doesn't open*. My famous temper flares. Rage, guilt, and despair bubble inside me. I dig the toe of my boot into the weeds that have built up around the bottom of the door, and I vigorously kick. Grass and stones go flying.

I clamp my lips against another scream that wants to rip out of my throat. My breathing is ragged, and my throat burns, and my chest hurts. I glare at the mess I've made, giving myself a minute before I sigh and gather the threads of my frayed temper together. To get my breath back, I lean against the garage wall. The red brick digs into my shoulder. I'll add fixing this shitty door to the list of endless shit that I've got to do this afternoon. I grind my teeth so hard my jaw aches and push back the ever-present anger I inherited from my vampire side.

I let out a bitter laugh. Shit, I am not even a proper pureblood vampire. No, I am a pesky hybrid. I am a born vampire with a twist.

Oh yeah, the best part. The twisted part... I have a little bit of shifter floating around in my veins. Ta-da.

Shifter.

It should be impossible. I shouldn't exist.

Grandad told me no one could find out about my hybrid nature, especially the guilds—it was our golden rule. If the vampires find out about my existence, I'm dead. If the shifters find out about my existence, I'm dead...

With a tired grimace, I step through the door into my new *home*.

CHAPTER
THREE

My eyes slowly adjust to the change of light inside the garage. The place is musty and damp.

On a positive note, it's slightly bigger than a standard garage.

On a negative note, the roof is probably asbestos, and there's a puddle on the floor from last night's rain.

The brick walls are solid enough, although the crumbling mortar looks like it's being held up by cobwebs. The whole place is full of dust, and with each breath it tickles the back of my throat, and the concrete floor only adds to the problem. The old surface is disintegrating, leaving craters of dust and loose stones.

It's not a palace, that's for sure. No electricity. No water. But heck, it will have to do.

My already-fatigued body aches as I eye the enormous pile of stuff dumped in the centre of the room, a mound of furniture and clothing. I shake my head.

Gah, my life in bin bags and boxes. I drop my car bin bag onto the pile to deal with later and spin in a circle.

"What the f— Look at that." I shake my head again, this time in disbelief as I spot the old garden shed that once had pride of place in my grandad's garden. Now in pieces, carelessly ripped apart and propped up against the far wall.

I rub my forehead as I take it all in—it isn't my things that upset me. Not really. What bothers me is I can pick out my grandad's things thrown on top of each other, dumped haphazardly.

Why would Uncle Phillip do that? They're his dad's things.

It's as if what Grandad left of his life, the things important to him, are truly meaningless. My heart hurts. I swallow to get rid of the tightness of grief that's now blocking my throat.

Keep going. I just need to keep going.

I roll my shoulders and twist my wrist to look at my watch. It's three o'clock—I worked the early shift today. My eyes drift to the open door as the welcome sunlight spills into the dank space. I have at least six hours of daylight left to get this place shipshape. Yay for British summer.

As carefully as I can, I search through the haphazard piles. "Please be here, please, please, please," I mumble. Bingo. *Yes.* Oh, thank God. That's one thing, one thing out of all this shit, that's gone right. I grab the old red toolbox.

At first glance, it looks like a piece of junk. But inside it holds so many treasures the toolbox is pure magic.

I've also never been more grateful that Grandad has so many little bits and pieces. Hinges, bolts, nails, and screws. The man never threw anything useful away.

I lug the heavy thing towards the wooden side door and get to work.

I hum. I wish I could play music with my phone, but I don't want to run the battery down needlessly. There's enough battery until I get to work tomorrow. My incessant humming used to drive my grandad crazy. He'd say, *Use your inner voice, Tru*. I snort at the memory. His moaning only encouraged me to hum more. He also didn't like the sound of chewing, so whenever I came across a video online where someone was obnoxiously chewing, I'd send him the link. I giggle. God, he'd get so mad.

I grab a screwdriver and attack the hinges on the door. *Lefty loosey.* In his day, my grandad was a badass fae warrior. He wasn't full fae, but he still had amazing magic. Grandad was an assassin. He was one of the best. A screw drops into my waiting palm, and I rap it against the door. Let's just say I didn't have a normal childhood, and my grandad taught me everything he could. He was the bomb. I don't care what creepy *not–Uncle* Phillip says. He was my grandad. I ignore the stinging behind my eyes. It doesn't matter that my mum never came back. It doesn't matter that Grandad found me on the side of the road.

So I guess she's dead... I guess all my biological family is dead.

Or... or they didn't want me.

I grind my teeth so hard my jaw aches. It's been a long time, eleven years, so it shouldn't hurt. Hell, I can't even remember them, even when I close my eyes. No, that's not quite right. Sometimes I have flashes of my mum's face, if that's even real. It could be from a film for all I know.

I grunt as I pull the door away from its frame and try to ignore the bleeding wounds reopened by the death of my grandad. At least he wanted me. I'm not a kid. I might be only seventeen, but I've been looking after Grandad and myself for years. Using my grandad's tools with care, I plane the door down, shave off bits of the damaged wood, and reposition brand-new hinges so it now sits perfectly in its frame. I smile with satisfaction when the door opens and closes smoothly without an issue. I also take a leaf out of Mr Gregson's book and install three solid bolts so when I'm here, I can lock the door from the inside.

Mental note: buy wood to secure the main rusty garage door when I get some cash.

I roll my shoulders, and with a scowl and a tired huff, I turn my attention to the leaky roof.

After hours of hard work and racing the slowly fading sunlight, I finish.

The now re-erected six-foot-by-eight-foot shed takes up a sizeable chunk of room, but it's an added layer of protection around my single bed. Using the plastic boxes that we already had, my clothing is now safely tucked away underneath. Battery-powered fairy lights wrap around the low beams, creating perfect lighting. A thick rug cushions the wooden floor, and I've nailed it so it reaches halfway up the walls.

It's August now, but winter is fast approaching. It's going to be unbearably cold in here, so I've used whatever I could find to insulate.

My eye twitches as I glare at my grim emergency toilet that sits in the far corner... It's a bucket, a squished loo roll, and an old bottle of antibacterial handwash. Go me.

I've installed shelves, and the old living room furniture is now the right way up and squished together in the corner—most of Grandad's important things are now off the dirty floor. A small space carved out within the mountains of things. It turns the garage into an odd space. But it works.

My hands throb and my back aches. I can no longer feel my feet. I've forgotten about eating, and I haven't any water to drink or to brush my teeth. So my gnashers are going to have to wait till I go to the gym in the morning. At least no one is around to smell my breath.

At least I have four months left of the gym, somewhere nice to get cleaned up. I'm a bit of a fitness fanatic—exercise helps with the whole grrr side of me. It looks like I'll be putting it to good use.

Plus the local launderette is only around the corner for my clothes.

"Yep, this is all gonna work out perfectly," I mumble.

Yeah, I'm Miss Positivity.

I have four solid walls—well, three out of four anyway; I'm going to ignore the entire wall of rotten garage door—a roof over my head, and a door that locks. If you add in the cheap rent, no utility bills, and the bucket—let's not forget my bucket—I'm living the dream.

Time for bed. I toe my boots off and leave them outside the shed. Like a paranoid weirdo when I set the shed up, I put the door so that it opens against the garage wall. I positioned it, thinking that if it's harder for me to get in, it's harder for anybody else to get in. Also, at first glance, it looks abandoned. No one in their right mind would think there was a bed in there.

So with some fancy manoeuvring, I hold my breath, suck in my already-flat tummy, and shimmy. I have to scrape myself against the walls to get inside.

Although if any creature wants in here, they will not come through the door. Oh no. They will just rip the shed to bits. *Little pig, little pig let me in. Not by the hair of my chinny chin chin.*

I duck and squeeze through the small gap—being tall sucks.

When I'm settled underneath the covers—God, I feel grotty—I look around the small space and take in the warm glow of the fairy lights.

This isn't so bad.

If I squint, I can almost imagine I'm in a log cabin.

I roll over and groan. My tongue is stuck to the roof of my mouth, and I can't even work up enough spit. My mouth is as dry as a bone. It's pathetic that I can't afford a bottle of water. Dehydration makes my head throb, and on an alternate beat, my stomach aches with hunger pains.

Thumping and fluffing my pillow, I silently berate myself for spending all my money on bills without setting some aside for emergencies. What was I thinking? Such a silly, naive mistake and not something I'm *ever* going to repeat.

I was so focused on struggling to get the bills up to date, so focused on patting myself on the back and telling myself how smart I was, how grown-up. I didn't even contemplate the consequences if something went wrong. Never again. I'm going to hoard my money like a squirrel hoards nuts for winter.

Exhaustion hits me like a wave. The lights become hazy and my eyes heavy, so with the last of my energy, I lift my hand and switch off the lights.

Tomorrow will be better.

CHAPTER
FOUR

Heavy, coarse rope binds my legs together. They don't release, no matter how hard I thrash. My body trembles, and a white foamy sweat clings to my fur. My hooves scrabble uselessly for purchase on the unyielding concrete underneath me.

On silent feet, he prowls across the room towards me.

I freeze, and my eyes roll with panic.

He has something terrifying in his hand.

I can't get enough air into my lungs, my heart pounds as if it's going to smash out of my chest, and before my eyes can roll in fear for a third time, he drops his considerable bulk onto my neck. My cheek hits the floor with a crunch as he pins my head to the ground.

"No! Mummy! I want my mummy!" I cry out, but the words come out as a terrified equine scream.

With his weight pressing against me fully and the ropes holding me tight, I'm unable to move. He grips my horn in his fist and the hand with the... the saw comes closer to my face.

I startle awake, and I groan as I push my hair back from my face and blink the crusty sleep residue out of my eyes. Gah, it must have been the stress from yesterday. God... I don't know why my head insists on torturing me with dreams like that. It's fucked up.

I roll onto my side and slide further under my duvet. I rub my forehead. It *throbs* with residual pain… which is ridiculous.

Someone removed my horn. I shudder.

Creepy as fuck.

I know—I know it's ridiculous… but the dreams always feel so real. I scoff. It felt real, but nothing in the dream makes sense. Shifters don't shift until they're older—at least in their early twenties. I know this. Everybody knows this.

In the dream, I'm little.

Also as a hybrid, there's no way I'd be able to shift. It's unheard of, and I've made peace with that. In the end, only purebred shifters change into animal form.

I glare at my hand that's gone back to rubbing my forehead. I yank the rogue hand away and stuff it back under the covers. Nope, it was a dream. I've got a vivid imagination, that's all.

Yep, it's 'cause I'm a wimpy unicorn shifter.

A *unicorn*. I snort with incredulity. I wish I was part wolf shifter instead. Now that would go well with being a vampire. Although being a unicorn makes strange sense. I'm a hybrid… so of course, I'd be the rarest of rare shifter type.

I'm a classic case of Jekyll and Hyde. I huff and grind my teeth with distaste. It's a horrendous joke. Each part of me is on either side of the creature spectrum.

The vampire-and-unicorn-shifter combo. The worst combination imagined—not that I know of any other hybrids apart from mixed humans—the ultimate predator combined with the ultimate prey. Yeah, it's a cosmic joke of epic proportions.

Sometimes I think the battling sides of me make me psychotic. A psychotic vegetarian unicorn vampire. Ha.

I grab my phone. It's tucked underneath my pillow—cooking my brain as I sleep. I squint at it. Five hours of sleep. Ugh, it'll have to do. I switch on my fairy lights so I can see and then drag myself out of bed.

Once I've wiggled into my—mainly clean—running gear, I pack everything that I'll need for the day into a small black rucksack.

On the way out of the garage, I catch sight of my unused emergency bucket. My lip curls with disgust.

I hoof it to the gym.

As I run, the weight of my heavy plait—that I've tucked underneath my top—rhythmically slaps against my back as my feet hit the wet pavement. I try in vain to dodge the worst of the dirty water and grimace as it splashes against my calves.

Oh, get in! I do a mental fist pump. *No puddles in the garage this morning and it rained heavily for the past few hours.* I can't help the proud grin that flashes across my face. *Yesterday's roof repair survived the deluge.*

It's a nervous eighteen minutes for me as I dash across the city. I'm glad the gym isn't too far. It's only three miles. Running makes the hairs on the back of my neck stand on end. A lot of creatures like to chase. *Walking at this time in the morning would be worse.* Sweat trickles down my back, and goosebumps rise on my skin at the feel of many eyes watching me. Especially when I have to run the last mile around the outskirts of Stanley Park.

It's like my pounding feet make the clang of a dinner bell.

I am not prey. The darkness inside me stirs, wanting to play. It whispers the suggestion to slow down, perhaps stop and do some stretches. The thought makes me uncomfortable. Who thinks like that? What type of person am I who wants to be attacked so I have a justified excuse to smash my attacker in the face?

Drink their blood.

Oh no, none of that.

I can look after myself—mostly. But being able to kick ass doesn't mean shit when you're outnumbered.

It's a relief to arrive without incident. I studiously ignore the wobble in my legs as I walk through the hotel's golden ward and pull open the door to the lobby.

My wet trainers squeak across the marble floor as I head for the stairs that will take me down to the gym. The night receptionist, Mike, is still on duty, so I nod an acknowledgement to him. He returns my sentiment with a nod of his own and a tired smile.

Like the nectar of the gods, water has never tasted so good. When the shit hits the fan, it all comes down to the small things in life being important. The simple joy of being squeaky clean and hydrated is high on my list.

With my hair and makeup on point—no way do I look homeless—and precious water sloshing in my stomach, I head off to work.

Luckily the café where I've worked since I left school at fourteen is only a short walk away from the fancy hotel gym. I arrive before six to get things set up for our early-morning breakfast rush.

I plug my phone into the charger in the back office, put my bag away, and come out into the café, tying an apron around my waist. Tilly, my boss, is staring mournfully at one of our tables.

"What's up?" I ask as I approach.

"Morning, Tru. Look at this table. Someone has vandalised it. Look at that. Just look at it." Her bottom lip trembles as she runs her fingers across the table's newly scarred surface. I lean forward and see the letters *L I Z* scored deeply into the wood.

"Oh, Tilly, I'm so sorry." I reach out and rub the dryad's shoulder. High on my DIY success at the garage, "I could fill it in?" I suggest.

"You could?"

"Yeah, I guess." I lean across the table and rub my fingers across the gouged letters. "A bit of wood filler and some sanding. It may take me a while, but I think I can fix it." They're deep but I can fix it, I think.

Tilly shakes her head, and the blossoms in her hair rustle. She squeezes my hand. "No, you know what? It's not that bad. I just hope it's not a new craze and no one else decides to do such a mean thing." She runs her fingertips across the letters a final time, and then with a whole body shake, she turns and meets my eyes with a warm smile. "Every scar tells a story... I'm being silly." Her gloomy mood dissipates. It peels away to reveal her normal, calm sweetness. I wish I could do that, swing from upset to happy within seconds. "I wanted to speak to you about your hours." My stomach drops.

Oh. Oh no. Oh please no.

My fingers twist together, and I rock from foot to foot.

"I know you asked for more, and I've tweaked it so I can give you an extra shift next week."

I sag in relief. Oh my god, she had me worried there for a second. I release the last of the tension in my shoulders with a roll and vigorously nod my head. "More hours would be amazing. Thank you, Tilly."

"I wanted to talk to you about something. My friend—" Tilly blushes. Huh, her *friend*. In response to her obvious embarrassment, I wiggle my eyebrows, and she slaps me on the arm. She glides behind the counter, washes her hands, and one by one she delicately places the pastries and cakes from the trays into the display. "My friend asked me if I knew of anybody who was looking for work. He's a shifter, and he is the manager of that club Night-*Shift* on King Street"—she holds her hand out to stop me from speaking—"I know they frighten you, but the money... The money is excellent. The hours might be a slight issue as the place is open late into the night, especially if you do the morning shift here. But I'm sure we can work it out. You'd be collecting glasses and clearing tables." She smiles and nods with encouragement.

My gaze drifts away from her face. I glance up in thought, and my eyes trace the pretty blossom tree that spans across the entire ceiling. Tilly's dryad nature keeps the tree alive and always in bloom. It's a hell of a feature. It adds such a unique touch to the café. The small lights dotted within the branches twinkle. I take a deep breath, and the comforting scents of cake, coffee, and apple blossom fill my nose.

A shifter club? That sounds like a reeeeallly bad idea. "How good? How much money are we talking?"

"Twenty quid an hour."

"Twenty? Crikey!" My head drops so fast my neck twinges in protest. Shit, that is good money. It's almost three times the rate that I get paid with Tilly. "Just glass collecting? I'm not old enough to work behind the bar." I narrow my eyes. "They don't expect me to work in my underwear, do they?" Tilly snorts and rolls her eyes.

Okay... So I might have a vivid imagination, but you never know in this city.

"Just glass collecting." She shakes her head and mumbles, "As if I'd let you anywhere public in just your underwear. Honestly, Tru."

I shrug. "Yeah, I didn't think that one through, sorry."

"The uniform is your own black pants and a club T-shirt that they will provide you. It's only twelve hours a week, Friday and Saturday nights. As Sunday is your day off, it might work? What do you think?" She twirls a strand of her green hair. I nod my head. "You love me?" she says in a sweet lilting tone.

Twenty quid an hour... I feel a rare and genuine smile flash across my face. "Yes, of course I love you. You're my favourite boss."

"I'm your only boss."

"Not anymore. Yeah, I'll do it," I say, a bounce in my step as I head towards the shop's door.

"Yay," she responds with a clap of her hands. She pulls her mobile free from her pocket. "Let me text him."

I watch on with amusement as her thumbs fly across the keypad. The blush is back. "Oh, can you work a double shift today?"

"Will you feed me?" I ask. As if my words are a signal, my tummy gurgles. Tilly giggles. "Are we ready to open?"

"Yes to both."

"Thank you for thinking of me." Heck, it's worth the risk of the shifters. What damage can I do working twelve hours a week? I flick the lock and turn the sign.

CHAPTER
FIVE

As I'm opening the door to my new *home*, a small body brushes against my leg and dashes into the garage ahead of me.

My mouth pops open with shock. "What the fuck was that?"

I glance down, and a bit of orange fur is stuck to my pants. It catches on the breeze and twirls in the air. I step inside with wide eyes and scan the space.

Movement. A stripey ginger tail disappears behind the ratty old sofa.

Huh. A cat. The sneaky thing ran so fast.

What a coincidence. I've had a niggling worry all day about mice getting into Grandad's stuff. They chew and nibble on everything. I had to shove the worrying thoughts to the back of my mind as I can't do anything about it. When I get paid, I'll buy proper storage.

There is nothing I can do in the meantime but be sensible and go through Grandad's clothing and take the quality stuff to the local charity shop. My stomach twists into a knot. It's going to be hard.

In all honestly, I don't want to get rid of his things. I want to hold on to them, hold on to *him* for a little longer. But I can't be selfish. If his things get damaged because of this damp garage and the vermin that are surely knocking around when I could have given them to someone who needs them... Yeah, I'd feel like a right dick.

I keep the door open in case it runs back this way and tiptoe towards the sofa and the hairy trespasser. *Having a cat around to scare off any mice would be helpful.* I groan. I can't look after myself, let alone a cat.

Even though I've brushed the floor, the crumbling concrete doesn't seem to want to behave. It will always be dank, smelly, and dusty, but I drop down anyway. Little stones dig into my knees and palms as I peer underneath the sofa. "Here kitty, kitty, kitty..." I smirk as I quote one of my favourite books. Two big yellow eyes return my gaze. "Hello there, little kitty cat, aren't you pretty? What do you think you're doing sneaking in here?" At the sound of my voice, the cat purrs. "Do you know how dangerous it is coming uninvited into a vampire's home?" I grin at my words and lie down on the garage floor.

Ew, the floor is disgusting.

I stick my hand underneath the sofa. "What am I doing talking to him as if he can understand me?" I mumble. The cat creeps forward and sniffs the fingers of my outstretched hand. "Shit. Please don't bite me." He rubs the side of his face against my skin, marking me with his scent.

Oh, he's cute. Oh, and I have an idea. "You hungry?"

I tug my arm back and wiggle my backpack off my shoulders. Guess I could share my dinner with him.

At the rattling noise from the tinfoil and the smell of the sandwich's tofu goodness, the cat appears in front of me. He places a paw on my leg, and his hungry eyes intently watch me as I carefully unwrap the sandwich and tear off a chunk of tofu.

"Purrrt," he chirps at me.

I interpret that as *for me* in catspeak. Though it might be more on the lines of, *If you don't hurry, I will eat your face*. Meh, he's friendly enough.

I offer him the tofu, and with a gentle paw, he carefully guides my hand to his face, and with sharp white teeth, he delicately takes it from my fingers.

As he eats, he purrs.

I grin and carefully stroke his soft ginger fur with my fingers. Once he's finished a few more chunks, I scoop him up into my arms and hustle to the door. He is lighter than I expected. The little fella is just bones and fur. Underneath my fingertips, I can feel little bumps on his skin—the poor thing is being eaten alive by fleas.

I gently place him outside and quickly slam the door.

"I know, I know. I'm sorry, I'm so sorry," I say in response to his pitiful yowls.

I lean my forehead against the wood. The darkness of the garage enfolds around me as the cat continues to cry.

"I can't look after you. I'm so sorry."

GROGGY after a restless sleep of worrying about the cat, I nearly step on the grizzly remains of a mouse outside the door.

A gift.

I lift my eyes to the sky to commiserate with the soul of the poor little mouse. Yet the implication of the cat's gift isn't lost on me. The starving skin-and-bone cat left *me* a present. A mouse that he could have eaten. Gross as it is, the mouse gift is the cat equivalent of teaching me to hunt. He sees *me* as his family.

I swallow a lump that's stuck in my throat, and my tummy flips. I rub the back of my head. Oh, the guilt I feel—the guilt of throwing the cat out into the night... yeah, it worsens.

I DON'T GET PAID until the end of the week, and I rarely get tips. People pay for their meals and drinks at the till. But today, today has been a good tip day. Although I have a sneaking suspicion that Tilly might have had a hand in my good fortune. I've scrounged up a tenner and a reusable water bottle.

In the discount supermarket, determined, I stomp right past the peanut butter that I should be buying, and instead, my feet take me to another aisle.

I glare at the varied assortment of cans.

The cats on the labels mock me.

After spending way too much time and contemplation on different flavours, I pay for a pack of cat food. I'm relieved to see I just have enough money to buy a single pipette of flea treatment from the vet.

I feel like such a sentimental fool. I'm an idiot.

As I am heading back to the garage with cat stuff in hand, I can't help looking at my old home as I pass by. My eyes fly over the familiar building, and my heart sinks into my abdomen when I see the FOR SALE sign.

I know it shouldn't be a surprise; it isn't a surprise, not really. I didn't think my uncle would stay in the house. Not when he moved everything out. But knowing and seeing are two different things. It makes it real, and it rocks me to my core. It rattles something deep inside me.

I pull my phone out of my pocket and do a quick online search... and there it is on the estate agent's website. I shouldn't look any further. *You're only torturing yourself,* I say, but I can't help it. I click the link for more details and scan the ad. Seeing the photos hurts.

I bet if I did a thorough search, I'd find everything that my uncle has inherited for sale all over the web. Including my car. I rub my forehead. Gosh, I wish I had enough money to at least buy my car back. Not that I'd want to give him a penny.

To buy the house would be an impossible dream.

I hate him.

The plastic case on my phone crunches in my tight grip. God, how I hate him.

You know, I didn't expect a free ride; I didn't think he'd be so cruel as to—I yank at the thought. No, none of that. I turn my phone off and stuff it back in my pocket.

I'll get my own back, I promise myself. When the time is right, I will get him back. I sigh. My head is so fuzzy with anger it makes my temples pound.

Back at the garage, while Dexter the mouse-killer cat—I named him while I was shopping—is stuffing his face with cat food, with some satisfaction, I carefully squeeze the liquid flea treatment onto the skin at the back of his neck.

As I listen to him purr and eat, I think about my work schedule and the need for Dexter to be able to come and go as he pleases.

I'm not about to lock him up or lock him out.

Heck, I don't want him to go outside. The roads are busy, and the predators would think nothing of making a snack of him. Also, if something happens to me and I can't get back... I need to know that he'll be able to fend for himself. That he'll be safe.

I spend a good twenty minutes fighting with a brick vent that I find at the back of the garage. Whoever designed this thing didn't design it with vermin in mind. The wide slats make an ideal mouse flap, a mouse highway. Why would somebody put a vent in a garage? I knock out the crumbling brick and secure a bit of hard plastic to hide the hole. Let's hope Dexter is the only animal that uses it.

The ginger cat joins me and inspects his new doorway. My empty tummy grumbles, but my heart is full and squishy.

CHAPTER SIX

It's Friday night, and Tilly told me to go to the club's back door. The metal gate that guards the road and the car park at the back of the club is huge. I stand on my toes and peer through a gap. *God, it's like Fort Knox.* What's with the gate and all the fancy security cameras? What type of nightclub has this kind of security?

With frustration, and the worry I'm going to be late, I slam my palm against the cold black metal. I guess I'll have to ring Tilly and see if she can get someone to come out to get me.

As I'm digging in my back pocket for my phone, my eyes scan the gate again, and this time my gaze lands on a fancy biometric scanner. A scanner I completely missed the first time I'd looked. Gah, I roll my eyes. It has a call button.

I've always been that type of person—something can be right in front of my face, and I'll not see it. I stab at the button with my thumb. The scanner lights up.

I tap my fingers against my leg as I wait and fight the urge to push the button again.

"Hello?" says a grumpy-sounding voice. I shuffle forward and lean my mouth closer to the speaker.

"Hi, I'm the new glass collector... You should be expecting me?"

"Miss Dennison?"

"Yeah, that's me." I nod my head, turn, and give the camera a little wave. The speaker crackles, and the man on the other end groans. My hand drops with a slap to my side, and I sheepishly tuck my hands behind my back. Yeah, I guess that was a little weird.

"Come through, head to the back door, and I'll get Luke to meet you."

"Thank"—the biometric scanner goes dark—"you." I roll my eyes. He was really friendly.

The gate clicks and ominously swings open. I quickly back away, and before it's fully open, I squeeze through the gap. As soon as I've stepped through, the gate's trajectory changes and it swings back and clangs closed. *Yeah, that's not ominous at all*, I think with a barely repressed shudder.

The surrounding area is well lit, and the parking area for the staff is clean and already half-full of cars. Silent high-tech cameras sweep the area.

I'm fifty percent impressed and fifty percent shitting myself.

I rub my sweaty palms on my trousers and continue around the back of the building towards where I hope the back door is located.

Another solid door with a fancy biometric lock. When I'm still a step away, the door buzzes and swings open. A blond-haired shifter meets my nervous eyes with a warm grin.

"Tru? I'm Luke... Tilly's friend." He rubs the back of his head, and I can't help my answering grin. In response to my smile, pink stains his cheeks. I can tell straightaway, even though this guy is a shifter, he's perfect for Tilly. "Come on, kid. Let's get your paperwork done and I'll show you the ropes."

The door opens into a large hallway. The carpet beneath my feet is soft and springy. The colour of crushed blackberries. Not quite black, not quite purple, but a cool mix of both. I'm surprised the nightclub has such an expensive carpet for its staff areas. *The underlay alone probably cost more than my car*. Pain shoots me in the chest with that thought. The loss of my car is still a sore subject.

Fucking car. I saved up for two years to buy that car, and look how it turned out. I owned it for three months. Shit, I regret not spending my money on teenage crap. At least I would have had something to show for it. *God, I hate Uncle Nobhead for stealing it.*

Luke points to the door far down the hall, "Owner's office." His tour guide finger points to another door. "Manager's office, security office and staff room. This door here will take you directly into the club, and there's another direct door in the staff room." He opens the manager's door and indicates for me to go in.

"All the doors have a spelled biometric scanner, so you'll be able to use them as soon as I've uploaded you into the security system. If you can't get into an area, then you're not supposed to be there. Please sit."

I take a seat, and as I tuck my long legs underneath the chair, I take in the room. The office has no personal touches. The walls are a plain white.

Luke leans on the edge of the desk and folds his arms casually in front of his chest. "Do you need to park your car?"

"No. No car," I say, trying not to snarl.

"Oh okay." Luke tilts his head to the side, and nostrils flare as he picks up the scent of my upset.

With a sad-sounding sigh, even to my own ears, I push the livid car thoughts to the back of my head and make a wall around them. Anytime I think about being homeless, about losing my car, I need to kick the thoughts away like I'm kicking a football. I need to keep those thoughts out of my head. I can't dwell or moan about the stuff I can't control.

I haven't got the luxury of being upset. It's a waste of time. A waste of my head space. It happened, and shit is bound to get better. Isn't it? I'll get my own back on my uncle. It's only a matter of time.

Perhaps my weird silence has made Luke uncomfortable, as he springs away from the desk. "Okay, I'll add you to the taxi list then. I don't know if Tilly mentioned it, but the club will make sure you get home safe. Working late is a risk that we want to mitigate as much as possible. So there are a few shared taxies for any of our staff that need them," he says a little robotically, as if he's quoting someone else word for word.

"When it's time to go home, I'll arrange that for you." He digs into a drawer.

"Thank you. That's very kind," I blurt out.

I'm glad he can't see my face. I appreciate the gesture, I really do, but inside I'm panicking. What am I going to say to the taxi driver? "Oh, it's the third garage on the left." Oh my god, will I have to pretend to walk to some stranger's front door? Maybe pretend to open the door so the taxi driver and other staff members know that I'm home safe. What happens if they don't drive away?

Gah, I rub my temple.

This is a great start to my new job so far. I know I'll have to go straight to the gym. It was something that I was going to do anyway, at least tonight's shift, as tomorrow morning I start work at six and it only gives me a four-hour break between.

My entire body groans with the thought. I know my work schedule is ridiculous. At least I have time to get in a power nap. Tilly has juggled the rotas for the next few weeks, so I shouldn't start Saturday shifts until the afternoon. Tomorrow is going to be hard like today. I have a double shift and then the nightclub shift. It's only a twenty-hour working day on maybe three hours of sleep… if I am lucky.

I have to keep Dexter in cat food after all.

Luke finds what he's looking for and slaps a fancy-looking datapad on the desk. He grins at me. "Complete the questions on this baby, and I'll get you hooked up with a club T-shirt and a locker."

I hook the corner of the datapad with my fingers and pull it across the desk towards me. "Okay, thank you," I say as I tentatively return his smile.

"No problem. I'll be back in a few."

I tap the electronic pad, and the screen comes to life. The forms are quite simple. I strum the desk as I take a few moments to ponder what address to put down.

I decide to continue using my grandad's address. It matches the information that Tilly has got for me, and it's the address on my identification.

I hum as I answer all the usual questions and fall into the flow of things: answer a question, click next—answer another few questions, click next—add my bank details, click next… so I don't even think twice about it when it asks me to put my thumb on a little nodule.

There's a sharp sting of pain as a hidden tiny *needle* sticks into my thumb and then disappears back into the device.

"What the fuck, fuckety, fuck."

I jump out of the chair and fling the datapad away from me. It clatters onto the desk. I rapidly back away, and I stare at the drop of blood on my thumb with growing fear.

The bloody thing bit me!

Pure panic hits me so hard my heart pounds and I feel dizzy. It's got my DNA. It's got my DNA.

Oh bloody hell.

Everything inside me is screaming for me to run away. Instead, I cringe and on wobbly legs stumble back to the desk. I drop inelegantly back into the chair. My knees tremble way too hard to keep me upright. The rapid beat of my heart yet to slow.

I huddle as my eyes dart about. I wait with dread for something bad to happen. A minute ticks by, then two as the datapad reads my freaky blood.

When the world keeps turning, I force myself to relax. No alarms sound.

Tru, you divvy, it's for the biometric security system.

"Damn it, Luke." I rub my sore digit. A bit of a warning would have been nice. Shit, I almost had a heart attack. I thought the biometric scanner was an eye scan or perhaps a thumbprint, not blood!

As a general rule, creatures don't give others access to their bodily fluids. Especially blood, a dangerous witch would have a field day. What the heck have I got myself into? The job is for a glass collector. Why the hell this business needs my blood to collect glasses... It's nuts. I have an almost uncontrollable urge to smash the crap out of the tech and scurry off home. But I refrain.

God, coming to work here might be the worst decision I've ever made.

I force myself again to relax. Well, relax as much as I can with my first-day nerves. I pick the datapad back up, and with now-trembling hands, I finish answering the questions.

As soon as I'm done, as if by magic, the door swings open to a smiling Luke.

"I've got you two sizes of T-shirt as I don't know if you like tight tops or baggy tops, so I've got you one of each." He slaps the two T-shirts that are still in their plastic wrap onto the desk, and he scoops up the datapad.

"The thing bit me," I growl and wiggle my thumb at Luke.

Luke's face pales, and he rubs a hand across his head. "Ahhh no, I forgot about that... I'm sorry." With supplication he holds his hands up. "It's so my fault. My bad, I should have warned you."

I wave away his apology. "It's fine." It really isn't, but normal people don't freak out over a small drop of blood. If I make any more of a fuss, all I'm going to do is raise suspicions and put a target on my back. He probably already thinks I am a weirdo. I don't want him or anyone looking closely at me. I need to remain invisible, a grey person.

Huh, being *grey* is hampered by my height and shocking hair colour. Girls with multicoloured hair are bright and bubbly. Aren't they? No one will look further than the smile on my face and the fake vacant look in my eyes. Smiling and being friendly to my new colleagues will help me blend in. No one will notice the quiet, friendly girl compared to the quiet girl that nervously skitters about glaring and beating the crap out of people. Aggressive Tru would stand out. I do not want to be standing out.

While he's feeling guilty, I can probably get a straight answer out of him. "So Luke." I lean forward in the chair. "Do you *like* Tilly?" I can't help grinning at his dumbfounded look at my change of subject.

"Yes?" he answers with a nervous laugh.

"Good. Tilly is one of the kindest people I know... so be good to her."

"Has she said anything about me?" Luke asks with an intense look as he leans against the desk.

I grin mischievously and clap my hands. "Maybe... Between you and me, there's a high chance if you asked her out on a date, she'd say yes."

Luke's smile overtakes his entire face, and his blue eyes dance. Miraculously, he forgets all about my faux pas and my weird behaviour. He taps the desk and nods. "Okay, thanks kid. Come on, let me show you the rest."

I trail after Luke into the club. The main overhead lights are on, and they're blazingly bright. The customer side of Night-*Shift* is impressive. The same plush carpet that's in the staff area covers the floor, with a fancy wooden sprung dance floor in the centre that breaks up the space. I'd been to a couple of clubs before my grandad got sick, with my older friends when I was about fifteen—it's hard to make sure people are old enough when lots of the clients are unageing—but they were never like this one. The combination of chrome, glass and leather makes the whole club look ultramodern, and once the main harsh lighting has gone down, I bet the place looks like something from a magazine. It's the very definition of an upmarket club.

Yeah, I can't wait to see what this place looks like when the lights are low and it's full of customers.

Like the outside, the security inside is just as impressive. Luke points out where the carefully positioned cameras are situated and where the security staff can be located if I need them.

I can see the deliberate use of magic. It is layered into the very fabric of the building. The multitude of spells cling to the floor, walls, the three bars, and the seating areas. Some of the spells I recognise. One will keep the floor magically clean—no sticky floor in this club. I don't know what the ones around the back of the bars do... perhaps protection? But I can hazard a guess that whatever that spell is used for, it won't be pleasant. It gives me goosebumps.

I get introduced to the prep staff who are getting everything ready to open. Luke allocates me an area to work from and explains my job. It's basic clean up. If there is a mess, I clean it. It's not rocket science, and it all seems pretty straightforward. Luckily, I don't need to touch anything behind the bar or go near those creepy spells.

I interact enough with customers at the café, so as a glass collector, not having to talk to customers is a bonus. I am going to be happy to mindlessly collect, wash glasses, and throw away the empty bottles in the concealed bins around the venue. Blend into the background unnoticed while earning a good wage.

The air-conditioning vent above my head blows wisps of my hair around. It's freezing. I rub my arms, brrrr. My goosebumps have goosebumps.

"When it gets busy, the air-conditioning is a godsend, not so much on setup though. It's always freezing," Luke says with a sympathetic smile. "We tried not having it on, and when we opened, it quickly became like a furnace. It was hell. So we keep it cold a few hours before we open." He points at the toilets. "Those are yours. Check them every hour. There's a maintenance cupboard with everything that you'll need. Fill toilet rolls and empty the waste bins. Just the ladies. You don't need to go into the gents." He claps his hands. "That's everything. Normally your shift won't start until we are open, so"—he flicks his wrist and checks the time—"go have a brew in the staff room. There is stuff in there supplied for everybody's use... um, unless it's got a name on it. You start at nine."

CHAPTER SEVEN

I'VE FINISHED for the day. I only did one eight-hour shift at the café, so I'm practically bouncing down the street. I have energy left to spare, hence the bouncing. With all this extra time on my hands, I hit the gym hard.

I find it hard to work out alone. I'm really missing my expensive fight training. It's been hard to stop something that has been a huge part of my life since before I can remember.

But as Grandad's illness got worse, our priorities changed. He couldn't work, and I had to step up to the plate and pay the bills.

Then there was his funeral to pay for.

After the whole homeless thing kicked in, the expensive one-to-one training became a thing of my past, a lost dream. I guess there have to be sacrifices.

So I settle for the gym classes that are included in my membership on top of doing my normal workout. Today I did an aerobic boxing class. I can't help my grin. The aggression and the grunts going on in that room... I will never see humans the same. Those ladies are scary. Talk about secret assassins—I'd rather spar with a shifter.

I'm surprised the combination of punching and dance actually makes me lighter on my feet. So I'm going to add a few more dance classes to my fitness regime. I'll try anything to keep my muscles toned and my body fit. Working every hour of the day isn't the same as working out. I need to keep my body in tip-top shape as I don't know when I will need it to get out of a hairy situation.

As I head for home, I enjoy the sun on my face. I'm sure I don't get enough of it. As a born vampire—well, half vampire—hell, any vampire—we aren't allergic to sunlight like some films will have you believe. I pass the park, which isn't at all creepy during the day. I take in the surrounding people, humans and creatures, all enjoying the pleasant weather.

There's a group of kids, teenagers probably around my age, messing around near the trees by the lake. They laugh, scream and tussle. I half-heartedly smile at their antics. What would it be like to have that kind of life, that kind of freedom? Spending time at the park with your mates, without a care, and the only thing you have to do is get home in time for dinner.

I had friends once. I growl and look away. I don't like the jealous feeling that spills into my blood like poison. My friends—I wrinkle my nose with disgust. They're long gone now; they didn't want to hang about when I suddenly became so serious. People are so finicky. The closest friend that I have now is my boss, Tilly, and wow, that's kind of sad.

I wasn't intended for an easy life, and that's okay. I shrug. I'd be bored to tears anyway. My steps continue, less bouncy and more like a shuffle, until the words "Let's set it on fire next" float on the soft breeze.

Without thinking—perhaps 'cause I'm nosy—I step away from the road and head into the park towards the direction of the lake. The grass crunches underneath my trainers, and I carefully step around some wild daisies. When I get closer to the group, I count nine boys.

My eyes narrow. What I see makes me break into a run.

Having vamp eyesight is a blessing and a curse. I wish I could unsee what those boys are doing, but I allow my growing horror to morph into a more useful anger. I've been good for so long I need to let off some steam. I barge my way through the group, putting a bit of power into it as I shoulder check two of them and they go flying. I'm not messing around. I stick my leg between another lad's legs and hook his ankle. I make sure to dig my boot into his Achilles tendon. He falls to the ground with a surprised wail.

I grab the knife from another boy's hand, and with a snap of my wrist, I throw the blade at his feet. It lands hard, piercing his trainer. He also drops to the ground, and with a scream that could wake the dead, he rolls around, clutching his foot in agony.

I growl at the other boys who are still on their feet. They must see something in my expression as a couple of them bolt. Two of the boys scrape themselves up off the ground and watch me warily. I turn away, giving them my back as I take in the tree.

"My name is Tru. They won't hurt you anymore." I keep my voice gentle. "Do you want me to call anyone? Ring the fae guild?" I ask even as I nervously swallow. I hate the idea of getting a guild involved, but this time it's not my decision. Yeah, it is the last thing I want to do, but this isn't about me.

It's about the pixie.

The pixie that's taped to the tree with duct tape shakes her head. The tip of one of her pointed ears narrowly misses the blade of a knife as she moves. I guesstimate she is around six inches tall.

Silver tears run from her large sapphire-blue eyes and sparkle against her cheeks. My heart drops to my feet. Something in my soul recognises her pain.

The knives embedded in the tree surrounding her tell me everything I need to know. One of them is so close it has ripped her trousers, exposing her sapphire-blue skin, and another has caught strands of her dark blue hair. The livid part of me swells to bursting. They've been using her for target practice—the evil shits.

I remember the words, *Let's set it on fire next*. I feel sick. What would have happened to her if I hadn't come over? Oh God. This is why I keep away from people.

My back is towards the reprobates, but my senses are on high alert, so I hear him approach. The ground crunches underneath his heavy footsteps, easily giving him away. He smells of sweat and something rancid. I wrinkle my nose and tug one of the blades—the one with strands of the pixie's hair—out of the tree. I turn my head and glare at him.

The blond boy is slightly older than his friends, and his attitude screams ringleader. His build is heavyset, but he's at least three—I narrow my eyes—maybe four inches shorter than me.

"Come any closer and I'll kill you," I snarl.

I don't look away from him as I flip the knife in my hand. It spins in the air, doing four rotations before I deftly catch it. The balance is off. His eyes widen a fraction, but of course he ignores his instincts and my warning and takes a swaggering step towards me.

The guy is an idiot.

I frown, and my head jerkily tilts to the side. Huh. He's also made a liar out of me. I should follow through with my threat of killing him... but my words were chosen wrongly. I can't kill him. Unfortunately, the park is too busy and I wouldn't get away with it. Next time I'll have to be a little bit more careful with the words that I say.

No, I won't be killing him today.

Even if he does deserve it. Unconcerned, I turn back to the tree. The way he moves tells me everything that I need to know. He's heavy on his feet, untrained, *human*. I keep him within my peripheral vision in case he does something else stupid, and I use the shit knife to carefully slice through the tape.

"What are you gonna do? There's nine of us," he says boldly.

I smirk. "I think you need a recount." I nod back at his group of friends. He follows my eyes.

"Five of us," he splutters. "And you're one girl. I think we should have some fun with you as well. Always wanted to *do* a giant." He finishes with a lick of his lips, and his hands dip towards his belt. Wow, he really is a filthy little beast.

I place myself between the thug—the now-wannabe rapist—and the pixie. "Am I supposed to be frightened? You aren't the predator here."

The guy with the knife in his foot takes that moment to wail, and I can't help my low chuckle. The blond human kid does a full-body shudder and steps back when he takes in my face, and he looks down at his friend who is rolling around on the ground. I don't think he expected me to laugh at him. He's so used to people being frightened of him I unnerve him.

"Ooh, I wouldn't pull the knife out just yet if I were you," I say helpfully to blade runner. My cheeks hurt as my lips tug into a crazy, bright smile. "I might have nicked something important. You don't want to bleed out."

I turn my attention to the other boys. "So is that what you are? Bullies and rapists?" Two guys flinch, so I aim my next words at them. "You got a mum? Sister?" I raise my eyebrows. "Girlfriend? How would you like your friend here casually saying that he's going to rape them?" I bare my teeth. "What do you think, shall we go grab them? Tie them to this here tree, listen to them cry and scream while your mate here throws knives at them? Or unzips his pants? Does that sound fun to you?"

They can't meet my eyes.

"She's not human, so it doesn't matter," the blond kid says.

"What the hell is wrong with you?" I shake my head and let my disgust show on my face. "You trust him, a guy like that, to have your back? What's going to happen when they find out what you've done? Torturing a pixie? Do you think they're going to be proud of you? If I were you, I'd put him down. I'd put him down before he puts you down."

I turn back to the pixie and drop my voice for her ears only. I'm conscious of the need to ask her for permission. She's already been through a traumatic experience, and I don't want to add to it. "I'm going to cut the final piece of tape. When I do, is it okay to hold you?" She nods.

"Okay."

With a final cut of the blade, the pixie is at least free of the tree. I hold her as gently as I can in my left hand. I cringe. I can scarcely see her underneath all that tape. How the hell am I going to get all the duct tape off her? I can see that she must have been struggling, so much so it's almost embedded into her skin. "Do you need me to drop you off at your burrow?" I ask gently.

"I have nowhere to go," she answers in a soft, lilting tone. Her face shines with more tears, and her eyes... She looks broken.

My heart hurts for her. "It's okay. I've got you." I raise my voice and address the boys. Two more have slinked off since I've had my back to them, including blade runner, who I'm amused to see is hopping away. I'm down to three. "You can't trust a guy who thinks it's okay to hurt an innocent creature. A tiny pixie. You know what that makes him—a psychopath. It makes you no better than him, his lackeys, and you're worse than he is 'cause you can't think for yourselves."

"We don't care," the blond kid says, puffing his chest. His blue eyes are alight with cruelty.

"*We* don't care. Oh you poor, silly puppets." I pout and shake my head at the two muppets. "Does it hurt with his hand so far up your arses?" I then smile back at the blond kid. Showing him my crazy.

Oh, he doesn't like that.

I almost want to rub my hands together with glee. He's the type of guy that I love to teach a lesson. Though you never know, my words might influence his so-called friends, and they might do the world a favour and take him out themselves.

"You will care. Especially when your muppet mates watch you get your head kicked in by a girl. Oops, how embarrassing." I fake giggle. His eyes glaze over with his rage. Look at that. I don't even have to go to him.

With a weird scream, like a bull, he drops his head and charges towards me, his arms flailing about madly.

I snort. This lad is used to using his weight to gain the upper hand. He's not even looking where he's going. I leave it to the last possible millisecond, then I step to the side and stick my foot out. As he runs past me, he trips and smashes his head into the tree. He's out like a light.

Huh, that's a little bit anticlimactic.

I poke him with my toe.

He's gonna have a right lump on his head. I peer at the knives still embedded in the tree. "Do you want me to stab him a few times?" I ask the pixie.

In response, she lets out a small shocked laugh. "No, thank you."

I give her a tiny smile. Her laugh gives me hope that she's going to be all right.

The rest of his motley crew have gone. They've left him. I shrug. He's not my problem.

If I could get away with it, I'd hunt those other boys down and hurt them. But they aren't worth the hassle of getting in trouble, and the pixie is my priority. "I have a friend that might be able to get this stuff off you. Is that okay?"

"Yes, thank you, Tru." She says my name shyly, as if she's worried she's going to say it wrong. "My name is Story."

"Nice to meet you. I'm going to run. Is that okay?" She nods again. "Okay. Let's get you sorted." I carefully hold the pixie in my hand and break into a jog.

I dash out of the park, down the street, and head into the city. I need something that will get between the tape and Story's delicate skin. I'm hoping Tilly will know what to do.

I fling the door to the café open, and the bell above clangs an off-tune protest. Tilly looks up from behind the counter, and as soon as she sees my face, she hurries towards me.

"Tru?"

"Tilly, please can you help my friend?" I ask, holding out my palm. Tilly frowns at me with confusion and then glances down at my cupped hand. As soon as she spots the poor pixie huddled in my palm, Tilly cries out with despair.

In response, Story drops her head and huddles further into herself. "It's okay. Tilly is a friend. Please don't be frightened," I whisper.

"Oh my Mother Nature... by the trees," Tilly splutters. Her horrified eyes meet mine. She rapidly blinks tears away, and a few blossom petals from her green hair float to the floor. "Of course, of course. We need to help this young lady immediately. Both of you come with me." Tilly pulls her apron off and leaves it on the counter. "Alex, I'm popping out. I'll be as quick as I can," she shouts as she hustles us out the door. "I have a friend, a witch. She's also a trained nurse. Please follow me."

A short walk away from the café is Birley Street. Smack bang in the middle of the street, sandwiched between an art gallery on the left and hairdressers on the right, in a modest-sized building is a witches' shop.

Tinctures 'n Tonics - Specialists in Portable Potions, the sign above says proudly.

My sensitive nose tingles. The shop smells heavily of herbs and magic, which makes me shiver. Tilly flings the door open, and we follow her inside.

I glance around the shop with interest. The wooden shelves are filled to the brim with magical artefacts, and a tingling hum of energy fills the air. The store is brightly lit—natural light filters through the enormous windows at the front, and fascinatingly, dozens of magical globes of light bob about in different corners of the room. I guess as the light in the shop changes throughout the day, the floating orbs will move to where they're needed. One is already bopping around above Tilly's head. Freaky.

"Jodie, Jodie," Tilly shrieks.

"Tilly? What on earth is wrong?" A pretty dark-haired witch looks up from a seat in the corner where she's reading an ancient tome.

"Oh, Jodie, I'm so glad you're here. We need your help," Tilly wails, rushing towards her friend.

As if a switch has been flipped, the witch goes into professional mode. She puts the huge book down and springs up from her chair and rushes around the counter. With a professional gaze, she assesses Tilly, and then her eyes fly to me.

"It's not me," I say. Once again, I hold out my palm.

Jodie gently smiles at Story. "Hello, my name is Jodie. You've come to the right place. I have just what you need to make you more comfortable. May I touch you?"

Story blinks up at the witch. Her enormous blue eyes then look at me for reassurance, and I give her a nod of encouragement.

"Yes, that's okay, I guess. My name is Story."

Jodie gently gathers her from my hand.

All of a sudden I don't want to let the pixie go. I watch with narrowed eyes as Jodie holds her in both hands. I nibble on my lip. I have to trust that Tilly knows what she's doing. "I can pay, so please do whatever you have to."

"Did you punish whoever did this?"

I guess... I nod.

"Good, that's payment enough. Come on, Story. Let's get you more comfortable."

Tilly and I follow the witch into her back room. The room is large but cosy, decorated in appealing warm tones. It has a proper wood-burning stove and a comfy seating area at one end and a beautiful, big, industrial-sized witches' kitchen at the other, with a table that can seat twelve in the middle.

Placing Story on the table, Jodie tells her everything that she's going to do and gets permission for every step. She uses potions to carefully remove the tape and to make sure that any scratches or sores are healed. Underneath all that tape is the most beautiful blue skin. Jodie even has clothing to replace the pixie's damaged ones.

"Thank you, thank you so much. I don't know what we would have done without you," I gush. I've never been more grateful. The witch's kindness has been humbling.

"Yes, thank you. You've all been very kind. I would have surely perished without all your help," Story adds.

"You're welcome," Jodie says with a gentle smile. "I am glad I could help. Story, if you ever need to talk about what happened, my door is always open."

"Thank you."

"Now Tru, are you going to take Story home?" Tilly asks. The pixie smiles, but her bottom lip trembles. "You do have somewhere to go, right?"

"I'll be fine. Thank you so much for all your help," Story answers quietly.

Shit, she has nowhere to go.

My heart jumps, and my own lip wobbles. Without thinking, I hear myself saying, "She can stay with me."

Nice one, Tru. She can stay in the garage 'cause that's the height of luxury. I want to smack myself on the forehead for being such a soft touch. But the look on Story's face, the way her sapphire eyes brighten, makes me realise I've done the right thing.

CHAPTER
EIGHT

"Is this your burrow?" Story asks. From the corner of my eye, I take in her perched form on my shoulder.

"Yeah, I guess... I'm sorry the place is—"

A dump. A garage. Shit.

"Amazing," Story finishes for me, her voice full of awe. She bounces down my arm into my waiting palm. Her delicate face could light the room with her excitement, her joy. Her bare toes dance on my hand as she spins. "This place is amazing," she whispers.

I shake my head and ruefully smile. All righty then. Who am I to argue with a pixie? Amazing it is.

I nervously wiggle and can't help but wince as I think about my negligible savings, yet I still open my mouth and hear myself say, "We need to get you some stuff." My new friend has to feel comfortable. She's already staying in a shitty garage, no matter what she says, I know what this place is, and she hasn't got anything. The poor girl needs things of her own. She needs necessities, and that at least is something I can do.

When I lost my home... When I got kicked out, I can only imagine how much harder that whole experience would have been if I hadn't had my things, my memories to cling to.

Story has nothing but the clothes on her back. And it hurts something inside me.

I don't want her to suffer, and if I can give her a tiny little piece of herself back, maybe... Maybe there's hope for me yet.

I grab my phone and start searching online; I find a few local stores that cater to pixies and, more importantly, have things within our price range. I want my new friend to have the freedom to communicate and to feel at home, so I find myself getting excited when I spot a dinky pixie phone. Oh my god, it is sooo cute.

It takes us another few hours to pick everything up—you've got to love click and collect, especially when you can buy items like a wardrobe and a bed and everything fits neatly inside a rucksack. Let's just say buying pixie-sized stuff is awesome.

When we get back to the garage, I gather my tools. I flip a screwdriver and give Story an encouraging grin. "Do you want to sleep in the shed with me, or do you want me to set something up so you have your own space in the garage?" Winter might be a concern, but I'm sure I can knock something up that will work.

"In the shed with you if that's okay. I don't want to be alone."

"Okey dokey, let's do this." I clap my hands. I have some wood left over from securing the garage's main up-and-over door, so at least this is within my budget—free. You've got to love free.

I hum as I knock together a wooden box, which will hopefully make a cosy bedroom. I don't, of course, say anything to my friend, but it's a bit like building Barbie's dream house.

Is it wrong for me to be enjoying myself?

I install a shelf in the top corner of the shed and secure her new bedroom. I cut a chunk from a bathmat as it makes a perfect carpet, and while Story watches, bouncing from foot to foot, I place her new bed and wardrobe inside.

"I wish I could brighten up the walls," Story says wistfully as she stands inside her room.

"Ohhh, I saw something. One sec—" I jump up and shimmy out of the shed, dive across the sofa, and dig into a bag of crap that I've been meaning to throw away. "Nope... nope... oh there." I pull out an old paint-by-numbers box that somehow got into Grandad's things. Let's just say the fae assassin I knew did not do paint by numbers. I grin when Story's eyes light up with excitement. The little pots of paint are pixie perfect, and I find a new mini lip-liner brush that will make a perfect-sized paintbrush.

Sat on my bed, I watch in awe as Story gets to work painting the most beautiful mural of a sunflower on her wall. She's so artistic. When she has almost finished, I go and grab dinner. Our time eating should give the paint a chance to dry, and then Story can clean up and organise her things.

"Oh Tru, this has been the worst, but also the best day of my life," she says, her bright blue eyes wide and earnest.

Wow, puff, my heart squishes. It's an addictive feeling.

We make a wonderful team.

After we've had dinner, I sit on the sofa and contemplate logistics. I need to think of the best way to make stairs, or perhaps even a ladder, so Story can access her new room without me. There's limited space in the shed what with all my stuff, and as Story's place hugs the ceiling, I might've caused an issue. I nibble my lip. Perhaps if I put a small door and erect something on the outside, that will make her more independent.

"Reow," my cat admonishes me, interrupting my thoughts. To prove to Dexter he's eaten every treat and to show him I'm not hiding anything, I present my hands to him like a human magician shows an audience that there is nothing up their sleeves. The cheeky cat waltzes across the sofa to me and sniffs my fingers to double-check.

"There's nothing left," I gripe.

I do not know how the hairy monster manages to make me feel so guilty. He eats better than I do.

I was hoping the treats would distract him and also encourage Dexter to be kind to Story. She's so tiny I'm worried for her safety. I don't want him to think it's okay to hunt her. But so far it looks as if Dexter will be on his best behaviour. I have a strong feeling that he already knows pixies aren't for eating, and he's shown nothing to prove he will be a danger to my tiny friend, which is a relief. I tickle him underneath his chin. "Who's a good boy? Yes, Dexter is. Dexter is such a good boy."

"I can't believe how blessed I am. I really am grateful for all my beautiful things. I mean you even have a *beithíoch* as a guardian. I know I will be very safe here." Story nods towards Dexter, who now has a back leg stuck in the air and is licking... urm... his bum. I frown. *Great first impression there, Dex.* I wrinkle my nose at his enthusiasm.

What Story said slowly registers. "A beithíoch..." They're huge fae monster cats, furless horrible eat-your-face-off things.

I look at Dexter's ginger fur. I've only seen beithíoch on television, and my Dexter isn't one. I hold in my laugh as I don't want to be rude to my new friend. I guess Dexter would look big to a pixie. "He's just a cat," I say as gently as I can with a smile and a shrug.

Story blinks at me, and then with a nod, she taps her tiny nose. "Oh yes, of course," she says as she adds a conspiring wink.

What the hell? My eyes flick about as I think, and my gaze lands back on Dexter. Nooo. No way. I narrow my eyes at him suspiciously. "Mert," he says and then goes back to his cleaning.

Huh, *mert* indeed. I shake my head and blow out my cheeks. I'm just going to ignore that whole conversation. I turn away and force myself to focus back on the problem of getting my friend to bed. I stare at the shed. Out of the corner of my eye I can't help but watch Dexter. Yep, I need to ignore that. He's just a cat. "What do you prefer to use, a ladder or stairs?" I ask Story, as ultimately she's the one that's going to be using whatever I knock up.

"Oh, um... I have something to show you. Please don't be mad."

I turn to look at her, and Story hops from foot to foot and nervously wrings her hands together. I give her an encouraging smile. Shit, things can't get any worse than the monster cat.

She gulps and closes her eyes. Sparkly pink magic appears behind her. "Oooh pink," I mumble appreciatively.

From one moment to the next Story has *wings*. I gasp and clap my hands. The pink magical wings flutter as she rises from the sofa and zips towards me. My eyes feel like they are going to pop out of my head, and I go a little cross-eyed trying to focus on her as she hovers perfectly in place in front of me. I rapidly blink with shock.

"Oh my god, Story, you have wings," I squeak out. The stunned awe in my voice makes her grin.

"Yes. My dad is a pixie, and my mum was a fairy. I inherited her wings." She spins in a circle, giving me an excellent view of her beautiful appendages.

I lift my hand, and without touching them, my fingers trace the air around the delicate wings. "Wow, they're so pretty. The pink rose gold against your blue skin is breathtaking. Why did you think I'd be mad?" Story's grin is wiped away with my words, and she slowly sinks down to stand on the arm of the chair.

"I'm an abomination," she whispers, and her wings disappear.

Dejectedly she plops on her bottom and crosses her legs.

What the fuck. I frown.

"When my wings appeared, my troupe threw me out. They said..." A tear rolls down her cheek, and a lump grows in my throat at seeing her pain. Wow, Story is different just like me. I knew there was something special about her. "They said—"

"They called you an abomination?" I finish for her gently, and she nods. My heart hurts for her.

"They threw me out, and I had nowhere else to go but the park as it's a free territory. I've been there for weeks. I thought I was being careful, and then those awful boys trapped me and I thought I was going to die. For a moment, just for a moment"—she lifts her eyes and looks at me as more tears stream down her face, and she hiccups as she rubs a hand across her cheeks—"I was glad. I wanted to die, as who would want an abomination like me?"

"You're not an abomination, Story. You. Are. Incredible," I say earnestly. "You're the prettiest fae I have *ever* seen."

"I am?" she asks in disbelief.

"Yes, you are," I reply. My voice rings with my conviction. "But don't tell Tilly," I wink, "as it will upset her." I see it when the truth of my words registers as her eyes widen. Story rushes towards me and jumps into my palm. She throws her blue arms around my thumb and... She *hugs* my thumb. I rapidly blink as my eyes fill up, and I have to swallow a few times to clear the emotion from my throat. Carefully, gently, I wrap my fingers around her tiny body and hug her back.

"I got you," I murmur.

I've got her back.

CHAPTER NINE

I HAND the customer her order, a pot of Earl Grey tea and a lemon pastry; she shuffles away with a half-hearted thank-you. The café is quiet. The city has been weird lately, and its inhabitants have felt the change in the air and are sensibly keeping away.

I yawn so big my jaw clicks. I am bored.

Story has finished her latest wedding cake. She unzips her protective suit—a hygiene precaution as she has to crawl all over the cakes to apply the delicate icing—and wiggles out of it. She ties the arms around her waist and stands back with her hands on her slim hips to survey her masterpiece.

"Hey, roomie, can you lift me? I need to see it from a higher perspective."

I nod and slap my palm down on the counter to let her jump on board. Her wings shed tiny particles of fairy dust, so using them inside the café is a big no-no.

I have no problem with being her elevator.

I lift her for a better view, and we both stare silently at the three-tier cake with its pink sugar petals and silver pearls.

"Nice," I say helpfully. It's a cake. If it tastes good, it's a good cake. If it tastes bad... I shrug. Yeah, I've no idea what I am looking at.

"It's perfect," Story says with a satisfied smile, and her sapphire cheeks glow with pride.

Story has proven herself to be super artistic. When I showed Tilly the photos of the sunflower that she'd painted on her bedroom wall, Tilly wanted to know if Story could do that design again but on a cake. All it took was some guidance and encouragement from Tilly, and Story rapidly clocked up some fancy skills in cake decorating. My friend has genuine talent, and her cake designs, I admit, are beautiful.

I've no idea how they do what they do. There's no way Tilly would let me near her cakes. She barely lets me near the pastries, ha. I can imagine what a mess I'd make. I am more a Hulk-smash kind of girl than artistic.

Although some fighting moves can be artistic, so I am not without skill. Fighting can be beautiful. A splash of blood, the crunch of bone... I lick my lips.

Vampire.

I might be a vegetarian, but I can still appreciate the grim details of a good fight and blood without having to partake. I scrunch my nose with the thought. Blood and me, we are soooo not friends.

Story taps her foot, her signal that she wants to go down. Obediently, I drop my hand, and she jumps back onto the counter. Even though she is getting a fair wage—she earns more than I do—Story still insists on living in the garage with me and Dex. She also didn't think twice about adding her wages to mine so we now have a growing pot of savings.

I'm so grateful.

It won't be long till we have enough money to move, and Story says she'll put the place in her name so we don't have to wait for my birthday.

How good is that?

Things are finally looking up.

"Storm winds," Tilly swears. "We're out of eggs. How can we be out of eggs? The new delivery company is diabolical." A cupboard door slams, and a harassed Tilly stomps towards us. She heads for the till and madly presses the buttons.

"Do you want me to ring them?" I ask sweetly while rubbing my hands together with glee.

"No, I'll do it. You'll only frighten them, and you're the reason that we have to use a new supplier and delivery company anyway."

Oh yeah, oops.

The till prints a receipt, and the drawer pops out with a ding. Tilly grabs the receipt and signs it, then stuffs it back into the till, swapping it for a twenty-pound note. "Would you take a trip to the shop and grab a few dozen?"

"No problem." I rip my apron off and throw it into the staff room without looking. Miraculously, it hits the counter and doesn't fall to the floor. I do a funky-chicken victory dance. What a shot.

Tilly tuts.

Story giggles.

I snatch the twenty out of Tilly's hand and head out the door.

"Don't forget to get a receipt," Tilly shouts after me. I wave my hand. "Oh, Story, that's the best one yet. I love the placement of the pearls..."

ON THE WAY back from the shop with the bag of eggs swinging in my grip, I see a vision. I spy wide shoulders, and I speed up my steps. I can only see the back of him, so I've no idea what has got me so intrigued. I guess you just know. When a guy is gorgeous from the back, you just know instinctively that he's going to be just as good-looking from the front. He has to be. Nature couldn't be that cruel.

Oh, and I'm also a sucker for hair-free necks. And whoever cuts his dark hair, they've cut it into perfection, short on the sides, floppy on top. He's also tall, like *really* tall. Which is a massive plus point. I'm lucky I can ogle all the supernatural guys as it's rare for human males to be taller than me. I like feeling strong, and I work out hard to have the body that I have, but sometimes I also like to feel feminine, and creatures do tend to come on the big side.

Yep, he's rocking the wide shoulder, narrow hip, bubble-bottom body, and with his jacket off and the sleeves of his dark grey striped shirt rolled up to show the most tantalising, incredible forearms. *'Ello, Mr Stripey Shirt.* I shake my head. I don't even like forearms. I had heard the term *arm porn,* and it was something I'd always sneered at. How can a guy's forearm be sexy?

Yeah, Mr Stripey Shirt showed me. Even from a distance, his arms are just... he is just—I cough. Those babies almost make me swallow my tongue.

His head turns, and I almost get a side view of his face. I tilt my head and—

—and I slam into a lamppost.

Ouch.

I keep my arm with the plastic bag out to the side; I saved the eggs, but I didn't save my embarrassment. Please God please... shit, I hope he didn't see that. I rest my sore forehead against the cool metal, and my eyelashes batter against it as I blink.

I peek in his direction, and he's no longer there.

Phew. I just hope he didn't see me go smack.

I'm not so lucky with the other shoppers on the street. Two teenage boys elbow each other and laugh at me. I'm sure I catch one of them mouth, *Ooh, that's got to hurt.* I groan. Why did I think learning to lip-read was a good idea? I wipe my hand across my red face and roll my shoulders. Okay. I better get back to work.

CHAPTER
TEN

THE CONSTANT FLASH *flash flash* of the lights is giving me a headache. The customers around me are happily dancing, drinking, and shouting to be heard over the pounding bass. The club smells of sweat and old beer and the occasional cloying perfume.

The first few shifts I was so excited to be working here, but after a few short weeks, the excitement dulled. Yeah, it got old real fast.

I'm not a naive person. Even though I'm young, I've always considered myself pretty worldly. Grandad made sure that I knew about every danger. But there's a big difference between knowing and *seeing*. Experiencing.

Yeah, a vast difference.

I don't know why—perhaps it's a club thing—but Night-*Shift* seems to bring out the worst in people. Their baser instincts are all on display for others to see.

To say it's been eye-opening so far wouldn't be an exaggeration. Working here is sure educational.

If I didn't already know that I wasn't a people person, ha, I know now.

I don't even take in the people having fun. They're just bodies in the way of getting my job done. When I started snarling at them with poorly veiled contempt, and I had visions of me committing murder, I flicked a switch in my head. Instead of annoying people, I imagine them to be objects, moving objects that I have to work around. 'Cause if they're people, I get irate with them, where if they are *objects,* they can't be held accountable for their actions and they don't matter to me. I know it's strange... but it works for me and my weird hybrid brain.

To help blend in, I wear baggy trousers instead of my leggings, and I've swapped out the tight club T-shirt for an oversized polo. Thank God I haven't inherited the perfect model looks of my born vamp side. There'd be no way of hiding then. My silhouette is shapeless. On my feet, I wear my old comfortable Doc Martens boots, and on my head a club baseball cap with the brim pulled down low. To stop my heavy hair from getting in the way—dipping the ends of my hair in a leftover pint isn't on my to-do list—I keep it in a tidy plait and stuff the end out of the way down the back of my top.

I blend into the background. I'm sure they think I'm a boy, which is fine by me. What I have found is it's rare for people to see beyond what you present to them. I am not here to look attractive, and I don't care what anyone thinks as long as I'm getting paid. I keep my head down and avoid drunk grabby hands like a pro.

I am invisible, just how I like it.

I'm finally getting used to my hectic schedule of balancing regular double shifts at the café with two nights a week at Night-*Shift*. Heck, who am I kidding... I close my eyes and shake my head. I feel like I'm sleepwalking from one job to the next.

Back behind the bar, in a side room, I robotically unload and then reload the glass washer, then I trudge back out. I weave around the customers, grabbing glasses as I go. I need to keep moving. If I stop, I might seize up. I am a seventeen-year-old badass hybrid, yet I feel like I'm an eighty-year-old human. I don't understand it. I'm supposed to be young, sprightly, bouncy—but I wake up in the morning, and my whole body aches and my bones creak. So I do what you'd expect a hybrid to do while in hiding. I ignore it. I just need more time to get used to these extra hours, that's all, and the early cold weather isn't helping. Summer has moved on, and it feels like we've skipped autumn completely. The garage is freezing, and it's messing with me.

I dodge out of the way of a stumbling, giggling *object* with sky-high heels. I try not to think about my own throbbing feet. About an hour ago, my boots stopped being comfortable—at some point during these last few weeks, my boots moulded to my feet. Even when I take them off, I feel like they're still on. Tonight the damn things have their own heartbeat. Thanks to today's double shift at the café, I'm entering the sixteenth hour of working.

Four hours to go. Yay. Then a nap at the gym—the spa has a brilliant area where I can lie down and listen to strange relaxing music—'cause there is no point going home. Then off I go to the café and do it all again.

I yawn.

One more full crazy day and then I have the whole of Sunday to sleep. Or I'll try. Dexter, after two days of surviving on dry cat food and no attention from me and no doubt bored with terrorising Story, will show his displeasure. I'll be lucky to sleep the day away what with all the howling.

I can't wait.

I smirk. There is no point in informing him that he was a stray before he butted into my life, and he isn't alone. He'll have none of it. Yes, my cat is smart, and like every cat owner, I know he understands every word I say.

The responsibility for the welfare of both the pixie and the cat keeps me going. At least I'm no longer on my own.

I avoid an *object's* hand as it tries to grab my arm. "Oi, mate, do you know where the gents is?"

I point.

"Cheers, pal."

A crowd of objects gather around the end of the main bar, staring at the big water feature. The fancy tank has an honest-to-God mermaid. Sometimes I wish I had her job. All she has to do is float in her tank and flip her hair. I smirk and shake my head as I see her rub her boobs against the glass to the delight of the male objects.

Huh, I guess getting stared at all the time might not be my go-to thing. I'd rather collect glasses and keep my boobs covered.

The nightclub is busy tonight. The atmosphere is buzzing with a strange excitement over and above the usual we-are-out-to-have-fun vibe, and it puts me on edge. As if my thoughts have trickled into fate's ear, excited energy ripples through the club like a wave. I lift my eyes and scan the crowd. It could be an indication of a fight brewing or a predator stirring the human herd. A lot of humans visit the club, as it's a relatively safe walk-on-the-wild-side environment. A lot of people seem to get brave after drinking copious amounts of alcohol, and they beg for the opportunity to gain some creature's attention.

Pick me, pick me. Bloody idiots. More like eat me, eat me. I snort. I find it strange. Humans are prey. Why would they want to play with the creatures that could kill them?

The buzzing energy makes my skin feel tight. The feeling is palpable, like a celebrity has arrived and everyone is vying for their attention. The objects around me freeze, and even in their inebriated states, they nudge and point.

I tilt my head to the side with interest. Seven huge shifters—they're head and shoulders above the regular customers—make their way through the club. As if moved by magic, the objects dive and scramble out of their way. The men walk in a box formation, two at the front, three in the middle, and two at the rear.

My whole world stops—it freezes. Nothing exists for me at that moment as my eyes greedily take *him* in. It is the seventh man, the one in the middle that holds my interest. He doesn't prowl like the shifters. No, he moves like liquid, he flows. I've never seen anybody move like him, and that's why I instantly recognise him. My heart thuds with excitement, and my body pings awake. I can't help grinning.

It's *him*.

Boom. I was right, the man is breathtakingly beautiful.

My guy. Well, urm, not my guy... He's obviously not mine. I roll my eyes. God, he must be important as he is in the middle of their protective grouping. He isn't a shifter, no. He is something else. As soon as I see him my tummy flips as if there's a creature inside me playing bongo drums with my organs.

I raise my eyebrows and I lick my lips. His power is exotic. It tickles against my senses. It's a testament to how strong he is that I can feel him from way over here.

He turns his head, and his glowing gold eyes look in my direction. I squeak, drop my head, and scuttle behind a pillar. Which I then peek around.

Yeah, my game is strong.

I rub the back of my neck with embarrassment. I can feel myself steadily going bright red, and I'm all of a sudden extra sweaty.

I'm not blind to the opposite sex, and I'm not an innocent fluffy virgin either. I've definitely disproved the rumour about unicorns and virgins. I scuff the toe of my boot against the carpet and kick the bottom of the pillar. And what an epic mistake that was. Boys? Men? Meh, I can take them or leave them, dismiss them without a second thought, no problem.

Boys are disgusting.

No, I haven't got the time or the inclination to pursue anything romantic with anybody.

But... this guy... does *it* for me.

To me, he is male perfection.

Yeah, he's absolutely beautiful. But he's an older guy. He is also a powerful, deadly unknown creature. That double combination spells trouble with a capital *T*.

I mean look at the way he affects me. I am having palpitations while hiding behind a pillar. I haven't even spoken to the guy, and if I'm honest, I probably never will. I mean good God, just looking at him freaks me out.

I rest my glowing cheek on the pillar. I know it's stupid to pant over some guy, some stranger who will never know I exist.

I haven't even got time to dream about him.

Huh, that's what he is... He's a dream. A beautiful dream—gorgeous and completely unattainable. Liable to mess with my head.

I can't be trusted. These feelings I have can't be trusted. I can continue to admire him from afar or... *Shut up, Tru*. No, he is better off far away from me.

I stare at his retreating, muscled form, my mouth watering for him.

BROGAN THOMAS

My life is one misstep into an early grave. There is no point going there, even if it's in my head. I can't have dreams past tomorrow.

I sigh as he smiles cordially at a shifter and—ouch. Someone bumps into me. I blink. I shake my head; I look back, and he's disappeared into the VIP area.

CHAPTER
ELEVEN

The VIP area needs cleaning, my inside voice whispers. My heart beats faster with the thought. He will be there, holding court.

I bet he likes to sit at the back in the shadows. No matter what dark corner he finds himself in, he will always stand out. As his golden eyes glow. I've never seen that before. Most creatures, if they have crazy eyes, they only start glowing or flashing when they're angry. His eyes seem to glow for no reason. I can normally taste anger in the air—it's my creature bread and butter—so I know he isn't angry.

I think I'll go and clean another area of the club.

I'm exhausted. If I stop and stare at every good-looking man, I won't be able to get any work done. I move away with less enthusiasm than I had before, gripping the grey plastic handle of the glass-collecting basket. It bounces on my thigh in front of me, and the glasses clink.

He is just another body, another *object*. My focus is on earning enough money so I can get myself out of the situation I'm in at the moment.

I can save myself. I have every faith in that... I have to.

I shuffle, and the varied pressure on the soles of my feet is almost painful. When I go to the gym, I'm gonna use the Jacuzzi and aim the water jets at my feet. The thought of a water massage on my aching toes makes me shiver. I can't wait.

I notice out of the corner of my eye a petite, curvy redhead. She pops a hand down the front of her dress and adjusts her boobs and lifts them so they're front and centre. I blink a few times. Wow, the girl has no shame. Shoulders back, she struts towards the VIP. Her hips swing like a pendulum. She struts like she's on a catwalk, her strides powerful and confident.

Her red hair flutters behind as she creates her own wind.

A doorman heads her off before she can get anywhere near. He quietly takes her to the side and starts talking to her. I watch her shake her head and point at my stripey-shirt guy. Half of me is impressed. The other half of me wants to rip her fucking head off.

She's really brave. I wonder what it would be like to be that kind of woman who can approach a man with all that sass.

"Mm-hmm, I didn't think that move would work for her, stupid cow. Some women have got to learn when men are completely out of their league." The female behind me snorts. "I bet she feels really stupid."

I turn to the girl who is talking to me. Jenny. She works behind the bar.

"I thought she was really brave," I say with a small tentative smile. I'm too tired for this shit. I hate small talk. "How's your night going? Not long to go now... I'm knackered."

Jenny responds with an impressive hair flick. Her blonde locks fly over her shoulder and hit a customer in the face. I think it also splashes into his drink. That's why I keep my thick rainbow hair in a tidy plait down the back of my top. It looks like Jenny doesn't care.

For the hell of it—to act like a normal person—I give him a small conciliatory smile.

He frowns back at me, looks at Jenny with interest, and then shuffles away when she glares at him.

"As if Xander would touch her."

"Xander?"

"Where have you been living, under a rock?" Garage. "The tall guy, with the glowing eyes. You know." Her voice drops. "Xander."

"Xander." I silently mouth. I'm feeling a little baffled.

"The angel? Our boss? He owns the club. God girl, you're dense." Jenny rolls her eyes and again flicks her hair.

A real life angel, here?

Wow. He'd have to be of a high level of power to be on Earth. They aren't native creatures of this world. Angels aren't like the religious depictions the humans cling to. Some believe that both races, angels and demons, had input into early human and creature history... poking their noses into our evolution, nudging us all in their preferred direction. Angels have *omnipotent* powers and are scary. I know they exist—according to Jenny I've just been ogling one—but they are super rare.

She continues casually talking as if she didn't drop a bombshell; I ignore her as my thoughts rattle around in my head. *His name is Xander, and he's an angel. An honest-to-God angel.*

"So new girl, what are you doing working here?" She throws me the same glare as she did the guy. I wonder how many times she's asked me that same question while I've been woolgathering. "What's your angle?" Jenny plonks her hands on her hips and leans forward, invading my personal space.

Is she trying to intimidate me? I hide my amusement and look back at her blankly.

"I'm just here to make money," I say, heavy on the fake confusion that interlaces my tone. "Urm... do my job and, you know... urm, go home." I tentatively smile. "My name is Tru."

His name is Xander, and he owns the club, my head screams.

"Yeah, I know that." She waves her hands in the air dismissively. "So Tru, you're not here to get turned?" Oh, okay, that's the reason that she's talking to me. She wants to know if I'm any competition. I know that a lot of staff and a lot of the customers come here hoping to catch a strong creature's eye. Looks like Jenny fancies herself a vampire.

Turned vampires are dead. Like dead-dead. When humans or even other creatures are turned, they die. They keep their age at turning, gain a rot smell and... perhaps a little extra strength and speed.

They also gain a little more time on this shitty planet, technically a few extra hundred years. Three hundred at a push before their body breaks down. *If* they live that long. Bitten vampires can be volatile and the Houses use the young ones as cannon fodder.

I shake my head. "Nope, I'm just here to earn money." I smile again. My cheeks pull and throb with all the action. I don't think I've smiled this much at one person in years. "I'm sure if that's what you want you'll have no problem as you're so pretty." Gag. I tell her what she wants to hear. Jenny smiles smugly.

"Oh," she says leaning closer, her eyes fixate on my forehead. "Look at that. Even your eyebrows are multicoloured." She flicks my hat up, and I knock it back down with a frown. "Who did your hair potion? Does it affect every hair?"

I blink. I don't understand her question. Every hai— Oh my god. Jenny crosses her arms and drops her eyes meaningfully to my crotch.

My pubes. She wants to know if I have rainbow pubes.

Ha.

I'm mortified.

"So?"

"So?" I squeak.

"The witch who did the potion?"

All my hair is natural. Bloody hell, do women actually ask each other these sorts of questions? If they do, I can't help thinking I'm glad I haven't got any close human friends. I rub my forehead. Who talks about pubes in public?

Gah.

"Tinctures 'n Tonics, Specialists in Portable Potions on Birley Street." I mumble the name and address of Jodie's store.

Jenny nods. "Thanks, I'll check them out. You know, new girl, you could be kind of pretty if you didn't hide behind those awful clothes and that hat. I mean even lesbians can attempt to look attractive once in a while."

I look down at my baggy clothing. Lesbian? Ha, I might have hit that last compliment a little bit too hard. I shrug. "Urm, nice talking to you, Jenny. I better get back. I don't want us to get into trouble." I give Jenny a wave as I rush away like my bottom is on fire.

I lose myself in the crowd. That woman is nuts.

I squeak and my mouth pops open in shock as a hand lands smack between my thighs, and the fingers wiggle.

They wiggle.

I act so fast, too fast to think. I step to the side, grab the offender's wrist, and thrust the hand in the air. He's made the worst mistake of his life in touching me.

When I turn to check out my quarry, I find the idiot touched me with his hand behind his back. Who does that? Not only did he touch me without permission, he thought it was a good idea to stick his hand out behind his back and touch me without looking.

Was he attempting to be sneaky?

Oh, somebody just assaulted me, so it can't possibly be the guy with his back towards me... Fucker.

Unfortunately for him, I now have his dirty hand in the air, and his arm is twisted in an awkward position behind him. He leans forward to alleviate the pressure. In his other hand he clutches a pint of beer. He's too stupid to live. He's also human.

"What kind of stupid human shoves his hand between a girl's legs in a shifter club?" I snarl in his ear. I have to tamper down the urge to rip his throat out. "You're a naughty boy," I say louder, condescendingly.

The men surrounding him laugh. With a flip of a finger, I tip the bottom of his drink. The beer splashes down him, leaving a nice wet patch on his crotch. His friends howl with laughter.

"I am not done," I whisper menacingly every female with a pulse. He screams when I add pressure to his arm, and with a vicious twist to his elbow, I break it. I don't give him any time to react as I grip the back of his head and unceremoniously slam it onto the table in front of him. "You do not"—slam—"touch women"—slam —"without permission" —slam—"that's assault."

I let go of him, and he slumps to the floor, unconscious. His friends are no longer laughing.

One guy holds his hands up, and the other two give me frightened nods.

"Take him and go home. Never come here again," I growl, my tone laced with compulsion. I don't wait for the impact of my words to see them go all zombie. Instead, I turn and stomp away, crushing the unconscious guy's fingers underneath my boot for good measure.

You know when you have one of those days when you think things can't get any worse? Of course it does.

Yeah, that's the story of my life.

"What do we have here?" Great. This one's a shifter.

My tolerance for bullshit is at an all-time low.

Why isn't my baggy disguise working tonight? I mentally whine. Have they been putting stuff in the drinks or is there a full moon that's making every man in the building crazy?

He leans towards me and takes a big sniff. "You smell nice," he groans.

He breathes in deep. Instead of it being sexy, it reminds me of a predator sniffing out its prey. Or worse, marking its territory. Fuck that. I give him an awkward nod. Men who over-the-top flirt like this make me feel uncomfortable. It's pretty obvious to me he's a shifter, so I don't know why he's sniffing at me. It's just weird.

I'll try my best to extract myself from this situation without being rude—I need this job—even if everything inside me wants me to punch Mr Sniffy in the face. I was lucky to get away with the altercation with the human before.

Now he's got my attention, he gives me a lecherous look that makes my skin crawl. "My name's Frank. What's your name, sweetheart?" He runs his dirty fingers through his greasy brown hair, pulling the mass away from his face. "I haven't seen you around here before. You're not dressed to impress, are you? Those long legs should be in a skirt and heels, not those"—he pulls a face at my baggy trousers—"whatever those are. You're so tall. Are you a model?" His tongue flicks out like a snake as he licks his lips.

I shake my head no, and it takes everything in me not to roll my eyes. *I'm working, dickhead. Sorry my ball gown is at the cleaners.*

Usually, when a person first meets me, they tell me how tall I am. What, really? I am tall? Nooooo, I didn't notice. Gah, I get that I'm tall. Thanks for pointing that out.

It's then followed by either are you a model or are you a shifter?

"You got a bit of shifter in you?" Bingo, there we go. Same old shit from a different mouth. It's so predictable that it gets boring.

I vigorously shake my head. Nope, not going there. I am not a shifter... As if I'm going to admit that.

My feet are killing me, and every time I look at my watch, only a few minutes have passed. I mentally groan. This shift is never-ending.

Freaky Frank licks his lips again. My nostrils flare, and I try—I really do try—to remain polite.

I need to talk my way out of this, but I have an itchy fist. It itches to meet his face.

"Do you want a shifter in you?" He smirks, cups himself, and thrusts his hips at me. Ew, no, he did not just say that. Screw being polite.

"Yeah, I get what you mean without the hip action, Grandpa. I'm seventeen, you perve." I tut at him with disgust and turn to leave. I give myself a mental pat on the back. There, see? Sometimes violence doesn't solve everything.

The idiot grabs me.

"Old enough to bleed—" he whispers in my ear.

My control snaps, and I take a swing at him. My knuckles smash into his throat, followed by a well-placed knee to the groin.

He drops like a stone.

"Oops, that's gotta hurt." I bring my foot back to kick him in the ribs, and a heavy arm wraps around my waist. I'm pulled into a muscly torso.

Shit, he's a big bugger.

I squirm in his ironclad hold. My baseball cap comes off and tumbles to the floor. "Get the fuck off me," I say as I wiggle.

I bring my elbow back and hit him square in his rock-hard abdomen.

Ouch.

"What are you made of, rocks? Get off me!" *Nice one, Tru. How the hell are you gonna get out of this?*

My eyes drop to the muscled, thick-like-a-tree-trunk arm that's wrapped around me. Golden skin with a smattering of dark hair.

Huh, a fine example of a veiny, hot-looking forearm.

I snap my teeth and growl as I viciously pull at the dark forearm hair while simultaneously attempting to hook my foot around his equally tree-like leg. I just need to throw him off balance. Or get my teeth into that meaty forearm.

"No biting," he murmurs, holding me tighter. The big bugger then lifts me higher and traps my flailing legs between steel calves. I continue to pluck at his arm hair, and with an angry grunt, one big hand swoops in and grabs both my wrists. I don't think anyone has ever made me feel so small before.

I can feel each of the hard muscles stacked along his body as they dig into my softness, even through our clothes.

Is this guy the perve's friend? Another shifter?

Why the hell didn't I watch my back?

This is poor form Tru, embarrassingly poor. I know bloody better. I lost my temper with the shifter, and this is the result. I throw my head back to headbutt him, but instead, my head smashes into his rock-hard chest. I groan as black spots dance across my vision.

Shit, he must be a few inches above seven foot.

He grunts and manoeuvres my body closer. I'm now plastered head to toe against him.

I'm trapped.

Wrapped around the massive monster of a man... like a person-shaped pretzel. I blow out a frustrated breath.

Well... This isn't embarrassing, not at all.

"Calm down." His voice is like fingers trailing deliciously down my spine. I can't help my shiver at the chocolaty tone. "What are you doing, attacking our customers?"

Our customers? Is this guy security?

With a growl, I turn my head to glare at the idiot. My cheek brushes against the giant's bumpy chest and soft shirt.

Oh no no no no.

My eyes widen as they meet the most incredible eyes, and my heart misses a beat, and I freeze. I can feel my cheeks go instantly pink.

Shit, it's *him*.

The one I've been stalking. I mean following... observing. Observing is a much better word than stalking.

Oh no no. Oh no no.

I cringe. Mortified, I slam my eyes closed. I've been plucking the arm hair, elbowing, and kicking the big boss.

Yeah, I'm pretzeled around my hot boss.

Xander. Jenny said his name was Xander. Oh boy. Now would be a great time for the ground to swallow me up.

Fuck my life.

CHAPTER TWELVE

I OPEN my eyes and peek at him through my lashes. My heart hammers in my chest for a very different reason.

Hecky thump. The guy is even more gorgeous close up.

Wow, he has the most incredible eyes. They're the colour of warm honey. My eyelashes flutter.

Dark hair, warm skin tone, beautiful eyes, wide forehead, high cheekbones, elegant nose, firm chin. Altogether it mashes into the most pleasant male beauty. My stripey-shirt guy is intently staring down at me.

All I can do is stare back.

More heat spreads across my cheeks. Crap, my face has got to be tomato red. I bet it's so red it's glowing.

Is my top lip sweaty? It feels sweaty.

My throat feels dry, I guess because all my spit is accumulated in my mouth. I wrinkle my nose and swallow the mouthful. Surreptitiously, I rub my lips together in case I'm drooling.

Belatedly, I realise I'm still staring.

His bright, seductive energy is intoxicating. His power heats my blood and curls my toes.

I slow blink. How the hell did I get here?

I bet this happens all the time; I bet he has women just throwing themselves at him. God, how embarrassing. What did I do? No, that's not right—he grabbed me 'cause I was beating up a shifter.

Crap.

My mouth pops open, and I take a fortifying breath to explain what happened just now with the shifter, but my vocal cords seem to be frozen, and instead of words, I make a strange gurgling noise. My eyes widen. He's going to think I'm a total idiot.

Crap, I still haven't said anything.

He's now staring back at me with total bewilderment and perhaps... if I'm not mistaken, a dash of contempt.

The energy coming off him sets fire to my nerve endings. I can taste the testosterone he exerts on my tongue.

My body trembles with fear as the full extent of his power and scent registers.

Wow, he smells good, whispers the inappropriate little voice in my head.

Sniff. Sniff.

Underneath all that anger is a deceptively alluring scent—an intense burst of metal mingled with sunlight—and my terror... and ahem... my *lust*.

"I lost my temper," I finally husk out.

His eyes shine like liquid honey, his mouth is in a firm line, and his jaw is tight. "I see that." His voice is soft and silky, at odds with his livid expression.

With some secret signal, two doormen appear from the sidelines, and the rude shifter is roughly scraped to his feet and escorted away.

"What I would like to know is how a slip of a girl can take down a twenty-five stone shifter?"

Oops.

My head pounds as I try to think of a good excuse. I can't think with him wrapped around me. "Pilates," I blurt out.

"Pilates," he says with some amusement.

"Mm-hm."

My body still wrapped around him is now warm, pliant. I could probably stay here for a few more minutes... It wouldn't be a hardship.

I think this is one of the best moments of my life.

If I can ignore my embarrassment. "Can I, urm, get down?"

"You good?"

"Yeah, I'm good," I say with a squeak.

His disbelieving grunt makes me shiver. He releases my legs from between his calves. Then ever so carefully, he slides me down his body until my feet hit the floor. Once I'm standing, he lets go of my wrists and steps away.

Suddenly I'm cold.

My body trembles like I just survived an encounter with a god. *A sex god*, my brain happily pipes up. When I try to walk, I discover my legs are barely strong enough to hold me up. I lean against a high table. I am shaking.

I peek up at him.

I have to tip my head back, he's so tall. My hands nervously twist together as I take him in. He's even bigger than I remember from stalki —observing him from afar.

Huge.

I take in a deep breath, and the tantalising whiff of metal and sunlight in his scent whizzes up my nostrils. The glorious smell is on my skin. I hug myself and hum. Hell, I won't shower until that scent all but fades.

The expression on his beautiful face is one of censure.

He is pissed.

Ah shit.

His anger is a heavy thing. I can feel it now, like a weight bearing down on me.

I feel suddenly awkward. Trapped in his golden glare. Overheated.

"Are you going to sack me?"

"No, he had it coming, but don't go all Xena like that again. I won't be so forgiving next time. You get one chance. I won't give you another. We have rules for a reason. Any issues with our customers, and you signal to security. You don't go around smacking customers in the face. Got it?"

Why is he calling me Xena? "My name is Tru," I grumble.

"I know," he says with a growl. "Got it?" His dark eyebrows raise, and if possible, his eyes harden.

"Yeah, I got it. No smacking customers in the face. Call security." I wave my hand in the air, and my arm twinges. I frown and rub my elbow.

God, and I thought my six-pack was impressive... The boss is built like a tank.

Shit, I was in his arms, held against his body. That was hot. I'm not too proud to admit to myself the boss is sexy as—*I want to lick him.*

My tongue hits the back of my teeth to double-check that it's still in my mouth, where it belongs, rather than waggling outside my mouth at him.

Want him. Want him. Want him.

The sweet blood that I can smell running through his veins appeals to me on an instinctive level. The vampire inside me pleads for a sample. I scratch my nose to cover my mouth as my teeth ache.

Both sides of me agree—even the unicorn—that I can have a little nibble on his neck. Which is why I have to stay the hell away from him. I want to snack on him... That's nuts.

Not that the hot man would be interested in me.

I know when a guy wants me and when they look at me as if they're just about to pat me on the head and tell me I have been a good girl, or in this case pull my head clean off.

Yet, I can feel the tension radiate between us. It's overwhelmingly sensual. My lips part, and a shiver racks me.

This is not how I wanted to introduce myself. I could have done something sexy... I lick my lips.

"Stop doing that," he growls out. He tilts his head to the side and looks at me as if I'm some new interesting-but-gross insect.

"Doing what?" I ask.

Should I flutter my eyelashes? I need to claw this situation back.

He sighs and rubs his hand across his face. I watch him intently. His hands are just as attractive, big but elegant-looking. "That." He points at my face. "That look."

I hold my breath as Xander leans towards me, and with a gentle hand, he tucks a wayward strand of hair behind my ear. His honey gaze feels like it searches my soul. He drops his voice to a gruff whisper that only I can hear.

"I don't fuck children."

I feel the blood drain from my face, and the whole world grinds to a stop like a skipping record. My breath puffs out of me as if he'd poked me with a stick. My stomach twists, and my heart jerks in my chest. Oh, and the female part of me cringes. *I don't fuck children.* I stare at him in horror.

He knows I like him.

He grunts with clear dismissal and then stoops to grab my hat from the floor. He slaps it none too gently back on my head.

"It's a crush. You'll get over it," he says, waving his hand dismissively.

Wow, that told me.

I set my jaw to stop it from wobbling. *I don't fuck children.* To give my trembling hands something to do, I adjust my hat and tuck my hair underneath.

Xander watches me intently, taking me in, in all my hurt glory. "Look, you're a kid. I'm a grown man, I don't need a little girl following me around like my shadow." He shakes his head and smirks. "I've got tins in my cupboard at home older than you."

Okay, I get it.

"Stop with the looks, it makes me feel sick."

"I make you feel sick?" I mouth. *Nice one Tru, make your boss puke, why don't you? The sight of you makes him nauseated. You are a real prize.*

Maybe it's not my age... Perhaps it's my face?

I nod my head and slink away from him. Before he can say anything else to damage what's left of my confidence. I grab hold of my glass-collecting basket. I won't say anything else to him. I am not an idiot. I certainly won't throw myself at him ever again. I'm not that kind of girl. I've got my pride. Ha, *pride*, that's all I've got. I rub my forehead.

Any... *any* thought about him other than him being my boss... I'm going to shut it down. Shut that shit down. I'm not the first person to be rejected by a *crush*. I won't be the last.

He's an angel. An angel, gah, what the hell was I thinking? The man is probably as old as time, and I'm a blip on his radar. I don't know what I was thinking; I don't want some *old* guy. If he wanted me, he'd be a perve, wouldn't he?

Yeah, keep telling yourself that, Tru.

I scrunch my eyes up. I fucked up. I allow myself a hot second to wallow in self-pity before I pull a mental shield around my tattered feelings.

Okay, Tru, that's enough. You know what? He's a total prick.

Aha, there we go. The hurt I'm feeling gets washed away with righteous anger. I know he's gorgeous, but strutting about telling *me* not to look at him? What a pompous dick.

I look over my shoulder at him. His mouth is still twisted with disgust. He shakes his head and prowls away. My eyes narrow. As I watch, he retreats, cutting through the club like a shark. People automatically scramble out of his way.

Man points minus ten.

It doesn't matter how pretty you are if you're so far up your own arse you can't be kind. That's not attractive. I bet he spends all his spare time kissing his biceps and whispering sweet nothings to his abs. I give my sore elbow another rub.

Granted, I admit there might have been drool at one point, and I also admit I did stare—I stared at him a lot. But to call me out on it... and *then* say I made him feel sick? I huff. All that lust I felt for him dries up faster than a sprinkle of rain in the desert.

Fuck him.

I have so much shit to deal with... without a bighead angel thinking he's all that. "I've got tin cans older than you," I gripe. "What. A. Cock."

Not only is he a horrible person, but he's also way too observant anyway. The man is way too smart. Bloody angel. I need to keep away from him. He's done me a favour.

If I didn't need the money, I'd leave this poxy job. I would leave this job right now and never look back. But I need the money; I need to save every penny. To get that deposit. To get that new place. To survive.

He will not stop me from earning a living, clawing out of the hole I'm living in. Fire ignites in my chest, filling the cracks. From now on, he does not exist in my world. I'll look right through him. I nod my head. Yeah, I can do that, no problem.

I want a man to look at me as if the sun shines out of my ass... or at least out of my vagina. I snort. I nod my head again, and my lips turn up in a bitter smile. I'm a one-chance person. Fool me once or make me feel like crap? You're not getting a second chance.

Does that make me a hypocrite? Yep, you betcha.

Is it a horrible way to live?

Abso-fucking-lutely.

But I ask myself *if* it's necessary... Hell yes it is. Heck, no one else is going to protect me. The one person who did... died. Grandad would cluck me underneath the chin and hand me some throwing knives, all the while telling me there are more suitable fish in the sea.

I peel him, Xander, from my mind. I pull the claws of the attraction I had for him, my stupid childish dreams, from my heart. I'm just a silly little girl playing with the monsters.

It's a lesson, the age-old thing when you see something, *someone* beautiful. You want them; you want them so much... I wanted him. I would have done anything to get him.

A man I knew nothing about. What did I expect? It shouldn't be a shock to realise he could never live up to the tainted expectations in my head.

Yeah, I can glue together my tattered feelings and pretend I never had those thoughts about him in the first place.

My wrist hurts. When I hold my arm out to a flashing light, I can see finger-shaped bruises on my skin where that idiot shifter grabbed me.

My lips part. What the hell? I'm a hybrid, and even if I have yet to come into my powers—if I have any—I heal, I heal, I always heal. I've never been ill, and I never get bruises. I poke at my arm, and naturally, it throbs. What the heck is going on? I know I've been working tons of hours and I'm tired, but it shouldn't affect my healing.

Shit.

I feel sick.

I dump the glass-collecting basket behind the bar and hurry to the staff room. I grab a long-sleeved top from my locker, whip the baggy polo shirt off, and pull the new one over my head, tugging so it covers my wrist.

Bruises. I frown. It's kind of worrying.

I've got twenty minutes left of my shift. The longer I can avoid going back out there, the better. No, stuff it. I'm done for the night. I've been assaulted twice, no... three bloody times. I've earned a break. As far as I am concerned, this shitty night is over.

I grab my bag from my locker and fill the kettle. I might as well do my flasks while I'm here.

God, I feel so exhausted.

I lean against the kitchen counter as the kettle roars to life. It angrily rattles and puffs out clouds of steam. How long can I keep going? I picture Dexter and Story in my mind. And I know I'll keep going as long as I have to. As long as I'm able. I rub my chest. The angel's callous rejection has knocked me for six. I feel...

"What are you doing?" a snide, accusatory voice says from behind.

I hunch and shake my head with barely held exasperation. What is it with Jenny always creeping up behind me?

What is her problem? Me in here ditching work or using the kettle? I've taken to using hot-water bottles to keep myself and Story warm or warm enough to at least fall asleep. I boil water and fill my flasks at every given opportunity.

It's working well. I could use magic. There are heating potions, but potions are expensive, and they aren't in my budget. Story insists that she doesn't mind the cold. That pixies don't have heating in their burrows. But I'm mindful that the ground temperatures are higher than the freezing garage air, and she is tiny.

I worry about her.

"Hi, Jenny, how's your night been?" I do what I do best. I change the subject. I straighten from my lean and turn to face her with a fake smile plastered on my lips.

What am I going to say? How am I going to explain the flasks? Not that I care what Jenny thinks. But changing the subject to her favourite one, herself, works, and Jenny talks and talks and talks.

I nod my head at the right places and secure the lids to the now-steaming flasks, popping them into my rucksack all while I continue to smile and nod my head.

"What have you done to your hand?" Jenny asks, her nose wrinkling with distaste. It certainly isn't from concern. I look down at my arm, and the bruising's got worse. It's spread across my knuckles.

I flex my fingers and do my best to shrug nonchalantly. "The glass basket got me on my knuckles."

Jenny easily buys into my lie because she doesn't care. "Huh, gross," she says with a flick of her hair. "That explains why you've finished early. I better get back. See ya later."

When the staff room door whispers shut behind her, I stare at my hand. Shit. That looks bad. Yeah, but who the hell am I going to tell? Ask for help?

No one. I have no one. I'm certainly not going to upset Story. *They're only bruises, Tru.* I don't know why I'm getting upset about them. Ha ha. Everything is fine. I slump into a chair.

Why do I not believe that?

CHAPTER
THIRTEEN

I DOUBLE-CHECK my hair to make sure it's secure. Gah, I have so much of it. It's so thick the wavy, multicoloured tresses get in the way. Once I'm reassured it won't, I drop to my knees and reach into the old red toolbox. Methodically, I empty the box of its contents and then carefully pull out the bottom tray and place it on the floor beside me.

Story perches on the sofa. Her blue skin blends into the seventies flower print. She kicks her legs, bouncing them against the cushion. "What happened at the weekend?" she asks. "You're upset more than usual." She pulls her legs up to hug her knees.

I narrow my eyes at my observant friend and shake my head dismissively. I haven't told her what happened with the angel.

I'm too embarrassed, too ashamed.

Not that I have anything to be ashamed about; it's all on him, I mentally grump.

I never tell Story much of anything. I'm a terrible friend.

"Thanks, Novel. So are you saying I'm always miserable?"

Story groans and flops back onto the sofa. I force myself to give her an explanation. "I liked a guy, and he was... horrible to me."

I don't fuck children. His voice echoes in my head, and I can't help cringing.

God, I wish I would have come back with something like *Good, 'cause I don't want to fuck you anyway.* Or called him out on it instead of standing there with drool on my chin.

Gah. I rub my face.

"Ah, I understand. I'm sorry... If you ever want to talk about it?" Story sits back up, pretty face scrunched up with concern, and she nibbles on her lip.

I shake my head. "I'll be fine." In twenty years. "I am fine, thank you."

She eyes the bruises on my right hand but says nothing more.

Which I appreciate. She's right. I am upset, and maybe it's why I'm going to do something crazy. It's earlier than I'd planned.

I need to do this.

Rolling my shoulders and wrists to limber up, I grab and turn on the small black torch. I shove it in my mouth—my jaw clicks as I grip it with my teeth. Heck, I so need to invest in a head torch.

I dip my hands inside the box. When they reach the bottom, they disappear into the magical void that the tray was covering.

Taking a few nervous deep breaths, I lean forward, and my shoulders rub against the smooth metal edges as I wiggle my upper body *inside* the small space.

It's a tight fit.

The toolbox acts as a small dimensional storeroom—a magical break in our reality, a rip in time and space. A tiny pocket world that's attached to the toolbox. I can't explain it any more than that... The magic and theory behind it is mind-boggling. All I know is that it works.

"Are you sure I can't help?" Story asks from outside.

"Oe-ay." *No way*, I tell her—or as best as I can with my mouth full.

The beam of the torch brightens the four-foot-square space that is lined with floor-to-ceiling shelves. My tummy scrapes uncomfortably against the lip of the box. Grandad packed the storeroom with everything he deemed important. The space inside here is limited, so he had to be careful. Priority has to be given to the most important stuff. So I can't throw everything I own inside it, which is a shame.

I groan. Doing this upside down makes me feel dizzy. I spread my legs wider on the outside to anchor myself, and I drop another few inches. The box digs into my thighs.

Grandad didn't have to dangle, I think with a grumble. No, he could place a hand inside and think of what he wanted, and the object, if it was in here, would appear in his hand.

The magic of the box doesn't work like that for me, and the toolbox didn't come with instructions. I don't know how to fix it, so I will continue to dangle.

It was one more thing that didn't come up for discussion when Grandad got poorly. When he was fighting for his life, it was the last thing on our minds.

Mmmh. I wrinkle my nose and tip my head. The light beams towards the floor. There's stuff on the lower shelves I will never reach. *I'm certainly not crawling inside here*. Goosebumps rise with the thought. *Nope. No way. I'm happy to keep my bottom in my own world, thank you very much.*

I really do need to invest in a head torch and perhaps a rope. If I secure myself with a rope, I might get down a little further and a little closer to the lower shelves. If I had a big friend to help me, that would also be easier. It's sad that I've got nobody but Story whom I trust to watch my back.

I haven't even told her about my hybrid heritage. It's the price of keeping myself safe, keeping her safe. I can't trust anyone to keep what I am a secret.

Above me, Dexter also meows his concern. The sound echoes around the storeroom, and soft, squidgy warmth fills my chest.

"Purrrt," he inquires. Story says something I can't hear, and Dexter yowls. Oops. I don't think he quite understands my disappearing upper body. I snort. Who am I to interpret what's going on in his kitty-cat brain?

He's probably hungry.

I'll run out of air soon if I don't get a wiggle on. This place is dangerous. I give myself a mental shake and rotate my torso to the shelf that has rows of carefully stored potion balls. I'll need these for my mission.

The mission I have dubbed Operation Get Your Own Back. I grab a handy cloth bag from a peg hanging off the shelf and start filling it.

Ouch. I wince. "Ickle... it... exter... hmmm-mm—" I growl out when a deliberate claw pricks against my calf. The torch rattles between my teeth.

I better get moving. It's already getting hard to breathe. I'm also unwilling to be a cat scratch post. Just in case, I grab one more potion ball for luck. There, perfect.

I squeak and almost drop the torch and bag as, with another dig of kitty claws, the little shit jumps up. Ginger pads and the occasional claw now knead my bottom.

Bloody cat.

Bag in hand, I clench my thighs and abs and wiggle my way out. Dexter drops to the floor.

I put the bag down, spit the torch out, and take in a lungful of fresh air. The ginger menace wraps himself around my legs and chirps away. He rubs against the bag of potions and then he *helps* me put everything away.

"Did you get everything you need?" Story asks.

I shoot her a grin.

"Are you sure I can't come with you?"

"No, but thanks for asking. I need to do this by myself. Dexter," I grumble as he smacks my face with his tail and a bit of fur finds its way into my mouth. I pull a face as I wipe my hairy tongue across the back of my hand. Ignoring me, he pokes his head into the toolbox, and I quickly close the lid. "That is no place for a cat."

"Come on, I'll feed you before I go. Today you have salmon. Yes, salmon. Yummy, yum-yum."

Story giggles.

I gingerly walk across the garage, dodging Dexter's winding form, and feed the greedy little monster. With that accomplished, I change into my sneaking clothes, say goodbye to my friends, and head to the bus stop.

Resting my full weight against the plastic bus shelter, I do a final check to make sure I have everything. I might be stubborn and impulsive, but I hope I don't fall into the trap of too stupid to live. What was that Friedrich Nietzsche quote? "Die a hero or live long enough to become a villain"? I shrug. I'm so up for that.

My grandad's house sold, and wow, it knocked me for six. God, it was painful. I avoid looking towards the house. Sometimes I wish I didn't live around the corner. The first time I saw the FOR SALE sign —it went up the day my uncle kicked me out—it made everything so real. Not that living in the garage wasn't real. It was just that I had a hope that maybe... Maybe my uncle would change his mind. I huff out a self-deprecating breath. How stupid is that?

I couldn't stop myself from going online daily and checking the listing.

To torture myself.

I dip my head and push my hands deep into my pockets. When the listing updated to say the house was under offer, and then a SOLD sign appeared... I was miserable. Then with all the angel bollocks on top of all that, something inside me snapped.

I huff and stare down the road. The bus should be here in a few minutes. I know it's ridiculous, and that it is just a house, but it was my connection to my grandad and my home. An end of an era. An end of my childhood and my innocence. Uncle Ph... I grind my teeth. The *Nobhead* had no right to throw me out like rubbish.

Heck, I've been contributing to the bills for the past three years. Nobhead could have given me a little warning, some time to prepare. I didn't expect any money from the house, and I didn't expect a free ride.

I scratch my nose. So I might have... urm... hacked into his computer system. He *really* should have changed his password.

I wave the number fourteen bus down, and the doors swish open. I smile at the driver and show him my bus pass. The bus pulls back into traffic as I walk down the aisle and settle on to a bench seat.

It's been a few weeks since the house sold, and I've been patiently waiting for the perfect time, for the ideal opportunity. While I've been working my ass off and living in a garage, the nobhead moved into a new fancy four-bedroom house at the end of a brand-new cul-de-sac.

Tonight he's taking his new girlfriend out for a night on the town, a meal, and some drinks. Quick to spend his newfound wealth.

When I finally get to my destination, I tug the baseball cap low and pull the hood of the shapeless black hoodie over my head. I hunch my frame and swagger along the street. I look like a teenage boy.

In the shadows, I watch the house. A taxi pulls up, and Nobhead leaves for the evening. I wait a few more minutes and then scramble over the back wall and use a glass cutter to carefully remove a square panel of glass from the back door. I slip my hand inside and grasp the key that he's conveniently left in the lock.

The door silently swings open. My trainers squeak on the kitchen tiles as I confidently strut into the kitchen, running my fingertips across the black granite surface as I pass. Fancy.

Diligently, I go through the house room by room to make sure that it's empty. The place is nice. Like most new builds in England, the room sizes are a tad small. They've painted the walls a clean magnolia, so everything is new-build bland. All so new, including the furnishings.

I set the countdown timer on my phone, dig into the rucksack, and grab a handful of the potion balls. I then repeat my walk-through.

In each room I visit, I whisper an incantation to activate the magic and then drop a glowing orange potion ball, which is the size of a marble, onto the floor.

I take nothing.

Just off the kitchen in the attached garage sits a thing of beauty, a shiny red Porsche. I run a fingertip across its perfect paintwork. Gosh, the nobhead was really having a midlife crisis.

Is this what my grandad's life was worth, a fancy house and a fancy car? With a sad smile, I balance the last potion ball onto the car's wiper blade.

"Sorry, little car," I mumble.

I head back to the kitchen—and with a last look around to make sure I've not forgotten anything and that this moment is ingrained into my memory—I smile and nod my head. I'm out of the door.

Within seconds, I'm over the wall and halfway down the street.

The timer on my phone goes off, and I pull it free from my back pocket. I swipe the screen, turning it off. I don't see, but I hear the explosions.

Wonderful things, those little potion balls.

A satisfied hum leaves my throat as I almost skip down the street. I force myself to hunch, and I keep my head low.

Nothing to see here.

Gosh, I'd love to see his face when he lays his eyes on his smouldering property. He put every penny into that house and car.

The guild will investigate and confirm it was arson.

"What a relief," he will say, "I have the very best insurance." The horror he will feel when he tries to claim on the policy he diligently set up. "But I am insured," he will argue.

"The policy was cancelled," the insurance company will argue back. His email to the company telling them he got a better deal with another supplier will be irrefutable proof.

His beloved car suffers the same fate.

What a terrible coincidence...

He really should have changed his password.

I get on the bus, avoid the seat with the chewing gum, and slump and lean my head against the window. The growl from the rumbling engine makes the whole side of the bus vibrate, and my teeth rattle.

I feel lighter than I have in months. Smoke rises in my peripheral vision. As the bus chugs past, I turn my head. Forehead to the glass, I watch the magically contained fire. The house is already almost ash.

I allow the wickedness I feel on the inside to show for a second on my face. He shouldn't have taken my youth and gender as a weakness.

Kicking me out of the house without giving a shit for my safety was his first mistake.

Stealing my car was his second.

I'm not a hero. If I have to be the villain—I shrug—so be it. My lips twitch into a smug smile. When I'm pushed, ha, when pushed, I refuse to be a victim—and I'm no one's fucking damsel in distress.

Welcome to homelessness, Uncle Nobhead.

CHAPTER
FOURTEEN

My shift is almost over when a visibly sweating bar manager waves me over. "Tru, would you go to the VIP bar and clean up that shithole? The staff there are swamped." I nod and head that way. When Xander is around, the entire staff get twitchy. I don't give a shit what he thinks. I do my best to avoid him. I won't even look at him, not wanting him to think I'm still panting after him. I have my pride.

When I get there, the VIP area looks like a bomb has hit it. With a sigh, I manoeuvre around the intoxicated customers, grabbing empty bottles and glasses, keeping my head down and my eyes on my task. The trick is to be in and out like a ghost; I hate dealing with these entitled dickheads. Somehow the VIP is always full of idiots.

On the other hand, the café is so interactive I like not having to talk to anyone when I am here. I reach for the last couple of glasses in a dark corner. They're on a low table that's surrounded by leather seating. A man grabs hold of my hand.

I roll my eyes.

It happens more times than you would think, people presuming that you're going to take their full or almost empty glass. I only take the empties or clearly abandoned glasses. I've even got into the habit of giving the bottles a little shake before I throw them into the bottle bins.

Drunk people get *really* miffed at the thought of you trying to take away any trace of alcohol. A mouthful left, and they think it entitles them to a whole new drink.

I don't even bother looking up. "I'm a glass collector, and I need to finish cleaning this area. If you will excuse me… Sir." I say *sir* in the tone I would use for arsehole. I attempt to pull my hand away, and the idiot tightens his grip. "Don't worry, I'll not take a drink. I'm just going to clear this mess away. I only want the empties." I sigh and try again to pull my hand away without being rude.

Xander's last warning is still in my head. Whenever he sees me, I get a snide, "Are you behaving yourself, my shadow?"

Yeah, *my shadow*. The idiot still thinks I'm stalking him. Talk about a huge, inflated ego. I'm sure he deliberately drops his tone into that rumbly, chocolatey cadence.

At least I hate him now. My heart rate goes crazy when he is near 'cause my body is gearing up to punch him in the face. I'm not his bloody shadow.

I need this job, even if I want nothing more than to punch him, or Mr Grabby Hand, in the face. What gives him the right to manhandle me? He grips harder. His hold on my wrist is painfully tight.

I grit my teeth.

No punching customers.

I don't even look at him. I just smile with lots of teeth and nod my head towards a group of girls outside the VIP who are desperately trying to get his attention. "I'm sure those lovely ladies would love to speak to you." I twist my wrist and knock his hand away with my basket.

No punching customers.

I spin, and I give myself a mental pat on the back. See there, sometimes violence doesn't solve everything. The VIP area is sorted.

"I'm talking to you, bitch," the customer growls. I lift my eyes and wrinkle my nose. Oh, hello. Just what I need, it's Freaky Frank. Yay.

Who says a good deed doesn't go unpunished? I shake my head, dodge him, and stomp away. I've been intentionally good, and I'm not having that idiot ruin it for me. I have ten minutes left on my shift. It is getting on to almost four in the morning. I've been working for nearly eighteen hours now. My poor body is done.

"Where do you think you're going? You owe me a kiss or I'll return that punch to the face," Frank the freaky shifter screams. Wow, he's now got everybody's attention. "Here, you didn't take my glass." I turn back around with a sigh. I can't help rolling my eyes up to the ceiling with exasperation. Perhaps there's some divine intervention up there hidden within the fancy club lights.

"Just so we are all clear." I stick my index finger up and circle it above my head. "Everyone heard him threaten to punch me in the face? Right?" I look around the group of fascinated objects. "Right?" I prowl back towards him.

I'm too tired for this shit.

Frank wiggles the full glass in his hand with a smirk. He then downs it in one go. I react on autopilot—*do not punch the customers*—and attempt to take the glass out of his hand. Frank grabs me and tugs on my hand. Like I'm a fish on a hook, he reels me towards him.

He lifts my hand to his lips and slobbers on my knuckles. I just stand there, horrified. Weirdly he licks between the webs of my fingers. Ew.

I'd prefer him to punch me.

I wrinkle my nose, and I purse my lips with disgust as Frank then licks down my fingers and sucks at the pad of my left index finger. His teeth scrape my skin, and I shudder with loathing.

Oh, that's just nasty. I don't want to be anywhere near this shifter's teeth.

I really should pull my hand away... Huh, it wouldn't be my fault if my hand slips and ends up breaking his nose. Total accident and nothing to do with me.

"I didn't wash my hands after I cleaned the toilets," I say helpfully. "I've just been sick in my mouth," I add for good measure.

Frank snarls. "Did you know a single bite from a shifter will kill a human female?" Funny enough, I did know that.

Is Freaky Frank threatening to bite me on purpose? I'm not human, but Frank doesn't know that. My heart misses a beat. The question bouncing around in my head is can a shifter turn a human when they aren't in animal form?

Has this shifter done this before?

Men turn, women die.

There's a movement to the side of me. "Frank, let the young human go. The reek of her fear is putting me off my drink." Frank snarls again. He squeezes my wrist so tightly I feel the bones grind together.

"Yeah, Frank, let me go."

Frank lets go, but not before he takes a good chunk of my finger. He smiles at me in triumph as my blood runs down his chin.

Can he tell I am not human?

Can he taste my vampire and shifter blood like a meat connoisseur?

I tuck my bleeding finger into my fist. I mumble a thank-you to the man who rescued me, and I get the hell out of there.

For fuck's sake, this is not the place to bleed. I'm surrounded by so many creatures. Creatures with heightened senses. Heart pounding and my hybrid blood dripping, I rush into the back area. My hands are shaking with fear and adrenaline.

I can't... I can't think.

My panic is overwhelming. I run the tap in the small sink and stuff my hand underneath the spray. With my other hand, I blindly search for bleach or any type of strong cleaning product. My hand lands on a bottle. I drag it from underneath the sink, bleach. I cringe, but I don't pause as I pour a good dollop.

I'm still shaking so hard I can feel every bone in my body rattle. Shit, I'm so frightened I am going to be sick.

I heave and scrub.

My finger is on fire, and my hand is going red. "Don't punch the customers, Xena." Bloody Xander. That worked out great. Where were your shit door staff when a shifter was chomping on my finger? Next time he's the one who bleeds," I grumble.

Oh my god, someone is going to smell my blood and I'm going to die. "He bit my finger. He bit my finger. He bit my fucking finger..." My panicked words run together like a drumbeat in my head.

"Are you okay?" a deep grumbling voice says from behind me.

I jump in surprise and let out a girly squeal. The water splashes me and the floor. "You scared the crap out of me. Thanks for that." I keep my hand in the water and grip the side of the sink with my other hand.

"Are you okay?" he asks again, this time with less patience.

"Oh yeah, I'm fine," I snarl at the nosy angel.

Fuck off. Fuck off. Fuck off.

Why does he pop up at the worst possible moment? *Please go away.* I don't need his help now. I needed his help when a shifter was chewing on my fucking finger. I never should have listened to him. Being polite with shiny customer service—is the worst thing ever—it's made me a victim.

I feel like a victim.

Hell, I hate this feeling... Gah, if I'd just knocked Freaky Frank out before the finger licking... I grab the bottle of bleach and squirt another load onto my hand.

Now I've got him asking stupid questions when all I want to do is cry. I won't cry 'cause I'm too stubborn, but him being here is making things worse.

This is all his fault.

Instead I pull on my anger. The anger I can deal with. It burns in my chest, and immediately I feel centred.

Also is the man blind? I think it's pretty obvious that I'm not okay, but I will not admit it. I turn my head and glare at him. "Everything's f—"

"Fine, I know." Xander prowls into the room. He makes the already-small space smaller. He's careful not to touch me. In response to his nearness, I hunch further over the sink and splash more bleach onto my hand.

I am glad I can't smell him over the eye-watering smell of bleach. My head is banging. I want to stay here with my hand in the sink forever, but I know logically it won't do any good.

The bleach won't do anything.

I take a deep shaky breath. The bleach fumes burn the back of my throat. God, did Freaky Frank just kill me? Do the creatures know who I am? What I am?

"Why are you bleeding?"

"A customer bit me. The bastard almost took the top of my finger off, so thanks for the protection. Consider this my notice. I'm not working in this shithole." I rub my hand. It's red raw and my finger is *still* bleeding. Why isn't it healing? This isn't right... I'm healing human slow. "I need backdated hazard pay," I grumble.

He moves closer. His massive frame towers over me. I hunch further into myself. The sink digs into my thighs.

"Who bit you?"

"Who do you think? Frank the pervert. You know, the guy I punched in the face? He came back for more." Droplets of water spray into the air around us as I wave my hand in the air. I point at my still-immersed hand. "This is what happens when I am polite. You'll be happy to know I didn't punch him, and due to the fact I didn't defend myself"—I swallow. *Don't you dare bloody cry*—"he"—*don't you dare*—"he bit me."

Xander's tree-trunk arm appears over my shoulder. He gently nudges me out of the way and turns the tap off. As I move away from the sink, I realise belatedly that I'm a sopping, bleach-covered mess.

I close my eyes with embarrassment; I lost my shit for a few minutes there. Thank God I'm never coming back to this shithole as my club T-shirt is ruined. If he expects me to pay for it, he can get lost.

"Were his teeth shifted? I don't think he's old enough or strong enough to shift his teeth. Do you know if his teeth were shifted, Tru?"

I shrug. How do I know what shifted teeth look like? Did he have a wolf head? No, he didn't. Who bloody cares?

Xander grips my shoulders and gives me a little shake. "This is important. Were his teeth shifted?"

"No?"

He grunts. Who knew a grunt could hold so much exasperation. His honey eyes flash with golden rage, and he drops his hold on my shoulders and leaves.

I take a deep breath in. He's seriously pissed. I can't believe he left me standing here, a sopping wet *bleeding* mess. "Good chat." I snarl.

I need a first aid box.

I'm sure I read somewhere that angels can heal. Huh, Xander must really dislike me. Nothing tells you more about another person's feelings than when they leave you bleeding. Perhaps he's worried I'll try to jump him.

"Angels make the best bosses," I grumble. My lip trembles, and I chomp on it in punishment. *None of that shit, Tru. Don't you dare cry.*

The only person I could rely on is fucking dead.

Even he didn't stick around. No, that's unfair. I take that back. I'm upset, and thinking like that is wrong on so many levels. *I'm sorry, Grandad.* I tug aggressively at the paper towel dispenser and wrap my finger in the blue paper. Not the most hygienic thing to use on a wound, but it beats bleeding all over the floor. Story would have helped me.

There's a full medical kit on the back shelf. I almost let out a cheer when I find it contains expensive healing potions. I grab a vial and pull the stopper out with my teeth. Tipping the liquid directly onto my finger, I watch with relief as the bleeding slows and the edges magically knit back together. My racing heart finally slows to a normal rhythm. I should've done this before the bleach fest. But I wasn't thinking. No, I was panicking, and that's something I can't afford to do.

Perhaps it's fate nudging me in a different direction. It might be time to get out of the city. Grab Story and Dexter and just go.

Nothing is here for me anymore.

I don't know if it was from the nip on my finger or the shock of getting bitten and bleeding everywhere. But the yuckiness I've been feeling on the edge of my consciousness for weeks suddenly hits me full force. Hell, it could be a bad healing potion for all I know. I've never felt like this before.

God, I don't feel well.

There's a tickle in the back of my throat, and my hairline is slick with sweat. My cheeks are red and hot, but inside I feel cold.

If I was human, what I'm feeling would be normal—it would be a sign that I was coming down with a cold. Perhaps the flu... terrible flu.

But I'm not human, and I'm not normal.

I've never had a cold in my life. On top of the bruises, it has me worried.

Instead of my routine of going to the gym, I clean up in the staff bathroom. I fill up my flasks in the staff kitchen, and a silent, worried Luke arranges for a taxi to take me straight home.

As I walk through the staff hallway and my feet sink into the carpet for the last time, I feel a sense of relief. I'm never coming back to this shithole again.

CHAPTER
FIFTEEN

The garage is freezing. The UK has been hit with a serious bout of cold weather. When I catch snippets of the news, they keep going on about an Arctic blast hitting the country.

Ha, of course. The year I'm homeless is the year we have record-breaking cold weather.

The bloody Arctic can keep its weather to itself, thank you very much.

Story flits about on my shoulder, making a fuss. Her worried voice fades into the background of my throbbing temples. I squeeze one of the bottles of water. The plastic bottle crunches underneath my hand, and a chunk of ice bobs about. I'm disappointed but not surprised to find the bottles of water frozen solid.

I rub my ice-cold hand across my sweaty forehead. "I'm so sorry about the water." I should have put them in a box to insulate them better. "Have you had enough to drink? I guess I could use some of the hot water we have to thaw a bottle, or you can have the boiled water from the flask when it's cooled. That might be better..." My voice fades off into mumbles.

My head is pounding, and my vision tunnels for a few seconds. The sensation is very much like being punched in the head.

Story rests her hand against my burning cheek. The light pressure makes me look at her. "We are both fine. Stop fussing, Tru. You don't look at all well, and you're so hot. I can feed Dexter in the morning. I think you should get in bed and stay there. Do you want me to call someone? Maybe Jodie, that nice witch?" she says, her voice full of concern.

I try to smile to reassure her. "I'm fine, it's just a cold," I lie. "It must be from this weather. I'll be better in the morning. I just need a good sleep."

Dexter also chips in and meows at me as I pour the hot water into the hot-water bottles and stumble towards the shed to get ready for bed.

"I'm not working at the club anymore," I say offhandedly as I tuck a hot-water bottle inside Story's bedroom and one underneath my covers. Not that I need one really... I'm radiating heat. I quickly change into my nightclothes. I've taken to wearing a sports bra, thick socks, jogging bottoms, and a jumper instead of pyjamas. I feel safer sleeping in clothing that I can run in. I stuff my shaking body underneath the covers.

Dexter, who is banned from the shed, jumps onto my bed. I groan. I left the door open. He proudly stands next to my head, front paws on my pillow, purring like a sports car engine. His ginger paws pad the pillow, rocking my head from side to side. I groan again and attempt to push him away, but he swipes me back and bops me on the nose with a pink toe bean.

I give up, and I hide my head underneath the covers.

"Dexter stop that. You know she's unwell," Story admonishes him. "You should do your duty and be on guard while she sleeps."

"You tell him, Story," I mumble from underneath my duvet. Instead of guarding—I roll my eyes, monster cat my ass—I feel the weight of him on top of me as he curls on my pillow and settles between my shoulder and my chin.

His soft purr lulls me into sleep.

When I awake he's gone, and I can't see Story anywhere. My eyes are almost stuck together, I can't find the energy to open them fully, so

I blindly reach for a bottle of water. My hand shakes as I drink a few frozen mouthfuls.

"Mert?" Dexter pads back into the shed.

"I'm okay, Dex, just feeling a little under the weather," I husk out as I take another few mouthfuls of water. The frozen bottle creaks when I set it down, and my hand throbs. I huddle back under the covers. Shit, I feel worse.

In the back of my head, the sensible inside voice tells me I need to check the time. I won't make it to work tomorrow, so I need to let Tilly know so she has time to plan a replacement.

Of course my phone isn't underneath my pillow like it normally is, and I don't know where my jacket is... I drift off before I can do anything about it.

DEXTER'S CONCERN turns into kitty outrage when I miss his breakfast, and when I don't respond quickly enough, he ends up dive-bombing my face and attacking the covers until I heed his demands. I drag myself out of bed.

"Where's Story?" I grumble. Perhaps she's gone to work? My shaking limbs feel worse, not better. First the bruises, now this. What the heck is wrong with me?

I clumsily pull myself through the tight gap between the wall and shed and stumble into the garage.

My panting breaths fog the cold air, and black spots dance across my vision as I top up Dexter's food bowls. I groan when I find the cat food in the can is frozen. It's the gravy that's icy. I have no alternative but to dish out the frozen chunks anyway, and I put extra dry food into his other dish. To finish, I squeeze out some bottled water.

Just from putting out Dexter's food, my hands are red, and they throb painfully. I pull my jumper down and cover them the best I can. My head pounds, and when I turn a little too fast, more black dots swim in my vision and my knees buckle. I catch myself from falling and hang on to the table where I store all the cat food. With determination and gritted teeth, I drag myself back into the shed and this time close and latch the door. Weakly, I lower myself to the bed and put my icy hands between my thighs, missing my hot-water bottle. The one in my bed is now useless.

With shaking hands, I change out of my damp sweaty clothes. I undo the stopper on the hot-water bottle, pour the lukewarm water into a small blue bowl, and then give myself a refreshing—so freezing I almost lose a nipple—wash.

I pull on some fresh leggings and another jumper and then crawl back underneath the covers.

I really should message Tilly... I hope Story is okay.

W

ITHIN THE SHELTER of my dreams—I must be dreaming—heavy footsteps, voices, crunching, and ripping is background noise inside my fuzzy head. With blurry eyes and no comprehension, I watch as my pretty, dangling fairy lights wink out, torn to shreds as the warm cocoon of my shed disappears with a crash. In my dream the wooden shed around me folds like it's made of paper. It folds away into nothing.

Scalding hot fingers touch my throat, making me jolt, and weak adrenaline gives me the energy for a moment to wipe the haze away from my mind. I blink my heavy eyes open and gaze into a pair of angry honey eyes. My heart jumps for a second then settles back into its sluggish rhythm.

"She's alive," says a relieved chocolaty voice.

My eyes flutter closed.

I don't like this dream.

"She must be freezing."

"You're in so much trouble, my shadow," a voice growls above me as a heavy hand gently pushes my loose, tangled hair away from my face. Then steel arms reach around me, and I am lifted from my bed, gathered into muscular arms. My cheek settles onto a solid chest.

"Grab all this shit. If she survives, she isn't coming back to this dump—"

"Reow."

"—and the cat."

"Her hair is beautiful, like a colourful waterfall," comes a gruff voice. "She's pretty."

"She. Is. A. Child," growls the voice of the man who is holding me. It rumbles through his chest against my ear like Dexter's purr. "If you look at her like that again, I will pluck out your eyes."

What a dream, I think as everything fades.

CHAPTER
SIXTEEN

I DRIFT in and out of consciousness; I dream of warm golden magic creeping through me like molasses.

When I wake up, I'm in a strange bed. I freeze, and my gaze skitters around a well-decorated bedroom.

What the heck?

The sheets pool around my hips as I sit up, and I run the delicate fabric through my fingers. Ooh, a super-high thread count. What the hell? I'm such a weirdo, why did I notice the sheets? Mmh. Apparently, I have a weird fascination with cotton. I shake my head and give my forehead a rub. Where am I?

I close my eyes and try to remember what happened. How did I get here? I rub my forehead again vigorously. I remember... being ill, and I remember being in bed and then snippets of time that don't seem quite right. I am not sure what happened...

Little pig, little pig let me in, not by the hair of my chinny chin chin. Shit, someone huffed and puffed and ripped my shed apart. I frown. There's a memory of incredibly angry eyes. The memory of them is burned into my very soul... and then the metal mingled with sunlight scent.

Xander?

I must be going mad. I swallow a nervous laugh. "Shit, where's Story and Dexter? I'm supposed to be looking out for them." My ears strain. I can't hear anything from outside the room. But... but I can hear the shallow breathing of the person inside the room with me. My eyes widen, and goosebumps rise on my arms.

This is like a horror film.

I slowly turn my head, and my eyes land on a silent, angry Xander. He is sitting in a chair by the window, watching me.

"That's not creepy at all," I mumble.

I guess a normal person would ask "where am I?" or "what's happened?" But I keep my lips clamped closed and return his stare.

Of course my silence isn't upsetting to him.

No, he stares right back at me, neither of us saying a word.

Daylight streams through the window behind him. I tilt my head to the side. Without the distracting lights of the club, I notice his eyes have a gold ring around the outside and little flecks of gold. His beautiful eyes narrow and he grunts. I guess he's seriously sick of my shenanigans.

He's pissed. Boy is he pissed.

Huh, that isn't a surprise. The angel is either angry or disgusted by me. I think those are the only two emotions I evoke.

Looks like I'm doing a grand old job of keeping myself invisible. What with the getting bitten by a shifter, bleeding in front of a couple of hundred creatures—oh, and telling my angel boss to fuck off. Did I tell him to shove the job up his ass too or did I imagine that? Ha. It's all adding up to a total and utter shitshow.

Yay, what a week.

Now to top it all off I'm in some strange bed having a stare-off with an angel. The dream... memory I have of him with his bare hands dramatically ripping apart my shed and pulling me into his arms must be the fabrication of an overactive imagination as the man glaring at me looks like he would be happier ripping me apart.

"The cat and the pixie are fine. You're here because a shifter bit you while at work and you're my responsibility." His voice is loud in the silent room.

"Okay—" I fidget. Thank God for that.

To break our intense eye contact and avoid looking at him, I pull the covers away and take a peek. Huh, new pyjamas.

"With rumours circulating about the incident that happened at Night-*Shift* on Saturday and out of concern for your well-being, your other employer went to your address on Ansdell Road and discovered that the property had been sold. When she couldn't find you, she came to me and requested"—I wince; that's a nice way to say *demanded*, knowing Tilly—"my help. With the help of the insistent dryad and finally a bossy pixie, I find you half-dead in a garden shed within a falling-down garage."

"It was far from falling down," I scoff.

Xander washes his hand across his face. "Give me strength," he says to himself as he leans forward in the chair, elbows resting on his knees.

He lifts his eyes, and I blink at him. This is... This is ridiculous. What the hell is going on? I keep my face as blank as I can as my heart leaps to my throat.

Xander is livid. I clamp my mouth shut. The angel who could probably smite me with lightning out of his fingertips is giving me the evils. My heart—still lodged in my throat—pounds harder.

I shiver. I don't know why I was poorly. I'm not human, but I can't tell him that, can I? And to be honest, I'm feeling okay. I pull up the long sleeves of the pyjamas and inspect my wrists and arms. No bruises. That has to be a good sign, doesn't it?

I ignore Mr Angry Pants and forge ahead with getting myself out of this situation unscathed. "Thank you for all your help. I feel so much better." I take a deep breath in, and my chest doesn't hurt. Yeah, I'm perfectly fine. "I am sorry for the inconvenience and for wasting your time. I'll be on my way." I slide towards the other side of the bed—as far away from the angry angel as I can get. "I'll clear everything up with Tilly, and I will also let her know I handed in my notice last night so she won't contact you again."

Xander holds out a hand, and I pause. "You've been unconscious for three days, and I'm afraid it won't be that easy. The shifters are demanding that I turn you over to them. I'm still waiting on medical results." He frowns.

What?

"The shifters are quite confident that the results will show that you are the very first turned human female in our history."

I rapidly blink at him.

"Tru, you are no longer human," he says, ending his speech with a splash of drama.

What the fuckety fuck fuck?

CHAPTER SEVENTEEN

My mouth pops open, and I can't stop the gargled laugh from leaving my mouth. God, I miss my grandad. He would have also found this whole thing hilarious and then sorted the problem out with a few choice words... well, after he told me off for getting bitten.

They all think I've turned? That I'm a bitten shifter? I slap my face with my hand and laugh through my fingers. I am poorly for a few days, and the entire world goes mad.

Hell, their imaginations, and this situation, are way *worse* than the reality of my hybrid status.

It is so much worse, and I never thought I would say that—shit.

The way the angel is looking at me, with false sympathy—he thinks he's connected all the right dots. When in fact he's gone off the page.

"I know it's a bit of a shock," he says.

I laugh harder.

I bet the hairy bastards—the shifters—are going nuts. I bet the angel has been shitting himself while dealing with his worst nightmare.

I guess it's a fitting punishment for him being such a dick with me.

Unfortunately, it messes with my life way worse.

They don't know I'm a hybrid. Getting poorly after that idiot chomped on my finger was a real cosmic coincidence. The timing couldn't be worse.

"You could have died," he grumbles.

My laugh cuts off, and my eyes widen.

Oh no.

It hits me.

It's not about what can happen to *me*. It's the implications for other women.

The realisation freaks me out. What if the shifters all suddenly think that they can turn women now? Everybody knows if a human female is bitten—hell, any female is bitten—by a shifter, they don't turn; they die. What if this whole thing sets off the shifters, and they go on a rampage and start chomping on everybody in a stupid attempt to turn them?

People could die.

I'd be responsible. Perhaps indirectly, but I'd be responsible. With a wobble, I slide back down onto the side of the bed, my back towards the angel. My temples throb and my heart pounds in my ears as my brain filters through the implications.

Female pureblood shifters are super rare, guarded as either precious jewels or as a commodity. Poor cows are seen as baby-making machines. If they think I'm a super-special turned shifter, my life will be a living nightmare. Bitten male shifters can't shift. But I don't know if they can pass the shifter gene down to their children. What if the shifters get it into their head that maybe a turned human can produce full-shifting children? Bile rushes up my throat, and I swallow it back down. No, I'm overthinking things without all the information. I never thought being a hybrid would be the best outcome in this situation.

"I know it is a bit of a shock," he says again.

That's the understatement of the century. I realise I'm shaking my head and rocking like a crazy person.

I've got to tell him. I've got to stop this.

When I still liked Xander, I might have googled angels, and on one site it said angels can tell truth from a lie. So whatever I say, I have to say it carefully.

The silence stretches between us.

A bit like an out-of-water fish, I open and close my mouth. Fuck. I shrug, have no idea what to say. *The truth, tell him the truth.*

I'm not a child no matter what he thinks. I know kids—teenagers —say that. But I'm not. I am the sum of my experiences like we all are, and I've seen things, dealt with things that would make most people— no matter what their age—crumble.

Come on, you can do this.

Everything happens for a reason. I screw my eyes closed and huff out an enormous sigh. I hate that phrase.

But... but I dunno having that theory helps. I guess if it is true, and fate pushes in a certain direction, and the push is so hard it rattles your teeth, maybe you need to go with it.

Maybe I need to go with it. Hell, hiding isn't working.

Fate has given me a massive kick to my bum. Getting bitten while already being ill? It's a crazy coincidence. This is more than me. More is at stake than my selfish self-protection.

All I need to do now is step forward.

"I am not—"

There's a knock on the door, and a guy in fatigues prowls into the room. "I have Miss Dennison's results," he says.

Results? Oh shit.

This guy doesn't look like a doctor. It looks as if he'd be happier with a silver sword than a stethoscope. Not that doctors use stethoscopes anymore. They have fancy magic tech for that.

"You'll not believe what I found," he continues, his eyes fixed on the medical tablet.

Double shit.

I wiggle on the side of the bed, then turn so I can see him better. His eyes lift from the tablet when he catches the movement. "Miss Dennison, you're awake."

I wave. "Yeah, I think I am... I'm in a sort of twilight zone at the moment, one where the world has gone mad. I think I might be still unconscious, and my brain is just having a fun time making unbelievable shit up," I grumble.

"My name is Dr Ross—"

"Okay, out with it, Ross. You can be polite on your own time,"

Xander interrupts. He waves his hand in the air for the doctor to get on with it.

The doctor shrugs at me apologetically and then turns his full attention to the angel. He puts his hand in his pocket and pulls out a potion ball.

Witches normally colour code their spells, red being dangerous, orange being fire or explosive. The one in his hand is pale blue. Asking for permission, he raises his eyebrows at Xander, and the angel nods his consent. The doctor flicks the potion ball onto the floor.

The air around us pops. I have to swallow a few times as the pressure hurts my ears. Silence. A bubble of silence so thick—it's an expensive potion.

Xander tilts his head to the side, and his face scrunches up with distaste. "Ross, if you can't trust my security over one pain-in-the-arse girl and her medical bullshit, we've got a serious problem on our hands. Do you need to waste a potion for this?"

Gosh, the guy reallyyyy does not like me. What a shame.

"I don't trust anyone else but the people in this room with this information."

I twitch, and my head throbs. I wonder if they'll notice if I go back to sleep. I lick my dry lips nervously. It looks like we're skipping my hybrid confession. I guess it's out of my hands.

My granddad died not even four months ago, and in that time... I've fucked up. I mentally give myself a double thumbs-up. *You're doing awesome, Tru.*

NOT.

I keep my mouth closed. God, I'm so bloody frightened.

"Okay, the good news. Miss Dennison is not a bitten shifter." Ah, shit. Here we go. "I checked the results myself three times. I even got another sample of blood to make sure."

Nice to know I've been prodded and poked while I've been unconscious. Among other things, I glare down at the brand-new never-seen-before pyjamas.

Xander nods his head. His face relaxes with relief. "That's the best news I've heard all day. I don't understand why you felt the need for the full cloak-and-dagger potion drama. Working with John's team has made you paranoid." Xander rolls up from the chair. "Send the results to the shifters. I'm sure they'll want to do their own tests to confirm."

Dr Ross holds his hand out and shakes his head. "I don't think we can do that. It's not that simple."

"Why not?"

I hunch and my shoulders brush my ears.

"The results show that Miss Dennison is half shifter." Both the doctor and Xander turn and stare. I force myself not to fidget, and I lift my chin. Half shifter is perfectly fine.

The way the shifters go about breeding willy-nilly. Practically every other human has some shifter DNA. There are thousands of half shifters out in the world.

"Okay," Xander scoffs. "No problem, we can handle that. At worst, it might look I've been harbouring a rogue half-breed." He scowls at me, and I glare back. "You will need to register with the guild."

Crikey, I don't know why he hates me so much. With all the angry looks he's shooting my way, he could seriously give me a complex. It's not as if I've taken a poo in his cornflakes. This isn't my fault. I didn't ask him to stick his nose all up in my business. He was the one who came to my home and ripped me out of my bed.

"I'm not finished."

No, really?

The doctor taps the tablet on his leg, and his hand trembles. He takes a deep, fortifying breath. "It's a whole lot worse than that, Xander. The results show that she is also half vampire." He doesn't look like a man who gets nervous. He looks like the guy who typically takes things on the chin and nothing bothers him. Which makes his next words so impactful. "I think we need to call in the hunters guild."

The doctor is freaking out.

"Half shifter, half vampire? That makes little sense... She doesn't smell dead."

"No, that's because she isn't. She's a born vampire, a shifter-vampire hybrid."

Oops.

Xander grinds his teeth.

"Check the results again," Xander barks out.

"I already did, three times."

Both men look at each other, and an entire conversation goes on between them with just their eyes.

Xander turns those eyes onto me. "Tru," he growls, using my name for the very first time. I can't leave the room because the doctor is blocking the door, so I do the next best thing like a total boss… I flop onto my side and pull the covers over my head.

Like a kid.

Look at that. I am rocking this. Maybe if they think I'm asleep, they will leave me the hell alone. I can sneak out.

Xander grunts. "Her illness?"

"I need to do more tests, but it looks as if she's going through her vampire transformation early. To me, it looks like both sides of her nature are conflicted. They're at war with each other. Her electrolyte levels are all over the place, her potassium levels are too high, and her sodium, vitamin D, and iron are critically low. From the data, both sides are losing." I hear a few taps, and I think he's showing Xander my medical stuff on his tablet.

"Medically, I don't know how she's still alive." It just gets better and better.

CHAPTER
EIGHTEEN

As I peek from underneath my covers, I watch the angel's finger weirdly *drip* with golden magic, which he then uses to wipe away the sound bubble. My top lip lifts with a silent snarl, and I shake my head at him. He is such a show-off. A normal finger poke would have done the job.

As soon as the bubble drops, sound rushes in, and straightaway there seems to be an issue. There's a ruckus in the hallway.

"I've come to collect my female!" some idiot bellows.

Xander groans and strolls from the room. The man sure knows how to move. If I couldn't see or I hadn't personally felt all the bumpy muscles in his torso, then I'd think he didn't have any. His movement is less like a walk and more like a liquid ooze.

The doctor goes back to his datapad, tapping the screen like a man possessed. I hope he's deleting my medical history.

Xander's quiet voice joins the conversation outside, and then the door shudders as something hits it. I roll my eyes; the angel is so diplomatic. What's happening now? I can't stump up enough fear to be bothered. I'm all tapped out. Yet self-preservation makes me tilt my head to the side and concentrate, using my hybrid ears to their advantage.

"She's only just woken up." Xander's voice drops to a scary growl. They must be right outside the bedroom now as I don't have to strain my ears to listen. "You are not permitted to interact with her." He sounds so ominous.

"I don't give a fuck what you think. She's mine. I bit her, so she's my property now. It's the law," the man growls back.

Ah, now I recognise the voice. It's Frank the freaky shifter from the club. So I am reduced to property now? I huff out a laugh. That guy needs a good kicking.

Suddenly I'm motivated to get out of bed and get dressed. I sit up and look around for something to wear.

The angel responds with a laugh of his own. It's a creepy, dark chuckle that gives me an entire body shiver. How can one laugh hold so much distaste?

"Listen here, Angel, you have no right to keep me from her. I have permission from the shifter council, so you'd better get out of my way."

There's a handily left-out pile of clothing on the dresser, so I spring out of bed, grab the bundle, and hustle past the doctor and into the en suite bathroom.

I don't trust the angel not to step out of the shifter's way and let him in.

I slam the door and hit the lock. There. I feel marginally safer. The fancy white bathroom has nice subway-style tiles, and the big tiles on the floor have speckles of gold—*just like Xander's eyes*. I grunt at my random thought and eye the glass shower wistfully. I'm magically clean. Even my teeth—I prod them with my tongue—are sparkling. But nothing makes you feel cleaner than a hot shower. I pout. Sadly, I have no time, and I don't feel safe enough to strip naked.

I rifle through the clothes to find underwear, black leggings, and an oversized red hoodie. I quickly dress.

"Well, you'll have to get in line," Xander says as I open the bathroom door.

Huh? What does he mean? The doctor has left the bedroom.

In case I have to fight my way out, I lift my arms above my head to stretch, and my wrists click as I roll them.

I feel great. Better than I have in months. Perhaps I just needed sleep? Yep, four days, or was it five? I'm so healthy.

I better plait my hair. As I section my hair, I hear the beep of a phone keypad and then ringing. "It's Xander. I have something that you might be interested in." He pauses as someone says something—I can't hear the other side of the conversation as the phone is spelled. "Yes, she's here—"

Forgetting my hair for the moment, I shuffle closer to the door and rest my fingers on the white wood.

"—no, not a bitten shifter. She's an unregistered half pureblood."

What the what now?

"Yes, a female... *the* female. I'll send you a temporary portal code."

The bloody angel sold me out.

Without thinking too much about it, I yank open the door and stomp towards him. Hindsight is a wonderful thing. My inner voice screams at me to not even attempt to beat up the angel. Even while lost in my temper, I know hitting the angel is not a smart thing to do. Go me.

Instead, I poke his chest.

"Fucking traitor." Poke. "Sell-out." Poke. "That was my secret to tell, not yours." Poke, poke. My finger bends awkwardly each time I prod him.

Bloody rock-hard arsehole.

Still on the phone, the angel eyes shine down at me with humour, and he responses to my poking by lifting a perfect eyebrow. "Yes, she is a handful. I'll arrange a meeting. See you soon. Stop it." Xander slaps my hand down and puts his phone away.

My nostrils flare with indignation, and I glare at him as I rub my hand. The ligaments ache. He was like poking a brick wall.

"You're coming with me," says a slimy voice. Behind me, a heavy hand thumps down on my shoulder, and what I think is a thumb digs into the joint. Ouch.

I turn my head and glare at the meaty, hairy hand. The fingernails are black with dirt. Underneath my hoodie, my skin crawls.

Shit, I did it again; I left myself exposed. Will I never learn? With a huff, I pull my heavy hair away from my face. Looks like my mind still gets fuzzy when the angel is around. I have to accept some part of me will always be drawn to Xander.

I wiggle my shoulder to dislodge the shifter, and Frank the dickhead digs his fingers in more. I can't help my wince as he tweaks a nerve. Xander's eyes harden as Freaky Frank tugs me back into his chest.

The entire situation flicks the angry switch inside me. I react like a woman possessed, and I respond with every angry part of my body. I twist away from him. The wooden floor beneath me helps me spin like a dancer in my socks. I don't even think. Muscle memory takes over, and once again I smack the shifter's face.

"That's for touching me." I hit his nose and feel the bones underneath crunch. "That's for biting me." I turn and hit his nose with my left fist to get at a different spot. I grin menacingly as his face crunches underneath my misdirections, and a well-placed knee to the stomach gives a satisfying *oof* sound from his bloody lips.

Just when I find a good ass-kicking rhythm, I once again find myself airborne, and I'm pressed up against stone-like muscle.

Mmm, bumpy, bumpy abs.

The bloody pretzel move. I'm going to kill him.

"Know that I allowed you to do that, my shadow. I won't allow you again. You're a guest in my home. I get you're frustrated, but violence isn't the answer."

"Oh, but allowing this guy to manhandle me is perfectly acceptable? Different rules for everyone, is that what you are saying?" I growl out as I try in vain to wiggle out of his hold. "He chomped the tip of my finger off, and then the dickhead comes to pick me up? I am not a fucking takeaway."

The shifter steps towards me, wiping his hand across his bloody face. I bare my teeth at him, flashing my itty-bitty fangs.

"Do not take one more step. You know my rules," Xander says almost conversationally to the shifter. Of course he completely ignores what I've just said. I realise at that moment my victory over Frank was too easy. Not once did he try to hit me back... I deflate. It looks like the angel has him on a tight leash.

Hmm. He's not the only one.

Xander gives me a little shake and whispers in my ear, "Settle down."

Settle down?

"HE. TRIED. TO. KILL. ME," I yell.

Frank stays right where he is, a smirk on his ugly face. I can tell he's trying to pretend he isn't affected by my attack, but his chest rapidly moves as he pants. Blood trickles down his face. "I can't wait till we are alone," he says.

"Yeah, neither can I, but not for the same reasons. You sick fuck."

He looks me up and down and his tongue flicks out to lip the blood from his lip.

Ew. I roll my eyes.

Even with my wrists secured in Xander's one-handed grip, I can still give the shifter both my middle fingers. *Fuck you*, I mouth in case he didn't get my point. A low growl rumbles up from his chest, and it's my turn to smirk back at him.

"What a creepy shit—"

Xander shakes me again in warning.

"He made me bleed, and as you said yourself, if I were human and if his teeth were shifted, he could have killed me."

"What do you mean *if* you were human?"

"You're not very bright, are you, Frank?" I say through gritted teeth. "Did you not hear the telephone conversation that he just made" —I awkwardly nod my head back to indicate my restrainer and almost brain myself on his pec—"to the vampires? The half shifter, half vampire? He was talking about me. You didn't turn me you, idiot; I'm a hybrid."

The tree-trunk arm around my waist squeezes me with a warning.

"No, I did. You're a lying whore," Frank says with a whine.

"Yeah, you believe that, Frank. I'm a lying whore, and *you* turned the first female in the history of shifters." I shake my head and curl my lip with disgust. "Fucking idiot," I finish with a mumble.

Warm breath tickles my ear. "I'm sorry I didn't protect you and that you were hurt. Please trust me to deal with this."

"Trust you?" I scoff. "Yeah, I'll get right on that. Trust is for *children* and dogs."

"Are you going to behave?"

"No," I spit out.

I make it a point to tell this guy the truth what with his sneaky angel tricks. Like hell am I going to behave! I tried that before and almost lost a finger.

The arm that he has around my waist moves. I squeak as Xander places his palm against a sliver of bare skin between the top of my leggings and hoodie, which has ridden up in our struggle. The hand on my side gets warmer, and my skin tingles.

"Sleep, my shadow."

"Not your fucking shadow."

Everything goes black.

CHAPTER NINETEEN

I BLINK AWAKE. I'm back in the bedroom. How embarrassing. I must have passed out. The doctor stands over me; it looks as if he's finishing a full scan of my body. When he notices I'm awake, he shakes his head with obvious exasperation.

"You're still not well, so stop running into battle without thinking. Fixing the mess you've made of yourself is still ongoing. Please stop making my job harder."

I scowl at him.

He scowls back.

Yeah, fair enough. "I'm sorry," I grumble as I sit up. "Have you seen my cat? And my friend, Story?" I'm officially a terrible pet parent and friend.

"The fat ginger one?"

I splutter. "He's not fat. He's super healthy." Fat, I huff. The man is a bloody doctor, not a vet.

"Yes, your cat and the pixie are both safe and around here somewhere. I believe"—Dr Ross coughs into his fist to cover a laugh—"the cat peed on the sofa. Our resident angel was not amused. I think he's already used two potion balls to clean up after him. You're costing Xander a mini fortune."

I cringe. Dexter is a stray; it's not his fault he isn't house trained. At least no one has said anything about Dex being a fae monster cat. I've been waiting for him to do something... but he's a normal cat. Perhaps Story got it wrong?

"Is Freaky Frank still here?"

"Freaky Frank?" The doctor's eyes narrow in confusion and then widen with realisation. "Oh, the shifter. Yes, he's in the living room with a group of important people."

My eyebrows rise. "Shit, how long was I out?" Oh, and great. The *important* people are here, I mentally scoff. "The vampires are here, aren't they? The vampire council?"

Dr Ross takes a peek at his watch. "Yes, the vampire council and *all* the other councils are here."

"All the councils? Here?" I squeak out.

When did the councils start making house calls? That bloody angel, he's a curse. This has his big dirty fingerprints all over it. This is worse than I could have ever imagined. "Oh shit." I groan and rub my forehead.

"Oh shit, indeed. You have the entire supernatural world wondering what to do with you."

I'm not reassured, especially when I can see the concern in the doctor's eyes. My tummy flips. Is today the day I am going to die? No, not without a fight.

"I'm not dead yet... so at least that is a positive thing."

"No, you're not dead yet. But you will be if you keep them waiting any longer. Hurry." He taps his watch.

I scramble out of bed, taking a moment to plait my hair and shove the end down my top. I haven't got a bobble to secure it, but it's so long even if the first few inches unravel, the rest should stay in place—that's if I don't do anything too vigorous. You know, like fight for my life, run...

I take a deep breath, push back my shoulders, and lift my chin. Grandad always used to say posture was important. I adjust my clothes; I should have had a quick shower. I keep catching whiffs of Xander's scent on my skin; it makes my stomach clench. I look like a total scuff bag, but it will have to do. I'm ready as I can be. At least I haven't got any of Freaky Frank's blood on me. That has to be a bonus.

My hand shakes as I grab the doorknob. If they're going to kill me 'cause of what I am, I might as well go down with a bit of dignity.

With that wonderful thought and the doctor at my back, I venture into the hallway. I pause to listen and then turn and make my way towards the sound of voices.

My eyes flick about as I clock the exits. The angel's place is nice; it looks super modern and expensive. It's next-level wealthy.

When I get to the massive living room, I freeze at the door. With wide eyes, I look back at the doctor. He's standing behind me and doesn't seem to be in any rush for me to enter. I puff out a shaky breath, and with trepidation and my heart hammering in my ears, I blink like mad and force myself to concentrate.

Yeah, the undoubtedly beautiful living room is a tad crowded. The important people, I presume, are the ones sitting down. The fae, then the vampires, are on the left; the shifters are on the right, and an empty seat—my empty seat—is in the middle. Huh, that sounds like the chorus to a song.

Dotted around the room are a plethora of bodyguards split into shifters, vampires, and the fae. The idiots are all focused on glaring at each other rather than watching the door. I swallow nervously. Thinking about it, the guards are probably not idiots at all... No other threat would be greater than the people in the room.

I peer down at my feet. I can't. I can't seem to make myself move any further. I can't do it. I rock from foot to foot, and frightened tears fill my eyes until my vision is hazy. I don't know if I can step into the room under my own steam.

Well, if you don't, I'm sure they'll drag you to that chair kicking and screaming and then any leverage you might have had will be lost.

Standing behind a chair is a dark-haired male witch—a rare sight. He's the only one who spots me, and he gives me a friendly, almost encouraging nod. As he's so polite, I nod back, and my lips twitch as I attempt a nervous fake smile.

My eyes drift back to the seated occupants.

Of course the seated bigwigs are arguing. What are they all doing here? My grandad made sure I had the truth about these powerful people. If they're current members of the council, I should at least know who they are. Knowledge is power, after all.

From what I can gather in the short time as I stand in the doorway, they seem to agree that they can't kill me.

Yay.

It sounds as if they won't kill me, but they're arguing about who will take ownership of me.

Yay.

The masculine power that buzzes the room cows me. How the hell can I fight against this? How can I protect myself?

I've never felt like such a floundering child.

I thought I was pretty fearless, but I was kidding myself.

I nervously swallow, and I blink the wet haze again from my eyes. I was playing, faking. I've been kidding myself this whole time, pretending I had some semblance of control when I'm just a throw-away cog in the creature machine.

The men in this room are on another level. It's a strange feeling to know without a shadow of a doubt you're completely out of your depth.

I smile sadly. Most of the time I'm confident bordering on cocky, and although I knew the councils would kill me if they got their hands on me, I never could imagine what that would look like.

I didn't see *this*—a meeting in the angel's living room. Watching through the door while the nightmare monsters that plague our world with their crushing power sit around arguing... while sipping tea.

I frown.

What would my grandad do? What would he say? *It looks as if the monkeys at the top of the tree have come down to the ground where the ants live. It's a right circus.*

"Not my circus, not my monkeys," I mouth his favourite saying.

When there is a break in the conversation, Xander, who has been watching me this entire time, waves me into the room. "Here she is, the child we've been talking about. Come on in and take a seat," he says with a nod at the empty chair.

I keep my mouth shut and try not to grind my teeth as everyone's eyes home in on me. I have to squeeze my legs together to stop myself from peeing my pants. Instead, I grab his words like a lifeline, and I also grab at the darkness and anger that is always present inside me. Why he insists on calling me a child, I don't know. It makes my blood boil. For a few seconds, the anger washes my fear away.

A few seconds is all I need.

I gather my tattered courage, and with a dancer's elegance, I strut across the room in my socks as if I'm a queen walking to her throne.

I settle on the edge of the seat, my hands in my lap and back ramrod straight. I shut my worries away, hide my fear deep inside myself, and deliberately ignore the little voice that is screaming inside me that these people are the leaders of our kind. I've seen them on television. This is surreal.

My lips pull into what I hope is a sweet, benign smile.

"So this is the girl who has caused so much trouble?" a man snarls in an irritating, posh voice. I turn my eyes in his direction. The guy is blond, dressed in an expensive fitted suit, and is Ken-doll creepy-looking.

Pureblood vampire.

He goes by the name of Lord Luther Gilbert—uh-huh, yep. *Lord*. He's a pretentious prick. I remember him from my grandad's files. I've seen a compilation of his greatest deeds. He's a scumbag.

"You could have at least dressed her in something respectable, Xander. She looks like a thug off the street, a little boy instead of a..." He shakes his head. "Whatever the hell she is."

As he talks, my top lip twitches into a snarl. I don't like him. I've never liked him. I've seen him on the news attempting to encourage human blood donations. Thank God the humans are protected. They give enough, the horrible arsehole.

The other vampire, Atticus, is the head of the vampire guild and the vampire council. He has a short, clipped-to-the-scalp, no-nonsense haircut, and his eyes are a solid black. The man is the complete opposite of the vampire sat next to him; he doesn't go out in public, and he certainly isn't a TV vampire. Apart from some basic information on what his job is, he's an unknown... a mystery. He scares the bejesus out of me.

Sat apart from everyone else, including the other shifters with only the male witch for backup, is a humongous man. Even though he's sitting down, he dwarfs the oversized chair and the other creatures around him. Hands down, he is the biggest guy I have ever seen. He just needs a sword to finish his look. It takes a few seconds to recognise him.

The dragon shifter.

Wow. They call him the General, and he's a total badass.

At school, we had an entire semester on him as he's that important to our history. He almost single-handedly won a war with the fae a bazillion years ago. He's the head of the hunters guild, and he controls the hellhounds —scary shifter warriors that have fire magic. You seriously don't want to meet a hellhound. They are scary—like really, really scary.

Yeah, the dragon shifter is huge. Must be over eight foot. Oh, and he's silver. Silver skin, long silver hair, and his eyes are dark silver, the colour of storm clouds.

He meets my gaze. "Miss Dennison." Heck, he's so polite.

"General." I gulp. He's so dangerous. "Councillors." I nod at the rest of the room. I might as well be polite and get my introductions out of the way. Not that they care. But now isn't the time to make enemies or piss these people off. I bet they're already annoyed about having to be here in the first place.

"Until we know the girl's parentage, the vampires should be responsible for her." Lord Gilbert continues his poor attempt at controlling the room. He pulls up a datapad that I presume has my medical report on it.

Yeah, thanks for that, Dr Ross.

"It says here she's deficient in various electrolytes and that she refuses to drink blood." He lowers his tablet and haughtily glares at me. "We need to assess her." He then looks down his nose at the dragon.

Whoa, I think I'm going to rename him Death Wish for fun. The man clearly has no self-preservation.

The dragon shifter grunts and dismisses him entirely.

"I think—" Death Wish's words abruptly cut off when Atticus

turns his head and narrows his eyes. Finally, he shuts his mouth. Death Wish bristles.

I almost smirk before I can catch myself. I have to keep my face blank. Even I can pick up on his unease.

"The girl is still a child and will not be bargained for like a piece of meat," the dragon shifter finally growls out. His voice is a rumble that has every hair on my body rising. He looks around the room as if daring the others to disagree. Of course no one does.

It's my turn to bristle at being called a child—again. I'm seventeen, not a toddler.

"I believe she should stay with me," says a chocolaty voice. "I know the girl, and I am impartial."

Xander.

My eyes drift to the side of the room where he casually stands, leaning against the wall, his arms across his chest. What on earth...

"I'm a neutral party, and besides, she's my employee and I have an obligation for her welfare."

I open my mouth to correct him as to why the hell not: I quit that stupid job days ago. But his eyes narrow at me in warning, and I sensibly snap my mouth closed. Perhaps that would be a stupid thing to do.

"Xander is more than capable to see to her medical needs," the dragon agrees.

"The shifters have already attempted to kill her," the quiet, mysterious Atticus says.

"We all know females aren't safe in their care," says a dark-haired man who has the most glorious Irish accent. Madán, representative of the fae winter court. Enormous pale blue eyes and pointed ears betray him as a full-blooded aes sídhe, a warrior elf. His black hair is long, as is their custom, styled into intricate plaits. Black fae warrior markings like human tattoos start at his right hand and go all the way to his neck. They link him to his court and give him crazy powers.

Sat next to him is Magnus, blond where his colleague is dark, with green eyes instead of blue. Both warriors protect Ireland.

Everyone in the room turns at once to a sweaty Frank who stands between two angry-looking shifters. He fidgets under the room's regard.

I allow myself a small grin when I get a look at Freaky Frank's face. Shifters heal fast, crazy fast. But they have to change into their animal form to do it, and if the swollen, broken nose and the specks of crusted blood around his nostrils are any indication, he hasn't been allowed.

I did that. The darkness inside me purrs with glee that he is still hurting.

"Yes, about that," says a deep voice, a shifter.

Why don't I know this guy? My heart squeezes my blood through me in fierce, urgent beats. His whole vibe sends shivers racing across my skin. Wow, I've never had such a visceral reaction to someone before. Sharp cheekbones set off a narrow nose and a severe jaw. Heavy-lidded eyes framed by dark blue lashes.

The shifter is oily; his entire power is off. I get the general impression he's the type of man who wouldn't think twice about kicking a puppy. Every instinct tells me he's wrong, bad. I shudder.

He's handsome. I shrug. If you ignore his evil vibe. But what freaks me out at this moment is that his hair is exactly like mine. It's not quite rainbow. It's shaded differently. Blue hues are broken up with slices of green. His eyes are pale, a pale grey that is almost white.

He's a *unicorn* shifter.

Aren't unicorns supposed to be all sweetness and light?

Not this... this man... God, I'm so confused. I gnaw on my lip. This man reminds me of the darkness that festers inside me. He has the same feel.

Sick rushes up my throat, and I force myself to swallow down the mouthful of bile. My throat burns. My mind gives me the answers, answers I hadn't wanted to see.

Nature wasn't wrong.

I wasn't unbalanced.

The raging dark inside me isn't the born vampire part of me. No, it's the unicorn.

Well shit.

CHAPTER

TWENTY

THE VILLAINOUS, skin-crawling unicorn stands. All at once, it's like the room holds its collective breath. Xander shifts slightly out of the corner, and the dragon's fingers, for a microsecond, tense on the cup that he is holding.

The unicorn stalks past my chair and heads towards Frank. I can't help the small sigh of relief.

"You dishonoured yourself," he says casually. "For the crime of attempting to murder a female shifter, the punishment is death."

"Whoa, hang on a minute. I didn't know she was a half shifter. I thought she was human. I didn't shift my teeth, I can't do that. I just bit her, that's all... I just wanted to make her bleed, frighten her a little. I wasn't killing anybody. But... b-but if you want me to volunteer, I can happily take care of her." Is this guy for real? "I'm a handy guy to have—"

His head rolls across the floor.

Blood sprays everywhere. I hear a tut from Xander and a mumble about having to clean.

Yeah... shit... urm, Frank is making a mess.

Frank's, urm, severed head stops rolling at my feet. His face is a mask of shock and his eyes are still open. I lift my feet off the floor, scoot to the back of the chair, and tuck them underneath me.

The unicorn has a silver sword in his hand, which disappears into nothing as quickly as I spot it. He prowls back to his seat.

Bloody hell.

I swallow and eye the head. Yeah, I'm so out of my league on this—these men—leaders in their own right are... Yeah, I have no words.

My grandad was an assassin, so as far back as I can remember my childhood was never rainbows and kittens. But I've never seen a dead body so close before. He didn't take me on his kills.

The blood from Frank's neck slows to a trickle. It's a lot of blood.

The dragon is watching me.

He's watching my reactions, analysing me. I meet his silver gaze with wide eyes, and his eyes crinkle with what I can only presume is concern. "Did you have to do that in front of the child?" his voice rumbles.

"Did you have to do that in my living room?" Xander grumbles.

While they argue amongst themselves, I see a flash of orange. My mouth drops open. Oh no no no. Dexter struts down the hallway and into the room. Eyes fixed on me, he prowls past all the guards and councillors without care. His whole cat vibe screams like he owns the place.

On the way past the scary unicorn, his fur stands on end, and I hear a grumbling, low growl. *Oh God, Dexter. Even I know not to pick a fight with that creature.*

"Reow," he says to me innocently as he jumps up.

"Hi, baby, I've missed you. Has Xander been feeding you?" I drop my hand, and my fingers itch along his spine. "Yes, you are such a good kitty. Yes, you are." Dexter stretches up on his hind legs so his bottom cups into my palm and his fluffy tail wraps around my wrist. "What a good boy."

"Breow," he says in agreement.

His ginger fur is so soft and thick. I'm so glad his skin is no longer sore. The areas of lost hair from the nasty flea infestation have grown back beautifully.

With each rumbling purr, he blows weird kitty bubbles from his lips; he swings his head to rub his wet mouth on my hand. I shudder. "Yuck, Dexter, thanks for the spit bath. Keep that shit to yourself." I wrinkle my nose and rub my glistening skin on my hoodie.

Satisfied with marking me as his, he drops to the floor, and with his tail waving in the air, he struts across the room to rub against the humongous *dragon*. An *eep* sound makes its way out from my lips.

Oh no.

I shuffle to the edge of my seat—I'm ready to run interference if needed. To make matters worse, Dexter *jumps* onto the guy's lap. I cringe and close my eyes. The dragon shifter grunts, and when I cautiously look back, a big silver hand gently strokes my cat.

The conversation in the room continues as I nervously bite my lip and watch the dragon with my cat.

"How can she have not been found before?"

"Some idiot has been slacking."

"Who was hiding her?"

"Which criminal was hiding her? I demand his head," the unicorn says. I lift my eyes from Dexter and can't help a little snort. *Yeah 'cause you're good with chopping.*

I try to avoid looking at the floor and the *head* that's still sitting there... gazing at me.

I hug my knees to my chest and pull my hoodie up over my mouth. I'm not willing to put them back on the floor. I don't think Frank's going to come back from the dead and chomp at me—although with necromancers... I shudder. I just don't want my feet to be near the goo.

"The fae responsible is dead," Xander tells them. His eyes track the top of my hoodie as I bury my face up to my nose. Grandad.

"Magic was keeping her alive. Strong fae magic. I can see the remnants on her. It's been fading for months," says Madán, the dark-haired fae.

Months since I became sick. Months since my grandad died.

"When that magic dried up, then the girl became ill."

"Wouldn't that take a lot of magic?" Atticus the vampire asks.

"Yes, the person would have to be full fae."

"If he wasn't?" I interrupt with a small cough to clear my throat. I lift my head so my mouth is clear of the red fabric. "What would happen if the person wasn't full fae?"

Madán turns his head and addresses me directly. "If the person wasn't full fae, they'd be using their life force to embed the magic. It's not recommended. If they did that for long enough, they'd die."

Oh, Grandad, what did you do?

I hunch. My heart feels like it jerks in my chest, and my tummy flips with the realisation. The man who was an assassin, the slayer of monsters, who should have had a warrior's death or lived a thousand more years, died slowly, his magic bleeding out of him.

Because of *me*.

Pain, guilt, grief clog my throat so tightly I struggle to breathe.

The illness that took him was him protecting me, giving his life force to keep me alive.

Despair rolls over me like a wave, and suddenly I feel like I'm underwater. The voices in the room become garbled. They reverberate. I can't make out what they are saying. All I can hear is the *thud thud thud* of my heart.

He shouldn't have done that.

Why the hell did you do that? My temples throb, and the lump of pain and guilt is lodged in my throat, now so thick I can scarcely breathe.

With a swallow, I lift my chin, and I stare up at the ceiling so my pain can't leak out of my eyes. I let out a deep, shaky breath, then another.

I will not belittle his sacrifice by moaning *why me, why me*.

No, I'm going to be grateful. I am grateful, and I'm going to make him proud. Is my life worth more than his? Hell no. But I will not throw away his sacrifice. *I love you, Grandad. I love you so very much.*

Small feet land on my shoulder, and I feel a warm, small body against my neck. In a sweet whispering voice, Story says, "It's okay. Don't let them see you are hurting. Stay strong for just a little while longer." My lip wobbles at the kindness of my friend, and I snap my spine straight.

The meeting continues, and they agree to run more tests. Until my family can be identified—if I have any living relatives—it appears we will stay with Xander.

Yay.

I'd rather they pop me into a nice quiet warm prison cell.

"Well, I've had an interesting day. It's been a pleasure to meet you, Miss Dennison, and your friends. You have been a pleasant surprise."

I let out a squeak and lift my eyes. The dragon shifter is standing in front of my chair. For a humongous shifter, he can sure move silently.

Dexter butts himself against the dragon's leg, leaving a smatter of orange hair—his calling card—on the shifter's trousers. My eyes widen, and I snap my head up.

Shit, I hope he doesn't notice.

"I haven't seen a beithíoch guardian for such a long time." The dragon drops that bomb of information almost offhandedly. "Xander knows where to find me if you need assistance. Have a good evening." He smiles gently at me and Story and bows his head in reverence to *Dexter*.

"It was nice to meet you, bye," I say robotically, pulling on my ingrained manners. I'm too busy staring at my cat to watch him go.

"Dexter," I whisper, "you've been very sneaky."

"He's not the only one. When were you going to tell me about you being poorly? You've been ill for weeks, and you've hidden it from me until you couldn't. You almost died. Do you know how scared I was?" Story pokes my shoulder with a jabby finger. "Oh, and were you ever going to tell me you're half vampire, half shifter? I thought we were friends." Her bottom lip wobbles, and her eyes fill with tears.

I hunch back into my hoodie. "I'm sorry."

"I love you. You're my best friend, so no more secrets."

"Okay... I am sorry, Story. I only didn't tell you to protect you. No more secrets."

Story jumps down into my hand and taps her foot on my little finger. "Pinky swear?" she says. Determination shines in her big sapphire eyes.

I can't help my chuckle. I wiggle my finger. "Okay, pinky swear."

Story twists around my finger as if it's a stripper pole. I wince as the agile pixie almost pulls my finger out of its socket. "Sooo Xander is nice," she says as she twists.

Oh crap, I promised not to keep secrets.

I lower my head and whisper tell her *all* about him.

When the angel comes back into the room from seeing his *guests* to his fancy portal—I say guests loosely—Story has a raging look on her face.

She stands on my knee with her hands on her hips. Radiating barely controlled fury.

"What?" Xander asks puzzled.

Story taps her foot in agitation. "Oh, I don't know... Perhaps I need to get someone to clean out your pantry. What with all the out-of-date cans in there," she snarls.

Oops, I really have been a terrible influence on my once-sweet friend.

Xander narrows his eyes in confusion for a few seconds, then his eyes comically widen, and he rubs a frustrated hand through his hair. "About that, I'm sorry. I wasn't very nice to you, my sha—" He scrubs his face.

Huh, has he forgotten my name already?

"Tru," I mumble.

"Tru," Xander says as he drops his chin and tilts his head to the side so I can see him clench his jaw. "Well, it looks like all the councils have agreed. I will be your guardian for the foreseeable future."

I snort. "You're my guardian? My guardian angel?" I slap my hand across my mouth as I giggle. Xander looks at me blankly, and I laugh harder. "Never mind, inside joke." I guff. He looks heavenward for patience. He closes his eyes and shakes his head.

When he reopens his eyes, I'm back in control, and I watch as Xander's attention goes to the floor and the congealed pool of blood.

Without thinking, I also glance down and immediately gag. There's a fly sat on Frank's eyeball. It's sat there... happily cleaning its front legs. I close my eyes and rub the back of my hand across my mouth. God.

"Right. Let me get this guy sorted, and then we can have something to eat."

I gag again, and my stomach churns. I vigorously shake my head. I am not up for food, no way. Thanks to Frank, I've lost my appetite.

"Don't shake your head, young lady. You heard the vampires and Dr Ross, you need a proper diet. You starving yourself will not help. Do I have to remind you you're going through a vampire transition? You need to practise better self-care."

Is this guy for real? There's a dead body on the floor.

"I know all that." I throw my hands in the air in frustration. "I'm just not hungry at the moment. Perhaps my appetite will come back when there's not a fucking body on the floor." God, I can smell it; the metallic scent of his blood has seeped into my clothes and skin.

"Go to your room. We will talk about this later."

"Okay." Arsehole. This whole situation is surreal. What does he expect me to say, pass the tomato ketchup?

Xander's foot knocks Frank's head closer to his body. I jerk back in my seat as I watch the head roll. It moves along the floor at a weird angle. *It must be the nose.* As soon as the head bumps to a stop, Xander's fingers twitch and glow gold. Waves of gold magic seep out from his hands.

I sweep Story into my palm and slide from the chair. I almost crawl over the arm to get away. I keep my eyes on him and take a hasty few steps back.

"Today has been way too much. The unicorn, the dragon, the council, the head chopping...," I mumble as I back away. *The revelation about my grandad's illness.* "This is all way too much."

Xander opens his hand over the body. There's a hiss and a flash of bright light, and the body that was Freaky Frank is gone.

Dissipated.

Shit, there's no way he's ever touching me with those glowing digits. No way.

"What are you waiting for? Go to your room," Xander says not even looking back at me as he directs his magic at the congealed pool of blood.

I suck a deep breath in. Is this guy so used to dealing with dead bodies, so used to dealing with the monsters, that he doesn't realise how inappropriate he's being? Has he forgotten how to treat people or does he not care?

I hate him.

Without another word, I turn and scurry away.

CHAPTER
TWENTY-ONE

LIKE A GOOD GIRL, I go to my room. A childlike part of me wants to stomp my feet and slam the door, but I keep my steps light as I prowl down the hallway with Dexter scampering at my heels. We slip into my allocated bedroom. The door gently clicks shut, it needs a lock.

Not that a tiny basic lock will keep the angel out. I can only hope he has a modicum of decency left in his body and he leaves me alone.

I need some time to process.

I feel a little heartsick.

"I apologise for grabbing you like that, Story," I say as I place her gently down on the bed. "He freaked me out."

"It's fine. I'm fine."

I slump down next to her, and Dexter joins us. I gently stroke his fur. "Okay, what can you tell me?"

"Your grandad's toolbox is in there with all your clothing." She points to the built-in wardrobes.

I nod with relief. That's a good start.

"Everything else is in the bedroom next to us. He left all the big stuff in the garage, all the furniture including your bed."

I wave away her worry. It doesn't matter as long as my grandad's stuff is safe... but how safe is it? Nothing will ever be safe again.

"Oh, Tru, I don't understand that man. When you were unconscious, he carried you like you were made of precious glass. He was so reverent, gentle." Story shakes her head and bounces across the bed as she waves her hands in the air.

Dexter follows her erratic movement, and his tail twitches. "Don't even think about it," I mouth. I poke him in his squidgy ginger belly with my finger. The not-fat cat rolls onto his back. All four legs stretch out. He lifts his chin and closes his eyes when I obediently stroke his spotted ginger tummy.

"For days he watched over you and he used his angel magic to help you. He saved your life. It was so romantic." She turns and stomps back. "Then you wake up and he turns into a complete dick. I don't understand it."

"It's 'cause he is a dick," I grumble. "I told you what he did."

"Nooo," Story wails. "He was like a prince storming a castle to rescue you." She dramatically swoons, falling back onto the bed. I watch as her body bounces. Story flips on her side and rests her head in her hand.

"He's still a dick," I say.

"He fought for you."

"Nah, he fought for himself."

Story groans and flops onto her back. I lie down next to her and turn my head in her direction. A claw pads my hand to keep on stroking.

"Look, he did all that before he knew what I was. I unintentionally made the angel look like an idiot in front of all the councils and the hunter's guild. Put it this way: I think he would have preferred it if I'd carked it.

"A dead Tru is better than a hybrid Tru in that man's eyes. He didn't like me anyway... Do I have to tell you again how he told me I made him feel sick?" I huff and rub my chest. Dexter takes that as an invitation and jumps onto the spot I just rubbed. I can't breathe for a second. Shit, he's heavy. He might be a little overweight.

"To top that complete shitshow off, I get bitten by a shifter and outed as a hybrid. A hybrid posing as a human working in his club. He's trying to save face."

"Gah, you are so stubborn." Story kicks her legs in the air. "Okay, I admit defeat. I will not win this as you've already made up your mind. What are *we* gonna do? Cause if you think I'm leaving you to deal with this on your own...," she growls out. "What's our plan?"

"Breow," Dex says as if in agreement as he butts me underneath my chin with his big head.

"The doctor says I'm still sick. According to the vampires, I'm going through a pureblood transition. So I guess I can't go anywhere until I get a grip on all this health stuff. I guess... We've got to play this by ear. One thing I know is these people aren't playing games. That unicorn shifter chopped Frank's head off for just taking a chunk out of my finger, a finger that healed in a matter of minutes with the help of a potion. They can do what they want."

What the hell are they going to do to me if I don't toe the line?

And how bad will a pissed-off angel be to live with?

It's been a few weeks, and nothing much has happened. Xander has avoided me, which has made things easier. It looks like he will be an absentee guardian. He at least allowed me to return to work at the café. Which brought me back to some normality.

Well, normal if I ignore my new bodyguards, who as you can imagine, love coming to work with me.

I've still not got my head around things. The big revelation about my grandad's death has caused me so much anguish I suffer from raging guilt. That kind of knowledge changes a person. I guess it's changing me.

I'm so grateful to have Story and Dexter to talk to. Story has been incredible, and I know Dexter is supposed to be a fae monster cat, but he's my monster cat.

Heck, cats are so damn sneaky anyway, so much so I do not doubt that they'll take over the world and we as their slaves will just watch them do it. Helping them out by making encouraging kissy noises. Or is that just me?

My questions about the unicorns have gone unanswered. Everyone believes the propaganda. I don't know if I'm right about the dark parts of me being connected to my shifter side. I'm not one hundred percent sure... but it feels right.

Wow, when I think about what evil, sneaky creatures unicorn shifters are, it's a serious public relations coup that they've had everybody believing unicorns are true creatures of light.

But then again, I'm learning that everyone has good and evil inside them, and nothing is black-and-white.

I wish in some ways I could wave a magic wand and be forgotten. Become the invisible girl again.

Even if it's temporary, we have a warm place to stay and a good amount of money accumulating in the bank. The weight of worry on my shoulders has lifted a little from us no longer living in a cold damp garage.

I thought... I thought things were finally working out.

Then bruises reappeared.

And *he* noticed.

CHAPTER
TWENTY-TWO

"I AM SORRY, Tru, but there are rules that I have to follow, and this is a vampire issue. By your own admission, you've been hiding things from me. It shouldn't have got to this stage. How can I do my job as your guardian if you don't trust me?" Xander adjusts the sleeves of his jacket. He's wearing an immaculate black suit and shirt. He looks sexy as hell.

And he catches me staring at him.

Red-faced, I stare at the floor.

Gah, I need to stop doing that. I fidget. I wish my body would stop betraying me. Every time I catch sight of him my brain short circuits, and... I want to jump him. Climb him like a tree. It's mortifying as it's pretty obvious how he feels about me... *the child*.

"What happens today is on you. You should have told me sooner that you weren't feeling well."

I scrunch my face. What does he mean by what happens today is on me?

Bloody hell, that doesn't sound good.

Xander's heavy hand lands on the back of my neck as he guides me down the hall to the portal. Why has he got to be so handsy? I attempt to wiggle away.

Him touching me is not helping my short-circuiting brain. Where does he think I'm gonna go? He squeezes my neck in a warning, and I take the hint and stop wiggling.

"I don't want to go see the vampires," I whine as I drag my feet. Undeterred, Xander uses his grip on my neck to push me forward. *Steady there, angel.* God, if he's not careful, he will be squishing my nose against a door.

This is my fault. I thought I was being sneaky. It was Story's idea to empty the bottles of blood into the loo when everyone dismissed my concerns. They wouldn't listen, so I lied. I pretended I was drinking the vile stuff.

I don't know how Xander found out I wasn't, but obviously, he did.

Hence this fun trip.

I guess no amount of makeup can cover my deathly pale skin and the purple bags underneath my eyes. Plus the horrendous bruises on my arms.

So yeah, I told Xander the truth... I can lie by omission, but I can't lie to that man's face—bloody angel mojo—and his response? He goes and immediately dobs me in to the vampire council. *Nice one, Tru.* I should have kept my gob shut.

I should never have trusted the tattletale angel.

Of course the sensible vampire Atticus is unavailable. Even though he's mysterious and a little bit of an unknown, I'd rather deal with that guy than Lord Gilbert, aka the fake posh prick.

I don't feel very sociable, and I should be at work, not playing at vampire diplomacy. I don't know what the angel thinks is going to happen. It's not like I'm gonna be enamoured by Lord Luther Gilbert and start chugging down blood like it's going out of fashion.

We should be really going to the doctor if Xander is so worried about my health.

We stand in front of a normal-looking door with a fancy rune keypad. The portal. Portals are a worldwide gateway system that takes you *instantly* to other places and sometimes other *worlds*. If you know the code to where you are going, you enter it and just walk through the door.

They're expensive pieces of kit, and I've never met anyone who's owned one personally. Xander has one in his house. He's such a show-off.

Xander doesn't bother to give me an answer and stoically inputs the gateway code. Together we step through the magical door.

The power of the gateway tickles the hairs on my arms, but it doesn't feel uncomfortable.

"Ha, Lord Gilbert hasn't got his own portal," I say with glee, instantly forgetting that I've been bullied into this visit. We've stepped into an alleyway.

It must rile up the vampire something proper to have his visitors pop out of a communal alley door—a spotless alley, but still.

I giggle.

Xander looks down at me with a soft smile. "Nice, huh?"

"It must drive the fake posh prick bonkers."

"Yes." He laughs with me. His eyes are perfect: honey flecked with gold, sparkling with fire, mirth, and intelligence. His strong jaw is shadowed perfectly by the light... My lips part.

And he catches me staring at him again.

Hastily, I avert my eyes. Oh, look at that... I recognise the area. It's a relief to know we're not in another city or, heaven forbid, in another world.

There's a bakery up the street that competes with our café. Their chocolate cake is to die for. I wonder if Xander will let me grab a few slices once we have dealt with this.

I giggle again when we arrive at a squat, grotty-looking building, and I see the sign VAMPIRE'S KISS plastered all over the building. What an original name. I clap my hands. A vampire that owns a nightclub, how predictable. I wonder if Xander sees this place as a competition to Night-*Shift*. From the look of the outside, I bet he doesn't.

"We're meeting him here?"

"This is where he lives."

Oh. So no fancy estate for Lord Gilbert. He tumbles down even further in my estimation. Not that he had far to fall. Not that I think money makes a person. No, it's their character. The man is a bully. But with all his pomp and attitude, you think he'd somehow be able to back all that up.

I snort when it registers that he's dressed his vampire guards—standing lazily outside the club as if they're waiting for a bus—in cheap red uniforms.

He's aiming, and spectacularly failing, at the impression of guard duty at Buckingham Palace. Yeah, Lord Luther Gilbert is all fur coat and no knickers.

"Lord Gilbert is expecting us," Xander addresses a guard. The guy nods and shuffles away as he speaks into his headset.

The other vampires stare menacingly at us. Which gets my back up straightaway. *How rude.* I dance from foot to foot. Xander's hand touches the back of my neck again, and the gentle pressure stills my movement and makes me shiver. What's with all the touching? I roll my shoulder and step to the side, knocking his hand away.

"Will you follow me," a creepy-looking butler guard says as he flings the door open. We follow him into the club.

You'd think the vampire lord would invite us into his home, which I presume is somewhere in this building, but no. We stand waiting for him to dazzle us with his presence in the empty club. Next to the bar.

Xander silently stands to attention, his hands tucked behind his back and his legs spread as if he's in the military. I don't blame him for standing like that. It means he doesn't have to touch anything. This place is as grotty on the inside as it is out.

I frown down at my boots and lift my toes... Ew, the floor is sticky. Every time I move my feet the soles of my boots squeak. Much to my amusement, I find myself composing a little squeaky tune.

Xander clears his throat.

Lord Gilbert glides into the room. He nods at his man, and like a well-trained puppet, the butler guard leaves. "The fewer people who know about you, the better," he says, running his hands down his out-of-place fancy grey suit. "Okay, Angel, you can leave her with me. Wait outside."

What? I look at Xander with pleading eyes. I try to silently tell him, "Don't leave me with the posh twat." What the hell am I doing here? I barely refrain from grabbing Xander's arm as he nods at the vampire and walks away.

Xander leaves. He leaves me alone with this strange vampire.

Thanks a lot, guardian, I mentally grumble.

I slump onto a nearby stool as Lord Gilbert steps behind the bar and pulls out a glass bottle from the fridge and gives it a shake. The liquid sloshes inside, and I wrinkle my nose with distaste.

"I'm a busy man, and I haven't got time for these childish games. They have informed me that you've not been drinking. We've made many exceptions due to your nature, and I won't force you to drink from the vein, but you must drink. Your refusal is a black mark on your character and offensive to our kind. You're not trying. If you don't drink this blood while I watch, I am going to force it down your neck." He undoes the metal lid, the top clicks, and the tamper seal pops.

Ah, now it all makes sense, why I'm here. I'm not feeling very well, and my brain has mushed a little. Who better than a vampire to encourage me to eat?

Lord Gilbert slams the bottle down onto the bar, and a droplet of blood hits my hand.

I stare at it as it spreads bright red across my skin.

I lift my eyes and meet his determined glare. Is he serious right now? Do people not listen to a word I say?

"Was I not clear when I told the council blood makes me poorly?" I snatch up a surprisingly clean cloth from the bar and vigorously rub my hand. The rancid smell of the blood is making me feel sick.

I chuck the cloth away and rub my forehead with frustration. "You wouldn't force me," I scoff incredulously.

He wouldn't force me... Would he? I wiggle on the stool and push myself back. The legs scrape against the floor. Huh. It's a miracle the chair moved at all what with all the gunk on the floor.

I need to get as far away from the bottle as I can. It's like somebody waving a packet of peanuts at someone with a nut allergy and shouting, "Just eat one. What will be the harm?" I'm not kidding when I say blood does not agree with me.

The man's an idiot.

"Drink the blood, girl," he growls. He leans forward and nudges the bottle closer to me.

"I'm a vegetarian, and blood makes me sick." I lean forward and push the bottle back.

"You're what?" Lord Gilbert scoffs, dismissively. "You're a vampire. A disgusting disgrace of one, but even I can admit you have pure blood running through your veins."

"I'm also a unicorn shifter," I say. I try to keep my tone reasonable. I wouldn't want to be accused of being a *child*. I clench my fists. Yeah, Xander might have given me a complex with that one.

For a millisecond, the vampire's eyes widen with surprise. Huh, my being a unicorn is news to him. Good to know.

I glance down at the bottle of blood, and my nostrils flare. The smell wafting from it is putrid. If he thinks this is him helping me—I shake my head—if he thinks this is a good idea, trying to bully me into drinking that rancid crap, it's not.

I'm done with this shit. I relinquish my manners. "You're being a dick," I say as I stand, abandoning the stool. His body tenses at my words, and he flashes his fangs. Eek, I really shouldn't have said that to the scary vampire, but fuck him. He started it. I cringe and take a step back.

Look at that. I am pissing him off.

It's kind of good 'cause I'm pissed off too.

"You're not listening." I throw my hands in the air and take another small step back. "I'm not doing this on purpose to myself, arsehole. Do you think I want to be ill?" He eyes my arm, which is almost entirely covered in bruises. I tug my left sleeve down. "Blood makes me sick."

His eyes flicker red, and his voice lowers dangerously. "This is something you've been avoiding, and it's a stipulation of the vampires. The only thing stopping us from taking you at the moment is the other councils and your age. As soon as you're eighteen, it's game on. That angel protector of yours can't take on all the vampires. All the shifters. Between us, we will rip him to shreds."

Crikey. When he puts it like that... I suddenly can't help worrying about Xander's health. I didn't realise the situation was so precarious. God, how selfish I have been. While I've been moaning about him being a crap guardian, he's been dealing with all this shit on my behalf.

"You feel comfortable being protected by that angel? Think about what your life will be like when we force feed you in a cell. *Breed you,* as that's the only way we can take advantage of your blood. As you, girl, are already a lost cause."

Breed me. Fucking hell.

I laugh to stop myself from throwing up. My entire body shivers with disgust. I guess that explains why I'm still alive. I bet he wasn't supposed to share that little titbit. I'll file it away to freak about later.

Shit, I knew things being quiet were a bad sign.

"You're hurting the bloodline by not taking blood. This stops today. You need blood, girl. The vampire side of you is *starving*, and you are no use to us dead."

My vampire side is starving.

"Sit. Down," he snarls with another flash of his fangs.

I don't.

I take another small step away, and my eyes flick to the door. Suddenly I'm airborne. My back thuds against the bar.

Shit.

"Get the fuck off me."

Instead of letting me go, he slams me again against the bar like I am a rag doll.

Ouch.

He drags me closer and forces me between his legs. My heart pounds in my ears, and inside my head, dozens of countermoves flash to the forefront of my mind. I have enough skill, enough training... but my body. Crap, I am so, so weak.

In one hand, Luther—I guess I can drop the lord title—grips my neck, and with his other hand, he grabs the blood from the counter. He shoves the cold bottle at me, and it smacks against my teeth. I squeak in alarm and quickly clamp my lips closed.

"Drink," he growls.

I shake my head, and I try to pull away, but his big hand against my neck holds me firmly. With all my strength, I jerk my head to the side, and the bottle hits my cheek.

I risk opening my mouth. "Get the fuck off me. You are hurting me." His hand continues to grip my neck, and his thumb digs into my jaw. I dig my nails into his wrist.

"Drink the life-saving blood. This aversion you have is all in your head."

"Fuck off," I say, my tone vicious.

Luther growls, and his cheek brushes against mine. "You say that like a child who's refusing to eat her vegetables."

Gah, child. I thrash about, or at least I attempt to; the vampire has got me so tightly against him I can't move an inch. "You don't understand. You're making a mistake."

"You'll be useless if you're dead."

"I WILL get sicker if you do," I yell.

I realise I've made a mistake as soon as the words leave my mouth. A finger slips between my lips, quickly followed by a thumb. The vampire prises my teeth apart.

Wide-eyed, I watch as the bottle of blood tips.

Blood fills my mouth.

CHAPTER
TWENTY-THREE

I TRY to shake my head from side to side. I try to spit the blood out. But the vampire's hand on my jaw keeps my head back and mouth open. I choke, and some of the blood splatters onto his face. I cough and the blood hits the back of my throat.

Oh God, no.

I swallow.

The first trickle of blood burns the back of my throat.

My throat seizes.

The empty bottle clatters to the bar, and Luther's hand slaps across my lips. The bastard forces my mouth closed, and his fingers pinch my nostrils.

I can't breathe.

The remaining pool of blood congeals in my mouth. The rancid smell of it overwhelms my senses. My throat is unwilling to swallow anymore.

Creepy, gentle fingers caress my neck.

"Swallow," he whispers in my ear. "It's okay. Everything's going to be okay. Swallow."

Liar.

The whole situation reminds me of when I give Dexter a worming tablet. Shit, regulated to pet status. *I am so sorry, Dexter.* I wonder if he needed worming what with being a fae monster cat. *I am lucky he didn't eat my face.*

Now this idiot thinks I have a blood aversion. That is psychological, psychosomatic. It isn't. Black wiggly lines fill my vision. "Drink, damn you."

I hate him. I hate him for doing this. Luther slams my head back against the bar.

I swallow the blood.

Cold claggy, congealed blood gushes down my throat. My stomach twists and turns. "Now that didn't hurt," Luther coos.

Ha, says the man who hasn't just had his head slammed against a bar several times. Perhaps if I returned the favour, it would knock some sense into him.

He lets me go, and I scramble to the other side of the room. I cough and wipe my mouth with the back of my hand. A lone tear runs down my cheek. I can't look at him. I have the strongest urge to go home, crawl into bed, and hide underneath the covers. Or kill him. I wouldn't mind getting my hands around his throat. Now isn't the time. My legs wobble as I step towards the door.

"Don't leave yet. Until I can trust you not to do something stupid, you won't be going anywhere. At least until I know the blood is in your system." He pulls out his phone with dismissal. He's all business. It's as if he hasn't just... My inner voice whines in my head... I feel violated.

Everything inside me wants to run away, but the thought of him touching me again is revolting.

God, I feel so vulnerable. I place my back against the wall, wrap my arms around myself, and hunch forward. I hide my face from him so he can't see the tears in my eyes.

I want Story. I want my cat. I want... *Xander.*

Not even five minutes after I've drained the bottle, my body revolts.

It starts with a tremble. My body seizes, and it shakes. A sharp pain hits my stomach as if a knife is stabbing me in the abdomen. The pain is excruciating. Unable to stand, I slide down the wall. My bottom hits the dirty carpet—thump.

"Xander," I groan. I need his help.

"I will call you back," Luther says. I tuck my knees to my chest, and a small whimper leaves my throat. Luther's lip curls, and he shakes his head. He tucks his phone into his jacket. "Don't be so dramatic. You can go in a minute."

Ants are crawling underneath my skin, and I'm now shaking so hard my teeth rattle and my head snaps back, smacking against the wall. For fuck's sake, my poor head. I'll be lucky if leave here without brain damage.

I slump to the side and roll into a ball. "Xander," I say a little louder. *I need you*.

Outside the room, my ears pick up the sound of a scuffle. I feel a wisp of a breeze rather than see the door fly open, and a familiar big warm hand touches the pulse in my throat.

He came back.

My eyes close with relief. Seeking golden magic glows around me. Instead of its usual flood, the angel's magic is just a trickle. Crap. It doesn't feel enough to battle through the conflict going on in my body. The magic inside me is going haywire, and even my angel's magic can't compete.

"Her eyes are bleeding." Xander tilts my head back, and I groan. Huh. Now he mentions it, my face is wet, sticky. "And her ears. Vampire, what did you do?"

"I gave her blood," Luther replies drolly.

"I'm not dying from this. Don't you worry, I'll be on my feet in a minute." I rasp. My chest burns and my heart stutters. I lurch away from Xander's warm hands and flop back onto my side. I cough and choke. A rush of hot liquid burns a path up my throat, and more blood violently sprays out of my nose and mouth. I can't...

Shiny shoes approach my head. Luther chuckles. "My, my. She wasn't kidding about blood making her sick. How unusual." Still chuckling, the bastard walks away. Unconcerned about the bleeding girl on his floor.

"Good luck with that," he says helpfully.

"Ross, Lord Gilbert gave her blood, and she's having an adverse reaction."

"Adverse, how adverse?" *Oh, hey Doc*. Look at that. I can hear him...

The doctor must be on speakerphone. This is all your fault, Mr Stripey Shirt, leaving me with that creepy-ass vampire. Would it be petulant to tell him I told him so? *You shouldn't have told the vampires my secret.*

"Did you just give her one bottle?" Xander asks the retreating vampire.

"Yes. Let it be known that the vampire council formally relinquish our claim. She's defective and useless. You have ten minutes to get her body out of my club," Luther says. A door slams shut.

What. A. Dick.

"She's bleeding from her eyes and ears, and she's vomited more than she drank. The blood is dark"—as if I am going to die, I violently cough out more blood—"with chunks. Her heart rate is rapid, and her breathing has become seriously laboured." Xander gently strokes my hair. "My healing magic has had no effect. I can heal everything. Why can't I heal you?"

I try to take a breath, but I keep on inhaling the blood, and I can't... My lungs aren't working; I feel like I am drowning. My chest burns, my eyes fly open, and panicked, I claw at his arm. Why can't I breathe? Fucking hell. I knew he'd be the death of me.

Blood has always made me sick, but I didn't think it would kill me.

"I am on my way."

"No time... Tru? Fuck, she's stopped breathing. What the hell have I done?"

My hands fall uselessly to my sides as Xander rips my top down the middle, and there's a splash of something on my chest. An empty potion vial lands on the floor by my hand.

"Healing potion?"

"As yet no effect."

"Give her your blood," the doctor demands.

"What? No. Blood got us into this mess... I'm starting chest compressions." Xander's warm palms settle on my breastbone. Liquid bubbles in my throat, and my chest rattles.

"Xander, give her your blood," the doctor growls. "Trust me."

There's a strange whoosh, and something soft, like a feather, tickles against my throat. Warm hands pull me up from the floor, and I'm back in his arms. My head flops to the side and Xander tucks me against his chest.

He lays a gentle hand on my cheek and traces my blood-covered lips with his thumb.

"Drink."

Urm, no, thank you. I have enough blood for a lifetime, more isn't going to do shit. The scent of sunlight and metal hits me. It's the most beautiful, delicious... What the fuck? How can I smell if I can't breathe? I can't believe even after everything I *dreamed* of being in his arms, and now that I am... Well, this wasn't what I meant.

Not this.

He cups my jaw and presses my lips against the crook of his elbow.

The taste in my mouth makes my eyes roll to the back of my head. Boiling hot, golden sunlight fills me while Xander's golden magic floods my chest and laps at my soul.

I feel full, warm. Safe.

I gasp. It's then that I realise my nose is clear and I'm breathing normally. I'm no longer shaking. No longer dying.

Yay, go me.

Feathers brush against me, and my eyes flutter open. I am cocooned in velvety darkness. A gentle hand brushes my hair away from my face, and I blink so I can focus on his worried, sad honey eyes. "It's okay, my shadow. You're okay. Take as much as you need."

Take as much as I need? What?

Oh... OH.

My mouth is clamped against *skin*. Warm glowing angel skin. A muscular forearm, to be exact. My teeth... my *fangs* are sticking in a vein at Xander's elbow. I am gulping the angel's blood down like a milkshake.

Ha. Oh crap.

CHAPTER
TWENTY-FOUR

"All right. It's been twenty-four hours, and we need to keep this on schedule." I greet the angel with a low groan as he prowls into my room. Obscenely, he rolls up his shirtsleeves. Oh shit. I look away, forearms are not for licking. "You need to eat."

Or perhaps they are.

Double shit.

Saliva floods my mouth, and I have to force myself to remain on the bed. I can feel my cheeks glowing a bright pink.

"I'm not hungry," I mumble as I stare intently at my phone.

Oooh, I'm such a liar.

I could so eat the Michelin-three-star-rated angel. The mobile in my hand makes little sense as my brain is currently fried. My heart thuds in my chest, and what feels like a colony of bats are smashing against each other while having a party in my abdomen.

"I'm just going to go watch some television," the little traitor Story squeaks out. She knows all about what happened yesterday.

She smirks at me, then zips out of the room as if her bum is on fire.

"Come on, Tru. You know angel blood is the only option you have at the moment. You don't want to be getting poorly again, do you?"

"Don't we have any other angels knocking around?" I ask him while peering over his shoulder. "Anyone?"

"I'm your guardian, and you're my responsibility. Dr Ross says my blood will keep you alive through your vampire transition."

"Dr Ross," I huff. "What does that guy know? He's a field doctor, not a specialist."

"So you want to see a specialist?" His eyebrows rise.

"No," I mumble as I abandon my phone on the bed and nervously play with the zip on my hoodie.

Xander licks his bottom lip, it glistens. And something feminine and interested raises her head.

"Show me your bruises."

Huh, since eating him... I briefly close my eyes before they roll out of my head. Even my thoughts are going rogue. I mean, since I drank his blood, shit. It's a lot to get my head around, but my crush on him has gone up to level one thousand.

I thought it was unmanageable before I tasted his blood, but now it's crazy. Last night I dreamed of him. The way I feel at this moment, the man could hold a knife to my throat, and I'd kiss him on the cheek and tell him he's adorable.

It's freaking me out.

I grip my libido with a mental fist and give it a shake. *Stop it, you horny bitch.*

I'm living my worst nightmare. Not only do I have to live with a man who spectacularly turned me down—even though I didn't make a move on him in the first place. Big-headed bastard. *Now* it looks as if he is the only person who can feed my *starving* vampire side. You know the irony isn't lost on me at all. There's mortifying, and then there's this. This is a whole new other level.

Okay, what did he want again? He wants to see my bruises. I huff as I drag my left sleeve up and show him in my arm. "I haven't got any bruises," I say as I rotate the limb. "I'm fine."

"Exactly. My blood is working. Look..." He rubs the back of his neck, and I watch the play of muscles under his shirt. His pecs pop, and his wide shoulders strain the fabric. I surreptitiously try to fan my face.

"I know I broke your trust, and my actions hurt you. Please believe it was not my intent." His beautiful eyes are full of pain.

At this moment he's never looked more like an angel. I can tell how conflicted he is and how guilty he feels. I have a sneaky suspicion that this man has been in my corner all along, fighting to keep me alive.

Crikey, does that mean I need to apologise to Story? She's been a strong advocate for him all along.

Nah.

"I heard you while I was snacking on your arm. Look, let's get real. If I tell you something, will you try"—I tilt my head to the side and hold up a finger—"no, will you promise to give me the benefit of the doubt and listen to me before you do something stupid like leave me alone with a crazy vampire?"

"I promise to discuss things with you."

"Okay, 'cause that's what friends do." I nod with conviction and then blush twenty shades of red when I realise what I've said. He's my guardian, the man that the council's put in place to keep me in line. He isn't my friend, and I shouldn't presume that he is.

Aah, why is it my head will not work when I'm around this man? I twist my hands in my lap. "Thank you for saving my life." I might as well get that out there while I'm on a roll. At least I can pretend later that we haven't had this conversation and that he didn't flash his veins at me.

"Just admit my blood is working, that you need more. But I won't force you."

Yeah, been there, done that.

I keep on thinking about the chunks that came out of my mouth. I am sure I coughed up an organ, perhaps a little bit of lung. I shudder.

Xander moves closer, and I can smell him, smell the blood in his veins, and my fangs ache. "Okay," I whisper as I fiddle with my zip. "Urm... Give me your arm..." Yes, stick out the hot delicious forearm with all those blood-filled veins for me to chomp on.

He sits down on the bed, and I shuffle next to him. Our shoulders brush, and my skin tingles. He holds his tree-trunk-sized arm out to me. The bloody thing is three times bigger than my own. I shouldn't like that he makes me feel so delicate, but I do.

My hands shake with nerves.

"Did you know," Xander says gently, his voice a rumble, the cadence so low I have to lean closer to hear him. "My blood isn't completely red like a human. If you look at a drop of my blood, even a human would be able to see that it has little golden flakes running through it."

"Oh, I didn't know that," I whisper back.

I don't know why I'm whispering, but it seems right, intimate. Logically, I know what he's doing. He's trying to make me feel better. He's trying to make me relax.

It's not working. My heart hammers in my ears, and I feel anxious and a little bit sweaty. I juggle his arm in both my hands. It's like lifting a log. Even though he's holding most of the weight, it's still heavy. I swallow and lick my lips as I pull his arm towards my face. My mouth waters.

I dip my head and inhale his sunlight and metal scent; it makes me feel dizzy. My eyelashes flutter. I force myself to look away from his arm and into his eyes. I need to double-check, ask for his permission.

Xander nods, my tongue darts out, and I lick the crease of his elbow with the flat of my tongue. The salty taste of his skin floods my mouth. Ha, I licked him. I wiggle as the feminine part of me clenches.

I peek up at him from underneath my lashes, and his eyes are closed, and his forehead is creased as if he is in pain.

"My shadow, I am not a chocolate bar," he grumbles. "Get on with it."

I snort. Licking helps with the pain. I think there's something in my spit, or that's the excuse I tell myself. Fuck it. I don't know how many times I'll get to do this, so I'm going to shelve my embarrassment and enjoy the moment. I mean come on. Who gets to lick an angel? My tummy flips, and I follow my instincts.

I bite down.

I groan as the golden blood trickles through my lips and onto my tongue. Wow. I only take a few mouthfuls. Any more and I feel like I'm being greedy. As his blood coats my throat, I can already feel power and energy flooding through me.

I lick the two tiny holes that my fangs have made, and whether it's my spit or the angel's natural healing ability, they instantly heal and disappear.

Like my bite never happened.

"Thank you. Are you okay?" I ask.

"Did you take enough?" the angel asks in a rough voice.

"Yes... I think so. Your blood is very powerful, so I only need a little. Well, that's what my instincts are telling me. I'm not completely sure. As you know, I'm new to all this." Following my newly found instincts, I lean forward and gently kiss his cheek. "Thank you."

The honey colour of Xander's eyes flares brighter, somehow, even as his pupils dilate, and the black circles that rim the outside of his eye that I've never noticed before expand.

He coughs and looks away.

The angel is careful not to touch me as he rises from the bed and rolls his sleeve back into place. I rapidly blink a few times. I'm sure I'm seeing things. Pink stains Xander's cheeks.

Is he... Is the angel blushing?

"Okay, my shadow, I better get back to it." He adjusts the cuff, politely nods, and then glides out of the room.

Huh, interesting. He's not so disgusted with me after all.

CHAPTER
TWENTY-FIVE

"I want to move out," I say without preamble as I storm into Xander's office with Dexter at my heels. I am sure the furry monster is trying to trip me. I deftly avoid a paw. The angel is sat behind his desk surrounded by paperwork. He's wearing a black crew neck jumper. The colour complements his golden skin tone and his eyes.

Those gorgeous eyes narrow, and he sharply shakes his head. "No," he says, and then he drops his eyes back to his paperwork, dismissing me.

I fidget and let out a little *humph* sound. Oh, okay. No explanation, no discussion, just a firm no. I can work with this. After thinking about it until my head feels like it's gonna pop off, I've come to the very sane and healthy conclusion: I can't live with this man.

The blood thing, it's too intimate. It makes me feel weird.

I don't want to feel this out of control. I hate it. I feel like someone has chucked me off a cliff and I'm forever falling. My hands scrabble for things to grab onto, but I'm failing miserably. I have to do what's right for me and for my friends to keep us all safe and before I metaphorically go splat.

I'm literally going insane with this man's mixed signals, and I have a plan. I have a plan to get me out of this complete nightmare. I need to be in control of my life. This plan does not involve being roomies with him. But I'm in a pickle 'cause my pride will not allow me to admit that I have a problem with him, an issue with drinking his blood, his life-saving blood.

So now is the time to hit two birds with one stone. I anxiously hop from foot to foot and then settle for crossing my arms underneath my boobs.

My badass pose.

"Look, Luther..." I huff and roll my eyes. I better knock that shit on the head. I am not friends with the vamp, so being so familiar and calling him by his first name is gonna make me look like an idiot. It just feels so stupid calling him by that silly name. "*Lord Gilbert* said some shit. He said the vampires were waiting for me to turn eighteen, and then they were going to lock me up and"—I pause for added drama—"*breed me.*"

Rage flashes across Xander's face and disappears just as quickly. A preternatural stillness sweeps over him.

Well... That was a little anticlimactic.

"Wait for it," Story mumbles in my ear. She's perched on my shoulder like a pirate's parrot. I frown. What is she... Then I see it... A vein in his neck pulses, and I think he's gritting his teeth. Xander sits behind his desk like a statue. We wait patiently for the angel to react. Even Dexter, who's been knocking about on the floor, rubbing himself all over the desk, is now sat, his ginger head tilted, and his tail wrapped around his paws, staring at the angel.

"Beow."

As if that's the secret signal, Xander grinds his teeth. "That will not happen. If they touch you, I will kill them all," he says in a deadly voice.

Oookay.

Story prods my neck with her bare toes. I swallow. "I don't think that's going to happen anymore what with Lord Gilbert officially withdrawing their claim when he thought I was dying... But what does history tell us about the vampires?" I'm on a roll as I paraphrase my grandad. "Vampires tend to kill first. They kill what they can't control. So I think the vamps will try to kill me, especially with the whole abomination thing."

I flap my hands in the air, and with another encouraging prod from Story, I hurry on. "Also, there's another thing... urm, while Lord Gilbert was doing his whole villain speech, he let slip that the shifters might want to do that as well. Not the killing, the locking up and"—I take a deep breath—"breeding thing." I wait with anticipation for his reaction.

"No vampire and shifter cock for you," Story says.

My lips part with shock, and I turn my head and stare at her. "Where the hell did that cute little pixie go?" I ask.

"Pixies age faster than other creatures," she says, looking at her toes.

"No shit." The mouth on the girl. She looks almost contrite until I catch her cheeky grin. "So," I say, turning back to the angel. "I'm thinking the shifters have that as their agenda." I tap my thigh rhythmically as the angel thinks it over.

Fuck it, I'm not that patient. "I'm not being funny, Xander, but you're tight with the shifters. Hell, my bodyguards are shifters. I need to live somewhere where they can't just pop in through the front door. It's obvious you can't watch me all the time, and I think you're in over your head."

"The vampires did officially withdraw their claim late last night, and this morning the shifter council requested a meeting," Xander says quietly as he rubs his temple.

Ah, no. Damn it, I'm already too late.

Story and I have discussed this and we have a plan B. The fae or the witches will not be interested in me, which means just the shifters. By our calculations, the clock is ticking until they reappoint a shifter guardian, and once I'm trapped in their corrupt system, there's no hope. I'll be fucked.

Go big, or go home.

"When is this meeting?" *How long have I got?*

"They're coming tonight."

My heart feels like it's in my throat, and my pulse hammers in my ears, that's not enough time. I vigorously shake my head. I need a little bit more time. "I'm working," I blurt out.

"Tru, this is the shifter council. I think they're more important than your little job."

"This is my life, Xander," I growl. "They can meet me at work after the café closes tomorrow night."

"My shadow, don't be ridiculous. You can't dictate terms to the shifter council." The angel scoffs.

Ha, I can't, can I not? "I think it's best for them and you to keep me pliant. Don't you think? Also, you made a promise. I'm asking you as my guardian to honour your promise to listen, to trust me."

Nothing. He gives me nothing. There's zero acknowledgement of my words, and the blank expression on his face gives nothing away.

I stand there feeling awkward. "I guess that promises an angel makes mean nothing." Okay, angel, you're playing hardball, time for the big guns. "They will meet me there or not at all. You'll have to drag me kicking and screaming to that meeting. Why not take the easy option... What does it matter to you?" I poke my chin forward and stubbornly glare at him.

I have a plan, a good plan that needs a public space and a little more time for it to work.

"Please."

"Okay, my shadow. I will see what I can do."

One hybrid girl... no, *two* girls and a monster cat—that doesn't *do* anything. Taking on the might of the shifter council. What could go wrong?

It's that time of the week when I have my medical check-up with Dr Ross. With Xander and the whole blood-drinking thing, the only person who is aware of me snacking on angel blood is Dr Ross. The poor guy isn't a specialist... I don't think anybody would be a specialist when it comes to dealing with me and the shitshow of my hybrid status. But Xander trusts him, so he's stuck with my care.

I wait for him to arrive, sitting in Xander's orangery, which is at the back of the house. With its large windows overlooking his pretty walled garden, the room is warm and bright. Story, Dexter, and I spend a lot of time here. I adore the glass roof lantern. On a clear night, if I lie on the floor, I can look straight up at the stars.

"I ran some more tests."

I turn my phone off and give the doctor a wave, but he doesn't lift his eyes from his notes.

"Hi, Tru. How are you?" I say in an overly deep voice. "Oh, I'm fine, thank you, Dr Ross. How are you doing, busy?" I answer myself in a squeaky high voice.

I smirk and he shakes his head and plonks his muscled bulk down in the chair opposite me, tapping madly on his datapad, which seems to be never out of his hands.

"I'm concerned. Even with Xander's blood and the magic, you're still not healing."

I shuffle to the edge of my seat, plant my elbows on my knees, and prop my chin in my hands. More tests? Oh goody. "Okay?" I say cautiously.

"Traces found in your blood show an impossible early childhood shift to animal form. Yet, you have shown no other signs of shifting, no other markers, and you have no shifting magic." Dr Ross taps his index finger on the datapad and scowls. "The data makes little sense. I might have to take some more samples, draw some blood the old-fashioned way. Perhaps your hybrid nature corrupts the magic tech?" He rubs his left eye with the heel of his hand.

I groan and slump back in the chair, pull my knees to my chest, and bury my head in my hoodie so it covers my mouth and nose. "Have you not run my DNA? What does the shifters database tell you?" I mumble through the fabric. I really need to get things back on track. My plan with the council rests on information, and if I haven't got everything I need, I'm doomed.

"The shifter council have not given me permission to do that."

"What? Why not?" Well, that makes little sense. Did Dr Ross just dip his head? I frown. Is he slightly hunching? Yeah, I don't think he's being deceptive... I think. I think the doctor's ashamed.

Shit, I need those test results.

My stomach jumps to my throat, and I focus on the doctor. What is he not telling me? What the hell has he been doing with all those scans?

Something isn't right.

The bloody council. I've got less than twenty-four hours to get my act together and save myself. Xander got them to agree to my meeting. I need that DNA evidence. Why is nothing easy? I thought it was important to everyone to find out who my family is, where I come from, but it looks like that's not part of the shifter council's agenda. That's... concerning. Alarm bells go off like the clappers in my head.

What are they trying to hide?

Me. It's all about me, and I have a sneaky suspicion that getting my DNA into that system to see if I have an ancestry match will mess with the council's plans.

Call me a rogue or a rebel, it doesn't matter. I'm going to do everything in my power to run those checks.

"You need permission?"

Dr Ross keeps his eyes on his tablet and doesn't look up. He shrugs.

Okay, I guess it's time to put my cards on the table. I'm sure I've already mentioned it... Perhaps I have, perhaps I haven't, but it seems a little bit obvious to me what with the multicoloured hair. Shifters instinctively know what other people's animal forms are—well, except me 'cause obviously the shifter inside me is broken. I read human. I smell human. All everyone sees is a powerless human.

"I'm a unicorn shifter. You know how rare that is." I drop my legs to the floor and tug at a piece of my hair to demonstrate my words, and then I point to my eyes. "The hair is all unicorn, and my amber eyes are a strange mix from my vampire side."

"But we don't know that for sure. It's just your word and second-hand information," Dr Ross whispers. For the first time since he came into the room, he looks at me.

"Yep." I fiddle with the zip on my hoodie. I bring it up to my lips and nibble on the plastic toggle. I nervously wiggle in my seat—this next part is gonna be uncomfortable. I pull the toggle away from my mouth, but I keep hold of it. "About the markers in my blood? The shifting when I was little... I have this reoccurring bad dream."

I take a shaky breath. Why is this so hard?

Probably because I've ignored the problem and buried it so deep into my subconscious.

Probably because I didn't even tell my grandad or anyone else about it.

And probably because I'm frightened that this dream isn't a dream but a memory.

"I have this bad dream of being forced to shift by a man, a really scary man, who uses a saw to cut off my horn." I dip my head, my hand on the zip. It trembles.

Crikey, even thinking about it freaks me out. I drag my knees back to my chest.

"The horn is the source of the unicorn's power. Unlike other shifters, a unicorn's horn contains all the shifter magic." Dr Ross gets up from his seat and paces. "That's the reason you've shown no shifter magic, but you have"—he points at my hair—"unicorn traits. I will have to speak with Xander as, from my understanding, without the source of your power, you will not be able to shift."

"So the horn removal messed with my magic?"

He runs his hand through his hair and flaps his other hand with the tablet about. "Yes. Although it's a little bit more than that. You're a medical marvel. It's a miracle that you're alive, unless… unless it's the vampire side of you, the pureblood strength, and Xander's blood, that's holding you together. Okay, let's think this through. The fae confirmed your grandad's magic got you through childhood. I have to be blunt, kid. A shifter stuck in wolf form can last decades. They might go slowly insane as the magic takes them over, but they can last *decades*. On the other side of the coin, a shifter staying in human form has got years, two, three years at the most, and your clock has already been ticking."

He slumps back down on the chair and meets my gaze. "The reason we've not seen any change to your health is that… Well, there's no easy way to say this, Tru, and it's only a theory." He holds his hands up, his face a professional mask. "It's only a theory, as your unusual nature is impossible to predict, but I think if you can't shift, no matter what steps we take, you're going to die."

"Okay." I dip my head inside my hoodie. I get what he's saying, and I might die tomorrow, I might die next week. "Okay." I puff out my cheeks and nod. "Back to the main issue. So if I got a higher-up to permit you access to the shifter database, would you be willing to run my DNA?"

For a moment the doctor's eyes widen. I can see the shock on his face when I don't freak out about my pending death.

Immortal creatures will die someday.

We all die. It's just a matter of when. We just have to keep fighting till the very end. A wonderful man gave his life for me, and I won't let him down. I bite my lip and rapidly blink. No, I won't let my grandad down.

So this is me, *fighting*.

"If you got me permission... of course," Dr Ross reluctantly agrees.

"Perfect." I hold up a finger, and I grab my phone from the side of the chair, where I left it, quickly search for the contact number I need, and hit call.

"Hi, could I please speak to the General? My name is Tru Dennison, and I need his help."

CHAPTER TWENTY-SIX

I NERVOUSLY TWIST MY HANDS, and Story pats my cheek. "Everything is going to work out, you've done as much as you can. It is now all up to fate."

I nod. Shit, I feel sick.

"Yeah," I whisper. I know Story's trying her best, but fate has never been my friend.

The bell above the door jingles, and the first of the shifter councillors prowls into the room.

It's showtime.

He glances around the café with disgust and makes his way to the table that I've prepared for this meeting. I can see his bodyguards outside through the café's large window. One of them gives me an assessing look. I give him my back.

The councillor doesn't even glance my way as he wipes down his seat with an embroidered handkerchief before he sits with a put-out-sounding grunt. Henry Phillips. He's a big cat shifter and a total slime ball.

The unicorn shifter sweeps in next. He at least gives me an acknowledgement, even if it is a look of contempt. He sits without preamble and quietly greets the other councillor. Outside, the guards have grown and we now have a magnificent collection.

The dragon comes in next. Considering his height and the breadth of him, you'd think he'd be noisy, but he isn't. Everything about him is silent. The bell doesn't dare make a sound as he opens the door and ducks inside. His silver eyes immediately meet mine. I greet him with a warm smile. Even with his scary reputation, I like this guy.

"Miss Dennison," he says, his voice a deep rumble.

"General, thank you for coming." I show him to the table, which is tiny compared to the size of him. Crap, I don't know whether to ask him to take a seat—it's not like you can boss an ancient dragon shifter around. The extra-large chair creaks a protest as he sits.

The rat shifter is next, Councillor Harrison. He doesn't say a word to anyone, and he looks uncomfortable as he takes a seat. It's clear from his body language that he doesn't want to be here.

Finally a wolf shifter prowls into the café. He walks through the door as if he owns the place, and his eyes land on me with a biting glare. Councillor Charles Richardson. He's a real piece of work and a real player. He doesn't think twice about using people as pawns around his game board. It's a shame he hasn't realised he stepped onto my board tonight.

Tilly bustles around, getting the shifters some drinks, and I shuffle closer to the table.

"Okay," the unicorn says. "We are here at your request, Miss Dennison. I don't know what you think the change of location will achieve, and although Xander insisted, we will not pander to you or your childish threats. You are not in charge here."

Okay, so the unicorn shifter isn't beating around the bush. That's fine.

I nod. Hopefully, my face looks gracious, and I am adequately hiding the fact that I want to leap across the table and smash the evil shifter in the face. I refrain, as that wouldn't be a good start to this farce of a meeting. I can feel anger pricking over my skin, and my entire body is stiff with nerves.

I feel like I'm already caged.

"We've decided," the cat shifter says, directing his words at Xander, "as the vampires have pulled their claim on the girl, we are no longer in need of your service. She will leave here tonight with me in my protective custody."

No, I will not. Who the hell does this guy think he is? I know his name and his history but only 'cause I checked him out online. You can find all sorts if you know where to look. He hasn't even introduced himself, yet he expects me to totter along and follow him home. I'm glad they're not looking at me at the moment because I'm livid. I can't believe I'm being treated like a child by a bunch of entitled men sitting at a table without a functioning brain cell between them.

I lock it all down. Thank God I've been doing that for years. I bite my bottom lip to keep my runaway mouth closed. *Not yet, Tru.*

Give them enough rope to hang themselves. That was another thing my grandad liked to say. I'll stand here and watch them wrap the rope around their own necks.

"Why is that? Why, Phillips, is she going with you?" the dragon asks the cat.

The cat shifter sniffs and fidgets in his seat. "She's an unusual hybrid. We want to see how that looks at a DNA level. The early tests are incredibly promising. I'm able to get that information better than anybody else. She will come for further invasive tests, biopsies"—ah, the lab rat approach—"then, when we have all the relevant information, we will match her with a mate." He nods at the unicorn shifter.

A not-Xander-like snarl rips out of his throat. "A mate? What if she is unwilling?" He moves to stand in front of me, blocking me from the view of the men at the table. "May I remind you that Tru is a child. She is only seventeen."

I roll my eyes and shuffle to the side, and there he goes, ruining it *again*. He was doing so well, so grrr and protective. Then the guy makes out I am a toddler. I guess to him, an angel, I am.

What a depressing thought... Unrequited love is a bitch.

Not that I love the big oaf. Nope, not at all.

I am just having a love affair with his blood, that's all.

"So the whole mating thing will not be happening until she is old enough to consent. She can stay with me until she's ready to make that decision. And I will accompany her for any of these tests." Xander attempts to get in front of me again, so I poke him in the ribs.

"Stop it," I whisper.

"She's no longer your concern, and her being willing doesn't matter," the cat shifter says as he sniffs again. The guy really should have used his posh handkerchief on his face instead of wiping down the chair. All that sniffing is gross. The creepy cat waves his hand in the air at Xander with clear dismissal. "We take what we want."

It suddenly feels like the café is too small for the disruptive energy rolling off the angel and the dragon.

"When does it ever matter? These females are becoming too uppity. They need to take a leaf out of Charles's book. His daughter Elizabeth does exactly what she is told," the unicorn says. "This one will learn to behave and will do as commanded. For the good of all shifters." He points in my direction.

Both the dragon and Xander growl. "It matters to me, and no doubt the populace," the dragon snarls. "You will not force her. You cannot force any female. Let me be frank with you, councillors, I will not allow it."

"Come on, General, the girl is not worth the fight. She's a nobody. We are well within the law, and the laws are there for this very reason." The wolf shifter smiles creepily. "You know you can't stand up to the might of the shifter council. You're powerful, but you're not that powerful." Charles Richardson, the wolf shifter, has royally fucked up. Obviously, the wolf shifter didn't take any of our histories seriously because he has forgotten what the silver dragon is capable of.

The rat shifter, who has yet to say anything, leans away from him, his eyelids peel back until the whites of his eyes are showing.

Crikey, the angry energy emitting from the dragon could boil a kettle. It almost makes me want to drop to my knees. He could cleave the guy in two with his power alone. Yet apart from the rat shifter, these men are so far up their own arses they can't see the very danger that they are in.

"We will match her to a strong mate. If she doesn't produce a child within a year, we will try another shifter. We have fair processes in place." The unicorn shrugs as if this is a normal conversation. I shiver and step closer to Xander. I grab his large hand. The angel holds my hand back like a lifeline and, for good measure, tucks me against his side.

"We could always pass her along even when she produces a child. The child, of course, will remain the property of the father. There are a lot of good shifters that need an heir who can shift. From our initial reports, there is a seventy-five percent chance the children will shift. That is incredible news. There is also a fifty percent chance the children will be female. *Fifty percent.*

"You know that's unheard of. With our female birth rate so low, for many years we've been on the edge of extinction. It seems whatever hampers the breeding of shifter females will not affect her. It's something to do with the vampire blood within her." The unicorn nods at the cat shifter. "I am sure Councillor Phillips and his medical team will give us the explanation."

"Look, General, this is for the greater good. Even you can see that. No one will miss her. No one will care. But she could be an enormous factor in helping a whole species—our species—and I'm willing to do anything, even if you're not."

Okay, that's it.

I wiggle out of Xander's comforting hold. "So you gonna what, rent me out, like rent a room? Put my uterus up to the highest bidder?" My nonchalant tone masks the fact that I'm speaking around a huge lump in my throat.

I'm proud of myself that my voice sounds so calm. The unicorn shifter turns his head and glances at me. The look on his face is as if he's forgotten I was even in the room.

This entire conversation is worse than I expected. *Sick, horrible fucks...* And to think I was feeling guilty about what I was going to do to them.

"Yes," he says, his voice firm. I maintain eye contact, but out of the corner of my eye, in my peripheral vision, I see Xander is taking a step forward. I hold my hand up to stop him.

I've got this. I have to believe I've got this.

"Just so we're clear, this is the judgement of the entire shifter council?" I ask the table. Three of the councillors dip their heads in acknowledgement, except the nervous rat shifter. He isn't for taking his eyes off the General, and I'm unsure if he's even heard a word that I've said. The man is frozen with fear.

"How far the shifters have fallen," I whisper. My eyes drift to the table behind them. I glance back at the unicorn. "Don't you even care that I'm a unicorn shifter?"

The unicorn shifter splutters. "You are not a unicorn." His tone is angry, adamant, and smattered with disgust. I can almost taste his disgust in the air.

"I'm not?"

"No, you're a wannabe with witch-coloured hair." He shakes his head, and his hands resting on the table clench. "I know all the unicorn shifters, and they wouldn't lower themselves to lie with a vampire to create an abomination like you."

Story—who is still perched on my shoulder—squeaks in despair. With a history of being a pixie-fairy hybrid and called an abomination by her troupe, I can understand why. I lift my hand, and she clutches my finger. I give her a gentle squeeze of reassurance. I'm not bothered about what this man thinks of me.

"Oh, okay." I nod, smile, and I drop my hand. "I see where you're going with that. If I'm such an abomination, why is it okay for me to be passed around? It seems I'm good enough for council-sanctioned rape—oops, sorry. What shall we call it"—I tap my lips and then point at him—"a council-sanctioned *breeding* programme? Rape is such a nasty word. I can tell you now while you are all here around this table." With my finger, I do a circling motion in the air. "I do not consent. I will *never* consent."

"Don't be stupid," the unicorn snarls.

"I'm not the stupid one," I snarl back.

"You don't have a choice. Are we going to allow this? Someone put her in chains and escort her to the lab."

"No one is touching her," Xander says.

At the same time, the dragon says, "Let her speak."

"While you were doing all the womb viability tests, did you idiots run my DNA through the system?" I ask pleasantly. "You know, the DNA that will say who I'm related to and what type of shifter I am." I want to rip the fucker's face off. "I can see from your face that you didn't. No, you didn't, did you? Not only did you not care, but you didn't want that little piece of evidence floating about, did you? You wanted me to remain a nobody. If I didn't have a family to care about me, there would be no one to make noise as I became your broodmare."

I wave my hand at Tilly, and she marches over with my prepared paperwork. She hands them to me and bravely takes a second to glare at the man at the table. She then marches away.

"Can you see where I'm going with this? I'm so glad that I took the time to have my ancestral DNA cross-checked on the creature database." I smile widely as I hand out copies of the report. "As you can see —I've highlighted it in pink so you can find it easily—I have a parental match. Oh, and I'm sooo blessed, I have a grandparent match here at this very table." I clap my hands.

Suddenly every man is frantically thumbing through the pages of the report.

I wait until the unicorn shifter reaches the final page of the document, and I drop my bomb. "Nice to meet you, Grandfather Denby. It looks like I'm Ryan's little girl." I wave.

The unicorn's composure breaks, and his hands holding the paperwork start to shake.

"That's impossible. I would have felt your magic. You can't possibly be a unicorn. It's not possible," he roars, ripping the paperwork in two. "Lies and fabrications."

This man who sends my skin crawling so much it wants to slither off my very bones is my grandfather. What a family reunion. Talk about fucked up.

"Are you talking about the magic that's linked to my unicorn horn? The same horn that was removed by this man when I was six years old." From my pile of paperwork, I throw a photograph of my father onto the table.

I lean across and poke at the man's face. "I always thought it was a nightmare, but when I saw this photo... when I saw his face. I knew... I knew it was him, the monster in my dreams.

"Like father, like son, eh? I was only six years old when your son, your precious Ryan, used magic to make me shift early. He tied my legs together with rope, planted his knee into my neck and, ignoring my frightened screams, used a hacksaw to tear my magic from me. He removed my horn. My magic, my fucking soul. My very identity."

A tear rolls down my cheek, and I angrily wipe it away.

"I don't know why he did it. Only he could tell you that. But it's the reason I'm still sick as I approach adulthood and the time my body should naturally shift. The doctors say without my horn I'll die as I can't shift without it. I'm a ticking time bomb. By removing my horn, my father killed me." I pat the table. "Sorry about that. Yeah, it sucks to find out your broodmare won't survive what you disgusting fucks have planned." My voice wobbles, and I swallow and straighten my shoulders.

"So Grandfather, out of curiosity, do you still want to pass me around?"

CHAPTER
TWENTY-SEVEN

THE UNICORN IS STILL STARING at the shredded paperwork. I think I may have broken something in his head. "I need to confirm... It's not possible... He removed your horn...," he mumbles.

"Oh, and that's something else." Oh boy. I haven't finished yet. Let's just say they might see a seventeen-year-old girl, but in my head... In my head I'm a trained tactician. Thanks to an incredible man that will always be my grandad. Not this unicorn dickhead.

I nod my head, and the magic at the table behind them shatters.

The expensive Don't See Me Now potion dissipates, exposing the table's single seated occupant, a sad and furious woman.

Dressed in a navy skirt and a crisp white blouse, her designer outfit emphasises her small waist and willowy frame, with her orange, red and yellow hair secured in an elegant chignon bun. Like mini rainbows, her livid eyes shine with a multitude of colours.

The lady rises from her seat and steps gracefully away from the table. Her sky-high heels rhythmically click on the floor as she strides towards the councillors.

Her hand whips out and slaps the unicorn shifter across the face. The crack echoes around the deathly silent room. The unicorn's cheek blossoms red from the impact. He doesn't move an inch.

The shock on his face... is crazy satisfying.

"When a rude young girl video called and told me all about her concerns, I laughed in her face. Her concerns were based on rumour and conjecture... They lacked facts. Evidence." She glances at me, and I see the regret shining in her eyes. She swallows, and her attention lands back on her mate.

"I told her she was a liar and that I would come tonight to prove to her how wrong she was." She shoots a glare at the other councillors, and every single one of them fidgets in their seats. "I came here to disprove her, to make her look like a fool. As there was no way..." She shakes her head. "There was no way that you, my beloved and moral mate, would *ever* lock a child up and use her. No way you'd behave like that... like the vampires." Her voice cracks. She swallows again and licks her bottom lip. "I know our race has our moments... but not you. Not you." Her hand flutters to her mouth.

"I told her you had integrity, compassion, and loyalty. The man I love, the man I have been with over the centuries, would never *ever* do that to a woman. Least of all a child." She coughs, and her hands ball into fists and drop to her sides. "She baited me and got under my skin, so I came tonight to shame her." She looks back at me. "What I didn't know is that she is my granddaughter. You know I don't even think she did at the time of our video call."

I shake my head. "I didn't," I whisper.

I only got the paperwork back an hour before the meeting. It is kind of karmic, fated, now that I think about it. She was the only mate that I could find that had a backbone.

I still didn't think the councillors would go so far, be so disgustingly open about their intentions as they did tonight.

"No, I didn't know that she was our granddaughter. I've just found out at the same time as you have. But even without the knowledge, I had to sit there—" She points at the table, and then the same finger swings around and points at her mate. She tilts her head to look down her nose at him. "I had to sit there and listen to your filth. You are not the man I mated. You are dirt. Even before she handed you those DNA test results, I was going to protect her. Protect her from you and your cronies. But now—by God, she's my blood. This boy's club you have going on is over. Times have changed. The shifter council is antiquated, outdated, and frankly, it's immoral. I will not stand by and let you ruin us, ruin our race anymore. How many of our women have to die? Tru was right. Look at how far we've fallen."

She turns and addresses the dragon. "General, you need to clean this shit up, use the hunters guild, use the hellhounds. This happening on top of what happened with your ward? When this all comes out, there's going to be anarchy. You must be ready. If the council do not step away from power quietly, *make them*."

To my shock, the General nods.

"Please Ann, we can talk about this," the unicorn begs.

"Absolutely not. Oh, and Denby, don't you dare even think about coming home. I'm done with you."

Her eyes meet mine. Tears now run freely down her cheeks, a mirror of the tears running down my own face. She gently lays a soft hand against my cheek. "Forgive me, child," she says, wiping away my tears with her thumb. "Please forgive me."

"There's nothing to forgive," I croak out. "You came. Whatever the reason, you came. I didn't think they'd be this bad. I'm sorry. I'm sorry I've made a mess of your life."

She leans forward, and the comforting scent of grass and wildflowers fills my nose. "This is not on you. It's not your fault that my rose-coloured glasses were pulled away from my eyes, broken, and ground into the floor." She huffs sadly. "Things happen for a reason. I have lost a mate, but I have gained an incredibly smart and brave grandchild." She kisses the top of my head. "I will speak with you tomorrow." Softer, she whispers, "You publish the video now, the whole thing." I nod. She smiles at Story and with a gentle finger clucks her underneath the chin.

My unicorn grandmother's heels click, the bell above the door jingles, and the door gently clicks behind her.

"Video?" the wolf huffs. He's the first to shake away the shock at my grandmother's tirade.

"Oh, you heard that, did you? Yes, Mr Richardson—"

"Councillor," he snarls. From what I know, the wolf shifter is a replacement, and he's only been in his new council role for a week. Sucks to be him.

"Not anymore," I say with a smirk and point to the surrounding air. "Micro cameras. I recorded everything you've all said tonight. If you look carefully, you might see the dozens of tiny cameras buzzing about." The magical and tech cameras have been incredibly handy. I am so glad my grandad had them in his pocket dimension storeroom.

"You will give me the footage," the cat shifter snarls, standing from the table and flexing his impressive arms.

"Or what?" I ask sweetly. "What are you gonna do? Sit your bum down." I snarl.

"So you're under the assumption that you're going to release a video, is that right? You will do no such thing, you insolent bitch. Let's lock her up," the wolf demands.

"You still don't get it, do you, Charles?" I shake my head and pout a little. "I couldn't leave anything to chance what with my whole life on the line. As soon as my grandmother gave her permission, the recording of this meeting started streaming. The footage is now live. Wave to your adoring fans."

"What have you done? You will incite a civil war," the rat shifter whines.

I shrug. "That's all on the council. I guess you have about five minutes to get somewhere safe." I drop my voice to a whisper. "The hellhounds are coming."

CHAPTER
TWENTY-EIGHT

"The General and the hellhounds are hunting all the corrupt shifters down. It's only a matter of time before they find me, and I don't have the heart to escape them or fight them."

I pull my mobile away from my ear and stare at it. My grandfather's words echo around my head.

This isn't my fault. This is all on him, his actions, his intentions. It's not my fault that his bad choices have bitten him on the bum.

Does he expect me to help him? Rescue him? He might be biologically my grandfather, but he isn't my family.

"The council has made a lot of bad choices," I say diplomatically. Seriously, they've pushed the entire country to the breaking point. Creatures were already up in arms about the suicide or unexplained death of a shifter girl, and now with my explosive video...

Shit, the timing couldn't have been better.

"I'm surprised you're not dead already." My chest throbs at my horrible words. *Bloody hell, Tru. Did you have to go there?* I shouldn't care how I sound. Kindness isn't a weakness, and I can't lose myself just because I'm related to this monster.

"I need to speak to you in person, tonight."

I groan and rub my face. "Okay. Meet me at Xander's house. I'll text you the new portal code."

"There's a witch that has more power than she should. For the past decade, her power has only grown." We're in Xander's fancy living room, sat opposite each other. When he said he wanted to talk to me... I didn't think this would be the conversation.

"Grey magic, it didn't concern us. But a few years ago, it came to my attention that she didn't use potions or spells. She instead used the power of a bone necklace." He raises his eyebrows meaningfully. "A multicoloured bone necklace."

"Multicoloured bone?"

"Rainbow."

Fuck.

My mind grinds to a halt, and I sit frozen and stare at him. *Multicoloured bone.* "Are you implying this bone necklace is made of horn?" The words come out mumbled from between my stiff lips. It's now my turn to raise my eyebrows, my heart creeps towards my throat, and I do my best to swallow it down. "My horn?" I whisper.

"Yes."

Wow. I cover my mouth with my hand and shake my head as I try to get around the implications of that revelation. Major revelation. The unicorn dropped a bomb.

Hell, perhaps we're more alike than I thought... Now isn't that a scary thought? I rub the back of my neck.

Shit, so there is a possibility that this witch may have my horn. My stomach flips, and I huff out a nervous breath.

It's my first lead, and although I don't trust this man, I know I have to at least check it out. I have no choice. The shifter side of me is dying. I wasn't lying when I told the shifters that—even with Xander's fancy angel blood and healing magic, without my horn, I'm a dead girl walking.

The unicorn shifter sits silently, patiently, watching as my emotions undoubtedly roll across my face. He lets me think.

Is this a setup? I narrow my eyes. Denby—my grandfather, ha, still can't get over that—places something gently down on the glass table between us.

"This is my show of faith."

I'm enveloped in its magic.

It resonates through me and buzzes in my ears. It thrums through my chest with gentle, almost painful waves. It takes a second. I blink. Oh my. I struggle to breathe... that's—that's a unicorn horn. The blue-green horn is *around the length of a Katana sword,* around twenty-four inches, my brain helpfully adds. My martial arts training always comes in handy at the strangest of times.

His horn.

I pull my gaze away from it and look back up, meeting his eyes. He sees my shock.

"I can't do this myself. My position will not allow me to, and what with everything going on, it would incite a war with the witches. A war we wouldn't win. For years the unicorns have been watching her, waiting for an opportunity, but without the owner of the horn coming forward, we could do nothing." He shrugs.

I thought the paleness in his skin tone was from the current political climate the riots and people hunting down the shifter council. But no, he's pale because he's missing the source of his magic.

"I believe, granddaughter, the horn the witch has in her possession is yours. It is your property, and you have every legal and moral right to get it back. But you need strength and power. I know without your own horn you are dying." He nods to the horn on the table.

"This is the only way I can help you." He chuckles softly. "Putting my horn on the line I know will not gain your trust. No matter what you think, I'm not a stupid man, and I know what I've done is unforgivable. But—"

His voice cracks, and he runs his tongue across his teeth and then takes what looks like a pain-filled breath.

"My actions broke your grandmother's heart. I've always been an evil man, and I've done whatever it took to get ahead. But your grandmother? She is the light of my life." He shakes his head. "And I ruined that. So please, please give me this... Allow me to be the man that she thought I was." Denby taps the glass table, and as if by its own accord his hand drifts towards his horn. He has to forcibly snatch it back. "I'd also like to make up for my son's failings."

We sit there for a moment in silence, the power of his horn thrumming.

"When you're ready, I'm sure your grandmother will help you find out more about your mother and that side of your family. You are so much like your grandmother," he says gruffly.

I clear my throat. "Yes, I'd like that."

"Let me help you. I'm trusting you." Denby reverently picks up his horn. "I hold my life in here in my hands."

Those things don't just click off.

I shudder.

I suppressed the memory of when my horn was removed for my own sanity. My hand can't help but rub my forehead. The truth has a way of creeping into your dreams. I remember everything of that day in my nightmares. The pain. The agony. It was like someone had broken all my bones at once.

I was just a little girl.

My grandfather holds his power, his magic, his *soul* in his hands.

I nod my head with consent and open my mouth to do a speech about how I will try my best, but before I get to say anything, Denby twists his wrist, and suddenly the horn is rapidly moving towards my face.

I can't help my squeak as I fall backwards into the chair. But he follows my movement. The flat end of the horn smacks into my forehead, and there is a whoosh of power that blows the loose strands of my hair back and a bright white light so fearsome I think for a second I've been blinded.

I groan and blink rapidly. When my vision finally clears, the world is a different place.

I can feel my blood moving in my veins. It's on fire with *power*.

I can taste the air around me.

All my senses have increased a hundredfold.

I feel like a superhero.

No. Not a superhero... I feel like a unicorn shifter. I feel like a vampire.

I swallow a lump in my throat as I realise the gravity of what my father did to me. What he destroyed. How could he have done that to me? Knowing what the feeling of being whole is like. Even though it's not my magic, it bonds with me.

I rapidly blink. I will not cry, not here, not now. I'll save this for later and deal with it when I've got time.

I focus on my grandfather with these new unaccustomed eyes. They let me see everything that I've missed, every detail. Denby's skin is deathly pale, and the pain he is in pulls down the corners of his eyes.

I understand his sacrifice more than anyone. Even if it's temporary until I deal with the witch and get my horn back. Every moment I waste, he suffers, and his body, without his magic, slowly dies.

It's a huge personal sacrifice.

"Thank you," I say, two meaningless words to a man who is giving me so much. I thought he was evil. Every time I've met him he's proven without a doubt he's not a nice man. But even he is redeemable. He might be the villain, but he's a villain with a family. My grandmother and perhaps... perhaps me?

"I promise to do everything in my power to get my horn back and return what is yours."

He nods. "I know you will. I know the reputation of the fae man who raised you." His eyes change, and his darker side peeks through. "You go get your soul back, child of my child, and you kill that witch. Punish her. Make her an example to protect the last of us. Let it be known what happens to creatures who steal magic." His eyes harden further. "You have to, no matter the cost."

I nod. "Yes, Grandfather."

As we walk back to the portal, he slips a piece of paper into my hand. "They will stop you if you give them the chance. Keeping you safe will end up killing you faster," he says. His voice is so quiet that even with my new super-shifter ears I struggle to hear.

I nod and stuff the note in my pocket.

Denby opens the portal door and leans heavily against the frame. "The fae assassin did an excellent job of protecting you." He visibly swallows. "Raising you... Tru, I know it's hard to believe, but nobody knew of your existence. Both your parents kept you a secret. There wasn't a whisper of a shifter-vampire hybrid." He shakes his head. "At the time of your conception, your father was off living this... double life that we weren't aware of. For what it's worth, I am sorry."

"Okay, well... urm... thanks. I will see you soon." With a tight smile, he steps into the gateway and disappears.

When I shuffle back into the living room, Xander peels himself away from the wall. His sneaky angel magic had been hiding him from the unicorn's senses.

"I wouldn't have believed that if I hadn't seen it with my own eyes."

My heart jumps, and I almost pat my pocket until I realise Xander is talking about the borrowed horn that's merged with my forehead. *Bloody hell, Tru. I don't think you're gonna have a career being sneaky.*

"I know," I whisper.

"How do you feel?"

I peer up at Xander, and even he looks different to my new eyes. He's even more handsome. His face becomes hazy as my eyes fill with tears.

"Whole," I whisper. "I feel whole, strong, normal." The first time in my life I feel normal, or what I presume normal feels like. My trembling hand goes to rub my forehead, and I stop myself midmotion. My hands curl into fists and drop to my sides, nails digging into my palms. Rubbing my forehead is... Heck, it's not like I'm gonna rub the horn off. But for now, it might be best not to touch the spot.

Wow, I feel seriously overwhelmed.

"This is—" I croak.

"It's a lot to deal with," he finishes.

I nod. I turn away from him, embarrassed.

I sniffle.

Xander sighs. His body comes closer, and his bumpy abdomen meets my back as he folds me into his arms.

"You're h-h-hugging me," I mumble.

Xander grunts a reply. I go limp and my entire body shudders as I try to keep my tears inside.

It's all been a little bit too much these past few months.

I've gone from being a circle of two... to just me, on my own. Fighting against the world and what I thought was my own rapidly encroaching death.

And now I'm alive, more than alive for now, and I have more creatures inside my quickly expanding circle, more responsibility than I've ever had before.

I don't like change.

I don't deal with it well; I sniffle and tilt my head to the ceiling. I know my choices have got me to this point, and I don't regret a thing.

I love Dexter and Story.

Heck, I love the stupid angel.

I don't want to go back to being on my own; I don't want to go back to feeling like I'm wasting away. Slowly dying. I don't want to go back to that feeling like I'm missing a huge part of my soul. I'm screwed. It's only been, what, twenty minutes? I feel complete in a way I have never felt before, and it's overwhelming.

Now I know what I was missing. I'm a hundred times more frightened.

What happens if I fail?

Fail my friends, fail myself, and what happens if I don't get my horn back... 'cause I will have to return this horn to Denby Jones. I try to swallow down my overwhelming fear, but too many emotions continue to bubble up my throat to drown me. A sob wrenches from my lips.

Shit, I'll go back to that darkness. I don't want to, I don't think I can. But I know I will 'cause that's the only thing I can do. A sad smile tugs at my lips, and a small whimper leaves my tight throat. I can only do the right thing.

Xander spins me so I'm facing him, and then he sits on the chair and drags me down with him into his warmth. My legs fall on either side of his hips, and I wrap myself around him. His big, heavy arms tug at me so my head rests against his chest, and a warm hand rubs circles on my back as his other hand cradles the back of my neck.

"You should be proud of yourself. You took on the might of the shifter council and won. You could have run. The General would have helped you." He gently tucks a wayward strand of my hair behind my ear and rests his chin on top of my head. "I would have done my best to hide you."

I'm not one for cuddles. I'm kind of miserable with human contact—less is more in my book—but I can't seem to stop myself from snuggling closer. I breathe him in as best as I can with a snotty nose.

"When you asked me to trust you to arrange the meeting, I had my doubts." Xander shakes his head, and the dark stubble on his chin musses up my hair. "But you did it... Granted you might have caused a countrywide mess and almost single-handedly destroyed the shifter council, but you did it, and you also gave other creatures a reason to fear you." He gently brushes my bare arm with his fingers. "And now, for the time being, you have your grandfather's horn, his power, and with it, you will go on an adventure to take back what was stolen.

"I do not doubt that you'll be able to get your horn back." He kisses the top of my head, and the angel continues to murmur, "But that is a tomorrow problem to solve. So if you need a moment to cry to let things fall apart? I'll make sure you won't fall alone. I've got you. I've got you, my shadow."

I cling to him, and the tears that I've been holding in for what feels like forever fall, drenching his shirt.

CHAPTER TWENTY-NINE

THE MAGIC in the shop hits me harder than the last time I visited. For a second it makes me dizzy, and floating black spots dance across my vision. In my haste to save myself, I grab hold of the doorway for balance and my bum slams against the shop's wooden door. I cringe as it crashes against the wall.

Crap, it sounded like I'd just kicked the door in. *Way to go, Tru*, a splendid start to ask for help.

I shake my head and rapidly blink to clear my vision. Once I'm confident that I won't fall on my bum, I peel my nails from their death grip on the doorframe—I'm sure I leave little indented crescents in the wood. My legs wobble. Crikey, having this borrowed unicorn power is an adjustment. Even in my human form it is a challenge. I can't even walk straight.

My tummy flips. *God, I can't believe this afternoon I'm going to attempt to shift*. I force the thoughts of shifting out of my head. That's a future-me problem, and now isn't the time.

With my knees practically knocking together, I enter the shop. A teenage girl—maybe a few years younger than me—turns from a shelf she's stacking and scowls. She looks me up and down with distaste while wiping her hands on her apron.

"We don't get a lot of female shifters around here," she says with a nasty curl of her lips.

I flinch back as if she hit me.

The girl huffs and turns away in dismissal and continues to slam jars onto the shelf. I want to smack myself on the forehead for being such a divvy. Of course she can sense the unicorn magic. I didn't even think about other magical creatures being able to sense the shifter magic inside me.

No, I didn't think, especially when I ditched my bodyguards. I didn't want to tip Xander off to the fact that I have no intention of letting him hunt this witch down on my behalf. After yesterday's cuddle fest, his words come back to me. *"Don't you worry about this witch. I'll fix this for you. Give me a few days."* Yeah, I interpreted that as "Don't worry your pretty little head. The big strong angel will fix all your problems for you." Well, he can bog off.

My eyes flick to the window and the empty street outside. I'm lucky that it's still early in the morning and that I didn't bump into any male shifters. Having to fight some idiot because he insists on taking care of me. Being kidnapped for my own protection would seriously ruin my day.

I guess I've got to think things through as for the time being I'm no longer able to mask myself as human. I now have a magical beacon composed of a unicorn's horn literally slapped on my forehead.

I'm lost in my own panicked thoughts, and when I don't say anything, the girl spins around and continues her angry spiel with a huff, "And especially rude shifters who think it's okay to try to take the door off the hinges." She hits me with a nasty closed-lipped smile.

God, if looks could kill, I'd be dead and buried. I sigh and rub the back of my neck. "Look, I'm sorry. I didn't mean to smash your door. Honestly, I didn't do it on purpose. It's just the magic in the shop hit me. I'm not used to such powerful witch magic all in one place, and I got a little dizzy." The girl narrows her eyes as if she doesn't believe me. "I will pay for any damages," I mumble.

"Heather, don't be rude," Jodie says as she comes out from the back room. "Tru? It is Tru, isn't it? You're a friend of Tilly's, and you brought the pixie here for help."

I relax slightly when I see her friendly face, and I studiously ignore the angry teenager.

"How is she?"

"Yes, Story, she is doing well thanks to you," I say, smiling brightly, glad for the change in subject.

"She's still living with you?"

"Oh yes. She's my best friend," I say as I vigorously nod my head. "Story is working at the café with me. Tilly gave her a job decorating cakes. Her designs are incredible."

I left Story at the café with the bodyguards. She's working on a huge cake monstrosity for a bridezilla who wants more of everything. One more tier, billions of more flowers. Story is having the time of her life, while I... Well, I want to punch the woman in her face. So while Story is climbing the Mount Everest of cakes, I thought since the streets were still quiet and the surrounding shops were still sluggishly opening, I'd sneak out and visit Jodie. Ask her a few questions about a certain unicorn-horn-stealing witch.

"That's lovely." Jodie's smile dims, and she tilts her head to the side. "I'm sure you were human last time you were here. How strange."

Heather huffs again, and her blonde curls bounce as she moves to Jodie's side. "Do you never watch the news? The entire country is going crazy. The shifters are rioting, and the shifter councillors are dying, and it's her fault. She's the hybrid who was on television." She points her finger at my face. "You know... the shifter-vampire mutt?"

"HEATHER," Jodie shrieks.

"Yes, that would be me." I slap my hands against my thighs and look away.

A mutt, wow. I focus on pulling a loose thread on my top.

"What on earth is wrong with you? Your behaviour today is disgusting. We both lost a friend, and I know that you're upset, and you are grieving. But that doesn't give you an excuse to be unkind and so... so cruel," Jodie continues to reprimand the girl.

If Heather's not careful, and she opens her nasty mouth and spews more shit about me, I'm going to kick the fuck out of her. Stuff it. I shrug and head for the door. I'll get my information off someone else. I'm not waiting to be insulted by some teenage witch and her rude speciesist shit. I also don't want to stand here listening to her getting told off for it.

What Jodie said trickles past my anger. *We both lost a friend, and I know that you're upset, and you are grieving.* I wince. Grief does strange things to a person... I should know.

"I am sorry for your loss," I mumble.

"Tru, please don't leave without getting whatever you came in here for. I am so sorry. She should not have said that. Heather, I have never been more disappointed in you." I turn my head and I watch as Heather deflates, and her eyes fill with tears. "Tru, I'm so sorry."

I shrug. "It's fine."

"No, it isn't. Please come into the back room and let me make you a cup of tea. You must be here for a reason to brave the unrest outside, and I owe you my help after my niece's rudeness." Jodie glares at the young girl, and her voice drops to a harsh whisper. "We, young lady, are going to be having a very unpleasant chat. Oh, and consider yourself grounded for the foreseeable future. Now apologise."

"I'm sorry," the girl grumbles.

Jodie narrows her eyes. I can almost hear her screaming silently *wait until I get you alone.* Heather fidgets.

"Please, Tru, follow me." Jodie marches into the back room, the same room that she helped Story in.

I meekly follow behind her. I don't want to rock the boat—and Jodie's pretty scary when she gets going—and slump down at the table. Jodie busies herself with getting the tea things ready. Eyes down, I absentmindedly run my nail against the grain of the wood, tracing its natural line. I think of Heather's words. *The entire country is going crazy. The shifters are rioting, and the shifter councillors are dying, and it's her fault. She's the hybrid who was on television.*

I didn't expect such a backlash, not against me, but at the shifter council. The whole world... *Don't exaggerate, Tru, although it feels like the world.* Okay, the entire *country* is going crazy. The shifters are talking about tremendous changes, new laws, and they're going to remove what is left of the council and put an assembly in its place.

Which is amazing. But what's not amazing is that my video has gone viral. Everybody is talking about it. My face is all over the news. It's enough to give me hives, and it's not going away soon.

Isn't it strange? If you have a fear, no matter what it is, you end up having to confront it.

In my head, I thought the worst thing that could happen to me would be being outed as a hybrid and killed, or being outed as a crazy person on television and social media for going nuts and then being killed. I can't believe my master plan for dealing with the shifter council was me outing myself on national television.

To show everyone what the council was up to, *I did it to myself*. I made that fear *real*. I brought it into reality, and overnight I've become a social media sensation. Yay.

Yep, and it is as horrendous as I thought it would be. It's nuts. Everyone knows it's me who took on the shifter council. Everyone knows what a total freak I am, that I'm half shifter and half vampire. That's something I'm never gonna get away from. It's always going to be online, and there's always going to be a record of it.

To top off the shitshow that is my life, creatures all over the world are now calling me *the rebel leader.*

Ha, the rebel leader. I groan.

Nobheads.

The video footage has made my mission to capture the witch harder. The urge to slump and smack my face against the wooden table is huge.

I'm an idiot... No, I'm not an idiot. That's being harsh. Hindsight is a wonderful thing. I didn't have all the facts, and I can only deal with the problems that are staring me in the face.

Gah, I even showed a photo of my father to add to the drama.

It doesn't take a genius to put two and two together and get four. Now I've got days to get this done, because if she runs... then I'm going to lose her forever. I've gotta get a wiggle on. So I will sit here and smile. I'll drink the witch's tea and get the answers that I need.

"How do you take your tea?" Jodie asks as she places a fancy-looking tray on the table. I was expecting a normal mug, not a full tea set.

"However it comes, thank you. I'm not fussed." I look down at my nails. I'm not really a tea drinker. After working in the café for such a long time, I quite like coffee.

Jodie sits down opposite me, and with her elbows on the table, she rests her chin in her hands and she stares at me. The silence stretches between us.

Her expression is open and honest, and dare I say kind. I trust this lady. "So tell me what happened…"

So I do.

CHAPTER
THIRTY

AFter I finish spilling my guts, I allow the steam from my second cup of tea to warm my face as I listen as Jodie divulges everything she knows about the witch.

"Her name is Karen Miller, and the witches have a standing open warrant for her arrest. The good news is she doesn't have a coven. The bad news is she doesn't have a coven because she killed them all." Jodie flinches as she talks. "Over the years she has only gotten worse, and Karen Miller has an ego the size of a small country." Jodie chuckles slightly, although it's clear to both of us there isn't anything funny about this situation.

I take a sip of my tea, willing myself to ask the question about the horn. *My horn.*

"She owns a unicorn artefact..."

Artefact.

I bite my tongue so I don't say anything that I'll regret. I can't be rude or angry when I know Jodie is only stating facts. But heck, it's so hard for a second to keep my mouth closed.

The witch has made a *necklace* out of my horn. And is using my magic to hurt people.

The witches really should have dealt with her years ago, but half the witches are nature-loving, peaceful, and wouldn't hurt a soul, and the other half won't get their hands dirty. I can understand why, as witch magic is about balance and nature.

Well, I mentally roll my eyes, unless you count ley line magic, which is used to make portals, and urm potions that can melt your face off... oh and if we ignore killer wards... yeah, I don't understand why the witches haven't done anything.

Perhaps it's because they can't.

That's a real helpful thought, ha, that so makes me want to shit myself. I'm seventeen years old, and I'm going after somebody older, more experienced people avoid.

What could go wrong?

Thanking Jodie for the information and the tea, I leave the magic shop with my brain buzzing and plod back to the café.

Maybe I should hide in a corner and let the angel fight my battles. *Ha, never going to happen.*

I guess it's time to break out my assassin training. I can use the skills my grandad cultivated in me. His training and the darkness inside me would make killing her easy.

Easy as breathing.

Taking someone's life, no matter who they are, should never be easy. I don't want to lose myself, so I'll refrain, for now.

Perhaps one day I won't have a choice, and I'll have to put my skills to the test, but I'm not at that stage yet.

Who's to say my father didn't just hand over my horn in a monetary transaction? Of course she shouldn't be buying unicorn horns—I kick a pebble off the pavement and watch as it skitters into the road—it's part of a person, for heaven's sake. But perhaps she didn't realise, and it would be unfair to go all assassin's adopted granddaughter on her ass. I know she's not innocent, but she might not be guilty of this particular crime against me. No, that particular honour goes to my father.

Rage bubbles up, and I stop myself from smashing my fist into the side of a building as I pass. Who knows what damage my new strength might do?

My father.

The unicorns might see possession of a horn as a heinous crime, but I'm not a unicorn... not really.

I hate Karen Miller, but not enough to kill her.

Capture rather than kill is certainly an interesting variant of my grandad's rules, and what I do know is capturing Karen Miller is going to be a lot harder than killing her.

I slip down the side street as I head for the back of the café, and when I get to our bins, I scoop up a piece of cardboard off the floor that must have fallen out. There's a whisper of the sound I almost recognise, a twang, and a change in the air, just as a silver knife whizzes past my face and thumps into the brick wall next to me. My instincts scream at me to move, so I dive behind the bin.

Fuck. The cardboard saved my life.

The sound was a throwing knife leaving someone's hand. The blade is buried to the hilt, and the red brick wall is now sporting a huge spiderweb crack. That takes a lot of strength.

My ears strain for movement, and when I hear it, I dart to the side, avoiding another knife. This is fun. The assassin has lost their element of surprise, so I think *fuck it* and get to my feet. I'm not hiding behind a bin while giving him an easy target. It's in my nature to fight.

"You need some training," I say.

The assassin, a male vampire, flashes his fangs. I retaliate by flashing my own blunt teeth and tiny fangs back at him.

Then I leap at him.

The shock on his face is priceless. "Ha, didn't expect that, did you, bloodsucker?" I hook my leg around his neck and ride him to the ground.

"I will kill you, abomination," he snarls.

"Yeah, yeah, get in line." I roll on my back, and with his neck still between my thighs, I grab hold of a chunk of his hair and lock my leg. The bastard grabs a silver blade from a holder on his leg, and before I can stop him, he slams it into my thigh. The pain is indescribable, it's excruciating. I bite off a scream that wants to tear through me, and instead I groan with the pain and then use it to fuel my anger.

I snarl and wrench his head to the left. "Lefty loosey"—and to the right—"righty tighty." His neck snaps underneath my hands, and his body flops against me. Nice to see the little rhyme works well with breaking necks and screws.

Unfortunately, bitten vampires don't need to breathe, so I couldn't choke him out, leaving me no alternative but to break his neck. I close my eyes for a brief second, then with a grunt, I push him off. The guy isn't dead, but he will sure feel like it when he eventually wakes up.

My leg is wet and sticky, and it hurts like hell. There is a bit more blood than I want to lose pooling on the floor underneath me. I keep the silver knife in my leg to plug the wound. I tilt my head as I look at my leg and contemplate the solid *silver* blade sticking out of it. I thought getting stuck with silver would hurt more. Zap my strength… It doesn't differ from a normal knife wound.

Huh, that's a pleasant surprise. It's nice to know that the effects of silver poisoning don't affect me. As I drag myself to my feet, I wonder if that's the same for all unicorn shifters. Or is it my freaky hybrid nature that gives me that wonderful little quirk? I think I'll keep that information to myself.

I shoot the still unconscious-vampire a dirty look. He'll be out for another five or ten minutes, depending on how old he is. I pat my pockets, looking for the black marker pen. I have to do the prices on the special boards today, so I had it in my pocket. I grin. I lower myself back to the ground and lean over the vampire.

Pulling the cap off the marker with my teeth, I hover the pen over his face.

"Oops, what a shame I haven't got any paper. Now where to put it…" I pick the perfect spot, and as I lower the pen, my tongue sticks out the side of my mouth in concentration. I neatly write on the vampire's forehead, "Send someone after me again, and I will kill them." I also artistically—I use that term loosely—draw a penis with hairy testicles on the right side of his face, and to finish on his left cheek I write, "Can't fight for shit."

I nod my head with childish satisfaction and cap the pen and stuff it back into my pocket. Humming merrily, I rifle through his pockets for any goodies and confiscate five more throwing blades and a handful of expensive-looking potion balls.

With a pain-filled groan and some colourful words, I scrape my bleeding body off the ground. I pull my phone out and take some photos of the vampire and scene, making sure I get a close-up of the guy's face for Story. I bet she'll love my artwork.

I hop carefully across to the café's back door, not wanting to disturb the big-ass knife that's still sticking out of my poor leg.

CHAPTER THIRTY-ONE

I BALANCE on one leg within the safety of the café's open back door and try to keep my injured leg as still as I can while I wait impatiently for the vampire to wake up. Blood trickles down my leg and into my sock.

I've not stemmed the bleeding because I don't know what to do. I know a tourniquet is an obvious choice, but I don't want to disturb the knife, and the silver blade is doing a good enough job, for now, of plugging the hole in my leg.

Sweat trickles down the back of my neck, and I grind my teeth as I do my best to ignore the pain. My leg is burning hot, and my hands are freezing.

A very nasty potion ball—once owned by the downed vampire—rolls in my palm, ready in case the vampire tries anything stupid. In my other hand is my mobile. My thumb hovers over Xander's number, ready to call in the cavalry.

It doesn't take long for the bitten vampire—he must be quite old—to recover from his broken neck. Bitten vampires get stronger with age until they don't, and then they fall apart. When consciousness hits him, he automatically springs to his feet; he stumbles, and he has to hold the wall to regain his balance. He rubs the back of his neck. I see it... the moment when he catches the scent of my blood. His nostrils flare, and his head whips around to look at me.

Our eyes meet, and I can't help my smirk as I creepily whisper, "An angel is coming to get you. If I were you, I'd run." I press Xander's number on my phone. I also wiggle the potion ball between my thumb and forefinger. The liquid inside the potion catches the light.

The angel answers on the second ring.

"Are you okay?" he immediately demands. He knows I wouldn't ring him if it wasn't important.

"No, not really. I have a bloody great knife in my leg from an assassin attack." I hear the small intake of his breath at my words.

"I'm on my way... stay on the phone. Where is your assailant now?"

The vampire runs.

I smile.

Looks like my walking message has gone to report to his master.

"He's gone," I can now say truthfully. I stuff the potion ball in my pocket and use the wall behind me as a guide to the floor; I bend the knee of my good leg and carefully squat as I lower myself. My jacket scrapes, and my top raises a little. I groan.

"Where are you?"

"At the café's back door."

"Where are your bodyguards?" In the background, I hear a door slam and a car engine roar to life.

"I presume they are at the front door."

"Stay on the line." The phone beeps as he places me on hold. I roll my eyes and end the call. I keep my injured leg bent and slump so the wound is higher than my heart.

Dark grey clouds float above the café, and an old spiderweb attached to the gutter flutters in the chilly breeze. I waited to call for help because I knew that if they'd caught him, he'd be dead. That wouldn't do. I wanted to send the vampire back as a message, a warning.

My grandad always said there's honour in a warrior's death. Assassins are a prideful, gossipy lot, so getting beaten by a teenage girl and *then* being humiliated in front of a client 'cause you didn't notice said girl had drawn all over your face, and to top it all off you get ridiculed by your peers when the photos appear online?

It will sure make other assassins think twice about coming after me.

The risk of losing their life is part of the job description, but failure and losing your reputation because you're a laughingstock? It will make them twitchy as hell. Yep, reputation is everything.

I don't have proof, but I'm sure the vampire council is behind this attempt.

Within a minute, a harassed, freaked-out wolf shifter bodyguard comes through the back door.

"I'm with her now. Yes, there is a silver knife in her leg... No sir, she hasn't removed it. Yes sir, there's a lot of blood."

This is why I need to learn to shift. 'Cause if I could just shift there would be no need to pull the knife out. I'd shift, and the blade would drop to the floor. Apart from the hole and blood on my pants, no one would be any the wiser, that's much better than all this drama.

STORY FREAKS out and then jabbers in my ear about how she knew I'd snuck out and that I'm an idiot. Tilly is manning the café. I told her not to come outside. The poor dryad would lose all the blossoms in her hair if she saw me with a knife sticking out of my leg and bleeding everywhere. I told her it was just a scratch, and I'd see her tomorrow.

I ignore Story's reprimanding lecture and instead open my photo app, and she almost falls off my shoulder with her raucous giggles when I show her the photos of my artwork on the vampire's face.

The two bodyguards look more alert than they have in days and slightly green. I feel a little guilty. Story is right. If I hadn't snuck out, they wouldn't be in trouble, but I keep my mouth shut.

I stuff my phone in my pocket as Xander's fancy car screeches to a stop. The door flies open and an angry, worried angel liquid prowls towards me.

"Why did you hang up? I told you to stay on the line," are the first words out of his mouth. I shrug. His honey eyes are everywhere at once, checking me from head to toe. His attention homes in on my leg.

He grunts, and I squeak as his enormous arms sweep me up off the floor into his arms bridal-style. It's as if I am made of feathers. He cradles me gently to his chest.

Story flutters above us, her hands in a praying position underneath her chin. She sighs. The bloody pixie is loving this.

"I will speak to you two later," Xander growls at the bodyguards as he heads towards the car. Without missing a beat, he pops open the back door, and without jostling my leg, which is an impressive achievement, he slides into the roomy back, keeping me on his lap with my injured leg across the seats.

The door snicks shut. The car has tinted windows, and it leaves us in an intimate cocoon. If my leg wasn't throbbing like a motherfucker, I'd be blushing, but as my blood is currently congealing on the street and stuck to my pants, my sock, and sloshing in my boot... I haven't got enough left to produce a decent blush.

"I'll get blood on your seats," I say belatedly.

"I don't care about the seats." Xander gently pulls me back against his bumpy chest. His fingers brush the bloody skin around the knife. I flinch. "Shush, you're okay. Don't move. I just need to..." Xander grips the fabric of my black work trousers with his thumbs and then rips the material, exposing most of my upper thigh.

God, that was hot... Shut up, Tru. You are such a weirdo.

"Why are you here on Earth? Surely it isn't to run a nightclub," I blurt out.

Xander looks up from my leg and frowns. Yeah, maybe now isn't the time to ask nosy questions. But in for a penny... I stick my bottom lip out and comically widen my eyes.

"Night-*Shift* is an excellent investment," he grunts.

"But what else do you do"—my lip quivers—"please I need a second, a distraction."

"I am the liaison between our worlds. I assess security threats."

"Shit, am I a threat?"

"You?" Xander's honey eyes dance with poorly veiled amusement and his mouth twitches. "You are a pain in the arse." His fingers gently brush the underside of my jaw, and he tilts my face up. Then his big naked forearm heads towards my face. I grip it with my hands before he knocks my teeth out.

"Whoa, warn a girl first."

"My shadow, you need to drink. While you do, I'm going to pull the knife out of your leg, remove the silver from your system, and heal you. It's going to hurt like hell, but I've got to do it now before your skin around the knife wound dies. Silver causes shifters rapid necrosis. I do not know how you're still conscious."

Should I tell him silver doesn't seem to affect me? I don't know... If I'm wrong, I don't want to look like an idiot.

I nod. I definitely won't say no to a snack, and the knife has to come out. "Thank you for looking after me," I whisper.

"Drink," he rumbles softly in my ear. His whispered word causes goosebumps to rise on my arms. I tug his forearm closer to my mouth. My fingers dig into his skin. I close my eyes and breathe him in. My tongue darts out, and I lick along the crease of his elbow and lave over my favourite vein. I pause for one second as the taste of his skin floods my mouth and his sunlight and metal scent fills my nose.

I bite down.

His incredible blood fills my mouth, and I get two big mouthfuls before Xander goes to touch the blade. *Damn, it must be lodged deep into the bone.* As the throwing knife was in the brick wall. I cringe. God, that's an awful thought.

"Okay, on three. One"—I take another gulp of blood—"two"—I remove my teeth from his arm and press my leg flat to the seat—"three."

A scream leaves my lips as the pain makes my head explode. I bury my face into his chest as his golden magic floods my wound.

Within moments the pain is gone, but I pant with its residual echo, and my heart hammers in my chest. My hands shake, so I hide them between us. The knife thuds to the floor, and Xander rocks me. "You're healed, my shadow," he murmurs.

I snuggle into his chest.

I'd love nothing more than to stay in his arms, but I can't. Once I feel able to, I pull away. Xander's hand grips my chin, and his thumb absentmindedly rubs my bottom lip. His eyes narrow. "Now, tell me what happened."

Ah, shit.

"Well, I urm, picked a piece of cardboard up..."

CHAPTER
THIRTY-TWO

I'M lucky that Xander's garden has a high wall circling its perimeter. Dexter winds himself around my legs, and Story, with a big grin on her face, sits on a purple plant pot, kicking her legs against its shiny painted surface.

"So we're doing this?" she asks, clapping her hands with glee.

"I guess so." I'm not feeling so gleeful. I wrinkle my nose and scratch the back of my head. "I've never been around shifters when they do this stuff, Story, so do I shift with my clothes on or my clothes off?" I pluck at my jogging bottoms.

Story shrugs. "I don't know."

"Okay." I nod. "I'll keep them on then." I bounce on my toes and roll my shoulders as I waggle my arms about to loosen them. "Okay, let's do this."

I feel strong. I'm like Rocky. You know, in the boxing movie when he runs up the stairs and punches his fist in the air, "Eye of the Tiger".

POW-POW.

I can take on the world. After the knife to the leg and Xander healing me, I'm fit as a flea. I cringe, and a nervous shiver runs up my spine. Well, for the time being, I'm no longer dying, and it's *amazing*.

Sooo amazing. I blow out a breath and wipe my sweaty palms on my grey jogging bottoms.

Crap, I'm scared.

Come on, Tru, you can do this. I rub my forehead with a frown. Of course the horn isn't sticking out of the middle of my human head, but I can't help giving my head a little rub. I didn't realise how sore my forehead was until it wasn't. It will take me a little while to get used to the feeling.

"Okay, let's take this baby for a test drive," I mumble. Story gives me an awkward thumbs-up. I fake smile and nudge some moss that's clinging to Story's flowerpot with the toe of my trainer. I don't know what a horse with a horn is going to do. The huge animal form will not help me track or help with the potential fight against a powerful witch. It's not like the form is sweet and compact. A horse is huge.

But shifter 101—turning into your animal form and popping back human—is how shifters heal, so I have to learn to do this.

I'd be naive if I thought I'd get away with hunting this witch down without sustaining any injuries. Hurting myself is a given. Not that I'm going to walk up to the witch and shout "hey you"—pointy finger—"give me back my horn." Nope, I have a much sneakier plan.

Yep, with that scary thought, I better hop to it. So I'm going to keep my clothes on, see what happens. I might have to do a naked dash back into the house later, but… Yeah, perhaps I need a spare set of clothes? I gnaw on my lip. If I leave to go grab them, I might not try again, so stuff it.

Let's do this.

I shouldn't be able to shift—I'm not technically old enough—but I can feel the shifter magic bubbling away underneath my skin. Either it's the fancy new horn, or with the unicorn power flowing through my veins my body remembers what my father did to me as a kid and it knows what to do.

I close my eyes and allow the power to whoosh out of me.

The surrounding air grows warm, and like a character from Star Trek being beamed up, my molecules separate… and… then they go back together in my other form.

Magic.

I stand on four feet, no, four *hooves*. I glance down, and the sudden movement of my head and neck makes my legs wobble, and my whole body tilts to the left. Ooh, I lock my knees. When I don't fall over, I take a steadying breath.

Oh heck, this is scary.

I don't move another muscle, I just roll my eyeballs to the floor so I can inspect my feet. Ooh pretty, my hooves are an iridescent colour, like the inside of a mother-of-pearl shell, and what I can see of my front legs —forelegs—they're white.

I brace my big body this time before I slowly lift my head. My head and neck seem to affect my balance. I swallow, and everything from my tongue to my throat feels *weird*. Isn't this supposed to feel natural? This does not feel natural, not at all.

My head moves, and I notice something flapping. Oh my god, what the hell is that! *Do not freak out, Tru.* Even though my heart is pounding in my chest and adrenaline is sloshing through my veins. I make myself look at the flappy thing. I almost go cross-eyed. As I slowly, ever so slowly, angle my head, the *fabric* flutters. I blink, are those... Are those my knickers?

I snort.

Yes, my knickers have somehow attached themselves to my borrowed horn.

Ha, my pants almost scared the shit out of me. I move just my eyes to see the rest of my clothing is intact on the floor, no ripping. That's handy. Maybe next time when I shift I might move to the side as I do to avoid spearing my clothes. I grin.

Dexter meanders across the limestone patio flags. He completely ignores unicorn me, and instead, he nimbly pounces on the bundle. He paws and sniffs my clothes, arranging them just so, and then the cheeky cat flops into the middle of the pile, closes his eyes, and tilts his head towards the weak autumn sun.

I brace myself, then violently nod my head up and down. My underwear drops to the floor. It lands on top of Dexter, and with an indignant growl, he rolls on his back, attacking the fabric with his claws and teeth. *Yeah, you killed it, Dex.*

Curious, I turn my head so I can see my fur, and my coat on both sides is the same fancy pure white as my legs. I'm so white I almost glow. I'm also big. If I stretch my neck, I can see easily over the ten-foot garden wall.

Okay, now movement. I lift my leg and take a tiny step forward. Wow, walking on four legs is a strange sensation. I glance at Story to see her reaction, and she's staring at me with her mouth wide open.

"Oh my god, Tru," Story squeaks, pointing behind me. I frown. Weird. Have I broken her? There's nothing behind me, I would have noticed. I'm too fascinated with this new form to work out what she is freaking out about.

I swish my bum... urm... hindquarters? I roll my eyes—whatever the term—and my tail whips between my back legs. It is the same multicoloured hue as my human hair.

Story continues to point frantically.

Yeah, I know, Story. I'm gorgeous. I waggle my ears—ooh, that's a weird sensation. They rotate—oh, and they go back flat against my head. I smile a toothy grin.

When I have time, I'll go somewhere where I can shift and run, where I can take my time to learn this new form... My excited thoughts grind to a halt. No, I won't. My heart sinks. I can't. This isn't my magic, it's on loan from a guilty man. I shuffle my hooves. Unless I can get my own magic back, I can't canter about in a field full of wildflowers while stopping to snack on lush grass and clover. I don't want to know what it feels like to be whole and free, to gallop about with the wind in my hair and my hooves churning up the ground.

Knowing what that feels like and then losing it would break me.

No, I've learnt to shift. That's enough to get my horn back. And if I don't, if I fail... Well, I look up at the sky. My eyes are doing their best to leak. That's why I know Denby Jones, my bio-grandfather isn't trying to trick me with the name and the details of the witch, especially with Jodie's confirmation. That man is doing serious penance. I've added him to my list of people I don't want to let down. Come hell or high water, Denby Jones will get his horn back.

A bouncing pixie gets my attention. "You have... you have...," Story sputters.

I have? I have what?

It's then that I see the feather.

My hooves clatter to the side, and with the jerky movement, I notice the heavy weight on my back. What the fuckety fuck? I turn my head, and my long neck helps me see... I do a double take and then an entire body shudder.

I have wings.

I blink. Wide-eyed, I straighten my neck, and my eyes swivel so I can stare down at the gurgling pixie. Unfortunately, I am not seeing things.

I let out a squeak, and a frightened equine sound echoes around the enclosed garden.

The back utility room door bursts open, and Xander clutching a sword storms outside. I weirdly hold up a hoof as if to stop him. We both look at my foot. I sheepishly place it back on the ground.

He prowls forward as he scans the garden for danger. When he finds nothing, the sword disappears into white smoke and his eyes land on me. His honey eyes soften as he takes me in, and then they widen when he notices my new appendages.

He moves to the side as he stares at my back, and my shoulder blades itch.

"That's interesting," he says.

No shit.

I never had wings before. When I was a kid, I never had wings. Urm, unicorns don't. They don't have wings... of all the freaky things to happen. Did my evil grandfather do something to the horn? Am I cursed?

I must be cursed. I wheeze. Oh God, I'm hyperventilating. Can unicorns have panic attacks?

Then it clicks.

The angel blood. I drank Xander's blood, and this is the consequence to my shifter side.

Shit, angel blood gives you wings.

CHAPTER
THIRTY-THREE

WITH MY HEAD and half my body stuffed inside my grandad's toolbox storeroom, I hunt around for the things I'll need. It's time to go after the witch. I've given myself forty-eight hours to get the job done.

"Okay, you have almost everything on the list. You just need the potions to counteract any wards."

I twist my hips and grab the final potion balls. "Got them," I say with a groan as I wiggle back out. I open my hand and let the three potion balls roll. They bump along the carpet towards the dedicated magic pile within the organised chaos of the scattered equipment on the bedroom floor.

Story sits out of the way on the edge of the bed, and she swings her legs as she taps her notepad with a tiny pen. "So let's try that naff-looking thing first." She points her pen at some random spot on the floor. She must be on about the magic necklace. I flop to the floor and cast my eyes around for the necklace she is talking about. Aha, it is near my feet, so without moving, I grab it with my bare toes and drag it across the floor. The necklace is a dark blackish-grey, the colour of fake silver. I hope it doesn't turn the skin on my neck green.

Story shakes her head and wrinkles her nose as I pull it from between my toes— What? They're cleanish. I smirk at her as I put it on.

"Gross toe juice."

I wiggle my normal-looking toes at her. "Ew, my toes aren't juicy. Who has juicy toes... I can understand flaky."

Story gags.

"I shifted. My toes are perfect and as soft as a troll's bum."

"Have you touched a troll's bottom?"

I snort and shake my head. "I haven't." The grotty-coloured necklace settles around my neck, resting just below my collarbone, and as soon as it touches my skin, it immediately activates. I can feel the low-level magic buzzing across my skin. I'm glad it doesn't need an incarnation to work.

Story zips into the air and circles me. "It isn't perfect, but it seems to do the trick as it masks your shifter energy, less like a beacon"—she does another few circles around me that make me feel a little sick when I try to watch her—"and more like a trickle. You feel like a normal shifter human half-breed."

"Fab, thanks, Story. It's an old spell, but as long as it makes it so I can blend in, it's perfect." I'm sure Jodie would have had a stronger necklace for me to purchase. I should have thought about it when I was at the shop, but I was so focused on getting information on the witch that *allegedly* has my horn and getting the hell out of there... I didn't think beyond that.

I am glad I have everything I need. *Thank you, Grandad*, as I'm not going back into that magic shop unless I'm being dragged by my hair, kicking and screaming. I appreciate it wasn't Jodie's fault that her niece was rude, but I'm seriously not a forgiving person and the girl is on my shit list. Unless it's a life-and-death situation, it's no go.

I've spent my life avoiding drama, and I'm not gonna start now. *Yeah, 'cause your face being on every media channel is low profile.* I roll my eyes.

I carefully remove the necklace, and on my hands and knees I slowly, methodically, pack my kit. Nerves bubble in my tummy, and I have to stop to fold my arms over my abdomen and hug myself to keep the crazy feeling inside. I puff out my cheeks. Wow, this is all getting so real. I let my arms drop and continue to arrange my things so they'll be easy to find.

Story ticks everything off her list like she's a military officer, and she makes a note of where everything goes. She's going to be running my comms, so if I forget something, I'm sure my scary and kind of control-freak friend will know where it is.

The girl is impressive. *I am so very lucky to have her,* I think with a side-eye when the pixie tyrant prods me with her pen to hurry up. I pick up my pace, and when I finish, I rub my nose and sit back on my heels.

"Is that everything?"

"Yep. I think so. I guess we'll know if you need anything pretty quickly." She nervously smiles.

I nod. "Yeah, let's hope it doesn't come to that. Thanks for your help."

Story zips towards me and lands on my shoulder. She rests a hand on my neck. "You've got this, Tru. From what you've told me, you've done hundreds of little recons like this over the years for your grandad. You can do this with your eyes closed."

I blow out a breath and roll my shoulders.

Showtime.

I leave Story in our bedroom and hurry down the hall to access Xander's portal, using the code my unicorn grandfather gave me. I take a deep breath as I step through.

The portal brings me out at the rear of a multistorey car park in what looks like a busy shopping area. I take only a few minutes of frantic searching before I get an idea of where I am. I don't know this city, but I've spent a few hours immersing myself online with Google Maps, and I've memorised enough to know my way to the witch's address from here. It's about a twenty-minute walk.

I'm dressed in black combats and a long winter coat that hits my calves. The outfit has so many pockets full of things I need I'm surprised I don't rattle with each step I take. If this recon mission goes wrong, I should have enough tricks to get myself out safely. The masking necklace buzzes along my skin. I tuck my hands into my pockets, and my fingers nervously jiggle the stuff jammed inside. With my baseball cap pulled down low, I hunch and walk with a little bit more of a swagger.

I have some leaflets for a local Indian takeaway to deliver as cover. So when I get to the witch's street, I ignore the battling moths bouncing around in my stomach, and I immediately open the gate and walk up the path of the first house and slip a leaflet through the letterbox.

So far, so good.

On to the next house.

My eyes flick about as I take mental notes: which of the houses are busy, and which houses aren't. Who are the nosy neighbours? I jump when the window next to me squeaks from a woman with her nose pressed against it. I give her an awkward wave. *Avoid the human granny at number six.*

The letterboxes scrape against my hand as I push each leaflet through. I decide straightaway I dislike the ones with the brushes inside and the ones that have two flaps. I'm sure they're good for the environment, but each time I try to stuff the piece of paper through, I end up losing a few skin cells as the letterbox either snaps closed on my hand or the paper gets stuck in the brushes and I have to give it an extra poke.

I keep going. Gosh, I don't know how the postal workers at Royal Mail stand it.

When I get to Karen Miller's house, I get my extra-special leaflet ready. I've already prefolded it, and it's full of little micro cameras. These cameras are expensive, and they're all tech without a sniff of magic. Hopefully, they'll be undetectable to the witch. I've programmed the cameras to go into different rooms, one in each corner. Their batteries will last a week.

I haven't got a week, and I'm on a deadline to do this as soon as possible, but before I take on the witch, I need eyes inside this house.

It's a risk, and when I step to the door, my hands shake, and I have to take a deep fortifying breath as I open the letterbox and stuff the leaflet inside.

Go, go, go little cameras.

I turn and stroll away, maintaining the same lazy teenage boy walk.

Nothing to see here. Then I go to the next house, all casual-like, as if my heart isn't beating out of my chest.

I feel like I'm going to puke.

I cringe and duck my head. My ears strain for any early indication that I've been caught. I keep mechanically delivering the leaflets as I wait for someone to catch me, for somebody to run out from the witch's house waving the leaflet and screaming about spy cameras. But nothing happens.

My heart beats madly, but the further I get from the witch's house, the easier it is to breathe. I finish that side of the street, then I cross over the road and put leaflets in the houses opposite.

Once my heart rate has gone back to normal, and I'm no longer panicking, I analyse what I felt when I went to her door. Karen Miller's house has a strong blood ward. The only way to get inside that house is to be recognised by the ward—yeah, that's not going to happen—or have skin contact with the witch.

Yay.

I pay particular attention to the house across the road from Karen Miller's. It's one of a set of three similar-designed houses in an art deco style. Sadly, the other two houses next to it have lost a lot of their art deco features, but the house opposite the witch has retained its almost-flat roof. I smile at the For Sale sign and grin when I have to knock the lodged post out of the way to get my takeaway leaflet through. The house is empty. It couldn't be more perfect.

When I finish, with a last look around, I quietly... like a ghost, leave the area and head back to the portal.

I ring Story's mobile on the way. "How's it going?" I ask as I rub my tender right hand. Within a few minutes, that should heal. I won't even need to shift now the vampire side of me isn't fighting with my dying unicorn side. I heal like a pureblood.

"Hi, the cameras are up and running. They're all working. She's alone watching television and eating breakfast." I sigh. Phew, that is a relief. "Tru, she has a chunky necklace on."

"Shit, God, I'm so nervous. That's good... perfect. Thanks, Story. I'm on my way home. I'll see you in a bit."

"See ya."

CHAPTER
THIRTY-FOUR

THE WIND WHIPS little pieces of my hair around my face, so I pull on a knit cap as I peek over the edge of the roof. My breath fogs. Tonight it's freezing, and frost glitters like diamonds on every available surface. When the time comes, it won't do me any good if I can't move quickly with my limbs stiff from the cold. So making sure I can function, I've sacrificed an expensive heating potion ball. The potion keeps me toasty warm.

It's the second night I've spent watching her house. I was too twitchy staying at home watching the cameras yesterday, so as soon as it got dark I came straight back and climbed up onto the flat roof of the art deco house. I could have broken in, but with the equipment that I'm using tonight, it's best to have a clear line of sight and not have to worry about any windows or anything.

Story is at home running interference with Xander, and she's monitoring the surveillance cameras inside the house. She'll let me know if anything changes as I don't want to split my attention right now. Dexter silently watches the quiet street, his head on his paws and his tail twitching. I glare at him.

I can't take him back. This has to happen tonight.

I groan. Don't ask me how he followed me here. One minute I'm walking through the portal and the twenty minutes to Karen Miller's street—avoiding the neighbourhood watch nosy granny house. The next, I hop over the fence of the house opposite, not wanting to use the noisy gate, and a furry body follows me. I almost shit myself.

A pitiful meow has me glaring at the floor, and lo and behold, it's *Dexter*.

More fool me as I didn't notice the hairy monster following me. So I pick him up, and lacking any kitty dignity, I stuff him in my coat while I shimmy up the side of the house to perch on the flat roof.

As I triple check my gear, I keep repeating over and over again to myself that he's not a normal cat and that he's going to be okay. But his presence adds to my worry.

Bloody cat.

"She's getting ready now, Tru. She's got a spell drop-off at midnight," Story says in my ear. Unfortunately, we didn't have any communication spells that would work with Story's size, so we are using our mobiles. I lift my hand and tap the earpiece twice, not answering her 'cause I want to keep silent. The signal tap will let her know I've heard her.

My hand reaches into my grandad's toolbox—I brought the heavy thing with me as it is part of my master plan—and pulls out a tightly rolled foam pad to lie on. I then carefully pull out the bolt-action sniper rifle, which has been modified to shoot high-velocity darts.

My grandad was a specialist in long-distance kills, and he had several weapons that made that possible. It's a fancy piece of kit, and it's a favourite of mine.

Creatures don't use guns, so they're super rare, and I could be killed on sight if caught using this weapon. I shrug, needs must. I'm certainly not gonna tap the witch on the shoulder and say, "Hi, you're coming with me." No, that would be a good way of getting your face melted off with a nasty spell.

Tonight I have sleeping darts. One dart will drop the witch and keep her asleep until I give her an antidote. I'm aiming for clean and quiet.

Karen Miller isn't a nice person. Yesterday we found out she was keeping a vampire in her basement. I lie on the foam pad in a prone position and make sure my body is perfectly in line with my rifle. This roof is perfect. It has a small art deco wall that hides me from the ground but doesn't impede the rifle. From our observations and listening to their terse conversations, the victim is there as a *spell ingredient*. He's young, recently turned, and so frightened. We think he's been there for a while, possibly since his turning as he doesn't look in the best of health. To keep him pliable, she's not feeding him enough. I swear it makes me want to kill her painfully.

So this mission has turned into not only a capture but also a rescue.

The bipod legs support the weapon, and I rest my cheek on the cheek weld and carefully adjust the scope. It's strange. As soon as I'm in position, my breathing gets easier and I get into the zone. All my worries flutter away as I settle down and wait. Tonight there is only the slightest breeze, and it's thankfully not enough to impact the flight of the dart.

"Okay, she's leaving now. She's at the front door."

Karen Miller steps outside.

I take a breath, then I pause as she turns to lock the door. I use the pad of my finger to gently squeeze the trigger.

The dart hits the back of her neck.

I wait and watch her through the scope; she wobbles. Satisfied, I get to my feet and quickly pack the rifle and the pad back into the toolbox. I use the rope I'd hauled it up here with to rapidly lower the toolbox to the ground. Then I scoop up a patiently waiting Dexter and zip him inside my jacket and quickly make short work of climbing down the side of the house. I tug the rope free, loop it around my arm, and snatch up the toolbox.

I hoof it across the street.

The witch drops to her knees and face plants halfway in and halfway out of her doorway. She tried to get back into the house. I grab hold of her ankle and pull her sock down. I cringe as I get a handful of her prickly, hairy leg. With the skin-on-skin contact, her blood ward lets me have access to her house. Unceremoniously, I drag the witch back inside.

I gently click the door closed behind us. Dexter meows, so I unzip my jacket and let him out, and he scampers away to sniff the living room. "Be careful not to touch any of her magic crap," I tell him. He flips his tail as he disappears.

I look down at the witch, and I flip her on her back. She looks so normal... a middle-aged witch with her dark blonde hair in a bun. Dressed in smart, middle-class mum clothing. An expensive winter coat. If I saw her on the street, I'd think she was a teacher or on her way to her coven. I wouldn't think, *Oh, that's a scary witch who kills people* and that she is a banned potion dealer. I systematically pat her down, and as I do, I empty her pockets and plop everything into a plastic evidence bag.

That accomplished, I stare at her neck. The professional numbness I was feeling before scatters. I nervously swallow, and my hands shake. *Thud, thud,* my heart pounds as I lean over her, and I undo the top two buttons on her coat.

I dip my fingers into the neckline. They tingle when my hand lands on the smooth chunky necklace... my horn. I recognised the power—and it *recognises me.*

I let out a small surprise laugh. My magic, my unicorn magic, playfully buzzes and dances over my fingertips. It almost makes my hand and arm feel numb.

Blinking a few times, I clear the wet haze from my vision, and I realise I've fallen onto my knees. I carefully remove my horn from around the witch's neck and, without thinking, I place it around my own.

I don't know how I'm going to return the necklace to its original form. There must be some magic that will help me do that, perhaps shifting with my horn in hand? I rest my hand on top of it and close my eyes for a second to allow myself to appreciate this moment. I did it.

Okay, okay.

I open the toolbox and dip my hand inside to find what I'm looking for, a special purchase. It's a small breathing regulator, and it has enough oxygen for about twelve hours. I clamp it over Karen Miller's nose and mouth and then flip her over and cable tie her hands. The dart will keep her unconscious, but I'm not taking any chances with the sneaky witch as I also slap a magic voiding bracelet onto her wrist.

Behind her, I sit her up and loop the rope around her torso. I then grab hold of her underneath her arms, and with a grunt, I lift her up so her legs dangle above the toolbox. With a smile, I stuff the unconscious witch with the breathing apparatus into my grandad's toolbox storeroom.

Slowly, I feed her body inside until she disappears. I then secure the rope so I can easily drag her unconscious ass back out.

Best body transport idea ever. I grab my rucksack, close the lid, and dust off my hands; I smirk down at the red innocuous toolbox. "The witch is in," I say conversationally to Story, who is still on the phone.

"Yeah, I saw that. That was some freaky shit. How on earth does your imagination think up these things?" she asks with a huff.

I shrug.

I leave the toolbox by the front door. It's time to rescue the vampire.

CHAPTER
THIRTY-FIVE

I LEAVE THE HALLWAY, ignoring the stairs leading up to the bedrooms as I know, thanks to the cameras—apart from her *guest* chained in the basement—no one else is in the house. Through the door where Dexter disappeared, I enter the living room. My boots sink into the soft carpet.

The house is nice—normal.

Magic buzzes around me. There are spells upon spells to keep the place clean, a cloying scent of fake vanilla and rancid magic fills my nostrils.

I take everything in and move with caution as I wouldn't put it past the witch to have something nasty set up for uninvited guests. The living room is homely, a bit too much cream for my tastes. The leather sofa is one you want to flop onto. It looks expensive. The room leads into a beautiful kitchen, more cream with fancy appliances.

Like the way she dresses; nobody looking at this house would even suspect that Karen Miller was anything but what she presented. When I first analysed the cameras, I thought there would be heads in jars proudly on display. But no. It's all so normal.

Thinking of heads in jars and scary witch paraphernalia, I drift to the side of the kitchen to an innocuous small narrow door. This is where she keeps all her creepy stuff. Without the cameras, I wouldn't even realise it is here 'cause it blends into the kitchen so well, hidden within plain sight. With a twist of the handle, the door pops open to reveal a basic golden ward; it wavers in front of dark basement stairs. I sigh. The ward isn't to stop someone from going inside, but more to stop whatever's inside from getting out.

I dig in the lower left pocket of my combats and find the potion ball I'm looking for. I lift it to my lips and whisper the incarnation, and then I flick it at the ward. The ward shimmers, and slowly the spell eats at it, the gold dulls and turns black, flaking away until nothing is left. I lean inside and switch on the lights; I pause.

"Shit, creepy basement time."

"It's all clear," Story says in my earpiece. "Just the vampire."

Yep, just the vampire. I adjust the black rucksack on my shoulder, and then I take a step.

Dexter appears from out of nowhere, making me yelp. He squeezes past me, butting my leg out of the way with his big head, and sprints down the stairs. "Dexter, bloody hell," I gripe. My heart pounds, and I clutch my chest. My fingertips brush my horn.

"Reow," echoes back.

"Shithead."

At least the furry ginger monster is in front of me instead of tripping me up from behind. Okay, let's rescue the presumably starving and possibly rabid vampire... Hmm, what can go wrong? I shuffle down the stairs.

It's the smell that hits me first, the smell of rot. It screams vampire, but more pungent than normal. Unwashed, sick vampire. It tickles the back of my throat and makes me want to throw up. But I swallow a few times and try to just breathe through my mouth as I make my way down the creaky wooden stairs.

Then with each step, the steadily growing magic batters at me. It must be the double unicorn magic what with my grandfather's horn and my magic now around my neck. Sweat trickles down my spine. If I didn't need the things in my coat, I'd remove it.

The basement is huge; it spans the full length of the house, rows of tightly packed shelves with illegal spell ingredients. I ignore everything as I head for the body tucked in the corner; he doesn't even look like a person as he hunches.

"Hey, my name is Tru." I attempt to keep my voice soft and gentle. "I've taken care of the wicked witch upstairs, and I'm here to get you out, get you home."

The body jerks, and a raspy voice answers, "Look, lady, I don't know who you are, but I'm not buying what you're selling. Leave me the fuck alone. Tell that bitch to fuck off."

Well, that's a surprise, even after everything he's been through. The vampire is feisty; I feel weirdly proud of him. "Okay. You hungry?" I let the rucksack slide from my shoulder and unzip it.

"I'm always hungry," he whines. His voice overflows with desperation.

"I've got you." I pull out a big plastic bottle of blood, give it a quick shake, and quickly remove the cap. His head snaps up when he catches the scent.

Red eyes within a gaunt face desperately follow my movements, and his fangs shoot out uncontrollably, piercing his bottom lip. I lean towards him, and he snatches the bottle out of my hand. I cringe when I see the state of his wrists; the scars are atrocious.

"I really am here to help you," I say as I crouch in front of him, my muscles tense and ready if I need to spring out of his way. "Steady, don't drink so fast. You'll make yourself sick." He doesn't listen, and he chokes, and the blood splatters across his lips and chin. "Can I undo your chains?"

He nods, his mouth full of blood.

I'm well aware that I'm putting myself in a hazardous situation since this young vampire could go completely rabid, but... but I don't know... I weirdly trust him.

I fish out the key that I got from the witch's pocket and undo each shackle. Carefully as I can, I peel the metal away from his raggedy, scarred wrists. It's painful to do, and I cringe with sympathy as the skin has grown over the embedded metal. It must hurt like crazy. But the vampire doesn't seem to acknowledge the pain as he continues to guzzle the bottle of blood. When the bottle is empty, he frantically pulls it apart, trying to stick his tongue inside the damaged plastic to get every drop. I grab another bottle, give it a quick shake, pop the top, and hand it over.

"I have another five bottles with me. So try to drink slower this time."

He drinks.

Eventually, he slumps against the wall, his belly distended.

"What's your name?"

"Justin."

"Okay, Justin. We have time for you to go upstairs and use the shower if you want to." I show him my bag full of clothes. "You can get clean and changed and we can get you out of here. Get you home or to a safe house. You're in control of what happens next." He meets my eyes. "I just want to help you. I don't think it's wise, and it would be unfair to you, if I let an untrained vampire out into the world."

His chin drops to his chest in defeat. "I can't do this," he whispers.

Shit. Dexter appears. He rubs himself against my knee, and then he sits in front of the naked vampire. Ignoring the blood still dripping from Justin's mouth, he rubs himself against him and purrs. "This is Dexter."

"Meow."

"You brought your cat with you?" Justin says with an incredulous shake of his head. "Is he your familiar?"

"Nah, he's my pain in the bum. I'm not a witch. I'm actually a shifter-vampire hybrid." I roll my eyes. Justin's hand shakes, and he strokes Dexter's fur.

"He's so soft," he mumbles.

"Yeah, he is." I know in that second, with him gently stroking Dexter, that Justin is going to be okay. "The reason we are here... urm, Karen Miller, the witch, had something of mine, and I wanted to get it back. When I was doing recon on the house, I noticed you were in the basement and thought I'd give you a hand getting out of here."

Justin rolls his head back against the wall, and his eyes drift up to the ceiling. "I don't think I can shower here. I know I stink." His voice drops. "What if she comes back?"

I smile softly in response to his frightened, whispered words. "That evil bitch is never coming back." In that moment I realise the truth... I had never any intention of handing Karen Miller over to the witches.

I can't.

No. I can't risk it. She's the ultimate bad guy.

But if I can't hand her over, does that mean I'll have to kill her myself? Am I willing to do that?

My eyes drift across Justin's emaciated frame. She chained him in her basement for a long time. I can see the damage that has been inflicted on his body. It paints a picture of horrendous abuse. Damage that is slowly healing, thanks to the blood.

I couldn't justify killing her for myself. But I watched the cameras, heard him cry. Worse, I see him now with my own eyes.

I'm a saviour, not a killer.

Looks like today I might end up being both.

A WOBBLY JUSTIN jumps into the shower and then gets dressed. I give him the option of either calling a taxi to get to the portal or walking; he decides he would like to walk, considering he hasn't been outside for a long time.

"Ready?"

"Yeah, I guess. This is going be a big adjustment." Justin shuffles awkwardly from foot to foot.

He definitely looks better. It is amazing the magical properties of blood when it comes to bitten vampires, and a shower and clean clothes also help. Although he still looks like a vampire and he still looks like... well, dead. He at least no longer looks like a walking zombie.

His face is fuller, and overall he looks less emaciated. His greasy hair that I thought was black is actually a dark auburn.

I crouch down next to the toolbox and pack away everything that I don't need, including putting most of the microcameras back in their box. I try to ignore the unconscious witch, who's slumped at the bottom of the storeroom, breathing like Darth Vader.

"Have you got somewhere to go? Family?" I ask Justin.

He glances down at his feet and shakes his head. "No, I've got no one. A female vampire turned me without my permission... She took a shine to me." He cringes.

"That doesn't sound good."

Justin shrugs, his eyes fixed on the floor. "She turned me on a whim, so I guess that means I'm an unregistered rogue vampire to add to my issues. When I refused to have a relationship with her 'cause I'm not attracted to women... Boy, she went nuts." He laughs bitterly. "I should've played the game and got safe before I rejected her. She hit me so hard... When I woke up, it was to find myself chained to a basement. She had sold me to the witch. I've been here ever since." His eyes drift unconsciously back to the kitchen and the basement. "Must be months... years... Hell if I know." He rubs the back of his neck.

"I'm sorry. I'm sorry that they did that to you." I get to my feet, and without thinking I take a miniscule step towards him.

He flinches.

The frightened look that flashes across his face makes my heart ache. So I take a big step away from him to respect his space and keep my hands where he can see them. "Look, I'm not eighteen yet, and I'm under the guardianship of an angel." I roll my eyes. "I'll tell you *all* about it when we have time."

I puff out a nervous breath. It's a risk even giving him this next bit of information, but... I am going by instinct. "So my friend Story, Dexter, and me, we have been living at the angel's house. He's called Xander." I fidget. "But as a backup plan, we have just rented a two-bedroom flat. I guess you could call it a safe house. It's not much, but it's safe, clean..." I pause and put my hand to my ear, tapping the earpiece. I hold up a finger to Justin. "I am just gonna check with her. Story? It is your home as well. I know we haven't even moved in yet, but would it be okay with you if Justin stayed until he gets back on his feet?" I hear Story inhale.

"Of course I was going to make that suggestion anyway. The guy needs us. He needs friends."

I grin. "You're the best, thank you." I give Justin a warm smile. "My friend, my roommate Story, said it's okay and you're more than welcome."

"You'd let me stay? With you? Why would you do that?" Justin asks incredulously. He narrows his eyes. I can see it in his face, mistrust. *If it seems too good to be true, it probably is.*

"'Cause I know what it's like to be on my own, and I know what it's like to be frightened. I know inside you are bleeding, but you are not broken. I'm not leaving you. Anything bad that happens to you happens to me too. So we're going to do this together." I shrug. "It feels the right thing to do." I shuffle my feet and look at the floor. In the café we have a pending food board, where our customers can buy a stranger a coffee and or a slice of cake. It's a small thing, but means so much to people who have got nothing. "Pay it forward when you can."

"Okay," he whispers.

"Okay." I drop the lid of the toolbox and heft it up. The toolbox looks and feels the same. It's so strange that a witch is stuffed inside there. Pocket dimensions are awesome.

Having Justin staying with us has pushed my timeline as I didn't want to move out of Xander's house until the guardianship was resolved, but after living on his own in a basement being tortured by a witch... I don't know if Justin wants to live alone. He might need somebody to talk to.

I might speak to my unicorn grandmother. Perhaps she might take over my guardianship? I need to live my life. Humans by law are independent at sixteen. It is so unfair... but when I think about it, it is understandable that creatures have so many more constraints.

At least I know Xander is a nice guy with an impressive moral compass. I just don't feel it's right to give him another person to look after and just invite somebody into his house.

"Come on, let's go. We can talk more on the way. Dexter," I yell back into the house. Dexter trots from around the sofa and gives me a look of distaste that screams *no need to shout, human.*

I open the front door and step into the front garden; the night is still frozen and fresh. I take a deep breath in to get the cloying vanilla scent and magic out of my nostrils. I'm so glad to be out of that house.

Everything went so well, I think with a satisfied smile. As soon as the thought bubbles up in my head, of course, everything goes tits up. The toolbox clunks against my leg as I catch the sound of rapidly approaching vehicles, and when I turn my head, half a dozen cars screech to a stop. Three come from one direction and three from the other. They completely block the street.

For fuck's sake, Tru.

Justin is about to step out of the house, and I wave him back inside. "Stay inside behind the ward please." I drop the toolbox to the floor, dig into my pocket, and throw a basic ward vial at the garden wall. It should hold long enough for me to speak to Justin and grab some weapons.

I look at the house. Or perhaps it might be best to head inside and call the cavalry. I flinch as two vampires jump from one of the cars and sprint towards me. They slam against the ward. The ward flickers and ripples. I have minutes.

"Is this about me?" Justin asks, his eyes wide with fear.

"No." Well, I don't think so. It can't be. This is about the witch or…

Bloody Lord Gilbert steps out of the lead car onto the pavement. He adjusts his suit jacket and shoots me a toothy grin.

Cocky pureblood arsehole.

CHAPTER
THIRTY-SIX

"I got your message," Lord Luther Gilbert says with a smirk and a hair flick. Ah, good to know I was right about him sending the assassin. "Come with us quietly, little girl," he says as he takes a menacing step towards me.

Creepy shit.

"Story, you getting all this? It's that dickhead, Lord Gilbert."

"Yeah, the cameras are still recording. Go back in the house."

I know when I'm outnumbered. I take a step back and nudge the toolbox back towards the door with my foot. I'm okay with running.

I cringe when four more vampires throw themselves at the ward. "Yeah, that would have to be a no, Luther." The posh vampire scowls when I use his first name. Oops.

"If you don't leave the ward, we are going to eat the neighbours," Luther says with a chuckle and a lick of his lips.

My mind goes to the nosy old lady at number six, and it takes three deep breaths to temper the hot surge of anger threatening to flood my head. I hate this; I hate him. "You know I can't let them hurt anyone," I whisper to Story. "If something happens to me, keep our new friend safe." I kick the toolbox over the threshold.

"Be careful. I love you."

"I love you too." I tug out the earpiece, pocket it, and throw Justin my phone. It slaps into his hand. "Good catch," I say with a wobbly smile. "Story, my best friend, is on the line. Please stay inside until she tells you to move. Don't come out here, Justin, no matter what."

"I can help," he says bravely.

"Thank you, but not today. Please promise me, whatever happens, stay inside the ward." The witch's blood ward will keep him safe.

He nods.

I tug my coat off and drop it on the floor; there's nothing in there that will help, and the bulky jacket will only get in my way. I have a dozen throwing knives and some nasty potions. I also have some epic weapons stuck in my grandad's storeroom, but I've got no time to arm myself. What I have will have to do.

The vampires are all out of their cars. My eyes flick over them. I have twenty of the buggers to play with.

Yay.

I'm fucked.

I roll my shoulders and my wrists. Looks like my morals are about to be tested, as if this is what I think it is I can't be messing around. I'll have to aim to kill.

"If you got my *note*, you would have got my warning. I'm not coming with you, and I'm warning you *again* if you continue to insist, I will give you and your boys here a true death..." Ha, ha. *Tru death*. I chuckle at my joke; even to my own ears my laughter sounds a little manic.

Only twenty vampires.

I gulp and grip my blades so hard my hands ache.

Finger by finger, I force myself to loosen my hold.

"Breow." Dexter rubs my calf. My heart misses a beat and sinks into my abdomen.

No. Oh God no.

I can't help the worried tears that fill my eyes, and internal me slaps my forehead. How stupid. I should have locked him in the house. *Please don't let them hurt my cat,* I beg the universe.

"You brought your cat?" Luther scoffs.

"Oh, he's not a cat," I reply. I drop my eyes to the troublesome creature that I love with all my heart. Mentally, I scream at the ginger monster. *Now is the time to do something, buddy. Do the fae monster thing or run and hide.*

"Kill them," Luther says with a flick of his hand. As soon as the words leave his mouth, rapidly one after another, my knives are out of my hands and flying towards him. The ward doesn't impede them as they fly perfectly on target. My heart thuds with anticipation.

Another vampire jumps in front of Luther and one of my blades hits him in the throat, the other in his heart. My heart misses a beat.

Oh.

Blood sprays, and the vampire falls to the floor. *I think he's dead.*

Luther brushes specks of blood from his suit and gives the downed vampire a dirty look.

"Wow, he saved your life and...," I croak out.

I killed him.

Lord Luther Gilbert steps over his saviour like his death is meaningless, and with clear dismissal, he turns his back and opens the car door.

He is leaving.

Like a living... urm... dead wall, a dozen of the vampires surround him while the four vampires continue to hammer at the garden ward. I shake my head and dip my trembling hand into my pocket.

His entire attitude to that man's death riles me. The bastard is more bothered about his suit.

I'll show him. I spot the perfect moment, then I throw a potion ball at Luther. It smacks him in the middle of his back, and the liquid splashes. I then watch numbly as it rapidly eats away at his expensive suit jacket.

Luther lets out a squeak, and he flaps his arms around. His men panic. They rush to help him tug his jacket off. All the while, the vampire lord is squealing like a pig. The destroyed jacket lands on the floor with a splat.

Yep, it's petty, and perhaps I should have thrown another knife, but a blade wouldn't have got past the wall of vampires.

I wanted to make a point. I also didn't want to kill anyone else unintentionally. If the pureblood vampire cares more about his suit... fine. I'll destroy his suit.

The garden ward crumbles, and with another two knives in my sweaty palms, I sprint across the witch's small front garden and jump over the wall. A vampire charges towards me as I land. I grab hold of his arm and twist it. Crunch, he grunts.

Shit, it snaps like a twig; I frown, that's not normal.

Concentrate, Tru.

I drag myself back into the moment and use his body as an anchor; I swing around him and do a roundhouse kick in another vampire's face. The guy goes flying down the road.

I blink. To be honest, that looked like a bad action film... *How did I do that?* Ah, the double-horn magic is making me crazy strong.

That's good to know.

I can't see, but I hear it when Luther's car leaves, and all the vampires converge on me at once, almost getting in each other's way. "Does it not bother you that your house leader doesn't care when one of you falls?" I block a punch. "That he cares more about his suit?" I do my best to scramble for some space, but it's useless as the vampires are everywhere. "He's running away, leaving you here to die."

A fist heads for my face. I block it and return with a hit to the guy's kidney. I block another two hits. But a fist makes it through my guard, and my head snaps to the side, and my lip splits. I get my right leg up and kick that guy in the face.

"Our master doesn't deal with vermin. He is pureblood."

Another vampire lands a blow to my temple. Then I'm grabbed from behind, and another vampire whips out a knife and stabs me in the leg with silver. I wince.

Bloody hell, it's the same leg.

Gah. Why has it got to be the same leg. Has it got a target on it? He flashes his fangs in a mean grin and rips the blade out. I bite down on a scream. My blood covers his hand and drips from the silver knife as he readjusts the angle, and this time he aims for my heart.

He thinks he's got me.

Without thinking too much about it, I shift. My whole body tingles, and I transform into my unicorn form.

Yay, I can shift after being stuck with silver.

Everyone around me freezes with shock. Smug, I get my hooves underneath me, and without losing sight of the surrounding vampires, I do a test wiggle.

Phew, the wings aren't anywhere in sight. I'm so glad as the delicate feathers would be a target. It looks like I can shift with or without them. That is kind of cool and something to practise.

The vampires are no longer attempting to attack me... and... They don't seem impressed with my gorgeous unicorn form.

No, it's not me they are looking at.

Instead, they are just staring over my shoulder in complete shock. I scrunch my nose up with disappointment. I then almost lose my balance as I jump in the air with fright, as a humongous *roar* echoes around the street.

I find myself as frozen as the vampires. My heart thuds like crazy in my ears. I slowly tilt my head and roll just my right eye back to investigate. My knees wobble.

The sight makes my mouth drop... and my hooves clatter as I clumsily turn.

The roar... Ha, it's Dexter, and he's... He's a *huge* monster cat.

Get in!

He is a gigantic version of himself. Wow. I narrow my eyes. His teeth are ginormous.

"Reow," Dexter roars again.

"Beithíoch!" a vampire screams. Dexter pounces on him and rips his head off. I blink. He then jumps to the next one.

Oh my god, he is ripping apart vampires quicker than they can run away. *I need to help him.* Heck, I haven't even learnt to walk in this form. Yet just as I'm about to shift back, a vampire knocks into my bum. I move without thinking. I kick out with my hind legs, double barrelling the vampires behind me, and then I stomp with my right foreleg. My teeth snap, and remembering I have a horn, I stab, 'cause why the hell not? My multicoloured rainbow tail gets in on the action, slicing through the air like a whip. This new body is fantastic.

A vampire comes at me. I rear up on my hind legs, and as I drop, I aim my front hooves at his head. The weight of my half tonne body cracks his noggin like an egg, Humpty Dumpty–style. Unicorns are badass.

It doesn't take long to finish the vampires. To be honest, it's all Dexter. The street is quiet, and my sides heave from exhaustion. I stumble away from the vampires and shift back into my human self. Mournfully, I look around for my clothes, but I can't see them. They're lost in a sea of vampire bodies.

This is horrendous. What a waste of life.

Oh no, the horn necklace. I frantically pat my neck and find it still around my neck. Some witchy magic must have allowed it to shift with me. There goes the theory that if I shifted with it, it would transform back into my horn. My shoulders sag with disappointment.

Dexter sits on a pile of... I cough and choke down bile. Rather them than us. But bloody hell, it's been a long night.

I carefully rub my face and check my leg. There's no pain, so at least shifting has healed everything nicely. I hear a rumbling purr and glance up from inspecting my leg. "Dexter don't you dare clean your paws. Ew." I have to look away.

Above me there's a crack of thunder—no, not thunder. *Wings*. Before I can focus, a small blue body smacks me in the face and hugs my nose. "Oh my god. I thought we'd be too late. You're alive. You got them all. Dexter is big... wow," Story screeches as she continues to hug my face.

"What... What are you doing here?"

"I wasn't going to leave you to fight alone."

My nose tingles, and I have to hold my breath so I don't sneeze. Damn fairy dust.

"We'd?" I tilt my head. She said, *I thought we'd be too late.*

She flies slightly back and squeezes my cheeks together and gives me a nervous toothy grin.

"Story," I growl.

"Urm... me and Xander."

Ah, that would have been the thunder.

When Xander spots me in all my *naked* glory, he tips his head, muttering words to the night sky. Then he prowls, moving like liquid towards me; he grips the hem, and he tugs his navy jumper over his head in a single motion, revealing slabs of muscle I can't pull my eyes from... until unceremoniously, his top covers my head and cuts me off from the incredible view.

Now all I can smell is him, metal and sunlight. I sniff, drawing his scent in like a crazy person. Deft hands impersonally pull the luxury fabric down, covering my bottom. His jumper is touching places he will never touch, and the girly part of me equally squeals and sobs at the thought.

Get a grip, Tru.

I make sure not to look at him and his glorious muscles, and instead, I check on Justin. Thank God he listened and he's still inside the house. He peeks out of the front door, and when he sees me looking at him, he opens the front door wider; his head swivels from me to Xander, and he stares at my angel in very much the same way as I do. Like a cartoon character with their tongue hanging out.

"Don't look at her," Xander grits out like he has to force the words past his teeth. He moves in front of me, blocking Justin's view.

I giggle. "I think he's looking at you," I say helpfully.

I peek around Xander and give my new vampire friend a wink, and he mouths, *Who the fuck is that?* and fans his face. I snort. Yeah, I know the feeling.

Angel, my guardian, I mouth back.

Seeing him react like that doesn't force me into a jealous, crazy rage. Instead, that little peek of Justin's personality makes me happy.

Xander turns back to me, and his eyes are glowing.

Ooh, he is mad.

Story zips towards Justin, abandoning me to my fate.

"Tru, what did you not understand when I told you I would handle the witch problem?" Xander's jumper hangs off my wrists, so I keep my head down and fiddle with the cuffs. He moves closer, tilts up my chin, and I meet his now-worried eyes. "Please explain to me what has happened before the hunters come."

I draw a raspy breath and fall forward, resting my cold forehead on his bare chest that feels more rock than flesh. "I'm sorry."

He grunts, and I squeak as he scoops me up into his arms. Xander quickly steps around the bodies and deposits me back in the witch's garden, which is free from blood and guts.

He grabs my coat from the floor. "Here, put this back on. You're freezing," he says gruffly.

With both Story's and Justin's help, I tell him what happened.

When we finish, he pulls out his phone. "Atticus." Oh, he is speaking to the head of the vampire council. "Can you explain why I am looking at the bodies of over a dozen vampires from Gilbert's house?"

"Twenty," I whisper.

"Twenty vampires attacked Tru this evening with no provocation… Yes, I have footage. Atticus, if you don't get a grip on that pompous little prick, I'm going to rip his head off. Is that clear enough for you? Come clean up his mess, and while you're at it…" Xander glances at Justin. "I need a young one registered and his sire put down for an illegal turning. I'll forward you the address and the nearest portal code. There are vehicles here for you to use." Xander ends the call.

"Now, apart from the unconscious witch and what sounds like an assassin's armoury, have you got spare clothes in that magical toolbox of yours?"

Wide-eyed, I nod.

CHAPTER
THIRTY-SEVEN

I'M on my second mug of tea. I yawn so big my jaw clicks, and my eyes water and sting. Gosh, I'm so tired. So much has happened, and it seems impossible for me to just sleep. My head is too full of thoughts buzzing around like a hive of angry bees.

On top of that, I need to ring my unicorn grandfather up and return his horn. The thought makes me a little sick, as it will not be a pleasant experience trying to get the damn thing off. I'm dreading it.

My lips pull down into a grimace. How selfish does that make me?

I fiddle with the bone necklace. It's warm underneath my touch. The power buzzes against my neck and fingers. I don't want to be selfish... but I can't help taking a moment to mentally prepare before I have to ring him. Also, it's five in the morning, and calling him this early would be rude. I should at least wait until the sun comes up.

I nibble on my lip and glance down at the necklace. When I look at it, my heart sinks. Oh, it is pretty enough. The rainbow colours make it look like colourful costume jewellery. At first glance, you'd have no idea that it was bone. I was so busy fighting to get it back I didn't have time to think, and I felt such joy when I finally had it in my hands. But now I've had time to think about it, my heart hurts.

It is heartbreaking to know what my horn should look like after seeing my grandfather's horn in all its glory. When I compare the two... It's *horrifying*. A part of me has been butchered and reduced to magical jewellery. It makes me feel sick.

It's worse than someone chopping off... say my little finger and wearing it as a necklace. The horn holds all my magic and pieces of my soul. It's not just magical bone.

I sip my tea. I'm also worried, worried that I won't be able to fix it and my horn will never go back to its original form. *The witch ruined it forever.* Will it still allow me to shift? My fingers drift back to the necklace. It feels powerful enough; the magic doesn't feel broken. When I give Denby Jones his horn back, if I can shift, will I be a unicorn without a horn?

I don't like the idea of having part of my soul around my neck, easy to remove, easy to steal. So even though I now have my horn, it'll be hard to let his go. A tear trickles down the side of my nose. I quickly swipe it away.

It's been a long night.

I won't be able to sleep until I make the call. Who am I kidding? Even when I make the call, the worry whipping around inside my head won't be conducive to good sleep.

Today has shown me I'm willing to kill to save strangers and to save myself.

My hand trembles, and I place my mug down on the side table. I rise from the chair and shuffle into the middle of the orangery. Near Justin, I lie down on my back. The bone necklace makes a faint clack when it touches the heated tile. I join Justin as he stares out through the glass roof lantern and into the dark sky.

Xander, who apparently is now running a hotel for misfits, insisted Justin come home with us. My angel took full responsibility for the young vampire after he got him registered with Atticus. Justin was understandably frightened of the other vampires, and Story's puppy dog eyes swayed Xander. I smile. That man has so many levels. The more I see, the more I fall for him. That thought makes me wiggle, and the hard floor digs into my spine.

Sunrise is still hours away, and with my enhanced shifter eyesight not hampered by the city lights, I can see the stars.

I don't know who said *when life knocks you down, roll over, and look at the stars.* Looking up at the night sky reminds me how insignificant I am in the scheme of things.

The vampire next to me is silent. He has been lying with his arms behind his head, staring out into the night, for over an hour. I leave him to his thoughts.

I know some people see vampires as dead creatures, and I also know other vampires see bitten vampires as expendable. But... I lift my chin to peek at him.

When I speak to Justin, all I see is a person. All I see is a guy trying to make his way in the world. So it would be hypocritical of me to see the vampires who died today as nothing less than people. People I killed.

The problem isn't that I feel guilty. I huff out a silent laugh. No, the problem is I don't. I feel nothing.

After the shock of the fight has dissipated, I find to my horror I don't care that I killed them, and it freaks me out.

It has me digging into my psyche.

What the hell is wrong with me? I know I'm not human, and there's no pretending anymore that I am. If I had to do it all again... kill them and protect the people on the street, protect Justin, I would. No, the only thing I regret is that Lord Luther Gilbert got away without a scratch.

The witch is alive; I guess it was only fair that Justin got to decide her fate, as she tormented him the most. While we had the attention of Atticus and his team of elite vampires, the hunters guild and the human police, Xander dragged out my unconscious prisoner from the toolbox. Karen Miller is alive, but her existence won't be pleasant, and without my unicorn magic, she is next to useless, and we've been told they'll bind the natural power she has. I've been told she is being sent off-world to a prison planet. Never to be seen again.

The sound of clicking claws drags me from my thoughts, and a normal-size Dexter struts towards me. He returned to his normal size once I was safe; it was a good thing too 'cause there was no way Dexter in giant beast mode would have fit through the portal. I let out an *oof* as the heavy cat leaps onto my chest. His claws dig in as he pads my chest to make sure I'm comfortable enough for his ginger behind. Satisfied, he lies across me.

"Thank you for saving my life today, kitty cat," I say, breaking the heavy silence of the room. I run my hands down his back, and he stretches out and then flips over. Grabbing my hand between his paws, he pulls me towards his spotty ginger-and-white tummy.

"If you hadn't followed me, I would've died. So thank you, Dexter. You are the best monster cat in the world." I gently stroke his tummy, and he purrs at my words.

When the sky lightens and the night recedes, I move a sleepy Dexter and get up off the floor. "Come on, Justin. You have a room with a bed. I think Xander has even put in a mini fridge for you with your blood supply. There's also a datapad and a new phone in case you need to ring or contact anybody." I drag him up off the floor and ignore his unconscious flinch at my touch. I keep my distance so as not to make him any more twitchy.

We wander out of the orangery and head towards the bedrooms. As I walk, I groan and roll my shoulders and swing my hips to alleviate the stiffness. Lying on the floor for a few hours wasn't my best idea. I drop him off at his room.

I pull out my phone and dial the number for Denby Jones. The phone rings and rings... He doesn't answer. I guess I'll give him another hour as it's barely seven.

I sit in the kitchen, yawning as I push jam around my plate. Gosh, I hope nothing has happened to him. Not that I didn't light the match of the shifter council being booted out of power and hunted down. I still find it strange that I can't seem to get hold of him. If it was me and I had lent some girl I don't really know the source of my power, part of my soul... Yeah, I would have the phone permanently stuck to my hand, waiting for her call.

At ten, when I still can't get hold of either of my bio grandparents, I ask Xander if he knows where they live and if he can take me to their house. I don't think Denby is staying there, as Ann kicked him out, but she might point me in the right direction. I need to give the horn back as soon as possible. I don't want to hang on to it any longer than I need to. I also have questions about my vampire mum and Ryan, her son, my father, aka the horn thief.

With the lack of a portal code, we couldn't use the gateways. We've been driving for thirty minutes. I pretend to stare out at the world whizzing past. Instead, I watch Xander in the window's reflection. He takes my breath away; he's so beautiful. He holds the steering wheel one-handed at the bottom, his arm resting on his leg. Like everything he does, he's a studious driver. I can't help my grin. Xander drives a little bit like an old lady going to church.

My smile fades and my stomach churns. I trace the outline of his face in the window. *Weirdo.* I curl my finger back into a fist, and my nails bite into my palm. This is why as soon as I deal with this horn business, the misfit gang and I need to move out. I rub my knuckle on the glass.

We have our flat; I need to ditch the angel.

Unrequited love is a real bitch. It hurts. My heart hurts, and living with him is not healthy.

God, I hope we won't walk into another problem. I don't think my head can deal with any more shit. I'd like a few months off. Even the vampire side of me is done with bloodshed. *Yet I still don't feel guilty.*

I lick my bottom lip and sigh. "I don't feel bad," I say, my gaze still fixed out the window. I avoid his reflection now as I don't want to see his face and his disappointment.

"You don't feel bad about what?"

I zip my coat up to my chin and nibble on the little plastic toggle. "I don't feel bad about killing those vampires," I mumble.

When he says nothing for a few seconds, I dare myself to turn my head. His eyes flick to mine. His beautiful honey eyes are soft and full of compassion before he looks back at the road and manoeuvres the car around a mini roundabout.

"If you weren't worried about not feeling bad, not caring, then I'd be concerned. It's when you don't reflect on the lives lost that is the time to worry."

"Or when you start to enjoy killing... What if I—"

"You are not a psychopath. Those men would have killed you without a second thought." He reaches over, and his big hand envelops mine. I look down at our innocent joined hands, and my heart flips.

"Tru, in life you can't control what happens to you, but what you can control is how it shapes you. You cannot allow the bad things to break the person who you are. Dent, mould, *shape*, but never break. Do you understand? You alone get to decide what each experience means to you." Xander drops my hand and gently taps my temple. "Only you get to decide what happens in here."

I sink into my seat.

Xander is right. I don't mind being a bit dented. We're all dented, some people more than others. The shadows in my eyes add character. It is up to me alone if I allow the bad stuff to break me. "Thank you," I mumble. Now I feel warm and squishy. Why does he always do that to me? God, it's going to hurt to walk away from him.

Some people write, create music, dance—I hurt bad people. I think it's what I'm made to do. I might as well put it to good use. I can be a saviour too.

Xander changes gear, and the car slows as it turns into a street where all the houses are huge. When we pull up to their house, it is obvious something isn't right. "Is this it?" The gate, which is a big solid wooden thing, is wide open.

"Yes." Xander's hand tenses on the steering wheel, and the golden stone rumbles up from the tyres as we slowly crunch our way down the drive.

I fidget with the zip on my coat, and my head swivels side to side; the place looks deserted. "Where are the guards?" I mumble. I lean forward in my seat and click my seat belt off. The alarm on the dashboard pings, so I grip the headrest and hover off the seat so it stops. "It shouldn't be empty, not with the unrest," I whisper.

"No, it shouldn't," Xander grunts out. "Perhaps I should take you home and return by myself. I haven't got a good feeling."

I haven't either. My instincts are screaming at me to leave. But Ann is family—new-to-me family, but I can't let that stop me from doing the right thing and checking on her. "We haven't got time." When the car rolls to a stop, I'm out the door, silver blades in my hands. I march across the stone.

The house is enormous. It's old and fancy-looking with pillars at the front. It's the type of house a period drama or a movie would hire as a location. All that is missing is a horse and carriage.

The car switches off, the engine ticking in the sudden silence. "Tru," Xander chides me. "Please wait for me." His door clonks shut. I stand still for a second and move as soon as I sense him silently join me.

I jog up the steps.

White smoke drifts in my peripheral—white with little gold flecks—Xander's magic. He is in warrior mode as he takes two big steps to overtake me, and with a nudge, he pushes me behind him. The magic bleeds out of his hands. And then Xander is holding a gigantic sword, bigger than a longsword. It is double-edged, with a straight blade. I don't recognise the design. It's the same one he had the other day in the garden. He twists the handle on the front door. It swings open on silent hinges, and with his sword arm blocking me from going ahead of him, we both look inside without stepping over the threshold... and perhaps avoiding a magic trap.

"Hello? Ann? It's Tru... Is anyone home?" I shout. "Grandmother?"

Calling her grandmother sounds so strange to my ears. I only called Denby my grandfather at first 'cause I was being sarcastic, and then I did it out of respect.

Silence greets us.

I glance at Xander, and he raises a heavy, dark eyebrow.

"Can you sense any magic?" I ask, dropping my voice to a whisper.

"No," he grunts out in a normal tone. "No ward, no magic of any kind."

I guess he doesn't need to whisper as I already announced our presence. I rub the back of my prickling neck with the hilt of my knife. "That's what I thought."

Oh heck, that isn't good.

CHAPTER
THIRTY-EIGHT

Xander takes a step inside, and when nothing untoward happens, he waves me forward. He closes the door behind us, and my boots squeal across the marble floor as he pushes me back against the wood.

"Stay here while I clear the house."

I blink at him and knock his hand away with an indignant huff. "Urm, no. We can do it together. It will be quicker."

I take a step forward, and he shoves me back with a low growl. My back hits the door, and it rattles. "Stay. Don't move."

He's more shifter than angel sometimes. Bossy bastard. I refrain from barking at him, as the stay comment was a bit much, but I settle for a salute... with both middle fingers.

Xander stalks off. I grumble as I wait pressed against the door, my silver knives gripped in my sweaty hands. We both know that he's being ridiculous.

The entrance hall—that's the only way I can describe it—is huge. It's more modern than the outside of the house would lead you to believe. White marble floor and wooden wainscoting three-quarters up the walls. Beautiful wooden stairs twist up in front of me. Xander clears the first room to the left. I can see it's an empty office, and

Xander then opens the door to the right. It's an empty sitting room. Another door and... It's a bathroom.

I groan and bump my bum against the door. This is going to take forever. "Waiting like a damsel in distress," I grumble, and then I grind my teeth.

Not even five minutes later, I might have to shift to replace the enamel on my teeth. Xander waves me forward. I rush towards him and follow him into a living room.

Ann is sitting silently in a chair facing a wall of windows that looks out onto a massive back garden.

"I'm going to arrange some security," Xander grumbles from behind me.

I turn my head. I belatedly notice his sword has disappeared, so I cram my knives into their respective holders and nod. "Okay, thank you." He grabs his phone from his pocket and steps away to make a call. I focus back on the silent woman in the chair.

"Ann?" I whisper.

When I get no response, I rush towards her, and I gently touch her arm to get her attention. She blinks up at me and smiles, but her bottom lip wobbles, so to stop it she firms her mouth. "Tru? I'm sorry. I didn't hear you arrive."

She doesn't look hurt, which is a relief. But her eyes are red-rimmed, as if she's been crying. "Are you okay? When both of you didn't answer my calls, I got worried. So... urm... Here I am. Why are you alone? Where are your guards?"

"Oh, I sent them away for the day." Her eyes drift outside.

Arseholes. They shouldn't have left her, I think with a flash of anger.

"I'm sorry, Tru. I'm not the best company." She takes a deep breath, as if fortifying her next words. "Are you here because you've heard the news?"

"News?" My pulse rockets. "Oh no. What the heck has happened now?"

Ann meets my concerned eyes. "Oh my dear, I'm so sorry. You haven't heard? Your grandfather Denby finally passed away." Ann's rainbow eyes drift back to the garden.

"What?" *Finally passed away?* "What?" I wobble on my feet. "But that's not possible... I have his horn. I came here to find him as I need to return his horn." My hand drifts up to pat my forehead.

He's dead?

Shit, no wonder he didn't answer his phone. My body suddenly feels heavy. I sink into a chair next to Ann.

Is this my fault?

My hands tremble, so I tuck them underneath my knees and I wait awkwardly for her to say something. Anything. But when the silence stretches and my nerves vibrate inside me like an elastic band pulled too tight, I clear my throat.

I guess I will have to prompt her.

If I don't ask and get an answer soon... I will think the worst.

Is this my fault?

"Ann, what... happened to Denby?" The question makes me feel bad because she's hurting. Even though she rejected him in the café, I can see from the grief written all over her how much she loved her mate.

Is it... Is it because he gave me his horn?

"That man. Of course he didn't tell you," she mumbles under her breath as she takes in my wide eyes and pale face. "He always enjoyed the drama. I should have realised he didn't tell you. I can guess if he did you would have refused. What did he say when he gave you the horn?"

"He said little, if anything. He told me to go hunt down the witch and slammed the horn into my forehead." I rub my head again with a grimace.

She lets out a bitter laugh. "What do you know of unicorns?"

"Nothing much." *Nothing at all.*

Ha, I thought they were the creature equivalent of light beings. But after meeting Denby, I changed my mind. There is nothing light about unicorns. I shiver. The way my body moved while I was fighting those vampires...

My leg bounces, and I have to press it down to stop it from jumping.

"Horns can be gifted. That's why no one went after that witch." She looks mournfully at my horn necklace, swallows, and twists her hands. "Our magic is so unusual compared to other creatures'. They classify us as shifters, but we're not, not really. We can pass our magic to others within the herd. It's inherited magic." Ann adjusts her pale blue cardigan and picks imaginary lint off her grey trousers. "When a horn is gifted... the bearer of that horn dies."

My mouth pops open. "Oh no." My throat makes a weird gurgling sound.

"We should only do the magic near death. Originally it was a practise solely used on the battlefield. Once your grandfather gifted his horn, it was only a matter of time"—her voice cracks—"before he succumbed."

Oh God.

A big warm hand wraps around the back of my neck, and the trickle of the angel's power anchors me to the chair.

I close my eyes for a second and then reach up and blindly grip his wrist. I need more skin contact. I'm so glad Xander is here. "This is a nightmare," I mumble. "Why would he do that?" I didn't know him. Hell, I didn't like him. He was bloody horrible... but has another man sacrificed himself for me?

Why would he do that?

Was it out of guilt?

My chest burns, and a heavy silence once again takes over the room as we both struggle through our emotions. I think I'd be a puddle wailing on the floor if it wasn't for Xander's grip on my neck.

"Frankly, I don't know how you survived without your horn. That's why it came as such a surprise that you are a unicorn. Perhaps it's your vampire nature that kept you alive for so long, or perhaps it was because you were just a little girl when your horn was—" Ann gets up from her chair and goes to the window. She leans her head on the glass.

It was a fae warrior. He saved me.

"You will not know, as he didn't tell you, Denby's horn has the power of his father and grandfather. Your great-grandfather and great-great-grandfather." She smiles thinly. "That's why you will feel so strong, even more so if you combine your power. And over time, you will only get stronger."

"I don't understand." I stare at her with utter confusion.

Inherited magic? It's just one horn.

Ann turns towards me and glides back across the room. "Three generations of combined magic transferred into a single horn." She places a delicate hand on my collarbone; her fingers rest against the necklace. Her smile is so sad, and her eyes shine with tears. "Now four." She drops her hand from the bone necklace. "You probably don't realise what a horrific thing the witch did to your horn."

"I know," I whisper, a lump in my throat.

Ann places her hand on my cheek. "Yes, I see you do."

"Looking at it makes me feel sick. Did R-R-Ryan"—gosh, my father's name sticks in my throat. It's a struggle to say his name—"take my horn to absorb my power?"

"That I don't know. The magic is sentient to a small degree. Both parties need to agree, to be willing. When"—she pauses and her face crumples with pain; she curls forward into her hand and rubs her chest—"Ryan stole your horn. When he took it by force, no spell in the world would have allowed him to absorb your power. The witch found a way"—she glares at the bone necklace—"to bastardise your unicorn magic. But the necklace only uses a fraction of your horn's magic.

"I am so sorry, Tru. What you had to live through doesn't bear thinking about. So you don't have to wear that disgusting necklace anymore. I know the magic to combine the power of your horn with the power of the horn your grandfather has gifted you."

"But... don't you want the horn back?"

"Oh, child, that isn't possible, not anymore. Your death would be the result if we removed the horn. It is yours by birthright, and it's a precious gift. It is your herd line, and I would never take it away from you."

"What about R-Ryan? Shouldn't he have inherited the horn? Is he even alive?"

"No," she says firmly. Her eyes flash with hate so visceral that it shocks me. "He's dead. He killed a pureblood vampire and was hunted down and executed. The vampires are vicious when protecting their precious purebloods. There was no protecting him from his fate. I can only presume that she was your mother. You'll have to compare her name to your DNA results. Denby got you a copy of the guild file; there's no mention of a child in the report."

"Oh, okay." Say it as it is, Granny Ann... Wow.

At the back of my mind it was always there... the knowledge that the man who haunted my sleep had killed her.

There's a dark corner in my head where the nightmares reside. Flashes of memory with dripping blood and brown hair. Something inside me whimpers and roars at the same time.

My leg bounces again. So my father is dead, and it looks like he killed my mum. I am glad I don't have to hunt him down. Wow, I truly am an orphan. I push my raging thoughts away to deal with later. Xander moves closer to me, offering his strength without saying a word.

"I'm sorry," I rasp out. "I'm being inappropriate. I can come back when it's more convenient."

"No, sweet girl. Now is a perfect time. You are my herd. I will do everything I can to keep you safe, and the thing around your neck needs to go."

Herd, I mouth. Ann has said that a few times. The unicorn equivalent to family. I have so much yet to learn. "If you're sure." I fidget uncomfortably in the chair, and Xander lets go of my neck. I squeeze his wrist in a silent thank-you and let my limb plop back into my lap. "So you think you can... urm... fix my horn? Combine the magic?" I get back to the nitty-gritty. The sooner I get out of this house, the better.

Ann nods, and before I think any further, my hands are reaching to take the necklace from around my throat. "Please, please fix it," I say with a hint of desperation as I hold the necklace out to her on a shaking palm.

Ann glides towards me, and with a nagging thought, I pull the necklace away from her reaching hand. "It won't hurt you? Please say it won't hurt you." I want to double-check before I agree to anything. I've already had two men die on my behalf, and I don't want anybody else to sacrifice themselves for me.

"No, Tru. It won't hurt me." I stare into her beautiful eyes as I try to ascertain if she is telling the truth. I can't tell.

"Xander?" I don't say it, but I'm asking him to use his mumbo-jumbo angel-power lie-detection skills.

"She believes her words." He answers my silent question.

I nod and release my hold on the necklace. Ann's eyes widen, and I viciously bite my lip to stop any words of apology from falling out of my mouth.

I'm not sorry.

"Okay," I say instead.

"Okay. I will warn you the power is great. You will have the combined magic of four unicorns. When you first met your grandfather, what did you feel?"

I tilt my head to the side as I think. I remember the feeling; I take a deep breath and aim for honesty. "Power, but also a darkness that made my skin crawl."

Ann nods, not at all upset with my answer. "Power and darkness. That feeling you had, remember that feeling because that might happen to everyone you meet once I combine your magic into the horn."

"Oh great. Skin-crawling power is just what I need." I cringe at my words. I don't want to be ungrateful. "Sorry," I mumble.

"Creatures are instinctive," she continues, ignoring my slipup, "and I will not beat around the bush, Granddaughter. If I do this, people will fear you." She shrugs her narrow shoulders.

Great, that's me not working in the café. *Do you want a dose of evil with your cappuccino?* The customers will love me, not.

Gah, you're still being ungrateful, Tru.

"Although power is subjective, and it could manifest differently. I can't remember a horn ever being gifted to a female of a herd, only the male line. Perhaps that is what went wrong."

Yet they can believe someone gifted one to a witch?

Perhaps the magic should have died with the unicorn. Perhaps the magic shouldn't be inherited at all. But what do I know? I'm only going off the bitter experience of a little girl and the horror of a hacksaw. Plus the burning need to get rid of this necklace and get my magic back inside where it belongs.

Ann shakes her head. "The amount of power you will have access to will be great. It will be a lot to control, a lot of responsibility."

"With great power comes great responsibility," I mumble, quoting Marvel Comics Spider-Man and the Peter Parker Principle.

I look inside myself. Can I handle it, and do I have a choice? The horn is already stuck to my forehead, and I can't deal with the worry of the bone necklace. I have Story, Dexter, Justin, and for the time being, my angel to keep me on the right path.

Fate has brought me to this point, this moment in time, and it feels right... as if it is meant to be.

"Please, will you combine the magic?" Ann nods.

CHAPTER THIRTY-NINE

With my horn in one hand and the other on my wrist, Ann closes her eyes and silently mumbles an incantation. The bone necklace in her grip glows and emits a humming sound. I look at Xander for reassurance. His focus is on Ann and the magic she shouldn't be able to create.

The more the necklace glows, the more my head feels fuzzy. I've dealt with angel magic a lot over the past few months, and I've also dabbled with witch magic along the way. I felt the unicorn magic when Denby smacked the horn onto my head, and the power of the horn has heated my blood for the past few days. But this is different. The unicorn magic Denby did was pure.

This... This is something else.

Panic rips through me, followed swiftly by a dose of adrenaline and horrendous PAIN. *Nice one, Tru; maybe you should have also asked if it was going to hurt you.* Ouch.

Crikey, this is not a pleasant experience, and vampires have stabbed my leg a few times, so I know.

My horn *shifts* into pink dust... No, not dust molecules. The same molecules that you see for a microsecond when a shifter changes shape. The pink stuff floats in the air, and when Ann's chant changes, it whips around and rushes towards me. My eyes widen.

Oh, bloody hell.

It slams into my forehead. The impact is so hard the back of my head cracks against the chair. Still the pain continues throbbing, twisting. My heart pounds; I go from feeling cold to boiling as my blood and nerve endings shoot fire around my system.

The pink magic seeps into me and wraps around my bones. Bile rushes up my throat, and I can't hold it in. I have to turn my head to the side and vomit. Then my body is completely out of my control. I slump to the side, and unable to hold myself up, I fall to the floor.

Xander is there, making sure I don't hit my head. *Oh, Xander, no. Don't touch me. Please be careful of the freaky unicorn magic*, I scream in my head as my body shakes. Crap, I'm having a seizure. A mumbling Ann keeps a tight hold of my wrist. Her nails dig into my skin.

"You're okay, Tru. Breathe through it," he says as he turns me onto my side and places his jacket underneath my head. "You should have warned her," he growls.

The room fades as the power rolls over me, and my life unfolds before me like the flickering pages of a book. I only get glimpses. In the past, I see my mum and her unconditional love for me. The present, Story and Dexter making me laugh, Xander with his compassion and strength. And the future... struggles, pain, joy... and love.

Love.

It's a future that cracks my heart open with equal fear and excitement at what it holds.

It's within those future flashes I somehow grab hold and—

Soft silken sheets, gentle fingertips caress bare skin as velvet lips kiss across my shoulder and into the curve of my neck.

"My beautiful shadow," he whispers into my ear. The rough cadence of his voice makes me shiver and goosebumps erupt. I groan and smile into the pillow.

Everything jumps, and I am harshly ripped away. My soul screams wanting to stay with him, but now isn't time.

I know what I need to do; I know which path I need to take.

The magic lifts, and the pain recedes. It's finally over. My muscles twitch and I moan. I take a deep breath in, and I lift a shaky hand towards my face. The damn thing flops, smacking me in the nose, but mission accomplished. I am able to wipe my mouth. God, I need to brush my teeth.

"I'm sorry I got sick. I'll clean it up," I say. My voice is so raspy it doesn't sound like me. It's then I notice Xander is on the floor with me. His big hand is running through my sweaty hair. Gross.

"I got it. Please stay where you are and get your breath back." Xander glares at Ann as he pulls a potion from his pocket and gets to his feet. He tilts his head to the side, and he looks at the door. "I believe backup is here. I will just be a moment."

Ann looks oddly disappointed and pale. Probably not as pale as me, but... hell who cares. "Are you okay?" I ask. "Did everything go okay?"

"I'm fine," she snarls. Whoa, okay. She seems to shake out of her anger, and she forces out a smile. Her sad mask slides into place. "That was harder than a normal transfer. Your magic stuck in the necklace was difficult to control."

I feel weird lying on the floor, so I roll onto my hands and knees. When nothing bad happens, I slowly use the chair to guide me. I get to my feet. I pick up Xander's scrunched-up jacket and give it a shake.

"I guess everything worked out?" I say cautiously, and sigh when Ann nods. "Thank you."

I excuse myself to use the bathroom and take the time to wash my face and mouth. I need a shower, and I think I could sleep for a week. At the moment, with my knees knocking together and my head pounding, I don't feel the power of four unicorns.

No, I feel like crap. When I step out, Xander is talking to some guys I don't know. They must be Ann's replacement security guards.

"Here." Ann is waiting outside the bathroom. She shoves a compact datapad at me. "You can take the whole thing. It has all the documents from your grandfather. Details of your mum, your vampire bloodline. There is also a signed emancipation order. I know he cares about you, the angel. But you have your herd to help you, so you no longer need him as your guardian."

Emancipation? Something... My instincts chime a warning.

Give a young woman the power of four unicorns and then remove her guardian. Wow, such a smart thing to do... especially when she waited for Xander to be busy before handing over the files.

"Welcome to the herd." *Welcome to the herd, my ass.* Why is she setting me up to fail? And then what? She'll sweep in and *inherit* the horn when I'm found incapable of handling the power. Or am I being completely paranoid?

I frown, and my fists curl at my sides, but I say nothing. Instead, I smile politely, showing her just how grateful I am. "Thank you," I gush.

Ann isn't the only one who can wear a mask.

"Denby also set up a new bank account, a house, a car." She hands me an envelope.

"Oh, how lovely. Thank you." I tuck the heavy padded envelope between my knees and log in to the datapad. With a few clicks, and using an encrypted code, I activate my online data and transfer the contents of the datapad to my personal server.

Ann scowls as I hand the tech back to her, but again, that sad smile covers up her genuine expression. "It's okay. I don't need the datapad, I transferred everything." No need for you to track my every keystroke. "Thank you for thinking about me and looking after me. When is Denby's funeral?"

Ann sniffs. "He has already been cremated what with the unrest."

Yet you still sent your guards home?

"Well, thank you so much, Grandmother. You've been incredibly helpful."

Ann's eye develops a twitch. Oops. She doesn't like to be called that. Good to know. I decide to call her Grandmother from here on out, as it's only proper. I dip my head to hide my grin.

Ticktock, Tru. I need to learn about this power that is bubbling inside me as quickly as I can, and without the angel's official protection, I'm on my own.

"OH MY GOD, what did you do? You obviously didn't get rid of the horn. Your power is intense... more intense. Oh, and thank Mother Nature you at least got rid of that awful bloody necklace."

"Is it bad?" I ask as I sit on my bed.

"Bad?" Story scoffs. "You were wearing your horn around your neck. I don't think it gets any worse. Unless you wore your ears..." Story rolls her eyes and gives Justin a look as if to say, *Can you believe this girl?*

I groan and rub my face. "No, not the necklace, my power. Does it feel terrible?" Xander didn't say anything in the car. I was tired from the transfer, so I didn't ask him. He just hung onto the steering wheel for grim death and kept sucking air through his teeth like an old man with dentures. Of course vampire me zeroed in on the vein in his neck that was intermittently throbbing with his stress.

"No, not bad... you feel—" Story zips around me, flying so fast she creates her own wind. I've learnt my lesson, so I don't keep a track of her frantic flight. I already feel a bit ropey, and watching her zip about always makes me dizzy. She stops and hovers in front of my face. "Your power feels incredible, like spring and new flowers or a freshly baked sponge." She flops back, and my heart misses a beat as she drops. Before I move my hand to pluck her out of the air, she catches herself and zips back to my face.

I don't feel bad, yay. That's great, right?

"Like a giant free blood fountain that I can dive in," Justin adds, licking his lips. I frown at the blood lust on his face.

Oh no.

"You are the ultimate unicorn, a goddess."

"Goddess," I squeak. My mouth hangs open, and my eyes flick between them.

"You know the rumours that we decided after meeting Denby Jones were untrue... that goodness, creature-of-light crap? You feel like... Heck, I could bow down and kiss your feet," Story says.

"But... but you hate my feet," I cry, hiding them under the covers. My eyes feel so wide they must be popping out of my head. Are they taking the piss?

"Yeah, I know," Story whines. "But your power is sooo nice." She flutters her sapphire-blue lashes at me.

"Yeah," Justin groans. "What the fuck... I don't even like girls..."

"Oh my god. Where are the evil vibes she promised me?" I wail. "This is a fucking horror show."

The door slams open, and Xander appears like a knight in shining armour. He liquid prowls towards me, grabs hold of my hand, and slides a gold bracelet onto my wrist.

Story, Justin, and Xander all groan simultaneously with relief.

I blink at the bracelet.

"It will mask your power, and it will shift with you," he grumbles.

"Oh thank you, Xander. Let me know if I owe you any money."

Huh, is that sweat on his brow?

"My shadow, you can thank me by never taking that off until you gain control." He points at the magic bracelet, his eyes slightly wide.

"Yeah, don't," Story pipes up, eyeing my hidden feet with disgust.

I giggle at her expression. "Aww, don't my tootsies get a kiss?" I say as I pull my feet out from hiding and wiggle my toes. I reach for the bracelet, and they all scream at once. I hold my hands up and chuckle. "Okay, okay. Don't freak out. I'll keep the bracelet on."

Outwardly, I'm sure I look as if I'm not also freaking out, but inside I frantically pat my own metaphorical sweaty brow.

That could have been so much worse without Xander's intervention—look what happened when my friends got a whiff of me. They know me. What would have happened if a bunch of creatures felt that power... Shit, they would have ripped me apart.

"You will be able to control your power with practice," Xander says. Correctly reading the horror in my eyes.

Phew, that's good to know.

Xander has crazy control. I wonder what he felt in the car? "How did my power feel to you?" I ask him.

"It didn't kick in until we were halfway back. I can only assume you were still recovering from the transfer. Dr Ross is on his way to check you over."

I groan. More poking, prodding, and tests.

"Let's just say your power didn't feel so nice." Xander visibly swallows. "I believe you can attract and repel depending on your emotions."

Attract and repel. Huh, handy.

"I'll leave you to it. Tru, meet Ross in the orangery in ten minutes." I groan again as Xander leaves the room.

Wasting no time, I tip the envelope from Ann out onto the bed and paw through its contents. Bank stuff including a card, address details for a new house, and various keys. I lean over and grab my datapad from the bedside table. Opening up my server, I thumb through all the new paperwork. "I need a solicitor," I grumble.

"So what happened?" Justin asks, poking at the items on the bed.

I tell them quickly about Denby's death, the generational power of the horn, and Ann's strange behaviour. But I don't say anything about seeing the future. How on earth do I bring that up without looking like I've lost my mind? Perhaps it was my brain misfiring with magic overload. But I doubt it.

Among the documents from Ann on my datapad, I spot my younger self in a photo. I don't know kids' ages as I've never been around them, but at a guess, I look about four years old. I'm peeking behind a woman's leg.

How did they get this?

The brown-haired woman in the photo is, of course, vampire beautiful. She has the perfect plastic look of a pureblood. Apart from her eyes. Her eyes dance with joy and happiness. As she looks down at me, her hand rests on my head.

Behind us stands a man. Seeing him makes my heart stop for a beat. Tears prick my eyes as I take in his handsome face.

We didn't do photos.

Dark skin, bigger-than-a-human's rich brown eyes, his hair is long and plaited in the way of the fae. His ears poke through with a delicate point.

Wow, I didn't know he was there from the beginning... He was our guard. He must have made a promise to my mum, and he continued to look after me after her death. *So many secrets.*

"Is that your mum?" Story asks.

"Wow, she's a pureblood," Justin says, moving closer to our huddle on the bed.

"Yeah."

"Aww, look how cute you were. You have the same face shape." Story hops down my arm and traces my mum's face. "Here around the jaw. Oh, and the colour of your eyes."

I nod. I see it now.

"And the guard?"

"That's him... my grandad," I whisper with a watery smile. "He kept me alive and safe."

"Why did you call him Grandad? He's fae?" Justin asks, leaning on me.

"I don't know." I shrug. "I guess kid me called him that, and it stuck."

"Do you know what happened to your mum?" Story asks.

"Yeah, there's a guild report buried in here somewhere. According to Ann, it doesn't mention me, but it says Ryan, my unicorn father"—my eyes drift back to the laughing women in the photo—"he killed her." Dexter jumps up and bashes me in the face with his tail. I bury my face in his soft fur. "I think when he removed my horn, my mum tried to stop him." I blink a few times. "Shit, I need to deal with all this later... when my brain is working and I'm not exhausted." I clap my hands. "Okay, listen up. Things have changed, and we are moving."

"To this new house?" Justin wiggles the address. "I know this area. It's posh, gated, warded..." His voice fades, and he pales.

I bump him with my shoulder and squeeze his hand. "No, we're moving to our flat that's been paid for by our hard-earned cash. It's time."

"No fancy house? No fancy car?" Story asks, poking at the keys with her toe.

I shake my head. "Nope, we are doing this our way. So pack your shit."

"Coolio." Story nods.

"Sounds good to me," Justin says as he drags himself from the bed.

"Reow," Dexter adds as his big head butts me underneath my chin. I glance at the time. Gah, I better go see the doctor.

CHAPTER
FORTY

I STROLL into Xander's office and close my eyes for a second as I inhale his scent. *Okay, Tru, focus. Be brave.* "Hey, I got a clean bill of health. Dr Ross even got me to sip some blood with no side effects. I'm cured."

I move towards his desk and run a finger across its shiny wooden surface. Xander looks up and places the paperwork he has been working on down. I tilt my head, a stock order for Night-*Shift*. How boring.

"So it looks as if angel blood is off the menu." I tap the desk. *This is hard*. "I, urm... emailed you a document, courtesy of the unicorns. I'm emancipated. Yay. Looks like you are finally free of me." I try to smile, but my lip wobbles.

Crap, this is harder than I thought it would be.

"You're leaving?" he asks, pushing his chair back.

"Yes," I whisper. I cough to clear my throat. "I know I've said it before, but I can't say it enough. Thank you, Xander. Thank you for saving my life."

"I'll miss you." He rubs his hand across his face. "I might not miss your mess."

I laugh, but it sounds painful. "What can I say? I'm cursed."

Xander moves away from the desk.

"Maybe we can meet for lunch? Catch up occasionally?"

Xander winces.

"Or not," I grumble.

"My shadow, you know that's never going to happen." A lump forms in my throat. Xander brushes my hair off my shoulder and runs his fingers through it almost absentmindedly. "I've watched you prowl into dire situations that would make most adults crumble with your head held high, and I couldn't be more proud of you." He bends and presses his forehead to mine. His breath whispers against my lips. I part them, breathing him in.

"You surprise and delight me. You also frustrate me to no end."

We gaze into each other's eyes, and his thumb traces my cheekbone and along my jaw. "But... but you are so young."

Look, there he goes again, being all moral and shit.

"We can't be together like you want, my shadow."

I duck my head so he doesn't see me roll my eyes. My angel can be really stupid. He might be right—I am crazy in love with him—but here he goes again, the big-headed bastard presuming shit.

I can't do anything naughty with you, Tru—I might be paraphrasing a tad—*I love you, Tru, but I shouldn't as you are a mere child and I am a mighty ancient angel...* blah, blah.

"I will always protect you," he says gruffly, pulling away from me.

My heart lurches as my gaze darts to his. Gorgeous honey eyes with their sprinkles of gold framed with thick, black lashes look into me like he is reading my soul.

There's pain in his eyes.

"Same here, buddy. Same here," I say with an ever-so-friendly pat on his forearm. His honey eyes narrow, and utter confusion fills his face.

"Sorry, chicken wings. Was I supposed to be all broken up?" Honestly, the man is sooo slow. I'm sure he has feathers stuffed in his brain.

I allow a little swing to my hips as I prowl away. I open the door. "I won't be seventeen forever," I say over my shoulder with a wink. "At the moment I haven't got time for romance and shit."

I continue walking down the hall, and with a wave of my hand I say, "I have an empire to build, vampires to piss off, and a rebel leader's reputation to cultivate."

I secretly smile.

I've seen a glimpse of our future, and it is *glorious*. He doesn't stand a chance...

THE END

CURSED WITCH

Her conjury was out of reach. But when she's flooded with strength, can she survive becoming a target?

Tuesday Larson thought she'd settled for normal. A disappointment to her mother for never taking well to magic, she deliberately put distance between her family and any witchery. But the supernatural destroys her barriers when a group of mercenaries tears through her home looking for blood.

Escaping with her cat-sized dragon to find her coven under attack, Tuesday's stunned when a hunky wolf shifter saves her from an elf abductor. But when she ends up at a quirky hotel that unleashes her abilities, she's shocked to learn she's part of a race that's being hunted to extinction.

Finally graced with formidable powers, will she outlive the shift?

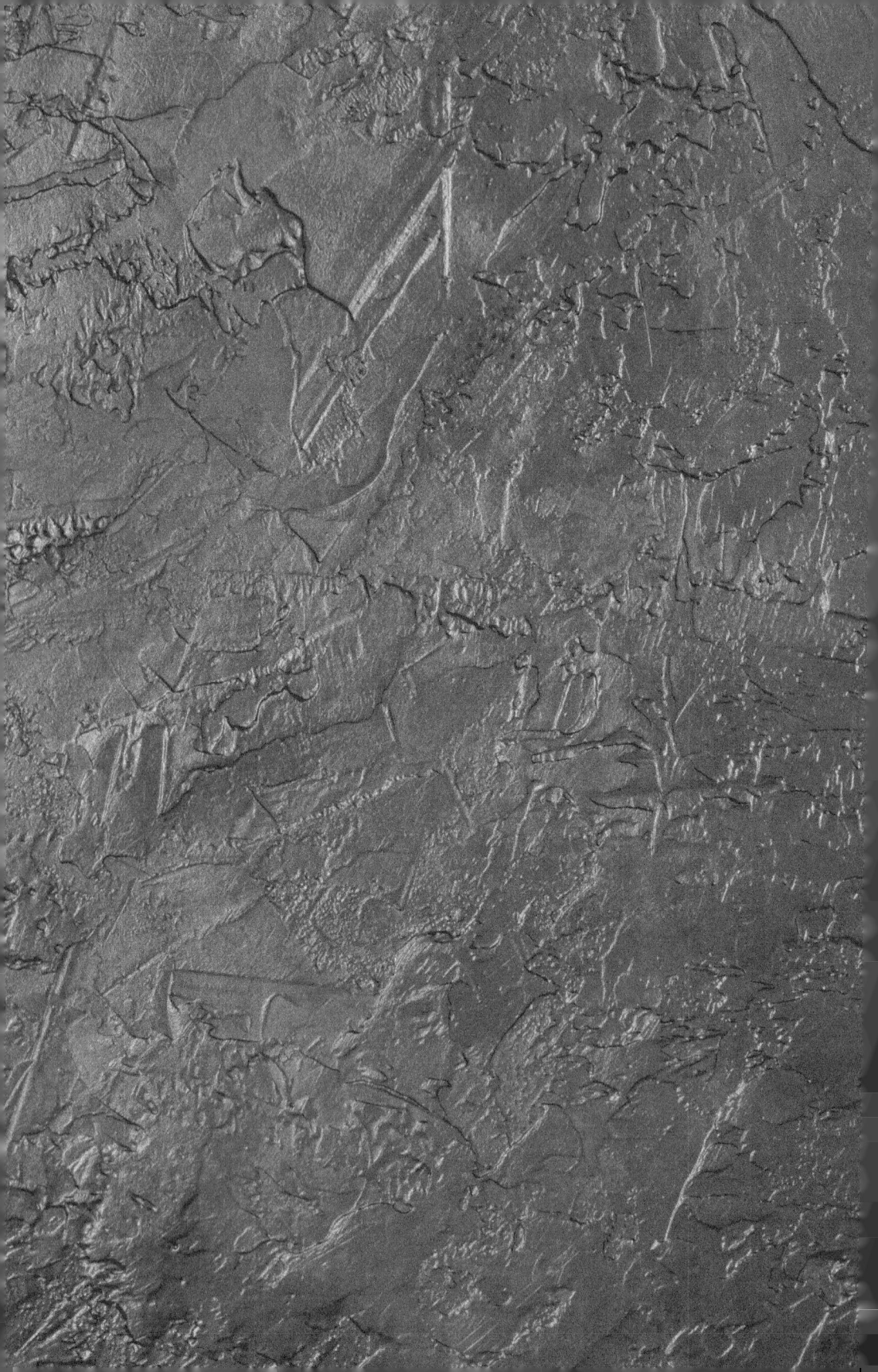

CHAPTER
ONE

Eight years ago

I SIT SLUMPED in the chair outside the headteacher's office as I wait for someone from my coven to arrive. My hands twist in my lap as I pluck at a ragged thumbnail. I wrinkle my nose. Every time I move, a whiff of my failure flies up my nostrils.

I smell like burnt toast and plastic.

I tug at the sleeve of my charred blazer. Parts of the navy jacket are yellowish brown, the polyester fabric has shrunk with the heat and the whole left arm is crispy. My once smart white shirt is smudged with black. I look a state. At least I wasn't seriously hurt; the quick actions of my teacher saved me—well, physically.

Mentally, I'm a mess.

The door leading to the corridor is wrenched open, and she stalks into the room. The door slams behind her.

Her violet eyes—the same colour as mine—scan the room until they land on me. "Tuesday," she whispers in horror.

My skin prickles uncomfortably and the secretary drops her paperwork and sits straighter in her chair. The woman standing before us is a tiny powerhouse, bubbling with authority.

The best witch in her generation. Dressed in an immaculate grey suit, her blonde hair is tied back in a severe knot.

"Hi, Mum." I drop my eyes to my lap and wrap my arms around myself. I feel like a ten-year-old.

"Are you okay? Did they heal you?" She leans down and her hands flutter in front of me. She finally tucks a strand of burned violet hair behind my ear. "I can fix your hair," she mutters as she pats my head. She drops her hand and roots through her big, brown handbag, which contains a plethora of potions.

"Mrs Larson?" the secretary interrupts. "The headteacher can see you both now." The lady smiles kindly at me.

Her kindness makes me uncomfortable—hell, everybody's kindness makes me feel uncomfortable.

Poor, poor Tuesday.

It's not anything they say, it's that look. The pity. Every day it gets worse—silent pity wrapped in poorly veiled disappointment. It seeps into my pores and messes with my head.

It coats my soul with its filth.

I am never going to be good enough.

Oh, and the witch community won't cast me out. No, they *love me*. Endless love and understanding. The whole "our love will fix you" thing. It's nauseating. It drives me fucking nuts.

I hate them for their kindness, which makes me a total shithead. Is it wrong to wish someone would just be angry with me for once? I think I could deal with the anger instead of facing the pity in their eyes when they look at me. *Ha! Says the sheltered girl who is yet to live*, my inner dialogue helpfully pipes up.

Mum doesn't pity you.

No, behind closed doors and away from prying eyes, she hates me.

I jump to my feet, almost running away from that thought, and beat my mum to the office door. I'm keen to get this over with. I rap my knuckle against the glass and when I hear the muffled reply, I open the door and head inside.

The headteacher sits behind a heavy wooden desk, and when she sees me, her brown eyes crinkle with concern as she rises from her seat. "Oh dear, the colour coded ingredients didn't work then." She nods at mum and thrusts her hand out. "Carol." A spark of purple magic zaps from her index finger. It meets mum's answering spark. The witch equivalent of a handshake.

It's another item on the long list of things that I cannot do. I tuck my hands behind my back and fidget.

"Please, both of you, take a seat." Once we're seated, the headteacher returns to her chair. She folds her hands on top of the desk and, with eyes full of sadness, studies me intently.

"Tuesday shouldn't be doing any dangerous magic," my mum angrily starts. "Why would you have her doing such complicated spells? She could have been seriously hurt—"

"It was a Don't Hear Me Now potion."

Mum deflates, and with a cringe, rubs her face. "Oh."

"There was no way to predict this would happen. It's unprecedented." The headteacher stares at my mum meaningfully and then both women scrutinise me. "I think we can agree that Tuesday's magiclexia is too much for spell work, and it gives me no joy to tell you her educational needs are becoming disruptive. Carol, it isn't fair to the rest of the class."

They are talking about me as if I am not in the room. It doesn't matter what I think, what I feel. My hand drifts to my sleeve and I pick at a particularly crusty bit as my thoughts drown out their voices.

Magiclexia.

I roll my eyes. It takes everything I have not to throw my hands in the air with exasperation. For them, it always comes back to my brain. It's never anything to do with my shitty magic. They are convinced I have cognitive difficulties and their poor witchy minds cannot conceive a *Larson* is simply low on power. That I am a magical dud.

No, there must be something wrong with my brain.

I'm sick of this shit. Sick of the whole "come on Tuesday, if you could just try harder" lecturers, followed swiftly by the sickly sweet "we believe in you, Tuesday."

If I try any bloody harder, my head is going to pop off. I wish they would all bog off.

Today just proves, yet again, how useless I am. Even with all the help in the world, I still can't get a simple basic spell correct. I rub my dirty face—crap, I'm missing half my eyelashes. Who's ever heard of such a benign potion exploding? I am bloody cursed.

I slump further and stare out the window at the school grounds beyond. *I wish I could go home and have a shower. I can't believe I'm sitting here, wearing my shame.* My left knee jiggles, and I grind my thigh into the chair to stop the movement. *I wish I never had to come back here again.* I hate this school.

A crunchy piece of my jacket crumbles in my fingers and flutters to the floor. What sixteen-year-old can pinpoint the exact moment her life fell apart? I can. Everything was going okay until I turned eleven and had to do the entrance exams for this damn school. Yeah, that went well.

For so long, I masked that I was struggling. Magic is hard. It isn't effortless like it is for my sisters—it makes little sense to me. I just can't get it. How everyone describes their power doesn't feel the same to me.

As a kid, I covered up my issues like a pro. I kept my head down, and no one noticed. Looking back, I don't know how the hell I got away with it. I must have been committed. I found ways around things. A new basic spell at school? I'd, urm, *borrow* an advanced one from home. The potions were all over the house. It was easy to do a switcheroo, and bam hey presto, my spells were perfect. I smile bitterly.

I only did it a few times. I didn't see it as being dishonest, not really. I just wanted to be normal. It was a knee jerk reaction. I was just a little girl. Disappointing my mum and being teased by my friends was the worst thing imaginable.

Or so I thought.

I frown and rub my chest. My coven was horrified I'd hidden my issues from them.

I made my mum cry.

They threw money at the problem and hired a specialist teacher. But my wonky, crappy, low powered magic wouldn't play ball.

Those first few years were so hard, and the damage was done in the eyes of my coven. I went from being a normal kid to a child with special needs.

Worse, I was a thief and a liar.

A rogue tear runs down my cheek and I surreptitiously rub it away.

I swallow and take in a deep breath. The smell of my scorched uniform tickles the back of my throat and I choke a little to stop a cough. What does it matter if my magic is crap? What does it matter in the scheme of things? Yet each failure gets harder to stomach. Each day gets harder to believe—to believe in me.

I hate it.

I HATE IT.

There's not a day that goes by that I don't wish I was human.

With these witchy expectations piled so high on top of my chest, I can't take a full breath.

As if I don't hear the whispers: *She was bred for greatness. What the hell went wrong?* Yeah, I am shit. I get that, thanks.

"We can put her in a different class. Perhaps we can try portals next?" With those words, I lift my head and focus back on the conversation. My mum sighs and leans forward as she runs her fingers through her blonde hair.

"Stop," I whisper. It is as if some demon has taken over my mouth. "Please, just stop. I can't do this anymore." My bottom lip wobbles and I viciously bite it, holding it still.

My mum casts me a withering glance. "Tuesday, don't you think—"

"NO!" I yell. The word echoes around the room as I throw my hands in the air in frustration. My entire body shakes. "It's like I'm a fish and you're asking me to climb a tree. I can't do it. I am a fish, not a... I'M NOT A FUCKING MONKEY!" I slap my hand across my mouth in an attempt to push the swear word back in.

Oh no.

The awkward silence in the room is palpable as both women sit open-mouthed and stare at me. The headteacher, with a shake of her head, snaps her mouth closed.

My mum visibly swallows, and her face goes red. "Tuesday Ann Larson, I will wash your mouth out with a potion if you swear like that again," she threatens. "I apologise, headteacher, my daughter has been brought up better than that." She scowls at me.

Doesn't she understand how frustrated I feel?

"I can't do this anymore. I won't." I vigorously shake my head.

"I'm sorry. I'm sorry that I've let you all down." The chair scrapes against the floor as I push away from the desk and stumble to my feet. "I'm out. I'm done. I give up." My arms flop to my sides and my chest and throat burns with pain. What they expect is suffocating me.

"I am a fish," I mutter as I back away.

"Tuesday, what on earth are you talking about?" Mum asks as her beautiful face scrunches up with confusion. She looks at the head-teacher as if she can interpret my crazy.

"Everybody is a genius. But if you judge a fish by its ability to climb a tree, it will live its whole life believing that it is stupid. It is a quote from Albert Einstein," I croak, as my vision goes hazy with tears.

I do my best to blink them away, but a sneaky one rolls down the side of my nose and plops onto my dirty shirt. Through a huge burning lump in my throat, I rasp, "Mum, I can't be your monkey. I can't do this anymore. I am not... I'm not good enough. I am not strong enough.

"I am not a witch." With that firm declaration, I turn on my heel, and with as much dignity as I can muster, I walk away.

CHAPTER

TWO

Crap. So much for the grand exit. I have to wait for my mum to finish in the office. I can't sit. I'm too wound up. So I stand in the corner by the window with my back to the room and the still smiling secretary.

Outside, it's a perfect winter's day, cold but with a bright blue sky. My eyes are drawn to a robin sitting on a fence post. His red chest is puffed with pride as he guards his territory. A gentle breeze ruffles his feathers.

With the way I feel inside, shouldn't it be raining? I sniffle and use my sleeve to wipe my nose. The burned bit scrapes my face.

I felt guilty for so long. It's the first time I've ever said no, the first time I've stood up for myself. I swallow as I remember the expression on my mum's face. I think people don't like it when you tell them no, especially parents.

I lean my head against the cool glass. I had to say something. I can't keep doing this to myself. I can't keep spectacularly failing. What about my self-esteem?

What everyone seems to forget is this is my life and I need to live it my way. I'm sixteen, so it is not like they are going to let me stop my education. I am not that naïve. But everything here is set up for me to fail. This path that everybody wants me to take isn't my path. I know it deep inside; I can feel it in my bones.

Every time I attempt a spell, a rune, or try to do an incantation, it feels wrong... like I'm on a greasy tightrope wearing shit shoes without a safety net. Splat. I fall to the ground every damn time.

They flush my self-confidence down the drain over again as they try to make me into someone I am not. Just once, I needed to be honest with myself, to be honest with them, even if I fail and they ignore me. *Please don't let them ignore me.*

I might as well flush my entire head down the loo. It would feel the same.

I'm drowning.

Fate must be pushing me to do something else—something I can actually do. One single thing I can excel at... Just one small thing. This can't be my life, forever the disappointment, forever on the outside. I have to believe there is something more. Some kind of purpose.

It's not giving up if your time could be spent doing something better.

Right?

I sigh and close my eyes.

Ten minutes later, the office door opens behind me and my mum exits the room. The little hairs on my arms rise as a wave of anger radiates from her. Her heels clack ominously towards me.

Oh no. I duck my head and hunch against the glass. I know there is no getting away from her. I gather the remaining scraps of my tattered courage and when I turn to face her, she glares. Her violet eyes are spitting mad.

"You're excused for the rest of the day," she snarls, and with stompy heels, she strides away. "Come on."

I nod, and like a good little girl with my eyes fixed on the floor, I scuttle behind her as we head outside to the car.

I sit with my arms wrapped around me as we drive home in uncomfortable silence. Wow, I suddenly understand the expression, "you can cut the air with a knife." My mum is livid.

With a sharp "go to your room" when we get home, I leave her at the front door, and hurry upstairs.

I strip out of my uniform and throw the whole thing in the bin before getting into the shower. Hours later, when Dad gets home from work, I sit on the stairs and listen to them whisper-argue about me as I fiddle with a piece of burned hair. I don't know why they don't use a privacy potion. I guess they don't care. After about twenty minutes of heated debate, I am called downstairs. I take each step as if I'm on my way to face a firing squad.

I peek into the room and my heart drops into my stomach as I take in Mum's still angry body language. Looks like she hasn't calmed down, and from what I've already overheard, it appears she also hasn't understood a word I've said.

"Matthew, tell your daughter that she will not be leaving school," my mum says as I enter our bright yellow kitchen.

With a shaky hand and fortifying breath, I pull out a chair and sit at the table. I'm getting a headache from the stress.

I clear my throat. "I didn't say that, Mum. I know I can't just leave school. I am asking not to do any more practical magic classes. It's for everybody's benefit, for everyone's safety."

"So, you've decided you don't want to do magic classes. Explain to your father that you, in your teenage wisdom, have also decided you are no longer a witch." I purse my lips and sensibly keep my mouth closed. "No longer a witch," she scoffs. "Have you ever heard of such stupidity? Did you blow that potion up on purpose?" she asks.

I flinch. Wide-eyed, I shake my head. "No. No, Mum, I did not."

Mum harrumphs. "What is wrong with being a witch? What's next? Are you going to decide you want to be a vampire?" She throws her hands into the air. "Your sisters are all outstanding. They are incredible. If you would just try harder—"

"Carol," Dad quietly reprimands. "That's unfair." He watches me with sad eyes as I hunch in the chair. "You know she didn't do it on purpose."

My mum sniffs and rubs her face. "Do I? Well, she has lied before. We have spoken about this, Matthew. She is not leaving that school. She doesn't get to do what she wants. What would the community think?" Her eyes widen.

Fuck the bloody witches.

This time, I say nothing. Acting out won't win me any prizes, and they have already made up their minds.

Familiar frustration bubbles in my chest and makes my heart hurt. It makes me dizzy. I take a deep breath as I battle with the overwhelming need to throw myself on the floor like a toddler and sob my heart out.

"No. It's not happening. It's. Not. Happening. Tuesday, I am your mother, I know what is best for you. One day, you will thank me."

I doubt it.

Come on, you ninny, say something. I try a different tack. "If you want to keep paying for me to go to school for the next four years to learn nothing, that's your choice."

She slams her hand onto the table and growls like she has a shifter trapped inside of her. Both Dad and I jump. "You are a witch. You will have a witch's education." The violence she excludes makes me wish I could take my words back. Pull them back from the air and let them dissolve on my tongue. "I cannot deal with her when she is like this." Her chair scrapes against the tiles with a screech as she gets to her feet and storms away. The cupboard doors open and slam closed.

Normally I'd get up off my butt and help her. But I'm not going anywhere near her today, not with the mood that she's in. The anger coming off her in waves makes me want to curl into a ball and protect my squishy bits. Oh, she's never hurt me physically—no, my mum's weapon of choice is her words.

The plates clack together as she shoves them down on the dining table in front of me. "No daughter of mine will quit." I cower. My dad winces, but he doesn't say anything to contradict her. When my mum has her back to us, he leans across the table and sketches a rune onto my hand. My eyelids tingle.

"To fix your hair and eyelashes," he explains.

"Thanks, Dad," I mumble.

Magic fixes everything, doesn't it? The bitterness I feel is like a rolling blackness inside me. I square my shoulders and lift my chin. "So, I must keep going to school, keep taking the magic classes that I can't do. Okay..." I nod. Oh heck, I am nuts. I don't know when to shut up. "If I sit there and refuse to do the practical lessons, what then, Mum?"

Mum stops viciously chopping up a carrot and points the knife at me. I sink further into my chair. "That is down to you, Tuesday. If you do not try, you will fail, and I will never forgive you."

Then I will fail.

It's going to be a long two years.

Thank goodness witches are legal adults at eighteen. As soon as I hit that birthday, I am out of here. Independence starts with money. This weekend, I plan to get a part-time job.

Fuck you, Mum.

"Another thing—your swearing." Uh-oh, it's like she can read my mind. "She said the F word, Matthew. At the headteacher. The *F* word. I have never been more embarrassed in my life."

"I didn't swear *at* her. Well, not really." I cringe and rub my mouth. "I'm sorry, I was upset. I didn't mean to. I'm sorry I embarrassed you."

"Upset?" Mum huffs as she throws the knife down on the chopping board and storms toward me. "*You* were upset? What about me?" She prods her chest. "I am upset. You—you do not know the meaning of the word. But I will give you something real to be upset about." She pulls something from her pocket. A potion vial clacks on the table and with her index finger, she pushes it towards me. "While I was waiting for your father to come home, I made this just for you. Drink up."

Made it with love, Mum?

The purple liquid inside sloshes. Purple is... I mentally flick through the catalogue of potions in my head. Mind control? A blocking potion?

Uh-oh. Purple is not good.

"It's an anti-profanity potion. I told you I would wash your mouth out with a potion," she says smugly. "So here it is."

Horrified, I stare at Dad for help. "Dad?"

He shrugs.

He shrugs. Thanks, Dad. I shake my head. No, this isn't happening. It's not bloody happening. I didn't think she'd—

In the past, she's always threatened me and my older sisters. But that's all it's ever been—a threat. An empty threat.

I swear a lot. It's a Northern English thing. Where we live in Lancashire, we practically use swear words as punctuation. I've never used a bad word in the presence of anyone distinguished before today. I'm not normally that much of a heathen. I understand why she is upset. But to magically gag me? She has finally lost the plot.

Mum impatiently taps her fingernails on the table and the expression on her face makes my hands tremble. *Looks like I don't have a choice.* I don't even bother to glance at Dad again—there will be no help from him.

I pick up the bottle.

"How long will it last?" I rasp.

"A few weeks. Just long enough to get through the winter solstice celebration. I do not trust you to behave and your father's job with the Hunters Guild is far more important than you, your potty mouth, and your silly tantrums."

Silly tantrums? Wow. Nice.

At school, was I really being dramatic? I don't think so.

Damn it, I should never have spoken up. I should have just kept my head down and my stupid fears to myself. Let the grown-ups sort things out.

I cannot believe I felt guilty all this time about hiding my problems with magic. Now I see my younger self was the smart one—smart to keep my issues to myself. All Mum cares about is her reputation. She doesn't care that, each day, I am dying a little bit more inside.

"I will not ask again. Drink the potion."

My eyes flick to Mum and then Dad. This is both my parents breaking my trust on a whole new level. I promise myself here and now that I will never ask for their help again.

I am done.

The vial in my hand is warm from being in her pocket. I roll it between my fingers, and with a sad sounding sigh, I dig my thumb into the cork. It comes out with a slight pop. Without preamble, I tip it to my lips and drink.

I gag when the liquid hits my tongue. It is vile. Potions do not have to taste bad, which means Mum has made it taste awful on purpose. I wipe my mouth with the back of my hand. She has gone out of her way to make it extra gross.

CURSED WITCH

Made with hate, right, Mum?
The potion will only last two weeks. It will not be that bad.

CHAPTER
THREE

Eight years later

There is a whoosh of magic that makes the little hairs on the back of my neck stand on end, and then the ward protecting the building fails spectacularly. Seconds later, there is a crash as the lobby door gets kicked in.

I sit up with a jolt and the crumbs stuck to my pyjama top spill around me. "Oh fiddle-dee-dee" comes out of my mouth instead of the "oh fucking hell" my brain was aiming for. *Umm, yeah, thanks for that, Mum.*

Bloody two weeks my arse. Eight years and counting and I still can't swear.

In my head, it is all good, but as soon as I open my mouth, those sweet, naughty swear words transform into torturous embarrassment. The quirk has made me odd, and with the weird way words bubble up out of my mouth, people apologise if they say a bad word around me. Apologise to *me* as if I'm pious.

Honest to God, they think I'm the swear police.

How can I explain that my mum magically gagged me? And that the spell is so strong, and my magic is so weak, it can't be broken?

I can't.

There is no way I am going down that rabbit hole to explain my coven drama. Oh, and I have this laugh—it makes me almost want to punch myself in the face. It's this small, fake titter, and I do this bizarre wave as if I am the Queen and I'm waving away their bad word. Absolving them. Yeah, I look like a right dick.

A crumb still stuck to my top catches my eye. Ooh. I hum the Hasbro commercial for the Hungry Hungry Hippos board game as I drop my chin to my chest and, without thinking, hoover it up. It takes me a second. Eww. I wrinkle my nose and cough—that wasn't toast. I prod my mouth with my tongue. I don't know what the hell that was. It was gritty and now it's stuck unpleasantly to my teeth. Gross.

Mental note: do not eat strange random crap stuck to you.

Bang-crash-bang. "Crikey. Stealthy, the intruders are not." It must be a heck of a fumble for me to hear them three floors up. And it is nothing to do with me. My neighbours are a rough lot and the building gets raided at least twice a month. It's no biggie.

I yawn and lazily stretch, my wrists crack, my left shoulder pops, and my lower back aches. Ow, I really need to get off this sofa and move around more. My sedentary lifestyle during my time off isn't doing me any good. I flop back and roll onto my side. The zip of the cushion digs into my hip as I glance at the dusty exercise bike rammed into the far corner. I will start an epic fitness regime... *next week*, I promise myself.

If I'm not here, vegging on the sofa, doing my version of a couch potato, I am working. I force myself to be manager Tuesday for over sixty hours a week. So, when I get home, I get to be lazy Tuesday in all her glory. I wiggle and point my toes. The evil cushion pokes at me again. Bloody thing.

My eyes drift to the floor as the ruckus downstairs continues. "Why can't people behave themselves?" I grumble. It's after ten at night. I shouldn't have to listen to this. No, I should watch instead.

I lean down and, with my tongue clamped between my teeth, I slap my hand about on the floor—without looking—in search of the remote. It dropped on the floor a while ago. I ignore the gritty texture of my carpet. Gross. I need to clean under there at some point. Aha, it's disappeared halfway under the tiny blue sofa, so I hang upside down and coax it out with my fingers.

As I sit back up, I spin it around, and with a *pew-pew-pew* sound, I point it at the television and turn it on. I'm so glad I don't have to get up to find out what's happening. As I am so nosy, I love the cameras my sister Ava installed in the building. But though I find watching random people fascinating, I have a rule: no camera time near bedtime, with a cut off at nine. But I have Sunday and Monday off this week, so a few extra hours are no harm. I click the app for the building's security cameras. *No one needs to know.*

Cross-legged, with an excited shiver running down my spine, I stare at the TV. The intruders are dressed in skin-tight black suits with stripes of colour along their shoulders and arms. Their faces are hidden behind full headgear. I can't help snorting. *What the heck?* They resemble evil Power Rangers. I lean forward. *How embarrassing.* A bad Halloween costume crossed with a military scuba suit.

"Those tight suits have got to chafe." I tilt my head to the side. No wonder they have their faces covered, as I can only imagine the ribbing they'd get from their friends if they were seen in those getups. Oh my, this is so much better than watching TV.

My eyes drift to my kitchen. I wonder if I will miss anything if I grab some popcorn...

"Flat eight, on the third floor. Harris, you take point," says the gruff voice of the Red Power Ranger. My eyes widen and with a squeak of shock, I drop the remote.

What? That's me. I live in flat eight. Uh-oh. Whoever they are, they are coming for me. "No-no-no." Adrenaline gushes through my bloodstream as I scramble up from the sofa and dash around my tiny flat as if my bum is on fire. *What the heck do I need to do? What do I need? What do I need?* I screech to a halt, panting.

"Stop freaking out." Helpful. When has telling yourself not to freak out ever bloody worked? I need to decide what to do first. My eyes flick frantically around the room as my hands shake. My fear and panic are making me dizzy.

I tuck a strand of violet hair away from my face. You would think they'd at least knock rather than destroy everything in their wake. How the hell did they find me? I have been so careful. I nibble on my thumbnail. Heavy footsteps and muffled voices are now *outside* the door, and my heart skips a beat. They are here. A flash of magic has me scrambling away. The flat's ward—done by my sister, Jodie, who's one of the best witches that I know—*groans*. Oh yeah, that's a great sign. I stare at it with wide eyes.

I bounce from foot to foot and mutter, "This isn't happening, this isn't happening." What the heck did I do wrong? Whom have I pissed off? It can't be about the old lady with the out-of-date fish. Even when she slapped me in the face with it, I gave her a refund.

I am way too young to die, I mentally wail. With that fun thought, I dash towards the huge safe room, which takes up a vast amount of space in my tiny flat. In living alone and away from the coven these past six years, this fancy safe room was something Dad had insisted on. It is one of the best on the market. I cringe when the front door is hit with another blast of magic and the ward lets out another awful groan. I thought this stupid, expensive thing was overkill. I guess they weren't wrong with all their warnings.

In the world I live in, magic is commonplace, with all manner of supernatural creatures: shifters, demons, witches, vampires, and an abundance of fae. Our world is all about the strong against the weak. It is all about power. If you're not powerful or you don't belong to a powerful group that can protect you, you're as good as dead. With a clank, I brace my feet and drag the heavy safe room door open.

This raid has got to be something to do with my dad. The next big war is brewing, and my dad is high in the Hunters Guild. The creature police. They oversee all the other councils.

I shimmy out of my red silk dressing gown and matching pyjamas, and then stuff my feet into my socks and wiggle into my beige thermal bottoms. Since I left home at eighteen, I am no longer protected by the coven. If someone wants to hurt my dad, well, I'm the easy target.

I cluck my tongue as I yank my sports bra on. My nostrils flare with indignation. It makes me so mad. Why can't I be left alone? I haven't done anything wrong. My skin is a little damp from my panicked state, so instead of the bra just sliding down, somehow the fabric sticks to my back and then twists.

I blink in shock. *Is it stuck?* "Cheese-on-a-cracker," I mumble. I tamper with the urge to scream as I attempt to tug the bra back up. I am bloody stuck. Ha. "Oh, this is bad. So-so-so bad." I wildly eye my flat door and the groaning ward.

Oh no. Any second now they're going to bust through the door and I'm going to be standing here, a sweaty mess with my arm stuck and my bra twisted, one boob in, one boob out.

Surprise.

I let out a wild, panicked laugh. What a heck of a surprise that would be! Who could think this stuff up? This? This is a bloody nightmare... This could only ever happen to me. *One step at a time, Tuesday,* I mentally berate myself. *Stop messing about and get your bloody bra on.* I wiggle and tug and just when I think I will have to get my feet involved, one good yank and I free myself from the sports bra.

Phew.

My arm throbs and with a quick glance down, I see I have a bright red line across my left breast and my head itches where I've pulled out a chunk of hair. *Good times.* I grip the evil bra in my fist, glare at it and grind my teeth. I take a steady breath and put the bra on again, *slowly* this time, giving it the respect it demands.

"There, okay, I got this." Boobs sorted, I put my top on. As the base layer slides down my torso, I hurry back into my living room and pull out the padded rucksack for my laptop. I use my bubbling anger at the mercenaries to wash away my fear. Frightened people do silly things and react without thinking. I can't let my fear rule me. I won't. This isn't my fault, and it isn't Dad's fault either.

No, it's the fault of the wanker who sent the bloody Power Rangers to break down my door.

I continue to layer my clothing and top everything off with yellow hi-vis waterproof trousers, a matching coat, and chunky boots. I catch myself in the mirror as I shuffle past and wiggle my eyebrows. Ha, I resemble a bright yellow version of the Michelin man or the giant marshmallow guy off the classic film, *Ghostbusters*.

A big, luminous body with a tiny, violet head sticking out.

Sexy.

My door shudders and I hunch. Bloody mercenaries.

I dump my discarded pyjamas on my bed and swing the heavy door of the safe room closed. With a blinding flash of magic that tickles my nose, the safe room protections engage. As I stand *outside* the safe room, I nod my head with satisfaction. The multi-layered ward crackles menacingly and the energy coming off it makes me shudder. That will keep them busy.

I smirk at the red sash of my silk dressing gown as it peeks out of the door. *Oh, looky here, Tuesday has run into her safe room. Please spend hours trying to crack it.* My lips twitch into a wide grin. It is perfect.

I shuffle back into my living room, and with a groan, drop to my knees. "Daisy, come on, we have to go." Thanks to the idiots breaking down the door, she's hidden underneath the sofa. With my cheek resting on the carpet, I can just see her if I squint. Yellow eyes with vertical pupils glare at me, and her third eyelid tracks across the eye from side to side. "Come on, zig-zag, let's get somewhere safe." I hold my hand out and wiggle my fingers.

A low hiss comes from between a mouthful of razored teeth.

"Hey, don't you hiss at me, young lady," I reprimand in the perfect, if not creepy, imitation of my mother. Her claws dig into the carpet, and she wiggles further back, out of arm's reach. "Look," I huff. "I'm not the bad guy here. The bad guys are currently smashing down Auntie Jodie's ward. Come on now, you scaly little beast, we have to go."

Daisy narrows her eyes and her nostrils flare. She must smell my desperation as, after a long assessing blink and a put-out sigh, she finally crawls towards me. I scoop her up into my arms and she puffs a smoky cloud of hot air into my already warm face. Her tail wraps around my wrist, front claws dig into my collarbone, and she wiggles underneath my chin. "What a brave girl."

I see a flash of red out of the corner of my eye. Blimey, the ward is struggling... Who the hell is out there? There must be a strong magic user. *Someone I do not want to meet.*

Oh no, the ward! I want to slap my forehead. My sister is connected to it, and she'll know that something is wrong. Goosebumps rise underneath my ridiculous outfit and I swallow down a lump of nerves that wants to crawl up my throat. I juggle Daisy into one arm and grab my phone. I quickly send Jodie a text that I am okay and to keep away from my flat. There are already a few messages that I've missed. But with what is happening outside, I haven't got time to read them.

I unzip my jacket and carefully pop Daisy inside. "What a smart, clever girl," I coo as she snuggles down into the specially made pocket across my chest. I can feel her heart beating with fear, so I take the time to rub the base of her horns and stroke her beautiful, soft scales. "There, that's better Daisy. You are safe."

Daisy was brown when we first met, her scales sore and flaky. But after a few weeks and a fortune on lotions and potions, the little dragonette moulted and her true colour emerged. Gold. Her scales are a bit tarnished on top and lighter on her abdomen, feet and underneath her tail. She is so beautiful.

My waterproof outfit rustles and squeaks as I hurry into the kitchen and grab a potion ball from a drawer. It's the size of a marble and it swirls with a goopy green liquid. My sister Diane is the genius behind this spell. It is a protective bubble for Daisy. It is designed to maintain oxygen, temperature and to cushion her from any blows. This fabulous little potion will make sure she is one hundred percent protected while I get us to safety.

I stuff a good handful of dragonette mix into my coat to keep her occupied while I whisper the easy incantation. The protective bubble pops around her. Perfect.

Then I load up. I stuff random potions that my sisters keep giving me and things Daisy will need into my pockets. I finish with a few good handfuls of dragonette mix. If Daisy has food and her water dish, it is all good.

The ward flashes again. I am running out of time. What I can't do is fight a dozen magical Power Rangers. I'm not a ninja. So it's time to get the heck out of here.

CHAPTER
FOUR

I scramble to the door that holds the flat's heating boiler and—being mindful of Daisy—shove myself inside. Gah, the space is tight. I barely fit. As I wiggle, air from my puffy coat tickles the back of my neck as it compresses. I press my thumb to the hidden panel on the left and the electric lock disengages, causing the panel to pop open.

With a groan, I drop to my hands and knees. I drag my laptop bag behind me as I crawl into the dark hidey-hole.

When my dad set this emergency exit up, I laughed and laughed. I mean, who needs a hidden exit? Not me. As I close the door, I burn my hand on the hot water pipe, causing me to hiss. *Bloody thing.* Yeah, I thought my dad was crazy, and along with the stupid panic room, it was a complete waste of money. I'm not laughing anymore. The escape hatch, as I lovingly call it, is now the best thing ever. It's a hidden ladder that runs perpendicular with my building's lift shaft that will take me safely down to the ground floor and into the maintenance room.

With a little more room to move and in almost total darkness, I strap my laptop bag onto my back. *Crikey, I wonder how many spiders are in this area at the moment?* Perhaps not being able to see is a good thing. I try to ignore the feeling of cobwebs tickling the top of my head and face. I shudder.

Oh shit, on top of everything that's happening, I am going to have to grovel to Dad. I will have to listen to an epic "I told you so" lecture. *Well, if I get out of this alive...* I roll my eyes at the thought. If all goes well, I should be able to sneak out of the building with no one seeing me. *Bye-bye, mercenary Power Rangers.*

I swing myself onto the ladder. My heart jumps in panic and I yelp as my clunky boots make me miss the step. As my left leg dangles into the black abyss, I scramble to curl my arms around the ladder and hang on for dear life.

Shit, what a time to find out that I don't *do* climbing.

I get my shaking foot back where it should be as my chin digs into the rung above me. Perhaps putting all my gear on before I escaped wasn't such a good idea. A bead of sweat runs down the side of my face and my cheeks radiate heat. Nope, not a good idea. Not at all.

Frozen in fear, I hang on the ladder. My heart thuds and my knees knock together. I lick my lips. My mouth is as dry as the Sahara. Gah, I feel sick.

I drop my eyes and peek at Daisy. She seems perfectly content. I can hear her nibbling on her food. I grit my teeth and force myself to move my right leg. I can't hang around here all night. As long as I don't look down and I take my time, I'm going to be fine.

I screw my eyes closed and blow out a breath. With a clang, I slide my right foot off the rung and toe the next one below. I make sure my boot is completely balanced on the rung and then I cautiously let go of my death grip on the ladder and allow myself to step down.

Okay. I am okay.

I keep doing it, counting each step in my head as I go. It seems like it takes forever. When my boots hit the solid concrete floor of the maintenance room, my knees buckle and my entire body shakes with residual adrenaline. I'm alive. I am alive. I want to cry and kiss the ground at my feet. But I refrain, 'cause that would be minging.

I look up at the never-ending ladder above me with a shudder. Nope, I never want to do that again. It's like I've just climbed down Mount Everest. My arms and hands are aching.

Fuck you escape hatch.

When I move away from the ladder, the whole thing shimmers and disappears. It's hidden by a long-lasting Don't See Me Now Potion.

With a cautious peek out the fire exit to see if the coast is clear, my boots teeter on the step as I pause on the threshold. Oh crap. *I hope there are no bad guys out there.* I take a deep—if not shaky—breath and coax myself to move outside. *You can do this, Tuesday.* My whole body tenses as I move, and the outside air whooshes around me. I am in a tight alley at the back of the building. I flatten myself to the wall.

No one is here. *I am okay. It's okay. No one is out here.* I push the door firmly closed and my back scrapes against the red brick as I hug the wall, my bright yellow trousers rustling as I move.

With a smile, I glance down the tiny gap of my jacket at my girl. "So far, so good."

Three doors down, the alley opens into a tiny, private car park. I dash towards the building and open the back door.

The smell of food hits me, and my stomach gurgles. Yum. Chinese. I wave at Wendy, who is standing at the front counter, taking a phone order. Adamantly, I point to the lockbox that holds the keys for the scooters that they use for the takeaway deliveries. Wendy nods and gives me a thumbs up. I grin at her and mouth, "thank you," then grab a helmet from the side and stuff it onto my head.

"Ew." I gag and wrinkle my nose at the smell. You haven't lived if you've not stuffed your face into the padding of someone else's sweaty helmet. My skin itches. I grab a set of keys and mince my way to the back door.

"Oi, Tuesday!" shouts a voice behind me. My heart jumps and for a second, I freeze. I turn to see Wendy as she hurries toward me with a bag of food. "I don't want you going hungry. Nice to see you. It's been way too long."

"Thanks, Wendy," I say, my voice muffled by the helmet. "I'll get the bike back to you tomorrow." She pats the top of my head and rushes back to the ringing phone.

Outside, I head to the yellow and red scooters. I jiggle the keys and squint at the number etched on the key ring. When I find the corresponding scooter, I open the storage compartment under the seat, grab the gloves nestled inside, and pop in my yummy food. I throw my leg over and insert the key.

While I am safe in the car park, I use my phone to book a hotel room nearby. I might as well hide out in style. With that all accomplished, and a last check on Daisy, I stuff my hands in the gloves and rock the scooter off its stand. I turn the key, twist the throttle, and zoom into the night.

I NIP the scooter into a designated motorbike parking space and grab my soon-to-be midnight dinner from underneath the seat. I slip inside the hotel and shimmy across the lobby like a proper weirdo, the helmet still firmly in place as I want to keep my face covered. The professional vampire on reception doesn't bat an eye and I check in without issue. Key card in hand, I head straight for the lift.

Once safe inside my room, my entire body sags with relief. I am proud that I made the three-mile journey to the hotel without freaking out. Buzzing down the main road on a scooter at night is scary. Wow, I've done something epic. For sure, along with the Mount Everest ladder, it's another fist pump moment. I evaded the bad guys, and both Daisy and I are safely tucked away.

The best escape ever and as a bonus, I have Chinese.

Whoop.

The hotel room is nice—full bathroom, a king-size bed and a seating area that leads onto a balcony. I tug the smelly helmet off and stuff it in the cherry wood wardrobe near the door, rubbing my ear on my shoulder. My head itches with the need to wash my hair and face.

Carefully, I unzip the jacket and gently pull Daisy out. Her nose twitches. "Look at this nice room, zig-zag." I place her on the floor and grin as she slowly stretches out one wing and then the other, then her back legs kick out with a thump as she excitedly bolts away to explore. She disappears around the side of the bed.

I shed my waterproof layers and throw them onto a chair. I'll use the thermal base layers as pyjamas—my outfit of choice.

I hunt down the welcome tea and coffee set, slide the tray from underneath and pop it in the bathroom with a handful of clean shavings for Daisy's loo. Then I quickly set up an area with her food and water. I turn the television on low and slump on the bed with what feels like a hundred cushions behind me, then I munch on Wendy's chicken chow main. I love that Wendy gave me a fork. As I am eating, I bite the bullet and ring Jodie. I need to check if my coven is okay.

"Tuesday." I scrub a hand down my face when Mum answers my sister's phone.

Great.

"Hi, Mum," I say through gritted teeth.

Mum is silent. That isn't a good sign. I hunch and stuff more food into my mouth. When she still says nothing after that first mouthful, I do my best to appease her. I don't enjoy silence. "Some mercenaries came to my flat. I have no idea why I was targeted. Please don't send anyone; they have a heavy magic hitter. I'm sure they'll leave when they find out I am not there. I'm urm... at a local hotel stuffing my face with Chinese." Silence. "Is urm... is everyone okay on your end?"

"Tuesday Ann Larson," she growls. Uh-oh, my full name. I almost choke on a noodle. Oops, I'm in trouble. "Your lack of planning for your emergency is not my crisis."

Okay, thanks for that Mum. My bad. I should have planned for a group of mercenaries to bash down my door with someone strong enough to rip away Jodie's ward. I'll get right on that and do an entire A-to-Z emergency plan next time. I groan. I work in retail for spell's sake. It's not like I'm a practising witch or anyone special. I thought I did quite well. I had a plan; it might have been Dad's, but it worked.

"You should have come home immediately." *Home.* Their house isn't my home. "Why did you not come home? I have called the full coven for an emergency meeting. You need to come home right now so we can protect you—Matthew, she's at a *hotel*." Her phone rustles as she huffs, and she drops her voice to an angry whisper. "I will not have our magicless daughter attacked by thugs."

I roll my eyes. Does she hear herself? *Magicless.* Yeah, and woe betides anyone who messes with me. It would be a lovely sentiment *if* she wouldn't take this as an opportunity to gain control of my life. She doesn't recognise that she is the worst offender and the reason I avoid everyone in my coven.

"Mum, I am fine. Please don't bother everyone. I didn't want to bring this minor issue home with me." The word *home* gets stuck in my throat.

"Well, it isn't just about you," she snarls. "Why are you so selfish? They also came here, but our wards and powerful magic kept them at bay. After an attack on our coven, do you think I have time to be running around after you? Selfish girl. Look Tuesday, I know it's not something you want to hear but being without magic makes you an easy target. I knew I shouldn't have allowed you to live on your own," she mutters.

Oh, so my older sisters who can stir up a potion are fair game? They sure as heck don't live at home. To Mum, it is like being able to mix a potion makes you a superhero. And as for her saying she shouldn't have allowed me to live on my own, I moved out at eighteen, on my birthday. She didn't allow me to do anything. I'm now twenty-four, for spell's sake. I have never asked her for a bloody thing.

Yet it is all my fault? And I am the selfish one?

Don't say anything, Tuesday.

"Another thing I shouldn't have allowed was for you to work in that shop," she continues. I am a general manager in a big department store. "You can work with Jodie." I wonder if she will ever conclude that she is wasting her breath. I mean, she is like a broken record. If I didn't take her oh-so-helpful advice the first dozen times we had this exact conversation, I certainly won't suddenly turn around and say, "What a great idea Mum!" after the hundredth.

"Heaven knows that girl needs a break. She works so hard. Honestly, I do not know why you insist on working with humans when you can help your sister." Perhaps it's 'cause humans are too busy trying to stay alive and keep their families safe than be bothered with me? It's so frustrating. I know Jodie is busy running the magic shop and working as a nurse, but I work hard too. Apparently, what I do isn't good enough.

I make a noncommittal sound in the back of my throat and stuff a piece of chicken in my mouth, so I won't say anything I'll regret. No wonder I avoid her like the plague. She can't help herself.

My lack of magic—she can't stand it. She takes it as a personal affront. I shake my head as I angrily chew. I've found it best not to argue, as what's the point? She never listens. The sad thing is, I don't care what she thinks anyway. Not anymore.

I lock away my hurt, channel my inner manager, and dig deep into my epic customer service training. I smile widely. I hope the shape of my mouth will be enough to change the cadence of my voice. "I am sorry, Mum. I didn't know that there had been an attack on the coven. I'm sure this misunderstanding will get sorted out, and I will be back in my flat in a few days. So please, don't worry."

"A misunderstanding?" my mum screeches. I wince. Oops, bad word choice. "Breaking down your sister's ward is far from just a misunderstanding, young lady. If you answered your bloody phone once in a while, then you would have known that there was a security issue. What you cannot seem to grasp is that we are witches, and our coven protects our weakest members. Now, you will come home this instant so we can protect you, while the Hunters Guild deals with the problem."

My fake smile slips and I stare down at my food. I'm always going to be the coven's weak link. I poke at my noodles, and with a sigh, I push the box of food onto the bedside cabinet. I am no longer hungry. I bring my legs to my chest and hug my knees.

"I must insist that you move back into the fold," she continues. "You need to come home." *I'd rather shove my head in a washing machine.* "We can get you a nice, normal job." A job suitable for a witch, she means. "And get you some help..." My mum continues and her words fade into the background, drowned out by my emotions.

My hurt.

I don't care. I don't care. I don't care what she thinks.

Yeah, right. I'm the only one deceived when I try to convince myself. The hurt makes my throat tight, leaving me to swallow against it.

Times like this, I wish... Gosh, how I wish I was super strong, my magic dramatic, with lots of bells and whistles. Instead of meh, non-existent.

I clear my throat. "I appreciate that you're only trying to take care of me, but Mum, you are smothering me. I have a well-paying job—"

"At a clothing store," she scoffs.

"That clothing store has paid my bills for the last eight years." I ignore her as she splutters and plough on. "I have never asked you or Dad for anything. I'm safe. I love you all and I will ring you next week." *More like next year.*

"Tuesday, don't you dare hang up—" I end the call. My tummy flips, and the Chinese food lies heavily in my stomach. I hug my knees tighter.

Today has been a nightmare.

CHAPTER
FIVE

DAISY'S CLAWS dig into the carpet as she scrabbles around the bed. How can one small dragonette make such a racket? When she gets to my side, she stands on her hind legs and her front claws rest against the box frame. She wiggles her nose. I smile, lean down, and gently scoop her up. She settles next to my leg in the centre of the crisp white duvet and the softness of her scales helps to calm me.

I close my eyes for a second and force myself to breathe. I survived another fun phone call—that must count for something. At least I didn't tell her to fuck off. Not that I can, with the anti-swear mind control.

"I love you, little zig-zag," I whisper. My voice cracks and I rub my face.

Gosh, I shouldn't have let the conversation end like that. Every time we speak, I always seem to mess it up. I love my mum. Guilt churns in my tummy like black sludge. I know she is worried, and rightly so. Gah, I sink into the pillows. I could have handled that better. Perhaps I should have gone straight to the coven? I glance around the hotel room and shrug. It is telling that my first action was to go to a hotel. Not a friend, or my sisters, but a hotel. *Okay, Tuesday, enough of the coven drama. You need to check what's happening at home.* I drag my laptop bag, which is at the end of the bed, towards me and log into my building's security cameras.

I start the feed before the mercenaries enter the lobby. The building's ward chimes with distress on the computer's small speakers and then the main door crashes open. A puff of plaster dust rents the air as the door hits the wall. Like I've seen in countless action films, the group of men—dressed head to toe in their odd gear, so they can't be identified—tactically rush the building.

My face scrunches up in a frown as one guy doesn't conceal himself. He follows behind the others at a nonchalant pace, his hands stuffed in the pockets of his trousers. It's as if he's out for a winter stroll window shopping. "What a cocky motherfudger." Where did he come from? I can't believe I didn't spot him when I was watching at home.

Heck, how could I have missed him? He certainly stands out, and it appears he is the boss of the motley crew. I pause the footage and take a few stills, then email them to my Dad.

Why does this man feel comfortable showing his face when his colleagues don't?

"Flat eight, on the third floor. Harris, you take point," says the gruff voice of what would be the Red Power Ranger.

Two men stay on the ground floor, while the rest head upstairs. They clear each floor—military style—and make their way slowly up the building.

They move fluidly, like shifters... or vampires? I rub the back of my head. To guesstimate their height using the door frames of the hallway, they are big, so perhaps I was right the first time and they are shifters.

The guy—the boss?—doesn't rush. No. He slowly makes his way, strolling along without a care in the world, still shopping. I grind my teeth as I follow him with the cameras.

Who are you?

I speed up the footage until the group of mercenaries finally get to my flat and I watch as they clear the way for the boss guy. Look at that—they move aside and let him deal with the ward. My eyes widen. He is the magic user who took down the wards?

Well, I am surprised. He's a witch? I lean closer until my nose presses against the screen. He doesn't resemble any witch I've ever seen. I tilt my head to the side. The witch community is small, and male witches are incredibly rare. I would have remembered this guy.

With my mouth slightly open, I watch as he rips my sister's ward apart. 'Ecky-thump, the guy is packing some power. The ward is complicated, yet he rips it apart like it's tissue paper. He could have at least made it look difficult. What should have taken him hours, took him, what, fifteen—I check the timestamp—no, twenty minutes?

Nerves flutter in my belly. Crap, I'm lucky I got out of the building when I did. With a swipe at my keyboard, I copy all the footage and again email it to my dad. The Hunters Guild will want to see this.

What the heck is he? Who is he? I nibble a nail.

I need to find out more about him, about all of them. Where did they come from? I skip the footage to the camera in the street before they entered the building, but—no, that can't be right. It can't. Something is blocking the security feed. I stab at the keyboard, but nothing I do fixes the issue. I growl in frustration and glare at the mysterious man. I send the entire file to Ava. Tech is her thing. I will have to let Ava, Dad, and the hunters deal with this. I'm okay with computers, but I am not an expert in CCTV.

I skip to the live camera inside my flat: Daisy Cam. I only have it so I can check on Daisy when she doesn't want to come to work with me.

Wow, they've already broken into the safe room. Shocking. It's also kind of disappointing that what should have taken them all night, took this mystery guy only forty minutes. I shiver. The other mercenaries I can hear through the camera are tossing my place. The laptop bumps against my abdomen as I wave my hands in the air and squirm on the bed. *Monsters.* They are breaking my shit.

"Nice to see the Hunters Guild has rushed to my flat," I grumble. *Everything can be replaced. It's only stuff.* I concentrate instead on the witch. He turns his head towards the Daisy Cam and smiles.

He smiles at me.

I yelp. What the friggity-fig-frig was that? I jerk away from my laptop and slam the lid closed. But not before I see him disappear.

The witch *Stepped*.

Stepping is an old, powerful fae thing. A teleporting thing. Witches don't bloody Step. "Not a normal witch," I squeak out. "Not a witch at all." With my heart pounding, I shove the laptop back in its bag and shoulder it. I scoop Daisy into my arms and cradle her against my chest as I scramble to my feet. "We need to get the hell out of here. We are not safe."

Every instinct I have is lit up and screaming danger. I don't know why, but I am sure he knows where I am. The guy is coming for me. Did he trace the security feed? My phone? Both are encrypted. It shouldn't be possible.

Yeah, it also shouldn't be possible for him to rip through wards like he's walking through cobwebs. Or Step.

Oh no. Oh no. Heart pounding, I grab my yellow jacket and trousers and stuff them underneath my other arm. I snatch my boots off the floor, the laces biting between my sweaty fingers. I will put everything on when I get the heck out of this hotel. I yank the room door open and narrowly avoid ploughing into a muscular chest.

"Where do you think you're going?" says a deep, heavily accented voice.

An *eep* sound slips out of my mouth and everything I am holding—except Daisy—thuds to the floor.

I scramble backwards. My bum hits the bathroom door, and it smashes back into the tiles with a crash.

Oh my. He is here.

He strolls into the room and, without taking his blue eyes from me, kicks the room door closed with his heel. I gulp. Without breaking his stride, he walks over my discarded outerwear.

My panicked heart pounds in my ears. *How is this possible?*

Daisy snarls and snaps her teeth at him. A puff of smoke comes out of her left nostril, and a lick of orange flame comes out of the right. I can feel how frightened she is with the rapid beat of her heart as it thuds against my palm. I love that she's being brave and trying to protect me, but I cannot put her in danger or allow her to be hurt.

Without taking my eyes from the stranger, I carefully squat, place Daisy on the tiled floor of the bathroom, and click the door firmly closed. I wince at her angry yowl. She growls and scratches at the door, then there are a few thuds.

"Hello, little lost witch," he says. His full lips tilt up with amusement. "I am told you're a dud, but you're more than that, aren't you? Your coven has hidden you well."

What? What on earth is he going on about? I haven't got a scooby. When all he gets in response is my dumbfounded expression, his mouth clenches and a muscle in his jaw jumps as if he's grinding his molars together. What is he expecting, a confession? My eyes drift away from his ticking jaw, and it's then that I notice his pointed ears.

Aes sidh, he is fae, an elf.

His short hair threw me. They normally wear it long with these pretty traditional plaits. He's a strong, old fae if he can Step.

"It's been over a century since I've met one of your kind in the real world. Stupid of you, really." My gaze darts from his ears and I take in the predatory gleam in his eyes. I smell bullshit. He is trying to butter me up. *One of my kind?* I wrinkle my nose.

It doesn't take a genius to work out I hate being a magical dud. *Nice one, Tuesday, that you know your place.* Yeah, I'm the secondary character, even in my own damn story. I swallow down a strange lump in my throat. I know I'm a silent internal badass. I don't have to be anything more.

But then why do I always feel so disappointed? My bottom lip wobbles, and I suck it into my mouth and chomp on it. None of that.

No. If this elf thinks I am going to fall for his total rubbish spiel of me being some kind of *chosen one*, ha. He has messed up. Boy, has he ever messed up.

A rush of angry heat washes away my fear and I see red. In the back of my head, I am utterly terrified, but I'm also too reckless to care. I've tipped over into madness. I don't cower like a normal person. No, when I am frightened, I get mad in a psycho way. It's another weird Tuesday thing, one that I presume is hereditary. Thanks, Mum.

I can feel my temper bubbling. It's warm in my chest and it spills out of my mouth with a vomit of words. "What?" I scoff as I narrow my eyes and lift my chin. "Are you nuts? Has your magic fried your brain?"

I hold my hand up and wiggle my index finger. "One, you and a bunch of mercenaries broke into my home and trashed it. Two"—a second finger joins the first—"you chased me across the city and forced your way into my hotel room." My hands go on my hips and I glare at him.

Shut up, Tuesday, a small voice in the back of my head begs. But I ignore it as I'm on a roll. My nostrils flare. At least my angry rant makes me feel like I am in control. "As if I would believe a single thing you say, sausage head."

Or not.

I meant dickhead. *Dickhead.* I groan.

He smirks and takes another menacing stride toward me. His bright blue eyes shine with mirth. "Yeah, that sounds about right," he drawls.

"You are delusional." I clench my fists. I've never hit anybody before, yet I'm struggling to tamp down the urge to punch him in his smug face.

Thumb out, right? Hit with the first two knuckles and twist your hips... I glance down at my small, balled fists then back at his smug face. I wince. It looks kind of hard.

"You're coming with me."

"Oh, heck no." I shuffle back and glance around wildly. There must be something in this room to brain him with. I'm not a victim. Mournfully, I glance at my heavy boots that are now behind his bulk. They would have made a fine weapon. The helmet would have also come in handy, but there's no way I can get past him to grab it. I tilt my head. He's a big bugger for an elf. He must be well over six feet, towering over my five-foot-four frame.

Lamp? I want to smack my forehead. *Magic. Bloody heck, Tuesday.* I have a knockout ball in the hidden pocket of my thermal trousers. It's a close contact spell and, well, we can't get any closer than this. One second, I'm about to grab it and the next, his weight is crushing me into the bed. Oof. I groan as his body knocks the breath out of me. His weight pushes me into the soft white covers.

'Ecky thump, this guy is built like a shifter. Crap, I wish I had listened to my dad about those self-defence lessons. He'd be snoring on the floor now if I'd used the potion sooner.

One hand grapples both my wrists together and slams them above my head. He reaches down between us... I panic. *Is he... is he reaching for his zipper?* A frightened whine escapes my throat, and I do my best to wiggle out of his hold. Before I can scream bloody murder, he pulls his hand back out, and in it is a nullifying band. It is made to remove every spell and shut down every trace of magic. It works on every creature but is mainly used on criminals.

Why does he want to use that on me? Why bother? My magic is non-existent. I try again to wiggle away, but his hand presses my wrists harder into the bed with bruising force and the clunky ring on his finger digs into my skin painfully. The damn thing is hot, and I wince as it burns me.

With a flick of his hand, the nulling band snaps out and wraps around my wrist. Something inside of me crashes. Disappears. Ouch.

What the heck? I don't have magic, but the jolt of the band hurts me down to my very bones.

"I don't feel well," I mumble.

"You'll get used to it," he says. His fingers sweep my tangled, dark purple hair away from my face. He tugs at a strand. "Huh. Not magic. I didn't expect that." The nulling band is making me batty. He didn't expect what? Did he expect me to turn into a frog? I hate magic. Why would I use a potion to change the colour of my hair? Everything is me.

"I can't breathe," I whisper. The elf smirks and digs his elbow into my ribs. I groan. Yeah, that helps. What an arsehole. Thinking I have been appropriately cowed, he lets go of my wrists.

With a scowl, I slowly lower my hand, the one without the null band, to rub my ribs. Inch by torturous inch, I work my hand down until I slip my fingers into my waistband. With my thumb and forefinger, I pull the potion ball out. Then slowly, ever so slowly, bring my hand back up, and I aim for the skin on his neck.

He jolts when there is a crash behind us, and the room's door is unceremoniously kicked in.

"Hey, welcome to the party," my voice slurs. "Ahh, here comes the cavalry." I hope.

He grunts, and his weight is yanked off me. There is a slap of a fist meeting skin—I hope it's his face—and the bed shunts to the side. The sharp movement of the bed whips me sideways and the potion ball flies from my fingertips and rolls off the side of the mattress.

Gah, for fuck's sake.

I try to move so I can find where the potion has landed. But I can't. What the heck? My head swims. Without his weight on me, I should be able to breathe, right? Yet each breath is getting harder. Like I am breathing through a twisted straw. It's too much... It is way too much. Why can't I bloody breathe? Did the bloody elf break something?

A body thuds to the floor. I hope that's the bad guy. My thoughts are fuzzy, and I can no longer open my eyes.

Come on, Tuesday, get up... darkness.

CHAPTER SIX

My aching bladder wakes me and, with one eye firmly shut and the other open the barest of a crack, I zombie shuffle to the bathroom.

The rules are: if I don't open my eyes, I'm still asleep.

To save me valuable seconds in the bathroom—the joy of living alone—I tug my thermal leggings down my thighs as I move. When I get to the toilet, I slam my bare bottom down on the seat and groan as I pee like a racehorse.

Once finished, with my eyes now firmly closed, I bump into the counter and quickly wash my hands, then without peeking—on my first attempt, go me—I grab the fluffy towel. Hotel towels are so fancy.

All sorted and with my leggings back in place, I continue my weird shuffle back to bed.

"Morning," says a gruff, amused voice.

"Arrahh!" I jump a foot in the air and clutch my chest. I tremble and my heart pounds as my now wide-awake eyes fixate on the strange man in the chair across the room.

I blink.

Oh no.

Some new guy is sitting in the chair like a James Bond villain. His long legs are spread wide apart, with Daisy and a small pile of dragonette mix on his abdomen.

"Don't worry. She is fine." His steady eyes are weirdly comforting. The light colour stands out against his dark hair and skin tone. His entire expression is kind, and I believe him. Daisy is fine.

Me? Yeah, not so much.

My now adrenaline-fuelled, wide-awake brain helpfully reminds me about what happened. The elf. I touch my empty wrist. The null band is no longer there. Huh. It's then my brain whispers, *did he see my bare bum?*

A small noise slips from my lips. I can still feel my body tremble, but my mind is oddly blank. I rapidly blink and then, in my head, I carefully run through my toilet shuffle, step by step. Then I factor in the chair's angle.

I allow myself a second to close my eyes. Mortified, my face heats and I want to sink onto the floor. Oh bloody hell, he saw my bottom.

My bare bottom.

Oh no, why me? I mentally whine. I rub the back of my neck and my hand catches on my long hair. Phew, my hair is down. It's long... It must have covered most, if not all, of my lily-white-arse.

Right? Right.

I open my eyes and cringe as I take stock of the situation. There is nothing I can do about it now. Hopefully, he will be a gentleman and ignore the whole thing. Like I will. It never, ever happened. I cough to clear my throat and examine the guy. Wow, if I thought the elf was big, this guy is on another level. He has got to be a shifter.

The man's massive hand strokes Daisy as she delicately nibbles at the food on his abdomen. She is happy, the little traitor.

"Never saw the appeal of a dragonette as a pet, but I have to say, I've changed my mind. She is absolutely adorable." His rumbly voice is like velvet.

"Yes, she is. Though she is less pet and more best friend." But that's beside the point. I rock from foot to foot. Who the hell is this guy? "The elf?" I husk out. Might as well get to the point. I need to see what he wants and then get rid of him sharpish.

"I'm sorry. He Stepped before I could get a good grip on him," he replies gruffly, his eyes apologetic.

I shrug. "It's okay, as long as I don't see him again." I hope the elf is gone for good. His strange comments about my magic threw me. When you've been told all your life you are the magic equivalent of a garden pea and some dickhead lies, making it out like you are some hidden marvel, it gets you questioning yourself. I am not too proud to say, shamefully, that I wanted to believe him for a hot second.

"He was creepy. Thank you for your help." I point to Daisy. "Urm... do you mind?" All my instincts say he's a good guy, but I still have a strong urge to rescue my dragonette.

The stranger nods. "Of course." I tuck my hair behind my ear and shuffle forward, intent on scooping Daisy off his flat abdomen. I hold my breath as I lean forward, doing my best not to stand between his legs or touch him.

It isn't until I get closer and study him that I get the full effect of this man. At first glance, he is humongous, and dare I say, forgettable. Just another shifter. A soldier with his black hair shorn close to his scalp. But then as my eyes trail over his perfectly symmetrical face—the words *ultra masculine* scream in my head—with strong elegant lines, high broad forehead, straight nose, good cheekbones, square jaw peppered with stubble, and a full mouth...

Carved without any weakness.

The shifter oozes raw alpha male. He is all testosterone and metaphysical fur.

Rich, dark skin and soulful eyes—a stunning grey—take my measure. Huh. I've never seen a guy with such thick eyelashes. He is incredibly handsome.

Ridiculously handsome.

I breathe him in. He also smells fantastic, of cinnamon and vanilla. I frown. That's right. I sniffed him like a freak. I don't think I've bothered to smell a guy before. Oh my goodness, I am so weird.

I have Daisy, but as I get lost in his pretty grey eyes, I stupidly gather up the remaining food. They are the kind of eyes that shine with intelligence and confidence. He doesn't look—he watches. My fingers brush against his bumpy abs. I gasp, and my heart misses a beat.

'Ecky-thump, now I am assaulting him. Oops. "Sorry," I mumble. I spin in my socks, and we hurry towards the bed. Red-faced, I perch on the edge and pop Daisy down beside me. Is it hot in here? I tug at the neck of my top. Thermals in a hotel room aren't the best.

"Your dad sent me."

"Oh." That was something I should have established. I guess I am still a little thrown from the bum incident. "Thank you for saving me. Are you a hunter?"

"Hellhound," he replies matter-of-factly. The carefully hidden hellhound power ramps up and hits me square in my chest.

I gasp and feel my red cheeks instantly pale. Born of pure instinct, fear grips me. This time, crazy Tuesday, who valiantly mouthed off at the elf, scampers away in my head and hides. Whoa, I feel woozy. I wobble to the side and grip the white cover to ground myself.

Shifters alone are a scary lot. It's not them turning into animals that produces the terror, it's that if you get bitten when they are in animal form, and you are a witch, a human, or even some of the weaker fae, you are so screwed. You will die.

Men have an over fifty percent chance of becoming a bitten shifter. They can't shift themselves, but they gain extra things like a longer life span, an eight pack, and strength.

But women always die.

There's something wrong with the magic. It obliterates the X chromosome. There's no healing spell, no medication, and nothing in the world can stop it from happening. So, when you add an old shifter and then the power of a hellhound to the mix... it's an *oh crap* moment.

Hellhounds are scary. Like a monster under your bed scary. They aren't from hell or anything like that. They are powerful old shifters with fire magic. Nature literally sets the strongest of the poisonous biting machines alight and gives them extra strength.

Yay.

The shifters reacted to the magical phenomenon by training these scary beasts into killing machines. Of course, they did. It really adds to the entire fear factor. They are the terminators of shifters and I have never met a hellhound before, as they are rare. They are the Hunters

Guild's elite fighters. Elite soldiers. They are the shit-has-hit-the-fan last resort.

And I have one in my room, a hellhound with pretty grey eyes and he is staring right at me. A predator, a fire wolf, looks at me from inside his eyes.

Hellhound. Hellhound. Hellhound.

Thank goodness I am sitting, and that I've already been to the loo. Why are the bad guys always mouthwateringly good looking? It doesn't seem fair.

"Hey-hey, you are okay." He takes hold of my hand and drops the potion ball that had fallen to the floor earlier into my palm. Gently manipulating my fingers closed, he holds my hand until he is sure I have it firmly in my grip.

A big-ass knife appears from out of nowhere and he places the hilt in my other hand. The blade is heavy; I know they do something technical to the silver to make the soft metal hard like steel. In seconds, in an attempt to make himself smaller, he is kneeling in front of me. The hellhound angles the knife in my hand, so the tip presses against his chest.

My heart misses a beat.

The hellhound has given me the means to protect myself against him. At least I can swallow down my chaotic, frightened thoughts and listen to what he has to say. I peek up through my lashes.

His grey eyes are so earnest.

"Hey, Tuesday, you are okay," he coos at me. "Sweetheart, you are safe. I am not gonna hurt you. Breathe, you are okay. I promise you are safe with me." His giant hands come up to cradle my face. His hands are so warm. "My name is Owen. I am a friend of your sister, Jodie. Your dad sent me to help you. I'm sorry if me being a hellhound scared you." It's a silly reaction but, I think, a normal one.

Why did my dad send a hellhound?

I take a deep breath and whisper. "My coven?"

"They are safe." I close my eyes and drop the knife. My hand is trembling so much, I don't want to risk catching him and cutting off his nose by accident.

No, accidentally stabbing someone is not on my to-do list.

"Everyone is safe. You are safe. I'm not with the guild anymore. I work in Ireland with the fae. I've been hunting your elf for the past three months."

"He's not my elf," I grumble.

"No, he is not. He's a bad man. When your dad received your emails, he got in touch with me. He gave me the heads up and instead of going to your place, I traced you here as I had a feeling the monster would come after you. I'm sorry I was late, and that he put his hands on you." Owen's thumbs brush gently against my cheekbones, and he huffs out a self-deprecating sound. "I thought my being here would be comforting. I'm sorry I got that wrong, that I frightened you."

I blink at him.

His eyes, this close, have a dark blue ring around the outside. So pretty. There's a knock at the door. I flinch.

"That would be for me," he says gruffly. Owen lets go of my face. With a tight smile, he pats the bed and then rises elegantly from the floor and prowls to the door.

I lean forward to peek around the jutting bathroom wall that's blocking the bed from the view of the door. I huff. I can't see, as the hellhound's bulk takes up the whole entrance. There's no getting past him. Saying he just has wide shoulders, a narrow waist, chiselled chest, and washboard abdominals does not do the hellhound justice. He is big. He must be almost seven-foot tall.

"I got the scuba guys," says a rough female voice. I cover a snigger with my palm. I'm not the only one who thought their combat gear was stupid. "Rat shifters. Where's the elf?"

"Stepped."

"Ah shit. What's the score, Nanny Hound? Ten-nil? You're slipping." Looks like I am also not the only one to pick up that the hellhound is on babysitting duty. *Nanny hound*. Great. "Old wolf, ya need to catch up. Next time, I'll handle the damsel and you grab the bad guys. What? Bad day at the office? Are you losing your touch?" The hellhound growls and the woman's throaty laugh threads through the room.

The laugh raises the hairs on my arms and an unshakeable sense of foreboding creeps along my spine. Along with that laugh, came the trickle of her power. She is so loaded up... My lips buzz.

"How's the girl?"

Fuck that. I scoop up Daisy and wiggle to the head of the bed, which is as far away as we can get from her without going through the window. To keep my hands busy, I scratch a finger between Daisy's horns.

"Safe."

"Good. I bought the stuff you wanted. You know I am no good at this female crap, so don't blame me if I got the wrong stuff. She should be able to brush her teeth and there are at least a few changes of clothes. I might have forgotten knickers..."

"Thanks, Forrest."

"Soooo, do I get to meet her?"

Oh no. No, thank you. There's a rustle of clothing and the floor in the hallway squeaks as if she is bouncing on her toes.

"Not today."

"Oh, come on, Owen. Jodie said I'd love her little sister. I've met everyone in the coven but this one. Please?" she throatily whines.

"No," he growls back.

Forrest. I am sure I've heard that name before, but not from my sister. There is a bump and a scraping sound against the door. I strain my ears at the sound of... wheels. He must have pulled a case inside the room. "I will see you in an hour."

"Nice to meet you, Tues—" Owen slams the door in her face.

Wow, rude.

And I am so glad. I shiver; I can understand why he didn't want me to meet her. Owen is on protective duty, and he's taking his babysitting seriously. His shifter nose must have caught the stench of my fear. The way my body reacted when she laughed. Oh boy, and the power she has. Bloody hell, it comes off her in waves. I've never felt anything like it. Instinctively, I wanted to climb out the bloody window. She is dangerous. I rub my arms and do a full-body shiver.

Crap, if she feels like that in the corridor, I can only imagine what it would be like standing next to her. I don't know what the heck type of creature she is, and I don't want to find out.

The fact she could arrest, um—I frown—take down the huge Power Ranger rat shifters by herself? Yeah. She is beyond scary.

I lift my eyes. Owen is standing silently in front of me. While I was stuck in my head, he brought me a suitcase.

"Thank you for all this," I croak.

"Are you okay?" I nod. "Did you hear all that?" I nod again. "Okay, find something to wear in here. You're going on a trip. While you were sleeping, your dad arranged a safe house. Oh, and the guild has contacted your work and explained what's happening. You're on emergency leave until this mess is sorted."

I puff out my cheeks. Great. I guess my department managers can handle things for a few days. Being hunted by some psycho elf takes priority, I guess.

"Okay, thank you," I mutter.

"Unfortunately, there isn't a portal nearby. So, Flash, if you think you're up for it, we are going to have to drive."

My brain grinds to a halt... Flash? Owen's face is carefully blank, but I can feel the growing horror race across mine. Is that a twinkle in his grey eyes? My chest and neck prickle with embarrassed heat. Oh bloody hell, he's talking about my bottom.

Flash. I'm a bloody flasher. Ha.

Once again, I am absolutely mortified. Daisy's scales rub against my hand, and I pick her up from my lap and gently clutch her to me.

"I can drive myself to the safe house. I'll be fine," I squeak.

CHAPTER
SEVEN

"I CAN DRIVE myself to the safe house. I'll be fine," I grumble as I grip the leather steering wheel so hard my fingers cramp. Yep, great job there, Tuesday. Leave the hottie hellhound with the biceps as big as your head to travel almost seven hours and three hundred and seventy-five miles, alone.

In my usual stubbornness to avoid help of any kind, I insisted I could drive myself. "What could go wrong? I will be fine." I sniff with self-disgust.

I have spent hours driving in a state of heightened alert, with my hands locked in a death grip onto the steering wheel in a ten-and-two driving position and a nervous sweat beading on my brow.

I dare to take my left hand—frozen claw—off the wheel for a second, to rub my tired eyes. I want my boring life back. I would rather deal with a nightmare shoe sale display, one where a kid has mixed up not only the left and right shoes but also the sizes. Matching hundreds of different shaded shoes is preferable to this.

I am so stupid. The last time I drove a car was the day I passed my test, and I never left my home city. Dad taught me to drive when I was seventeen. Once I had my pass certificate, as a rite of passage and for my first and last solo trip, I drove my dad's car through a McDonald's drive thru. That was seven years ago. I rub my thumb against the steering wheel and swallow. I loved learning to drive with Dad, but the whole car thing tainted the experience. All three of my older sisters were gifted their first car. With blatant unfairness, and in a sweeping statement by my mum, I was informed that if I wouldn't behave like a proper witch—I was refusing to attempt any magic—I had to walk.

I lift my stiff shoulder. It was fine. Who was I to dictate how my parents spent their money? I enjoyed walking and school wasn't far.

I am sure it was a naff attempt at reverse psychology by Mum, but instead of pitching a fit, I drifted further away. I wanted nothing from them anyway, so it was probably a good thing. In my teenage mind, it only highlighted again that my parents and magic just brought me pain. It made me more determined to be successful on my own terms. *Away from magic.*

I didn't drive a car again until today. I push the unhappy thoughts to the back of my mind. It's in the past and I am no longer a teenager. I'm an adult and I am adulting perfectly.

I quickly peek at my phone. According to the driving app, I am only thirty minutes from my destination. *Nothing is going to go wrong.* As if fate is listening to my thoughts, the fancy hire car shudders, and the headlights dim. *Oh, no.* There is a burst of warm air from the heater, and then the dash lights up, blinding me. I take my foot off the accelerator just as the car goes dark. Slowly, we roll to a stop.

"Motherclucker."

The engine ticks and my heart pounds as I sit wide-eyed in the dark on a country lane in the middle of nowhere Scotland. I gulp and my shoulders creep towards my ears. The fear that is rolling inside me makes me feel sick. I was pooping myself just driving. This is on a whole new level. The dead car is on a bend with no lights, and we are surrounded by thick hedges.

Oh no.

With shaking hands, I put the car in neutral and let go of my death grip on the wheel. *Get a hold of yourself, Tuesday, and think about what you need to do. Don't you dare freak out,* I berate. Crikey, the voice in my head sounds like Mum.

If I can deal with sixty-two staff and our wonderful array of customers, I can deal with this. I am the best problem solver. My not-so-sneaky staff call me Scary Poppins when they think I'm out of earshot. I roll my tense shoulders and flex my sore fingers. I am spoonful-of-sugar nice until things go wrong, then I can get a bit bossy. *I am a retail manager badass.* I snort.

I unclip my seat belt and, channelling my inner Homer Simpson, I frantically push every button on the dashboard, but nothing works. The phone Owen gave me is also dead. It must have cut out at the same time as the car did.

Uh-oh. That is not creepy. Not at all.

Magic normally raises the small hairs on my arms and tickles the back of my neck. I don't feel that sensation. But that doesn't mean much. Why would the car and the phone die at the same time? I shiver and then turn my head to scrutinise the passenger seat. My girl, who is safe in her fancy extra-large protective travel bubble, is fast asleep. I think. I tilt my head and narrow my eyes. Damn it, I can't see her. My eyes can't pierce the thick darkness. Why does tonight have to be so dark?

"It's okay, Daisy. I'll get us out of this," I say, in case she is awake and is looking at me. I aim for brisk confidence, but my voice wobbles at the end.

With a disgusted huff at myself, I crack the car door and the sound of the night rolls in. I blink into the darkness. I am so used to city sounds and the never-ending artificial light. I have never seen the outside world so black, so vast. It's jarring. I hold my breath and listen.

There are strange clicks from random insects. I frown and tilt my head. Wow, I didn't even know we had clicky minibeasts in the UK. I have no idea what the hell they are. I strain my ears for any other signs of life. The wind rustles in the trees and that's it. Absolute silence.

At least I will hear if a car comes, well, urm, unless it's electric. Great. I nibble on my lip and wince. I've been chomping on it for hours and desperately need some lip balm. My bottom lip probably looks a chapped mess.

"I wonder if this car has a warning triangle?" Gosh, my voice sounds loud to my ears. I grab the keys, rotate my stiff body, and boldly shove the heavy car door open. I use the door frame to help me clamber out onto the road. My knees knock together, and I whimper as I straighten. I've been driving for so long, my poor body has moulded to the shape of the seat. I was too nervous to stop and take a break in case I had to turn the car around or drive in a small space. The thought of reversing gives me heart palpitations and makes my top lip sweat.

My feet crunch on the ground as I head for the back of the car. When I reach it, I trip on the uneven road surface and almost go down, but a wild grab with my hands and my fingers dig into the roof trim. I hang on a second longer to steady myself and then squint down at my feet. What the heck is that?

"Oh my goodness, please don't tell me I hurt some poor creature." I toe something squishy and I squeal. "Oh no, oh no, am I a murderer? I was driving super slow." I feel sick.

No, it's not a dead body. Is that… Is that grass? I stop myself from dropping to a crouch and touching the ground as a trickle of memory tugs at my brain. A flash of the road before the car died. I lean against the car with relief. The rural road had a strip of grass running down it and I now distinctly remember I had been mindful to keep the tyres straddling it while praying no one came the other way.

Now, will the boot open with the key alone? These new cars are so fancy and reliant on technology. I feel along the back of the car, the dirt from the road gritty underneath my hand. I aim for the middle and… Aha! I find the lock. I trace it with my fingertips and then blindly aim the key.

The boot whooshes open and I puff my cheeks out as I methodically feel my way around the boot. Nothing. It's bloody empty. No crappy triangle, no warning spell. I haven't got anything to light up the car. I drop my head in defeat.

I am doomed.

I slam the boot closed and shuffle my way to the front. Hands on my hips, I peer at the road ahead. Why is it so bloody dark? As I turn back to the car, the moon peeks from behind what I can now see is thick cloud cover.

As the clouds break, the full moon shines down, granting me much needed light. I tip my head back in thanks and give the moon a grateful smile. Between the heavy clouds, I can see a slice of the night sky and a smattering of stars. Wow, they are so pretty. I quickly glance about before the light disappears and I see—I tilt my head—is that a break in the hedge?

Just around the bend... Is that a driveway?

I dash forward, being mindful of the uneven road, and I find a driveway and a sign: THE SANCTUARY HOTEL.

Well, isn't that convenient? A warning bell in my head is going off like the clappers.

Creepy. Creepy. Creepy.

But what choice do I have? I glance back at the dead, stranded car and pull a face. Creepy hotel or wait until it gets light? The way the car is positioned on the road, I could kill somebody if another car comes around the bend.

Mind made up, I ignore my screaming self-preservation instincts and turn back to the car. It shouldn't be too much of a push. Right?

As I hurry back up the grassy road, I realise there is a slight incline I didn't notice. That's handy. I might be able to freeroll the car into the driveway. That's if the fancy car's steering works without power. Otherwise, I'm going to overshoot the driveway and find myself stuffed into a hedge.

So much fun, I think with a manic smile as I clap my hands. "In for a penny, in for a pound," I mutter. I will say a lot about Mum, but she raised me and my sisters to be tenacious. All the Larson women are stubborn as hell. So, thanks to Mum, I am not a damsel in distress.

I dump the keys in the closest cup holder so my hands are free, and I take a peek at Daisy. Her hot breath fogs in adorable puffs against the travel bubble. She is curled in a ball, and thankfully fast asleep.

Then, like I've seen in films, I brace myself against the open door frame. *Come on, Tuesday.* My boots dig into the uneven tarmac as I give the car a good push.

Nothing happens. I groan, jump back into the car, and put the car in first gear. That might help. I get back into position. *Films make this look so easy.* I growl, get a little mad, and *push* the car with all my might. Just as my poor shoulder begins to scream in protest, the wheels move, inch by tiny inch, and then the car is rolling.

Yay, it is moving!

It quickly picks up speed. Crap, it's rolling pretty fast! I squeak and fling myself into the driver's seat. I am almost settled inside when the car door slams closed, cracking against my right shin, which is still dangling in the road. Ouch. The stupid bloody thing. I stuff my leg inside and ignore the urge to give it a rub.

Instead, I grit my teeth and tug like mad on the steering wheel. The wheels dry grind on the tarmac and the car *eeks* its way to the left. *Come on. Come on.* Without meaning to, as my eyes are firmly on the looming menace of a hedge, I clip the kerb and the bounce puts us dead centre on the hotel's driveway.

We roll into the empty car park. The front wheels bump into another kerb, stalling the car's now slower momentum, and the car settles into a parking space. Perfectly between the lines.

Wow.

CHAPTER
EIGHT

My heart is pounding from the adrenaline of my epic car push and coasting antics. I lift my arm and kiss my bicep. I am so She-Ra. I have the urge to bellow "I have the power" while wildly waving my arms about. Oh, or was that He-Man? My face scrunches in a frown. Meh, who cares? I bet few people have pushed a car by themselves.

The car park is dimly lit with ground level lights that highlight the crumbling path up to the hotel. Why didn't I see the lights from the road? The hedges weren't that thick. Even though the lights are dim, they should have been visible.

I vigorously rub my forehead. I find this all hard to deal with. Nothing makes sense. I know something wacky is going on, but I have no idea what, and interpreting this shite is beyond me. I am almost at my limit. I've spent hours driving, frightened half to death that I am going to crash the car, and my whole body aches. The need for a locked door, a bath, and a good night's sleep thrums through me.

In the light of day, everything will be better.

Hottie hellhound mentioned my coven will meet me at the safe house, so my mum is at the end of this wonderful drive. Yeap. I huff. I am not in the mood to deal with her, and I can't be arsed with her passive aggressive bullshit. So, if I can leave that confrontation until tomorrow... now that would be a billy bonus. I can so risk a stay in a creepy hotel to avoid Mum.

Perhaps Dad can come and get me in the morning? Something inside of me dips and I rub my thigh and pick at some imaginary fluff on my black jogging bottoms. No. No, he won't. I will ring the hire car company in the morning and get them to fix the car. I lean across, and from my yellow jacket hung on the back of the passenger seat, I grab a handful of potions and stuff them into my pockets. I need to be ready for anything.

Typical spaghetti western music *bow-wow-bow-wow-wow* chimes through my head as I then pull out a plastic blue and orange toy gun and blow on it.

No longer She-Ra, I'm now Clint Eastwood.

Instead of underwear, Forrest left this and a bunch of weapons in the suitcase. With a helpful scrawled note to add a sleep potion to the foam bullets.

Wow, just wow.

The woman is a scary, evil genius.

I am glad I added the potion before I left, so the gun is good to go. Many creatures carry weapons, but not guns. Guns are licenced and heavily regulated. There is also this strange thing of honour between creatures where it's all blood and blades. Oh, and not to mention the many spells and nasty potions that will melt your face clean off and turn you inside out. Go witches.

For all our technological advancements, I don't think we've ever made it out of the dark ages. So, guns are a big no-no. Not that this is a real gun. My grip tightens on the plastic. I have no idea if a toy gun wielding a sleep potion is illegal. If caught with it, I might be in a huge amount of trouble. Like I care. I don't know how my aim will measure up anyway, but I am willing to try anything if the shit hits the fan. I'm not a fighter, and I am a crap magic user. But after meeting the scary elf, I will take whatever I can get.

I slide out of the car, and as soon as I put weight on my right leg, my poor calf throbs. I glare at the offending car door and slam it closed a little harder than necessary. *Bloody door.* I nod, feeling vindicated with the car now suitably chastised. I hobble around to the passenger side to get Daisy.

Like I've seen in films, I stuff the toy gun within easy reach behind my back, tucked into my waistband. When I take a step, the elastic pings and the gun slides down the back of my trousers and clocks me on the ankle. I roll my eyes, stand on one leg and jiggle until it pops out of the bottom and clatters to the ground. I tighten the string on the jogging bottoms and put it in my pocket.

"I have the power," I grumble as I struggle to lift the small suitcase from the footwell. With a grunt, I drag it out and then tap Daisy's travel bubble. The magic swirls and it rises from the seat. As I move away from the car, it floats in the air behind me.

I wish I had the same magic for the suitcase, I think as I hobble down the wonky path. I hobble, smack, hobble, smack. With each stride, the damn thing bounces in the ruts and smacks against my leg. The sore one. I grit my teeth, lift my eyes, and take in the hotel. The Sanctuary appears to be a gatehouse to a stately home. A squat, mini castle. It even has—I'll have to Google the name—a flat roof with the castle-like square spikes along the pitch. I bet it once had a turret.

Even in the dark, I can see the rundown state of it, which makes me sad. The place could be incredibly beautiful, but it would take some serious money to restore it and give it the modern twist it needs, while retaining its history. That might be why someone turned it into a hotel, in an attempt to get it to pay for itself. But the whole place screams money pit.

About twelve feet from the door, the heavens open and I am pelted with freezing cold Scottish rain. I'm instantly drenched. I can't feel my face. With rain dribbling down the back of my neck, I mournfully think of the warm waterproof coat I left in the car as I scurry the final few feet to the door. With relief, it opens and I hurry inside.

I wrinkle my nose as I am instantly hit by the odour of feet. Nice.

The interior is as sad as the exterior; they have ripped the heart out of this poor old building. I see touches of grandeur peeking out, screaming for restoration. I shake my head and hobble to the wooden reception desk and ring the bell.

As I wait for someone to come, my eyes drift back around the room. What a waste. If I could draw, or had an aptitude for math, I would have loved to have been an architect or a designer. I guess life impedes your passions.

I smile and shake my head. Whenever a new housing development pops up, I can't help having a nosy at their floor plans.

I can spend hours on the internet going through the drawings and analysing the room shapes, mentally redesigning the layouts or appreciating clever designs. I know it's nuts. Looking at building plans is a weird hobby, but I like it. I once spent an entire month studying a manor house that had been converted into fancy apartments. Wow, they did an incredible job.

Building my own home is definitely on my bucket list. Sometimes to get to sleep when my brain is too busy from work, I build houses in my head. It's a quirk. I guess everyone has some strange thing they do. I haven't got the skills to build a house, but it doesn't stop me from mentally doing it anyway. It comforts me enough to sleep. I drum my fingers on the desk and try to peek through the tucked away staff door. I'll give them a few more minutes before I ring the bell again.

There is this one particular building I design over and over again. I've landscaped it into a perfect world. It has beautiful windows and a lake and mountain views. I turn and slump against the desk and... funny, I can almost see it being adapted to this hotel. I rub my face and groan. Look at me in a smelly hotel reception area, dreaming.

A throat clears behind me. I squeak and spin around.

"Hi." I wave. "I didn't hear you." Rainwater drips from the sleeve of my jumper and plops onto the floor. Oops.

"It happens all the time." The receptionist, or night manager—whatever his job title—smiles.

He could be between thirty and sixty. His age doesn't show clearly on his face. That isn't unusual in this world. As a witch, I will age the same as a human. Quickly. Witch's lives are fleeting compared to the creatures that live alongside us. Shifters and born vampires are practically immortal. So meeting someone with an unageing face and ancient eyes isn't far from the norm. But my wacky magic is screaming at me that something is off about this guy.

That is disconcerting.

I surreptitiously check his ears for the tell-tale point of an elf. But his ears are rounded. He isn't a shifter and there isn't the distinctive smell of rot that I associate with turned vampires.

But still, he feels off.

Fae? His dark red hair gleams under the lights and the longer I stand there, staring at him like a proper weirdo, the more his dull green eyes brighten. They sparkle with excitement. This isn't him putting on a show and being polite to a customer—no, it is genuine.

Joy.

Maybe that's my problem? I am so used to people not being impressed when they see me. Perhaps his beaming smile is throwing me off completely.

The negative voice in my head that I usually associate with my mum tells me to sleep in the car. But my inner voice, the one that I always stubbornly listen to, purrs with contentment. It's like I have come home.

What the heck is that all about?

"Hi." My hand flaps again in a feeble wave. It's as if my limb has a mind of its own. I pin it to my side and smile sheepishly.

"You're here. Finally," he says with poorly veiled glee. He claps his hands. The guy is practically bouncing on the spot. He is positively glowing. "I can't believe it—"

"Oh no, you must have me confused with someone else," I quickly interrupt. Oh heck, now I feel bad. I don't want to be the reason that his glowy smile leaves his face. "My car broke down." I point lamely over my shoulder, in the direction of the car park. "Yeah, the power of the car got sucked right out. Even my phone stopped working." I narrow my eyes.

"Oh... well, okay." He scratches his nose. "That explains a lot," he mutters, but then he beams a warm smile at me and claps his hands again. "Let's get you booked in. I presume you're staying and don't want to just use the phone?"

"Yes, please. I'll stay for the night."

"Perfect, that's perfect." He spins and pulls a key from the old-fashioned key hooks hanging on the wall. Twelve rooms. The key from the number one hook is missing, which means there might be another guest. He places the key to room twelve on the desk and then drops to a crouch.

My hand strays to my pocket with the sleeping gun. What is he doing? As I rise on my toes to peer over the desk to see what he is up to, he pops back up with a—I frown—I can only describe it as a tome. It smacks down so hard that the desk vibrates.

What the heck is that?

Has this guy never heard of a computer? No wonder the place is so quiet. Wide-eyed, I stare at the enormous book.

The old spine creaks as he opens it to a blank page, and as he spins it towards me, dust and god knows what sprinkles onto the desk. I wrinkle my nose.

"If you would just pop down your name and sign here." He points to a spot and places a pen next to the book.

I shimmy forward and glance down at where his finger is indicating.

"Here?" I ask with a frown.

I read fiction; I don't read tome or whatever the heck this is. *Should I really be signing my name into an ancient-looking book?* Urm, no.

No, I should not.

Crap. I can feel my whole body ache with disappointment. It seems we will be sleeping in the car. I wish I had a human-sized version of Daisy's travel bubble. I open my mouth to make an excuse and then—

I'm signing the stupid book.

What the fuck? What happened?

I blink a few times and take the offered key. I blink again and then I am standing in a clean but shabby room. Which thankfully doesn't smell of feet.

What the heck just happened? Was that magic?

The same magic that messed up the car and the phone? I sink to the bed and put my head in my hands. "I've gone and done it now. Signed my life away. Demons. I bet demons are involved." I shudder. "My parents are going to kill me." Ha, the first thing that comes to mind is the inevitable "I told you so" lecture from my parents, not dying horribly. "I am seriously fudged up."

Then there is this feeling, an inner feeling of being safe, of being home.

I've never felt that.

Wow, now that's sad. I've never felt safe or content, no matter how successful I have become professionally. I've always felt something is off, missing, and that I am... in the wrong place. Now everything inside me screams I'm okay. Here is where I am meant to be.

I flop back onto the bed. I know a lot about magic. Even though I am a dud, I'm still a witch. I have felt the worst kind of magic as it trips my tongue and controls my words. My fists clench. Yeah, thanks to my mum, I have had years of a potion working on my mind, so I can tell when I am artificially being controlled. I can feel it. This isn't that. No matter how powerful magic can be, it can't alter what you feel inside. Your inner voice.

I pluck at the covers and my eyes trace the lines of a dark blob on the ceiling. I need to be honest; it wasn't magic that made me sign that book—well, not outside magic anyway—it was something inside me. My face scrunches up. I think it was like, inner me took hold of my body, took me for a joy ride for a few minutes. I shake my head and blow out a breath.

And isn't that freaky?

What I feel about this place is genuine. It must be. But that doesn't mean I am going to be an idiot and walk around blindly. No, it just means I am going to find out what the heck is going on. Tomorrow.

With a tired groan, I get up. I pull the plastic gun from my pocket and pop it on the bedside table within easy reach.

Even though I feel like crap and my head is swimming with fatigue, I'm also feeling icky from the long car journey, so I run myself a bath. I don't have a bathtub in my flat, so having a long soak is a well-deserved treat.

Before I strip off, I dig out a temporary ward and set it up to protect the entire room. It's a strong one, with both Diane and Jodie's combined magic. At least if anything untoward happens, I will have a warning as the ward will wake me up.

I check the floor for safety, making sure there's nothing hidden that could hurt Daisy, and then I touch her travel bubble and the door opens. Inside, my little dragon is adorably snoring.

When she wakes up, she'll be able to come in and out as she pleases.

Though, knowing Daisy, she'll wait till the very last moment to pee, so I set the bubble close to the bathroom and use another tray and remaining shavings for a temporary dragon toilet before also setting up her food and water.

I then fiddle with the phone. Miraculously, it works.

Hi Owen, it's Tuesday. I am safe, but the car died. I think it's an electric issue. I didn't crash it! I'm staying the night at The Sanctuary Hotel. It's about thirty minutes from the safe house. Will you do me a favour and let my coven know? The phone you gave me also has an issue and it keeps dying. I will use the hotel phone to ring my dad in the morning. Thank you x

I quickly press send before the phone can decide to quit and the message wings its way into the ether.

Ah crap. I wince when I re-read it. The kiss at the end. *A kiss.* I groan and rub the back of my neck. Why did I do that? I added it on without thinking. I nibble on my nail. Of course, it's gone now. *Then* the stupid phone flashes and the screen goes grey. It shuts down. Dead.

Gah. I tap the phone against my thigh as I rub my face. At least he knows where I am, right? In my mind's eye, I see Miss Piggy dramatically blow a kiss to an unimpressed Kermit while saying kissy-kissy-kissy. A kiss on a text is friendly, right? With another wince and a helpless shrug, I stuff the phone away.

I groan at the splash in the steamy bathroom and the echoing flap of wet wings. "Oh, it sounds like it is dragonette bath time," I grumble. "I hope they've given me a lot of towels. We're going to need them."

Before I enter the bath battlefield, I drop to my knees and open the suitcase. I push the knives Forrest has packed for me to the side. Who needs six silver blades and two iron ones, but no underwear? That woman has serious issues.

I pop a knife on the bedside table and empty my pockets of all potions, lining them up for easy throwing, just in case.

A small giggle of disbelief slips from my lips as I grab some fluffy, pink *unicorn* pyjamas. Although they are adorable, I would never in a million years buy them for myself.

Knives and unicorns. Forrest seems really weird.

CHAPTER NINE

I DREAMED of a world that I painstakingly pieced together using my architect visions of perfection, from elegant rooms to the minute detail of a single blade of grass. It was glorious.

When I wake up in the cloud-like bed, I feel odd and heavy. As if my conscience has returned to my body. I am so comfortable, I immediately want to go back to sleep. There is a clink next to my ear as if a plate has been carefully set down on the bedside table, the one closest to my head.

That is when I smell the bacon.

I groan and turn my head to where the smell originates. I wiggle like a worm as I unbury myself from underneath the covers. Peeking out, I sniff, and the scent of delicious, crispy bacon flies up my now flaring nostrils.

On the bedside table, placed carefully between potions and the plastic gun, is a toasted bacon butty, and a mug of steaming tea.

I blink.

A bead of tomato ketchup rolls down the crust and plops onto the plate. Oh my, that looks amazing. That has got to be Warburtons Toastie bread.

Where the heck did that come from?

I hold my breath for a second and wait for movement. Empty. No one is here. "Has someone been in my room? I knew this whole place was sketchy." When you freakily sign an ancient tome to stay at a mysterious hotel and later almost have a panic attack 'cause you might have signed your life away, nowhere in that nightmare scenario would I have expected crispy bacon and a cup of tea.

My tummy gurgles as if to say, *mmm bacon*. I blink a few more times and rub away the pool of drool before it reaches my chin. It is then that I notice the room. My drool hand flops onto the bed and my mouth falls open in shock. My head swivels. Instead of it being a rundown nightmare, it is like I am in a six-star hotel or a gazillion pound apartment. My entire face scrunches up with a frown. Well, this is unexpected.

Bloody hell. I fling the covers away and scramble up. But I forget how to use my legs and instead sort of roll out of bed. I slide ungraciously to the floor, the soft spongy carpet cushioning my bottom. Wide-eyed and with my heart pounding, stomach forgotten, I stare at the room.

The room that is mine.

Mine.

More than mine—it's bloody what I made up in my head. What I have dreamed of for years. Outside, through the new floor-to-ceiling windows, are familiar rolling hills, a distant forest and... a lake.

"This is fudged up."

In my sleep, I reshaped a world.

I gasp.

Then wheeze.

Woah, I cannot get enough air into my lungs. I rub and slap my palm to my chest. *Breathe, Tuesday, you will not lose your shit.* Black dots appear in my vision, dancing in front of my eyes. I am losing my shit. *Calm down and just think.* I viciously pinch the skin on the top of my hand and wince. Ouch. Yeah, I'm awake. This isn't a dream—no, it's magic.

My whole body shivers.

"It's not like you are being attacked by Power Ranger mercenaries," I reason. I am not in any immediate danger, and no one is breaking down my door. Instead of jumping up and running around the room like a chicken with its head cut off, I take a deep breath, hold it, and slowly breathe out. I concentrate on breathing until my heart rate is back to a regular rhythm and my body has stopped twitching with the need to run. *Panicking only gets you hurt,* I remind myself.

I grab the plate from the side and take a big bite of the breakfast sandwich. Why the heck not? The bacon crunches, and as the greasy taste hits my tongue, I groan. It's made perfectly.

As I chew, I do my best to push away my initial shock. I don't know how I know it, but I do. Now that I can think a little bit clearer, I can *feel* the magic. Somehow, I did this. This is *my magic.*

Bloody hell.

I've gone from a magic dud to being full to the brim. I can't work out if this is a dream come true or my worst nightmare. Magic that I have never had is pounding through my chest, zipping down my arms and legs. The hand not stuffing my face taps my head to make sure my hair isn't standing on end. It is like I have stuffed my finger in a light socket, and I'm being electrocuted. It is as if I am now part of an electric circuit.

I grab the tea and take a big gulp. I think back to what the fae guy said. The elf. *Hello, little lost witch. I am told you're a dud, but you're more than that, aren't you? Your coven has hidden you well.* I pop the last bite of the butty into my mouth. *It's been over a century since I've met one of your kind in the real world. Stupid of you, really.*

"Your coven has hidden you well," I mumble. Well, he got that wrong. My coven—my parents—didn't hide me from this. Oh no, this would be the equivalent of my mum winning a rollover in the National Lottery. "Real world?" I sip the tea and lean back against the bed. As I roll the words around my head—*real world*—I rap my fingernails against the mug and stare down into the tea. The remaining liquid dances to the rhythm of my fingers. Perhaps he wasn't blowing smoke. Perhaps he got something right.

Daisy's claws dig into the soft carpet as she moves toward me, a piece of cucumber gripped between her teeth. It's her favourite snack. A snack that appeared just like my breakfast. She climbs into my lap, joining me in the impromptu picnic on the floor, and noisily crunches.

A world I created. Like... like *a pocket realm.*

No.

There is an odd, unpleasant little jump in my chest. No. Whoever made pocket dimensions didn't make them this big. I huff in disbelief. Small rooms and bags to hide equipment. Not... I lean forward and stare out at the forest, at the hills and the bloody lake. Acres and acres of land. Whatever the heck this is, it cannot be that.

Yet, I know every inch of this place. For years, I have been building this in my head. There's no getting away from the fact that I made this.

I rub my face and shake my head. They are a myth.

World walkers, world makers.

Godlike power.

My stomach is suddenly full of butterflies, and I can't help shivering as the small hairs on my body all rise at once.

Everything about them has been conjecture.

Witches—we can make portals, fixed doorways linking places together using the Earth's ley lines. But someone before us made portals to other worlds. That knowledge was said to be lost. Some people said it died with some extinct creature. Others, mainly the witches, said it was a branch of magic that had become extinct.

The only sign of their existence was what they left behind: pocket dimensions. Which are coveted and go for vast sums of money. I stare back outside. To think, as soon as my car rolled down the driveway, I wasn't in Scotland anymore. Goosebumps erupt along my arms. Portals, pocket dimensions, and artificial magic worlds are strange places. If a creature is strong enough and magically tied to it, the dimension can shift and change. But not to this extent. This is so far beyond the small, sad hotel and scrabbly patch of land of last night.

My tummy flips again. I rub my arms, the fluffy pink unicorn pyjamas rise with the movement and my breath catches as— "What now?" I whine.

I stare at my arms. My skin is covered with magical tattoos.

Glowing tattoos.

I gently place the still munching dragon on the carpet and scramble up. I hurry into the bathroom, pull off the unicorn top and peek into the opulent mirror. Glowing silver lines curve complex patterns across my entire body. I cautiously lean into the mirror and trace the delicate dancing swirls on *my face*.

In shock, I stare at myself for several minutes.

Instead of detracting, they highlight my cheekbones and light up my eyes like the best kind of makeup. I don't hate them. *It is like they always should have been there*. No, that is crazy thinking. I back away from the mirror and my naked back hits the cold tiles.

I am frightened but I can't escape the facts. This hotel, this place, this world? Has made *me* magical.

Ha.

My mum is going to shit a brick.

CHAPTER
TEN

I DECIDE to explore the hotel and get some answers. I have my trusty sleep pistol after all. Which will probably be useless to anyone who can wield magic that can change a world and procure bacon on toast with Heinz tomato ketchup.

Tuesday, it's you. It's your magic. I ignore that pesky inner voice for a moment as I need to hunt for answers, and although this fancy apartment is amazing, I can't stay here and hide. No, I need to get dressed. Find answers.

The wardrobe has changed from the hotel's basic one to a full walk-in, and it's full to the brim with clothes.

Like the bacon butty, I don't know where these clothes came from. I glance back at the mug and plate I left carelessly on the floor. They've disappeared. The hotel is self-cleaning. Aha. That is perfectly normal.

With wide eyes and slightly hunched shoulders, I turn back, and without going inside, I cautiously poke at the clothes. They sway, and the wooden hangers rattle and screech against the rail.

Has someone, somewhere, found their clothes missing this morning? Do they disappear from individuals? Is this where missing socks go? Or is some poor retail manager going to find that they have missing stock?

It's. Magic.

It's got to be magic. So, that then begs the question: if I wear magic clothing, will it leave me naked in the outside world? What happens if someone slaps me with another null band again? Will the clothes disappear like magic hair colour? Gah, so many questions. I am developing a headache.

I blow out a harsh breath that ruffles a strand of my hair, then push all my questions to the back of my mind. I shuffle into the wardrobe and take a proper gander at the clothes.

I work in a department store that's full of designer gear. I have an eye for quality. I can't help the excited shiver that runs down my spine when I see my favourites. Favourite styles, brands—this is clothing that I could never afford or stuff that I have talked myself out of buying.

I pull out a drawer. It is filled to the brim with expensive underwear.

Within moments, I whip off my unicorn pyjamas. I dress in soft, black trousers and a beautiful, long-sleeved but lightweight top that has a colourful butterfly print. Girly, but also professional, and the trousers are a perfect fit. There is no need for me to dress so smartly; I could put on the jogging bottoms I wore yesterday and a hoodie. But what I am wearing feels right. Power dressing? I shrug. Perhaps.

To finish the look, I grab a pair of black, sparkly trainers. Practical footwear in case I need to run. I think I have already established that I won't be doing any Kung Fu fighting. So getaway shoes are a must. As I stuff my feet in them, I notice they are Gucci. Gucci trainers.

This is nuts.

I leave Daisy to nap. I need her safe in the room. As I close the main door, I double-check the ward. Again, I have no idea how it's still up. What with the room being about six times bigger and all. But it is still there, still working. It will stop any creature from getting inside.

Not for the first time, I fret about leaving her alone. One day soon, I will get my girl a friend.

I PULL the heavy door and step into a very different lobby. My heart makes a quiet leap in my chest. Old and new now mash perfectly together, leaving a breathtakingly beautiful entrance to the hotel. If this magic is all me, I reeeally have outdone myself. Seeing in real life what I have dreamed of for so long is seriously perplexing.

"Where's the guy?" I mumble as I take in the empty reception.

"Larry? He's gone," says a refined voice behind me. I barely refrain from jumping out of my skin and instead, hunch like a tortoise as I try to disappear into a non-existent shell. I spin around.

"Oh," I say when I see the man who is sitting in a chair behind me. Where did he come from? I don't know what to say. I presume this is the guest from room number one. He seems oddly familiar. Short, black hair that matches his black eyes, his skin is almost plastic in its perfection. He looks alien, like he is a walking mannequin.

Pureblood vampire, my frightened inner voice whines.

A born vampire.

I lock my knees so I don't take a step back. *Show no fear, Tuesday. You're his walking, talking version of a bacon butty.* I swallow and try my best to control my breathing. In my mind's eye, I can see myself covered in ketchup and slapped between two slices of bread. I shudder and push the freaky image away.

These past few days have been an eye-opener when it comes to creatures. An elf, a hellhound, and now a pureblood vampire.

I so didn't need to add vampires to the crazy mix.

I have definitely seen him before, but where? TV? Born vampires are rare and most of them are famous. They are the elite, often the top movie stars of our world. *Atticus.* My eyes widen when his name comes to me. What is the head of the vampire council doing here? This guy is super old, super powerful, and way above any experience I have in dealing with all things creature.

I am getting a little freaked out by his cold, expressionless, black eyes as they take me in, his gaze tracing the swirls on my face. I rock slightly from foot to foot and tamp down the urge to hide my face with my hair. Thank goodness I dressed nicely. When he has finished his appraisal, he politely holds his hand out to me.

I automatically shake it. It's warm and silky smooth.

"Atticus," he says with a little bow of his head. I barely stop myself from checking his feet to see if he clapped them together.

He is so formal.

"Tuesday. Tuesday Larson." I cough slightly to clear my throat. My voice is several octaves higher than normal. "You are the head of the vampire council," I point out like a divvy, but I can't stop now as I am on a roll. I decide to wing it even more like I always do. "What are you doing here?"

Has he been lured here too? Or did he do the luring? Crikey, now that's a thought.

"I'm your guest," he purrs. "The Sanctuary is my permanent residence, has been for over a thousand years. With you here, your realm should finally be able to return to the collective of dimensions."

Blood rushes to my head, and I wobble. What? My realm? The collective of dimensions? Crap-on-a-cracker. I have so many questions that I am practically bursting. I guess I need to start small. If I don't, my brain is going to explode.

Should I even trust this man? "It's a pocket dimension?"

"A pocket realm." *Ah, I was close then; one point to Tuesday.* "This is your world, your dimension. It became yours as soon as you arrived and took control. You control the air we breathe, the seasons, and everything we see and hear. There is nothing you can't do."

Atticus moves closer, and I watch, dumbfounded, as he slowly reaches out his hand and gently, with just his fingertips, touches my collar bone. My skin crawls. I barely refrain from slapping his hand away. "The well of power that laps like an immense silver ocean inside of you has been untapped. After a few scant hours of being here, it has come to the surface. A single drop of power while you slept and look what has already happened." He waves his elegant hand in the air. "See what you have achieved without even trying. You are incredible."

This isn't happening. It's not happening. This can't be real, can it?

An incredulous laugh bubbles up in my chest and spills from my lips. I shake my head as I move away from his fingers, and twitch with the urge to wipe away the feeling of his touch. I don't like the strange vampire touching me. His head tilts to the side with a snap and my laughter dies. Friggity-fig, he is scary.

I suddenly wish I was staring into the soft grey eyes of the hellhound, instead of this creature. His black eyes remind me of a shark.

"How is this realm mine? Oh, and have you by any chance got a contact I can speak to about this?" I know I can't quiz a pureblood vampire like I would a random man from the pub. But the desperate words will not stop. "The collective dimensions?" I squeak out with a wince. *Shut up. You are being rude.*

Atticus's black eyes narrow. "I have to say, your cluelessness is endearing." He nods at the tome that still sits on the now fancy reception desk. This one sure appears steadier than the last. "You have a lot of reading to do. When the last host died"—I mouth the word *host*. Huh. Interesting —"the magic allowed me to continue to make The Sanctuary my home. There are other hosts, other worlds, and a guild."

"A guild?"

"The details will be in the book."

I glare at the book. Do I really have to read that thing? It will take me a year. I rub my temple. The heavy tome twitches. I narrow my eyes. What was that? The pages flutter and, with a creak, the ancient-looking thing rattles harder against the wood. Woah. The book wobbles and then, with a flash of blinding white magic, a fancy tablet appears in its place.

I rapidly blink.

The vampire grunts. "Interesting," he mutters. I cringe and give him a hapless shrug. Done with our conversation, he dismisses me with the same nod he greeted me with and prowls away.

I watch him leave with growing panic. "Oh, urm... sir? Urm... Atticus!" I yell. "Do I need to do anything? For you, I mean... I've never run a h-hotel before. Do you need t-towels?"

His head turns and his lips sort of tilt in a semblance of a teeny, tiny smile. "Your magic will meet my needs. Read the—" He shakes his head. "That." He points to the desk and disappears down the hallway.

"Okay, thank you." My hands flap to my sides and I turn to take a hesitant step toward the innocuous-looking tablet. "Ooookay," I grumble.

I shuffle closer to the desk and scoop it up. It is a datapad, a ZS-T, which is the latest model. I turn on the screen and wait impatiently, drumming my fingers on the desk. "Thanks for explaining everything, *Larry*." My top lip lifts in a snarl. Is this place so bad that he did not want to stick around to tell me what's what? Not even a basic handover. As soon as I got my room key, he must have scarpered. No wonder he looked so happy.

The screen of the datapad remains blank. Did I break it? I press the power button a few more times.

"I broke it," I mutter. What the heck am I going to do now? My heart feels like it drops through my chest. What do I do now?

I'm playing with this magic—unknown, powerful magic. I have no idea what the hell I am doing.

The magic just randomly does shit.

I'm so out of my depth... The datapad brightens and a cursor blinks. My mouth pops open as I watch the letters appear.

It writes: *'Hello, Tuesday. What would you like to know?'* The cursor blinks and my hand hovers, frozen over the screen.

Uh-oh. If that isn't the creepiest thing I have ever seen.

CHAPTER
ELEVEN

I STARE at the datapad as I nibble my lip. Huh, now that's interesting. I trace my bottom lip with my tongue. It's not sore like it was last night. I frown. When I went to sleep, it was a chapped mess. I must have healed overnight. I rub my chest, puff out my cheeks, and ignore it for now. It's such a small thing when compared to all the magic stuff.

Now back to the tablet that knows my name. What the heck do I type? I huff and strum the desk. "I need to know everything," I mumble.

'You need to be a bit more exact.'

I almost drop the datapad with shock. Wide-eyed, I gently set it down. I can't help the small, manic laugh that spills from my mouth. I poke and pull at my healed lip, squishing it between my thumb and finger. I don't even have to type; the tome slash datapad is listening and has a sense of humour.

Good to know. Clinging to the reception desk, I shuffle stiffly sideways from the haunted tablet. The cursor on the datapad blinks a little faster.

I clear my throat. "Um, is someone here trying to hurt me?"

'No,' is the curt reply.

I clear my throat again. My mouth is so dry, the salty bacon from breakfast has made me thirsty. I have bacon tongue. The tell-tale clack of a cup and sudden heat next to my hand causes me to drop my eyes to the desk to see a fresh, steaming mug of tea.

Oh boy, they really do pop out of thin air. "Thank you," I say with a nervous squeak. I shrug, pick up the tea, and take a big gulp. Fun fact: I regularly thank inanimate objects. Like cash machines. I've even been known to have entire conversations with a difficult mannequin at work. Unless you've dressed one of those things, you have no idea how awkward the limbs are. So, saying thanks to the magic—magic that works for me for the first time in my life—is the polite thing to do.

Oh! Am I a genie? Is this pocket world like a genie's bottle? If my magic can just make things appear, does that mean hotel guests get three wishes? I huff out a strangled laugh. A genie isn't a creature that exists in this world. I rub my forehead a little too vigorously. Now I know I'm overthinking things. If I am not careful, it won't be long before I'm rocking in a corner and crying.

I clutch the mug and take another mouthful. The tea is delicious.

Oh crap, another thought hits me. I hope I'm talking to the magic, or what was once the book. I don't think I could bear it if Larry, the manager guy from last night, is hidden in a secret room somewhere, watching me and laughing his arse off.

I lean both elbows on the desk. Staying here wouldn't be too horrendous. I'm an introvert at heart. A homebody. I like to be in my own space, doing my own thing. But that still doesn't help the worry in my chest. I have commitments. I mean, what about work? I've been the company superstar since I started at sixteen. I have the lofty accolade of being the youngest general manager in the company's history.

Eight years. Eight bloody years. So much time and effort wasted if I walk away. I huff. I've never even taken a sick day. What are they going to think when I give them zero notice? Oh, this is just awful. Maybe I can somehow take the magic with me? I take another sip of tea.

Yeah, I like being at home but there is a big difference between choosing to stay at home, and not being allowed to leave.

"Am I trapped?"

'No, you are not trapped.'

Okay. So, no one is saying I can't leave, and it's not like I'm stuck in a room on my own. The realm is beautiful. There is an entire world outside the hotel, miles and miles to explore. That's kind of amazing.

Out of the corner of my eye, the damn datapad cursor blinks impatiently.

But... I hate change. I hate the unknown. I hate bloody magic. I hate this entire situation.

"If I leave, what will happen?"

'The realm will go into stasis to wait for another host. Over time, it will slowly crumble until nothing remains.

You will live the life you had before as a mortal witch. The magic that you have inside you will be untouchable on the outside. If you stay, power beyond your wildest dreams, omnipotent magic, and immortality.'

Oh. I blink in time with the cursor. Isn't that how supervillains are made? *Great.* Or superheroes...

'If you leave, so does your new magic.'

If I leave, I return to being the dud witch. Well, that is not something I want to do. Does that make me a bad person? I also don't want to be trapped in a pocket dimension forever. And immortality? That's a scary can of worms.

Maybe I am in a coma, and this isn't real. Maybe it's some wacky, made up dream. I rub the reception desk with my index finger and finish the tea. It feels real.

It feels right.

Leaving all this behind is unfathomable. I tilt my head back and take in the beautiful lobby. I don't need to gaze outside to know this place is perfect. I put myself—my soul—into the fabric of this realm. Even if I didn't know what I was doing at the time.

This is where I'm meant to be. I can run away back to my flat, back to my not-so-perfect life, or I can be brave, explore this strange new magic, and find out who I am.

Grab a hold of my destiny.

I shiver. Wow, I'm not so much a sidekick anymore, am I?

"How does this work? How do we get guests?"

'You help the people who are in search of sanctuary.'

"That simple, huh?" I gripe. "What about bad people? Can my magic handle creatures popping in all willy-nilly?" *It could be millions of people.* I'm twenty-four. I don't think my retail management training covers running an entire world. Nervous sweat trickles down between my shoulder blades.

'It's your dimension, your rules,' it types. The words run together in my mind. The whoosh and thud-thud of my heart overwhelm my senses. I feel sick. How the hell am I going to do this? A whole bloody world. This magic isn't supposed to exist. I can't do this. I hate magic.

The reality of everything hits me with the force of a double-decker bus. I ignore the magic tablet and push away from the desk.

"Fuck." The swear word echoes around the lobby, and I slam a shaky hand across my lips. What the heck was that? Did I just swear out loud? Crikey, the anti-swear spell my mum had forced upon me must have broken.

My brain must have healed like my lip.

A painful hiccup jolts me. The spell is *broken*. "The spell that's been the bane of my life is gone." I flick my fingers. "Just like that."

It's not the only thing that's broken.

A strangled half laugh, half sob bubbles up my throat along with another blasted hiccup that rattles my chest. "This is wank," I whisper. The naughty word feels alien on my tongue. "Wankity, wank, wank, wank." With each swear word, my voice gets a little louder, shriller, until the last word and I'm screaming. "WANK!" I shove both hands over my mouth to hold the craziness in. Oh my, I'm going mad.

My legs are so wobbly, I can't take a step. I can't get away. Instead, for the second time today, like a sack of spuds, I sink to the floor. I slam my back against the desk and clutch my knees to my chest.

Why me?

I have learned to live with my lack of magic. I came to terms with my mediocrity years ago. I have finally got a handle on my life, and I am content with the person I am. So what if I don't have a talent? I've never been good at anything, but that's okay. I'm good at my job. I'm a wonderful manager. A nice person.

Now everything has changed again. The goalposts have moved to another bloody dimension.

Why? Everything was going okay. Why did I have to have a sneaky hidden power that comes out of nowhere to ruin my perfectly boring life? Why did I get hit with the weird shit? *I will always be on the outside of the supernatural world. Always the freak.*

I shake my head, and my hair rustles as it rubs against the wood at my back. *Magic.* It will always misbehave and cause me no end of frustration. There is no escape. There has never been an escape. I am doomed.

Most people presume I'm human. I still get the odd, "Oh, you're a witch. What type of magic do you do?" How do you answer that? Say, "Yeah, I am the famous Larson witch who can't do magic, so nothing." It embarrasses them, or worse, the opposite thing happens, and they use that knowledge to belittle me.

In the real world, magic is used for everything. Technology, medicine, silly frivolous things like altering your hair, down to the fit of your clothes. Even as a non-practising witch, my life revolves around it. I cannot avoid it. I must use it in everyday life as it is integrated into the fabric of our society. It's an essential thing, like electricity.

I have learned to grin and bear it. But every time I use someone else's bottled magic, I get this crawling sensation in my gut.

Disgust.

Every time, I hate myself a little bit more. 'Cause the obvious screams at me: *I am not good enough. I never have been good enough.*

It's torture knowing if I had been born a little differently, I'd be capable of creating my own spells. Not buying them—and sure as hell not blowing them up.

I rock a little and rub my forehead on my knee. I thought I'd escaped. I thought I could ignore it. Embrace my beloved outcast role in life. I had that false smile fixed to perfection. "People can only hurt you if you let them" was my mantra. I isolated myself from the witch community, my parents, and my super talented sisters. I put myself in an emotional bubble. All safe.

"I was doing okay. Everything was finally going okay," I whine into my knees. Well, until those damn Power Ranger mercenaries bashed in my front door.

Now here I am, *buzzing with power.*

Buzzing with enough power that I can alter a magic realm with a single thought and make food and drink appear from thin air. Do things that even the strongest witch can't do and would probably kill for. It's a lot to take in.

Instead of being fixed, I am different again. "Is it too much to ask that I be a normal witch?" With a thud, I smack my head against the desk. I do it again to punish myself. To knock some sense into my stupid broken head.

Why does it have to be me? I swallow down my frustration and the festering pain that sits inside me. I've gone from being the witch who is an embarrassment to this…

A host. A world maker.

How the hell can I do this? I can't. There is no way. Fate chose the wrong person. I'm not strong enough. I'm not brave enough. I've spent my entire life so far running away from magic. Running away from everything. To do this, I will have to embrace everything I hate. The magic I hate. I can't do this. I can't. Not when I can't move from being a frozen pathetic lump on the floor.

Bloody hell, Tuesday, woman the fuck up.

I would but I'm so frightened. I wipe at the stupid tears that are streaming down my face. I am so bloody frightened.

The mobile Owen gave me rings, and its shrill tone scares me half to death. I almost ignore it. I almost sink into the pity party I'm throwing myself. Almost. I sniff and robotically drop my knees and lift my bum from the floor so I can get my fingers into the tight pocket. I answer, and with a shaky hand, put the phone to my ear.

"Hello?" I croak.

"Where are you, Flash?" His voice is rough. He sounds worried. Listening to him and that silly nickname somehow centres me and smashes through the dark layers of my panic and fear. Without knowing it, he lends me a little bit of strength.

"I'm in a pocket dimension," I rasp.

"A pocket dimens—" He blows into the receiver and the sound rustles. I think he rubs his face. "Wow, you have been busy."

"Yes." I hiccup a sob.

"Okay, do you need help? Do you want me to come and get you? Tell me what you need."

Do you need help? Unless they're being paid, no one has ever asked me that before. *Woah there, don't make it something it's not. Don't forget Dad sent him.* I sniffle. It has been so long since I asked anyone for help. "Please," I say through the lump in my throat.

"Ah shit, Tuesday, you're killing me here. Are you safe?"

"Yes." I think so.

"Can you get out?"

"I don't know... Y-yes, maybe?"

There's a pause as he thinks through what I'm not saying. "Do you want to leave?"

"Things are... complicated."

"We can fix complicated together. So the entrance to this pocket dimension is in Scotland?"

"I think so." *I wish I could wave a magic wand and bring him here.*

My hands and feet tingle, and the swirling patterns I can see etched on my skin begin to move in time with the pounding of my heart. *What?* I have the urge to scratch at my arms and tear the marks off my skin. *I don't like this.* I draw in big, panicky gulps of air, but the oxygen in the room has thickened, and it is almost impossible to breathe. My chest aches and my throat burns. *Something is happening.*

"Tuesday? Tuesday? Flash, talk to me." The phone slips from my hand and clatters to the floor. My ears buzz and whoosh like I am underwater.

Pain shoots across my chest and the magic—my magic—floods out of me. My back bows and my head smacks against the wood. A terrified scream leaves my lips. With frightened tears streaming down my face, I watch as the magic hits a spot in the centre of the room and spreads out.

The area gets darker. It shimmers. Then, like it is made of glass and I have just taken a hammer to it, reality splinters.

The very fabric of the world cracks. The crack widens and a black hole appears. It's round and so dark, it is like I have made a black hole into the universe. A black, endless hole that will suck me inside.

My feet scrabble against the floor, and I press back against the wooden desk. My shoulder blades and spine dig into the ornate surface. *What the fuck is that?* I have never felt this frightened. An ominous feeling of impending doom is screaming through my bones. I feel so bloody helpless. Even when the mercenaries came and the elf attacked me, what I felt was child's play compared to this.

I don't know how I know—perhaps some inbuilt thing inside me recognises the sensation—but the pocket realm adds its magic to the mix until the rippling hole solidifies. The colour changes from black to dark green, and it stabilises. There is movement. A massive shadow appears in the centre of the hole and a person walks through.

"Oh my goodness, this isn't happening. It is not happening," I mutter as I slam my eyes closed. I'm done. I'm not brave enough to look upon my impending death. There is a whisper of movement, and instead of eating my face off, a big warm body smoothly sits on the floor beside me.

"Hey, Flash, you're okay. I'm here." The hellhound tucks me into his side. A warm, solid, enormous arm folds around me, enveloping me in the best kind of hug.

Owen.

It is Owen.

I let out a relieved sob and I sag into his arms. "What? How? I don't understand," I say, mumbling into his very solid chest.

"You sent a portal."

"No... I didn't. That is not possible." I pull away and gape up at him in disbelief. "I sent a portal?"

"Well, I presumed it was you."

"But that is impossible. No one can make portals out of thin air." *No one can make a cup of tea appear from thin air either.* The magic is omnipotent. "So, I opened a portal? I guess it makes sense as I drove here using a magical driveway, so of course, I can open gateways to friends in other worlds without thinking about it." Why not? "Wait... You just hopped into a random portal?"

"You needed me," he says earnestly, looking down at me with those beautiful grey eyes. "You were crying, and you screamed. Of course, I jumped into the portal."

I shake my head in disbelief and hold him a little bit tighter. "Thank you. Don't do that again for me though; that was so dangerous. But thank you so much for coming."

"I never should have left you. I should have driven you my damn self. I'm an idiot. You're not getting away from me again until I know you're safe," he grumbles into my hair.

"It's not your fault. It's mine." It was me. I was super insistent that I could drive myself. The thought of driving hours in the same car as Owen was... Let's just say, after I'd embarrassed myself so fully with the bottom zombie shuffle, I had a huge motivation for me to drive alone. When it comes down to it, at my core, I'm too introverted and awkward.

"What about the elf?" I say into the fabric of his chest.

"Forrest is hunting him as we speak. I'm here for you." It should feel weird that I'm allowing this man, a *hellhound* I've only just met, to manhandle me and offer me comfort. I ignore the voice of my mum that screams impropriety and instead snuggle closer into his warmth. "Don't you know?" His pause makes me lift my chin to peek at him. "We are bottom buddies." His eyes dance with mirth as I groan.

I tuck myself back into his side and let out a horrified laugh. *Bottom buddies*. Oh heck. I can't believe he made me laugh.

How can I not fall instantly in love with this man?

CHAPTER
TWELVE

Love, I scoff at my silly thoughts. What would the hellhound want with me? I don't know him. I lean against him anyway, and we sit quietly. There is no give in Owen. No softness in his body. It is all hard muscle and bones, wrapped in a harsh, predatory strength. I have never felt so safe.

Tuesday, he is an unattainable dream.

How can I expect anybody else to love me when the people who should love me unconditionally don't? They don't even like me. I am an embarrassment. I don't even make a good friend. All I want to do is stay at home, play games on my computer, watch TV, and read. I'm boring. My tummy flips and I move away from Owen's heat.

I'm a throwaway person.

I've been picked up and put down so many times that I now expect it; I expect to be thrown away. So, when I see this powerful, handsome man, my life experience up to now tells me he is so far out of my league that there is no point in even trying.

Yet, each moment I'm with him, he cradles my fears in his gigantic hands and he smothers me with genuine kindness. I've never met anyone like him. He is special. That is why I know when he gets a full look at the person I am... he'll be appalled. He will no doubt walk away like everyone else.

What would he want with me?

I have come a long way from the little girl who used to steal spells.

Sure, I have days when I wobble, when my heart hurts so much it's hard to get out of bed. The days when I'm starved for affection, and even when I am surrounded by people—I am alone. It's always been easier to hold myself back, to keep part of myself tightly wrapped, hidden away, so when the time comes, there will always be a small part of me left that will pick up the pieces and be there to stick the broken bits back together.

The only person who is going to be with me day in, day out, is me. So, I will temporarily borrow his strength, and when he leaves, which he will, I will be okay.

I will keep plodding on.

I roll my eyes. Bloody hell, I am annoying myself now. Boohoo, no one loves me. Other people have it way worse. I peek up at him through my loose hair. The silence has become awkward. I need to say something. "The datapad," I blurt out. My hand points to the tablet still on the desk above us. "It said if I stay here, I will be immortal."

"Oh. Well, you shouldn't believe everything you read."

"I know. It just freaked me out. This whole situation is scary. When I got here, this was a rundown hotel." I wave my hands wildly. "Does it look like that to you? Rundown?"

"No."

"I did this, Owen. I changed the pocket dimension somehow and now I don't know what to do. I'm a freak, a powerful freak, and perhaps immortal. Will I have to watch everyone die?" I bite my tongue to stop any more frantic words from spilling out of my mouth.

"Tuesday, everyone dies. There is no such thing as true immortality." I wince and blink at him through my scratchy and undoubtedly red eyes. That means a lot coming from a shifter.

Everyone dies. I guess being immortal is a subject he is aware of. Shifters are one of the so-called immortal races. But everyone knows shifters are a predominantly violent race.

"You are ancient, aren't you?"

The hellhound smiles down at me and shrugs. "I wouldn't say ancient. I've not hit a thousand yet, but I'm close."

"Wow." It's hard to get your head around that. I am so out of my depth with this guy, it's not even funny. Young shifters struggle to survive adolescence. To live to a hundred is an achievement, to be almost a thousand... Well, that means Owen is a very dangerous man.

I scramble up. I suddenly feel uncomfortable and a little silly to be sitting on the floor. I grab my phone and without discussing it, we both move away from the reception area and into the lounge. I sink into one of the comfortable chairs.

I watch as the hellhound circles the room, peeking through windows and checking behind doors for threats. If I relax my eyes to the point of my peripheral vision being hazy, I can see the hellhound's power as it wafts about the room. A shiver runs down my spine. I've never been able to do that before.

Finally, Owen chooses the vacated chair that the vampire sat in. I guess it gives him a perfect view of the room and all the doors.

"If you need help and I'm not around"—he takes the phone still clutched in my hand and inputs a number—"ring Forrest. She's the only one I trust to keep you safe. Even though she comes across as..." Owen sighs and rubs his eyebrow. "She's an amazing person and she'll die to keep you safe."

My eyes drift to the ceiling as I picture the just in case arsenal of knives next to the bed. The ones she packed in my bugout luggage along with the toy gun. Calling scary Forrest would be a last resort; I hope I'm never in such a dire situation to need her help. "Thank you. I'm sure I will be fine. I'm already feeling better. I am so sorry you had to see me like this. I don't normally..." I fake smile and shrug. "It's a lot to deal with."

Owen nods with understanding. He sits forward in the chair and his kind grey eyes trace the glowing tattoos on my face. "Are you going to explain?"

I nod and wiggle in the chair. My mouth is dry as a bone, probably more from nerves rather than the bacon. I don't know where to start.

Will he believe me?

There's a clack and a cup of tea and a mug almost overflowing with whipped cream and little marshmallows appear on the table in front of us. I frown at the unusual choice.

Owen picks up the froufrou drink. A pink marshmallow escapes the mountain of cream and rolls off the edge of the mug. His hand whips out and he snaps it from the air and pops it into his mouth. He grins at me and my insides twist. I have never had such a visceral response to another person. It is terrifying. He settles back in the chair, and as the hellhound takes in my incredulous expression, he sheepishly smiles.

"Thank you. That is one handy trick. Hot chocolate is my favourite drink." I blink at him. "Forrest's fault," he mumbles in explanation.

With the steam drifting from the cup warming my face, I animatedly tell him about what has happened so far. I finish with a flop of my hand. It's not even ten in the morning and I'm exhausted.

"The book you signed was the one you turned into a datapad?" Owen asks as he runs his hand through his short hair.

"Yes."

He nods. "I don't like this. But sometimes magic can't be explained logically, as you know." The hellhound leans towards me. "I don't need to tell you to be cautious." His warm breath breezes over my face and I am enveloped in his scent of cinnamon, vanilla, and the taste of chocolate on his breath.

He smells like the best cinnamon bun ever. Weirdly, my tummy rumbles and—clack. Mortified, I stare at the plate that appears. A huge, square cinnamon bun with lashings of white icing and a sprinkle of chocolate sits on the table between us. I have no doubt my face is bright red.

I shove the pastry into my mouth with a mumbled "thank you" to the magic. Yeah, thanks soooo much.

The hellhound watches in amusement. "Do you want one?" I ask after I swallow the mouthful. He shakes his head and laughs as he leans forward to pluck a piece of bun from my top.

Oh wow, did he just do that?

I huff out a small, mortified laugh. I can't believe I missed my mouth. With a whoosh, my entire face glows with an embarrassed heat. I wiggle and surreptitiously scan my top for any other surprises.

"You are adorable."

While I finish the pastry as quickly as possible, more cat than wolf, the hellhound slumps back in his chair. Each muscle is deceptively relaxed. Owen rubs his bottom lip with his thumb as he thinks. I avert my eyes as my stomach does a weird flip flop. Gosh, he is sexy.

And now I'm blushing again. My entire face is on fire. He is only here to keep me sane and to deal with this nightmare. It's not an opportunity to pant after him. I need to drag my mind out of the gutter. Be professional. I take a deep breath and ignore the fact that all I can smell is him.

I'm annoying myself.

I plant my elbow on the chair's arm and rest my warm cheek in my palm as I wrangle through the magic problem.

First, it's bloody day one of this freakfest. I need to stop being so hard on myself. I've always been an overachiever. I ignore the nasty voice in the back of my head that wants to point out that my so-called overachieving attitude never helped me with magic. I mentally give it the middle finger. The voice that still sounds distinctly like my mother can bog off. Now, I know for sure, I never was a normal witch. No matter how much I tried, I'd have never been able to achieve anything in the real world.

This whole thing is like starting a new job. I don't know anything, so I can't be cocky. I slump back in my chair, mirroring Owen's relaxed pose. Instead of looking at what I don't know, I need to change my thought process and focus on the things I do.

I nibble my lip. I don't feel trapped—it's like I'm at home in this pocket realm. My eyes drift to the phone in my lap. "It's cowboy time," I mutter. I narrow my eyes with a stray thought that makes my heart race. "Was the time the same when you left?"

"Ten to ten. Cowboy time." Owen barks out a laugh, and his grey eyes sparkle as he puts his empty mug onto the table. "I haven't heard that in years," he adds with a grin that would melt the knickers off a nun. I feel my cheeks heat again. "Yes, the time here is the same as home."

I give him a thankful nod. Phew. "Okay, so no time changes." That is a good thing. I've heard of some pocket dimensions where time is faster or slower and no one wants that.

What else? Okay, I also know my magic here is as easy as breathing. I can practically do whatever I want. I mean, I made a portal door out of nothing just to get Owen here. Not that it was easy—I thought I was going to die. Portals are supposed to be attached to ley lines, but I produced one out of thin air and stabilised it with my magic. That is unheard of crazy, and sort of ticks the box on omnipotent power. Now that I've opened a portal, something tells me it will be easier to open one again. I tap my thigh. I guess I'll have to practise these new freaky powers.

Yay. Great. Something to look forward to.

Without warning, Owen's nostrils flare and his hand shoots out towards my face. The empty cup in my hand slips from my grip, but before it hits the floor, it disappears. I let out an *eep* sound in terror and, wide-eyed, I jerk away from his massive limb.

"What the heck?" Did I say something wrong?

CHAPTER
THIRTEEN

Behind me, there's a panicked squeak and I turn my head to find a man wiggling in Owen's grip. "Larry?" It's the guy that checked me in, the missing staff member.

Owen's muscles are tense as he drags Larry around the back of my chair. The smaller man's hands claw desperately at the hellhound's wrist. His shoes squeak on the floor as he tries to scrabble away, and his eyes roll in his head like a frightened rabbit.

My hands shake uncontrollably from the adrenaline rushing through me. I wobble to my feet. Sitting makes me feel vulnerable. For a moment, I thought my new friend was going to hurt me.

Crikey, my heart is having palpitations. He scared the shit out of me.

"Tuesday, I'm sorry," Larry wails as our eyes meet. "I thought you'd be mad, so I used the tablet you made to talk to you. It was me." I knew it! Was he laughing at me too? "My job is to help you. But I don't know you and I didn't want you to kill me. Tuesday, please don't kill me."

"Tuesday kill you? I'm the one with my hand wrapped around your throat, dickhead," Owen says with a growl as he gives Larry a rough shake in emphasis. "He's not what he pretends to be," he grumbles. "I don't know what this thing is. He doesn't make a sound, and he doesn't have a scent. He was invisible until I grabbed him."

Larry's face is getting redder and redder.

"Don't pretend you need to breathe. She is not doing it to save you." The carefully hidden hellhound power ramps up and hits me square in my chest as Owen's other hand lights up with a blue flame.

I gulp.

Apart from the scuffle in the hotel room when I was struggling with the effects of the null band, I haven't witnessed the full effects of his power. Not really. I haven't seen Owen's grrr side. Not like this. The violence is shocking. The fire magic is shocking. The hellhound has been nothing but kind to me. But going from his sleepy, relaxed state to aggressive in the blink of an eye, even when it's not directed at me, makes my heart race crazy fast. The alien magic inside of me flares and my pounding heart misses a beat.

Oh God.

My magic doesn't like it. No, not mine. The realm's magic doesn't like this confrontation. The word *sanctuary* screams inside of me over and over. It echoes till the word is running through my blood and stamped on my very bones.

Okay, I get it. I grit my teeth and slam my eyes closed. The magic is like a living thing. I mentally grapple with it and it rushes out of my useless grip like a waterfall. No, like a tsunami. It hurts as it smashes inside me, wanting to get out and wreak havoc.

None of that, I growl in my head. *Settle the fuck down.*

I can't do this, a small part of me whispers. This is way too much. I can't do this.

A whimper slips from my lips. Oh no, I can't do this. I am not going to be able to stop it. My hair is moved to the side and a warm hand wraps around my neck and massages it gently. "You are okay, Flash. I'm sorry I scared you. Just breathe." His voice sends a soft rumble through me. With his touch, goosebumps rise all over my skin, and I can't help the shiver that racks me.

The hellhound is lending me his strength.

I swallow and then take a single deep, shuddering breath. Then another. His hot, heavy hand on my neck grounds me, and with an aggressive prod from me, the magic of the realm dissipates—no, it retreats and allows my magic to settle back into a pool in the middle of my chest.

I cautiously open my eyes and I nudge Owen with my elbow. "You are hurting him. The realm doesn't like it. It doesn't like the violence." The big hellhound immediately lets go of Larry and he stumbles a few steps away.

Larry stands there, wide-eyed and shaking as he rubs his neck.

"The truth," Owen spits out.

Larry swallows and his Adam's apple bobs. His face screws up as he tries to think of an answer that will satisfy the growling, terrifying hellhound. "I was created by the first host." His eyes implore me, and he presses his hands together as if in prayer. "Please don't kill me, Tuesday. I didn't mean to desert you. I was frightened. I thought you'd be mad that I lured you here. Then when you started crying..." He throws his hands up in the air and his lower lip wobbles. "I felt so bad. Then the big guy came and tried to strangle me." Larry plucks at his fingers, his green eyes wide with fear. "Only the host of the realm can destroy me. I was only made to be temporary, but I've been here for over a thousand years, looking after the hotel. I feel pain." He scowls at Owen and rubs his neck. "I'm as real as anybody. Please, I can help."

"You're a magical construct?"

"Yes. Yes." Larry points at me as if he's a teacher and I answered a question correctly in class. He even gives me a double thumbs up. His eyes crinkle with relief and he nods his head so fast, I worry it's going to pop off. "I direct the magic to where it's needed. I was made to keep the world functioning until a new host could be found. But the host never came and as Sanctuary slowly crumbled, I got worried. In desperation, I put feelers out into all the worlds. I was so sure I could find a new host. I found you." He grins.

A realisation pokes my brain as I make a connection. "Ah, it was you. You stopped the car." I narrow my eyes.

Larry's happy face creases with worry. He nods and twists his hands. "And the phone. I didn't want you to call for help until after you'd entered Sanctuary. I knew that once you got here, you'd find your home. You need this pocket realm, just like we need you."

I stare at him. I should be so mad. I should be raging mad. But... I'm not. I guess he has a point. As soon as I stepped inside the hotel, my non-existent magic took over my body and got to work. I lift my eyes to take in the beautiful lobby. I did this.

I just wish I had a way of knowing he was telling the truth.

"Alright, magic man, say we believe you. Which I don't. What about Tuesday signing the book? What was that all about?" Owen drops his voice to a threatening growl. "What did you do?"

Larry takes another step back and holds his hands up in front of his chest as if to ward off an attack by the angry hellhound. "Wow, he really doesn't like me, does he?" he mumbles. Owen takes a menacing stride toward him. Larry frantically waves his hands. "Everyone, every guest, has to sign in," he squeaks. "It is a normal procedure. She didn't sign her life away. I did nothing but get her here. I swear, I wouldn't hurt her. I would never hurt you, Tuesday."

My magic oddly chimes inside me with some sort of creepy magical confirmation, as if agreeing with his words. Crap-on-a-cracker, what now? What the heck was that? A weird magic lie detector? I shake my head and blink rapidly. That was freaky. It felt like my brain was tickled.

"He isn't lying to us," I mumble as I rub the side of my head.

Owen takes a deliberate sniff, perhaps smelling for a lie. Can shifters do that? He grunts in acknowledgement.

"Okay?" I whisper.

"Okay." The hellhound agrees while giving Larry the stink eye.

Larry grins and claps his hands together. It is like the sun has come out from the gleeful expression on his face. Then his smile disappears, and he slants his head to the side. In a monotone voice, he says, "They know you're here and request an audience."

"Who?" I ask at the same time as Owen grumbles.

"Oh, for fuck's sake. What now..." He washes his hand across his face. "Who?"

"The collective of dimensions."

Oh. Now this sounds like a whole new level of fun.

Arrrah.

"Do I have to meet them in person?" I whine as I brush my hands down my black trousers.

"Not in person. None of you will meet in person. Hosts, as a general rule, don't leave their pocket dimensions. Here, you are at your strongest, and the longer you stay, the less inclined you are to leave," he says with blatant honesty. "The conference call will start in ten minutes. Come, let me show you to your office."

Oh heck, talk about short notice. What a bunch of twats. Don't they know how to schedule meetings properly? They're doing it on purpose to throw me off my game. Well, we'll see about that. The idiots probably don't realise I'm already floundering. What's one more thing to add to the overflowing bag of crap my life has become?

CHAPTER
FOURTEEN

Owen gives a low whistle of appreciation. Yeah, the office is better than I imagined. While the reception area came from the five minutes or so of dreaming while I was waiting to be checked in to the hotel, the office nestled behind and to the left of the reception took me years to lovingly construct in my head.

My office at the department store is tiny, stuffed in a corner within the main stock room with its puke green paint. It's only big enough for a desk and two chairs. With one wall full of CCTV monitors and the other walls plastered with schedules and planners. I do my best to avoid the cramped space and try to be anywhere else in the store.

So, it stands to reason I've dreamed of something a little fancier over the years. It is the amalgamation of an office and a library. An ultra-modern space with white walls and glass shelves. Huge floor-to-ceiling bi-fold doors look out onto a patio area overlooking the lake. Huh. Technically, the view of the lake shouldn't be possible.

"With the position of this room within the building, these doors should have a partial view of the car park," Owen says, pulling the words right out of my head. He slides the door open and steps out. I lean against the glass and watch him prowl to the side of the building.

With each stride, he runs his hand against the wall, perhaps searching for illusions, or an obvious explanation.

I hope he can tell me. I take a moment to breathe in the sweet air of a perfect spring day. Which is strange in itself as... isn't it supposed to be winter?

"We are in a pocket world and Tuesday can bend reality to her every whim," Larry scoffs an explanation. "Of course she wants a pretty view from her office. Come now, stop messing about. My mistress needs to get settled in the conference room."

I shudder. "Oh no, please don't call me *mistress*." I follow him to a door that wasn't in my original design. Larry pushes the door open and the familiar smell of feet wafts into the air. I wrinkle my nose. He smacks at the wall a few times and there is a click. The pale glow of the ceiling's single bare bulb highlights a sad and drab room.

The conference table has seen better days. No windows. The cream paint on the ceiling is coming off in strips and the corners have clumps of black mould. Debris from the peeling paint and plaster litters the table.

Owen, like a shadow, follows me inside. His boots crunch as he circles the table. "Nice."

"I didn't make this," I mutter.

"I can tell," he says as he flicks at a piece of blown plaster. It immediately breaks off and crumbles to the floor.

"The room only opens when a council session has been called. If you try, you should be able to fix it before the meeting." Larry bounces from foot to foot and twists his hands. He wants me to do just that.

I shake my head, vetoing the idea of making the room pretty. Until I can see for myself who is friend or foe, I will give them nothing. I will not paint an irresistible, bright, shiny target on my head. I don't want them to realise my strength, and nothing brings out the worst in people than someone else's weakness.

Not that I have any strength... I don't know what the hell I'm doing. But I am going to go with my gut. As an obvious underdog, it will show their true colours faster. These people are—if Larry can be believed—immortal, and immortals have all the time in the worlds. A hundred years to them is probably a day to a witch. I can't be arsed playing a long game. Either they will help me or attack me. I might as well get it out of the way sooner rather than later. At least while I can hide behind the hellhound's bulk.

Fun times.

"Will they know how much this world has changed overnight?" I ask Larry as I pull out a chair.

He shakes his head. "No, they won't, and they'll never come here. They can't. Hosts don't go to each other's dimensions. It imbalances the realms and confuses the magic."

So that means the possibility that they will send in spies, so my ruse will not last for long.

I might be wrong, and these people might be lovely and helpful. But I've learned over the years to expect the worst. Most creatures are selfish and predictable.

So, if I'm playing the role of the underdog, I need to dress the part. I glance down at the pretty butterfly top with its delicate colours and flowy sleeves. It's not the ideal outfit… I need to show them what they expect.

A frightened mess.

A hair bobble appears in my hand. *Thank you.* I scrape my hair into a sloppy ponytail. Since I woke up this morning, my hair has been like silk, it's so smooth and shiny and it seems longer, the length now hitting my waist. My skin is the same. If I ignore the swirling magic for a second, I can feel the difference as it glows with health. Even my nails are harder and appear as if I've had an expensive manicure.

The plastic gun clacks onto the table as I pull it out of my pocket. The hellhound does this sexy enquiring thing with his eyebrow. "Forrest," I murmur in explanation. He grunts. I haven't got time to run upstairs and change, so I close my eyes and think of the clothes that I arrived in. The fabric on my skin changes. It goes from the light, floaty fabric to the heaviness of cotton. When I crack my eyes open, almost unwilling to look, I see a black oversized hoodie and jogging bottoms. I puff out my cheeks with relief. Perfect. I silently thank the magic yet again.

The sleeves slide over my hands, and I pull the hood up, shadowing the glowing marks on my face, and I shove the gun back into my pocket.

As I sit in the chair, it creaks underneath my weight and lists slightly to the right. Whoops. I push a little bit more of my weight into my left bum cheek to keep the chair level. I hope this meeting doesn't drag on.

Across the room, beautiful grey eyes watch me. The hellhound gives me a nod. He knows what I'm doing without me having to say. Smart wolf.

I place my phone on the table and raise an eyebrow. "Larry?" He gazes back at me blankly. It takes everything in me not to headbutt the table with exasperation. "What do I do now? Are we video conferencing?" I wave my hand to incorporate the entire room. "There is no technology. Do I use the phone?" Larry opens and closes his mouth, while Owen growls. This time, the growl is deeper and rumbles from his chest.

I shouldn't find his growls and grunts so fascinating, but I do.

"What? Oh yes, sorry, the magic will bring them. It'll beam them into the room. Well, um, not them exactly. But a magical version. So, you can, you know, speak." He flashes his teeth in a too-white smile.

I sigh and close my eyes. I understood that completely. Not. This is beyond my comprehension, and for my sanity, I should run away as fast as I can and go home.

Owen mutters something under his breath as he prowls around the room and settles behind me. Everything in me is hyperaware of him as he stands at my back. His shifter power, along with the heat of his hellhound magic, makes shivers randomly zip up and down my spine. *Instead of frightening, his hellhound power is...* Nope. I yank on that thought. *Hellhounds aren't yummy.*

The room buzzes and the little hairs on my arms rise as the sudden change in room pressure makes my ears pop. My guests shimmer into existence. Oh-uh, here we go. *Showtime.*

CHAPTER
FIFTEEN

Four creatures—two men and two women—sit across the table. It's the oddest thing to see them magically projected. I have to blink a few times to get my eyes to focus. *"Help me, Obi-Wan Kenobi. You're my only hope."* Princess Leia's voice from Star Wars pipes up in my head, and I smirk.

I'm glad they can't see my expression. Smirking wouldn't make the best first impression. I might appear to be a sullen teenager with my hood pulled up and my face hidden within its shadows, but I instinctively know I did the right thing as I notice another obvious thing about my guests.

Their fancy, glowy markings.

While my face is covered with pretty swirls, the creatures opposite me have a swirl here and there. The marks must indicate power, and I am covered head to toe. It's not something I need to be highlighting to a bunch of unknowns.

Thank goodness I hid my face.

Underneath the hood, I give them a sweeping glance, my eyes trail from left to right. The first man has white hair that's cropped close to his scalp. He is painfully thin and everything about him is white, from his lips to his skin tone. Even his eyes lack pigment.

Next to him is a woman. Her skin and long hair have a slight green tinge. She has a single, prominent swirl across her sharp cheekbone. The second woman is the most human-looking of the four. She has a round face, brown hair, and hazel eyes that shine with intelligence. The last man, a male version of the woman sitting next to him, has this sneer on his handsome face—a sneer that he's aiming at me.

Oh, and they all have the familiar tell-tale pointed ears of the *aes sidh*.

Elves.

Huh. I frown and shift slightly, and the dodgy chair creaks. I don't know what I was expecting. Aliens perhaps, not the fae. Something inside me chimes a reminder, and a memory flashes of the elf who attacked me. He also had short hair. Perhaps he wasn't an elf from Earth?

Great.

"How delightful. A hellhound bodyguard." The green skinned lady purrs as she runs a finger against the swirl on her collarbone, highlighting her impressive chest. She smiles at Owen like a crocodile.

Whoa, the woman has waaayy too many teeth.

"Maybe after this meeting you can guard me." She licks her lips.

Eww.

I wrinkle my nose and I can't help myself, I swivel, being extra careful not to unbalance or break the already wobbly chair, so I can see Owen's face. The hellhound has taken up a guard position behind me. He stands with his legs wide apart, and his hands rest almost casually at his sides.

Ever the professional, he doesn't react to her words. Though his soft grey eyes have hardened like flint. *The dead eyes of a killer.* I take in a shuddering breath. *Stop it, Tuesday. That's unkind. All Owen has done is try to protect you. That's his game face.* I'm lucky to have his help. It's not like I'll be able to fight off four alien elves when I couldn't handle one. Thank the stars they aren't actually here.

The poor guy promised to protect me, yet we don't know from what. Thanks to this strange world, and now this impromptu meeting, we've both been dropped right in it. I feel sorry for him.

In good conscience, I can't allow this to continue. He's a hellhound, for spell's sake. He's the best of the best, the ultimate soldier, and instead of going out and rescuing people, he's here, playing bodyguard for me. It's a joke. I need to tell him he is free of his promise, as it's not his job to stand with me. This isn't his fight. It must be a helluva favour he owes my dad.

I'm not worth his time.

I do my best to give him a small, reassuring smile. His left hand clenches. Yeah, after this meeting, I'll send the poor guy on his way.

Reluctantly, I turn my attention back to the creatures across the table. The elves—no they aren't elves, are they? They are hosts, and thinking back to first impressions, a sexual proposition doesn't make a good one. It seems like I'm in for a fun meeting. The hellhound isn't the only one who needs a game face.

"Poor little lost host, you must have been so lonely in a world that doesn't understand you. Earth, isn't it? Peeking out of that hood, you appear human." Crocodile lady smiles at me and I shudder. I can't help but count my teeth with my tongue. Yeah, crocodile lady has at least double the gnashes in her wide mouth. Freaky.

"You are earthborn?" The man on the right sniffs with distaste. "Earth is full of scavengers. It's a backwards world. For many centuries, it has not been advantageous for us to trade with the snivelling, vile creatures that roam that planet. The last time I checked, they treated humans like slaves and hosts like witches. Can you believe that? Witches? We are gods."

Next, he'll be pounding his chest. I blink as he continues to rant, and he waves his hands in the air. *Some god,* I mentally scoff. I use that title very loosely—his words. Witches on Earth can't be so bad if at one point in history some host dipped their DNA into the gene pool.

I must have a recessive gene.

Should I tell him? Nah. I keep my gob firmly closed and allow his rude comments to fly over my head. What does it matter to me? Who cares what these aliens think? I'm not an ambassador for Earth. I'm also numb to this type of game, thanks to my mum. No one can play it better than her. I still rub my hand down my leg in a self-soothing motion. I've trained for this. This exact moment. Dealing with my mum, my coven, and dealing with nightmare customers and colleagues has led up to this.

"Little human host," crocodile lady continues with a toothy smile, "is there something wrong with your face?" She drops her voice to a creepy whisper. "We don't mind scars."

Gah. It takes everything in me not to roll my eyes. Now they are calling me out. I have no choice. I must drop the hood, as I need to show my face.

"My apologies," I say in a fake timid whisper as I reach for the hood with a trembling hand. "I didn't think, and the room is cold." As the fabric slips away from my head, my heart jumps. I duck my head and screw my eyes tight as I ask the magic for its help. A push of power answers my call, making the skin on my face tingle. As the heavy fabric slaps against my back and loose hair from my ponytail settles around my face, I feel all but one mark fade, like a mask. They disappear underneath a layer of magic.

Phew. It'll do. I lift my chin.

The crocodile lady smiles with satisfaction as her eyes scan my face. They all appraise me and take in the lack of markings.

"Are you sure she's even a host? Just look at her. A single measly marking. She isn't powerful. The human blood has ruined her," says the brown-haired fake god with a dismissive sniff.

Witch. The words *witch blood, not human,* scream in my head. I lift my chin higher and keep my mouth firmly closed. They are pissing me off.

"Look at this room. She can't even do a basic change. She's not one of us. Thank the rivers I can't smell this place. It's disgusting. She's disgusting," crocodile lady pipes up.

Nice.

It takes everything in me to hold in a sigh and a nostril flare. Losing my temper now would be a huge mistake. This is something I'm used to. At least she's direct and saying it to my face. Meh, her words won't trigger the Mum gene. I've heard worse.

I smile.

"Look at that." Crocodile points at my face. "She doesn't even know she's being insulted. What a waste. She is such a pretty little thing to look at, those big violet eyes… she'd make beautiful babies. Tendris, you always said you were waiting for a host mate." She elbows the white-haired elf, and he grunts with dismissal.

A low growl sounds behind me. Owen's boots creek against the wooden floor as he shifts his weight. I wave my hand frantically below the table and the growl cuts off. I don't think they heard him as they've continued to talk about me as if I'm not in the room. I've seen what I wanted. My eye twitches and I give it a rub. Sorry, but the hosts are a bunch of pricks.

I haven't even had a chance to explore the realm yet, as these creatures demanded an immediate meeting. Without asking. What is it about my face that gets everybody up in arms? They go from nought to sixty with insults. Even when I haven't said anything to warrant it. Not yet anyway.

I loudly clear my throat. "Excuse me," I say as I tap on the table to get their attention. "I'm sorry. I thought you could help me, advise me. Now I see that's not the case. If you'd excuse me, I have things to do." I rise from my chair. As I stand, I tuck a strand of hair behind my ear and deliberately allow the baggy sleeve to roll down to my elbow, flashing the silver swirls on my arm.

"Oh Jupiter, her arms," the brown-haired lady squeaks. "Please, please don't leave." Something in her tone makes me pause. I groan as I see the genuine panic in her brown eyes. What's one more minute? I tug the chair back and go to sit, but the poor chair has had enough, and it crumbles into pieces. I stare at the sad chunk of wood in my hand and puff out my cheeks. Without thinking, I drop the wood and wash my magic across the room. The power hits the room in a wave and from one breath to the next, everything changes.

Whoa. Seeing it happen in front of my eyes is a trip. It's like I've gone full on Disney.

The conference room now mirrors the office next door with white walls and floor-to-ceiling windows that also overlook the lake. A fancy glass wall now separates the two rooms, letting in lots of light.

That's much better. I nod my head and the protective mask of magic peels away from my face as I casually pull out the now solid, elegant chair to take a seat.

The hosts' mouths are open.

"My name is Tuesday Larson. The hellhound gentleman behind me is Owen, and Larry here is the previous host's magical construct. Gosh, look at that"—I narrow my eyes—"I have manners. Not bad, I guess, for a vapid Earth savage."

For a few moments, the only response I get is silence.

Wow, awkward.

So much for keeping your gob shut.

Yay, nice one, Tuesday.

"She is feral." Crocodile lady recovers first. She snaps her teeth and takes a deep breath, to prepare for what will be an epic rant. "She doesn't understand the rules. You can't just—"

"No. She's magnificent. I take everything I said about Earth and the humans back. She doesn't know the rules, so she isn't confined to them. Her magic is wild." The brown-haired guy leans forward and points his finger at crocodile's face. "Don't you dare ruin that." He's a brave man. I wouldn't point a precious digit anywhere near those teeth.

Crocodile lady proves me right when she tries to take a chomp out of it.

Yikes.

Their images combine for a split second, and he smirks. Oh yeah, they're not really here. He leans back with a smug smile on his face. Thinking about what he said, I'm happy for once that the host magic is a complete unknown to me. It's refreshing I don't have to conform to someone else's version of perfection. I can listen to what my magic is telling me and do it on the fly. I have to bite my lip to stop myself from grinning like a loon. I like the idea of being wild.

The lady with the brown hair clears her throat. Her cheeks are flush with embarrassment. "I think we need to apologise to Miss Larson. I'm sorry that we didn't introduce ourselves. It's a little overwhelming finding a new host. My name is Nyssa. This is my brother, Nestern. The lovely lady next to me is Zaina, and last but not least, the gentleman at the end is Tendris."

I huff. It's a little bit too late for polite introductions.

"You deliberately mislead us," Tendris says with a white-eyed scowl.

"Yes," I reply with a sharp nod. His eyes widen, and I shrug. What?

I'm not going to lie. Well, not entirely anyway. I neglect to tell them I hid my markings 'cause I was shitting myself.

"It was a test," he says as he rubs his face.

"Yes."

"A test we failed," Nyssa says in a mournful tone. I shrug again. I need to wrap this meeting up.

The way Zaina, aka crocodile alien host, is now glaring at me is making me feel uncomfortable. If looks could kill, I'd be dead and buried with a pretty headstone. She pointedly brushes a chunky gold ring on her right ring finger with creepy reverence and then glances at my empty ringless finger and smirks.

I notice each of my visitors has one. Nope, I'm not in the ring club. The rings must be powerful artefacts. I guess I will add that to the list of things I have yet to find out. Zaina is now smiling at me. Some psycho part of me wishes she was corporal. I stroke the toy gun in my pocket. I'd love to shoot a foam sleeping bullet into the middle of her green forehead. I duck my head and grin at the thought. Shame it would pass straight through her. *Look at me, a plastic gun in my pocket and I've turned into a right rebel.*

Okay, back to getting answers. "So, you are the council for hosts?" What did Atticus call them? "The collective of dimensions?" My eyebrows rise with my question, and I plaster what I hope is an encouraging expression on my face.

"Council—" Nyssa lets out a strangled laugh and turns to her brother for help, finding something interesting on his hand. Did I say something wrong?

Nyssa abandons her chair. On the way to the window, she walks through the table. The magical projection of her flickers so much it makes me want to vomit. She takes in the view and her hand hovers against the glass. "Beautiful view," she murmurs. "I can see for miles." The other hosts quieten their bickering as they also take in the view.

Zaina grinds her teeth and snarls. "You're powerful then. So what?"

"And you've learned quickly," Tendris says in a low voice. His white eyes remain focused on the lake.

"If you would like, I can teach you, help you with your magic. I can give you the tools to keep yourself safe," Nyssa offers.

"Thank you."

"Well, I won't. Her power will bring out the sealgairí and I'm not killing myself to protect a baby host. She will be a magnet for trouble," Zaina snarls.

"Who are the sealgairí?" I try to pronounce the word the way crocodile lady did, but I make a mess of it.

"Just keep out of my way, Wednesday."

I roll my eyes. As if I haven't heard that one before. "No, my name is Tuesday," I say with a sad shake of my head. "Wednesday is my sister."

"What?" Her green face scrunches up with confusion.

"Boy, it doesn't take much, does it?" I mumble.

"Your sister's name is Wednesday?" she splutters with incredulity.

I snort. "No. But you should have seen your face." I grin. All three of my sisters have lovely, normal names. It's only me who has a wacky one. Talk about tempting fate. I think my mum was so sure that I was a boy she didn't even think about picking an alternative, so when it was revealed that I was a bouncing baby girl, she let my dad name me. I was born on a Tuesday. Yes, really. *Thanks, Dad.*

"We are the hosts," Nestern says in a low voice.

"Pardon?" I rapidly blink. Oh, he is answering my question that upset Nyssa before about them being part of the council. I don't think I quite understand. Did they not send the council? The guild?

"There are four of us, well, five of us now." Nyssa returns to her seat, waves at the others and smiles warmly. "That is the reason we arranged this meeting so quickly." She leans forward with enthusiasm, but her smile doesn't reach her sad, hazel eyes. "Miss Larson, you are in danger. The hosts have been hunted to extinction. We are the last."

Five of us? "Oh." Well crap.

CHAPTER SIXTEEN

After I arrange a training session for the following morning with Nyssa, I cut the magic to the room. It is so easy to do, like flicking a switch. *Bam* and they are gone.

"Extinction. Bloody hell." *Gah, Tuesday, why did you show them your magic so quickly? Why am I so impatient?* I flop my head down on the table and groan. My quiet life as an outcast was preferable to being hunted. "I don't want to be an alien elf," I whine.

"You're not an alien elf," Owen says with gruff amusement. "You are still a witch, but with host magic."

I let out an unladylike grunt. I'm far from being a witch. My sweaty forehead squeaks against the table as I attempt to press my pounding head into the wood.

"Was that wise, to show your markings and magic like that?" Larry asks, voicing a polite version of my own scattered thoughts.

"You tell me, Larry," I grumble. "Probably not." I sit up and rub my face. Great. Even the magical construct thinks my move was a bit pre-emptive. *Nah, it was worth it just to see their faces.*

I get up, and with wobbly knees, I leave the conference room. The two men follow silently behind. Not thinking, I trundle through to reception. Aw heck, I should have kept this conversation private. Before

I can turn and retrace our steps to the office, a sound bubble pops up around us. It's similar to a Don't Hear Me Now spell. Wow, that is kind of neat. Freaky, but a cool piece of magic.

Larry prods the bubble with an approving nod. I shrug. It's not like I did it on purpose. This magic stuff is nuts. I'm throwing magic around without a chant or spell in sight. "I needed to do something," I continue. "They were walking all over me. Did you hear what they said? What a bunch of d-dicks," I stutter. For some reason, perhaps because I'm tired and I'm a little jittery, the word *dick* is heavy on my tongue. My brain misfires slightly at the odd sensation of finally being able to say out loud whatever is in my head. I rub my leg. I don't think I will ever get used to it.

My head goes back to the big reveal. I have thrown all my cards down. I hope I made myself look stronger than I am. This all feels like fate is pushing me aggressively forward. I still don't know if this is going to blow up in my face. I hate not knowing if I am doing the right thing. Although I think the hosts are frightened and have more problems on their plates than my existence, my gut says any future ordeals I have will unlikely come from them.

"No, I had to reveal myself. I had to claw that meeting back and now they think I'm an evil genius," I add with heavy sarcasm. The lie detector inside me pings. The thing even works on me. Oh shit, I hope there is some way to turn the damn thing off. I white lie to myself frequently. At least it's good to know that during that meeting I had lie detector backup. They didn't lie. "When you're as weak as me, you learn how to bluff," I finish lamely.

"The sealgairí. Have you heard of them?" I ask Owen with a wince as I know I am again butchering the pronunciation.

"No. But the word means *hunters* in Irish. I will ask my contacts."

"Host hunters." I shake my head. "Thank you. I'd appreciate that." A wave of dizziness hits me, so I lean as casually as I can against the desk. No one needs to know that it's holding me up. If I ignore it, it'll go away. I sigh and rub my temple.

I blink away another rush of dizziness and meet Owen's concerned gaze. He hasn't been fooled by my casual lean. "I'm sorry she was rude to you. I should have said something."

"No," the hellhound replies gruffly. "You did the right thing."

"No, I didn't. I should have called her out. She was being inappropriate. I'm sorry you had to listen to that." I'm ashamed of myself. I reach over and squeeze his warm hand. Then I turn my attention back to Larry. "Larry, one thing I wanted to ask: why did you get a notice of the meeting, and I didn't? Are you, like, a magical personal assistant?"

"You just need to let the magic know."

"Great. Is there anything else I must let the magic know about?"

"Yes." I tilt my head to the side and wave my hand in a "get on with it" gesture. *Come on Larry.* "Oh, there's so much to tell you, it would take me weeks and weeks."

"Right." I narrow my eyes. Larry rocks from foot to foot. "You know you don't have to keep things from me. I will not kick you out or, heaven forbid, kill you. Just be honest, yeah? I need your help. I need a friend."

"A friend?" Larry blinks at me.

"Well, yeah..." Embarrassed, I casually pull the phone out of my pocket and tap it on my hand. I turn the phone back on and it works perfectly. "I always need more friends," I whisper.

"I am your friend!" Larry giggles with childlike glee. I lift my eyes, and he beams a smile at me and bounces on his toes. "I've never had a friend before. That's amazing."

"Friends." I smile at his antics and hold my hand out. He bounces towards me and gently shakes it.

"You just have to open your senses and the magic will tell you everything you need to know."

I nod and try it. To focus, I close my eyes. He is right. It is so weird, like I am touching a phantom part of my consciousness. I can feel everything in this pocket realm if I only reach out with my senses.

With a mental nudge, against the blackness of my eyelids, a map appears. "A map of the realm!" I gasp. *That is nuts.* I push my surprise away, wrinkle my nose, and keep my eyes firmly closed. "I guess it's not *everything* I need to know, but it's a start." Owen grunts an acknowledgement. Somehow, everyone in the realm shows up like coloured blobs on the map. And if I poke the black blob, I just know the vampire is quietly working away in the library. Gold. Daisy is playing with some friends. My entire face scrunches up, and what I am doing grinds to a halt... Woah. What? Friends? Um, that is new. I know she's safe and content, so I will refrain from charging off and going all mama bear.

Thinking of mama bears, I open my eyes and squeeze the phone in my hand. No time like the present to knock something off my horrendously long to-do list. With a deep breath and my stomach flipping with nerves, my thumb hovers on the keypad, ready to dial my dad, which will no doubt entail a conversation with Mum as well. I swallow.

Nah, I think I'll leave that fun call for another day. I should check on Daisy and her *friends*. Uh-oh. My eyes widen. I have no idea what a dragonette will conjure up with the realm magic listening to her every need. "I need to check on Daisy." I move and then stagger to the side. A strong hand grips me underneath my elbow. "Oh, thanks," I mumble. "What the heck is wrong with me?"

"You've just used a shit load of magic. Magic that you have never used before last night. Of course, you are wobbling around like Bambi. When did you last eat?" The hellhound gazes down at me with a frown.

"The cinnamon bun?" Owen scowls. "Oh, and I had a bacon butty this morning."

"So, a magically made pastry and a breakfast sandwich? It might feed your future guests, but do you know if it's nutritious for you?"

I groan, shaking my head and barely refrain from slapping myself on the forehead. *Oh, Tuesday, why do you not think things through? The man is going to think I am a complete moron.* "I've no idea."

"Okay, so you need to eat some proper food before you do anything."

"Yeah, okay, sounds like a plan. But... urm... I don't know if I made a kitchen. I'm guessing there's no actual food here." We both turn and stare at Larry, who shakes his head. That's a no to the food idea then.

Owen growls. Larry waves his hands out in front of himself as if to ward off an attack. I roll my eyes and the hellhound drags his hand across his face. "There is no need to panic," Larry squeaks, continuing his dramatics. "The food here will sustain Tuesday." He turns to me, his green eyes pleading. "It doesn't come from your magical source.

The pocket realm can fulfil your every need. Owen is right; you have used a lot of magic. You just need to eat more."

A nutty protein bar appears in the palm of Owen's hand. "I could get used to this; the magic is incredible." The wrapper rustles as he opens it. "When you're feeling better, perhaps we should open a portal and get some fresh food delivered, just in case." He glares at Larry and hands the bar to me.

I nod as I stuff it in my mouth. "Have you been to a pocket dimension before?" I ask when I finally finish chewing.

"Yes, several. None this big. I can't wait to explore."

"Me too." After I've eaten two more protein bars, I already feel better. "Oh, I really need to check on Daisy. She's up to something." With my energy levels restored, I hurry for my room. Owen follows silently behind me. It's strange having such a huge but silent man following me around. The shifter sure pumps out some heat. No wonder Daisy likes him.

His warm breath tickles my ear. I close my eyes in exasperation and suck in a shaky breath before shuffling faster away from him. "Where are you going?" I grumble.

"With you."

I spin around to face him. I have to tilt my head way back to meet his eyes. Heck, I still cannot get over how big he is. With a huff, I put my hands on my hips, ready to argue. I can't have him following me around all day.

He already makes me feel awkward, and the crush I have needs to be squished before I shame myself any further.

"I'm safe. You don't need to do the whole guarding thing. No one is going to get in here without me knowing about it."

"Really?" he says, raising an eyebrow and folding his muscly forearms across his chest. "You know that for a fact, do you?"

I groan and rub my face. "No," I mumble underneath my hand.

"Well, you let me know when you know everything about your magic in this world. Then I will leave you alone."

I blink.

The hellhound grunts.

Ahh, we are at a stalemate.

Gah, the hard-headed hellhound. Nothing I say will convince him. "Fine. I just think an elite hellhound's time could be better spent than babysitting me." He grunts. I huff and spin on my toes. Now stomping my feet, I continue walking. I am sure he needs a break. I know I do.

I open the door to my snazzy room and wander inside. The whole place is about three times the size of my flat back home. It has three extra bedrooms. I rub my face and groan for what feels like the millionth time today. That's another thing I need to do—cancel my flat's lease. Every minute I stay here, it looks less likely I am ever going to go home. I bet my landlord will be thrilled to see the back of me, what with the Power Ranger mercenaries smashing apart his expensive building ward.

"Daisy?" I say in a cutesy voice. I search the entire apartment and when I have to look a second time, panic bubbles inside of me. She isn't here. Why isn't she here? "Daisy Duco? Oh, no, oh my goodness, did the magic take my dragonette?" If this bloody pocket realm hurt my Daisy...

Owen opens a door and I want to shout at him that Daisy couldn't possibly be in there, behind a closed door. She hasn't got thumbs. But his rumbling voice stops me. "Tuesday, you need to see this. I think she's here, and she's... got friends?"

The friends. I rush to him and take in the world beyond the door. I thought I'd seen everything but this—this is nuts.

"Dragonette utopia," I mutter in shock.

Did I wish for Daisy to have friends? I think I did this morning at some point when I was leaving. Oh heck. But I also remember her eating a cucumber snack, so she might have done this herself.

The room isn't a room, but a lava field. The rocky area has lava pools interspaced with volcanic hot springs. The eggy odour of sulphur fills the air. There is a tree in the centre that must be fifty feet tall. A deep-looking hole within the root of the tree hints at a cave underneath. When Larry said the magic could bend physics, he wasn't kidding.

But what has my mouth flapping open is all the dragonettes.

It's dragonville.

A bright blue dragonette takes a big bite of volcanic rock and noisily crunches it. "Oh no, what has she eaten? She must have gorged herself silly. Daisy is going to have a tummy ache." I rub my abdomen in sympathy. "I'm normally so careful with what I feed her." Daisy is only young, and we've focused on a special dragonette mix diet, with the perfect number of rocks to help her digestion.

We stand and stare at all the dragonettes running, flying, and playing. My heart breaks a little, to think Daisy has been lonely. It makes me feel like I've been selfish. Keeping her all to myself.

Daisy scrambles around the tree and dashes towards me. I drop, ignoring the bite of uneven ground on my knees and can't help but smile as she charges into my arms. "Are you having fun? I hope there aren't any boys."

As I stroke her golden scales, her excited heart flutters underneath my fingers. Instinctively, I let a sliver of my magic trickle its way through her. I don't know what the heck I'm doing, but for my sanity, I need to check that she's physically okay. After only a few seconds, my magic dissipates happily. I sigh with relief. Daisy is perfectly healthy. Her tummy is fine, she's just exhausted from playing and overdue a nap.

"They don't smell real," Owen says in a low voice. "They smell like Larry." Oh. I nod. That makes sense. Fake dragonettes are safe dragonettes.

Done with my fussing and using my knee as a springboard, the little gold dragon springs away from me. With her wings flapping, to add an extra oomph to her run, she scampers off towards a hot pool. It will be a few more years until the bones in her wings are strong enough for her to fly.

I stand, wiping dirt and stones off my jogging bottoms.

"Hey." Owen nudges me. "You okay?" I swallow a few times and twist my hands together. I don't think I can answer as my emotions are all over the place, so I nod and then shake my head almost at the same time.

I'm not okay.

His heavy arm settles around my shoulders, and he pulls me against his side. I melt against him. After ten silent minutes of watching the dragonettes play, his big hand cups my chin and his grey eyes find me. I expect him to say something poignant. "Best pocket dimension ever." He grins. His smile involves his eyes, and he practically lights up.

Wow. My heart misses a beat.

"Do you want to go for a walk?" I rasp out. Staying inside is making me anxious. I need to get out of the hotel and get some fresh air. Not that I know if the air is fresh. I know nothing about this strange realm. It's scary.

Owen grunts a confirmation, and I shuffle along beside him as we head down to the ground floor. I'm sad. It's that feeling that you get when your best friend has a group of new pals, and you don't fit in. I know it's daft. Most people would say Daisy is only a dragonette. But for the few months that I have had her in my life, she's become important to me. I love her.

Now it appears I've been cruel, selfishly keeping her to myself. I rapidly blink so I don't cry. I've never seen her so happy.

It's a good thing and I shouldn't be feeling sad. What an ass I am. I should be happy for my little dragon.

CHAPTER
SEVENTEEN

We leave through the main door. The path that was cracked and bumpy last night is smooth at our feet. I can't believe that was only last night. So many things have already happened. No wonder my head feels like it's going to explode.

Owen takes one step for every three of mine. I try to widen my stride, but I slip and almost pull a muscle. Out of the corner of my eye, I catch the hellhound's lips twitch as he represses a laugh. Thankfully, the big oaf slows down.

As I walk normally, each step I take is lighter. The air smells sharp and crisp, a far cry from the pollution in the real world. If I relax my eyes, tiny floating filaments spark and crackle with magic. Full of energy. This pocket realm is more real to me than the world I come from. Everything around me buzzes with magic. The feeling of being home thrums through me. It builds up through my legs and zings into my chest.

Home.

"Do you feel welcomed, as if you have come home?" I ask him.

"Peaceful. There's a level of safety here that I haven't felt before. Welcomed, yeah, but not like I've come home. Is that what you're feeling?"

"Yeah, it's weird." I rub my chest. "I've never felt it before."

"But—" He stops his words and rubs the back of his neck.

"What?"

"Well, you are from a big coven. Don't you feel like that when you go to your Mum's?"

I laugh. It sounds bitter to my ears, and I shake my head. Without thinking, I overshare. "I'm the coven's embarrassment. The lack of my power rubbed my parents the wrong way." I inwardly groan. I've said too much. The hellhound is practically a stranger, and worse, my dad sent him to help me.

It's my turn to awkwardly rub the back of my neck. He must think I'm a proper cow. "It was my fault. I was... urm... a troublesome child." I shrug and fake a smile.

The hellhound narrows his eyes. I trust Owen, and I have a huge crush on him, but he's friends with my well-respected dad. I don't even want to go near who he'd believe if I told him the truth.

Nah, even I wouldn't believe it. Reputations are broken in moments, and with a little digging, he'd find mine is way past the dust age. Broken and ground so fine, it's just sand. I am seen as beyond nothing. A day of being a fantastical host doesn't change any of that.

I will always be the defective witch.

A small sigh of pain slips from my lips and I pull at a piece of rock that's embedded itself into the fabric of my jogging bottoms. I'm a nice person—unless I am channelling my mother—and if there's one thing creatures don't understand, it's niceness. It freaks them right out.

But it doesn't matter if you are a nice person when your entire coven thinks you are a waste of space. That is why I am terrified for him to get a full look at the person I am. He will be appalled and will no doubt walk away like everyone else. I thought I got over this. I know better than to live in the past. Now there's an awkward silence between us.

The path changes to a crunchy golden stone. It's the real fancy stuff I admired at a country estate. My eyes drift across the empty car park. It seems bigger than it did last night and there's a signpost that wasn't there yesterday, directing people to a leisure centre, to the swimming pool and gym. Crikey, there is also a sign for the stables. Heh, I can't remember that one.

Something nags at me, something is missing... My eyes scan the empty car park.

Oh. Hang on a minute. The car is missing! "The hire car is gone," I squeak. "I was thinking about sending it back... Did I?" *Oh heck, what did I do with the car?* I bounce from foot to foot. Goodness gracious, if that happened, this place is even more dangerous than I thought.

Owen frowns and fishes out his phone. It appears tiny in his hand. I don't know how he doesn't press all the buttons at once, his fingers are so big.

I can't even bloody think without the magic doing something wacky.

Stop doing that, I internally whisper. The breeze playfully tugs at my hair, and I stare at the crunchy stone underneath my trainers. If it's listening to my thoughts, then it can listen to this. *If I need your help, I will ask, but you need to stop reacting to my every thought. It's creepy. I may not be talking to you, so double check first, yeah? Thank you for being so smart and helping me, but just ask or wait until I'm more direct. Okay? It's freaky. You are freaking me the hell out.*

And now, now I'm going crazy.

"The car is back at the hire company. It appeared out of nowhere with the keys in the ignition." Owen lifts his sparkling eyes from the phone and raises an eyebrow.

"Oh." My hands flop about in a "what can I do?" gesture.

"Handy, eh?" he says with a grin and a friendly nudge that makes my silly heart flutter.

"Very," I mumble.

I tuck a strand of hair behind my ear as I desperately search for a change of subject. "Urm, do you like being a hellhound?" I blurt out. Yeah, hit him with a nice simple question. I roll my eyes. I guess I want to know more about this man. He has this whole masculine energy thing going on, yet his kindness seeps through. It is a heady combination.

Owen tips his head to the side in contemplation and we continue walking. "Yes, I enjoy stopping the bad guys and helping people. It's not a nine-to-five job, and a time or two, things have got so hairy, I didn't think I'd make it. I miss being out in the field with the lads. I've been watching Forrest's back in Ireland and that girl..." He smiles. My heart squeezes in disappointment that the smile isn't for me. "She can get herself into a hell of a lot of trouble."

Forrest again. Not only do they work together and have a relationship where he can guarantee her help without having to ask, but he also drinks what I'm guessing is her favourite drink. No way I can compete with a friendship like that. My heart sinks and I force my face into a normal expression. Jealousy doesn't suit me. *I have lost the plot.* The sooner this guy leaves, the better.

"I've never been so busy. I don't regret what I am, what I've done. It's in my blood. The only thing I regret is not getting to a bad situation quicker, being too slow to save an innocent. That can eat you up if you let it. When you see the worst in people over and over again, it gets old. It gets old real fast. I guess I have always been destined to be a soldier."

It's his calling. I can appreciate that. His honesty floors me. I was lucky to have lived a privileged life for as long as I have. I might have been an outcast, but at least I was safe. The horrible things Owen must have seen, had to do. Yet, he'd do it all again to keep people safe. The hellhound is a hero. I reach over and rub his forearm, and he smiles at me.

With an *oof* of surprise spilling from my lips, Owen pulls me to his side and wraps his heavy arm around me. I dip my head to hide my smile. *Only friends,* my inner voice screams. *He is out of your league.* With that single thought, the smile is wiped from my lips. I can do friends. I can push my feelings away and be friends with this man. It's not his fault that I am hopelessly in love with him. When we come to a turn in the path, I take the chance to slip from underneath his arm. It is the right thing to do.

It isn't until we walk for a while that I realise something else is making me uneasy, and I take a few minutes to pinpoint exactly what it is. There aren't any birds or insects. No signs of life. There is only the sun and the breeze.

The tickle of wind and the squeak of the branches from the trees above us, along with our footsteps, are the only sounds. Wow, it's freaky. Now I recognise it, the environment around us is so fake, and unsettling.

Like we are strolling through virtual reality.

I close my eyes and ask the magic to fix that. I don't want this place to feel odd. There is already the fake sun and weather. I open my eyes to see a fat bumblebee buzz pass my nose and a monarch butterfly settles on a patch of bluebells underneath the trees. I don't know if they would be about this time of year, but they aren't real, and it's not like I'm going to create a hard frost and kill them. They are perfect.

A giggle escapes me as a bluebottle smacks against Owen's cheek. He frowns. "Your handiwork, I take it?"

"Yes."

"I like it." He rubs his face. "Perhaps not the kamikaze bluebottles, but I like the signs of life."

When we turn the corner, and the trees fall away, the path slopes down towards the lake. I stand and take in the view. The lake is huge, and it is so much bigger than what it appears to be from the hotel. There are a dozen or so ducks, noisily quacking. I smile as we get closer and I watch a duck bob upside down in the water, his bum bobbing up and down as he snatches at some duck delicacy below.

"Do you want to go out on the lake?" Owen asks.

"Huh?" I eloquently reply. My full attention is now on a male mallard duck who is chasing the females around and getting nowhere. They are so lifelike. It's kind of like I ate the red pill and I've joined the Matrix.

"The boat," Owen says, giving me a gentle nudge. His big hand points to a pale blue rowboat that's moored to the side of a quaint wooden dock.

"Oh, I'd love to. I've never been in a rowboat before." I clap my hands and bounce on my toes. I'm excited to explore the lake that spreads endlessly before us.

Owen grins as he holds the wooden boat steady and with a hand, he helps me in. The boat doesn't dare move an inch with the big hellhound gripping it. Once I am sitting, Owen gets in, showing for a big guy he has the balance of a fighter. He settles on the bench seat opposite me and unties the rope, flinging it onto the dock so it doesn't get wet. He then picks up the wooden oars. I nod with encouragement as he digs them into the water.

That's when things get a little confusing, a little bit strange. The boat bounces forward and then lists to the side. It circles back to the dock and bumps into it.

Wood grinds against wood and the oars splash.

They splash a lot.

Owen swears under his breath. *Don't you dare laugh.* I suck both of my lips into my mouth and bite down as we continue to go around in a weird circle. *Don't you dare laugh.* I rest my elbows on my knees and politely pretend to watch the ducks. The poor guy doesn't need me staring at him as he increasingly gets more and more frustrated. I casually slap my hand across my mouth to hold in the laughter that is trying to bubble out.

After about five minutes of him rowing and a pool of lake water at my feet, I must ask him. "Owen, have you ever rowed before?" I mumble the burning question through my hands.

Don't you dare laugh.

He must have, right? Owen's ancient. He is from a time long before modern technology. Perhaps he has forgotten?

Owen growls down at the oars. He tightens his grip, the muscles in his forearms tense, and the wood creaks. I think any normal oar would have shattered with the pressure he is exerting. He sighs and lifts his head. He gazes back at me, his grey eyes earnest.

"Well, um... I've used the rowing machine in the gym."

That's it. I lose it. Laughter rips out of me, and I'm howling.

The man is adorable.

"I thought it would be easy."

Tears stream down my face, and the boat rocks violently as Owen's laughter joins mine. "Y-you've used the rower at the gym!" I gasp out. Laughing so hard, I have to hold my abdomen as it's hurting. "Oh, Owen," I say when I can. I wipe my eyes. "I needed that. Thank you." I beam a smile at him, so big my cheeks hurt. He blinks at me with a stunned expression.

"I like it when you are happy," he says gruffly.

CHAPTER
EIGHTEEN

When we get out of the boat, I'm still grinning like a loon. I secure the boat before Owen can and laugh at his growl.

"You need to eat a proper lunch," Owen insists. "Let's have a picnic." As soon as the words leave his mouth, a picnic blanket appears on the grass and then one by one, plates, glasses, a basket of food, and a bottle of what appears to be freshly squeezed lemonade appear.

You can say a lot about the host magic, but it's incredibly handy. I have a feeling it's going to make me lazy.

I secretly smile and we settle on the grass. I've never had a picnic before. Owen loads up a plate for me. I blush and mumble my thanks.

As I nibble at the beetroot and feta cheese salad, the sun filters through the trees. It's warm on my skin but not burning. I guess if I can control the weather and the sun isn't real, I can probably also sit outside all day and never burn. I tilt my head up and smile as a welcome breeze flutters across my face.

"Back home, I bet it's freezing," Owen rumbles. I nod and stab at the salad to get another forkful. "I like that your favourite season is spring. The weather here is lovely."

"Huh. I didn't even realise I loved spring so much. Everything I do seems instinctive. I guess I need to think about the weather more if people are going to stay. Maybe it needs to mirror the outside world. Perhaps something I can try later? When I've got more of a grip on the magic. Not that I'm going to go crazy with the rain or anything." I do a full-body shiver and stuff the salad in my mouth.

"You don't have to do that. Like the fae lands, the different courts have the same weather all year round."

"That's a good point."

"I think what you are doing so far is impressive. I've never seen anything like it before." I drop my eyes and poke at the salad. *He thinks my magic is impressive.* My heart sings.

Owen's mobile rings and I wave away his look of worry with a smile and a nod. "It's fine," I mouth. "Answer the phone." Smoothly he gets to his feet and prowls away.

I turn away to give him some privacy.

After a few minutes, he returns but doesn't sit down. A sad yet determined look takes over his handsome face. "That was Forrest. She needs my help."

Oh.

He looks worried, torn between helping me and his duty. I can't have that. Lives are probably at stake. So, like I did when I drove off in the hire car, I again decide to convince him I'm happy to be alone. This isn't his fight, and it's unfair of me to manipulate his time.

"Look at where we are; nothing is going to happen. I will be perfectly fine. Do you need to go now? Where would you like me to send you?" I don't want to do the entire Exorcist opening the portal malarkey that I did to get him here. But I somehow think if it's my idea, using my magic without being forced by the realm, it should be easier... I should be able to do it, easy-peasy. It will be a piece of cake. I hope I will be able to send him to where he needs to go. *Gosh, I instantly feel sick.*

"Yes, please, if you don't mind. Back to where I originally came through will be fine. Flash, I'm sorry I have to leave you. I know you're dealing with a load of—"

"It's fine," I interrupt as I snap open a portal behind him. *Wow, I did it.* "I understand. I didn't expect you to be here long anyway. You have a very important job to do. Thank you so much for helping me. I appreciate it." I drop my eyes from him as my stupid heart hurts. I'm being ridiculous. I fix my gaze on the picnic blanket and thread a tassel between my fingers. "Please be careful."

"I'll be back. I shouldn't be long," he says gruffly.

My magic pings with his lie.

"Sure." My lips pull up to show the fakest smile he's probably ever seen. I don't need magic to tell me I'm also lying out of my ass.

Everything inside me screams, "Don't go! Please don't leave me!" But I have my pride, and those words would never leave my lips. I cannot be that selfish. My problems are minuscule compared to others. Creatures need him, and Owen does not owe me anything. He has already done so much. He doesn't need to do anything more or be involved with any more of my shit.

"Make sure you eat. You've got to aim to eat at least double what you normally do."

I roll my eyes. "Yes, Dad." I wave my hand towards the portal. "Go. Be careful and I'll see you soon." Owen nods and steps into the portal, then with a final look back at me, he is gone.

Everybody leaves. I am, after all, a throwaway person.

A sad sounding whine comes from my throat and I slam my hand across my mouth to absorb the sound.

It's okay. I'm okay. I am just being a bit daft.

I force a forkful of salad into my mouth. It tastes like ash on my tongue, but I finish every bite. Once I finish the desert, I roll my shoulders, and with a wave of my hand, everything is gone. As I crawl up from the ground, I look at my hands. I don't think I need the hand gestures. The entire waving my hands about is kind of weird. If I'm ever in a situation where I do not want to show my intent, I need to stop doing the weird wave. Otherwise, I might as well get a fake wand and glitter.

I turn to walk back to the hotel, and cold encompasses my limbs. The sensation is eerily odd. The magic tingles a warning and then my entire existence folds around me. Sunlight, starlight, the magic explodes, and everything that I am is violently ripped away.

Oh no!

CHAPTER NINETEEN

I HOLD in a terrified scream as I'm swept along like I'm caught in a rip current. As the dizzying world settles around me, I attempt to school my face into a serene expression. A group of strangers is staring. I so meant to do that... Did I *Step*?

I bloody teleported. Unbelievable.

I think I left my stomach back at the lake. I'm in reception and at least a dozen dryads are standing before me, the remnants of a portal fading behind them.

"Gracious host," a lady says, stepping forward from the group. She drops into the most incredibly low curtsey. I blink a few times and my mouth flops open. What the heck? How do I react to that? I internally groan when all the dryads follow her lead. Fourteen of them, my magic helpfully supplies.

I wave my hands in the air and a "Hi" squeaks out.

My frantic waving encourages them to return to normal, and the lead lady continues what must be a readymade speech. "We are here for sanctuary—our trees are in peril. The humans and the dwarfs demand progress, so they have been ripping out our forests and ignoring the environmental protection orders the fae council put in place. No one will help us, and we are dying." The willowy lady leans towards me, her pale blue eyes glimmer with tears. I swallow and have to pin my arms to my sides so I don't fidget.

"I'm sorry to hear that."

"With your permission, mistress host, we would like to bring our trees to be rooted in your pocket world. We will lend you our strength, and you will allow us to live without fear so all branches can flourish, and leaves can nurture the ground."

Ah, that sounds completely ceremonial, and I have no idea what to say. My eyes flick about nervously like I'm a cartoon villain. I need Larry. "Well, okay." *Nice one, Tuesday. Real eloquent.* I give myself a sarcastic mental thumbs up.

The surrounding dryads all seem to breathe a sigh of relief at my words. Encouraged, I try again, hoping for the best. "You are all more than welcome." Better. This is all a bit of a shock. What more can I say? The poor dryads are dying. I can't have that on my conscience. And who doesn't love trees?

"Thank you, mistress." I inwardly cringe. The whole *mistress* thing is weird. It's something that we can work on once they've settled in. The other dryads join in with their thanks as I frantically look around for Larry. Where did he go? It's not like he needs a toilet break.

"Here is our sacrifice."

The—what now? Sacrifice?

The dryads part and a girl is unceremoniously dragged between them. Her dirty clothes hang off her painfully thin frame. When the dryads let go, I see the skin on her forearms is cracking. I look closer and see it's not just her arms. Like the bark of a tree, her skin sloughs off from her face and neck.

I worry even a slight touch will make it crumble. She needs urgent medical help. My heart ricochets off my ribs as they roughly push her towards me. The momentum of the push is too much. Her left leg drags behind her, and her right leg can't keep her weight. She flops to the floor in a tangle of limbs at my feet.

I silently yelp, my eyes widen with horror, and I drop to my knees. Without thinking, I reach out my hand and she flinches away.

Of course, she does. She's a sacrifice.

Her eyes roll about like a frightened horse and, with the last of her strength, she drags herself away from me. My heart flips. It cracks in my chest.

"You'll take her remaining life force as payment for our relocation?" the dryad asks.

A strange gurgling sound leaves my throat. My tongue is numb, frozen, and I don't know how to respond. *"You'll take her remaining life force as payment for our relocation?"* The leader's voice keeps echoing in my head. This whole situation is beyond me and my life experience. I mash my lips together. Oh no, I'm going to puke. I dry heave into my fist.

Maybe I should try to make my face into a villainous snarl, try to convince them I'm an evil creature. The threat that they undoubtedly imagine I am. *This is all too much.*

Everything around me instantaneously drifts away. Dimly I realise I'm in shock. For a few moments, I can't see or hear anything and it's like my brain shuts down and reboots. What happens if I am sick or I give in to the floundering panic that lies in wait beneath the shock. If these creatures are willing to sacrifice one of their own, what will they do to me if I act like prey?

Where the heck is bloody Larry when I need him?

As if answering a summons, the redheaded construct pops into existence. He takes in my wide-eyed form on the floor with the girl and casually steps over us.

"Welcome to The Sanctuary," he says in his friendly, jolly tone. I scowl. Can't he see everything is going to shit? "If you will all sign our terms and conditions, I can get you settled." He grabs the check-in datapad. "Are you okay to sign on behalf of your party? Excellent. If you just sign here and here. I see you brought a sacrifice. Lovely."

Lovely?

I realise the fae creatures are politely ignoring us. It's as if a family member and a friend isn't rasping with pain and fear on the floor at their feet. Like a piece of rubbish, they ignore her. Acting as if I'm going to suck the remaining life out of her while they check in.

What the hell is wrong with these people?

"Wonderful. Now, are we relocating your trees?" Larry herds the dryads away and they make their way outside.

Leaving the girl to her fate.

Anger ignites and the magic in my chest bubbles with the violent emotion. This is supposed to be a sanctuary. Sanctuary shouldn't require sacrifice. I need to get away from these parasites before I do something I'll regret. With a single thought, this time controlled, the magic twists around us and, with another gentler wave, sucks us into the ether.

WE ARE at the top of the hill, at the edge of the forest. The lake is far below us and we are sheltered from any wind. The dryad pants next to me, on the verge of hyperventilation. Her breath wheezes through her cracked lips and rattles her chest.

The girl rolls into a ball. "Please, make it quick. Don't let it hurt," she whispers.

I brush away the loose forage and then sit down next to her. I hug my knees. "What's your name?" Whoa, my throat is so damn tight. The girl's rapid breathing pauses. I can see her confusion at what she must think is an odd question. Murderers don't ask people their names, right?

"E-Erin."

"Well, Erin, my name is Tuesday. I know what you've been told, but it isn't true... Well, it isn't true of me. I will not hurt you. In fact, I'm going to try my best to help you." I rock slightly and nibble on my lip. "I'm thinking that you're struggling because of your tree?" Erin moves, so I take that as a nod. "Okay, so I'm going to—somehow—fix you both."

Erin lifts her head. Hazel eyes blink at me with utter, desolate confusion. "Is this some kind of joke?"

"No." I've never been more serious in my life.

"You're not gonna kill me?"

"No, but I need your help. You see, I've been a host for a day, and I've never done this before." Unless I count sending my magic through Daisy.

"A day? And you're willing to try to save us—me and my tree?"

"I want to try."

A tear dribbles down the side of her face and another follows.

Oh.

Erin buries her head in her hands and sobs. I wiggle on the ground and my hands uselessly flutter. I want to comfort her, but I don't know if I can. A minute ago, she thought I was going to suck the life out of her. It isn't every day that your friends and family attempt to sacrifice you to a *monster*.

I'm the monster.

I tuck my hands underneath my knees and rock a little as she cries. The dryad's pain is infectious, I want to ugly cry too. But I hold it in. I desperately hold off my thoughts. I can't dissect all this now. Erin is too important; she is the priority. So, I force myself into a blank state, a professional numbness.

When I think about this later, or if I dare to tell anyone, I will probably rage. But now, with the dryad crying, beyond the forced numbness... I feel so sad.

I hope Owen comes back soon. I need a hug.

When Erin's sobs are but a whisper, I clear my throat. "Are you ready for me to try?"

"Yes, please," comes the muffled reply.

"Okay, I need to urm... touch you." I cringe. "Can I please hold your hand?"

I can't even imagine how brave Erin must be as she takes in a shuddering breath, unfolds herself, sits up, and places a delicate hand in mine. Even though her hand feels like I'm holding a piece of wood, and slivers of bark-like skin sprinkle into my palm, I give it a gentle and what I hope is a reassuring squeeze.

"Okay." I take my own shuddering breath and close my eyes. I don't have to call my magic; it's there.

The tattoos glow bright white, painting patterns on the trees behind us as they swirl and dance on my skin. I can imagine I look a little like a disco ball.

The magic knows what I want, I guess 'cause it's a part of me. Like my heart, the beat pushing blood around my body. The magic is the same. It's a part of me. How quickly things have changed from visceral hate of magic to comparing it to an organ. Never in my wildest nightmares would I believe that could happen.

The silver magic flows into the dryad. Oh. Oooh, I can feel the rot. The pain of her tree, the agony from the very top of its branches down to its roots. Something heavy has crashed into it, and the tree has been ripped carelessly from the earth.

They are connected. Symbiant. And both are dying. Through that connection, my magic enters the real world. It crawls through the earth. With pinpoint precision, I free the crushed branches from the ground and gently unwind the roots that are buried in the mud. I ease the tree's pain as I call it to me. I pull it through a portal.

The portal opens behind us, and I pick the perfect spot. Where the soil is full of nutrients, sheltered from the elements, but where the light from my sun will hit the tree perfectly.

The ground gently parts, pulling the tree into its warmth. Each root is unravelled and repaired. The magic creeps in a spiral around the trunk, healing all wounds, spreading out inch by inch across the branches and encouraging new spring growth.

My forest is already full of magic and as connected as I am; I can hear the hum of the wood's joy at having such a beautiful fae tree join its company. Erin's tree sings back. No longer in pain. When it can do no more, my magic gently and reluctantly swirls away.

Erin groans and my concentration wanes. I blink and sweat rolls in my eyes, making them sting. I screw my eyes shut and dig deep into myself. I'm only half-finished. Now comes the scary bit: healing Erin.

I can do this. I must.

My magic gently creeps inside of her and immediately starts repairing her cells. It heals to the point where her body can then take over. I can almost see the red and white blood cells rush into each area. My magic collects the toxins and the rot as it goes, repairing and syphoning. My breath becomes laboured as Erin's breathing stabilises, but I push on. I just need a few more minutes.

There, it's done.

I slump to the forest floor and Erin rests against me.

"You did it. You saved us. Oh, Tuesday, thank you. Thank you so much... Oh, are you okay?"

"I'm fine," I slur. The two paltry words get stuck in my throat. *It is not safe to lie here*, warns my inner voice. I force myself to roll onto my side and I blink up at Erin. I don't have to force my smile. "Hey, you look great." My eyes swivel to her tree. "You both look great." Erin's short brown hair is glossy, and her skin has returned to a soft, healthy shade.

My head is a little floaty, like I have low blood pressure as I sit up. I can't look at Erin for this next bit. I trace the soil with my finger. "The other dryads, urm, they're on the other side of the forest." I can feel them. "I didn't know if you wanted to be closer. If you can give me a few days, I can mov—"

"No," Erin quickly interrupts. "If it's okay, I'd like to stay here. This spot is beautiful. If it's okay with you, I don't want to see them. Not for a while. Not ever, if I can help it." A fat tear runs down the side of her nose.

"Take all the time you need. Do you need somewhere to stay? I'm tapped out, but you can stay at the hotel overnight. I could build you a cabin? You don't have to see them."

"I will stay with my tree. Do you mind?" Her hazel eyes shine with unshed tears. "I'd like to sleep now."

"Oh, of course," I squeak out. I do an undignified roll onto my knees and somehow, with pure will alone, I scramble to my feet.

"Thank you. Thank you so much, Tuesday. You saved my life. I can't quite believe it." With each word, Erin steps back towards her tree. When they touch, her human form fades, and she becomes part of the trunk.

"You are welcome," I rasp.

CHAPTER TWENTY

After the overwhelming trauma of the day and with horrible thoughts bouncing around in my head, I thought I would never sleep soundly again. But I slept like a log. As soon as my head hit the pillow, I was out. I can only attribute it to using all that magic. My brain might still be actively freaking out, but my body was done. I slept so hard that when I woke up, I almost felt hungover.

Daisy stayed with her dragonette friends, which made me kind of miserable. Then I had to deal with my conscience, telling me I was being unbelievably selfish. I need to be happy for Daisy and be here if or when she needs me.

I'm up bright and early. I have already stuffed my face with breakfast. Taking Owen's advice to heart, I ate more than usual. I dress carefully in a high-neck, cap sleeved, navy cashmere midi dress and knee-high boots.

I've left my hair down, and it swishes against my waist as I make my way to my office. I need to have it cut, but I know if I do, I will hate the shorter length. So, I will refrain until it really needs it. Although, with the new magic sloshing through me, that might be some time.

I'm startled when I see Atticus sitting in the lounge area of reception, casually drinking a mug of something. I presume coffee. *Not blood. Gag.* He assesses me with those black eyes of his, and once I've passed some vampiric test, he greets me with a silent nod.

"Morning," I say, returning his nod.

"Good morning. I see we have more guests, the tree fae."

"Yes. I hope they won't disturb you. Your privacy and comfort are important."

"Not at all. I like the changes you have put in place. It makes for more of a pleasant stay. Don't worry, I won't eat any of them." He flashes his fangs.

I roll my eyes at his theatrics. He's not the first vampire that I've dealt with, even if he is the first pureblood. But the guy is super old, and he has a reputation to maintain.

"That's good to know. Although I should warn you, my magic will not allow you to harm another guest. Please let me or Larry know if we can help to make your stay more pleasant, or if you need anything."

"I will. Thank you, good lady."

"If you'll excuse me." Atticus nods and I spin away. I head to the back of reception and my office. But a stray thought stops me in my tracks. Burning curiosity. I turn back to the vampire and the nosy question spills from my mouth. "What are you doing here?" I wince. Yeah, I said that so beautifully. "You can tell me it's none of my business, but you are..."—I point to his immaculate suit and the whole 'grrrr I am a pureblood vampire' thing he has going on—"and this is..." I wave my hands at reception and bug my eyes meaningfully. "The hotel was not a nice place to stay before I arrived."

Atticus tilts his head to the side, and his black eyes take me in again. I'm almost positive he's going to tell me to get lost. "I loved a woman once. She went missing and all I could find led me here. To this hotel."

"Oh," I say eloquently. Well, that's deep. I wasn't expecting that. I shuffle from foot to foot but maintain eye contact. I've inadvertently asked a painful question and now I must see it through. The least I can do is look him in the eyes. "I'm sorry."

"I will stay until I can find what happened to her."

Oh. My stomach twists when he allows me to see the pain in his eyes. It is like a real-life tragic love story. My lower lip wobbles in sympathy. "She must be a very special person." I can't imagine being loved that much or loving someone so much that I can't move on. My eyes nervously flick about reception. "There is something not right about this place."

The vampire's black eyes narrow. I take that scary look as confirmation. I think little of what goes on here will get past him. I'd love to pick his brains. I'm sure, in talking to him, I'd get the nitty-gritty of this pocket realm.

But you have to give a little to get something back. Build trust.

So I aim for honesty, hoping sometime soon, the vampire will help me.

I nervously lick my lips and plough on. I need to trust my instincts. "When the dryads arrived, they brought a sacrifice. They wanted me to drain a girl of her power. Her life force. Erin... She's nice... She's alive," I squeak out as I wave my hands in the air. "I didn't, you know, urm, drain her. I'd never hurt an innocent." I shrug and scratch the back of my head. I drop my voice. I should have put a privacy bubble in place, but my magic tells me there is no one else around. "Look, it's only day two, but no matter how long it takes, I'm going to get to the bottom of everything. If I can, you know, find answers about your lady friend... Help..." My words come to a stumbling halt when he scowls.

His anger rents the air around us. My heart jumps a beat and my stomach flips. Shit, this creature is scary.

He takes a deep breath in, and it's like a mask falls into place. "Your kind words mean nothing. I've given up hope. I know she is dead." He taps his chest, and his voice drops darkly. "I just can't seem to move on. That's what happens with old things. Change is hard."

"Not just when you're older. I hate change." I wrinkle my nose and scratch my wrist. "It gives me hives." Atticus's top lip moves in an awful semblance of a smile, and with a dismissive nod, he takes his mug of *coffee* and prowls away.

I sigh with relief and wipe my sweaty palms on my dress. That wasn't a conversation I thought I'd be having with the vampire council leader. I think he is the European leader, actually, not just Britain.

I shiver and scamper to my office. Let's hope the knowledge of his lost love doesn't bite me on the bum and he kills me. I puff out my cheeks and la-la in my head for a few seconds.

CURSED WITCH

I have a meeting with Nyssa, the nicer host. Hopefully, I'll find some answers. I don't know this lady. I know I can't blindly trust her. I can't blindly trust anyone. So even though she was nice to me when we first met—well, nicer than the other hosts—I must remind myself she is not a friend.

I debate on where to take the meeting. I don't need to be showing her any more than I already have. So I decide to use the conference room again. Larry said the conference room only opens for council meetings, but I find no issue.

I take the same seat and strum my fingers against the glass table as I wait. The time ticks. I'm early. In the end, I don't have to wait long. The meeting magic pulses in my chest, in the rhythm of a telephone. When I acknowledge the weird sensation, the air in front of me shimmers and there she sits.

"Hello, Tuesday." She greets me with a warm smile that I instantly don't trust. I've seen the same look reflected on my face.

"Nyssa, thank you for meeting me." I smile back with my own professional but fake warmth.

"I am happy to. Now, you must be bursting with questions. Let's start with you asking me everything you need to know."

Wow. That is blunt. I have the almost overwhelming urge to word vomit everything that is going on in my head. I smack the eager words back down my throat and prioritise what I want to discuss. What is the most important?

My mouth is dry. "Thank you. That's a kind offer." I swallow and a mug of tea appears on the table. I mentally thank the magic and wrap both hands around it. Nyssa watches the whole thing, a flash of greed in her eyes. Interesting. Can her pocket dimension do that? Or is it unique to mine?

It's not important. I need to come to grips with this entire power sucking thing because if I don't, it's going to drive me crazy. "Do they pay? If you have a hotel in your dimension, do they pay to stay as a guest?" What I'm getting at is, do they pay with people? I still can't get over the whole situation with the dryads. It is sinister. The entire host thing is so snide.

"Well, there's only ever been one hotel in our history, and that's yours. No one else has strangers coming into their dimension. The security risk is immense. I would never put myself in that situation. My pocket dimension is small, with no outside space. I use my magic to build magical spaces—trinkets like bags, storerooms, nothing too elaborate. My clients love the fact that they can buy a magical bag. It weighs next to nothing, yet inside it holds their entire wardrobe." She leans forward in her chair as her eyes assess me. "The host that created your dimension wanted to help people. Can you believe that?" She titters into her hand. "He was the first to die. He wanted a world that could be a sanctuary." She wrinkles her nose. "But he didn't have the power. It was in a time when communication with the other worlds was difficult, not like it is now. I'm sure with your connection to Earth you'll be able to get enough guests. To answer your question, people do pay, and not all ways are monetary. To maintain the bonkers idea of keeping a sanctuary, you'd have to leech off your guests' power."

Stealing people's power seems to be a common theme.

I hunch in the chair and hug my arms around myself. I'm uncomfortable. It looks like my disgust in the dryads was unwarranted. They were so desperate, and they thought they were offering the right thing.

No wonder hosts have been hunted down, the snarky voice pipes up. This time I must agree; it doesn't look good.

Nyssa continues, seemingly not aware of how uncomfortable I am. "I guess you can charge money. Many a host has become exceedingly wealthy from our gift. That's what I do. But in running a pocket realm, energy matters. If you ignore the risks, the whole hotel idea has merit. Say you have guests—their essence adds to the magic. It's different with every host and every dimension. A small dimension like a storeroom can be powered for a thousand years with a few seconds of someone's life force—a drop of blood. A realm the size of yours"—she looks out of the window—"with the way it has grown, you might require years."

I'm unable to cover my horrified expression. I blink rapidly. Is she for real? I've given up my career in retail management for a hotel, a realm, that will cannibalise its guests.

Oh my goodness, what have I done?

No, there's no way I'm allowing it to do that. What about Owen? Has this bloody hotel been eating him? I think I'm going to be sick.

"Look at your face. You don't have to do that, Tuesday," Nyssa says, her eyes bright with understanding. She waves her hand across my arm, like an air kiss. "Close the hotel if the idea is so terrible. Keep your magic to yourself. You don't have to worry if you think about yourself. Why would you waste your magic on helping others anyway? No one else cares we hosts are dying. Take the power back, shrink the world to a manageable level and live your life." Nyssa narrows her eyes. "You want to help people?" She smirks at the idea and at what she sees on my face. "But you hate the idea of a power exchange. Think about it another way. You're from Earth?"

I do an odd little shrug of acknowledgement. My shoulders and neck are so tight.

"You spend, say, eight hours of your life a day working to earn wages to live. Your time in exchange to pay your bills. Yes?" She stares at me meaningfully and I nod. "Staying in your pocket realm, your sanctuary"—her nose wrinkles and she snarls the word with disgust—"the guests pay in power rather than money." She leans back in her chair and does a little stretch. She rotates her wrists in a way that, if I was with her in person, I'm sure I'd hear the click of her joints. "Both ways suck a little on the soul. At least this way, the hypothetical guest doesn't get sore feet and the hours in the day are their own.

"The balance is up to you." She holds her hand out and tips it like a scale. "Which way the needle falls. Too much and you hurt people. Not enough, and the pocket dimension disintegrates around you." She wiggles her fingers. "This balance doesn't make you evil. It is just a different payment system than the one you're used to. You wouldn't get much power from a pixie, barely a drop. But you could take a sizeable chunk from an immortal, like your hellhound. He wouldn't even notice the exchange."

Her explanation makes me breathe a little easier. It makes sense in a freaky, horrific way. Not that I'd touch any of Owen's power. Or anyone's power without permission. It's not something I could ever condone 'cause I'm not a psychopath.

This conversation highlights the difference between the hosts and me. I'm never going to belong, and you know what? I'm happy with that. I don't want to.

I think what hurt me about Erin's entire situation was that I could see myself in her shoes. I've always been seen as the weak person in a group. I do not doubt that in a reverse of fate that involved witches, it would have been me up for the role of sacrifice.

"I could pay the cost," I mutter.

"No, that's not possible, and it's completely unrealistic. The magic doesn't work that way. As I said, magic requires balance. But you don't have to keep The Sanctuary open. You don't have to have a hotel. You can just close your doors and pretend this has all been a bad dream." She smiles with satisfaction, happy with her advice.

Huh. Maybe a little bit too happy.

CHAPTER
TWENTY-ONE

I GET a warning tingle that a portal is about to open and then Larry's frantic voice comes from reception. "Tuesday, come quick."

"What now," I groan. I slam my hands on the desk and spring up, abandoning my business plan to see what all the fuss is about. I guess I need a break.

I stride into reception. The hotel is in chaos.

Everything slows down. It's like I am on the set of a film as smoke billows from the portal and heart-stopping moans rent the air.

The cloying smell of sweat, burned hair, and blood permeates the hotel and makes me gag. I cover my mouth and sway as my feet root me to the wooden floor. All I can do is stare in shock at the frantic activity before me.

A huge portal is open. It almost spans the entire room, and messed up looking creatures are getting spit out onto my floor. Dressed in tattered black uniforms and overspilling with weapons, the creatures' oversized eyes, pointed ears, and long hair announce these new *guests* are elven.

Not just elves, as I see the tell-tale black warrior markings peeking between the ripped fabric on their arms. Aes sídh warriors, to be exact, not normal fae. Two of them look to be seriously injured and they stay where they've landed, although one is rolling about and groaning, so he can't be that bad.

"I am not trained to deal with this shit," I mutter. It's like I have woken up into a lucid nightmare. An average, if not strange, day has inexplicably changed to this. What the heck am I supposed to do? *I am a soon-to-be ex-retail manager, now a reluctant hotelier. I can adapt.* I square my shoulders, lift my chin, and calmly track my unexpected guests.

The elves are setting up defensive positions.

In *my* reception.

That will not do.

When one of them shunts a sofa away from the window and goes to break the pane of glass with the hilt of his knife, my brain goes into instant emergency manager mode. I need to get control of this clusterfuck. Now.

"STAND DOWN! THIS IS A SANCTUARY, NOT A BATTLEFIELD!" I bark.

The elves stop what they're doing for a second and eye me like I'm nuts, then continue as if I haven't spoken. At least the elf that was going to break the window refrains. "Naughty elf," I magically growl in his ear as I shove the sofa back to its rightful place. He jumps, rubs his ear, and looks about wildly.

An episode of a medical drama comes to mind and the theory behind basic triage. "ANYONE WITH CUTS AND BRUISES BUT WHO DOES NOT NEED IMMEDIATE MEDICAL CARE, PLEASE WAIT OVER THERE!" I yell, pointing to the left of the room. "EVERYBODY ELSE GO WAIT IN THE LOUNGE AREA!"

I puff out my cheeks and rub my temple. When I ran from my home, I brought at least four vials of Jodie's healing potion with me. Forrest also stuffed in another six bottles. I am not prepared for war... but the aftermath of a skirmish? Yeah, that I can do.

Larry scurries to my side. "Larry, please, can you make sure they have everything they need?" With a tug of magic, I pull the potions from my room and shove them at him. "Start handing out healing potions."

"Of course."

"Thank you."

Larry clutches the potions to his chest and rushes away. I rapidly move through the elves towards the quiet one I had seen on the floor. The elves ignore me. "Now people! Get moving!" I clap my hands and shove them with my magic. "The more time you stand about staring at me, the less time I have to help your friends!" They grumble and hobble to their allocated sides of the room.

Better.

A few of them flick their long hair behind them as if they are fashion models. I roll my eyes. Now all but the seriously injured elf remains in the centre of the room.

Oh, and his scary-looking friend. Yay. Her dark hair, which is as long as mine but decorated in intricate plaits, glares at me. Her big, brown eyes are full of hate. Gee, it wasn't me who kicked her arse and hurt her friend. She needs to reign all that hatred in. I stare her down. I am pissed. The anger, combined with fear, makes me brave.

"Move," I tell her.

"I don't know you," she snarls.

I shrug. "Yeah? I don't know you either, but it didn't stop you and your fellow warriors from crashing into my hotel lobby, did it? You came to me, so move out of my way so I can help him." For a second, I think she's going to throw down and start stabbing me with the wicked-looking knife she is clutching. But she must think better of it. Not getting up, she shifts on her knees, allowing me barely enough room to see what I'm working with.

The unconscious elf is at least alive and bleeding profusely from a stab wound in his abdomen. I place both hands on his wound, and his hot blue blood squishes between my fingers. I wrinkle my nose. Gah, I should have thought about gloves.

This is gross. I am not trained for this shit.

At least the healing magic will deal with any cross contamination. He won't get ill because of my hands.

No, I am more at risk from the unfriendly elves.

If this is an entire court of warrior elves, popping through the portal, I'm in serious trouble. This is supposed to be a hotel, not a hospital. Why on earth did they decide to come here? I've got no idea.

I hunch and brace my hands so they don't shake. *Gosh, I feel vulnerable.* With that thought, I erect a barrier around reception. Not only to stop any of the dryads or Atticus from stumbling into this nightmare but to stop the elves from wandering. I don't want them to cause any trouble while I'm busy and my back is turned.

The realm's magic shudders, and more people come through the still open portal. In my peripheral vision, the portal spits out another bloody mess. Then, with energy that makes my hair flutter and stick to my sweaty face, the portal snaps closed. Thank goodness for that. I didn't want to close it in case I trapped anyone.

I blow at the hair stuck to my cheek and focus. I haven't got time for finesse. I need to heal him quickly. Sinking into the magic, his life force flutters. It is barely hanging on. I throw my magic into his body, using what I learned from healing Erin. Was that only yesterday?

My patient groans. I wince, and the female elf's hand drifts to the hilt of her knife. My eyes narrow on her fingers, and I grind my teeth. *What a cheek. I don't have to help her friend. These guests are taking the piss.*

With a mental snap of my magic, her weapons disappear. All the weapons in the room disappear. I should have done that as soon as they arrived tooled up to finish a war. That was a mistake I won't be repeating.

I wonder if I can make it so the portals won't allow weapons to come through? That might be a superb idea. Most creatures are, in themselves, walking weapons, but at least it limits the risk of being stabbed.

The noise in the room intensifies as my *guests* notice the missing weapons. Their shouts grow in outrage and the angry energy in the room peaks. "You will get your stuff back when you leave!" I yell. I lift my eyes and glare at the woman. "That was your fault," I mumble churlishly.

"I don't need a blade to kill you," she spits.

I roll my eyes. "Good to know. Neither do I. If you twitch a finger towards me, I'll send your arse back to where you came from. M-kay?"

She narrows her eyes at me and nods. "Wonderful." I grin manically, showing too many teeth.

Owen would be proud.

More magic and the elf's gnarly wound closes. I pat him on the chest. "There you go, Mr Elf, as good as new." Feeling exhausted, my hands drop to my sides, and I sag back onto my heels. My leather boots dig uncomfortably into my knees.

"I apologise. Tensions are high from the battle. Thank you," the female elf says, surprising me. The old fairy tale about the fae and their thanks is unfortunately exaggerated. Some say if you thank the fae, you gain a life debt, and vice versa. That isn't the case. But I appreciate the apology.

"No problem. Glad I could help." She pulls her now semi-conscious friend to his feet and guides him to the lounge area where the others are chugging down water. I drag myself to my feet and stumble to my next patient.

Gosh, I am drained.

A humongous black wolf lies in the middle of the floor and a petite girl with a mass of pink hair holds his shaggy head in her lap.

Shifters can heal from anything. Their cells regenerate every time they shift. That's why they don't age once they've hit their biological age of majority. Well, unless they encounter silver, which halts the shifting process completely, then all bets are off. After all they need to be alive to shift. Silver. That's what's happened to this big fella. He is riddled with silver and is bleeding out.

I drop to my knees next to them. "A silver bomb," the petite girl rasps and then violently coughs. "The dust... It's in our lungs. He knocked me out of the way and took the brunt of the shrapnel. You bloody idiot, Nanny Hound. Why did you do that? I would have been fine." Her voice is so raspy, it's like she has smoked two packs of cigarettes a day. I'd have put it down to silver damage, but I've heard her voice before. I recognise it instantly.

Forrest.

"You will help him?" she begs, lifting her eyes to implore me.

Her eyes hold a deep, haunted sadness with an edge. They whisper of death. My heart bounces and nerves twist my insides. One eye is yellow, and the other is too but with a hint of green pooling at the bottom. It makes her wild gaze difficult to hold.

I knew Owen's friend would be fierce, and also pretty, but I did not expect her to be so tiny and innocent-looking.

So bloody powerful.

She's a shifter. A formidable one. I tilt my head; her magic is weird. It bites at mine. Not with aggression, I don't think, but almost playfully. I ignore it and the goosebumps that spring up.

A female shifter in my hotel, covered in blood.

Oh heck. If anything happens to her... it doesn't even bear thinking about.

Female shifters are super rare. There are about ten in Europe. Ten. Wars are fought over them. They are coveted and squirrelled away like precious jewels, and yet, I have one covered in blood, kneeling next to me as she coughs out silver particles. *I should heal her first.*

But if I do, the black wolf will die. While I know she will not die anytime soon, the indecision wears on me. A niggle in the back of my head tells me I know this wolf, but I push the painful thought away. It can't be him. Surely fate wouldn't be that cruel? I sit back on my heels and try to steady my hands, which tremble with fatigue and nerves. *You're spiralling. Snap out of it.* I need to think of triage.

"Please try to heal him," she rasps.

This is a little more than repairing an open wound. "I will do my best. Come on, wolf, let's get you better." I don't know anyone who could fix this. I mentally roll up my sleeves, take a deep breath, and get to work.

With my heart still hammering, I thread my fingers through the wolf's beautiful, densely packed fur. His outer layer is coarse, and the downy undercoat super soft. I gently probe his wounds. He has chunks of silver sticking out of him. Like a furry pin cushion. I know if I don't get the silver out, and he doesn't bleed to death first, the metal will poison him and cause necrosis.

I can do this. Yes, it is a complicated procedure, but I can heal him. I'm the only one here who can.

This time, I close my eyes. I need all my concentration as I reach out with my magic. Cautiously, I touch the shifter's energy with the intention of not disturbing it. I imagine the pad of my finger brushing a pool of water so softly the tension breaks and the water ripples out. My magic is the ripple.

Gently, oh so gently, I follow the ripples through the tissues of his body, hunting out even the minuscule amount of silver nanoparticles. Destroying any trace of the dangerous silver oxide while also repairing his cells. Each cell vibrates at a slightly different frequency. I must match it.

On and on my magic travels, destroying and repairing until... there is nothing left.

Everything inside of him is normal.

"I did it," I whisper. I gently stroke him and then turn my attention to Forrest. "Okay. Now you."

"You are exhausted. I can wait."

"No, you can't. Please?" I hold my hand out, and with a scowl, she places her dainty, pale hand in mine. I do the same thing. This time it is much faster as the silver has settled only in the places where she has breathed it in. Her nasal passages, trachea, and the delicate bronchial tree of the lungs. "There," I say with a satisfied smile.

"Thank you."

"You are welcome."

"This is your fault. If you hadn't encouraged him to work for the fae, this would have never happened," an angry voice snarls. I sigh and lift my head.

"Arsehole, can't you just, you know, like, not be a prick for five minutes?" Forrest growls at the tall, fierce-looking blond man standing above us.

Another shifter.

"Forrest," he growls back, his green eyes flashing.

"Fuck you." She flips him off with both middle fingers and turns away. When she catches my eye, she smiles sheepishly. "Sorry about my brother. He's a dick."

I give a small chin lift in acknowledgement and duck my head back down to assess the black wolf. He still hasn't woken up, and I am worried I have done something wrong.

Forrest's brother prowls around us, and in response to his aggressive body language, she gently lowers the wolf's head to the floor and stands. Using her tiny frame to block her brother from getting any closer, she herds him away from us. With each step, she pokes him in the middle of his chest. My lips twitch. I like her style.

"Yeah, 'cause he isn't in any danger while working with you," she scoffs. "What a load of crap." Poke, poke. "Next time, use your own guys and leave my friends alone. The fae don't need your kind of help, arsehole."

"No fighting at The Sanctuary," I mutter. I ignore them as they continue to bicker. With growing panic, my magic washes over the wolf. Again, I check him, his blood, his cells, and I can't find any trace of silver in his system. I scrape my messy hair back as I think. He should wake up... any second now. It is then I notice that I'm still stroking the wolf's beautiful fur. I am too tired to blush. What a strange thing to do.

I reluctantly pull my hand away. As soon as my fingers leave him, the gorgeous black wolf shifts. It's a blink-and-you'll-miss-it transformation as he changes shape.

Beautiful, rich dark skin and a naked, muscular torso greets my suddenly wide-awake eyes. I've never seen anyone this well-proportioned in useful muscle—ever. I almost swallow my tongue. Mesmerised, I follow the rise and fall of his chest with each of his shallow breaths. I force my eyes up his torso instead of down... The wolf's grey eyes find me. He grins.

Wow. My heart misses a beat. Thank the stars he is okay.

"Hi, Flash."

CHAPTER
TWENTY-TWO

"Owen. You're okay!" Forrest drops to her knees beside us, her brother long forgotten. My gorgeous hellhound beams a smile at her like she hung the moon. My raging libido screeches to a halt and my addled heart hurts. My soul cracks a little.

He loves her. I can see it.

With a delicate hand, she pats his chest and I can't help but grind my teeth as my eyes fixate on the motion. *Get off him.* Everything inside me cries. My magic whips out with fury. Forrest doesn't even blink when the naked hellhound she is petting is suddenly dressed from head to toe in his normal black combat gear. *Better.*

"You had me worried there for a second, Nanny Hound. Never pull a stunt like that again. If you had died, I would have gone after you and dragged you from death, just to beat the crap out of you." She huffs and then grumbles, "I'm glad you're okay." Then she hugs him. She loves him too.

Warm grey eyes catch mine over her head and he shrugs as if to say, *what can I do?* My face contorts into a brittle smile and, with determination and a total lack of finesse, I scramble to my feet. "I need to organise this mess. Please excuse me." I turn on my heel and wobble away. "See Larry if you need anything," I say over my shoulder.

Owen is just someone my dad paid to help me. There is no need for me to be upset and I am not the girl who will go after another girl's man. That is the worst thing to do to another person and now that I have seen Forrest in person, felt her power, it would be immoral, and frankly suicidal, to step on her toes. *They love each other.*

My stupid heart is eviscerated.

Instead of running away, like I want to, I reaffirm that I have a job to do. I need to focus on what's happening around me. Owen must have opened the portal here for the warrior elves while he and Forrest tackled some big bad who uses illegal silver bombs. I hope this wasn't anything to do with the elf they were hunting, the one who tried to kidnap me.

As I stomp towards Larry, with each step, I feel more and more like hammered shit. I am quite sure nobody can tell. I'm sure I am pulling off the hundred-percent-in-control-of-the-situation-vibe. I have my manager face plastered on. Crikey, using all that magic in such a short span of time has drained my energy dry.

If this is going to be a typical day in my life as a host, I'm probably going to be dead before the end of the week. I shake off the macabre thought as a high energy protein bar is slapped in my hand.

"Oh. Thanks, Larry."

"No problem. The way you wobbled across the room, I thought you needed it." Well, there goes the idea that I'd nailed my getaway. I scowl and, with trembling hands, carefully unwrap the bar and stuff my face. *I should wash my hands. They are still kind of gooey from the first elf.*

As I chew, another man swaggers over to chat with Larry. He is a shifter, with light hair. He is also dressed in black. Huh. The shifters must work closely with the elves. Which is strange. From my history lessons, working nicely together is unprecedented. Shifters and elves have a nasty intense history of hating each other, and if I remember correctly, shifters may not set foot in Ireland.

It appears things have changed. I shrug. As long as there isn't a ruckus at the hotel and they aren't trying to kill each other, it has nothing to do with me.

On our walk, I remember Owen saying he and Forrest were working in Ireland. I guess I was too busy drooling at Owen to put all that together.

"We will be out of your hair in an hour," he tells Larry in a soft, lilting Irish accent. "I didn't even know this hotel existed. This is a pocket realm, right? With the power buzzing around the room and the fact nobody can wander off as there is an impenetrable force field in place, all evidence points to the fact you must be a legendary host." He slaps Larry on the shoulder. "That's incredible."

My eyes flick between them, and as I chew, my jaw aches. Why are these extra nutty protein bars like chomping on concrete?

"I've never met anyone alive with your branch of magic before. My boss would be interested in working with you."

"Me? Working with me?" Larry splutters. His bright green eyes widen. "Oh, no, sir. You must have me confused. I am but a lowly servant of my mistress." Larry presents me with a flourish of his hand and a click of his heels.

Cute.

"Hi," I say, as I cover my mouth to hide my chomping. As my mouth is still full, the word comes out garbled. The empty wrapper crackles in my grip as I give the shifter a tired wave. The shifter stares at me as if I've got two heads.

"You? You're the host?" he scoffs. "But you are just a girl."

Dick.

I ignore his faux pas. Frankly I can't be arsed. On the plus side, at least I've finished the protein bar without getting any blood on it. Go me. Larry hands me another. "Thank you. So an hour?" I ask, waving the protein bar as if trying to hurry the shifter along. I have important things to do. Like... cry. "You said you will all be leaving within the hour?"

As I unwrap the new bar, my hands no longer tremble. My energy levels have already increased. My lip curls at the state of my hands and in response magic washes across me, cleaning my navy dress and skin of any residual sweat, goo, and blood.

Handy.

I bite down on the new bar as the shifter chokes on his own spit. Oh dear, I have unintentionally shocked him with my quick clean up. I refrain from offering to pat him on the back. Perhaps Larry should, as they are so chummy.

"Yes, um... mistress?" the shifter mutters, his tone full of disbelief.

The word *mistress* coming from him hits a little bit below the belt. I wince and shake my head. "Oh no, none of that. Ignore Larry, please call me Tuesday."

"Tuesday?" His hard brown eyes narrow. I can almost see his mind churning as he rolls my name around in his head. "Don't I know you? Aren't you Matthew Larson's daughter? The younger one?" He raises an eyebrow.

Oh no, he knows my dad. Can this day get any worse?

"The dud." He nods sagely. "Your lack of magic has been truly exaggerated."

"Can't fool you, can I?" I fake titter. *I need to get out of here.* "Yes, I'm Tuesday Larson, and yes, I have host magic. You are? I know we've never met." I drop the fake smile and narrow my eyes.

"Mac. Pleased to meet you, Tuesday." He holds out his hand. After transferring my snack into my left hand, I reluctantly shake it. "No, we haven't met, but I've seen a photograph of you in your father's office."

Oh. I nod wisely. Insinuating I know about the photo. I didn't know Dad had a photo of me. It must be a group one. I clear my throat.

"So this is *your* pocket realm?"

"Yes."

"Impressive."

I back away from the shifter. "Well, I will just—"

"Our weapons?" Mac taps his thigh and narrows his eyes.

"Will be returned once you've entered the portal."

"Thank you for your help," he says reluctantly. "We wouldn't have survived if it wasn't for your timely portal and assistance. Please give your father my regards."

"I will. Well, thank you for visiting The Sanctuary Hotel. I hope you visit us again, under less exciting circumstances. Larry will help if you need anything. If you will excuse me." I don't wait for confirmation and instead spin on my heel and hurry away.

I fixate my eyes on the door behind reception, not trusting myself to search out a certain hellhound. As I beat a hasty retreat, I catch the raspy voice of Forrest as she tears into Mac. "Sexist much? You'd think being my friend you would have learned not to be a dick."

CHAPTER
TWENTY-THREE

Lightning flashes across the sky as thunder booms so loud it rattles the glass. It becomes so dark outside as angry grey clouds roll in and a torrent of rain smashes against the floor-to-ceiling windows.

I made it rain.

Without conscious thought, my mood has affected the weather. I refused to cry, so the realm does it for me. I stare at the sheets of rain, matching what I feel inside, and my guilty thoughts go to Erin and the other dryads. I'm sure the trees will welcome a drink unless I flood the bloody place. I push the clouds apart and release the odd energy in the atmosphere.

What I need to do is work. It's what I am good at. I drag the datapad towards me and click back to my business plan. I studiously make a note that I need to improve the residential suites. It will take me a while to gather the power needed, those damn fae warriors and their power sucking visit. I absentmindedly brush my magic against the realms. *I can't...* my thought trails off.

It should be almost empty from the giant portals and everything, but it is full to bursting. That is not right.

What has it done? Have I accidentally hurt someone?

Oh no, no-no-no.

My overwhelming panic makes me shake like a leaf. I feel sick. *I knew. I knew I should not have trusted this cursed place.* With a pulse of power that I will no doubt regret, as it makes my head spin and my heart pound in my ears. I close my eyes and spread my magic out as I would when healing a body.

Against the blackness of my eyelids, the realm's map appears. As each guest pops up, I urgently do a mental check on them. I start with the elves and the shifters in reception and work slowly outward to the fae in the woods. My entire body sags against the desk as I discover each person is safe and accounted for. Thank the stars.

The realm has not stolen a smidgen of power. In fact, all my guests are glowing a little more with each second that passes. Huh. While my magic is still doing its thing, I tap into the realm's magic a little harder.

I need to know more. I discover an immense bubbling pool of power at its centre. It was not there before. I frown. As tentatively as I can, and with the same creeping delicate fingers of magic I used with Owen, I explore the edges of the deep well. I see where the trickles of power and rivers of magic are coming from.

A relieved laugh spills out of me as I realise what I am seeing: the dimensional realm does not need to steal power. The power, kind of like the formation of clouds, happens naturally. The invisible energy that radiates off every living creature sheds naturally into the air. I can somehow see it. Under normal circumstances, I would only feel the power when someone like Forrest is scarily powerful. But on my mental map, I see it. I see Forrest glowing like the sun and all my other guests moving stars around her. Their power saturates the air, condenses, and forms into invisible droplets. Which then pool into the realm's well of power.

The varied creature presence alone is enough to replenish the magic. The magic then meets the guests' needs, including my own.

Magical symbiosis.

It never needed to take any power by force. The entire revolting sacrifice saga was a complete farce. Did the other hosts know? Gosh, this changes everything.

Unless... I open my eyes and blink as they re-adjust to the bright light of my office. Unless the magic is fooling me. My stomach dips, and I groan. I sink my head on the desk. Perhaps I need some time out in the real world to get my head on straight. I need to think without any interference, as it's obvious the magic wants me here.

I don't know what is real.

I don't know if I am being manipulated.

I can't trust myself.

Of course, I can't trust myself—I convinced myself that I was in love with a complete stranger, and all the while he was in love with another girl. I turn my head and my cheek presses into the frigid glass of the desk. First, I need to eat to replenish my energy, then wait for the elves and shifters to leave. Then spend a few hours away from this crazy place.

There is a rustle in the hallway, of scales rubbing together, then a scrape of claws on the wood. With a grin, I leap from the chair and fling open the door. Daisy scampers in.

"Hey, pretty princess, this is a pleasant surprise," I say in a singsong voice. "How did you get down here with the magic blocking reception?" I firmly close the door behind her and sit back down. I wouldn't put it past her to Step. I hold out my hands and wiggle my fingers. Daisy jumps, her wings flap, and she gains enough height to land on my lap. "Perfect landing. You are getting so good," I praise.

With a deep contented purr rumbling in the back of her throat, she tucks in her wings and curls into a ball. I gently stroke along her spine and sniff. This is nice. Normal. I blink a few times. I am not crying.

A MUG of hot tea is balanced on my tummy. I grab the individually wrapped piece of Terry's Chocolate Orange. The chocolate normally comes in a bar or in a fancy orange shaped ball that you have to tap on a hard surface to unleash the orange milk chocolate segments. But this packet is special. It has all different flavours of chocolate mixed with the famous orange.

I narrow my eyes and my mouth waters as I fiddle with the wrapper one-handed as my other hand precariously balances the cup. This one is white chocolate. Daisy, who is now sitting on my desk, watches my antics with interest. She juts out her head and with her left nostril, sniffs at the chocolate. She wrinkles her muzzle, completely unimpressed. "No? Good. Chocolate isn't for dragonettes," I tell her wisely.

The plastic wrapper rustles and the piece of white chocolate jumps. A sound of dismay leaves my lips as, with only the one hand, already encumbered with the wrapper, I'm unable to catch the runaway treat in time. The chocolate falls. "Noooo," I groan, horrified as it falls the wrong way, plopping into the cup with a splash.

My poor tea.

I like my tea super-hot, so I can't just stick my fingers in and fish it out. Jodie, my sister, says I have an asbestos mouth, that no tea can be too hot for me to drink. I shrug and strum the porcelain. What can I do?

I stare down at my cup mournfully. I tip it, but I'm unable to see past its brown watery depths. Never mind. I was going to dip it in any way. I guess now I will have to wait to eat it.

I take a sip. Like a tea connoisseur, I tilt my head to the side and smack my lips. *Huh, the tea tastes the same.* I wiggle my fingers over the bag, and with a dramatic flourish, I close my eyes and reach inside. I crack my left eye open. Oooh, this one is dark chocolate. This time, I unwrap it well away from the cup.

Once I take the last sip of my brew, I grin when I spy the white blob nestled at the bottom. I tip the cup to my mouth and give it a shake. "Come to me, my sweet," I mumble. The white mass doesn't want to move, so I bang the cup on my bottom lip to encourage it. I watch in cross-eyed fascination as the blob oozes towards my mouth.

Slowly, oh so slowly.

"Gah, come on." I stick my tongue into the cup to give it a prod of encouragement. I grin when the melted goo hits my taste buds.

Yum.

I'll have to remind myself to do this again. I could become a superfan of tea-melted chocolate goo.

When my tongue can't reach the remaining chocolate, I stuff my entire hand into the cup. I hum as I use my index finger to scoop up the chocolate trail. Once collected and the evidence from the chocolate mishap erased, I lick my finger clean.

Still humming around the finger in my mouth, I lift my eyes. The hellhound is leaning against the wall. Staring at me. My finger comes out of my mouth with a pop.

I wince.

His grey eyes dance with amusement. "Here you are."

"Here I am," I say as I duck my head and play with the empty cup. I ignore Daisy's happy yip as she greets the hellhound. The traitor. My fingers trace the handle, and my eyes fixate on the movement. I can't look at him.

"Why did you run off?" he asks gruffly.

Owen isn't wearing his normal combat gear. Instead, the hellhound has on grey suit trousers and a black shirt and tie. He looks gorgeous. My stomach flips as if I have got a load of fairies bouncing about in there. Bouncing around drunk.

His big body moves, and he prowls across the room. He stands next to the chair. The heat and the masculine smell of him fills my senses. My mind flashes back to his nakedness and I feel my cheeks go instantly red.

Ah shit.

"I..." *Tell him the truth.* My heart hammers in my chest and my stomach feels as if those stupid drunk fairies go *crazy* inside me. I lick my lips. "I wanted to give you and your girl privacy."

"My girl?" Owen's voice rumbles. "What? Who? Do you mean Forrest?" He laughs.

It's not bloody funny. I can feel the red from my cheeks spreading down my neck and onto my chest. Anger bubbles inside me. Women should build each other up, not tear each other down. Yet, this hellhound thinks the entire thing is hilarious. I will not mess with another girl's man.

My hand tightens on the cup, and I hunch into myself. I must seem so pathetic.

"Hey. Hey, Tuesday, look at me."

I shake my head. His big hand cups my chin and he tilts my head so I meet his eyes. "I haven't got a girl. Forrest is like my adorable, crazy, annoying little sister. I love her; she is pack." I freeze and my breath sticks in my throat. "I'm single, Flash."

He. Is. Single.

The magic doesn't ping. He isn't lying, not that I think he would, but... Oh my, he isn't with Forrest.

"You are? You are single?" I whisper.

"I am. What about you?" His dexterous fingers of his other hand knead the area behind Daisy's horns, and she wraps her tail around his wrist.

"Urm... single. Very, urm, single," I squeak out as I do a bizarre movement with my hands.

Owen chuckles. "Are you now?" He moves so close that I can see little blue flecks dancing in his eyes. I gasp and breathe in his warm, minty breath and the fresh scent of soap. He's had a shower.

"Yes," I croak.

"That is good to know." My heart almost stops at his breath-taking smile. "But you won't be single for long. Not if I have any say in it. I am gonna make you mine, Flash." My mouth pops open, and Owen brushes his thumb across my bottom lip. The taste of him fills my mouth.

"You are?" I rasp against his thumb. "Me?"

Oh.

My entire body is on fire. He is so close I can feel the whisper of his breath on my lips. I squirm in my seat as he closes the scant inches between us. I go cross-eyed as I watch him. He kisses the tip of my nose. And then the left side of my mouth. Then the right. Not quite a kiss. I have the sudden desire to feel that full mouth on mine.

"Can I kiss you?" he whispers roughly.

"Oh, thank—" Before I can say more, Owen swoops in and wraps his arms around me. He lifts me from the chair and into his body. He growls. The sound is so deep, it rumbles in his chest. My heart skips a beat. Dumbfounded and so turned on, I think I'm going to explode. I close the gap between our lips.

I'm kissing him! I am kissing him! And he's kissing me back!

Bumper cars, my addled brain whispers strangely. Wow, the hellhound has fried my brain. It's like an impact of pillowy bumper cars. His lips are firm, but also so soft. Owen tilts my chin to get a better angle to pillage my mouth. His tongue nudges against my lips and I open. Oh my goodness. Our tongues twirl together.

This is an epic kiss.

Way too soon, he pulls away from my mouth, and I follow his lips with a tiny, disappointed moan. "Your dad gave me a heads up—he had an interesting conversation with our friend, Mac. Your coven will arrive any minute."

Dazed, I blink at him and rub my lips together. They are tingling in the best way. "Okay…" I say dreamily. "Can we… at some point… urm, do that again?" My voice comes out breathless, as if I've run a mile.

"Abso-fucking-lutely."

CHAPTER
TWENTY-FOUR

I collapse back in the chair in bliss, then my kiss-addled brain starts firing, and the words, "Your dad gave me a heads up; he had an interesting conversation with our friend, Mac. Your coven will arrive any minute," finally sink in and echo around my brain.

Oh no.

No-no-no. My eyes widen. I bend forward and wrap my arms around myself as dread fills me. My mum and dad are coming. They are coming and my time to get a grip on this situation has run out.

Bloody Mac. That damn shifter has gone and dobbed me in to my dad.

My mum is going to flip out. She is going to be a thing of nightmares. I sink back into the chair and my hands shake as I imagine her face when she found out about my new, shiny magic. Not from me, oh no, but from one of my dad's associates. I cringe. She's had time to work herself up into a frenzy, and now they are coming to visit.

Yay.

"What is wrong?"

"Nothing," I whisper.

"Tell me what you are thinking that has such a sad, frightened look on your face."

"They are my thoughts," I grumble in a petulant tone.

What is it about our parents that can reduce us from perfectly normal functioning adults back to little kids?

"I am fine."

Owen chuckles, making me feel even more silly. His grey eyes narrow, and he places his hands on my desk and leans toward me. Our faces are so close, my eyes cannot help but drop to stare at his beautiful full lips.

Crikey, the man is beautiful.

"You are a terrible liar." He taps his nose. "The fear wafting from you burns."

"Oh." *Oh crap.* I look down at my hands and cringe. "I'm sorry." I don't want his sensitive shifter nose to have to deal with my stink.

I try to roll the chair away, but the frustrating hellhound just follows me, concern and determination written all over his face. He grabs hold of the chair and wheels me back towards him as he sinks to his knees. *He is trying to make himself smaller.* My tummy flips.

I take in a deep breath and blow out a series of short breaths to gain control. My knee bounces.

Somehow, I know he will respect my privacy and let this go. But he's earned an explanation. Am I brave enough to be honest? I've never told anyone. He is going to see my coven in action for himself. There will be no hiding it.

Forewarned is forearmed, I guess.

But then… she's always so lovely around strangers, and even with my coven, she hides her nastiness so well. They see me as the bad penny. I'm her scapegoat. If I tell him and she acts all loving, then he's going to think I'm a liar. I don't want to see the distrust or distaste in his eyes. It would break me further. This is why I don't let anyone close.

I chomp on my lip, and then the words blurt out. "I'm worried about what she will say, what with the whole host thing…" My voice trails off and Owen's eyes soften. I drop my voice to a bare whisper. "She can be a bit much, my mum." I twist the cashmere fabric of my dress and thread it through my fingers. "It's stupid, but she can be scary. I-I didn't ring her when I should have and now Mac—"

"Hey. Hey, Flash, I got you." His humungous hand comes up and his thumb brushes away the stupid tears that are trickling down my face. *No, he doesn't.*

"You are only here 'cause my dad asked you."

"Is that what you think? I'm not staying 'cause your dad asked me. Tuesday Larson, you intrigue me. I have an overwhelming urge to be around you." The hellhound smiles down at me. I lean into his hand and close my eyes for a second. "I am on your side. I will always be on your side. If you want me to, I can meet them and send them back on their way. You don't have to do anything you don't want to do. I've got big shoulders; I can deal with your mum. I can be your rock, your shield."

Wow.

No. One. Has. Ever.

"Or if you don't want me as a shield, I'll be here to pick you up, dust you off if you ever fall."

Oof, my heart just doubled in size, then exploded. I am done for.

"T-thank you," I rasp. The hellhound kisses my forehead, and I turn my head and kiss his hand that was holding my face.

I am so in love with this man. I don't care if it's only been a few days. Soul-deep, I feel overwhelming love. He is *mine*. I might not be his, but I don't care, even if it makes me a fool. He is worth it.

"What you need is to stick with people who pull the magic out of you, not the madness." I blink at him and sniffle.

"I hate magic," I whine.

Owen chuffs. "It is a quote, and I meant it figuratively. You need to be around people that bring out the best in you, not people who drive you crazy or frighten you."

"She is my mum."

"Doesn't matter," he says gruffly. "You hate your magic? Huh. Really? From what I can see, you were made for this. Your use of magic is effortless. For you, it is as easy as breathing. Do you think the other hosts find it so easy? Do you think I've seen anyone do what you do? Forrest told me how you dealt with the warriors. How you bossed them all about." His eyes twinkle. "How you saved Sebastian and healed me. You are so incredible, unique, and so damn brave. Stop doubting yourself. I believe in you."

I sniff again, and my lips curl up into a tiny smile. Owen is super old. He must know what he's talking about, right?

"Are you going to be okay?"

I nod. "I think I am."

"Good. Okay, I am gonna go have a little chat with Mac," he growls.

The hellhound kisses my forehead and prowls out of my office to go deal with his friend who Owen thinks is still loitering in reception. I think, from his expression, he is also planning to put Mac in a headlock and punch him a few times in the face. Ha. I want to put Mac in a headlock and see if I can punch him in his face. I'm so mad at him. I knew the shifter was a dick. I didn't know the extent of his dickishness. If I had, well, I would have charged him for the use of the hotel. I huff and get up from my chair.

I rub my arms. I need to think of a way to get Owen the hell out of here, at least for a few hours. I don't want the man I love being brought into my coven shit. We have this special thing going on. We've had our first kiss and now... Now my mum, my dad, and whoever else from my coven are coming to ruin everything.

Ah shit.

My hands flutter as I firmly tug and then smooth out the fabric of my dress. From what I can see, it looks immaculate. I tuck a loose strand of violet hair behind my ear and sigh up at the ceiling. *I'm a horrible person.* I know it's not Mac's fault, and he isn't a dick. I shouldn't blame him for my mistake.

It's my fault. I should have told my coven before anyone else had the opportunity. This is on me.

I'm glad then that Mac has already left the dimension with the last of the elves, including Forrest, and her brother.

"Come on Daisy Duco, our pain in the arse coven is coming." Daisy gets up from the desk with a stretch and an enormous yawn. She waves her wing at me, her way of asking me to carry her. I roll my shoulders, scoop her off the desk, and shuffle into reception. With a flick of magic, I drop the barrier around the front of the hotel and—

Gosh, everything inside me wants me to lock the portals down and run.

CURSED WITCH

I love my coven, but I don't want them here. This entire situation is going to end up being an embarrassing mess. Different versions of this moment have played out before. It always ends with me the loser.

Owen's phone rings. "Hello. Yes, sir. I will ask her." He puts the phone to his chest. "It's your dad. He asked for you to send the portal. He has tried asking for sanctuary without success."

No, they don't need sanctuary; they never have. It's me that has needed it from them. *Get a grip, Tuesday,* I mentally snarl. *Other people have it worse and your witch girl problems aren't even that bad.* I need to count my blessings.

I picture my dad in my mind and visualise opening the portal at his location. With a snap of magic that crackles the air and makes the little strands of hair on my nape raise, there's the familiar warning tingle, and then, with swirling green magic, the portal rips open into my realm.

CHAPTER
TWENTY-FIVE

Great, my panic is making me sweaty. My heart thuds and I fidget. The first to come through the portal is Dad, followed swiftly by the rest of my coven. Cool as a cucumber, Dad strolls into the middle of the room, his hands behind his back as he takes everything in with a raised eyebrow.

I also glance about and try to see the hotel from his perspective. It is exquisitely beautiful. I am so proud of the changes I've made.

In the exact spot my dad is now standing, an elf was bleeding all over the floor. Now, the entire lobby is immaculate. You could not guess a massive group of elves and shifters had stomped their way through here only a few short hours ago. For someone who doesn't like to clean and who has, in the past, given her dust bunnies names, a self-cleaning hotel is epic. Like a mega jackpot lottery win.

I take a deep breath, move my neck from side to side, and shake out my hands. My poor fingers are cramping as they have been balled so tightly into fists. A light breeze ruffles my hair and cools my sweaty cheeks. In my next breath, vanilla and cinnamon invade my lungs. The hotel somehow smells of comfort, like I have burned a dozen cinnamon and vanilla candles for their visit.

It smells of Owen.

I huff out a surprised sound. Whoa, it does. I sniff again. It smells just like the hellhound. How strange. It is like the hotel is trying to calm me down.

Thank you. I hope the realm's magic knows I'm grateful. It is also a reminder that if this all goes tits up, I can always stuff them back in a portal and send them home. For the first time in my life, I have the power here.

Daisy flaps a wing and I wince as her long claws dig into my shoulder and arm. My dragonette nuzzles me, the scales of her muzzle brushing against my cheek. I cluck her underneath her chin and kiss the extra soft skin between her nostrils.

"Hi, sweetheart," my dad says to me, then nods politely at Owen, who is standing directly behind us like a sentry.

"Hi, Dad. Thanks for coming," I mumble awkwardly.

My mum doesn't say hello. She doesn't say a word. At first, I think she is giving me the cold shoulder as I watch her sashay across the room to the seating area. Her heels click ominously on the wooden floor. Each clicking step she takes tries to drag me back to my childhood, and the helplessness I felt makes me cringe. When Mum gets to the window, she pokes at the curtains, flipping the fabric between her fingers as if to check the thread count. She then looks out at the lake with a satisfied sigh.

Oh no, she's not mad at me. She is proud. It took me a moment 'cause I didn't recognise the contented expression on her face.

"Hi, Auntie Tuesday. Hi, Daisy. Hellooo, hot bodyguard," my fifteen-year-old niece Heather says as she barely glances up from her phone. She manages a half-hearted wave as she bounces towards my favourite chair.

"Heather!" Ava squawks.

Heather's curly blonde hair flutters around her shoulders as she collapses into the chair. "Great. You have fast Wi-Fi," she mutters, ignoring her mum as her thumbs rapidly move across the screen.

"I am so sorry, Owen. She's at that age. Thank you for looking after Tuesday. It is nice to see you again," Ava says.

My mum is fluffing up all the loose cushions. She is practically buzzing, overflowing with joy.

My other two sisters break out of their shocked trances and, as a unit, turn and rush towards me. Jodie gets to me first, and I'm engulfed in her strong perfume as she hugs me. Daisy sneezes and then lets out a hiss when Jodie doesn't immediately let go. Daisy's tail whips about like a cat. She dislikes the intrusion into her body space.

"Hush, mini monster. I am allowed to hug my sister," Jodie chides. "Little sister, I've been so worried." Within the hug, she shakes me. Daisy wraps her tail around my arm and grumble-growls her disapproval in my ear. "When you didn't get to the safe house, I thought something awful had happened to you."

It had.

"I am sorry. As you can see, I'm okay." I hold my arms out for a visual inspection, but Jodie hugs me tighter. "I'm sorry I worried you."

Jodie, out of the four of us, is the spitting image of Dad, just a tiny female version. I have to look away from those brown eyes when she finally lets up her hug-fest and meets my gaze. They radiate with equal parts hurt and concern. "You have a lot of making up to do." Jodie lowers her voice. "I understand why you didn't message me. It just makes me sad you avoid us because of her."

My dragonette is done with another angry grunt as if she is highlighting just how much Jodie has ruined her day. She pushes off my shoulder and jumps. She is airborne for a few seconds until she smacks into the centre of Owen's chest.

The hellhound lets out a surprised grunt and then allows the golden dragonette to snuggle into the crook of his arm.

"Oh. Well, now that is interesting," Jodie says as she eyes the pair.

I can feel the redness heat my cheeks as I see her brain working overtime. Daisy hates everybody—everybody but me, and now Owen. "Afternoon, Owen," Jodie says with a huge grin.

"Hey, Owen," Diane says as she unceremoniously shoves Jodie out of the way. Then it is our older sister's turn to pull me into an embrace.

"Ladies."

Diane is five years older than Ava, six years older than Jodie, and that makes her fourteen years older than me. She's the spitting image of our mum, with her dark blonde hair and violet eyes. When I see her, my heart always does this silly little jump, and I can't help but be cautious around her, which is entirely unfair, as she is nothing like our mum.

Diane is incredibly sweet, unlike her creepy boyfriend. I can't believe he is here.

Andy, the boyfriend, loiters behind her like an unpleasant smell. He pulls his hands from his pockets and scratches the back of his neck. His dark hair is all over the place. It's only been a few minutes, and he already appears to be bored with our coven reunion.

"What have you been up to?" Diane whispers as she hugs me fiercely. Squished against my sister, out of the corner of my eye, I frown as I watch Andy trundle over to the nearest wall and tap it with his knuckle.

What a weirdo. I don't know if he thinks that's a manly thing to do or thinks the walls are made of paper. *Everything is real, dickhead.* You'd think as a shifter, he'd know a little about magic. I do my best to ignore him as his dirty trainers squeak-stomp across the floor. But then the cheeky sod attempts to go behind reception! Before I can say anything, Owen is suddenly there, in his way. My hellhound narrows his eyes in discouragement. Daisy adorably snaps her razor-sharp teeth, providing backup.

Andy puffs up his chest, scowls, and stomps back to my sister's side. He mutters under his breath about elitist shifters and something about fire extinguishers.

"You've had some big changes," Jodie says as Diane finally lets go of me with a sniff.

"I can't believe you didn't ring and ask for help. How on earth have you dealt with all this on your own?" Diane says almost at the same time. She crosses her arms and shakes her head.

It is not as if I can say, "Oh, you know, it's me against the world," so I shrug and mumble, "I didn't want to bother anybody."

"She's not been on her own," Jodie says with an eyebrow wiggle and salacious grin. She drops her voice into a sexy cadence. "The hot hellhound has been guarding her body."

Diane snorts.

Crap, I hope he hasn't heard her. Uhm. Owen's silent amusement dances in his eyes and he coughs suspiciously.

I clear my throat, my damn face going red. The blood rushing to my cheeks is practically vibrating. "As you can see, I am okay."

"Okay," Diane tuts. "You are more than okay. The magic is off the charts strong. I can't believe you sent us a portal! A portal! Out of nowhere. Do you know what level of magic that is? No, of course you don't. Witches would kill for that level of skill, and you do it without a spell or a potion in sight. I can't believe how much you've blossomed, Tuesday. I am so proud of you."

"Oh, urm... thanks."

"What the heck is the magic on your face?" Jodie asks in a way that only a sister can.

I shrug. "It's a host thing."

"It's pretty," Diane says, her eyes tracing the swirls across my skin.

"Thank you, though you should have heard me scream when I first noticed them and the light show started. They freaked me out."

"I bet. Beautiful, but scary, huh?"

"You've had a hell of a long weekend." They continue talking over each other and I can feel the start of a headache.

"I wonder if you'll be able to make small pocket dimensions. Those things are crazy expensive. It would be great practice for your new magic and fantastic revenue for the shop," Jodie says.

"I guess I can give it go."

"Wow. You have your own pocket dimension." Diane lets out a squeal and spins in a circle. "This is so cool."

"It's a pocket realm," Ava says.

I smile at her and nod. "Yes, it is."

Ava has our mum's violet eyes and our dad's dark hair, which is a striking combination. She is a tech witch—the proper term is technomancy. Her magic is so unique. She can combine magic with technology with breath-taking results. She is more at home with computers than people, so she doesn't hug me, which I appreciate. But I get her thousand-yard stare in reprimand.

I groan. "Again, I am sorry. I have only been here a few days, and you cannot believe what a nightmare it has been. It's been a lot to deal with."

"Yeah, we heard about everything," Jodie replies. "We just didn't know it was *you* until a few hours ago."

"What?" My entire face scrunches up with a frown. "But how could you have—"

"Heather!" Mum snarls at my niece. "Stop sulking and get off your phone. This is a coven meeting, not time to talk to your friends. You need to step up, child. We have only just risen from the shame of having the worst witch in Europe."

"Mum, don't speak to Heather like that. She is nothing like Tuesday," Ava says, blocking her daughter from our mum's sight. Ava's wide eyes meet mine when she realises what she just said out loud. "Oh, Tuesday. I didn't mean... I'm sorry."

My magic pings with her lie.

I rub my chest and drum up my best fake smile. "No, it's fine," I rasp. I duck my head, but I am not quick enough as Ava sees the hurt in my eyes. She moves towards me. I am quick to hold up a hand to keep her at bay. "Honestly, it's fine." My bottom lip wobbles.

Talk about putting me on a pedestal and then kicking it away. Yeah, wow. It's always a guarantee my coven will keep me humble.

"We heard about the elves," Ava says quietly.

"And the dryads," Jodie says.

"The entire UK is talking about you," Diane adds.

"What?" Horror fills me. "No. No. It's supposed to be a secret."

I am not ready.

"It was Mum," Jodie mumbles.

"I informed everyone I could," Mum says as she clicks back across the room towards us. She snatches the phone out of Heather's hand and drops it into the bag that is nestled in the crook of her elbow. Heather whimpers.

My sisters unconsciously move out of her way and Ava grumbles under her breath. Heather looks a little lost as she stares at her empty hand.

"You told people?" How could she have in such a short timeframe? "You told others what I am? Mum, how could you? You don't understand. There are these hunters—"

"Of course, I did. I made a magical announcement."

I sag in defeat. A magical announcement is a huge expensive spell, mostly used in wartime to send out a message to *every witch* in the United Kingdom.

Yay...

"Your power should be celebrated. Your magic will make the history books..." she continues, crowing on about how elevated the coven has become. I rub my forehead as I silently freak out.

How could she do that without speaking to me? I knew keeping my identity secret would be impossible, but I thought I had a little bit of time. Time to perfect my magic, time to learn to protect myself, protect the coven, and now I've got no bloody time at all.

Oh, bloody hell.

I can't think, what with the metaphysical knife that is sticking out of my back, biting against my shoulder blades. I swallow down what feels like a lump of lead in my throat and for a few seconds, my vision goes hazy and my head spins.

I feel the warmth of the hellhound, a trickle of awareness as he moves closer behind me like a rock turning the tide of an ocean. "Breathe," Owen murmurs, the spearmint of his breath caressing my cheek. His soft lips brush the shell of my ear. His hot hand slides down my body to rest on my hip, and he gives me a small reassuring squeeze. Lightning rushes up the back of my legs and, all at once, my knees are weak. My arm slides against his hand and his thumb traces the soft skin on the inside of my wrist. Ha, goosebumps are traitors.

I take a shuddering breath, and I lift my chin. For the first time in my life, I know what it is like for someone to have my back against my mum.

"You shouldn't have told anyone, Mum, it's way too dangerous." My voice is firm. I become the woman who competently scaled the career ladder at work. The woman who dealt with a massive group of warrior elves. "Do you realise you've put the entire coven in danger?"

"Danger?" my mum scoffs. "I've put the coven on the map more like it. Oh, my darling girl, you do not understand our world as you've been squirrelled away for years with the humans in your shame. You don't have to do that anymore." When I continue to stare at her, she tuts. "Honestly, Tuesday, you are so dramatic."

She turns her head to bring Dad into the conversation. He is eyeing Owen's hand, which is still resting on my hip. "Matthew, you agree, don't you? We needed to get ahead of the situation. What with the fae in Ireland going on and on about the great dryad rescue."

The great dryad rescue? What on earth?

"We had to make sure everyone knew the return of a legendary host was, in fact, a witch. A Larson." She nods her head at Dad, and he noncommittally shrugs back. "Wonderful. Oh, Matthew, you should have seen Patricia Cordell's face. I've waited years to put her in her place."

"Dad, are you listening to her? You have got to understand—"

"Don't you try to manipulate your father," my mum spits. Her hand whips out and she points a jabby finger at me. My heart jumps and I can't help the minuscule flinch.

There you are.

Her *oh darling girl* charade didn't last very long. Her mask just keeps on slipping. A boom with a flaming sound effect chimes in my head. *Burn.*

In response, Owen's hand on my waist gets a little heavier. His chest rumbles behind me with a barely repressed growl.

"I'm your mother and I know what is best for you. If you had listened to me in the first place, we would have figured out this whole host magic thing years ago. What did I do to get such a disrespectful and stubborn daughter?" Mum's tone implies me being stubborn is the worst possible trait one can possess.

Mum, I learned it from you. It's a coven trait.

She throws her hands up in the air and turns her attention to my sisters. "I brought you girls all up the same, so I don't understand why Tuesday is so... Anyway, let's get back on track. As soon as I found out the news, I announced it to the community. I have already had two marriage offers." Mum claps her hands with glee. "Two!"

What?

I've never seen her look so excited. It's freaking me out. More so when she beams a smile at me.

CHAPTER
TWENTY-SIX

Confused, I shuffle my feet. I tilt my head and peak up at Owen. His lips are pinched, and his jaw is tight. Nestled in his arm, Daisy lazily blinks at me. One of her wings is flopped, daggling across his muscled forearm, the other against his chest. She is lying belly up with legs akimbo, toes pointed as the hellhound tickles her tummy. *I'm glad one of us is having an enjoyable time.*

I rub my temple in an attempt to relieve the huge stress headache that is building. He must have worked out what's going on. I wish he would fill me in, as I haven't got a scooby. Why is my mum talking about marriage proposals?

"Margaret Harris's son, Peter, who is only a few years younger than you. Twenty-two. The best witch in his class." She nods smugly. "The other man is fifteen years your senior. It's all very sad his wife died during the riots. He has two little girls and has been holding out for a powerful new wife."

Is she... talking to me?

My mum grabs hold of my wrist and tugs me away from Owen to deftly manoeuvre me around my sisters. She snaps her fingers at Dad, and he obediently places a datapad in her hand. She waves it in my face.

CURSED WITCH

I look at Owen in alarm. It might be the light tricking me, but his shoulders look even broader, and *blue flames* flash within his eyes.

Whoa. Flame on.

"This one is Peter." I wince as Mum pinches the inside of my arm to pull my attention from Owen as she points at the image of a nice-looking guy. She flicks the page to a *long* list of the stranger's attributes. Of their own accord, as my eyes drift down the page, they seem to cling to a highlighted section and a notation about his sperm. I squeak and wave my hands in the air; my panicked flailing makes her drop her hold on my arm. Mum scowls and tries to make another grab, but I skilfully avoid her and rapidly back away.

"That guy? You want *me* to marry him? Are you kidding?"

"No? Oh, well, the older one—"

"Neither. No way." I wildly point at Jodie. "Jodie would make an amazing wife."

"Oh, thanks. Shove me under the bus instead," she mumbles.

Uh. "Sorry," I mouth.

Witches, like many humans, marry. But I never knew that there was a weird underground arranged marriage thing going on in the background of our society. Male witches are super rare, but we don't need male witches of our kind to procreate. Heather's dad is fae. The magical gene is incredibly strong, and it seems to produce powerful witches, no matter the bloodline. Strong, full-blooded witch parents don't necessarily make a strong child. Look at me.

Before this mess all started, everyone thought I was a dud, or I had magiclexia. In the scheme of things, fate and a creature's DNA does what it wants. Again, look at me. Where the heck did the host magic come from?

Magic is weird.

Unless you are from a coven with super old-fashioned rules and a fanatical need to keep their bloodlines *pure,* I presumed no one else in the community cared.

I guess from the manic glow in my mother's eyes, landing a rare male witch as a husband is considered a great honour.

"Don't you think I've tried?" Mum whines and throws her hands up in the air. "I've been working away for years to get one of you girls a decent match. Years. Now, out of everyone in this coven, it's you. And *you* have the gall to say no? I don't think so, young lady. It is a great honour. Don't you dare ruin this for me. You will do as you are told."

A great honour out of my nightmares.

I am in love with a hellhound. As if I'd say okay to marrying some random guy. Even if my soft heart did not belong to Owen, I can only imagine having another coven as in-laws. Gosh, more random witches sticking their oars into my life. I'd have permanent hives.

"Mum, I will not marry a stranger. Why would you ever think I would?"

"I neither have the time or the crayons to explain how important this is," my mum snarls. Wow. I'll have to remember that insult, as it was a good one. Even after all these years, she still has the ability to hurt me. Never underestimate the power of words. "You will do as you are told!" she screams.

My ears ring. I am so angry, for a second, I lose my good girl filter. "This is bullshit."

"Language!" Mum yells.

Jodie's mouth pops open and then she grins with understanding.

"Wow, Tuesday. I haven't heard you swear since you were a kid," Diane says with narrowed eyes as she blinks her long lashes at me.

"You can swear?" Mum gasps.

Yes, Mum, the nasty anti-swearing spell you made me take is finally broken. Ta-da. Go me. "Yeah, well, it's hard to swear when your mother puts a gag spell on you," I blurt out bitterly.

The silence is deafening.

Shit. Did I say that out loud?

"A what?" Diane squeaks. "No... You wouldn't." She laughs awkwardly and looks around. "Mum, she is kidding, right? Mum?" When Mum says nothing to contradict my statement, Diane narrows her eyes. "That is abuse."

"Mum?" Ava says.

"It was a strong, illegal potion," Jodie says as she looks down at her feet and toes the floor.

"Jodie, you knew?" Diane elbows her in the side. "You bloody did.

Why didn't you tell me? Mum, I don't understand why you would do something so awful." Diane's hurt but angry stare is laser focused on Mum.

Mum shrugs and looks at Dad for help.

He remains silent.

"When? Mum, when did you put... a what?" Diane tilts her head to the side and her violet eyes flash. "An anti-swearing spell? When did you put an anti-swearing spell on my little sister?" My feisty blonde sister steps in front of me while holding her arms out wide, almost as if she can protect me from something that happened years ago. "When did you do that?"

"I was sixteen," I say helpfully. I shuffle forward and place my hand on her shoulder and squeeze it. "It's okay. It is in the past. Jodie only knows 'cause she tried to help me a few years ago."

"Why didn't you ask me?" Diane spins around, pointing at her chest. "You know potions are my speciality. I could hav—wait. What? Back up at sec. You were sixteen? Sixteen," she whispers.

"Mum," Ava snarls.

I can't believe that my sisters are sticking up for me. Perhaps it is Owen's presence that is motivating them? Or maybe I've never given my sisters enough credit.

Wow, they love me.

"You always said she had a stick up her arse." Andy chortles and slaps his leg.

Hilarious.

"Andrew, now isn't the time," Diane chides. She turns back to me and grips the top of my arms. "Look, I did say that. I said it a lot, but I didn't understand. You hid it so well. I used to think you not swearing was ridiculous. I used to think it was an adorable, weird quirk." Her voice drops and her eyes fill with tears. "I used to laugh at you, Tuesday. All this time I thought because you couldn't do magic, you were bitter, twisted... jealous." She swallows.

"But you weren't jealous, were you? You were just trying to protect yourself from her." An angry tear runs down her face, and she wipes it away. "From our mum." She spins, blocking me again from our parents. "Mum, how could you? What else have you done?"

"I did what I had to do." My mum lifts her chin stubbornly and glares back at my sister. "And don't use that tone with me. I'm still your mother. When you have children Diane, you will understand—"

"I have a daughter and I don't understand, Mum," Ava interrupts.

"It worked out in the end, didn't it? I was right. Tuesday just had to learn to apply herself. Look at this place. It must be worth a fortune. Once we get a grip on her magic, there's no telling what she can do."

"You won't be going anywhere near Tuesday and her magic," says a menacing voice.

Owen.

CHAPTER
TWENTY-SEVEN

Owen is watching me. His eyes glisten as they stare, and I see about a million questions hiding in his beautiful grey eyes. *What is he thinking?* I unwillingly stare at the way his muscles seem to ripple with his every movement as he prowls toward me.

He'll be the death of me.

He reaches across and takes my hand in his. My skin throbs with the contact. Tiny sparks pass where we touch, and they careen up my arm until the silver marks dance like a disco ball.

Whoa.

The awareness of his body from mine is like a living thing inside me.

"What? Who are you?" *Knock it off, Mum. No one believes you didn't notice the seven-foot hellhound.* "Why are you even here, pawing my daughter? Keep your hands to yourself. She. Is. Taken. This is coven business, shifter. So why don't you"—she flicks her fingers at him—"hurry along. Matthew, get rid of him. He shouldn't be here for coven business."

My dad hunches and makes a sad sounding sigh. Dad learned a long time ago not to interfere with the women of our coven. His words, not mine. I think he thought it was best, as he was—and again, I quote him—outnumbered. For a man who is always professional and in control of his work life, he's really under the thumb when it comes to his wife.

"Hellhound," Owen corrects. "And I hunt people who break our laws," he says in a dark warning.

Mum makes an unimpressed humph sound. You have to hand it to her. She really doesn't give a monkey's.

I don't know what Owen will do if she roots around in her bag for a nasty potion.

"No, he is staying. He is with me," I tell her. "But don't, you know, kill off my mum," I mutter out of the side of my mouth.

Owen squeezes my hand in reassurance.

Mum glares at me in a way that screams, "Wait until I get you alone." "I can make him forget if needed," she says with a malevolent smile.

"Mum! Don't you dare." My breath seizes up in my throat. There is a hallow silence that raises the hair on my arms. The hellhound is preternaturally still, and his face is carefully blank. Is she trying to get herself killed? His hellhound power floods the room, battering my mum's weaker magical signature out of the way like a battering ram.

"Wow, you are racking up illegal magic use, Mum," Diane mumbles.

"Power hungry bitch," Ava says under a breath.

The hellhound's power has nothing on mine. I drop Owen's warm hand and move. I glare at my mother, and with each stride I take toward her, the livid magic inside me floods the space. "You will not touch him. You will have to go through me first and I'm not a little girl anymore," I snarl.

The room goes dark, and outside, thunder cracks. Heather screams in fright at the lightning strike that follows. It hits the roof of the hotel and travels down through the building, dancing and crackling against the windows. The sweet, pungent aroma of ozone and magic fills the air.

Owen's tree-trunk sized arm wraps around my waist and he boldly lifts me. He moves me away from my coven, away from my crazy mother. He puts me gently on the floor. *Is it time for them to go home yet?* I willingly shuffle behind him, and I rest my cheek against his back.

Crikey, Tuesday, that was a little bit dramatic.

It has been a long day; that is my excuse. I glance at the clock on the wall and groan. *Is it only two o'clock?* I yawn so big my jaw pops. It has been a crazy day, and I need to keep my wits about me, but soon, I will need sticks to hold my eyes open. I could sleep for a week.

I push the clouds away and take a deep, cleansing breath to settle my magic. I breathe deep until all I can smell is his scent. Oxygen has vanished, replaced by cinnamon. "Sorry," I murmur.

With flaring nostrils, Daisy peeks over Owen's shoulder. She chirps and a little puff of smoke spirals from her nose. With cat-like agility, her claws stab into Owen's shoulder and back as she scrambles down to me. Owen grunts. "Gentle," I reprimand. I then smile when her scaly little body wiggles into my waiting hands.

I move to stand next to Owen as Daisy clambers up my arm and then balances between my shoulders, her back legs on either side of my neck. Her front claws dig into my head, pulling out wisps of hair. Her tail whips from side to side and her wings flutter for balance. I don't bat an eye, used to her antics.

Luckily, at the moment, she's all smoke, but I have it in the back of my mind. I could always use a hair potion to fix any accidents if my cute little beast set my hair alight. Owen's hand drops to envelop mine and we thread our fingers together.

"Don't make a choice just yet." Mum's pointy finger is back, and she draws an imaginary circle in the air around us as she moves forward, seemly unaffected by my outburst or the quietly livid shifter.

"I see where this is all going. A hellhound? Really, Tuesday?" Her eyes take us in with pity, and she shakes her head in disappointment. "You will change your mind when you get bored with his muscles."

She looks at Dad and narrows her eyes. "Thinking about it..." She taps her bottom lip. "The longer we take to decide on the lucky husband, the better and the more offers we might get.

"If we rush in and pick a witch, others might think we are too keen. It makes sense to wait. I can make them work for it." My mum beams a creepy, satisfied smile.

I am glad Owen is here to grab a hold of me, otherwise, I'd be going with my urge to knock my head against the reception desk, while wailing, *why me, why me?* Why won't she bloody listen? Nothing I say is going to change her mind. In her head, she's finally hit the magic jackpot.

Mum wets her thumb with her tongue, then leans forward and rubs the spit-coated digit on my face. On. My. Face. I throw myself back away from her as I make a sound of disgust. "Mum, gross." I wrinkle my nose and scrub at my cheekbone. Ew. I can smell her spit and it makes me want to gag. "Why would you do that?"

"The marks are real?" she asks. "I thought they were some frivolous spell."

What? Marks? Oh, the glowing, swirling magical marks all over my face and body. "Of course, they're real."

"Mum, I don't think a spit bath is going to remove powerful magic," Jodie says with exasperation.

"Unless there's something in your spit that we don't know about," Diane snarls. She still hasn't let off her glaring.

"Tuesday, are you not going to offer us refreshments? I think we will be more comfortable sitting down in the lounge area. If you will all follow me."

Yeah, why not. Make yourself at home, I think as Mum sashays across the room and Dad, my sisters, and Heather obediently follow. Andy and his trainers squeak along at the rear.

"Andy has been so helpful while we've been dealing with this nightmare. He has really stepped up, hasn't he, Dad?" Diane says to change the subject. Dad makes a noncommittal shrug and mumbles what I think is an agreement beneath his breath. As if on cue, my magic pings with the lie. Huh. Interesting. I'm not the only one who thinks Andy is a dick and my sister is waaay out of his league.

But Diane is an adult and if she wants to love a man-child, that's up to her as long as he doesn't hurt her. I hope the creepy shit doesn't hurt her.

The shifter must also be on Owen's shit list, as when Andy attempts to take a seat next to me, he has to scramble out of the massive hellhound's way. Instead of standing behind me like an anonymous bodyguard, Owen sits down on the sofa, placing himself between me and my coven. He tugs me against his side.

This is all nice and cosy.

I let the magic of the realm pick my coven's brains and an assortment of food and drink clatters on the surrounding tables.

"What? What is this? I have never seen magic like this before."

"This is all very special."

"Whoa, can we eat this?"

I can't help but grin at my coven.

"Yes," I say, shuffling a little in my seat. "The magic of the realm can be a bit jarring. I woke up to the smell of bacon and fell out of bed."

"You know that this is beyond the coven's expertise, beyond anything we've experienced," Dad says, his voice soft.

"I know. I think it's beyond anyone's experience. I don't even think the other hosts know what they are doing."

"Oh my, afternoon tea," Jodie whispers at the full tea set and fancy tower of plates overflowing with mini sandwiches and cakes.

Heather squeals and gives me a toothy grin at her bowl of spaghetti. "Auntie Tuesday, your magic is epic."

"Perhaps we can sit in the dining room?" I ask, frowning at all the plates. Gosh, they are hungry.

"No, we are fine here," Mum replies. Dad grunts when she pulls the massive bacon cheeseburger from his hand and then loudly lectures him about his cholesterol.

"Yes, dear," he grumbles.

I roll my eyes as if Mum couldn't knock up a potion to counteract anything negative in his diet. Another burger appears next to his outside hand, with a pint of Carlsberg lager to wash it down. I snort and Owen's lips twitch. Without my mum noticing, Dad bites into his new burger. He closes his eyes on a silent groan. I help him out by getting Mum's attention as I feed Daisy a slice of cucumber with a "here comes the aeroplane" noise.

"A dragonette familiar," Mum declares as she takes a delicate sip of coffee. "It has been staring me in the face this entire time. I cannot believe the most important thing in the history of our coven, and I did not see it. Mainly because you avoid spending time with your coven."

Yes, yes, it's all my fault.

"Familiar?" I frown. Familiars are scarce, to the point of being sacred to witches. Even in my coven, no one is strong enough to have one. There hasn't been a new familiar bond in over a century. I might be out of the loop with the witch community, but I know that.

"Do you think dragonettes are that friendly? It's a wild animal, girl. Of course, Denny is your familiar."

"Daisy."

"Oh yes, Daisy. Lovely creature." Daisy lets out a hiss and tries to bite Mum's finger as it waggles in front of her nose. Dad swiftly pulls Mum's hand out of the way of her snapping maw.

Mum's eyes are glazed over, so she doesn't seem to notice, and even after the close call of almost getting bitten, she doesn't drop her manic smile.

"You have a point. The dragonette is showing actual signs of a familiar bond. How interesting." Mum nods at Jodie's words and her smile grows even bigger. "She also adores Owen. Which is wonderful. She must see you, Owen, as Tuesday's mate." Owen grins and Mum's smile vanishes as Daisy hops onto Owen's chest and rubs her muzzle underneath his chin with a happy chirp.

"Jodie?" I ask.

"Hmm?" She places a hand over her mouth as she chews a delicate-looking sandwich.

"Is it okay if I try to link a portal gateway to the shop?"

"You can do that?" Andy's nasal voice pipes up, butting into the conversation. He bites into an apple and peers at me over the shiny green skin, his face a mask of disbelief as he chews obnoxiously. *Chomp-chomp.* I wince at his mouth sounds.

"I think so... I'd like to try it."

"You aren't a gateway witch." My nose crinkles as I get a glimpse of chewed up apple as he speaks. "Someone is getting a little bit full of herself." He chuckles mockingly and opens his mouth to say something else, but then thinks better of it when Owen turns to stare at him. He looks away and takes another bite of the apple.

"Of course. That's a wonderful idea," Jodie says.

"I think it would make a good escape hatch, in case anything were to happen again, you know, like the mercenaries."

"That's a great idea," Dad says. He leans forward in his chair. "So, did you use the escape ladder when the mercenaries came to your flat then?" I nod and Dad looks all too pleased with himself.

"Yeah, yeah," I groan and wave my hands in submission. "Yes, Dad, you were right about having an alternative exit." Dad grins but doesn't rub it in. "I am reformed and from now on, I solemnly swear to always have an alternative escape route."

"Why the shop?" Mum asks. "You should put one at the house so I can come here directly. I don't want to have to wait around for your wonky portal service."

Wonky portal, have you heard her? Yeah, that's never going to happen. A doorway directly to her house? Gah, I have to repress a shudder.

"So, I am going to do that today if that's okay?" I ask Jodie.

"No problem, the wards will let in you and anyone with you of your choosing," Jodie replies with a not so subtle nod at Owen. Andy grunts and we ignore him.

"You can always make your own portal, Mum," Diane says sweetly. Uh-oh, her smart mouth is going to get her into trouble. Mum can't make portals, only a gateway witch can, and only with fixed gateways that are attached to ley lines.

Mum ignores Diane's dig.

As a host, I don't use ley line magic. I think I just rip a connection through the dimensions as I make portals out of thin air. If my school's magical theory books are right, I should be able to open and fix a portal to go anywhere. That is a cool piece of magic.

I guess I have only just scraped the tip of the iceberg on things that I can do. My tummy flips, and suddenly, I am overwhelmed and a little bit sick.

Another thing that is making me sick is all this marriage malarkey. Distance and running away has always been my thing, a simple but perhaps unhealthy way of protecting myself. I learned long ago no one was willing to listen to me, so there was no point in opening my mouth. Now, here is Owen. We've just had our first kiss and I am already head over heels. This time, I can't sit back and nod my head when my mother says I will marry a stranger. Owen doesn't know that I will agree, only to avoid my coven for as long as it takes for my mum to give up her wild notion. Another eight years if needed. But instead of it being me and Daisy against the world, I must take another person's feelings into account. I've got to think of him.

What does he think?

What would I think if his pack insisted he marry… mate with somebody else? I'd be devastated. It would break my heart.

To not say something would be the worst thing I could do. Disrespectful. What kind of person would I be if I did that?

So, I do something I haven't done since I was sixteen years old. I fight my corner. I get a bright idea and send a blast of magic out into the real world.

Huh, it worked. I sit back, feeling a tad smug. Ah, heck… I might as well get this over with. I don't want this hanging over me and Owen.

I have the urge to roll my neck like a fighter going into a ring.

Ding, ding.

"So, Mum, this whole marriage thing…" Owen's thigh brushes against mine. I nibble on my lip. This will be like removing a wax strip, unpleasant but worth it in the end. But like a wax strip, it must be done quickly. Not that I've used a wax strip. We have spells for that. Even though I hate magic—or I did—I'm not opposed to cheating when it comes to body hair.

"Not this again." Mum groans and dabs her mouth with a napkin. "I have decided you will marry one of those boys. There is no choice, no discussion. You will, for once in your life, do as you are told."

Well, there might be a teeny tiny problem. I try again, doing my best to hold in my smugness. "I appreciate the time you have spent on this, and I understand how important it is to *you*, but I am not marrying a stranger just to make you happy."

"I'm right about this. You'll see. I know what is best for you. I am your mother."

Owen grunts.

"How dare you interfere?" she snarls at him.

Owen just sits there and stares back at her. His silence will drive her bat shit crazy. She isn't his mum or his coven leader, and he doesn't have to learn her rules or play her games.

"Mum, you are being rude." Diane puts her steak knife down on her plate, abandoning the huge steak she is eating as she stares Mum down like she is dealing with a charging minotaur. "You have to stop." Mum blinks at her and then slowly takes in the angry faces of her coven.

"Carol," Dad growls. "That is enough."

"Well, it's a good thing then that I have magic," I say as I blow on my nails and then buff them against my dress. "'Cause I sent a magical announcement to both men, thanking them for their kind consideration, but I'm not and never will be available for an arranged marriage." Mum grows pale. Diane grins at me with approval, picks up her plate, spears a piece of steak, and chews happily.

"Oh, and I also sent an announcement to the rest of the community, so there will not be any further misunderstandings." For the first time since they arrived, my smile is genuine.

"You did what?" Mum croaks out.

A packet of crayons and a colouring book pop out of the ether and slap onto her lap.

CHAPTER
TWENTY-EIGHT

Everyone gasps and Heather snorts out a laugh. Mum opens and closes her mouth a few times. I have rendered her speechless. *This might have been the best thing I have ever done in my life. Or the worst!*

Mum, seemingly no longer interested in the conversation, fiddles with the corner of the colouring book. The strange expression on her face makes me feel guilty. No doubt her brain is going a hundred miles a second. I cringe. Psychological warfare is her thing, and I am sure she will get me back, and oh boy, it will be a doozy. I gulp. It is the first time I have acted on the naughty voice in my head and... it felt amazing.

Which, of course, is very, very bad.

So now I have the overwhelming need to get the hell out of here before the shock wears off and she screams.

Uh-oh.

"I, erm, have lots of things left to do today," I say, as I jump up off the sofa like my bottom is on fire. I can't even look at Owen in case he thinks I behaved like a brat. "I am sure you also need some time for yourselves. Larry?" My voice is slightly squeaky. Larry appears at my side with a bright smile. *Run-run-run!* My head screams as I quickly introduce him to my coven. "This is my friend, Larry. He is the heart of the hotel."

If Larry could blush, I am sure his freaked face would be rosy red. He beams a smile at me, and I smile a shaky one back.

"I will get everyone settled, mistress," he says with a clap of his hands.

Jodie mouths the word *mistress* at me. I roll my eyes and shake my head. I quickly turn to Owen and grab his hand, tugging the huge hellhound to his feet.

"...we have a wonderful pool, and the leisure centre is divine..." Larry continues. His red hair glows from a strip of sunlight that beams through the window.

My mum lifts her head, and my heart misses a beat.

The last thing I hear as I fold the air around us is Diane's shocked voice. "Whoa. Did she just Step?"

"You Step, huh?" Owen asks when we arrive in my living room. I smile and look at my feet, suddenly shy. I should have asked him first instead of just grabbing him and running. "That's pretty cool."

"Yeah, it happened when the dryads came. It almost scared the poop out of me."

Owen grins. "Are you going to explain the dryad story?"

"You heard that, huh? Yeah, I will. It was horrible and sad... But first, I want to say sorry about beaming you out of there without asking and also thank you for... for you know... I am sorry about my mu—"

"It doesn't matter," Owen interrupts and wraps his arm around me. "She loves you." I want to deny his words, but I can't. I know she loves me. It's just hard to believe it sometimes. The hellhound hugs me to his chest and kisses the top of my head. Between us, Daisy licks my face. Her barbed tongue takes what I'm sure is a tongue's width of the skin off my cheek. Ouch and ew.

Thanks for that, Daisy.

"I didn't want to interfere too much, as I know they are your coven. I hope you don't think I overstepped."

"No, no, of course not." I can't help feeling all warm and squidgy. "You were amazing. It was nice to have you in my corner." Someone who genuinely cares. Although my sister's outrage on my behalf was a big surprise.

Yeah, he's amazing until he sees what you are really like, the nasty voice pipes up. What if that is true? What if he leaves?

I cannot control what Owen feels or does. All I can do is be me and if I am not good enough, well, it was not meant to be.

"Talk about amazing. I had to bite my tongue and channel nine hundred years of military training to stop myself from laughing when you slapped down those crayons and that colouring book." Owen guffaws. I huff out a mortified laugh at his expression. "That was priceless."

"It was mean," I whine. "She's going to kill me."

"Worth it." Owen's eyes sparkle with mirth and we both grin at each other. I drop my head and giggle into his chest. "Nah, she will not kill you. I think she was quite proud of you. It was an epic comeback." I shake my head, then lean back in his arms and take him in. The poor man looks exhausted. I sweep my thumb across his cheek.

"You're not going to lick it first?" he asks.

I giggle again and comically widen my eyes. "I can't believe she rubbed her spit on my face. When is that ever a good idea?" Owen smiles down at me.

My laughter fades and I bite my lip. He almost died a few hours ago. And after all that trauma, he then gets roped into my coven mess.

"When did you last sleep?"

"A while," he grumbles.

"Let's get you settled. Maybe you can have a few hours to catch up."

"No, it's okay. I can wait until tonight." Daisy, who is snuggled up against his chest, yawns, and Owen catches her movement and automatically yawns back. He sheepishly rubs his face. "Perhaps a few hours might do me some good. What about your coven?" *He doesn't want to leave me alone. My heart puffs.*

"Larry has got them, and I promise to keep out of their way while you sleep. Okay?" I reassure him.

"Okay," the hellhound says gruffly.

"Right then, well, let's get you to bed." My horrified eyes shoot to his. Oh crap. "Urm... I mean, show you to your room, on your own to, urm, sleep." I close my eyes. *Oh, for crying out loud. Shut up, Tuesday.*

Owen chuckles.

I really need to leave.

I show Owen into one of the spare bedrooms. Daisy wiggles out of his arms and throws herself down onto the bed. I stand awkwardly as I watch him remove all his weapons from magic only knows where. He's wearing trousers and a shirt you would think he wouldn't be able to hide anything in, but they just keep appearing. It's as if he is carrying enough weapons for ten men.

I run a finger across the hilt of a pretty but sharp-looking silver knife. "Silver," I mumble. I think I've seen enough silver for today, especially when I was pulling it out of him, dragging it particle by particle out of his bloodstream. I still can't believe I did that.

"Yes, it's a throwing blade."

"Why do you carry silver? Doesn't it make you tired? Why would you use a weapon that could also hurt you?" The hellhound pulls out another two blades. They clink against the bedside table.

"Over the years, I've become immune to some of silver's effects." He gently pulls me into his body and his arms wrap around my waist.

I could get used to him holding me. I'm not a tactile person, but I think being in his arms is now my favourite place to be. The fabric of his shirt rustles as he leans down and oh so gently kisses my neck.

My heart slams in my chest and I shiver.

"Oh," I say eloquently.

"Every weapon can be used against you"—kiss—"no matter what metal it is made from"—kiss. Oh, my... He makes a good point about the *weapons*. My skin is on fire, and I want nothing more than to spin around and jump his bones. Climb him like a tree. Tackle him onto the bed...

I cough to clear my throat. "I will leave you to sleep." I reluctantly slip away from his arms. "Come on, Daisy." I wiggle my fingers at the sleepy dragonette, but she turns her nose up at me and snuggles more into the duvet.

"It's okay. She can nap with me."

"Are you sure?" Owen nods. Wow, that is sweet. "Okay. Well, I will get out of your hair and see you both soon."

I smile. The sexy, beautiful hellhound unbuckles his belt and smiles back at me.

Bloody hell.

CHAPTER
TWENTY-NINE

I STEP to the office and frantically wave my hand to fan my fiery face. Whoa, the look in his eyes when he undid his belt... I dreamily sag against the desk and swallow the copious amount of spit in my mouth. *That was hot. So hot.* The urge to go back and help him take off the rest of his clothes is huge.

I want to snuggle with the hellhound.

I groan and look up at the ceiling for divine intervention. Fate only knows I need help. Loved up, I might be, but I am annoyingly cautious. Stepping away from him—I shake my head—is a moment in my life that I will no doubt regret. Forever. On my deathbed, I will tell anyone who will listen, "I should have banged the hot hellhound when I was in my twenties." I snort and groan again.

No. I know I am impaired with this magic battering at me. I cannot think straight. My head is full to bursting with everything that has happened these last few days. It has been nuts, and here I am, throwing a new relationship into the mix. There is no way, no way, I can *nap with Owen*. It is unfair to him, and I can't do anything naughty until I sort my head out. I roll my eyes and rub my face.

Okay. I clap my hands like Larry does. I want to see if I can figure out a permanent portal to the real world. If anything happens to me, people in this dimension need to be able to leave. I have been reprimanded already by Mum for not having an adequate emergency plan in place, so an emergency exit is a priority.

Jodie also wants me to make her mini pocket dimensions. I know she only mentioned it in passing, but it would be lovely to give something back. She is always helping me, so I might as well work on that. I mean, how hard can it be? Nyssa makes them... I can Step. I should be able to stuff some magic into an object and make it its own dimension. No biggie. I slump against the desk.

I sign and grab the datapad that was once that giant, dusty book and do a quick search and... there is nothing. Nothing.

Great.

I throw my hands in the air and push the datapad away. What is the point of this thing if it doesn't work? I will have to do this the old-fashioned way, by trial and error. Yeah, I am going to wing it. Magic on a wing and a prayer. What can go wrong?

I need to keep listening to my magic. Trust myself. I didn't know how to heal, I didn't have a bloody clue and yet, I did it. I saved three people. Three. With no training. That is amazing. If I take the time to listen, the magic tells me clearly what I need to do to get it to work.

I tug at my dress. First, an outfit change. With just a thought, my clothes change from the navy dress into a comfortable, soft-knit jumper and jeans. I roll up my sleeves and I open a portal to Jodie's shop.

I wander into the stockroom. Behind me, I keep the portal open; I have no idea if I can re-open it. *Shit.* I huff out a self-deprecating laugh. *I would look like a proper idiot if I couldn't get back in.*

The room is stuffed to the brim with witch paraphernalia—all things recognisable from my childhood. Instead of happy memories, the sight invokes a sickly sense of fear.

Everything in here has a terrible memory attached to it. I dig my nails into my palms to stop myself from being unwillingly dragged into a nasty memory. I do a full-body shudder to shake the feeling off as I push the thoughts away.

I scan the shelves and find what I need, which is a plain black drawstring bag with the shop logo. Ah, it is perfect.

I grab it, slip back through the portal to my office, and throw myself into the chair. *How the heck am I going to do this?* I turn my full attention to the cloth bag in my now sweaty hand.

Okay. I wipe my hands on my jeans. *What do I need it to do?* The bag needs to expand to store things, so the person using it can put things into the dimensional space and, with just a thought, bring them back out again when needed.

The weight cannot change, and the shape of the bag in the real world can't change either. I puff out my cheeks. No biggie. My leg bounces and my hand trembles as I fiddle with the bag's string. *What if I mess up?*

Oh no. I really don't want to blow up the cotton bag, myself, or the realm. I drop the bag and lean away.

Whoa, Tuesday, don't freak out. You improvised an entire realm. I think you can deal with one small cloth bag. "I just need to have a good imagination, that's all," I mumble. "Oh, and completely ignore physics." My other leg jiggles.

Stop it.

I have all this negativity swimming around in my head. I flick the bag. I cannot let my past magical prejudice interfere with what is happening to me now.

I can't let my old fears impede this strange new version of myself.

But it is so bloody hard.

I blow out a breath and twist my fingers. I have been doing some snazzy things, impossible things. I don't think what I can do has really sunk in. Snapping magic out on the fly with all the crazy life and death pressure. It is okay and perfectly natural to be a little nervous.

Okay, back to the pocket dimension and basic rules: living creatures are not allowed inside. I give the bag a poke. I know it is only a bag, but it could be the width of some kid's shoulders. I can't be responsible for asphyxiating some poor sod. I don't mind people stuffing their limbs in. That's understandable. But not an entire air-breathing person.

I nibble on my thumbnail. Size... the size inside. Does it need to hold stuff like an immense bag? Or does it need to hold the contents of a house? I tug the bag open and stare inside. It can only fit things under about ten inches wide, so there is no way anything big like a sofa will fit.

My mind immediately goes to Mum's magic bag. She lugs that thing everywhere. I click my fingers. *Magical wardrobe. No, that's not right.* My heart jumps with excitement and my eyes widen. *A stockroom.* A grin tugs at my lips. So, a magical stockroom, a pocket dimension roughly four-foot-square, should do it.

Once I get to grips with this, I will have to make Mum a replacement bag, or add a dimension to her existing one. If she will let me.

Okay. I narrow my eyes. The top of the bag will act as a mini portal, and the items will be stored inside the storeroom. What if items are small or super big? I don't want to put a limit on the pocket dimensions usage. So, I won't. I don't need to design things like shelves. Instead, why can't the person using it make it how they want? Self-designing. Oooh. I explore the idea of adding a choice. Once the owner bonds with the bag, their intent can shape the room within the original footprint and design rules. Oh my gosh, that is so cool.

To bond, the owner will need a drop of blood, and if anything happens to them, a simple incantation, like a pin code, will re-set the bag.

I nod. Yeah, that will work. I blow out a breath.

No pressure.

Sweat tickles my neck. I feel like I'm disarming a bomb. Small beads of sweat dot my upper lip. I use my sleeve to wipe them away. *It's okay, Tuesday, you can do this.* I press my jiggling legs into the chair to keep them still as I concentrate. I stare at the cloth and unfocus my eyes. I see the little filaments of realm magic float around in the air like energised dust motes. As they drift around me, I allow myself to zone out and drift with them.

It's as if I am not in control of myself, but a higher power is helping me, guiding me. My pounding heart settles into a steady rhythm, along with my breaths. I am in a weird, magical zone where nothing exists but the magic. I do what I have done for years. I first build the storeroom in my head.

When I am ready, I go with my gut and pull the magical dust towards me and the bag. I feed the magic, both my magic and the dust, into the black fibres with the intent to allow the space I am creating to be flexible. But also strong enough to hold the walls of dimensional space. When I feel like it is working, I expand the walls, making them wider, bigger, and stronger. I set my rules into the magic, layer by layer. When I think I have finished, I test everything. then come back to myself with a sigh and flop back in the chair with a satisfied hum.

Phew, it's good. I did it. I eye the bag and let out a huff of surprise. *I bloody did it.* I squeal and do a little wiggle. The chair squeaks, and I do a full bum dance on the seat. I did it!

I carefully fold the bag and stuff it into my back pocket. I will give it to Jodie later and let her test it out to see what she thinks. I am sure my smart sister will have ideas on how to improve my design.

In the hallway outside my office, but closer to reception, I add a random door so I can use it to make a fixed portal gateway. I've seen these in a few posh houses—a portal room. Using the doorway as a guide, I open a new portal, this time to the inside of Jodie's stockroom.

I search the shelves and grab a finger prick lancet. I twist the top to break the seal and hold the plastic lancet with trepidation over my poor, innocent index finger.

"It's like a hole punch," I whisper. "A teeny tiny skin hole punch." I roll my eyes. Yep, that makes me feel so much better. Not.

A hole punch. Bloody hell, Tuesday. A hole punch? Really? Now all I can see and hear in my head is the crunch of the round metal prongs cutting through the paper and leaving those perfectly cut, *large* circle holes behind.

I gnaw on my lip and, with a gasp and a full-body cringe, I press the lancet down. A teeny tiny bit of pain derives from my finger. That's it.

I blow out a breath. That was a little anticlimactic. I then sternly remind myself to squeeze my digit. I squeeze until I have a good drop of blood balanced on the tip. I don't want to be doing the entire hole punch thing again today if I can help it.

With blood drop balanced, I carefully shuffle to the empty back wall of the stockroom.

Now comes the gross bit. I smear it onto the wall, tracing around the still open portal, but being careful not to touch the magic or get the blood inside the dimensional gateway. I have no idea what nightmare situation that would cause. I know it's gross and wiping an open wound onto the wall of my sister's magic shop is not exactly hygienic, but I am again going with my gut and what I am doing feels right. With another few squeezes, I finish the freehand rectangle.

A doorway.

I move back to eye the now fixed doorway that leads into my pocket realm. Perhaps I should say some witchy words? My lips twitch. A fancy incantation to lock it all into place. I know there is no need. My blood has done the trick. I stand and stare at it. Huh. My mum said my portal was wonky and look at that. A real wonky portal. It's like what she said was a premonition. I tilt my head. Yeah, it might not be the best thing I've ever done. Mum will moan that I should have outlined it first in chalk and perhaps used a ruler. The shape will irritate her.

It couldn't be more obvious that I made the portal unless I scrawled "Tuesday was here" in blood. I grin and shake my head. Yeah, I'm not going to do that.

Am I nuts, giving my coven direct access to me and my pocket world? Maybe. Although, it could be worse. I could have gone with Mum's suggestion and put the doorway at my parent's house. I snort and dramatically shudder.

I will have to pop a ward on the door at my end to make sure no one comes through to do some sneaky shopping. The shop has enough wards. No one but coven can access the portal, so at least I don't need to mess around with it on this end.

Blood is one of the scariest ingredients in witchcraft. Even trace amounts can be used against you. I press and hold a small button on the side of the lancet, and something hidden inside the plastic breaks. With a puff of smoke, the entire thing vaporises. I brush the ash off my hand into the bin. I should now use a medicated wipe to clean the wound, but with the portal open, there is no need. My finger has already healed.

I shuffle away and direct the pulse of magic that emanates from my chest at the portal. The blood trail around it glows, and with a flash of light that momentarily blinds me, the gateway seals.

The fading buzz of power tickles my skin, and then the portal closes, sealing the doorway into the very fabric of the building. The room transcends into darkness.

CURSED WITCH

All I can hear through the pounding of my heart are my raspy breaths.

Dizzy, I sag against the wall and a few unseen items fall to the floor. I rapidly blink. *Whoa, that was a bit of a shock.* I have to lock my knees so I don't fall over.

It is not the power I used to make the doorway that is affecting me. To anyone else, using power like that would be a momentous challenge, if not an impossibility, but the power I used to make the fixed portal? Well, it didn't even register.

No, the reason I feel like a wet balloon that's been popped is that I have gone from immense power to *nothing*. Nada. Without the doorway open, I am back to being plain old me, and wow, I do not like it.

Staying in my pocket realm, I can see, will be addictive.

I was right. I do need to gain some perspective, take that fresh air break I promised myself. I will also not let this powerful magic control me. I need to make a decision that is right for me and not just go along with everything like a proper numpty.

I am no one's puppet. I need to be here. I need to think with no magical influence and be reminded of what being normal feels like. *Crikey, if I feel like this after a few days? What am I going to feel like after years?* What a terrifying thought. That is why I am going to stay here for at least a few hours.

I force myself to move my feet. The wooden floor creaks underneath me as I leave the dark storeroom behind. I come out into the homely-looking backroom, which I ignore, and instead, I enter the shop.

The smell of magic is more potent. The strangeness of the foreign energy wiggles across my skin like ants crawling. It tickles the back of my throat and I have to breathe in shallow gasps to stop myself from gagging. It is so gross.

I hate this shop.

Yet, I cannot stop my fingers tracing across the shelves, shelves packed to the brim with magical items and artefacts. The store's name is everywhere. 'TINCTURES 'N TONICS' - SPECIALISTS IN PORTABLE POTIONS. My lip curls with deep-rooted disgust.

This shop is the accumulation of everything that was wrong in my old life.

All I see when I come in here is my failure.

And I need to make peace with that. It is not the magic in this world's fault that my strange host magic was not compatible. I have blamed magic, school, the witch community, my coven... I swallow against the growing lump in my throat. *Everyone. I blamed everyone.*

Diane was right. I was bitter. I was jealous.

Those imaginary fairies bounce around in my abdomen as I come to a horrid realisation. *What type of monster would I be if I had all that power to begin with?*

I have been given a unique perspective that I would have never had if I had not lived it. *A gift.* I have had years of being weak and powerless. Perhaps I needed to learn through my experience to gain empathy and compassion. *Perhaps everything does happen for a reason.*

I roam around the shop, the retail manager in me mentally rearranging things to make more sense of the higgledy-piggledy way items are stuffed onto the shelves.

I itch my arm. The layout is going to give me hives.

There is an enormous mirror alongside a display of pretty jewellery. According to the labels, they contain powerful disguise spells that can change appearance, Diane's speciality. I glimpse my reflection and notice the lack of glowing marks on my skin. My stomach dips.

They mark me as different, alien, so how can I miss them? Of their own accord, my eyes drift back to the hidden portal. A sharp urge for *home* thrums through me. I need to get my head on straight without the pocket realm's magic mojo messing with me.

CHAPTER
THIRTY

The door to my sister's magic shop clicks closed and I wander down the street. I take careful note of the people moving around me. Somehow, I am almost convinced some creature will stop, point and shout that I am the host everyone is talking about. I shake my head. I know the idea of that happening is ridiculous. Witches are incredibly private. They might be the worst gossips imaginable, but they keep what happens within the community to themselves. It's like some unwritten rule. Security is important.

I avoid the shopping centre where my department store is located. I don't want to see anyone. *My old department store,* I amend with a frown. I know the Hunters Guild already did a lot of the legwork, but I will still need to give them a call and officially hand in my resignation. No matter what, I can never go back. I would be too much of a security risk.

There is still a huge amount of guilt. I think I will always feel guilty. I know it is only a job and that everybody is replaceable, as bad as that sounds. At least I know I established a great team who will step up; it will be like I was never there. My tummy dips. Gosh, these changes are so hard.

Running feet have me turning. "Stop where you are!" bellows a male voice. I flatten myself against the glass of a shop as three hunters barrel toward me. Their weapons glint and jingle in time with the beat of their feet.

I only breathe a little easier when they run past. The wind stirs my hair in their wake. Everyone on the street has also frozen. Well, everybody but one guy. He takes off at a loping run.

"Stop. Niles Bradbury, you are under arrest!" The yelling hunter pulls out a potion. The crowd ahead parts and people scramble, disappearing into shops and doorways. The man, of course, doesn't stop, and with impressive aim, the potion hits his shoulder and bursts open.

The man takes a few more steps, seemingly unaffected, but then he falls to his knees with a muffled groan.

Like a well-practised team, one hunter steps forward and a null band is slapped onto the guy's wrist. The other hunter slaps silver handcuffs on him, pulling his long arms behind his back. *Long arms?* I let out a shocked gasp. His arms are super long. The null band must have erased the guy's appearance-masking spell.

His arms and legs are now super long, with his trousers halfway up his calves.

"You are here on Earth illegally, Niles Bradbury, and you will come with us to be processed."

"Nooo. Click-click." The prisoner's speech becomes garbled and his—mandibles?—clack together. His face now resembles an insect.

An unmarked van pulls up from the closest alleyway and the guy is hauled to his feet and shoved unceremoniously inside.

I must make a noise as the hunter that threw the potion ball turns his head and looks straight at me. He closes the van door, and the bang makes me jump. The hunter narrows his eyes and glares.

My eyes dart about. Oops. I am the only one stupid enough to be left on the street. With a squeak on the glass, my hand frantically searches for the door of the shop. If I am not careful, my nosiness is going to get me killed.

The back of my left hand smacks into a handle. I grab it, push the door open, and I stumble gracelessly inside.

The bell above the door chimes a cheerful welcome. I hunch as I wait for the hunter to come and get me. But he doesn't, thank goodness. Self-consciously I stand a little straighter and look about. The delicious smell of cakes and coffee hits my nose and my eyes widen.

I BALANCE the plate in one hand and keep one eye on the full mug as I shuffle across the room. I am conscious that if I am not careful, I will splash a trail to my seat. My hand-eye coordination is horrendous. I find the perfect spot for people watching—no, I have not learned my lesson—and I settle down next to the window with the bookshelves at my back.

The bright, winter sunset is hitting the table just right. It slashes across my arm and face. I lean back in the chair a little, so the light doesn't blind me. With a deep breath, I lift my eyes to the tree above my head. It has branches across the ceiling. Glorious pink blossoms entwined with twinkling fairy lights. *It's a dryad's tree,* I think with recognition. *I wonder if she's related to or knows Erin?*

If I breathe deeply enough, I can just about smell the sweet scent of blossoms above the coffee and cakes. The café is enchanting. I can't believe I've never been in here before. The smell of pastry alone makes my tummy grumble.

I turn the mug so I can get at the handle, and it catches on some bumpy lines on the table and wobbles. I move it to the left and run my finger across the gouged marks.

Huh. It's a name. I tilt my head as the words are upside down. Liz. I wonder why someone wrote that? Perhaps this is a favourite table of someone's lost love. What I wouldn't give to be a fly on the wall when the person wrote that. I grab the spoon to start on the hot chocolate.

I bought Owen's favourite more-dessert-than-drink, with marshmallows, whipped cream, *and* a chocolate flake. I'm hoping it and the enormous slab of chocolate cake will pep me up. I guess it's over the top and will probably make me sick with a chocolate overload rather than fix my mood. But the cake looks amazing and I couldn't resist. I'll do my best to finish it all, as it would be a crime to waste it.

Across the road, a troll scratches his bum and shoots me a glare when he notices I am watching. I shift my eyes and let them go unfocused, hoping he thinks I am staring into space. I am a pro at people watching. No way do I want an argument with a troll. With an angry, if somewhat confused glare, he stomps down the street. I smirk when his hand goes back to itch. I bet that is the work of a potion.

From inside Jodie's borrowed coat pocket, I pull out my mobile, a notepad, and a pen. I slap them down on the table. Writing helps me think, so I've gone all old-fashioned as I enjoy jotting down my thoughts. If it all goes wrong, at least I will get some pleasure from ripping the page up into tiny little bits. Much more satisfying than a datapad.

I plant my left elbow on the table, lean over the pad, and I plop my head on my hand. *Okay, let's do this.* I draw a wobbly line down the middle of the page and scrawl on the top of the two columns: To stay. To go.

Okay, that's simple enough. I tap the pen against the pad. My rogue left leg bounces, and I puff out my cheeks when I catch myself humming the song *Should I Stay or Should I Go* by The Clash. With a groan, I sit back in the chair and rub my face. This is harder than I thought it would be.

I look about, hoping for inspiration. The café is almost empty, with only three other customers.

My eyes drift to the two human ladies sitting near the toilets. Their heads are close together as they enjoy each other's company. I can't help my smile at their raucous laughter. They giggle over a flowery blue teapot, and their words drift towards me. The conversation is about a dog called Tobie peeing on a nightmare neighbour's leg. *Go Tobie.*

Movement in the cake display area catches my eye. A sapphire blue pixie, in a protective suit, clutches a small paintbrush in her tiny fist as she climbs a wedding cake, like she's scaling Mount Everest.

Wow, the thing has got to be seven tiers. I can just about make out she is painting each flower with gold glitter. The attention to detail is astonishing, and I find her fascinating. I dig into my drink and pop the spoon loaded with a pink gooey marshmallow into my mouth.

The girl next to the pixie, the one with the rainbow hair who served me, groans. Hands-on-hips, she looks around the café—at us, her remaining customers, and then back at her watch. Her face scrunches up with a scowl.

I guiltily nudge my phone to check the time.

Phew, I'm okay. There is still an hour left until close. I am not keeping her from going home. From her expression alone, I am guessing it must have been a long day.

Crikey, how many times have I done that myself, looked at my watch with my feet and body aching. My poor brain buzzing with overstimulation and the overwhelming need to go home. A minute feels like a lifetime, like the working day will never end and when the second hand of the watch doesn't move, it's the worst. Especially when you are finally about to close the doors and a random customer strolls in. Why? Why do they do that?

"I'm so bored," she grumbles at the pixie.

"Well, no wonder," the Pixie huffs, wiggling her paintbrush at the girl's face. "You are so busy with the excitement of saving the world, no wonder you find being stuck here boring. I know you want to help Tilly out with a couple of shifts, but you have better things to do." She climbs up another tier.

"Yeah, I guess. I just wanted some normalcy, you know."

"I know you don't want to let things go," the Pixie says as she raises a tiny blue eyebrow meaningfully. Ooh, I bet there is a story there.

Heck, Tuesday, you are so nosy.

I lean forward in my chair and tuck my hands underneath my chin.

"But sometimes you've just got to move on. You live in the past too much." The pixie shakes her head when all the girl does is scowl at her words of wisdom.

She opens her mouth—

Clink, clink, clink.

Ahh, nooo! The lady furthest away sure likes to stir her cappuccino. I rub my forehead as she irritably cracks the spoon against the cup a few more dozen times. I can't hear what they are saying. *I think you got it. What is she doing? Digging to Australia?* I hope she hasn't got anything to eat. She is probably one of those people that chews really loudly.

I glance down at my pad of paper and the simple words I've written scream at me. To stay. To go.

I say I'm a throwaway person, but if I'm honest, I run away before people get the chance. I keep away from people, so I'm less likely to be hurt. I glance down at the pen in my hands. I've picked at the rubber grip so much, it's falling apart, and the little yellow pieces are scattered across the table.

Emotional pain is my nemesis. It wiggles inside my brain, turning, twisting, rotting my sense of self. I sigh as I put the damaged pen down and slowly pick up each tiny, ragged piece of rubber. I collect them into the centre of my palm and then drop them into the coat pocket.

I think my mum always knew that there was something wrong with me. Something about me she didn't like. Even before she found out I had cheated at school, she treated me different. She dotes on my sisters.

I love her.

I love her, but I hate her too. How horrible is that? How can I hate my mum? I'm not even sure if she consciously knows what she is doing. I hope not. No, I don't hate her. I just hate some things she does. There is a difference.

The noisy cappuccino drinker stomps across the café and leaves. The girl with the rainbow hair moves like a dancer. In a few short silent strides, she is at the cappuccino lady's table, removing the cup and giving the table a quick wipe.

She goes back behind the counter as I take a huge bite of the cake. I groan as the taste of chocolate fills my mouth. I should really use the cake fork. I am eating like a savage. Oh, but this cake is divine. No wonder they boast the best chocolate cake in the city. This is—

I jump when the door cracks against the wall and the bell above chimes in distress. I close my eyes for a second and then place the cake gently back on the plate. My hypervigilance kicks into overdrive.

Uh-oh. I hope this isn't about me.

CHAPTER
THIRTY-ONE

A DARK-HAIRED VAMPIRE angrily strides up to the counter and points at the girl. No, it's not about me. "You, abomination," he snarls.

"You just had to say it, didn't you? You had to say you were bored and tempt fate," the pixie says in a singsong voice from the top of the wedding cake.

In response, the girl rolls her eyes, casually leans against the counter, and crosses her arms. With her top hand, she dramatically points her thumb at her chest and flutters her multi-coloured eyelashes. She manages the best 'who me?' face I have ever seen. I can't help snorting.

"Yes," the vampire snarls. His teeth elongate and prick against his bottom lip. "Prepare to die."

Whoa. My eyes widen. That escalated quickly; things are about to get real.

The girl, seemingly unaffected, smirks and holds a hand up. "Hold on a minute. That's against the health code. Sorry, they are pretty strict with the no dead bodies in the café rules. We'll have to take this outside."

Wow, how cool is she? My eyes automatically drift to look outside and I frown at the busy street. It's bustling with people going home after a busy workday. She must spot what I have seen as she huffs, "Perhaps we can go out the back."

"No," the vampire bellows.

It appears he has had enough of the conversation and to make a point, he swipes his arm across the till display, sending things flying. Leaflets scatter, and an empty sounding tip jar crashes to the floor. His fist then heads for her face.

Oh no.

I watch as she blocks the vampire's strike with an almost lazy movement, as if fighting is so easy for her, she could make a cup of coffee while she's doing it. The vampire *really* does not like that, and he lets out a dramatic roar. She rolls her eyes.

Then his hand heads towards the cake masterpiece. My eyes almost pop out of my head. *No, not the cake!* The pixie squeaks out in horror. "Tru, stop him!"

The girl, Tru, grabs his wrist. "No. Bad vampire," she scolds.

Gone is the amusement and in its place, with a flash of red eyes, the girl transforms into something *other*.

What the heck is she?

I thought she was human. She must have him in a bone-crunching hold as the vampire winces. Like Owen's friend, Forrest, who has all that crazy power packed inside her, this girl has a serious hidden strength that makes me feel a bit like wet lettuce.

Two more vampires aggressively crash into the café.

Double oh no.

It's a full-on party. Like a wimp, I sink lower into the chair, and with shaking hands, wipe my chocolate frosted fingers on a napkin. I puff out my cheeks and try my best to control my rapid heartbeat. It's all going to kick off and I don't want to be ringing the dinner bell with my heart racing and my tasty blood rushing through my veins.

Not that vampires are allowed to go around chomping on people, but I wouldn't put it past them to say my neck got in the way of their teeth.

The old ladies also sink in their seats. We are all scarcely breathing. They look so frightened.

CURSED WITCH

I grind my jaw. The rainbow girl is going to struggle against three vampires. I don't want to see her get hurt.

The first guy smiles smugly at his backup and puffs out his chest. He yanks his wrist out of the girl's grip as the other two vampires spread out about the room with the bigger of the two blocking the door. He cracks his knuckles.

Err, I hate bullies.

When I was younger, I always expected people to have the same level of morality as my own. To understand wrong from right, to value life. It was a shock and a big lesson to learn. Other people do not play fair. They do bad things and sleep well at night. As long as they are alright, the world they live in is perfect.

I can't do that. I cannot sit back and watch bad things happen when I can do something, try to help. I think my life would be easier if I minded my business. The problem is... I care too much.

Gosh, after everything I have been dealing with, I'm going to die by vampire in a tiny café.

Boy, my mum is going to be pissed.

All I'm missing is my raging temper. I didn't realise how much of a buffer it was. I think I prefer to be angry than feel this kind of powerless fear. *If only I had my magic, if only I had access to my power...* An idea tickles at the back of my head. It is such a silly thought. I have to be in my realm to use my magic, but perhaps I can use it another way. I do have an item coated with magic in my pocket. The portable dimension. Nah, I shake my head. No, it will not work. It can't be that easy.

Can it?

Tru might not even need my help. My eyes flick back to the vampire as he continues to shout out murderous threats. But we all know what happens to witnesses of a crime and if she fails... she isn't the only one who's going to get hurt, or potentially die. I can't help looking at the two old ladies. One whimpers and the other shushes her, reaching over to hold her hand.

No, I will not sit and watch this happen without at least trying to help. I make sure the vampires are busy and, millimetre by millimetre, I lift my hips and from my back pocket, pull out the empty storeroom bag. With a hope and a prayer, I unravel it and without giving the game away, I stuff my left foot into it.

My leg tingles with pins and needles. Okay, that is something.

The vampire grabs hold of Tru's hair and, at the same time, sticks his dirty finger into the cake. The pixie, with a kamikaze scream, throws herself at him and bites his hand. He hisses and bats her away. Her tiny body flies across the room and hits the café window with a bone-crunching crack.

"No!" Tru cries.

Oh my.

"That's enough!" I yell as I slam my hands on the table and stand up. The chair scrapes the floor and rattles as it impacts the bookcase behind me. My leg continues to tingle as familiar energy zips across my body and settles into my chest. Relief makes me almost dizzy as my glowing tattoos reflect in the window. It's working! The two vampires turn and one of them, the big one, rushes toward me.

Oh heck.

With a fancy parkour move, the rainbow-haired girl leaps over the counter and spins on her toes. With unnatural speed, a blade appears in her hand and she stabs the closest vampire in the chest, just as I throw my hands up to cover my face.

There is a moment where it feels like time slows down as I wildly fling out my magic.

The seconds tick.

When nothing happens, I peek from behind my quivering arms. The knuckle cracking vampire's fist hovers inches from my face.

Ooh.

I don't know why, but I reach out a shaky hand and poke at the dinner plate sized fist. *If he had hit me with that... Hell, look at it.* I gulp. *He would have mashed my face.*

Luckily, I have frozen the vampires in place.

Tru circles the frozen vampire she stabbed and pokes his cheek. "Huh." His blood didn't freeze with his body, and it drips down his chest onto the floor. "Shit, Tilly is going to kick my arse. I hope you have got some cash on you," she says to the now presumably dead vampire. "You're paying for the clean-up spell, buddy."

CURSED WITCH

I wince.

She moves, graceful and lithe, like a dancer, to the next vampire. When she isn't leaning against the counter, the rainbow-haired girl is super tall. Beautiful but... with a sleek predatory quality I didn't see when I first spoke to her. All I saw was the girly hair. I guess that was all she wanted me to see.

I shiver.

With a shrug, she grabs hold of the next vampire's head. With one hand gripping the back of his dark hair and the other on his chin, she breaks his neck with a crunch. She does the same with the third. The one near me. I swallow down bile. I'm not used to this kind of violence.

My wide eyes meet the girl's.

"It's okay," she whispers. "Vampires can't be killed by a broken neck. They will heal. Well, those two will. The one I stabbed..." She pulls a face. "I hit his heart. You can let them go now." I release the freezing magic, and like puppets with their strings cut, all three of them flop to the floor. I shiver.

"Thanks. Shit, are you okay?"

I nod.

Across the room, there's a tiny rasp. Even from here, I can see blood bubbling between the pixie's lips with each of her struggling breaths. "Oh no. Please, no." The despair in Tru's eyes makes my abdomen clench as she spins and hurries back across the café toward her friend.

I don't know how long the power in the bag will last, so without losing time trying to move and worrying I'll dislodge the bag from my foot, I direct the magic to heal the pixie.

I cringe and cross my fingers. I am all so new to this, and I've never healed without touching someone before. My magic flies like an arrow from me to the pixie without issue. It takes seconds to heal her. Then because I can, I fix the beautiful wedding cake that the vampire damaged.

With a wobble, I lift my foot and pull off the bag. My trainer smokes. It also looks a completely different colour than the other one now. Whoa, I must have pulled in some power. I scrape it against the floor, and it leaves a rubber residue. At least it didn't disintegrate.

The bag still bubbles with power. I can feel it, but I have got no energy left to access it. Working magic in the real world is exhausting.

Dizzy, I slump in the chair and, with trembling hands, take a mouthful of the now cold drink. Black spots dance across my vision. I need to eat something. My stomach growls and aches like it's eating itself. I take a big mouthful of cake.

"Hey, thanks," the pixie shouts. Standing on the glass dome that surrounds the cakes, she grins and waves. "You healed me and saved the cake. Thank you so much. It took me so many hours to make."

I finger wave, finish my mouthful of cake and wipe my lips. "Oh, you're welcome. I'm just glad you're okay." The bell chimes above the door as the old ladies leave without a word. I try not to watch as Tru unceremoniously drags the dead and unconscious vampires outside.

I duck my head and shovel in more cake.

"He will know about this. I bet he's already on his way," the pixie whispers.

"Yeah, I know. That is why I've texted Tilly that I'm getting the hell out of here. I'm so done for the day. I need to go to the gym and smash things."

"We can close early. It's almost time."

I jump in my seat when the rainbow-haired girl appears. Crikey, she is freaky quiet. She must have glided over the floor like an apparition, making little to no noise at all. I know 'cause I was listening so hard to their conversation. It's another little detail that affirms her deadly nature.

"I owe you one. You stepped up even when you didn't know us. You saved my friend's life. Thank you." I blink. Her warm orange eyes take in my trembling body.

I must look pathetic.

I shuffle uncomfortably in the seat. "It's no bother," I say with a shrug. "It was the right thing to do."

"Yeah? Well, thank you. You are a total badass."

"Me?" I squeak. I point at my chest and shake my head in disbelief. "I was so scared."

"You could have fooled me. I loved the whole 'that's enough!'

scream. It was very scary. Here. It's on the house." She slides a replacement hot chocolate on the table.

"Thank you," I mumble.

"My name is Tru." She taps the table twice and raises a rainbow eyebrow.

Oh, she wants to know my name. "Tuesday," I splutter. Seemingly satisfied and finished with our conversation, with a nod and a warm smile, she pirouettes on her toes and goes back to cleaning up.

Huh. Tru didn't ask any awkward questions. She didn't even care what type of creature I was. She just appreciated my help.

That was nice.

My trembling disappears, and my pounding heart settles. Bloody fate. Looks like I'm exactly where I need to be. Back in my pocket realm, helping people like Erin. For the first time since this wacky adventure started, I can take a full breath. This vampire fight has settled something inside me.

I'm enough. I am strong enough, and if I can pull magic out of my arse to deal with raging vampires, I can deal with my mum and running a hotel in another dimension. I dab my finger onto the plate and sweep up a dollop of chocolate frosting.

Perhaps I can be a badass. *Yeah.* I grin at the plate. *Piece of cake.*

CHAPTER
THIRTY-TWO

"Jodie." I knock. "It's me. Have you got a sec?" I love using my magic to pinpoint my sister's location—I can't seem to find Larry but I'm sure he will pop up—and the more I use the magic, the more natural it feels.

Coming back from the real world, I am energised and emotionally lighter. Gosh, who knew this ordeal could be so cathartic? My head is clear for the first time in years.

"Tuesday." The door flies open, and Jodie blinks at me, then peeks over my shoulder with a salacious grin, which then promptly drops. "Oh, no hunky hellhound?"

"No, he doesn't follow me around all the time."

"Could have fooled me," she says under her breath. Louder, she says, "I've known that man for years and how he looks at you..." Jodie grins and fans her face.

"I like him too," I say softly.

I can feel my face going a nice, bright red. I guess I will have to get used to many shades of red when conversation steers towards Owen. I rub my damaged trainer against the carpet and the rubber peels back.

Oh, yeah, the reason for my visit. "Here." I shove the mini pocket dimension into her hands. When I returned, I checked the mini pocket dimension over in case I had damaged it with my foot. Strangely, the power inside had increased, so much so that the bag was practically vibrating. Whatever I did in the real world, it liked it.

Freaky magic.

Jodie's smile dims. She tilts her head to the side and frowns at the bag. Visibly confused, she opens it and peeps inside. "Oh," she gasps. "Oh my, Tuesday this is... wow." She looks up at me, dumbfounded.

I rub the back of my neck and chuckle. I then quickly explain how to use it with the blood and stuff. "It's a tester, so let me know what changes or improvements you need."

"I will. Thank you so much."

"No problem. I made the fixed portal too. I placed it on the back wall of your stockroom. But now I am thinking it was a stupid idea, what with all the wards in the shop. If anyone unauthorised goes through, they are going to get a nasty zap. So, I might see if Dad has an alternative location, and we can just use that one for the coven."

Jodie nods and waves a hand; she's not listening to me. She's staring at the pocket dimension bag with gobsmacked awe. I roll my eyes when she hugs it to her chest. "Mum is on the warpath," she mumbles between bag hugs.

"She's always on the warpath," I scoff. "Okay, see you in the morning. I'm going to hide out in my roo—" As I am walking away, I stumble, and full body smack against the wall.

Oh! Well, that isn't good.

"What's wrong?" Jodie asks, rushing towards me. "Tuesday, you've gone white as a sheet."

What the heck was that?

I press my forehead against the wall and groan. Jodie grabs my elbow and I lock my knees to hold myself up. The magic inside me is screaming a warning. "Someone has just ripped a bloody big hole into the realm," I say in disbelief. Horrified, I stare at Jodie, my eyes wide. My ears ring, and my head pounds from the attack. "I don't know what's happening. No one should be able to come here like that," I rasp. "You aren't safe. I don't think anyone is safe. I need to lock down the portals. Please grab our coven and get to the new emergency exit while I deal with this. It's the door behind reception, near my office. I will let you know when it's safe."

"No, no, I can help you." I shake my head and somehow send her the location of everyone in the coven. I can't find Andy, which is strange. I hope he is okay. "No. Come with me. We can get them together." Jodie tugs at my arm.

"I can't. I am so sorr—"

"Please," she begs.

I made a choice in the café. I chose this new life and the realm. Now here is some wacky cosmic test to prove my mettle. I will not fall at this first hurdle. I won't.

Lives are counting on me.

"I have a responsibility to my guests, to the realm. I know where this person is. I still have strong magic, Jodie."

Jodie takes in my determined face and, for a second, she closes her eyes and sags in defeat. "You are so bloody stubborn."

"If Owen won't go with you, tell him to head East."

"Okay, okay, go kick their arse. I've got this, sis. I will get everyone to safety. Go. Go!" Jodie runs to my parents' room and bangs on their door.

With the magic's insistence pulling at me, I Step.

CHAPTER
THIRTY-THREE

I ARRIVE at a dark place that I didn't even know existed. It looks like a dead corner carved out in the world. The surrounding air is heavy and stagnant.

The elf who tried to kidnap me is standing in front of me. "You," I say in shock. When he sees me, his overlarge bright blue eyes widen with surprise.

Yeah, I can Step just like you. I might not be able to in the real world or use my magic without a bag on my foot, but in this world, I'm golden.

"Hello," he says politely. "What a lovely surprise. It's nice to be greeted."

"You," I sneer. "Did you think I wouldn't notice you ripping a hole in my realm? What the heck do you think you're doing? What are you doing sneaking about? You are so not welcome."

"I seek sanctuary," he says in a low, smug tone.

My lip twitches into a snarl. "Sanctuary denied. Go away."

"Okay, you got me." He holds his wrists out together mockingly as if I'm going to whip out some handcuffs. "No, I don't want your stupid sanctuary. But thank you for making everything so much easier. You've Stepped right into my hands."

I huff and roll my eyes. "Do you know what the definition of insanity is, elf?" My hands go to my hips as I channel my mum. "According to Einstein, it is doing the same thing over and over again and expecting a different result. Have we not done this song and dance before? It was only a few days ago." The massive elf looms menacingly over me and I instantly regret my snarky words, and I quickly scramble back.

"Don't you dare come any closer." I wave my hands in the air to frantically warn him away. His deep chuckle makes me want to bop him in the face.

Oh my goodness, could I be any more pathetic?

I have magic. I have an entire dimension at my fingertips.

Why do I always forget? I pause my retreat. I gather my magic and feel more confident. "I have friends coming who are going to lock you up." I continue with a little bit more bravo. "You made a huge mistake coming here. By doing so, you've handed yourself over to the fae warriors." Smugly I freeze him in place like I did the vampires.

"Do you mean the useless group of fae warriors and shifters that I iron and silver bombed? Those friends?"

Oh no. That was him?

The elf smirks and itches his nose. *Wait... what? That isn't right.* How is he talking, moving? My heart misses a beat when I realise the magic has done nothing. Nothing. The elf isn't frozen.

I try to grab the magic of the realm as this guy is strong and I need the big guns. But it's kind of unwilling. Sluggish. I huff, and nervous energy skitters down my spine, as goosebumps erupt on my forearms. Perhaps I can't use the magic so soon after I've Stepped? Or maybe there is an issue after he ripped his way into the realm?

I swallow my panic and continue talking to keep him busy. "What do you want with me? Why did you attack my coven?" I ask as I wrangle the unwilling magic, I need to restrain him. The fine strands of magic finally slide ever so slowly around his body like I'm a spider and he's a fly in my web. "Is it because you knew what I was? A host?" There, sorted, he shouldn't get away from that.

Phew, I was worried there for a second. Then it clicks in my head. "Are you a member of the sealgairí? Are you a sealgair?"

He chuckles annoyingly, and with dancing blue eyes, drops his head to observe the magic as it wraps around him. "Is that what they are calling me a sealgair? A hunter? How fitting."

"If you know what I am, that I am a host, why are you attacking me here, where I'm the most powerful? What is wrong with you?"

"Are you? Are you really?" He lifts his chin and smiles manically. "Are you really the powerful one here, little lost host?" He drops the smile, and my tummy drops along with it.

"The magic isn't playing ball with you, is it?" He waves his hand and the magic web crumples away.

'Ecky-thump, that's not good.

"You think I dumped you here for you to ruin everything I created?" His eyes narrow, and he slinks closer. I want to move away, but the ground underneath my feet will not let me. Oh my goodness, my feet are glued to the floor.

"THIS IS MY DIMENSION, YOU STUPID GIRL!" he screams. His face is so close to mine droplets of spit spatter against my cheek, and his voice echoes around us. I tremble. His nostrils flare as he takes a deep breath, and once he is back in control, his voice drops. "You are here because I brought you here to drain your magic." I stare at him with absolute horror, and he wrinkles his nose. "Not for you to play hotelier and set yourself up as a benevolent fucking hero. You shouldn't have made it through the first night. Isn't that right, Larry?"

Larry manifests next to the elf. He stands, head down, hands in his pockets, and kicks at the ground.

"Larry?" I rasp.

I catch the horror and worried expression as it crosses Larry's freckled face. His green eyes meet mine and the light in his eyes goes dead.

Oh Larry.

The elf reaches out. I finch away but he grabs the back of my head. His hand tangles in my hair and he violently yanks my head back. I wince as my scalp burns and my neck aches. At a painful angle, the elf holds my head still and brushes away an escaped tear that was rolling down my face.

With an unnecessary slurp, he licks the tear off his finger.

"He was supposed to get you here so the realm could drain you dry," he whispers into my ear, pressing his face against my cheek. "Not make friends with you." The elf's other hand whips out and Larry stumbles sideways as the elf cracks him across the back of the head.

"Larry, you lured me here to drain me?" I rasp around a growing lump of terror in my throat. I have never in my life been so frightened. I strain my eyes to the side. The way I am being held means I can only move my eyes to look at him. "You're a bad guy?"

No shit, he's a bad guy, Tuesday. Didn't the incident with the dryads not teach you anything? Why did you think he acted as if it was same old, same old? Because it bloody was.

I didn't see it.

I didn't want to see it.

I attributed it to him being non-human and his construct nature. Why did I assume? I'm such a fool. How could I be so trusting? *Unless he doesn't have a choice and he's being coerced?* Gah, there I go again, making excuses. I am so bloody stupid.

Oh gosh, I hope my coven has left. I can't feel them anymore. My connection to the realm has been ripped away. I cannot believe I brought them here. I presumed the place was safe. Even when my instincts knew something fishy was going on, with everything thrown at me, I didn't have the time to work it out. If something happens to them, it's my fault.

It's then I notice that I can thankfully still feel Owen. He is in his wolf form and rapidly heading this way.

"I thought we were friends?" I whisper.

"He's a magical construct, you stupid girl." The elf gives me a shake and yanks my head sharply to the side and I can't help whimpering. "He is my magical construct. He isn't real. The red-haired guy you see before you is what works to lull my victims." He lets go of my hair and grabs hold of Larry's face and drags him towards me. The elf squeezes Larry's cheeks till his mouth bulges. "Everyone loves this handsome, freckled face." The elf speaks in a cutesy baby tone and pouts his lips, mirroring Larry's squeezed face. "His bright smile is the perfect lure." With a dark chuckle, the elf slaps his hand against Larry's face and roughly palms him away.

It's all been an elaborate trap.

"If you are a host, and if this is your dimension, why was it dying?" I need to keep him talking. I need to give Owen time to get here and help me. My hellhound will rip him to shreds.

"The power is mine, silly girl. I control the dimension; it doesn't control me. I used way too much magic making this world. I will not spend energy making it pretty. It's a tool."

"But… but Nyssa told me about the man who created this sanctuary, that he made it to help people."

"That old spiel?" he scoffs. "Smoke and mirrors, girl, smoke and mirrors. I wanted to help myself, not other creatures. Now, this little chat is nice and all, but I'd prefer to drain you now. You will make such a pretty husk."

Husk.

Oh God.

CHAPTER
THIRTY-FOUR

"There is nothing sweeter or more powerful than draining a host. Our magic is delicious." He licks his lips.

"You cannibalise your own people." To understand what this creature does is an alien concept in my head. It is horrific. Another realisation comes to me. "There are no sealgairí, is there? No big bad killing hosts. It's you, isn't it? It has always been you. You have pulled the wool over everyone's eyes." I shake my head. "Not only are you a mass murderer who has taken our race to the verge of extinction, you have been draining other creatures, while blaming it all on the realms."

"Not so stupid after all." He creepily tilts his head and taps his lips. The man is a bloody psychopath. His expression is thoughtful as he shakes his head. "Tell you what, I will indulge you just this once, as what does it matter? A last wish. The hosts left alive are too wily, too embedded in their little realms, hiding like little mouses. So, I hunt the young ones. The ones like you."

He bops me on the nose. "Baby hosts, yet to get their power. I scare them enough that they run and I trap them in my dimension. It activates their magic and then... bam! I simply drain them dry." He shrugs as if he's not talking about ending innocent lives. "It all worked perfectly." He scowls. "Until you."

He leans closer again and breathes me in. A shiver of revulsion trickles down my spine. "So much magic," he whispers. His tongue flashes out of his mouth as he gazes at me like I am an extra delicious cheeseburger. "You know, it has happened once or twice when the magic hasn't drained my prey completely overnight." He smirks. "They spent the time they had left flapping around, panicking, crying, freaking out. They couldn't even leave their room. After a day or so, when I finally got to them, they were practically basket cases. So deliciously frightened."

I feel sick. This guy is a monster.

"What they didn't do is take over. YOU TOOK OVER MY FUCKING WORLD! LOOK AT IT!" I flinch as he roars, sweeping his arms around to encompass the realm that peeks out from behind this dark horrid corner. He lowers his voice and, somehow, it's more menacing. "Trees, flowers, butterflies, a lake? I left a rotten hotel and a barely functional car park. You've been busy making yourself a true sanctuary when you should have been a good little girl and laid down dead. This isn't fucking Disneyland," he spits. "This pocket dimension is not yours. It is mine. *Mine*. This place was made to be a prison."

In a panic, I send my magic out and try—like I'm pulling strands of string that are tangled—to gather the realm's magic, but it is as if I'm trying to touch through glass. I keep hitting a wall.

"Girl, stop trying to manipulate the magic. You have had days to try and learn something I've been doing for millennia. Quit it. This pocket world is not yours."

It wants to be.

"That's the problem though, isn't it?" I rasp. "This realm *likes* being a sanctuary. It does not enjoy being a trap." *Sentient.* I know it sounds crazy. The magic is sentient, and that is the reason I am still alive. He's been killing people for centuries, sucking out their life force, abusing the realm's magic. Like me, the magic doesn't want to hurt people, it wants to help, and perhaps it found that spark of possibility within me. We align. The magic stepped up and protected me. "That is why you are so pissed. The realm locked you out." My released host magic combined with the dimensional magic healed the world and pulled it right out of the rogue host's hands.

"Oh, will you just shut up? What does it matter, Nancy Drew? Just shut up and die already." He groans. "It will take me years to get your stink out of this place. Do you know what? I'm going to drain you slowly. It will take weeks." He runs his finger across my lips. "I will cut out your tongue to halt the incessant chatter and put you in a tiny pocket cell, safe and away from my realm. While I drain your magic, I will enjoy watching you slowly go mad."

Pain screams inside me. *Is he draining me already?* Ouch.

"You feel that, don't you? The tickle underneath your skin." A tickle? More like my stomach and bowels have been put into a meat grinder. "Danger will do that. The magic doesn't like it. So finicky in its attempt to be so pure."

My vision flashes to black and I am forced to close my eyes. Creatures pop up on the magical map inside my head, and it pounds with the overload of information. I take the opportunity to frantically check on Owen, Daisy, and my coven. For the moment, they are safe. I can feel my hellhound's concern and determination. But then I see what the rogue host wanted, the reason why he is allowing me to see, to torture me with the truth. Eight—no, ten people that shouldn't be here. Mercenaries.

The first thing I did when I felt someone rip a hole in the realm was lock down all the portals. He has yet to re-open them.

I locked down every portal, except for one.

I didn't lock down the emergency one leading to Jodie's shop. Nobody but a member of our coven could gain access to her shop. *Yet they have.* Perhaps the rogue host destroyed the wards? But Jodie would have known.

"I brought along some friends." Despair fills me. His *friends* are surrounding my coven. They didn't make it out. I failed. The magic screams at me to do something, but the rogue host cuts my connection. It is down to just a whisper.

My voice cracks. "How?"

"I didn't even have to pay them," he says, all jolly. "You killed a dryad, and some guy loved her. He went a bit nuts when her tree disappeared. The poor love-blinded fool thought he had a hope of saving her —save the tree, save the girl."

Erin.

"When the whole clan up and left, he knew something bad had happened. So he did a little digging. A kind-hearted soul—that would be me—whispered your name in his ear. I helped to stir him up and push him in the right direction. Towards you. I also helpfully gave him the number for an excellent mercenary firm as professional backup. The rat shifters are wonderful soldiers and so much easier to manipulate than the wolves."

Yeah, the same rats that ransacked my flat.

I don't bother telling him that Erin is still alive and well. It's not something he'd understand. Undoubtedly, he thinks everyone is a soul-sucking monster like him.

"I needed a backup plan in case you were more difficult to deal with. Waste of effort, really. I thought you would have at least offered me more of a challenge, but…" He huffs. "Never mind. By now, the rats will have gathered all your guests, including your pathetic little coven, for me to eat. Even if they kill everyone before I get there, the power, their souls, are mine."

I force my face to look appropriately horrified. The host has made a mistake. He should have used a null band on me. He should not have left the tiny little spark of access to the realm's magic.

Using that magic, I initiate a change of plan. Instead of letting Owen come to me, I need him to help the guests, help my coven. With the access to the realm's magic drifting ever so slowly out of my grip, I get a message to Owen, to tell him what is happening and to give him access to the realm map and the location of all the mercenaries. Within the message, I lie and tell him I have got everything under control, and with a blast of magic, I Step him back towards the hotel. I breathe a silent sigh when it works.

The host does not notice, as he is still waffling on with his villain speech. "…I must say, I do so enjoy the thought that so many creatures will add up to a real feast."

"Can you remember who you've killed?" The host scoffs and tightens his hand in my hair before wrapping the other one around my throat. "What about Rebecca Lynch? She was a—"

"Dead." He squeezes my throat. "Any creature that stumbles into the hotel and isn't useful is dead. A mere snack. Unlike you. I'm going to feast on your power, little girl. I will be careful to drain you so slowly you'll be kept alive for months."

"What about Atticus? Does he not care about you killing hosts, killing guests?"

He laughs. "No, you naïve little fool, of course not. He doesn't know. What do you take me for, an amateur? I control everything he sees. Pureblood vampires are selfish. He doesn't care about others."

"That's where you'd be wrong," says a cultured voice behind us. "I care, and I quite like having a swimming pool."

CHAPTER
THIRTY-FIVE

Atticus's fangs flash, and he buries his teeth into the host's neck. His black eyes glisten with satisfaction as they meet mine. The ground beneath my feet lets me go and I stumble away.

When I sent a message to Owen, I also sneakily sent a message to Atticus with two questions: what was his girl called, and did he want to meet her potential killer? My magic brought back his answers: Rebecca Lynch—and if I gave him Rebecca's killer, he would be eternally grateful.

When my magic moved Owen to where he was needed, it yanked Atticus here.

I look away from the vampire and block out the noise of his feeding. I don't like violence, but I understand justice.

Even if justice makes me a little queasy.

My knees knock together, and I rub my throat, then my aching neck.

I never want to be in that position again, with an enemy's hand wrapped around my throat.

I need to be better, stronger.

"Tuesday, I did what I could to protect you. I am sorry I could not tell you," says a pained voice. I raise my eyes from a spot on the floor and meet Larry's pleading green gaze.

Oh no, Larry! The magical construct is *translucent*. "Larry? What's happening?" Why does he no longer appear real?

"You freed me from a monster. Please forgive me for my treachery. I am glad you are safe." I watch him fade into nothingness. "Thank you for showing me what it was like to have a friend..."

"Oh, Larry, of course, I forgive you." I reach out and brush the empty air. My hand trembles. I fold my arms underneath my chest, so I am hugging myself.

I hear a thump, like something heavy falling to the ground. Like a body. I gulp, hunch, and keep my back turned. I have already seen a dead person today. I do not want to see another. A second later, the magic of the realm floods into me. My connection to the realm is restored, and it is stronger than ever. The feeling is so powerful, I stagger. I have to peek at my feet to double-check I'm still on the ground, as I could swear that I am floating. My hair follicles tingle and when I pat my head, my hair crackles with power. *Freaky*.

Oh gosh, what am I doing? I need to help my coven, is my next urgent thought.

Eagerly, the realm's magic hunts down each trespasser. The mercenaries do not stand a chance. Removing their weapons, we pluck them up as if they are just pieces of a board game and Step them to the hotel reception, where they are frozen solid in place while they wait for me to deal with them.

"Tuesday," Atticus says.

I can't. I can't turn around. I'll vomit. I hunch into myself. "Yes," I answer him with stiff lips.

"Here." His hand reaches over my shoulder and a heavy bronze ring settles in my palm. "He was wearing it. It is rightfully yours as it is full of magic—your realm's magic."

My precious, Gollum from *The Lord of the Rings* coos in my head. *Crikey, I am such a weirdo.* The ring is so heavy in my hand. I frown down at it and give it a poke with my index finger. The power inside gives me a little nip.

"Thank you, and thanks for coming to my aid." I decide to put the ring in the little pocket of my jeans for safekeeping. I flip it between my fingers so I can slide it inside. When it touches the fabric, the ring comes apart and becomes a single piece of metal. I freeze. *Oh, that's not...* The ring, like something from a horror movie, jumps and wraps itself around my right ring finger. It tightens.

A whimper leaves my throat as I come out of my strange paralysis and then, as if my hand is on fire, I flap it about like a crazy person. *Get off, get off, get the fuck off!* Yeah, as if shaking it will dislodge it. I go to yank it off. I yelp. The little bugger shocked me! Ouch, that was more than just a nip.

My hand shakes as I hold it as far away from my body as I can. I hiss and brace it with my other hand when what feels like a thousand barbs dig into my skin, muscle, and then the bone of my poor finger. "Ouch, ouch, ouch." My stomach twists and the pain makes me want to vomit.

When I am about to hyperventilate and do something stupid like, I don't know, grab a blade out of the ether and chop my damn finger off with the sheer overwhelming panic I'm feeling, the pain stops.

I lick my dry lips.

"I have seen nothing like that before. Jewellery is not normally that rambunctious," Atticus says.

My wide eyes swivel towards him. "Yeah, no kidding. It really wanted on my finger." My chest aches. Cautiously, as if the ring is a dangerous animal, I remove my stabilising hand to rub my chest. My heart pounds underneath my palm. "Crap-on-a-cracker. That was scary." I clear my throat and blow out a breath.

After a few more seconds and no further pain, the previously inert silver swirls on the back of my hand get in on the action.

Uh-oh.

They pulse in time to my pounding heart and then they change direction. They straighten and flow towards my abused finger and the ring. Like an electric circuit.

"Do you want me to cut it off?" Atticus asks matter-of-factly.

"No!" I squeak as I tuck my hand against my chest. "I don't think so. No. At least it's no longer hurting me." It's not draining my power either. Somehow it makes me feel more centred. The power of the realm is now crystal clear. Honestly, can this day get any crazier?

Atticus tilts his head as he stares at my hand. "I believe this might be how he used his magic outside the realm."

"Oh." Atticus is right. The ring is packed full of magic, and things that were bugging me now make sense. Answers slide into place. "I forgot he was Stepping in the real world." And smashing powerful wards in minutes, destroying magic that would have taken anyone else hours, if at all. I then remember crocodile lady smirking at me when she noticed I didn't have a ring. "The other hosts have the same ring," I mutter.

The silence stretches between us.

"Do you urm... want the body?" I ask awkwardly.

What the feck, Tuesday?

Well, I don't know what the hell I am doing. This is stressful and I have no idea about revenge protocol!

"No. No, thank you." Atticus smirks.

I rub my face. "Okay." I then nod my head like a nodding dog and allow the magic of the realm to absorb the dead host's body. Without looking, I somehow know he's disappeared.

I stare down at the ring. As he was the original host, the realm should technically die with him, but because of me, the realm is stronger and healthier than ever.

Gosh, I still have so much to learn. Everything written about hosts seems to mislead or be outright lies. I have so much to do... Wow, it is going to be an adventure.

"I need to deal with everything."

"Of course. Oh, Tuesday, I would prefer you not transport me. It makes me want to vomit," Atticus says, looking a little vulnerable trusting me with his honesty.

I nod. "Okay."

I wonder if my Stepping makes others sick or if my new friend, the big bad pureblood vampire, has got a weak stomach from all the blood. I will have to ask Owen.

Owen. My mind and magic automatically go to him. He has tracked the mercenaries back to reception and is guarding them, still in his wolf form. I can feel how anxious he is, so I send reassuring thoughts through the magic.

Right. I better get to it. I need to deal with the mercenaries. The longer they stay, the more at risk we are of them combating my magic. Boy, they have some questions to answer. I already know, or can guess, most of what's happened. The host's slimy fingerprints are all over everything.

"Tuesday, thank yo—"

"Think nothing of it," I rudely interrupt, my voice squeaky. "Really don't."

The scary pureblood vampire chuckles, and I turn and hurry away. I leave him standing there to make his own way back.

Just before I wrap the magic around me to Step, I send a magic call to everyone in the realm to let them know everything is safe, and the emergency is over. I then send another magic message to my coven, for them to meet Owen and me at reception.

CHAPTER
THIRTY-SIX

The foliage crunches underneath my feet as I carefully pick my way between the trees. I have to make a quick stop to collect Erin before I deal with the mercenaries.

I am glad it's only my coven, Atticus, and the dryads staying. If I had more guests, the reputation of the realm as a safe place would be ruined after today. The dryads have made zero sign they even heard the warnings, as they didn't stir from their trees. They must be in some kind of deep, regenerative sleep. I will have to check on them in person. My anger over Erin's situation has made me negligent and I let Larry deal with them... Shit, what was I thinking? Yeah. I shake my head. *I wasn't thinking.*

Yep, good call there, Tuesday. I give myself a hearty mental thump on my back. *Great job.*

Hindsight is a wonderful thing.

At least the realm's magic tells me they are safe. Otherwise... I puff out my cheeks as something inside me cracks. This entire situation with the rogue host will have me waking in the middle of the night for years with thoughts on what could have gone wrong and what I could have done better. I can't believe it has worked out so well, unless he has more surprises waiting for me. I glance at my right hand. As soon as I think about it, the ring on my hand weighs a tonne. I squeeze between some branches, and shuffle around a thorny bush.

The realm was a bloody prison, so it is only up from here, right? Ah bitterness, my old friend. A prison. Then there was me, all lah-di-dah and butterflies. I thought the realm would be a fabulous safe space while knowing nothing about it. Like I invented the wheel and a brand new six-star resort. Crikey, I allowed my coven to come. I put them in danger.

Right, shut up with the self-flagellation. Now isn't the time.

I mentally duct tape my insides and tuck away the horror and panic I feel until I am ready to deal with it later.

"Erin." I reach out a finger and brush the rough bark of her tree. I then instantly feel weird. Is touching a dryad's tree like touching them? I don't know the protocol, so I drop my hand and scoot a little further away to what I hope is a more appropriate social distance.

Erin's tree looks amazing. It is even healthier than when I first healed it, and the entire forest appears to be better. Yesterday, the forest was more open. Now it has grown thicker, like a protective barrier has grown up around Erin's tree.

"Erin?" I try again. "I know you want to be left alone, but something has happened. I need your help. I haven't spoken to him yet, but from what I have been led to believe, a man you know, a man who claims to be in love with you, has infiltrated the realm with mercenaries looking for justice as he believes you are dead. He thinks I killed you. Erin? Please, I need your help."

I feel stupid talking to a tree, and when nothing happens, I doubt she has even heard me. Then the tree shimmers, and Erin's pretty face appears. Her long eyelashes flutter and pieces of bark attached to them drift into the air with each blink.

She yawns. "Pardon? Did I hear you correctly? A man claims to love me and has tried to kill you?" Erin pulls away from the tree with a pained gasp. First, she wiggles her arm free and then her left leg. She has to forcibly yank herself from the tree's clutches as if it does not want to let her go. "Mercenaries?" She stares back at me with frightened, horrified eyes. "Jeff came to find me?"

Jeff. I file his name away. "It is more like he came to kill me. I have not had the pleasure of his company yet. Fortunately for him, he hasn't hurt anybody, and I have him detained." I add on quickly, "He is safe," in case she is worried about him.

"He came to avenge me? He thinks I'm dead? Oh, no." Erin rubs her forehead. "What was he thinking? We split up over a month ago. We are not together. He... he told me he couldn't deal with the whole tree thing, and he wouldn't let me explain that without my tree, I am dead." She presses one hand to her heart and the other behind her on the tree. "He said I was overreacting and that my dramatics were interfering with his game time. He was more interested in his game console than my life. Can you believe that? Overreacting to my pending death. I'm so dramatic.

"We had a huge fight, and I left him. Then everything happened. My tree got knocked down, and that was that. As my tree slowly rotted on the ground in our decimated forest, I slowly rotted alongside it. The other dryads panicked. They had no choice but to ask for help as they could see what was happening to me and they knew they were next.

"An elf pointed us in the hotel's direction and said it was a safe place for our trees. As we are earthborn, we are not allowed in any of the fae realms." Erin frowns and rubs her head. "I don't know why I didn't tell you any of this before. It's... it is like my tongue was tied and it didn't seem important. All I wanted to do was sleep." She drops her hand and shakes her head. "The elf told us we would have to make a sacrifice. I was told I would be that sacrifice, as I was already dying. Friends, creatures that I had loved and known my entire life, turned on me. I was told my death would have meaning.

"But when we got here, you healed me and saved my tree. I didn't have time to let Jeff know what was going on. Not that he would have cared." Erin laughs bitterly. "So, now he loves me? What is that all about?" She gazes down at the ground and toes a few rotten leaves. "I didn't think he cared. I am so sorry; I can't believe he came here. After everything that you have done for me, I pay you back by bringing trouble to your door. I'm so very sorry, Tuesday. Geez. Did he think playing combat computer games made him a mercenary?" Erin pulls away from the tree. "Love?" she huffs. "I didn't think he even liked me."

"It is clear the elf set you all up. That is why your friends acted out of character and why you did not tell me what had happened. Until now. The horrible guy is dead, so he can't manipulate anyone anymore." *I hope.*

This is why asking questions is important. If I had not been so shocked when the dryads arrived, I might have saved myself some heartache. If I had asked them simple questions, I might have realised things didn't add up.

"Will you come with me to speak to him?" I ask, holding out my hand.

"Of course, I will come."

I drop my offered hand as a thought enters my head. I need to tell her now before she sees him and perhaps changes her mind. "I must warn you, even if I think Jeff was manipulated, I have to treat him like a threat. He came here intending to hurt people, so he won't be able to stay with you in the realm."

"I completely understand. Believe me, I don't want him to stay either. I don't know why he thought coming here with a group of hired thugs would be a good idea. Avenging my death... when he left me to rot." Erin looks up from the ground, her eyes pleading. "Y-you won't kill him, will you? Please don't—"

"No, I won't kill him," I say, horrified. I feel a little disappointed at her insinuation. Although I can see why she would be concerned, she can probably see the anger radiating from me. I'm pissed. But that anger is aimed at me. I am so disappointed in myself. "I also don't blame you for his actions." And in all honesty, I don't blame Jeff either.

That host was a master manipulator.

"Come on, let's get this mess sorted out." I hold my hand out again and Erin takes it.

CHAPTER
THIRTY-SEVEN

Erin and I are the last to arrive. The frozen mercenaries immediately draw my attention. My magic has just plonked them together in a rough grouping. A couple of them are even facing the wall. Seven are standing, and three are unconscious. *The Power Rangers.* "Has no one ever told you guys that your Power Ranger outfits are ridiculous?" Of course, the frozen men can't reply, they can't make a peep. For extra safety, and not willing to encounter any more surprises, I lock the entire reception down.

The huge black wolf's grey eyes land on me, and he shifts. What I can only describe is a look of pure relief crosses Owen's handsome face as he prowls toward me. His entire focus is on me. His enormous hands land on my hips and he lifts me into his arms. The cinnamon and vanilla scent of him fills my lungs. One arm is underneath my bottom—like the best kind of seat—and it holds me up against him while his other hand cradles my face. My tummy flips as I am engulfed in his heat and his perfect bumper car lips find mine.

He kisses me sweetly, reverently, as if I am the only person who matters to him in the entire world.

When I reluctantly pull away to take a breath, my breasts brush against his chest. His pecs are hard. Steel beneath silken skin, reminding me of the power of the man that holds me. We breathe in unison for several seconds and unfortunately, my head screams a warning that we are not alone.

Oops.

I am now very aware we are kissing in the same room as my parents and a bunch of mercenaries. I glare at him ruefully. Owen returns the look with a soft smile, so I allow myself the luxury of leaning against the hand that is cupping my jaw for a few more precious seconds.

When I finally lift my eyes, I peek over his shoulder. My coven is milling around; they appear relaxed considering the current situation and the earlier excitement. My attention lands on Mum. She isn't so relaxed. Her eyes are politely averted, and her hand is firm across a grumbling Heather's face, blocking her view.

In the back of my head, I acknowledge my hellhound is, um, naked, having just shifted. Even though I love his soft skin underneath my fingertips, and I know he isn't shy, nor does he mind everyone checking out his bare bottom, I tease, "I'm not the only one who should be called Flash.'" I wrap him in his combat style clothing and include his weapons for good measure.

"I was so worried," he whispers. "I am so glad you're safe." The rough stubble on his jaw scratches against my hair as he kisses the top of my head. Owen gently places me on the floor and pulls away just enough, so he can check me over.

The bruising on my throat where the host grabbed me must have faded. But it still doesn't stop my hellhound from homing in on the area. Probably scenting the host on my skin. "Where is he?" he growls.

"Dead." My mouth goes dry with the words and my throat aches. "He is dead." Owen's eyes soften with compassion.

"Good. Did you kill him?"

I shake my head. "Atticus."

"I owe him."

I don't bother correcting him that the vampire still owes me, but it is a long story and I'll tell him when we have privacy and not an entire reception full of frozen but listening mercenaries.

"Daisy?" I don't wait for his answer as my magic finds her automatically. She is swimming in a lava pool with her fake dragonette friends. "Found her," I mumble.

"She kept trying to bite your mum."

"Oh." I can't help but grin and Owen's eyes sparkle. "I will have a stern word with her to not bite grandma." As if we conjured her, Mum tugs me away from Owen and hugs me.

Oof.

"The dragonette is not my grandchild. I am so glad you are okay. Please don't do that again. I was worried. Tuesday, you don't have to prove you are the strongest person in the room. We all know it. Next time, let us help you. You don't have to do things alone." She gives me a shake and then Diane, my protector, pulls me away from her tight grip.

"Now is not the time, Mum," Diane chides. "Glad you are okay, sis."

I expect Mum to say something else, to reprimand me, but she doesn't. She gives me a small smile and... is that respect in her eyes?

Nah. Now I know I must be seeing things. Her concern has shocked the stuffing out of me.

"Is everyone okay?" Andy, as usual, is scowling.

"Yes, we are fine," Ava says.

"Hellhound"—Mum clears her throat—"perhaps we need to discuss a spell that will retain your clothes while you shift. While you are a fine-looking man, we do not need to see you in all your glory. Especially when there are children present. We are witches, not wolves, and we have standards."

I snort and Owen and I share another look.

"I don't know," Jodie whispers to Diane. "I don't mind." Diane shushes and elbows her, while Andy looks appalled.

I turn back to our prisoners. "So, you got three?" I ask Owen, acknowledging three of the mercenaries who are unconscious and a little bit worse for wear. I look a little closer and spot the odd man out. I should say, two mercenaries and one lovesick young man are unconscious and frozen on the floor.

"Oh, hello, Jeff."

Erin's takes that as permission to hurry towards him and drops to her knees beside him on the floor. Her hands flutter about as if she doesn't know where to touch him. "I don't know whether to ask you to slap some sense into him or help him," she whispers. When she catches my eye, she blinks back tears. "Please, please help him. I know it's wrong of me to ask, but can you please heal him as you did me?"

I can see he's a little beat up. Claw marks rend across his chest and his abdomen. The eyes of my coven and the frozen mercenaries track me as I shuffle toward them. As I kneel in front of Jeff, I whisper, "Erin, will you please stay out of the way for a second? Just so I can talk with him without interference? I promise I won't be long." Erin nods and scrambles out of Jeff's sightline.

"I am going to heal him first." I keep him frozen as I send my magic into him to heal the superficial wounds. Well, superficial to a creature. But not to the pale young man before me, who has the markers of a person who spends all his time inside.

Jeff is human. Which makes what he did, coming here for revenge, more impressive—I frown—if not more stupid. What was he thinking? Was the host's influence that substantial? Or is Jeff the gamer a closet Rambo?

Gosh, he has been very lucky to have only got away with a few nasty scratches. As my magic finishes healing him, his eyes flutter open.

"Hey Jeff," I say, all friendly-like.

I remind myself that the rest of Jeff is frozen, so I unfreeze his mouth, allowing him to speak.

"Bitch," he snarls. Erin gasps. I wave the hand that he can't see at Erin, in a silent request for her to keep her mouth closed until after I have finished talking to him. Thankfully, she listens. "It's you, isn't it? He told me you had freaky purple hair. You killed my girl and I'm going to end you."

I slow blink. He is going to *end* me. My lips twitch. That was kind of adorable.

"I am going to rip you apart with my bare hands and shit down your neck."

Ew. Lovely. That was not quite as cute. "Are you now? Well, alrighty then," I say with zero aplomb. "That is kind of a dramatic statement, Jeff, considering you are frozen to the floor. I healed you and you are so welcome." I rub my eyebrow and wrinkle my nose when Jeff roars.

He grits his teeth and grunts with a bold but bizarre attempt to prove me wrong. I watch as his face goes bright red and a little blood vessel in his temple throbs as he struggles to make good on his threat.

Gah.

I tilt my head to the side and wait him out. After a few more grunts and groans, he settles. "Are you done?" I quietly ask. He glares at me and then looks away. "So, Jeff, who told you I killed Erin?" The same eyebrow I've been scrubbing rises with my enquiry.

"Everybody knows. Everybody knows that you're a murderous bitch. And if I don't get you, someone else will."

"Okay, that's nice." I nod sagely and then ask the same question. "Who told you I killed Erin?"

"An elf did."

Ah, now we're getting somewhere. His explanation doesn't seem to differ from the host's villain speech. "What did he tell you?" Jeff clamps his lips closed, and he stubbornly closes his eyes. I sigh at his childish antics. "The elf lied to you, Jeff. He used you and you put Erin in danger by coming here all potions blazing."

"Liar!" Jeff yells. "You're a lying evil bitch." Owen growls, so I freeze Jeff's mouth before Owen can come over and pull his head off.

I get off the floor and wipe my sweaty hands on my jeans. I am so completely out of my comfort zone in dealing with this. I know I'll get nothing out of him. He is too angry. At least it is easy to prove I'm not lying. "Wow, Erin," I mumble, "you have a real winner here. No wonder you broke up with him." I nod and wave my hand in a "have at it" gesture. She falls forward, shuffling on her hands and knees towards his inert body.

My eyes go to the mercenaries. Perhaps by speaking to them, I will have more success?

"What did you do?" Erin cries as she grabs hold of his shirt. The shock in his eyes is worth taking his vitriol for a few minutes. "Tuesday saved my life, you idiot. She saved my tree, and you want to shit down her throat? Are you for fucking real? What the hell did I see in you, you weasel?"

CURSED WITCH

Jeff's eyes almost bug out of his head, and I again allow him to speak.

"What? You're alive? How? What? Erin! Erin, I love you so much. I had to come here, as I couldn't live without you." I sigh as he blubbers. I don't think Jeff will want to kill me anymore, so I unfreeze him. His arms snake around the dryad and he clutches her to his chest, raining her with snot and tears as he cries.

I catch Erin's mortified look. I wince.

While trying to push him off, Erin tells Jeff about how I saved her and her tree. Jeff tells her about finding her missing and then being unable to find the rest of the dryads.

And *then* he talks about meeting an elf who offered him a chance for revenge, which he couldn't pass up.

To give them privacy, now that I've got what I need, I move them to a new build cabin in the woods, close to Erin's tree. I make sure that Jeff cannot go wandering about, confining him to the cabin. After all, he hired a bunch of mercenaries and led them to my realm to kill me. I'm not a horrible person and they need privacy to sort stuff out. So, I will give him an hour and then stuff him in a portal. Then the human police can deal with him.

I flick my magic over the two injured mercenaries, rapidly healing them. As shifters, they'd be able to heal themselves completely if I let them shift, but there is no way I am unfreezing them to allow that. Hands on my hips, I check out the mercenaries. Well, the ones that are facing in my direction. You can tell a lot about somebody's character from their eyes. One guy in particular makes nervous shivers run down my spine as his black eyes glare at me with uncontrolled hatred. He has the whole 'rough leader' vibe going on. Perhaps he might be the best person to have a little chat with.

Like I did with Jeff, I unfreeze his mouth and ask him a question. "Who do you work for?" He continues to glare at me. "Do you know what? Like you, I have had such a horrid day." I sigh and shake my head. "Today has been nothing but drama. All I want to do is have a nice bath and go to sleep.

"I could sleep for a week. I am sure you're the same, Green Power Ranger, what with getting set up, being treated like bait, and then getting your arse kicked. I bet you want to go home, get out of your little rubber outfit, and have a beer and relax." The rough mercenary's left eye twitches. "Please don't make me kill you," I whisper.

When I look back at this conversation, I'd like to think it was the soft appeal in my voice that made the green Power Ranger answer me. But I know him opening his mouth is probably more than likely because of the growly hellhound at my back. The world I live in is sadly patriarchal to its core, and no matter the power I have, I will always be viewed as a mere woman. Not that I care.

"I work for Rattan and Sons." *Bingo.*

"Perfect, thank you. Have you got their phone number?" I pull my phone out of my pocket. With an incredulous tone, green rattles off a number, which I promptly dial. The phone rings. "What's your boss's name?"

"Henderson," he growls.

"Thank you."

As the phone rings, I give the steely-eyed hellhound behind me a chin lift in appreciation. *I see what you did there, handsome.*

The phone connects, and a bored sounding receptionist rattles the company's name, with a not-so-pleasant "How may I help you?" added at the end. I guess it is getting late.

"Good evening, please may I speak to a Mr Henderson?"

"Mr Henderson is not available at the moment."

"I think he would *really* like to speak to me."

"Mr Henderson has finished for the day."

"Oh, okay. I just thought he'd want to know where his missing team was. I'm sure nine lives are easy to throw away, what with mercenaries being so abundant and easy to come by. I understand they must be such pesky employees, and not worth Mr Henderson's precious time." I pause and stare at green as I listen to the woman gasp and splutter.

"I will transfer you now. Please hold." Music plays in the background and I put the phone on speaker and tap my foot to the beat.

"Who is this and what do you want?" comes a gruff voice.

"Mr Henderson?" He grunts an affirmative. "My name is Tuesday

Larson, and you must have been informed I have nine of your men in my possession."

"Are they alive?"

"Yes, and healthy."

"What game are you playing? What do you want?"

"I'm not playing a game, Mr Henderson. I will give your men back to you out of the goodness of my heart, but I need something from you first."

"What do you want?" he snarls.

"Mr Henderson, let me be clear on this. Their lives are on the line. All I ask for their safe return is for you to give me a promise, a single promise that for as long as you live, for as long as your firm exists, you will *never* accept a contract for my realm or a member of the Larson coven. Oh, and I'd like to add my boyfriend to that list. Owen—he's the hellhound. We are on your 'do not touch' list, do you understand? If you don't have such a list, you make one tonight. In exchange, I will return your men to you unharmed."

"So, I make a promise and you return my men? Is that it? Just like that?" He laughs. "And you said you weren't playing any games, Miss Larson."

"If you make this promise to me, Mr Henderson, let's just say I have the power to enforce it."

"Yes, yes. I am sure you do. Okay, we have a deal, for whatever it's worth," he finishes with a grumble and a disbelieving scoff.

"Perfect. Oh, and as a punishment and safeguard, every person linked to your company, including their families, they have a lifelong ban from The Sanctuary realm. If they try to enter, they will be refused admittance and if they somehow get inside under false pretences, I will kill them. Is that understood?"

Whoa, I am sounding very bloodthirsty this evening.

"Okay. Whatever. Who cares?"

"I have your word?"

"Yes." I feel the realm's magic pulse, and I watch as filaments of the magic shoot out like arrows and disappear into the mercenaries' chests. Oh, now that is handy. A magical tag, just so I can keep track of them. "What the fuck was that?" Mr Henderson yelps.

I open a portal behind the mercenaries and shove them through. As soon as I hear the thuds over the phone, I release the frozen spell holding them captive and snap the portal closed. Owen moves away from behind me with a relieved sigh.

"Nice speaking with you, Mr Henderson. Have a pleasant evening." If that didn't scare the shit out of them, I don't know what will.

"Oh, Miss Larson, don't go just yet. Don't you want to know who let my guys into your realm?" Oh, I do. There I go again, forgetting the important questions. "As you have returned my men safe and sound, I can afford to give you some free information."

"Call me pleasantly intrigued."

"Your rat—pardon my pun—the wolf with access to the magic shop and your fixed portal, was your sister's boyfriend, Andrew."

CHAPTER
THIRTY-EIGHT

Owen's eyes widen, and my world slows down to microseconds.

A weight slams into my back, knocking me off my feet and sending me flying as a fifteen stone wolf hits me from behind. The phone clatters to the ground, followed swiftly by me. I hit the floor with a crunch and my ears ring as my head bounces off the wood. Ouch. I roll to avoid a heavy paw to my face, and bring my hands up just in time to protect my throat from the wolf's savaging teeth.

Bloody hell.

Underneath the wolf's snarls is the sound of Mr Henderson's tinny laughter.

Even though the wolf attack feels like forever, it is only a matter of seconds until the shifted wolf goes airborne and is yanked off me.

"Andy? That was Andy, right?" I say dazed.

My vision is hazy, and I can see actual squiggly lines in front of my eyes. I must have really cracked my head if I am showing signs of concussion. I watch as a black fuzzy blob rushes toward me.

"Tuesday, are you okay?" Mum cries as she helps to sit me up.

"I am fine, Mum," I rasp with a fake smile as I move my head to knock her icy hand from my cheek.

The bloody magic lie detector pings. *Great.* The stupid magic won't even give me the peace to lie to myself.

I blink a few times and my head clears. "He just knocked the wind out of me, that's all. The realm magic will fix me right up." My tone is light and even, but my heart is slamming against my ribs. I lick my lips. Blood coats inside of my mouth and the back of my head aches.

I duck my head to cover my horrified expression, and madness bubbles inside of me. The shock I'm feeling right now makes me want to roll back onto the floor and laugh. Laugh like my entire world has not fallen apart.

Up. Get up.

My stomach churns with fear, and my body is rubbery with shock. My limbs are like a day-old Pot Noodle. I scramble to my knees and, with my left hand, I stretch out and grab the fallen phone. "Thanks for the heads up, Mr Henderson," I say pleasantly as I end the call.

With Mum's help, I stand. I fist my right hand behind my back.

"Flash, are you okay?" Owen asks over the ruckus of the brown thrashing wolf. He has a good grip on the wolf. He holds him by the scruff of his neck.

"Yes." I get the single word out before my throat locks up.

Liar, liar, broom on fire. The old nursery rhyme echoes around my head.

With Owen's attention on Andy, it is easy to pull the wool over his eyes. Plus, this is my realm, and reality can be altered. I make sure the scent of my blood goes nowhere near his keen shifter nose. The hellhound lets out a hair-raising growl and shakes the wolf like a puppy. His arm bulges with strength, but Andy's weight doesn't seem to affect the big man.

"Andy?" Diane whispers brokenly. "Why, Andy? Why would you do that?" I clamp my mouth closed, as it takes everything that I have not to say, "'Cause he is a dickhead."

Jodie tries to comfort our sister while looking back at Mum and me with frightened eyes. Ava and Heather are nowhere to be found. I don't need to ask my magic where they are as Dad is guarding the way to my office.

"Shift back, or I'll break your neck," Owen says. His voice is a deadly whisper in the snapping wolf's ear. Then it's as if Andy comes back to himself. He finally pauses his struggles, tucks his tail between his legs, and cowers.

With puppy dog eyes and pink spit dripping from his jaws, he inspects our angry coven. The realisation is dawning on his wolfy features. He has seriously messed up.

The wolf shifts.

I'm glad to see Andy isn't naked, having been gifted the coven's expensive clothing retention potion. I stand there quietly. I don't have the heart to interfere with this interrogation.

One thought keeps screaming at me. It bounces around in my head and I have to push it away, so it doesn't come spilling out of my lips in a devastated scream.

"You brought in the mercenaries," Diane says, shrugging off Jodie's arm and surprising probably everybody in the room as she steps up.

Her voice is clear. Gone is the pain, and it is replaced with anger. "You brought mercenaries here to hurt my coven. Why? Why would you do that?" Andy winces as Owen applies pressure to his neck. There are flames in my hellhound's eyes and is that... yes, his free hand is once again engulfed in dancing blue flame.

I love that I can see his magic. I am not in love with the circumstances, but I'm glad I get to see him like this again, for what undoubtedly will be the last time.

"I am sick of you and your fantastic, amazing, incredible coven looking down at me as if I'm scum. What are you without your potions? What can you do really? It was easy to make you think I loved you." Andy winks. "Any hole is a goal, am I right?"

Beside me, Mum lets out a disgusted sound.

Diane blinks a few times and then laughs. "You narcissistic, little shit. To think I thought your weirdness was endearing. You are a joke. Who told you any of this would be a good idea? When did you decide on this brilliant plan?" She waves her arm in the air and then nods at Owen. Owen's fiery hand drifts closer to Andy. A droplet of sweat from his hairline rolls down his face. Andy lets out a whimper.

"It was all Mr Henderson! He knew I was dating you and when you included me on the trip to the safe house, it gave the ideal opportunity to set things in place. It was a nice little earner. Kill two birds with one stone. It meant I was finally rid of you and wouldn't get my arse kicked by your bitch of a mother." Mum huffs. "Win-win. Until you all decided to move location and come here." He toothily grins at me.

He knows. He knows what he did.

"So, when your useless sister mentioned fixing a portal to the shop at lunch, I got on the blower and made the plans. It happened quickly after that."

Ah, this wasn't the work of the host. Good to know Andy was not a victim, brainwashed into doing something that was out of character.

I keep my injured right hand behind my back and a small droplet of blood splatters unnoticed on the floor. The realm's magic whisks the evidence away.

Andy looks again at me with a triumphant grin. I didn't get away unscathed and no magic on Earth will heal me. Andy bit me in his deadly wolf form.

He bit me.

"Tuesday. Will you open a portal?" I must have missed some of the conversation. Mum gently strokes the back of my head to get my attention. "Your dad and Owen are going to take Andy to the Hunters Guild."

I nod. "Sure," I croak. I need to mask what I am feeling, suck it up until they've gone.

I open the portal.

"Please don't take me there. I don't want to be locked up. Diane, tell them to kill me. Are you not going to kill me?"

"Kill you? No, that would be way too easy. Where you're going, pal, they will keep you alive for a very long time." Owen shakes Andy like he is a rag doll to get his point home. I am glad I've not said anything about the bite. Owen would rip Andy's throat right out.

Andy must have the same thought. "Tell him, Tuesday—"

I freeze his stupid mouth.

My breath shudders. It's probably my imagination, as I've always been a tad dramatic, but as the painful bite on my hand burns, I can already feel the poisonous shifter magic running through my veins.

"Love you, Dad."

Dad kisses me on the cheek and whispers, "And I love you. Please look after your sister." I can't speak the lie, so I nod.

I shuffle towards Owen and quietly mumble a goodbye. "See you in a bit. Be careful. Thank you for your help." Owen smiles at me in that way he does.

"Always."

My heart wails.

Why? Why couldn't I get my happily ever after?

I'm dead, my body just doesn't know it yet. The small bite will kill me within seventy-two hours, and this is the last time I will see my hellhound. I don't want him to see me suffer like that.

I stubbornly lift my chin as they step into the portal, dragging Andy between them.

I love you. I love you so much. I scream inside.

Before the portal closes, I squeeze my eyes tightly shut and turn away so I cannot see the budding confusion in his beautiful grey eyes.

I can't watch him leave. I just can't.

When the portal closes, I lock everything down so he can't return. I am so proud that I held it together.

Now I have a decision to make. I can run, like the million times I have done before, or I can be honest. Tell the truth. Everything inside me wants to run away, wants to find some deep, dark hole to fall inside. But the selfish part of me wants my mum. It also wants Owen. But he is gone. It wants to be greedy, to have my coven and Daisy at my side.

My heart aches for my brave, beautiful hellhound to somehow fight this for me, to chase away the poisonous magic in my blood and rescue me.

But he can't.

A sob wrenches out of my throat. I cover my lips, and beneath my hand, an inhuman wail comes out of my mouth.

I never knew grief and horror had such a sound.

"Tuesday, Tuesday, please tell me what is wrong."

"Mum, I'm sorry." Blood dribbles down my wrist as I hold up my bitten hand.

CHAPTER
THIRTY-NINE

The silence is so strange, ominous.

It is a silence that will stretch through time and be a clear memory for the rest of their lives as it implants itself into their soul with a vicious crack. They stare at me, shell-shocked, and I do not know how to comfort them. Diane is the first to react. She sinks to the floor as if her legs have given out, like she is a puppet with her strings cut. She pulls her knees to her chest and rocks. "No. This can't be happening. It's a nightmare. It's not real."

Mum freezes. Her violet eyes narrow, and then a look of horror and pity flashes across her face. "No. Please, no."

I bet you are glad it's me and not them.

Jodie goes into nurse mode. She is suddenly there in front of me, holding my cold wrist between her warmer hands. She gently palpitates the skin around the bite. It is numb to the touch. I am glad the wound doesn't hurt. Though not hurting is probably a terrible sign. She then pulls the sleeve of my jumper up to my elbow, and there is a hitch in her breathing, and she visibly swallows. I glance down. The only reason I do not swear up a storm is 'cause of my respect for Diane. I don't want to upset her any more than necessary. I hold in my horrified gasp.

A spider web of red spreads from the bite. It wraps around the

CURSED WITCH

silver swirls on my wrist. It looks horrendous against my pale skin. And where the red web touches the silver swirls, they blacken. That isn't good. Jodie's compassionate brown eyes meet mine, her gaze holds such heart-wrenching sorrow that for a split second, it feels like I am already dead.

Diane wails behind us.

"Help her," I whisper underneath my breath.

"Okay," Jodie whispers back. We both know there is nothing she can do. I'm sure she has seen different versions of this scenario dozens of times before. I shake my arm until the jumper slips back over my wrist.

Jodie crouches next to Diane. She pulls out a familiar black bag and I can't help my small smile. It is the pocket dimension I made for her. She quickly pulls out various potions. "I am going to give you something to help you cope."

"Why are you not helping Tuesday?" Mum whispers.

Jodie shakes her head and pops the top off a pale lilac vial. Diane, between sobs, obediently sips.

I move toward her to help and—

It is then I recognise his heat. Before I can spin around, a solid arm wraps around me and gently grips my right arm. "Did you think you could hide that from me?" he says against the shell of my ear as he rubs the skin above the bite. "That I wouldn't see the overwhelming pain and fear in your eyes? That I wouldn't notice the woman I love is distraught?"

"Owen." My voice cracks, and I turn and bury my face into his abdomen. *He didn't leave me.* The indifferent, stupidly brave mask I'm hiding behind shatters. I thought I could only remain brave if I held on to pain and sorrow. *I was wrong.*

He holds me as I cry. His massive hand threads through my hair and the other rubs my back as he makes soft comforting sounds in the back of his throat. When I've thoroughly dampened his shirt and I don't think I can cry anymore, I lift my eyes.

"Y-you love me?" I whisper.

His eyes crinkle at the corners. "Since you shuffled to the bathroom with your trousers around your ankles." I laugh, and I don't care that, even to my ears, it is a retched horrid sound.

"I love you too. So, so much," I gush. And then I remember that isn't going to be enough. "I don't want to leave you."

"Do you think I will let you die without a fight?" His thumbs wipe away the remaining tears from my face, and he crouches so we are eye level. "Listen to me, Tuesday Larson, I've seen you do things that are solely confined to the history books. I've seen you do things—impossible things. You learned in days magic that would take anyone else a lifetime to master. So let me be clear, so you understand, and there's no mistaking my words.

"This. Is. Your. Realm. With your rules. The rules of Earth don't apply here. That is why you can create the things that you do, why you can pull things out of thin air. Why you can *heal* creatures when all hope is lost. You will *not* die."

"I won't?"

"No. I have so much faith in you. I know in my heart you have the power to heal yourself. This is not the end." He rests his forehead on mine. "I want our happily ever after," he growls.

Bloody tears. I swallow the enormous lump in my throat. What he says makes a strange kind of sense, but... the bite is a hundred percent fatality rate.

How can I beat that?

"That is an amazing idea," Jodie says, suddenly becoming animated and standing. A subdued Diane flops almost casually against Jodie's legs. "You use the shifter magic, absorb it and mix it with your own. Owen is right. No one has ever seen anyone like you before. I bet you differ from the other hosts, too."

"I do differ," I mumble. "They resemble our elves. While I'm all witch."

"Exactly."

"You are way too stubborn to die," Mum snaps. I take in her red eyes from her silent crying and puffy face. Her hair is listing to one side. I have never seen her so not put together. Softer, she pleads, "Tell us what you need. We will help."

"Mum, what's happening?" Heather whispers. "I don't understand."

Aw heck.

I wince. I missed their return to reception, and the realisation wraps me with guilt. I didn't want Heather to find out like this. I did not want her to know until I was gone. She deserves to know from her aunt; she deserves to see, even in the face of such fear, I have dignity. "I'm so sorry, Heather. I have been bitten by Andy in his animal form. As you know from school, the bite is deadly to women."

Again, everyone is quiet while Heather absorbs this information.

"You are going to fight, right? You will not let the shifter magic win."

I shake my head as determination fills me. I need a little faith, belief. "No. I will not let the shifter magic win. I am a Larson."

Heather nods. "Okay."

"Forgive me. Forgive me for not being fast enough." I spin on my toes and look up at my hellhound.

"Forgive you for not having a crystal ball, you mean? Owen, bad things happen. This"—I wave my wrist underneath his nose—"was not your fault. It wasn't Diane's fault either. It was dickhead Andy who attacked me. He went for my throat and ended up chomping on my hand. Stop blaming yourself and put the blame firmly on him. The jumped-up little prick. Right..." I clap my hands. "Coven bedtime. Come on, everybody. Let's get some sleep. I know I'm exhausted and I cannot think clearly with all the snivelling."

Diane huffs out a laugh. "You are unbelievable. Do you ever take anything seriously?"

"Never. I will need your super smart brain and your witchy talents. You need to be at your best in the morning, so go and relax. I will see you soon." I unlock the portal so Dad can get back after dropping Andy off. I also check to confirm that Jeff has gone.

"You won't do anything stupid, will you?"

"No, Mum." I ignore the magic ping. "I am sorry about the crayons, Mum."

"I'm not. I find colouring relaxing. Perhaps the swear word colouring book was a tad much. But you made your point."

"It was a swear word colouring book? Wow, is that a thing?" I grin. "Well, I am glad you will enjoy it." Mum nods as she helps a swaying Diane to her feet.

"I'm sorry. I am so sorry my horrible boyfriend hurt you. Killed you. I love you, little sister," Diane says as her head flops oddly from side to side.

"Stop that. I am not dead yet, so you can stop looking at me like that. Otherwise, I am going to moan the word *brains* and do the zombie shuffle." Heather opens her mouth. I hold up a hand. "No, I am not turning into a zombie. It was a joke. Sheesh. Diane can't control another person and what he did was on him. It was my fault for getting my hand in the way." I'm so glad that they are all safe, as it could have worked out so much worse. "I got some bad luck, that's all. Now please, go get some sleep."

"I'm going to kill him," Diane viciously whispers as she is sandwiched between Mum and Jodie as they wobble away.

"No, you are not. Think about how miserable he is going to be locked up. He doesn't deserve a quick death," Jodie tells her.

"I would not make it quick," Diane huffs back.

"Not tonight. You're going to get some sleep and then you are going to help our sister."

"Of course, I'm gonna help Tuesday. I'm going to fix this, but there's no way I am going to be able to sleep."

"Naturally, no, but I've got another wonderful spell you can chug."

"See you in the morning, Auntie Tuesday."

"Night, Heather."

The hallway door swings closed. "Now you've got rid of your coven. What are we really going to do?" Owen says once we are alone. "I know you will not have a nap. You have that expression on your face."

"What expression?"

"Mischief. Trouble."

"Oh." I shrug. What can I say to that? Although I'm less mischief and more shitting myself, what with dying and all. But my hellhound's attempt to lighten the mood is sweet.

"What are we doing, Flash?"

All the way through this rollercoaster journey, I have always felt as if the magic was guiding me. And I've concluded that the realm needs me just as much as I need it. So why not ask the realm what I need to do? The answer comes to me.

"I'm going to the heart of the realm and you're going to help me."

"Together?"

"Yes, together."

He gently kisses my cheek. "You haven't had a normal few days, have you?"

"No." If I survive this, I don't think I will have normal ever again. "I can feel the foreign magic, Owen. It is eating me up inside." I rub my shoulder and puff out a breath. I roll my sleeves up and the red spider web has already spread further up my arm. It is itching along my shoulder, pulsing as it threatens its way towards my heart. "There is a war going on inside of me. I think I have less than an hour."

"An hour?" Owen rubs his forehead and then presses his palm over his mouth. "How can I help?"

"Can you go get Daisy?" My voice breaks as soon as I say her name. I swallow a few times and cough to clear my throat. "Then can we go to the lake?"

I worry that Stepping will only exasperate the poison.

So, after Owen comes back with Daisy, he carries us both outside.

CHAPTER
FORTY

THE NIGHT IS STILL and warm. With my arms wrapped around his neck and my legs around his waist, I nestle against him as he holds me with reverence to his chest. Daisy curls across his shoulders, watching me intently. She chirps her concern and, every so often, nudges my arm and face. I find it hard to look at her.

I have never seen a night sky like this. I tip my head back to investigate the blackness of the night sky, and, of course, there are millions of beautiful bright stars. Pinpricks of burning flame, circling overhead in a spiralling vortex. The stars, it is like they are almost following us. Perhaps they are? They are my stars, after all.

Even with me in his arms, his footsteps are silent. The hellhound moves like a ghost, like he is floating. His feet barely touch the ground.

With my eyes on the sky and the smooth, but fast movement of my hellhound, it isn't long before we reach the lake. He has chosen the spot well, where we had our picnic, close to the dock and our rowboat. Owen settles down onto the grass. My legs slide on either side of his hips.

My hellhound carefully arranges me. My body is so floppy, I have zero control over my limbs.

CURSED WITCH

My thoughts wildly scatter. *Ah, fear, my old friend, so glad I can't make a fool of myself, as my body is now too messed up to deal with you.* My heart is sluggish and doesn't even pretend to care as my mind freaks out.

In the last few minutes, I'm finding it harder and harder to breathe. Each new breath is more laboured than the last. I am not in any pain. It's just the spreading numbness that is disconcerting.

If there is ever a time to keep my cool, it's now. If I don't keep calm, I'm going to spend my remaining time freaking out instead of finding a solution.

When I was a little girl, I had appendicitis and had to have surgery to remove the defective organ. I remember when the nurses used the anaesthetic potion. I could feel it burning and spreading through my veins. I could taste the spell underneath my tongue. Flooding my mouth with its bitter tang.

It is kind of similar to that, wrapping like a monster around my lungs, rushing its poison through my blood. A coldness.

Owen cradles the back of my head and Daisy quietly creeps as close as she can, her golden wings touching the both of us.

"Tuesday," Owen says, breaking the raspy silence.

"Just hold me. Please, if it doesn't work—"

"It'll work," the hellhound growls.

"I love you," I gasp out. Gosh, talking without being able to breathe is hard. "I am sorry we didn't have enough time." I wheeze. "I know... it's a lot to ask but please will you take care of Daisy? She is my heart."

"Please, Flash—"

"Thank you for not leaving me when you could, for staying..."

"You don't have to thank me, and this isn't the end," he whispers gruffly. His grey eyes shine with tears. "I believe in you. You can do this." He is so strong, my hellhound.

"Okay." I flop against his chest and listen to the steady beat of his heart. With his heart showing me the way, I close my eyes and let go.

I fall.

I fall into the magic and the life force of the realm embraces me. My soul peels away from my dying body. I perceive my essence as it shifts between dimensions to a crossroads linking all the worlds.

It is so dark here. Like how I imagine a sensory deprivation chamber would feel. The silence is so vast, it is never-ending and no matter how hard I strain my ears, I cannot hear a thing. No matter how much I strain my eyes to pierce the blackness, I can't see even the smallest pinprick of light. Nothing exists.

Have I made a mistake?

I was supposed to go to the heart of the realm, not here. Not this lifeless place. Then there is a whooshing sound, and I brace the body that no longer exists, but instead, my battered soul flutters, as vast power flows over my incorporeal form and... that is when the pain comes. Every previous hurt finds me, and I am torn apart.

Judgement.

My life flashes before me and everything I have done wrong is plucked out and put on display. Analysed. Set out before me is a loathsome, macabre exhibit of my past wrongs.

I see moments of small hurts that I caused, moments of long forgotten unkindness. There aren't many, thank the stars. But the careless words bite, and the careless actions sting. It's a wall of shame and it makes me ashamed.

I'm being judged, and I am found... *lacking*.

I am not good enough for the mystical heaven. Not bad enough for the mystical fires of hell. Some higher power communicates to me in feelings rather than simple words. I still have so much left to do. Two choices: purge the shifter magic or embrace it.

The choices come with knowledge, a knowing of future issues, and a knowing of future pain. I am stubborn, so of course, I choose the hardest, but most rewarding path.

I am remade.

Remade into something different, something that I was always meant to be. More than just a host, more than a simple witch.

The knowledge of my choice and what I learned fades from my mind, leaving no trace. And then, with rough dismissal, I'm thrown back into my body.

So much bloody pain.

A colourful array of magic bombards me; it oozes through my veins. Strangely, the taste of fruit fills my mouth, then the fresh almost tasteless coolness of cucumber, and the bitter taste of volcanic rock. Daisy? When flavours in my mouth fade, green magic joins that of the realms, washing away the pain and some of the darkness that is still clinging to me. Familiar magic. Daisy's magic mixes with mine and the realm's. It combines to batter the remaining numbness away.

Everything stops, it grinds to a halt when I hear a voice. "Come on, breathe. Damn you. Don't you dare die on us."

What is that?

There is pressure on my chest. "Please don't leave us. I love you." The ring on my finger burns a fiery path up my arm.

My body jolts.

The magic explodes inside of me and finally, the shifter magic is now *mine*.

I gasp.

"I've got her back. She's breathing," says a raspy voice. Jodie. My sneaky sister must have snuck out and followed us here, knowing I would need her help. My eyes flutter open. "Never do that again!" She slaps my arm weakly and then bursts into tears. "Three minutes. You stopped breathing for three minutes." She sniffles.

"Sorry..." I croak out.

"The ring on your finger started glowing, and it was as if the entire realm held its breath. The bite on your wrist healed and the red marks faded almost straight away, but they didn't go away fully until Daisy touched you. Tuesday, your little dragonette glowed like a freaky green star and then... that was about the time you stopped breathing..."

My sister continues to ramble. My hellhound is right next to me, stroking my face and hair. I cannot focus on his expression yet, as my eyes are kinda fuzzy. "...I did chest compressions, and I was about to use a spell to shock your heart."

I move my fingers; at least I am no longer feeling numb. I take a deep breath, ooh, and I can breathe without issue. Sweet oxygen fills my lungs. I am alive; I did it.

So why do I still feel a little spider webby? I frown.

The sticky new magic zips through me, vibrating the very cells that hold me together. The cells that make me, me. I sit up with Jodie and Owen's help and lift an unsteady hand to my face. The vibrations in my body are getting worse, and my right hand is tingling.

Time seems to slow, and goosebumps raise on my skin. My vision becomes clearer, and I watch in morbid fascination as tiny pieces of skin detach from my hand and float off. I blink. *What the heck is that? Does anyone else see that!*

The shape of my fingers is the first to disappear. It doesn't hurt and the cells don't go far, they hover above me in some sort of magic swarm.

Time speeds up, and it's not just my hand, it is my entire arm and then... it's as if I am made of sand. Everything crumbles.

And then there is nothing.

Blackness.

With a strange pop echoing in my ears, everything is normal again. *Well, that was weird, and a little bit anticlimactic. Did lack of oxygen do something to my brain? Has everything that has happened made me mad?*

I move my hand back in front of my face to check out the bite on my wrist, and... Oh boy, that's not a hand. Uh-no. That is a fluffy, violet *paw*.

I yeep. Jodie squeaks.

Beside me, I can hear Owen's shocked laughter and I kid you not, my left ear swivels toward the sound. It is the weirdest sensation I have ever felt. I am not even going to say anything about my tail. When I look at him, the stupid thing wags!

I clamber to my feet, all four of them. My ears fatten to the side of my head as I wobble.

"You are purple! Your fur is purple. I can't believe you are a bloody wolf. Oh my god. Wait until mum finds out!" Jodie splutters.

That last comment has my cells zipping and vibrating with panic. Mum is going to kill me. Then I am standing naked and shivering.

Did that just happen?

CURSED WITCH

A warm top is slipped over my head, and the body heat clinging to the fabric engulfs me. While the scent of cinnamon and vanilla wafts around me, the smell makes me dizzy. My sense of smell is... wow. It is like I had a cold with a stuffy nose my entire life, and now I can finally breathe. Owen stands there, his gorgeous dark skin and rippling muscles on display.

"Hi," I whisper.

"Hi," he says gruffly. I force my eyes to leave his bumpy abs and his beautiful sparkling grey eyes capture mine. He has been crying. Oh, Owen.

"I am sorry I frightened you. Did that just happen? Did I—" My words abruptly stop. I stare at my hands as if I have never seen them before. My thumb picks at the ring still on my finger, not even changing shape will dislodge that sucker. *Change shape.* My bare feet wiggle into the grass and I blurt out a weird-sounding manic laugh.

"Shift? Yes."

"Oh. Crap-on-a-cracker," I mutter.

Daisy does a running jump, and she hits me in the chest so hard I grunt—I'm so glad shifting has fixed my remaining aches and pains—then I am hugging her and kissing her scaly, adorable face. "Who is a clever girl with fancy green magic?"

"You're alive. I can't believe you're bloody alive! And you turned into a wolf!" Jodie says as she tackle-hugs my side. Daisy snarls. I hold my hand out to the side, and Owen's massive, warm hand engulfs mine. I squeeze and he squeezes me right back.

Jodie pulls away with a pat on my arm. "I think I need a shot of the same potion I gave Diane. It's going to take a full year for me to calm down." She rubs her face. "Blinking heck, I feel like I have aged ten years." She spots our clasped hands and smiles softly. "Okay, well, I am so done. I have had enough excitement for the night. I will leave you guys to it. I'll go get some sleep." Daisy yawns so big I can almost see her tonsils. Jodie giggles. "She is so cute. If you want, I can take her with me. Do you want to stay with Auntie Jodie for tonight?" she coos.

I shrug. Daisy lets Jodie take her out of my arms. Head in the air, she holds herself as stiff as a board, and more amusing, she keeps her wings and tail stuck out at awkward angles. *"I will allow you to touch me, but I don't have to like it."* Mournfully, her eyes roll in our direction. She wrinkles her snout and makes an unhappy sound at the back of her throat. Once Jodie hugs her, that is the extent of her objection. She yawns again and relaxes, bestowing her temporary permission.

Aw, my little dragonette is completely tuckered out. "Thanks, sis. See you in the morning." We watch as Jodie and Daisy trudge back towards the hotel. I don't want to Step them until I have tested my magic.

Owen pulls me into his arms and hugs me. I bury my face into the silken skin of his chest as he rests his chin on the top of my head. "You are a beautiful wolf."

"I am a bitten shifter who can shift, the first woman known to survive a bite," I whisper. "The first of my kind. It's going to be a nightmare when people find out. They are going to lose their shit."

"They will wonder if The Sanctuary Hotel solves our dwindling numbers, if what happened to you will be the shifter's salvation."

I groan.

"It will not. This will likely bring evil into our lives. Owen, the crazies will come."

"Let them. Between us, we can take out the rubbish. The predators are more than welcome. You are not a simple shifter, and neither am I, and I am not going anywhere."

"Are you sure you don't want to tap out?"

He grins. "Hell no."

"So, are we going to do this? Run the hotel? What about your job?"

"You are my priority. So yeah, we are going to run the hotel."

A safe place for all the misfits and the rebels. I like the sound of that.

"Hey, Flash, will you do me the honour of coming for a run?" What? I pull away slightly and blink at him.

"A-as... as wolves?" I stutter.

Owen's grey eyes dance, and he smiles brightly. "Race you!" And within two breaths, his clothing flutters to the floor and a big, black

CURSED WITCH

wolf is bounding across the grass. He stops and turns his head; his tongue lolls out in a wolfy grin and he playfully yips.

I shift, and on wobbly violet paws, I join him.

THE END

Dear Reader,

Thank you for taking a chance on my books. I hope you enjoyed them. If you did and have time, I would be *very* grateful if you could write a review.

Every review makes a *huge* difference to an author—especially me as a brand-new shiny one—and your review might help other readers discover my book. I would appreciate it so much, and it might help me keep writing.

Thanks a million!

Oh, and there is a chance that I might even choose your review to feature in my marketing campaign. Could you imagine? So exciting!

>Love,
>Brogan x

P.S. DON'T FORGET! Sign up on my VIP email list! You will get early access to all sorts of goodies, including: signed copies, private give-aways, advance notice of future projects and free stuff! The link is on my website at **www.broganthomas.com** your email will be kept 100% private, and you can unsubscribe at any time, with zero spam.

P.P.S. I would love to hear from you, I try to respond to all messages, so don't hesitate to drop me a line at: brogan@ broganthomas.com

ABOUT THE AUTHOR

Brogan lives in Ireland with her husband and their eleven furry children: five furry minions of darkness (aka the cats), four hellhounds (the dogs), and two traditional unicorns (fat, hairy Irish cobs).

In 2019 she decided to embrace her craziness by writing about the imaginary people that live in her head. Her first love is her husband and number-one favourite furry child Bob the cob, then reading. When not reading or writing, she can be found knee-deep in horse poo and fur while blissfully ignoring all adult responsibilities.

facebook.com/BroganThomasBooks
instagram.com/broganthomasbooks
goodreads.com/Brogan_Thomas
bookbub.com/authors/brogan-thomas
youtube.com/@broganthomasbooks